SHATTERED

A HIGH RISK NOVEL

SHATTERED

JOANN ROSS

THORNDIKE
CHIVERS

This Large Print edition is published by Thorndike Press, Waterville, Maine, USA and by BBC Audiobooks Ltd, Bath, England.

Thorndike Press, a part of Gale, Cengage Learning.

The text of this Large Print edition is unabridged.
Other aspects of the book may vary from the original edition.
Set in 16 pt. Plantin.
Printed on permanent paper.

LIBRARY OF CONGRESS CATALOGING-IN-PUBLICATION DATA

Ross, JoAnn.
  Shattered : a high risk novel / by JoAnn Ross.
    p. cm.
  ISBN-13: 978-1-4104-1435-9 (hardcover : alk. paper)
  ISBN-10: 1-4104-1435-3 (hardcover : alk. paper)
  1. Hostages—Fiction. 2. Search and rescue
operations—Fiction. 3. Iraq War, 2003—Veterans—Fiction. 4.
Central America—Fiction. 5. South Carolina—Fiction. 6. Large
type books. I. Title.
PS3568.O843485S53 2009
813'.54—dc22   2009002570

BRITISH LIBRARY CATALOGUING-IN-PUBLICATION DATA AVAILABLE

Published in 2009 in the U.S. by arrangement with NAL Signet, a member of Penguin Group (USA) Inc.
Published in 2009 in the U.K. by arrangement with NAL Signet, a member of Penguin Group (USA) Inc.

U.K. Hardcover: 978 1 408 44132 9 (Chivers Large Print)
U.K. Softcover: 978 1 408 44133 6 (Camden Large Print)

Printed in the United States of America
1 2 3 4 5 6 7 13 12 11 10 09

As always, to Jay.

And with heartfelt appreciation to all the troops and their families, including my personal favorite military men: deployed sailor Keith, airman Trae, and PFC Jason.

ACKNOWLEDGMENTS

Again, a huge shout-out to the fabulous team at Penguin/NAL, who make this job of storytelling a joy. What fun that the twisting yellow-brick publishing road has brought me full circle, back home to where my career began so many years ago!

■ ■ ■ ■

PART ONE

■ ■ ■ ■

The only easy day was yesterday.
— U.S. Navy SEAL saying

1

Gardez Air Base, Afghanistan
April 1

Like all warriors, Army SOAR pilot Shane Garrett had contemplated death. He lived with it, even expected it at times, but had always been a fatalist — when your number was up, it was up, and there wasn't a damn thing you could do about it.

Still, although he'd never considered himself the least bit psychic, he'd had bad feelings about this mission from the beginning.

Night Stalker missions were complex, daring, and totally out there. In the six years he'd been wearing the red SOAR beret and unit crest, he'd taken part in missions no one — not even other members of the military — would ever know about.

Give a SOAR unit an impossible scenario, and they would put their heads together, train like demons, and then go off and execute it. Although it might not get as much press as Iraq, Afghanistan was pretty much the Wild West of the war on terrorism. SOAR was the Army's cowboys, and having grown up on a ranch, Shane fit right in.

Tonight they were "deep black." They had no reporters with them, no one back home knew where they were, and they'd cut off all communication with the outside world.

Having initially joined the 160th to fly AH-6 Little Birds, which were the Porsches of military copters, or at least Black Hawks, which were considered the Cadillacs, Shane understood how people could look at his forty-thousand-pound Chinook and see an ungainly, flying refrigerator box, or as smart-ass Navy SEAL Zach Tremayne was always calling it, a Winnebago with rotors.

They also weren't exactly designed for stealth. While the bad guys might not hear a Black Hawk or Little Bird until it was directly overhead, when a Chinook was anywhere nearby the earth would rumble like it was about to blow apart. If he'd still believed in Santa Claus, at the top of Shane's Christmas list would have been a noise-cancellation system, which, although currently the stuff of science fiction, was being seriously studied in the aviation community.

But from the moment he'd climbed into the cockpit, Shane forgot all about those smaller, sexier birds. Where others looked at the helo and saw fat, ugly, and slow, Shane saw charm. And durability. And when you absolutely, posifuckingtively had to have something moved overnight, the Chinook jockey was who you called.

The bird had legs. Incredibly reliable, it didn't have to land to refuel every couple hours. It also had the respect of its customers — Spec Ops guys who were interested in working with only the heavily armed and powerful birds that could get them to their targets, bringing the fight to the enemy anytime, anywhere, in any kind of weather.

Because of the altitude and temperature extremes, flying in Afghanistan, where peaks soared more than sixteen thousand feet and the high altitude made engines run hot, was intense, nonstop, over-the-edge combat flying in a place where only the huge, sturdy birds could venture.

It was the Chinook pilot's war, and Shane was damn glad and proud to be part of it. Nothing was ever routine or remotely mundane; he was shot at every night, but it was flat-out the most fun he'd ever had, and, in his view, loving his work kept him in the game and on his toes, which could just be another reason he was the most requested pilot in the unit by his customers.

Although this mission had originally planned for a SEAL team he'd flown with so many times that they'd become as close as brothers, since everyone wanted to play, a bunch of Rangers, Marines, and even some CIA guys had joined the full load he'd be ferrying up into the mountains.

The string of bad luck had begun when he'd gotten the go, only to have flames shoot out of the exhaust when he'd fired his engines, essentially burning one up. Which required them all to sit around on their asses, waiting for a replacement to be flown in from Bagram. There'd been more delays while they waited for the newly arrived bird to be refueled.

Then, just as he'd been readying to take off, damned if the delayed timeline hadn't gone crashing into a B-52 bombing raid, keeping them on the ground even longer.

While last week's earthquake may have shaken things up, the mountainous land in the lawless Waziristan area along the Afghan/Pakistan border had already become destabilized as various factions struggled for supremacy.

One al-Qaeda leader had begun a move to control the entire region. According to the latest intel, the terrorist was holed up in one of the many subterranean tunnels, and the SEALS that Shane was ferrying tonight had been tasked with locating the "bat cave," then calling in massive amounts of ordnance down on it.

Given that the Night Stalkers flew in the dark, without lights, the Chinooks were outfitted with a technical system called Terrain Following/Terrain Avoidance Multi-Mode Radar. Having never been used in combat before Afghanistan, it required "flying the cues," which meant the MMR would "paint" the terrain, which appeared as a three-dimensional image on a display on the cockpit console.

Shane never looked out the windshield — something that had seemed more than a little weird in the beginning when he'd switched from the Black Hawks he'd flown in Iraq — but he'd keep his eyes glued to the VSD (vertical situation display), avoiding trees, power towers, buildings, and, most importantly, the sharp, thrusting peaks of the Hindu Kush.

It was just like playing a video game, except you couldn't hit the pause button, and if you screwed up you couldn't just turn it off and start over again, because you and everyone else on board would be dead.

Because of the delay, rather than landing farther down the mountain, the decision had been made to land near the peak. Which, given the lack of flat spaces, damn well wouldn't have been Shane's choice, but since no one had died and made him head of central command, well, like the Duke (whose movies his dad was always watching on the Western channel) said, sometimes a guy had to do what a guy had to do.

Like all pilots, Shane was good at multitasking. Which was why, as he flew over the mountains, he thought about the recent earthquake that had further destabilized the region, and wondered if Kirby Campbell might be down there.

He'd met the army physician when he'd been brought into the 28th CSH — Combat Support Hospital — in the Green Zone, after the bird he'd been using to ferry SEALS looking for Saddam had been shot down outside Fallujah.

Unlike everything else in that country, which was covered with fine desert sand, the white tile floor, walls, and windows of the hospital that had once served as a private clinic for the former dictator's relatives had been sparkling clean. With five operating theaters, ten emergency room trauma stations, and seventy-six beds, it could've been a top hospital in any major city back home in the States.

It also boasted the sexiest military medical officer Shane had ever seen. Her wheat-blond hair, which she wore in a short, practical, no-nonsense cut, had contrasted with the deep midnight blue of her eyes.

Unlike the tall, tanned, and toned whip-thin ranchers' daughters he'd grown up dating, Captain Kirby Campbell barely topped five-feet-two, and even the baggy desert cammies she wore couldn't hide the kind of curves Monroe had boasted back in her *Gentlemen Prefer Blondes* days, one of the few movies his old man would watch that didn't have a single cowboy in it.

Shane been smitten — a stupidly girly word, but it was the only one that fit — at first glance. Which was why it had been even more humiliating to spend their first thirty minutes together with him lying on his stomach on a metal table while she picked pieces of shrapnel out of his ass cheeks.

While he might have felt like a damn fool, apparently she'd taken the incident in stride, because the next time he took his pants off in front of the sexy captain, she'd been naked, too. They'd spent the next six weeks getting together whenever they could between missions, eating pulled-pork barbecue in the cafeteria of the former Republican Palace, drinking near beer while hanging out at the pool, and screwing each other's brains out.

After she'd been rotated out to Heidelberg, they'd kept in touch by e-mail, but eventually life intervened and correspondence drifted off. He'd heard that after finding the staid confines of the European army theater boring, she'd left the service and signed up with a medical relief organization. Knowing how she loved being in the midst of the action, he wouldn't be at all surprised if she was currently on the ground, bringing order to the additional chaos the earthquake had visited upon the border region.

Just as Shane flared to land the big bird, he saw a flash of orange.

The RPG blinded him, but that didn't stop him from shouting out a warning an instant before the grenade crashed into the side of the Chinook.

Someone on the ground began raking them with machine-gun fire, shattering the windshield and sending a bullet through his copilot's forehead.

An instant after the RPG hit, creating a

chest-wrenching blast, a fireball of heat, and a bitter chemical taste in Shane's mouth, the helo lost power, which he knew would cut out the door guns. At the same time, the VSD screens in the cockpit went dark as the navigational systems shut down.

With the instruments gone, Shane began flying by feel. The Chinook, which was lurching from side to side, began to lift up.

That was the good news.

The bad news was another flash from the ground.

Shane ducked instinctively as the RPG came roaring toward them, only to land — thank you, Jesus! — in the snow twenty yards away.

The machine gun was still blasting away and small-arms fire was peppering the fuselage.

"Go, go, go, baby," he coaxed the heavy Chinook.

There was shouting from the back. Shane couldn't allow himself the distraction of wondering who else might have been hit.

"That's the girl," he crooned, using the same warm tone he'd used his seventeenth summer when he'd coaxed Heather McFarland into letting him make love to her in the bed of his old F-150 pickup. It had worked then. And it seemed to be working now. "Lift it up, darlin'."

They were flying.

Okay, not exactly well; the huge copter was bucking like some of the Brahma bulls Shane had grown up riding. But they were nearly airborne again.

"Nearly" being the definitive word, as another fiery RPG came sailing by.

This time the hit felt as if they'd just had a head-on collision with a freight train.

Overhead, Shane could hear the rotor blades, which must have gotten peppered with shrapnel, whistling.

It was not a merry tune.

The communication system, which worked on DC, fortunately hadn't been taken out with the first grenade.

"We've got smoke coming in from overhead, flames from the hydraulics, and a big chunk of metal, which I'm guessing is part of the back rotor, just flew by the open ramp," Zach Tremayne reported over Shane's headset.

Giving credence to the SEAL's guess, the Chinook began to spin.

"I suggest you put her down." Zach's voice remained as calm and collected as if they were out for a little Sunday Afghan sightseeing tour. "Now."

"Roger that." Trying to stay upright in a

sky that felt as if it'd suddenly turned to ice decidedly upped the pucker factor.

Shane pulled back on the power controls. No way this giant bird would be able to hover, letting him ease her down gently. She had one landing left in her, and it had better be a good one.

A bedlam of bullets hammered against metal walls and pinged like balls in a pinball machine. The tortured shriek of the right engine's turbine blades ensured that once down, they weren't going to be getting back up anytime soon.

"Tell the guys to brace for a hard landing," Shane said.

Damn, he thought, as he prepared to slam down at what had to be fifty knots, this is going to hurt.

2

Pakistan
April 1

Kirby Campbell was clearly in hell.

She wasn't precisely certain which circle she'd landed in, but if this wasn't what Dante had been describing, she'd definitely misunderstood the narrative poem she'd labored over during her freshman English Lit course.

It wasn't that she wasn't used to chaos, having spent the past years working first as an Army trauma physician, and more recently, working for Worldwide Medical Relief.

As relief groups rushed to this dangerous region on the Afghanistan-Pakistan border from all corners of the globe to provide aid after the latest earthquake, WMF was already on the scene, fortuitously having set up a maternal health care clinic just last week. While they were currently working in a tent, an inflatable hospital had been promised and was supposedly on the way. Kirby could only hope that was true.

A last-minute replacement for a male doctor who'd bailed to take a teaching position at Johns Hopkins, Kirby was disappointed but not surprised to discover that no one was at Kabul's airport to greet her. Of course, it was only six o'clock in the morning and a bloodred sun had barely begun to rise over the mountains. But still . . .

Accustomed to making her own way, within five minutes, she located an Afghan driver who not only knew the location of the refugee camp she wanted to visit, but was also willing to drive her there.

And best yet, he actually spoke English. While she'd learned some Arabic during her posting in Iraq, other than "hello," "goodbye," "please," and "thank you," her Farsi was nonexistent.

Also unsurprisingly, the promises that had been made to WMF about military protection into the mountains had been swept away without explanation or apology from the government.

She'd been traveling from Darfur for a grueling thirty-six hours, but by the time she'd traveled two kilometers from the airport, even discounting climate change from the desert to the snow falling from a leaden sky, Kirby realized that this trip could be more challenging than most.

The bullet pockmarks in the white sides of the armored UN vehicles they passed suggested more problems than Mother Nature had provided.

Grim, silent columns of refugees struggled to make their way down from the mountains, all their worldly possessions heaped high on the backs of shaggy donkeys; panhandling victims of land mines sat on empty brown pants legs in the dust alongside the road; heavily draped women, babies clutched against dirty burkas, begged for coins with outstretched palms.

The level of misery increased the farther they got out of the city. They passed what looked to be a vast parking lot filled with vehicles that had been cluster bombed into fused, fire-blackened metal.

"You maybe go back?" her driver, Hasan, asked hopefully.

Kirby shook her head, which she'd covered with a traditional black *hijab* scarf. The scene, as dark as it was, only deepened her resolve. "We'll keep going."

Hasan sighed dramatically. Muttered something beneath his breath, which she suspected was along the lines of "Crazy

Americans."

At the moment, she couldn't argue the point.

The sixty-mile trip, which back home on a decent freeway would've taken less than an hour, was excruciatingly slow. The higher they climbed, the steeper that only the most optimistic person could consider a road became.

The snow turned grittier. The mountains they were entering were draped in a pall of campfire smoke. The biting-cold, coal-colored air pressed down on Kirby's chest and made breathing an effort. Small flags — the scarlet hue of the poppies that grew at lower elevations — dotted the landscape, warning of buried land mines.

In the distance, from the direction they were headed, Kirby heard a series of thuds, then a tearing sound overhead.

"Al-Qaeda," Hasan said. "They are firing salvos at the Americans."

"But those trucks are bringing aid," Kirby pointed out, instinctively ducking as another batch of shells went flying, luckily too far away to prove a threat to her team. At least not yet.

"They are not welcome," he said. He shot her a glance. "There will be those who don't welcome you, either."

"There will also be those who do," she said mildly, as low-flying jets began strafing the mountain peaks where the salvos had originated. The shredded trees added a pungent scent of pine to the smoky air. "And those are the ones I've come for."

She wondered if, just perhaps, Shane Garrett was somewhere up in those skies. He'd always enjoyed being in the thick of things, and it hadn't taken her long to realize that SOAR pilots were not only every bit as smart and skilled as the fighter-jet jocks, but also, perhaps due to their Special Forces training, even tougher.

If a Night Stalker pilot asked for a vitamin M (Spec-Ops speak for Motrin), it was likely he was trying to conceal a fracture that might just cause him to miss some action.

Shane had been the toughest of the bunch, and although they'd lost track of each other, that hadn't stopped her from thinking of him. And from comparing every other man she met to him.

Although she'd worried about crossing into Pakistan, where the camp was located, during what appeared to be a raging battle, they passed through the unguarded border without incident.

Finally, three hours after leaving Kabul,

she arrived at the refugee camp set up amidst the ruins of a quake-damaged village. The sight that greeted her was not encouraging.

First of all, "camp" was definitely a misnomer. Unlike the rustic yet tidily pleasant Girl Scout camp in the mountains outside San Diego Kirby remembered so fondly from childhood, scores of people, packed together like sardines, hunkered beneath bits of dirty plastic sheets that fluttered forlornly in the wind.

A mangy donkey chewed at a straw mat making up the side of one shelter. The single source of water appeared to be a half-frozen stream, whose icy blue color belied the bacteria she knew would be swimming in it.

A few had tried to improve their lot, carrying stones to build rough shelters, and she could see the evidence of drainage furrows meant to carry off sewage.

From the stench, they weren't working.

Still, proving the resiliency of the human spirit, others were getting on with their lives, selling vegetables, breaking boulders with sledgehammers, even getting haircuts while perched on a battered barber's chair along the side of the road.

Several men appeared to be repairing damaged weapons and oiling others, while children foraged for loose bullets, gathering them into plastic bags. One boy, no older than six or seven, struggled beneath the burden of ammunition belts that tumbled out of his small arms and dragged on the frozen ground behind him.

Even as desolate as the scene was, when she spotted the familiar six-pod white inflatable field hospital, Kirby felt a surge of adrenaline that wiped away the exhaustion and aches of the long, hard trip.

Two women who must have heard the truck arrive came out of the tent. One woman's cloud of white hair and round-cheeked face gave the impression that she should be home in Iowa, baking cookies for her grandchildren, rather than working in a war zone. The other's tanned blond surfer-girl looks belied the fact that she'd been working in ERs for the past eight years

"Hi." Kirby held out a hand. "I'm Kirby Campbell."

The blonde's brown eyes narrowed as they swept over Kirby's face, then looked past her. "Where's Dr. Otterbein?"

Yet another wrinkle in a challenging day. Obviously they hadn't been informed of the change in plans.

"I imagine he's over the Atlantic on his way to Baltimore about now," Kirby said mildly. "Headquarters sent me instead."

"You're a physician?"

Kirby lowered her hand, which had remained ignored, and offered a reassuring smile. "Yes. I am."

"Dammit." A frown darkened the woman's brow. "Look, this isn't anything against you," she said. "But we were promised a male doctor."

"Well, I can't do anything about my gender. But if you're worried about my qualifications, you needn't be. I spent six years in the Army, two in the 28th Combat Support Hospital in Bagdad. I've worked in the bloody mess of the Sudan, where I was held captive for five hours while militiamen fought over a bar of soap and two Power-Bars I had in my pack. And I'm very, very good at my job. Maybe the best, in a crisis situation, you've ever worked with."

"And modest, too, I see." The woman's lips quirked, just a little. Then she held out her hand. "I'm Lita King, BSN, CCNS, CFRN. Along with claiming that alphabet soup of credentials, I've done the gambit of relief acronyms, including a stint with Doctors Without Borders. And I'm sorry for the rudeness, but this has been a rotten forty-eight hours, and having Otterbein bail on us was the proverbial last straw."

"We all have our moments." Kirby shook the doctor's hand.

"I'm Anne Douglass," the white-haired woman introduced herself. "CRNA. This is my second posting as nurse anesthetist. Before this I spent six months in Mogadishu."

"That must've been a tough initiation," Kirby said.

Although Somalia had pretty much faded from the public spotlight, medical relief teams remained in the country, fighting disease and starvation suffered by a population forced to live in a continual state of political crisis.

"It sure as hell was a long way from working in the surgical unit at Seattle's Children's Hospital for thirty-five years," Anne agreed.

There was a murmur of voices. The crowd that had gathered to watch Kirby's arrival parted to allow a dozen men to approach.

Beneath coats made of some sort of animal skins, they were wearing *perahan-o-toman,* the long tunics and baggy pants favored by the males of the region. From their automatic weapons, pistols, huge curved knives, and grenades hanging from their heavy belts, and grenade launchers slung over shoulders, Kirby guessed they weren't from the camp Welcome Wagon.

Their beards were filthy, their dark eyes — as hard as the rocks that made up these mountains — burned with something resembling scorn.

Which was why the AK-47, with its attached blade that looked sharp enough to shave with, pointing at the three women did nothing to bolster confidence.

3

Even with Shane babying the bird, the Chinook still hit the mountain with a jolt. Rocked hard to the left. Then settled.

Into a big, empty field of snow.

Okay, so the landing might not have been the softest he'd ever pulled off. But then again, he'd managed to keep the bird upright.

Shane cut the engines, jacked a round into the chamber of his M4, set the selector to semiautomatic, then reached up and yanked on the yellow-and-black emergency exit handle at the top of the door. But when he tried to kick the door open, nothing happened.

Thinking his flight suit must have caught on something, as another round of fire hit the instrument panel, which began to smoke, and the heavy rotor blades overhead slowly coasted to a stop, Shane tried again.

Again, nothing.

Puzzled, he looked down at his leg, which was spurting blood like Old Faithful.

The material had been blasted away, revealing flesh that — and this was really weird — looked to be glowing green through his NVG.

"Shit." The familiar, amazingly calm expletive had him looking back over his shoulder at Zach Tremayne, who was crawling like a diamondback rattler toward him. "You've been shot."

"It appears so." Time had seemed to take on a slow-motion replay feel as Shane stared down at his eerily smoking flesh.

"You've caught a tracer round." Before Shane could brace himself for the attack, Tremayne ripped off a glove and dove into the wound with his bare hand.

O-kay.

That he felt.

He hissed through clenched teeth as he fought against the vomit trying to rise in his throat as the SEAL pocketed the tracer and tied the lanyard from his 9 mm around Shane's leg as a makeshift tourniquet. No way was he going to give his best friend the opportunity to claim that flyboys weren't as tough as frogmen.

Tremayne handed Shane back his M4. They both ducked as another round of machine-gun fire tore through the cockpit.

Pulling himself forward by his arms and one leg, dragging the other behind him, Shane managed to crawl back through the companionway and into the back of the bird.

Which was even more of a mess than the cockpit.

It was also on fire. Again.

Not a good thing, given that they'd topped off the fuel tank before leaving Gardez.

As wires jumped and sparked around them, and bullets pinged around as if they were inside a giant pinball machine, this second fire, even more dangerous than the first, began greedily eating its way up the side of the bird.

Having always been a quick study, Shane decided that even the Duke would figure it was time to blow this pop stand.

4

The man pointing the weapon at the three women began rattling off a stream of words in a sharp, bulletlike rat-a-tat to Hasan.

"What did he say?" Kirby asked.

"He wants to speak to the doctor," the driver said.

"Tell him that's me."

The way Hasan rolled his dark eyes needed no translation. But he proceeded to pass on the message, which earned a darker scowl and an even more rapid-fire response.

"He prefers a male physician."

"Too bad." From the flush in the driver's cheeks, Kirby suspected that wasn't all he'd said. She folded her arms. "Tell him what he sees is what he gets."

Hasan hesitated.

"Tell him," she repeated.

With obvious reluctance, which Kirby suspected might be due to fear for his life, Hasan started to translate when the armed man, who seemed to be in charge, cut him off with a sharp command.

He made a slicing motion with his hand toward his men, two of whom moved forward, carrying the stretcher on which lay an adolescent boy who looked no older than thirteen.

He was conscious, but just barely, his face twisted with pain. His eyes, fiery with fever, were deeply sunken in their sockets and moved restlessly, unseeingly. His right hand was swathed in a blood-soaked bandage.

Rather than the dark tan that came from living so high beneath the harsh Afghan sun, his complexion was the color of ashes drifting down from the sky. The color of impending death.

"Bring him into the tent," Kirby instructed.

As Anne quickly began gathering up supplies, Kirby knelt on one side of the stretcher, Lita on the other.

Kirby pressed her fingers against the boy's throat. "His pulse is thready."

So thready, she could barely detect it. His hand, despite the fever raging through him, was ice cold. The lax skin on the back of his hand revealed severe dehydration.

She snapped on a pair of gloves, and as she unwound the bandage, her confidence plummeted at the sight of the oozing, dirt-encrusted, mangled mess.

After a bit of back-and-forth between Hasan and the leader, they discovered that the boy — who'd undoubtedly never been allowed to be a child — was a jihadist who'd been holding a grenade when it exploded.

An examination revealed that the explosion had torn apart his hand, which was swollen with pus and turning a deadly black hue.

"How long ago did the injury occur?" Kirby asked as the boy moaned at her touch.

"Two weeks," Hasan translated yet again.

Even worse. Proving himself one tough kid, he'd survived shock and blood loss, but she couldn't guarantee he wouldn't die of infection. Even if he survived the surgery, the dressings should be changed each day under sterile conditions.

Like that was going to happen.

"Let's get some fluid and potassium in him," Kirby instructed Anne, who'd already set up the IV. The good news was that they were already working well together; without waiting to be instructed, Anne added antibiotics and morphine to the drip bag.

"In a way, he's lucky he hasn't had enough fluid," she murmured as she and Lita began scraping the grit out of the mutilated hand with a nail brush, while Anne kept track of his respiration.

Contrary to civilian medical care, Kirby's CSH background had taught her that dehydration could be useful in battlefield conditions.

"It's kept his blood pressure low," Lita agreed.

"Dangerously low, but higher would have increased his bleeding." Kirby moved on to snipping away torn flesh and bits of bone shards.

"I'll admit I was annoyed when I found how short-staffed we were going to be," Lita said.

"And having the guy who was also supposed to be here back out last week and leave you without a male physician in a place not known for women's equality didn't exactly make your day," Kirby said understandingly.

"That's an understatement." A jagged piece of bone clunked like a stone into a metal pan. "But I think we've got the perfect team."

Although it would have been inappropriate to smile under these grim conditions, Kirby had been thinking the very same thing. The leader began speaking again to Hasan in Farsi.

"He wants to know what you're doing," their driver/translator said.

"I'm going to have to amputate at least three of his fingers." Kirby held up a hand, anticipating the argument. "If I don't, he'll die."

"Life or death is Allah's choice," the leader said through Hasan. He frowned darkly. "Do you know who this is?"

"No."

And she didn't care. If relief medical teams started getting to know the people they were sent to care for around the world, they'd find themselves embroiled in politics. Which was something they couldn't allow themselves to do.

"This is the son of Imam Jalaluddin."

While the name didn't cause the expected fanfare of trumpets his tone suggested, it did ring an instant bell. Even down in the Sudan, Kirby had heard of the terrorist leader the United States had been hunting for the past two years.

Kirby didn't care if the kid was Allah himself, but knowing that saying it aloud would be considered blasphemy and get her — hell, all three of them — killed, she tried again.

"If he doesn't have surgery, short of a miracle, he's going to die."

"It's important that he live."

He really was getting on her last nerve. "Then I suggest you be quiet and let me concentrate."

There were more looks exchanged. A rapid-fire discussion Kirby couldn't begin to follow. She could tell they were conflicted. But no one made a move to stop her and Lita from continuing to clean the wound.

"There is one more thing," the leader said as they continued their ragged work.

"What's that?" Kirby asked, allowing herself a bit of optimism at the way the IV Anne had started had begun to bring a bit of much-needed color into their patient's boyishly smooth cheeks.

"If the son of Imam Jalaluddin dies at your hands, he will not die alone." As Hasan translated, the leader swept a hard look over all three women, his meaning clear.

Kirby believed him.

5

By the time the gun battle was over and the bad guys had been eliminated, bodies were lying all over snow that had turned the color of strawberry margaritas.

Although it was bad, the worst Shane had ever experienced, he had managed to get in some decent shots of his own. And while he might not be as good a shot as Tremayne or Quinn McKade, the SEAL team's sniper, he'd sent his share of terrorists to paradise, or wherever it was that they went to retrieve those forty virgins they'd been promised.

The sun had risen bloodred and was beginning to move across the sky when Tremayne called McKade and SEAL medic Lucas Chaffee out of the bunker they'd taken and were now huddled in. Tremayne's excuse was that now that the gunfire had stopped, they could take the opportunity to retrieve some ammunition and other needed supplies from the downed Chinook.

41

Which made sense.

But Shane hadn't just fallen off the potato truck. He knew that another reason they'd left the bunker was that they were trying to come up with an evac plan. Because although everyone was continuing to act all business-as-usual, they were sitting ducks for any reinforcements those dead tangos might have called in before being sent to their heavenly reward.

He'd also begun to lose feeling in his left leg. Shane didn't need to be a medic to know that couldn't be a good thing.

One of the CIA guys, who'd been studiously avoiding Shane's eyes, cursed beneath his breath, climbed out of the bunker, and trudged through the thigh-deep snow over to where the three SEALs were holding their confab.

Although it took a major effort, Shane managed to pull himself up onto his good leg so he could watch what looked to be an argument going on.

Tremayne had taken off his black balaclava and looked less than thrilled to see the spook. More words were exchanged. Deciding they were now discussing him, Shane ducked as all four heads turned in the direction of the bunker.

The quick movement put him off balance.

"Shit, shit, shit!" he cursed as he landed on the cold ground in a heap, his wounded leg crumpled beneath him.

He'd just managed to untangle himself when the group returned from their confab.

"Good news," Tremayne announced with what, even if he hadn't known him so well, Shane could have recognized as false cheer. "We're taking you to the hospital and letting some sexy hot-lips nurse kiss your boo-boo."

"As appealing as that sounds — especially the sexy hot-lips nurse part — I'm fairly familiar with these mountains," Shane said.

Actually, he'd gone over every square inch of flight charts and topo maps to make sure he didn't crash into a damn peak some night. Computerized gizmos were cool, but they'd never replace a pilot's knowledge of the region he was flying over.

"And I sure as hell don't remember a decent-sized village in this part of the country. Let alone one large enough to have a hospital."

"There wasn't until last week," Tremayne said. "Our resident spook here" — he waved a gloved hand toward the CIA guy — "says that there's already a relief medical group in the area." He named a small village Shane had seen on one of the maps.

"That's across the border," he felt obliged to point out. Even though the SEALs obviously already knew that.

"And your point is?" McKade asked.

"Not only would we be breaking the rules of engagement, if we go into Pakistan on our own, we'll be breaking international law."

Which, despite being a Black-Ops team, there'd be no way they could keep that out of the report. Which meant they could well be looking at headlines, even congressional hearings.

And every man there knew it.

"That's not your problem," Tremayne said. "You may call the shots when we're in the air. But we're on the ground now, and since we lost the LT, I'm in charge of this mission, as fucked up as it is. And I say we're going. Now."

Shane folded his arms. "I'm not letting you guys risk being court-martialed on my account."

"Bite me," McKade ground out. He'd no sooner spoken when the Chinook, which had been leaking fuel and smoldering since the crash, blew.

The earth rocked so hard, they could have experienced another earthquake. Blinding flames of red and yellow shot into the sky, and the ammunition the fire-fight had kept them from being able to offload exploded like Fourth of July fireworks.

"Damn it all to hell." Shane glared up at the black smoke billowing into the sky. "I loved that bird." A fury even hotter than the fire burned away his pain as he thought about how a lousy fifty-dollar RPG had managed to destroy a forty-three-million-dollar helo. "Now those bastards are really going to pay."

Unsurprisingly, nearly everyone wanted in on the adventure, which left Tremayne drawing lots to choose which Rangers and Marines would be coming along and which would stay hunkered down at the site, guarding the dead — which, as they were gathered and laid side by side, boots up, looked eerily like they should've been making snow angels — and waiting for nightfall and the exfil copters that would be coming to take them back to camp.

Lucas Chaffee got busy triaging the survivors. Those categorized as "walking wounded" — men unlikely to deteriorate before the exfil copter arrived tonight — were green tagged and would remain behind.

As would those dubbed yellow tags, who, although their injuries could be potentially

life threatening, weren't expected to deteriorate in the next several hours.

That they were risking what could be a
deadly climb, along with breaking the rules
of engagement, told Shane he fell somewhere between a yellow and a critical red.
The good news was the fact that they were
taking him to get help revealed that Chaffee
thought he had a chance of survival.

At least a lot better than the guy who, even
Shane could tell, with his massive open head
wound, was probably going to end up a
black tag. Nevertheless, Tremayne assigned
four Rangers to pull the SKED that would
take the Marine with them.

Because you just never knew.

At least the SEALs had their PEPSE —
personal environmental protection and
survival equipment — consisting of a sleeping bag, sleeping shelter, boots, balaclavas,
ground pads, cooking utensils, water bottles,
a water-filtration system, a shovel, folding
saw, climbing harness, a portable stove,
several hats, gloves, mittens, snowshoes,
crampons, and folding ski poles. Loaded for
bear, they were pretty much set for anything
the tangos might throw their way. Shane
wouldn't have been surprised if given
twenty-four hours, they could have built an
entire village.

Unfortunately, the Rangers dragging the SKED he was strapped onto weren't SEALs.

It wasn't easy making their way straight up the steep mountain to the border, especially without snowshoes. Which was why Shane didn't blame the Ranger who stumbled.

Which immediately caused the other three to lose their grip, and the next thing Shane knew, he was skidding back down the mountainside at what seemed like sixty miles an hour.

At least he was no longer on the verge of passing out, as he'd been only moments earlier. Every nerve ending in his body was on high alert and screaming, *Get me the hell off this fucking tobaggon!*

Just when he was sure he was about to sail off the mountain into the void, the SKED slammed into a jagged granite boulder with a force that caused his bones to jangle.

It tipped over, burying him in a drift.

Then, hotshot SOAR pilot that he was, Shane checked out.

6

The men were not going to leave.

Although this was not the first high-risk situation she'd been in, Kirby wasn't wild about the idea of operating under gunpoint.

For the first five minutes, she expected to be shot any moment. After that she became so focused that a bomb could have exploded right next to her, and as long as it didn't blow her off her feet, she wouldn't have noticed.

Although it was not yet noon, black clouds covered the sun, making the inside of the tent as dark as dusk. The lights, run by a sputtering generator, kept blinking off and on.

Although Hasan had tried to leave, the terrorist leader had insisted he remain as translator, which came in handy when Kirby instructed four of the men to beam their flashlights onto the patient's wounded hand.

Although she could tell they disliked taking orders from a mere woman, the men did as they were told. She suspected their obedience was due more to their fear of failing their leader than any authority they might be willing to grant her. The others sat cross-legged nearby, silently observing every move the women made.

She ended up amputating the three fingers she'd thought would have to go when she'd seen the wound, but managed to save the young insurgent's thumb by pinning fragments of bone together with syringe needles, which with his index finger would allow some use of his hand.

If he stayed alive long enough for it to heal.

Which, given his occupation, wasn't all that likely.

Kirby swiped iodine over his hand, wrapped it in gauze, then put a heavier bandage over that, in some slim hope of keeping it clean; then followed up with penicillin and tetanus injections.

"I've done all I can," she informed them as she stripped off the bloody surgical gloves. "He should recover, but I'll know better in the morning."

"We are taking him back to camp," the leader said, over the thud of more mortars hitting somewhere in the distance.

Kirby shook her head. "That's too dangerous." If infection didn't kill him, the mortars and strafing runs well might. "He needs to stay here, so —"

"What he needs is to be with his father." His tone was clipped. Precise. "Where he will, *Inshallah,* survive to fight another day."

Inshallah. God willing.

The three women exchanged a look. Kirby knew they were all thinking the same thing. That if matters had been left entirely to God, the boy wouldn't have survived until morning.

"May I at least suggest a compromise?" Kirby asked.

The man lifted a dark brow.

"Give him three hours post-op. That way, I'll be able to make sure he doesn't have any reaction to the anesthetic. Then you can take him to his father. It would be tragic if he survived the surgery, only to die because he wasn't given proper aftercare."

He stroked the long, unkempt beard favored by jihadists. From his dark frown, she could see that he was imagining breaking that news to his terrorist leader.

"Two hours," he said finally. "After *Dhur.*" Which was, Kirby knew, the noon call to prayer.

His steely tone assured her it was his final offer. He turned and left the medical tent, the men carrying her still-unconscious patient behind him.

"Welcome to Wonderland," Lita murmured.

The description fit, since Kirby felt as if she'd fallen down a very dark hole.

As a steady flow of men, women, and children began flowing down the mountainside toward them, she wondered again, briefly, if that hottie Night Stalker she'd spent so many nights tangling the sheets with in Baghdad was in the midst of the battle obviously being waged.

And prayed that if Shane Garrett was up there in that tracer-lit sky, he'd stay safe.

7

There had been times when Shane had ragged the SEAL team medic about carrying everything but the hospital sink. Today, he was grateful that Lucas Chaffee believed in the old Spec-Ops axiom "Hope for the best; prepare for the worst."

Shane didn't need a medical degree to know that the loss of red blood cells reduced the oxygen-carrying capacity of blood to the brain. Fortunately, Chaffee had dragged some oxygen tanks off the helo before it blew. Better yet, he'd also brought some whole blood along, and when that had run out, he'd hooked Shane up to a bag of Hespan, a plasma volume expander. Which unfortunately ran out, too.

Shane had always prided himself on being at his best when things were the most fucked up. He'd go into what he secretly called his cone of chaos and kept his head cool while others around him might be losing theirs.

Not that he'd ever seen that happen with SEALs, but still . . .

Which was why he absofuckinglutely hated the fact that he was forced to lie useless on this damn SKED while the other guys were plowing through the deep snow, up the steep mountain grade, propelled solely by sheer willpower.

Two FNG (fucking new guy) Rangers, who hadn't been in the country long enough for their bodies to adjust to the altitude, were suffering from mountain sickness. The base at Bagram was almost a mile high, and at nearly twice that, they stumbled along, lungs searing, stomachs roiling, tossing their cookies along the way.

Except for the panting of labored breaths and the unrelenting whistle of the biting wind, the mountain seemed deceptively calm.

Almost peaceful.

Then suddenly, *bang!*

They'd come under intense fire.

The first few times it happened, the FNGs, this being their first time in battle, would dive face-first, burying themselves in the snow. The more experienced Rangers, Marines, and SEALs didn't so much as flinch.

After three gunfights in approximately thirty minutes, the FNGs were quickly becoming seasoned soldiers. Had it not been for the high potential of bleeding wounds and possible death, they could have been playing paintball.

"Thank God for pray and spray," Tremayne said as one guy madly shot down from above, the bullets hitting harmlessly around them, sending up small geysers of snow.

"Roger that," McKade said.

He calmly lifted his rifle, put the shooter in the cross-hairs of his scope, and effectively took the bad guy out.

Not long after that, they came across a group of stone-and-mud huts set in a small valley on the side of the mountain. Three were standing; the rest appeared to be rubble.

"What do you think?" Tremayne asked, scanning the huts with his field glasses.

McKade eyed them through his rifle scope. "The place looks deserted to me."

"Either it took a hit from one of our bombers or the quake got them," Tremayne decided. "Odds are that a refugee camp isn't going to be overrun with friendlies. Let's see what we can find."

They dragged Shane and the unconscious

Marine past a dead cow and two goats who'd survived whatever had taken out the huts. Tremayne instructed one of the Rangers to build a fire in one of the hut's fire pits while the rest went out scavenging.

"We need some local clothing," he told them. "We've already got the Afghani hair-and-beard thing going, but those Ranger high-and-tight haircuts stand out like red flags."

It took fifteen minutes to round up what they needed. Including some thick wool blankets.

"So long as you don't mind the fleas, they'll help keep you warm," McKade said, piling three on top of Shane just before they took off again.

And walked straight into a wasps' nest of machine-gun fire and mortars.

"Goddamn it!" Tremayne shouted as they all ducked behind a fortuitously close outcropping of rocks surrounded by trees. Momentarily ignoring the risk, he yanked off his helmet and threw it on the ground. "I am starting to get fucking tired of these guys!"

"At least now we know where all the people from the village went," McKade said with his usual calm.

"I don't suppose you can get around

behind them, like you did at the crash site?" Tremayne asked.

The sniper looked out from behind the rocks, immediately drawing another burst of gunfire. Fortunately, these tangos' aim turned out just as bad as the earlier ones; a grenade, obviously shot from a launcher, hit about twenty feet away, creating a small avalanche.

"The problem is, they're shooting from what appears to be a fortified location from up above," McKade said. "My guess is that it was built back during their fight with the Russians. Or, hell, maybe it goes all the way back to the days of British occupation. Without some heavy air support, I can't see any easy way to get past them."

"The only easy day was yesterday," Tremayne reminded him of the SEAL axiom.

"True. Though some days are tougher than others. And despite our well-deserved reputation for chewing nails and spitting out bullets, getting blown away by tangos isn't exactly going to be completing our mission."

"How far away would you say they are?" Tremayne asked, looking through his binoculars toward the fortification.

McKade shot the distance with his sniper scope.

"Three hundred and fifty yards."

Tremayne turned to Dallas O'Halloran, an Air Force combat controller who'd been on the mission and had come with them. Geniuses when it came to coordinating weapon-laden aircraft, because the selection process was nearly as daunting as it was to become a SEAL, CCTs fit in well with both SEALs and Delta Forces on the ground.

"Well?" he asked.

"I could call in and see if we could get us an F-15E Strike Eagle," O'Halloran said. "But I gotta warn you, Chief, it's awful close. If one of those five-hundred pounders hits the wrong coordinates, we could end up nothing but boots and mangled guns."

Everyone was looking at Tremayne, obviously waiting for an answer.

"Damn," he said, as another round of gunfire split a tree behind them. "We sure as hell can't stay here. On the other hand, having my ticket punched by friendly fire isn't exactly my favorite way to spend a snow day."

He rubbed his chin.

Everyone waited.

SEALs were known for their ability to improvise. And Zachariah Tremayne was one of the best Shane had ever worked with.

"What we need is a Reaper," he decided.

The upgraded version of the pilotless Predator was the military's hottest new toy. Able to fly three times as fast as its predecessor, it was also capable of carrying eight times more weaponry. Including HELL-FIRE missiles.

"I'll see what I can do," O'Halloran said.

He dug into his rucksack and pulled out a radio with a whip-thin antenna, which he'd already explained he'd learned about from a female sailor he'd met while on shore leave in the Green Zone. Unlike many military radios, it allowed him to talk to anyone in the joint services, whatever the frequency.

After making the connection, he handed the radio to Tremayne, who explained their current condition and their coordinates. His expression, while he listened to command, gave nothing away.

"Yessir," he finally said. "Roger and out, sir."

He handed the radio back to the CCT.

"Well?" McKade asked.

"It's on its way."

Rousing cheers drew another round of attack from the bad guys. This time the grenade landed closer, but exploded in a puff of snow.

Within minutes, the propeller-driven unmanned drone came flying over the mountain peaks. Every eye in the group was on it as it fluttered into position, using the target coordinates Tremayne had given command.

The first missile hit ten yards from the stone bunker, causing a wild round of fire into the sky from the enemy, who didn't seem all that happy about the change in tactics.

McKade re-marked the target, adjusting for the wind speed; Tremayne called it in.

The Reaper circled back. Fired again, this time blasting the bunker.

Once.

Twice.

A third time.

A cloud of snow filled the air as another small avalanche came roaring down from what had once been the bunker, just missing the copse of trees.

Then the mountain went still as everyone waited to see if the tactic had worked.

"Fire a few rounds at them," Tremayne instructed the Rangers, who were more than happy to take a break from dragging the SKEDs.

They shot off their M16s.

Then waited.

Again, nothing.

There were more "hooahs" from the Rangers, who were definitely feeling their oats.

Although their luck had momentarily changed, as they continued their trek up the mountainside, Shane, who'd seen things get a lot worse before they got better, wasn't prepared to celebrate yet.

The sun, which had caused several of the guys to toss aside their body armor earlier, disappeared behind black anvil-shaped clouds, causing the temperature to plummet. The sweat that had soaked their clothing froze to ice.

Despite the blankets, the same thing was happening to Shane, but instead of sweat, it was the blood from his leg freezing and stiffening his pants.

Now he couldn't just not feel his wounded leg; he couldn't feel either of his feet.

And he figured he must have kept passing out, because every so often he'd wake up from some dark place to McKade throwing snowballs down at him.

"You guys oughta just leave me here," he argued between clenched teeth as Chaffee stuffed more and more of the cottonlike Curlex into his wounded leg. If someone had given him a bullet to chew on, he would've gnawed it in half hours ago, but at least thanks to the cool-headed medic, he wasn't bleeding out. At least not yet. "Before you all get killed."

"What?" Tremayne turned on him. "You think you SOAR guys are tougher than a SEAL?"

"I didn't say that."

"You implied it."

McKade stood over him, arms crossed, huge in the too-small white tunic and billowy pants that had him looking like an oversized Frosty the Snowman. Not that Shane would ever dare accuse the sniper of that out loud.

"Whatever happened to that Night Stalker Creed y'all make such a fucking deal about?" Tremayne demanded. "The part about about never surrendering? Or never leaving a fallen comrade to fall into the hands of the enemy? That you'd rather fucking die than quit?"

"No way would I fucking surrender!" It took more energy than Shane wanted to expend to shout it, but he wasn't allowing that accusation to go unchallenged. "Just give me my rifle, set me up against a damn rock, and give command my coordinates so a bird can pick me up tonight."

"That's the stupidest fucking idea I ever

heard," McKade ground out.

Of all the SEALs Shane had worked with, Quinn McKade was the least likely to lose his temper. But right now his jaw was clenched so hard Shane wouldn't have been surprised if his teeth shattered.

"It also pisses me off that you'd even suggest that any of us, but most of all us SEALs, would leave any man behind," McKade continued. "There is no fucking way that's ever going to fucking happen!"

He knelt down in the snow. At six-feet-five, even on his knees, he towered over the SKED, so he bent down until they were nose to nose. "You fucking get that?"

Shane set his own jaw and glared up at the man who'd become as close to him as a brother. "It would be a little hard not to," he yelled back, the effort causing the icy air to knife his lungs. "Since you're fucking yelling in my fucking face!"

"Well, you fucking deserved it." McKade stood back up again, huge hands braced on his hips.

"At least unfasten the straps," Shane said, his own hot flare of temper cooling. "If we come under really heavy fire and things go south, I don't want to be tied down."

McKade stared at him hard. And long.

All around them men were holding

their breath.

Finally, the SEAL sniper crouched down and sliced through the straps with his KA-BAR. "You fall off this thing, you're going to have to crawl your skinny butt back on by yourself," he warned.

"Roger that," Shane shot back.

"Coffee break's over, ladies," Tremayne called out to the others who'd been watching the conflict. "Let's get humping."

There was not a single muttered word of complaint. Shane wasn't sure whether that was because they totally agreed with the SEALs, or they were afraid if anyone opened their piehole to say anything negative, McKade would shoot them.

Chaffee walked alongside the SKED as they continued on up the mountainside. "You want some morphine?" he asked.

The offer wasn't real encouraging, given that he'd already told Shane that since morphine lowered the heart rate, it would be risky to give it to him at this altitude. He wondered if the medic's change of heart meant he was already close to dying, like the Marine who hadn't even stirred during any of the firefights.

Besides, if he'd really wanted morphine, he could've used his own; no SOAR pilot or crew member ever went on a mission without a morphine Tubex tucked in their first-aid pocket. Just in case.

"Hell, no," he said.

The medic nodded. "Good."

As they trudged back up the mountainside, a single refrain kept repeating over and over again in Shane's head.

"Night Stalkers don't quit!"

8

Baghdad, Iraq
One year earlier

Having been up in the north, flying Special Forces members of Task Force 20 around in their search for Saddam, Shane had been away from Baghdad for three weeks. And during much of that time, he'd spent a lot of time thinking about Captain Kirby Campbell.

He'd been lying on his stomach, his butt ignominiously bared, waiting for treatment in the cubicle the triage nurse had stuck him in. The moment Kirby had opened that white privacy curtain, the air in the small space had turned instantly electric, like heat lightning shimmering on the horizon.

Her lips, the petal-pink color of peonies in his mother's garden, were bare of any artificial color or gloss. The urge to taste them hit like a bolt of lightning from a clear blue sky.

And that was just for starters. Shane wanted to taste the rest of her, too. Every lush, womanly inch.

She hadn't really given him any sign that she might be interested. In fact, she'd been brisk and efficient. Of course, being an Army officer, she knew better than to flirt on the job.

If she'd stuck around long enough for him to have gotten out of that undignified position on that steel treatment table, he would've put a move on her.

But before he could get a chance to even suggest they might go out for a pizza, she'd been called out to treat a soldier wounded by a tank gun barrel that had swung around while he'd been driving by atop his Humvee. The barrel had smashed into his face, and from what Shane could tell, it had shattered every single bone.

So he hadn't even gotten to say good-bye before heading out again. But even while he flew over the miles of desert, he couldn't stop thinking about the sexy military doctor, who in no way resembled *M*A*S*H*'s Hawkeye Pierce.

Which was why the first thing he did when returning to the fortress that was the Green Zone was to head to the CHS.

He'd just reached the hospital when two

Humvees came roaring up right next to the hospital doors. The driver of the front one, obviously the top dog of the pack, shouted instructions to the others before tearing into the hospital.

Thirty seconds later, he'd returned with CSH medics, who, with the other soldiers' help, loaded four injured men onto gurneys, then raced back into the ER with the team members bringing up the rear. There was a lot of cursing and yelling, and adrenaline pumping so hard Shane could almost smell it over the sweat, dust, and blood.

Their long hair and lack of identifying patches revealed them to be Special Forces. Shane might not know them personally, but being a SOAR pilot himself made them his brothers, so he didn't hesitate to go in with them.

While the team leader — so furious a vein was pulsing on his forehead, making him look in danger of stroking out — yelled about goddamn delays at the goddamn gate leading into the goddamn Green Zone, the medical team began to triage their new patients.

Shreds of clothing, equipment, watches, dog tags hit the floor, jettisoned in the attempt to save lives.

Unable to leave, Shane backed up against

a wall next to an American flag, staying out of the way as he watched the woman he'd come here to see do chest compressions on a soldier who had more gaping wounds than Shane could count, exposing bones and torn muscle tissue embedded with dirt and shrapnel.

Meanwhile, one of the uninjured, who'd picked up a bloodied envelope that had fallen from his buddy's shirt pocket — probably a letter from home, Shane thought — was shouting for him to "Keep fightin'! You're gonna to make it!"

He screamed the words, as if shouting them could make them true. His accent was from below the Mason-Dixon line, maybe Mississippi or Alabama. But the frantic tone was a long way from a soft Southern drawl. "You're gonna be okay, Jimmy boy!"

The second soldier's leg was barely attached, causing blood to gush onto the floor, turning it red.

When a medic asked the third soldier if he could move his hand, he couldn't.

No shit, Sherlock, Shane thought. Since it looked as if it'd been broken in about a hundred pieces.

Outside the hospital, a series of thuds from insurgent bombs erupted, sounding like massive, backfiring engines. Apparently accustomed to such sounds, and utterly focused on their patients' wounds, not one of the doctors or nurses bothered to look up.

The fourth soldier had taken a bullet in the head, but after being quickly stabilized, he and the guys with the bloody leg and broken hand were rushed out of the ER, destined for Balad, the Trauma III Air Force theater hospital sixty miles north of Baghdad.

Shane had been in Iraq long enough to know no one stayed in this place long. Medical care downrange worked like a conveyor belt. Any wounded soldier injured in Baghdad would probably land here first, with the more serious being coptered out to Balad.

After Balad, they'd be flown on a C-17 to Landstuhl Regional Medical Center at Ramstein Air Force Base in Germany.

Then, finally, back home to the United States.

Those less severely injured were usually sent to a U.S. base in Kuwait for a few weeks' convalescence. After which they'd return to duty.

One of the soldiers who'd stormed in with his unit had been triaged and was sitting in a chair, waiting patiently for someone to stitch up a slash down the side of his face. His eyes were open but glazed, and in that thousand-yard stare, Shane could see whatever horror they'd experienced out there beyond the relative safety of the Green Zone.

The electronic beat of the heart monitor attached to the soldier Kirby was working on suddenly turned into a long single note as he flatlined.

She shook her head. Briefly closed her eyes, then called the time of death.

Turning to the soldier's buddy, who had tears pouring down his cheeks, she touched his arm and said, "I'm sorry."

"Thank you for doin' your best to save him, ma'am," he choked out.

From the floor she plucked the dog tags that had been ripped off him and checked the engraving. "Corporal Tyree was Protestant?"

The soldier nodded. "Yes, ma'am. A Methodist. He'd always go to services whenever we happened to be in some camp when they were bein' held."

"Well, then, I think we should say a prayer together, soldier," she said, stripping off her latex gloves.

And as Shane watched, she gently took the grieving young man's hand in hers, and although he couldn't quite hear all of what she was saying, he did pick up on her asking that both the corporal's life and tragic, too-early death would help hasten a much-needed peace and bring the war to an end.

The leader, who'd been the first off the Hummer, came over for the prayer, as did the rest of the unit. And for those brief couple of moments, silence descended over the ER.

And then, just like that, the moment of peace was over, and everyone got back to business as usual.

Except for Kirby, who turned toward Shane. She seemed unsurprised to see him, making him wonder if she'd been aware of his presence all along. Even though he'd always considered himself an expert at compartmentalizing, that impressed the hell out of Shane.

"Well, isn't this is a surprise," she said, coming over to stand a professional three feet from him. "What can I do for you, Captain?" She skimmed a look over him. "You don't look like a man who needs any more shrapnel pulled out of him."

"I've managed to stay out of trouble," he responded.

She was wearing a boxy blue scrub shirt over BDU cammie trousers she'd tucked into a pair of bloodied combat boots. She wasn't wearing a bit of makeup, and the dark shadows beneath her eyes told of a lack of sleep. But she was still the sexiest woman he'd ever seen.

"I'm glad to hear that." She folded her arms, still waiting for the reason for his appearance in her ER.

With his hands sweating and his ears actually burning like a sixteen-year-old nerd's while he was trying to get up the nerve to ask the head cheerleader for a date to the prom, Shane said, "That was real impressive." He waved a hand around the room. "The way you all kept so cool."

Her eyes, the deep purplish blue of meadow wildflowers he'd grown up with back home, saddened.

"It's our patients' emergencies, not ours," she said mildly. "Our job is to try to establish calm from chaos. Much as I imagine you Special Forces types do when you're out on the front lines."

He'd been so focused on the sexual punch the first time they'd been together, he hadn't stopped to consider that, other than them both being in the military, they might actually have something in common.

"I'm here for the next forty-eight hours," he said. Because he was unreasonably tempted to skim a finger beneath those fatigued eyes, which he feared would just lead to a lot of inappropriate touching, he stuck his hands in the pockets of his BDU to keep them out of trouble. "I was hoping to spend some of them with you."

She tilted her head. Narrowed her eyes. "How many hours, exactly, were you hoping for?"

"As many as I could get."

"Well." She glanced around the ER, where medics, nurses, and other doctors were treating the less severely wounded patients. "As it happens, I have some time saved up myself."

She reached into a pocket of her trousers, pulled out a set of keys, and took one off the ring. "My trailer's not all that large, but it's home." She gave him instructions on how to find it. "My shift ends at sixteen thirty hours. I'll meet up with you then.

"Meanwhile, no offense, Captain, but you look as if you could use a shower and some sleep. Oh, and there's a bottle of Glenfiddich in the cupboard above the bed."

Despite the seriousness of what he'd just witnessed, Shane grinned.

"Not only are you spectacular-looking, a great physician, and, from the way you prayed with that poor corporal who's probably going to have survivor guilt for a very long time, a very warm and caring person, you also managed to get hold of single-malt Scotch in this country. My admiration, Captain, knows no bounds. I don't suppose you'd marry me?"

"I'll take it under consideration," she said mildly. "After I check you out in bed. Wouldn't want to find myself stuck for life with a dud."

She pointed toward the door. "If I'm going to arrange for some R and R, I need to get back to work. So go."

He saluted briskly. "Yes, ma'am."

She sure as hell hadn't been kidding about her hootch being small. Shane figured it was about a hundred and fifty, maybe sixty, square feet, tops. But it had a bed, a shower, and in just a few hours, the sexy captain would be home.

Life, he thought, as he located the bottle of Scotch, didn't get much better than that.

9

Unable to slow down enough to catch her breath, Kirby had sent Lita to check on the injured teenager twice, and each time the nurse reported back that he was regaining consciousness and seemed to be doing as well as could be expected under the circumstances.

With the clock ticking down, she was about to go examine him herself, when the tent flap opened and a bearded man with long hair walked in.

"We need a doctor," he announced.

He might be wearing native clothing, but his accent was definitely Southern. One of the Carolinas, perhaps. From the square jaw you could park a Hummer on beneath that dark beard, rigidly defined muscles beneath the snug tunic, and steely, gunmetal gray eyes, he had SPECIAL FORCES WARRIOR written all over him.

"I'm a doctor." She dug into her supply

kit and handed a lollipop to the child she'd just treated for minor burns on the leg from when a cooking pot had tipped over. "And you're in the wrong country."

"We've got wounded."

"And the military's got hospitals." It wasn't that she didn't care. But treating an American military man in this camp would only undermine her mission.

"Nowhere closer than Gardez. Which we can't get to until the command sends a helo to exfil — that's —"

"I know what it is." She held out her hand. "Former Captain Kirby Campbell, at your service. My last Army posting was in Baghdad."

He blew out a short, quick breath she suspected was relief that he didn't have to go through the entire song and dance, and shook her extended hand. "Good to meet you, Doc."

He did not, she noticed, give his name, rank, or affiliation. "You do realize you've crossed the border?"

"Didn't have any choice. Our pilot was critically wounded when our helo got shot down. We've already lost too many men today, including a Marine who checked out on our way up here, and this one will god-damn die if he doesn't get more treatment than our medic — who's damn good, by the way, but there are limits — can give him. And, like I was going to say, CENTCOM's refusing to exfil us until dark."

"Because they don't want to risk another copter."

"Roger that." He gave her an admiring look. "Damned if you aren't the real deal."

"Don't tell me anything," she said. There was no other decision to make. A patient needed her help. End of story. "Not rank or serial number. For any of you."

If they didn't exist, she wouldn't have to be specific in her report.

"That's cool, Captain," he said. "But even though we're black, now that we've shown up here, it's going to be real hard to keep our presence a secret, especially with Al Jazeera television so eager to broadcast any negative stuff they can get about U.S. forces. Which means we're going to have to put it in our report to our own command, anyway."

They both knew the shit was going to hit the fan when that happened. Yet she wasn't surprised at their behavior. She'd been in the military long enough to know they lived by the "Leave no man behind" axiom.

There wasn't one of them, from any of the services, who wouldn't risk death — or, in this case, court-martial — for one of their own.

"Bring him in."

A quartet of exhausted-looking men, a couple whose faces beneath the turbans they'd managed to pick up from somewhere didn't look old enough to shave, let alone be fighting a battle in these deadly mountains, carried in the SKED.

Her patient was beneath a pile of blankets that smelled like wood smoke. Although the filthy wool was white from the snow that had fallen on it, she could practically see fleas doing a happy dance at having latched on to a new human host.

"It's his leg," one of the two men who'd followed the patient in said. "He got hit with a tracer round. I've stuffed the wound with Curlex, given him Heparin and oxygen, but . . ."

The man, obviously a medic, looked both frustrated and a little bewildered. As if he couldn't comprehend the idea of anyone dying on his watch.

And didn't she know that feeling all too well?

She knelt down and pulled off the blankets — her eye drawn directly to the bloody and mangled leg wound as she pulled on a pair of gloves.

"The leg's probably going to have to come off." She'd seen too many of the same type of wounds from IED blasts. "Above the wound."

"That's what we brought him here for," the first man, who was obviously their leader, said.

"Look around," she said, waving a gloved hand at the interior of the tent. "This isn't exactly Johns Hopkins. Hell, it isn't even County General," she named the fictional television hospital.

As serendipitous as it might sound, she'd decided to become a doctor because of *ER,* which had debuted while she was in high school.

The army had helped pay her way through medical school, and Kirby's only regret was that she'd never gotten to work with George Clooney.

"Military injuries are more complex than those in civilian life," she said.

"That's why we risked coming here," the medic entered the argument. "I've done all I can. And without getting exfil before dark, you're our only chance."

"And how, exactly, do you plan to get evacuated out of here?"

"Don't worry. We've got that covered."

"There's something you need to know,"

she said. "Something that will probably cause a problem."

"That's pretty much been the kind of day we've had so far. Feel like sharing?"

ER work had taught Kirby to impart a great deal of information quickly, in as few words as possible.

"Where are they?" he asked after she'd told him about the terrorists.

"At the far edge of the camp." She described their location.

"And there's a dozen?"

"Thirteen, counting the boy. Who won't be in any shape to help."

"Hell," the big guy, whose name she'd probably never know, said. "I thought you were talking about a *real* problem. Not a mosquito-sized one. We'll handle them. After you take care of our guy."

It wasn't as if she hadn't done preliminary amputations before, back in Iraq. Munitions focused destructive forces on extremities, creating a particularly complex wound with fragments of the weapon and other debris being driven into it.

As in this man's case, it had also blasted away clothing and soft tissue, leaving exposed bone, a flap of skin, and all the unsterile debris — and she didn't even want to think about those fleas — forced between the membranes that connected the skin to the muscle.

"We'd be risking systemic infection, which would lead to a multisystem organ failure. Which, even if he didn't die, would only result in the need to reamputate at a higher and less functional level."

"In case you haven't noticed, Doc, he's not exactly functional right now," another man, who'd come in with the medic and was larger than any Afghan she'd ever seen — which resulted in his obviously borrowed pants stopping several inches short of his boots, revealing Thinsulate long underwear — pointed out.

She folded her arms and looked a long, long way up at him. "You don't look as if this is your first rodeo, so you should know that battlefield wounds are initially left open because of a high risk of infection."

"Leave it open much longer and he's not going to have any blood left," the man, who, from his long hair and beard, she took to be another Special Ops guy, argued.

"I can clean out the wound. Debride it. And get some whole blood into his system, which should help stabilize him. But I spent enough time dealing with the same type of injury in Iraq to know that a staged amputation is honestly the best way to go. You need to get him to Gardez."

"Terrific." He folded arms the size of oak tree limbs and gave her a hard stare she suspected proved intimidating when inter-rogating captured terrorists. "Why don't you just get out your magic carpet and we'll fly him the fuck out of here right now."

Knowing that they must have had a hor-rific day, and understanding the band-of-brothers bond that existed among military men, Kirby didn't call him on his sarcasm.

"I thought you had a plan to get him out of here."

"We do. But if something isn't done, like, now, he's not going to make it long enough for us to pull it off."

Not wanting to waste any more valuable time arguing, intending to take vital signs, she moved her gaze from his shattered and bloodied leg to the wounded man's face.

And couldn't prevent the gasp from escap-ing her lips.

"What's wrong?" the medic and the team's leader asked at the same time.

Still stunned, she ignored them.

"Shane?" she asked.

Since he'd been wrapped up in the blan-ket, they hadn't tried to change his clothes. Like all Spec Ops guys, he'd torn all the insignia off his uniform and was wearing only his last name and blood type. But even as bad as he looked — which was dreadful — she instantly recognized the SOAR pilot.

"You know him?" the large man who'd argued with her asked.

"I met him while I was posted at the twenty-eighth Cash in Iraq," she said, pronouncing the acronym. She pressed her fingers against his throat, counting out the thready, too-weak pulse.

"Hot damn. You're —"

The leader slammed his mouth shut.

But not soon enough.

Kirby was not going to allow herself to be embarrassed. She knew that men in war zones were the same as men everywhere. But more so. Conversations invariably ended up being about women and sex. Which meant that there was a good chance these men knew all about her crazed time with Shane Garrett. Maybe they even knew about her tattoo.

So? At the moment, embarrassment was way down at the bottom of her priorities list.

"How long has he been unconscious?" she asked.

"He's been drifting in and out for about an hour," the medic responded. "Which is why I didn't want to give him any morphine."

"And he wouldn't have asked."

"Would've bit his tongue off first," the big guy agreed.

"He needs to be stabilized before surgery."

"If you've got some trick up your sleeve on how to do that, I'd like to hear it," the guy obviously in control of this mission said. His quiet tone was more forceful than the loudest shout. "Otherwise, it looks as if you've drawn the short straw today, Doc."

Having been in Baghdad during the worst days, Kirby had never imagined wishing she were back in Iraq. Since joining WMR, she'd grown accustomed to working under the most primitive conditions. But at this moment, she'd give anything for even a bit of the high-tech equipment she'd had back at the CSH.

She touched his face, preparing to pull back his lids to check his pupils, when his Hershey-brown eyes suddenly opened and looked directly into hers.

"Kirby?" She watched as the man she'd never been able to get out of her mind tried to focus. "Wow. That's funny. I was just dreaming about you. Maybe I still am?"

He tried to lift a hand but lacked the strength. She told herself that it was only exhaustion from jet lag, along with a trying day, that caused her eyes to well up.

"Or is this one of those near-death things, and all my friends are here to tell me good-bye?"

"Don't talk like that," she said quickly. "You are *not* going to die." Granted, the prognosis was not good — okay, it was flat-out lousy — but there was no way Kirby was going to allow herself to think other-wise. "We won't let you."

He looked up at the others. "Didn't I tell you she was the best?"

"Yeah." The big guy smiled. Oh, it was forced, and Kirby knew it was only done to reassure. But it was real and had her liking him.

"You're in luck," she said, turning her at-tention back to her patient. "Of all the relief hospitals in all the world, you just happened to end up in mine."

10

"So, what do you think?" Quinn asked Zach.

They'd left the tent to talk in private. Countless eyes were on them, none of the refugees seeming fooled by their native outfits.

Some looked too stunned by their circumstances to give a shit that a bunch of American military men had landed in their midst. Some looked suspicious. Others looked downright hostile. Unfortunately, every man in the place appeared to be armed. Including those terrorists the doc had told them about.

"The deal was I'd have O'Halloran call the spook when we were ready for that helo to get us out of here and back to base," he reminded Quinn.

"There's a good chance we might have to fight our way out."

"So what else is new?" Zach looked around. "Okay, maybe this isn't turning out as good as it could be. But it sure as hell beats Garrett dying while waiting for exfil." He looked down at his black dive watch. "It's eleven thirty-five."

Quinn grinned, immediately catching his drift. "I knew our luck had to change."

11

Kirby had done all she could. She'd cleaned the wound — and poured in hemostatic material designed to control high-volume arterial bleeding. Because she was afraid to give Shane too much morphine at this altitude, she'd stuck as much as possible to injecting local anesthetic.

Except for a few muttered curses and the occasional flinch, he'd remained amazingly stoic.

"This is really weird," he said, after she'd finished pumping him full of blood to replace what he'd lost. "I was thinking about you right before my helo got hit with that damn RPG. Wondering where you were and how you were doing. I was even planning to track you down after this mission. And, wow, here you are."

"News flash, Captain," Kirby said as she wrapped his leg in sterile bandages, "getting yourself shot out of the sky just for a reunion was overkill. Even for you."

"What can I say?" Somehow, through the pain he managed that cocky, flyboy smile that had always had the power to melt. Oh, it might only be about a third of the wattage she remembered, but it was still damn effective. "I figured you'd appreciate the grand gesture."

"You're incorrigible."

"Yeah. I remember you saying that a time or two. Especially that time —"

"Shut up." She put two fingers over the lips she could still, in her dreams, taste. He'd always tasted like cinnamon, from the Big Red gum he chewed. "You need to conserve your strength."

He looked inclined to argue, when the all-too-familiar *whomp, whomp, whomp* of a helicopter's rotor blades drew her attention.

In Iraq, that sound had meant incoming trauma patients. Even now, it spiked her pulse rate and sent adrenaline surging through her.

"Stay here," she said, immediately realizing how stupid that sounded. Like he was going to get up and go crawling out to do battle on his one good leg?

Unfortunately, knowing him as well as she did, Kirby wouldn't have been at all surprised if he'd tried to do exactly that. "And stay quiet."

12

She went outside, looking up at the incoming copter. Given that the Iraqi government had bought a lot of helicopters from Poland, as it grew closer, she recognized it as Russian.

Was it, she worried, Imam Jalaluddin, come to collect his injured son?

And wasn't that just what they all needed?

"Relax," the leader, who'd been outside conferring with the larger man, said. "It's ours."

"Ours, as in CIA," she said.

"Hey." His grin was quick and belied the seriousness of their situation. "Surely you've heard of 'Don't ask, don't tell,' Doc." His expression sobered. "I'm sorry to bring this down on you," he said. "It could make your work here more difficult."

And wasn't he just the master of understatement?

"Maybe you can have one of your baby

soldiers put a gun on me when you leave," she suggested. "At least make it look as if I didn't have any choice."

"That's a good idea," he said. "But they're not *baby* soldiers. I don't know what they were when they climbed on the helo. But they definitely became men today."

"Point taken." Kirby felt duly chastised.

The men worked well together, which was what they were trained to do. Still, the way they'd gotten Shane back on the SKED, this time wrapped in a non-flea-ridden silver space blanket she'd contributed, and out of the tent, was impressive.

As the copter hovered to land on the outskirts of the camp, blowing down a handful of tents created from blue tarps, people scattered.

Guns were drawn. Kirby prayed there wasn't going to be a battle.

Damn. The Americans weren't the only ones who had use for that copter. The men who'd held those guns on her would un-doubtedly rather fly back to wherever the father was hiding out than carry the boy back into the mountains.

"This could be bad," she murmured, not wanting to think of what could happen if bullets started flying. "In case you haven't noticed, you're a bit outnumbered."

"Don't worry, Doc," the big guy said. "We're only talking about, oh, a hundred of them against each one of us."

"Piece of cake," the leader said cockily.

"You realize that you're all crazy," she said. But her voice held both the respect and the affection she had for these brave men. There was a reason they called them *Special* Forces.

"Spoken by someone who should know," a deep voice from the SKED said, with what, amazingly, given that he'd been unconscious when he'd arrived, sounded like humor.

One of the things she'd loved about the SOAR pilot was that he'd always managed to find something positive in any situation.

"The sane thing for you to have done after leaving the Army was land yourself some cushy job in a big-city hospital where you could get beaucoup bucks. But instead, you ended up here in what's gotta be one of the lower rings of hell," Shane said, unwittingly echoing her own thoughts this morning.

Had it been only this morning? It seemed a lifetime ago.

"Not that I'm not real glad to see you," he said. "And not just because you're the best doctor in these mountains."

"I'm the *only* doctor in these mountains."

"Well, there is that," he allowed. His brown eyes, which had been hazy from the pain and the scant amount of morphine she'd risked giving him, suddenly and unexpectedly cleared, like a camera lens coming into sharp focus.

"But if I had to get blown out of the sky, there isn't any other hospital I'd rather land in than yours, Captain."

Kirby was a physician. Not only that, during her years as an Army CSH doctor, there wasn't much she hadn't seen. And while she'd never been able to close her heart to her patients, she'd learned early in her internship to save the tears for when she could weep in private.

But that didn't stop the mist from blurring her vision as she crouched down beside the SKED and tucked the shiny blanket more snuggly around him.

"Gotta move out," the leader said abruptly, saving her from having to come up with a response.

She stood up. Folded her arms.

"Good luck," she said.

"SEALs make their own luck," the big guy said.

"Rangers, too," one of the younger soldiers said.

She knew Spec Ops guys believed in their

invincibility. Most of the ones she'd met believed they could outrun locomotives and leap tall buildings in a single bound. Not to mention that myth about bullets bouncing off them.

As she watched them head toward the waiting copter, Kirby could only hope that would prove true today.

13

The situation, which had been bad from the beginning, really sucked.

Except for the part about fate landing him in Kirby's medical camp.

Shane had thought, at the time, that would have done it. That the torch he'd been carrying for her while ferrying those SEALs all over northern Iraq, hunting Saddam, would be doused.

He'd been wrong. In fact, just the opposite had happened. The more he'd been with the sexy captain, the more he'd wanted her. And although she'd continued to play the affair, or relationship, or whatever the hell it was they had going, as if it'd been an extended spring break in Baghdad, he'd begun to think they'd connected.

In more ways than just the what-fits-where physical part of their relationship. Not that they hadn't fit perfectly. In fact, the sex got more mind-blowing every time they were together.

He'd just decided that he was the luckiest son of a bitch in the universe, and was going to suggest taking their *thing* to the next level and see how it went, when damned if Special Forces hadn't found Saddam in that spider hole, causing him to be shipped out to Afghanistan.

Then a month after that, she'd been rotated out to Heidelberg, and suddenly his e-mails seemed to all land in a black hole. He'd even used one of those phone cards USO handed out to call her, but her tone had been distant. Almost remote.

No. Not almost. Really, really remote.

Which could only mean that his feelings had been one-sided. Oh, he didn't believe she'd just been a Night Stalker groupie. While they might not get the press that the SEALs or D-Boys did, a SOAR pilot never left a bar alone unless he wanted to.

No. Captain Kirby Campbell hadn't been a groupie.

But, apparently, all she'd wanted from him were a few laughs and a lot of sex.

The ironic thing was that at any other time in his life, he'd have been singing hosannas to find a multiorgasmic woman who only wanted his body.

But, dammit, Shane had wanted more.

Which was why he'd decided to find her and convince her they belonged together.

Bygones, he told himself as he dragged his mind back to her refugee camp he hadn't even been aware of being carried through when they'd arrived.

Jeezus. There was a reason this was regarded as the most armed region in the world. Instead of Game Boys or basketballs, even the kids were lugging around AK47s and ammo belts. It only took one look at the all the guns in the camp to totally wake him up.

And, here was a big plus, all the adrenaline racing through his veins numbed the pain.

"You gotta give me back my gun," he said as they began forging their way through the crowd.

Not a single person moved to stop them. But their eyes were hard. And deadly.

Tremayne looked down at him. "You sure?"

"Do tangos shit in the woods?"

Tremayne shrugged and handed him back his M4. "That doc's good," he said.

"The best," Shane said.

"And hot," McKade volunteered, even as his head kept moving, scanning the crowd, watching for the slightest movement.

"Which explains why, when you woke up

enough to recognize her, little red hearts started doing the South Carolina shag in your eyes, flyboy," Tremayne said.

"Ha ha ha," Shane said, even as he suspected that accusation might be true.

Like every pilot who'd spent thousands of hours listening to radio traffic, he'd learned to tune out what was unessential, while immediately catching what affected him. He'd been drifting in and out of consciousness, only vaguely aware of people talking around him when that one all-too-familiar voice cut through the clutter.

Shane decided that the little spurt of lust he'd felt when Kirby had bent over him was proof he was going to live.

"Tangos at nine o'clock," Tremayne said quietly.

Quinn's head didn't move, but Shane knew they both were checking out the terrorists Kirby had told them about.

"You going to try to snatch the kid?" Shane asked.

"Any other time, I would," Tremayne answered. "If I could manage it without getting the doc killed. See what he knows, maybe even use him for a bargaining chip. But right now our mission is to get the hell out of here without any more lives lost."

"What if they shoot first?"

"We shoot back. But I don't think that's going to happen."

"Why not?" Shane tilted his head just enough to the left to see the group of tangos in question. They sure as hell didn't look harmless.

"First of all, they've got the kid to protect. If we try to grab him, they'd go off, all guns blasting. Then again, if this place turned into the O.K. Corral, which we'd make damn sure it did, how'd you like to be the guy who has to explain to Imam Jalaluddin that you'd gotten his kid killed?"

"Heads would probably roll."

"Literally," McKade said.

"Besides," Tremayne continued, "the guy in charge realizes that all we want is the same thing they want. To have our wounded patched up and get the hell out of here."

That made sense, Shane decided. But . . .

"What if one of the so-called civilians in the camp decides to open up?"

"That's when the second reason we're getting out of here alive kicks in," McKade said.

"What's that?"

Tremayne looked down at his watch. "It's eleven fifty-nine hours."

"So?"

Before either of the SEALs could answer,

somewhere in the crowd, someone with a megaphone began calling the *adham,* the call to prayer devout Muslims were required to answer five times a day.

Every man in the camp knelt for the *Dhur,* the noontime prayer.

All except one. The tall, armed-to-the-teeth man Kirby had pointed out as the terrorist leader.

Tremayne lifted up both gloved hands, palms out, a universal signal to show he wasn't looking for any trouble.

After a moment's hesitation, the man did the same.

"Next time," Tremayne murmured.

Although he was too far away to hear, the man must have sensed the SEAL's words, because he slowly nodded.

Still embarrassed as hell that he couldn't make it on his own, Shane allowed the Rangers — who'd definitely earned their Spec Ops cred today — to lift him into the bird.

The helo was a Russian M17, which Shane considered inferior in every way to his beloved Chinook those damn tangos had shot down. The manufacturing was Russian-cheesy; it only had the capability of carrying thirty troops, compared to the Chinook's fifty-five; and its speed was a mere one hundred and thirty-five knots, compared to his Chinook's one fifty-four.

Still, as the bird lifted off, he decided that he wasn't exactly in any position to be picky.

Once they were safely in the air, the burst of adrenaline wore off. Shane closed his eyes and drifted back into the void. And just as he'd been doing earlier, right before he'd come to and found himself in that hospital tent, he returned to dreaming of hot, mind-blowing sex with former Army Captain Kirby Campbell.

14

Shane wasn't the only one taking a stroll down memory lane. Since the appearance of the Americans, the entire camp had suddenly gone quiet. Those who had shelters had gone indoors, and the terrorists with Imam Jalaluddin's son had disappeared back into the mountains.

Telling Lita and Anne that she was going to try to steal twenty minutes to see if a nap could do anything for the jet lag that crashed down on her, Kirby went into the green tent next to the hospital tent, lay down on one of the narrow cots, and closed her eyes.

But she couldn't sleep. Instead, her mind kept spinning back to that time in Iraq. Especially that day Shane had surprised her by showing up again at the CSH.

Kirby had never taken sex casually, but she hadn't been able to get the handsome-as-sin Night Stalker out of her mind.

Which was why, even though he was the

kind of man mamas the world over warned their daughters about, and even though she could be the poster girl for safe sex, without allowing herself to consider all the reasons it might be a mistake, she'd given him her keys.

Then, in case he hadn't gotten the message of the keys, which certainly hadn't been the least bit subtle, and worried he might mistakenly believe she was just feeling doctorly toward him (and giving him a private place to rest), she'd flat-out assured him that he was about to get lucky.

Later, as she walked from the building — which had once been a private hospital for Saddam Hussein and his friends and family — to her trailer, she found herself wishing that she'd instead suggested meeting for kung pao chicken and fried rice at one of the two Chinese restaurants near the Imperial Palace.

That would've given her time to clean up. To get the stench of disinfectant, blood, and death out of her skin, hair, and clothes.

"Stupid, stupid, stupid," she muttered.

But she'd always been a pragmatist, and since she doubted that some fairy godmother was suddenly going to appear in the Green Zone with a pumpkin coach and turn her scrub shirt and cammie trousers into a sparkly white ball gown, and her blood-stained boots into glass slippers, she was just going to have to make the best of it.

Kirby needn't have worried.

She'd no sooner walked in the door when he stood up from the too-short couch he'd been lying on, pulled her into his arms, and before she could utter a word of welcome or protest, took her mouth.

The shock was instant and reverberated through her like a nuclear blast.

"I need to take a shower," she managed to say as his ravenous mouth created havoc with every cell in her body.

"Later." His teeth nipped at her lower lip.

"Later." Refusing to stop to think, Kirby twined her arms around his neck and pressed her body even tighter against his.

While she might not indulge in one-night stands, Kirby was no virgin. She'd had sex. Good sex. Even, on occasion, great sex. But she'd never experienced such instantaneous, raw, hot need.

Her mouth turned as greedy as his, as desperate. Swamped with sensations, drowning in desire, she let her head cloud and surrendered to the sensations caused by his hungry mouth and wickedly clever hands.

He was kissing her like he wanted to eat her up.

Which was exactly what Kirby wanted him to do.

"God, I want you." His voice was thick and harsh as he roughened the kiss.

Because she was on the verge of coming — from a kiss! she thought through her spinning senses — she dragged her mouth from his.

"I can tell." She drew in a deep breath that was meant to calm, but didn't. "I just have one question."

"I'll tell you anything you want to know." His hands moved down her body, skimming over her breasts before tackling her belt.

"Do you have any blood left in your head?"

He laughed, a deep, rumbling sound that vibrated through her. He pulled the belt through the loops and tossed it onto the floor. Then unzipped her BDU trousers and slipped a long, dark finger between her distressingly practical cotton nude-colored panties and her flame-hot skin.

Two fingers replaced the one, combing though the curls between her thighs before probing moist, feminine folds.

Somewhere in the distance, a mortar exploded, causing the trailer to shake.

As his thumb began doing incredible things to her tingling flesh, Kirby didn't care.

Wanting to make him as needy as he was making her, she snaked her hand between their bodies and ripped open his own trousers. He was going commando, which made it so much easier to wrap her fingers around him.

He was hard as marble in her hand. But much, much hotter.

"You keep that up, Captain," he groaned as her hand began to move, "and we're going to have an early blastoff."

"That works for me." She tilted her head back, giving his wickedly clever mouth access to her throat.

"But not for me." His tongue dampened the hollow where her pulse was hammering like a rabbit's. "I've been thinking about this a long time and decided that I want to be in a bed the first time I'm inside you."

"Ah." Her body ached for release. "A traditionalist."

"I'm a country boy." His teeth closed on the lobe of her ear. "We're real big on tradition."

He was stroking her, inside and out, causing her legs to tremble and begin to go weak. "Though I'm up for swinging from the chandeliers in the Imperial Palace," he said, "we've got forty-eight hours to work our way up to the kinky stuff."

The idea of getting kinky with this man, along with the final flick of his wicked thumb, sent her over the edge.

Before the last of the ripples had faded, he pulled his head back.

Desire burned like flames in his eyes as he looked down into hers. "I'm considering changing my mind."

That wasn't what his body, which was grinding against hers, was saying.

"Oh?"

"Maybe the first time, I'll take you in the shower."

"That's not too far from traditional," she said breathlessly.

He released her, going down on his knees, his tongue creating a hot, wet swath up her thigh.

"Or maybe I'll take you this way in the shower."

His arrogance was pure Night Stalker. But as his mouth clamped on the damp crotch of the panties he hadn't yet taken off, the heat alone nearly making her come again, Kirby decided it was well deserved.

"Then, after I wash every inch of that delicious covergirl body, and make you come with just my mouth, I'll carry you, wet and slick, to bed."

He stood up and scooped her off her feet, bloody boots and all.

"Then," he said, "after I helmet up, I'm going to come inside you."

"Oh, God." She never realized she was multiorgasmic, but just that promise was nearly enough to push her over the edge.

"Did I tell you I grew up on a ranch?"

"I believe you mentioned it."

It was then that the image of that tight butt in boot-stacked Wranglers, smelling of sweat and hay and horse, had become permanently emblazoned on her mind.

"Well, we have a saying out West," he said as he carried her the few feet into the bathroom that was scarcely large enough to turn around in.

"Save a horse."

He bent his head and gave her a deep, tongue-tangling, soul-stealing kiss she could feel all the way to her toes.

"Ride a cowboy."

"Oh, God," she practically whimpered as he sat her on the undersized trailer toilet, turned on the shower, then got busy unlacing her boots.

It was the last thing she would say for a very long time.

15

Landstuhl, Germany

Although it wasn't easy finding out information on any member of the Special Forces, Kirby called in some markers throughout the military medical community.

It took a while, but eventually she learned from an Army captain, who'd heard it from a SEAL, who'd heard it from a member of the 160th Airborne, that the Russian copter had taken Shane first to Bagram, where he'd been stabilized, then to Ramstein Air Force Base, and then to Landstuhl Regional Medical Center.

Using a bit of political pull from her Army days, aided by the lucky fact that one of the surgeons at Bagram had been her superior officer at the 28th CSH, two weeks after Shane had shown up at the refugee camp, Kirby managed to hitch a ride on a C-17 carrying six wounded soldiers — one who was unconscious from a head wound, two with shrapnel wounds to the legs, lying on litters, and three ambulatory, one of whom told her he was suffering from severe headaches and PTSD — and the attendant medical crew.

Landstuhl was not only the largest military hospital in Europe, it was also the best. With a survival rate of nine out of every ten soldiers who reached the LRMC, Kirby took heart in the mere fact that Shane had made it here.

After landing at Ramstein, she and the others were loaded onto bulky American buses. The buses, painted dark blue with white crosses, looked like toys next to the gigantic cargo jet.

Weaving in and out of rows of parked aircraft, the buses made their way across the tarmac and through a base the size of a small city.

After passing though the gates, they continued down a long, wide highway off-limits to the public, then beneath the autobahn, on through the wooded mountain hamlet. Unlike Heidelberg, her last posting, which had been a bustling German city of one hundred forty thousand, Landstuhl was charmingly picturesque, with winding, narrow streets befitting its fourteenth-century beginning. There were several stone churches, houses were mostly whitewashed with red tile roofs, and a few trees were beginning to sprout early spring green leaves.

At any other time, Kirby might have enjoyed the scene that could have appeared on a postcard from the local tourism bureau.

But not today.

With nerves in a tangle, she waited until the wounded were helped off the bus and met by waiting medical teams clad in cammie BDUs and purple latex surgical gloves.

There was also a woman chaplain, who, Kirby noted, greeted each patient — even bending down to the unconscious soldier — by name.

"Your work is done for the moment," the chaplain told each of them soothingly. "You're in Germany now. And you're safe."

As eager as she was to get to Shane, Kirby paused to comment about the greeting.

"We always call them by name," the chaplain, who said she was an Episcopalian priest, explained. "And assure them that they don't have to worry anymore. Knowing that they're safe is an important part of the healing process. We welcome the unconscious ones, as well, and tell them the same thing, because you never know what they might be able to hear."

As a doctor, Kirby knew that was true. Although civilian visitors were not encouraged at Landstuhl, her former superior had called ahead. A nun, obviously one of the many civilian employees, told her in German-accented English how to find Captain Shane Garrett's room.

After walking what seemed a five-mile-long corridor (which, one of the medical team on the C-17 had informed her, was actually a mile and a half long), she reached his door.

She took a deep breath to calm her jittery nerves. It didn't work. As a physician, Kirby was familiar, even comfortable, in a hospital setting. But it was so much more difficult being here as a woman concerned about a man she'd begun to think she might be falling in love with.

He was watching television. Feeling uncharacteristically shy, not wanting to just barge in on him, she knocked on the open doorjamb.

He glanced up from the screen. A range of expressions moved across his face before he could garner control of them. First surprise, then something that looked like happiness, then discomfort, then . . . nothing.

"Hi." Since he hadn't invited her in, she

113

stayed in the doorway.

"Hi, yourself." His cautious tone was one she'd never heard from him before. "This is a surprise."

"I had a little time off from WMR." She didn't share how many strings she'd pulled to find a doctor willing to take her place at the Pakistani relief camp.

"So you figured, hey, why go to Cancún or Paris or even back to the States when you can spend your R&R at a military hospital?"

"I didn't feel like going to the beach, my French is about as strong as my Farsi, which is to say barely functional, and there's no one in the States I wanted to see."

She paused.

Nothing. He just sat there in the bed — his eyes a little glazed from pain meds in a gray and haggard face, his newly amputated leg heavily bandaged — looking at her as if she were a stranger instead of the woman he'd spent so many hours having hot, crazy sex with.

Maybe even making love with.

"May I come in?" she asked finally.

"Sure."

He shot another glance up at the TV, then muted the sound. But did not, Kirby noticed, turn it off.

So far, this wasn't the most encouraging welcome she'd ever received. It wasn't even as heartfelt as that unconscious patient had received from the chaplain. But reminding herself that depression was to be expected with new amputees, Kirby forced the smile to stay on her face as she crossed the room to stand beside the bed.

"You're looking a lot better than last time I saw you."

"Yeah. I've been told I clean up well."

She wondered if he remembered that she'd been the one to tell him that. Their first night together.

"I was talking about your color."

Her hand itched to brush some sunstreaked mink brown hair off his forehead. Since he didn't look all that thrilled to see her, she linked her fingers together to keep her hands to herself. For now.

"You were the color of chalk the last time I saw you. Obviously, you're receiving excellent care."

"You know what they say." He shrugged the broad shoulders that had filled out his flight suit so well. "If you make it to Landstuhl, you're good to go."

"That's certainly true."

She and Shane had always been amazingly comfortable with each other. Their relationship, while revolving mostly around sex, had also been easy.

Even natural.

This was not.

"I owe you a huge debt of gratitude," he said with a distressing formality she'd never — ever — heard from him before. "The doctors at Bagram said I could've had my ticket punched if it hadn't been for what you did for my leg in that camp."

"You don't have to thank me, Shane," she said. "I was —"

"Just doing your job," he cut her off.

"That wasn't what I was going to say." She untangled her fingers to rake a hand through her hair, appalled when she realized it was shaking. "I was going to say that when I saw you lying on that SKED, so horribly wounded, although I know it's medically impossible, I thought my heart had stopped. I've *never* been so nervous working on a patient in my life."

There. She'd given him an opening, let him know how much he meant to her. Not just professionally, as his doctor. But personally.

"Well, I guess that just shows what a super doctor you are," he said. "Obviously, the nerves didn't affect your work, because the surgeons in Afghanistan and here both said you'd done a bang-up job."

They could have been two strangers stuck sitting next to each other on a plane.

This conversation also wasn't getting them anywhere. It was time to try a different tack.

Rather than hold her own hand, she took away the remote, which he was still holding, from his. Then linked her fingers with his on top of the crisp white sheet. The gesture, which she'd done countless times before, now felt uncomfortably awkward.

"You've no idea how worried I've been about you."

"Well, as you can see, short of losing half my leg, I'm just doing jim-dandy."

The Shane she'd once known had been self-deprecating. Although it seemed he intended for her to take his words lightly, she knew they were no jest.

"Unfortunately, I knew you'd need amputation the minute I saw it." She lifted their joined hands and pressed her lips against his knuckles, which were still bruised and scraped from the crash. "But they're doing amazing things with prostheses these days."

"Yeah, that's what my therapist keeps telling me."

"So. I guess it could be worse."

God. How could she, a doctor used to discussing bad news with a patient, have said anything so ridiculously trite?

"I figured that out back at the crash site. When I didn't die like my copilot, or the LT. Or all those Marines and Rangers."

He pulled his hand back. Picked up the remote again.

"This isn't going well, is it?" she asked.

He sighed. Pinched the bridge of his nose. His eyes — framed by thick, long lashes that most women kept cosmetic companies in business trying to duplicate — were flatter than she'd ever imagined they could be.

"What do you want, Kirby?"

"I'm not sure," she admitted. "But I've been thinking about those days in Baghdad a lot lately, before you showed up at the camp — in fact, even on the drive up from Kabul, when I was wondering if you were flying up there above me — and I think maybe we were wrong."

"About what?" He could not have looked any more edgy if she'd tossed a grenade with the pin pulled into his lap.

"About our relationship just being about wartime sex." She took another deep breath. "I know that's what we used to joke about at the time. And what you'd reminded me the night before you flew off to Afghanistan."

Which had admittedly stung. Which was

why she'd been uncharacteristically remote with him when he'd finally called her. She still regretted that display of feminine pique.

"But what if it was more than that?"

"Kirby —"

"I think it *was* more," she cut him off, determined to finish what she'd come here to say. "I think maybe I'd begun to fall in love with you. Which was, to be perfectly honest, even scarier than those mortars being shot into the Green Zone.

"But then you got transferred to Afghanistan, and I was sent to Heidelberg, and, well, I don't know about you, but I convinced myself that it was better if we didn't try to muck up what we'd had with emotions, and maybe I'd been wrong, anyway. About our feelings."

"If there'd been anything there, we would've made it work," he said gently. "It wouldn't have just faded away because of distance."

That was precisely what she'd told herself. But it had become more and more difficult to believe. It was true, she'd discovered. You regretted most in life those things you *didn't* do. Much more than the things you *did*.

"Are you sure?"

"Dead sure."

She hated the finality in his voice. Wondered how many times he'd given the same "Hey, babe, it's been good, but it's over because I have to go fight the bad guys, and doing the wife and rug rats thing would get in the way of me saving the world" speech to other women.

Always having prided herself on her tenacity, Kirby wasn't prepared to throw in the towel quite yet.

"Landstuhl looks like a really nice town," she said.

"Since I was unconscious when I arrived, I haven't seen the place," he said. "But I'll take your word for it."

He couldn't have been any farther away if he'd suddenly been beamed to a base on Antarctica.

"It's really nice," she repeated. "Quaint. And picturesque. At least, what I saw of it driving over here from Ramstein. The bus driver told me there's a large American community living in town. Plus, a lot of the people working here at the hospital are civilians, so I was thinking —"

"No."

"Well, that certainly sounds definitive," she managed to say past the lump that had risen in her throat.

It took a major effort, but because he really did look as if he'd been through the wringer, she managed, just barely, to keep from pointing out that Captain Shane Garrett was not the boss of her and that now that she was out of the Army, she could work wherever the hell she pleased. Including Landstuhl Regional Medical Center.

He sighed again and looked at her with what actually appeared to be regret, or even pity, which Kirby found more hurtful than his earlier distance.

"What we had in Badghad was great, sweetheart," he said. "Better than great. It was one of the best times in my life, which is kinda weird when you factor in that I was also having bad guys trying to blow me out of the sky on a regular basis. But I enjoyed the hell out of it. And I liked and admired and respected you a whole lot —"

"You also screwed me six ways to Sunday," she reminded him.

"That was part of what made it so great." His grin was forced. "But it was more than that. I cared about you, Kirby. A whole lot."

"Me, too. About you."

"I know."

His gaze softened.

Oh, God. That *definitely* looked like pity.

"But we were living in our own insane sandbox universe," he said. "What we had in Iraq would never hold up in the real world."

"You don't know that."

Kirby had never begged for anything in her life. But she was willing to beg now, if that's what it took, for him to at least open up to the possibility that they might have a future together.

"Yeah." That distant look returned to his eyes, which drifted to the door, as if suggesting she might just want to take this opportunity to walk away. "I do."

"Well." Kirby was an intelligent woman. She had, after all, graduated in the top ten percent of her medical school class at USUHS. There was also the little fact that he couldn't have made himself more clear if he'd started waving semaphores in her face. *Go. Away. Now.* "So . . . I guess that's that."

"I really am sorry." He glanced up at the TV, which was broadcasting some stupid baseball game from the States.

Boston was losing to the Yankees in the eighth inning.

And she was losing him.

Again.

This time, Kirby realized, forever.

She blinked to fight off the mutinous tears stinging at the back of her lids. "Well, I'm really glad you're doing so well, and I've no doubt you'll be fit as a fiddle in no time at all."

Fit as a fiddle? Oh, shit. Had she really said that? The last person she'd ever known to use that expression had been her grandfather Campbell, who, as an Army Air Corps tail gunner, had flown thirty missions over Germany during World War II.

"So, I guess I'll be going."

In a perfect world, the cowboy SOAR pilot would've said, "Dammit to hell, Kirby Campbell, you're the only woman for me, so let's get married and we'll go back to the States and start our lives all over again. Together.

"Maybe we'll raise ourselves a passel of little cowboys and cowgirls on a ranch back in Oregon." He hadn't told her much about growing up, but he had mentioned riding bulls in local rodeos.

"Or if you'd rather go back home to San Diego, we'll buy ourselves a tidy little cottage somewhere close to the beach with a picket fence and a swing in the backyard for our kids. Because if you walk out that door, you'll be taking every reason I have to live right along with you."

That was what Captain Shane Garrett would say in a perfect world.

Unfortunately, as Kirby had learned the hard way, there were no perfect worlds.

"Thanks for coming all this way just to

123

check on me," he said instead. "And hey, again, thanks for saving my life."

She forced a brave smile as she wavered between leaving while she still possessed some small shred of dignity, or climbing up on that bed and strangling him with her bare hands.

"Hey." Opting for dignity, she forced a light note into her voice. "I was just doing my job."

She bent down to kiss him. So they'd been lovers. Surely they could leave this emotional train wreck as friends. What could be wrong with a simple good-bye kiss between friends?

Apparently, a lot.

He turned his head at the last second, causing her lips to brush his cheek.

It took every ounce of self-restraint Kirby possessed, but she managed, somehow, to keep from weeping until she was walking back down that long, long hallway.

It was only after she was gone that Shane, proving that even hotshot SOAR Night Stalkers could cry, put his pillow over his face.

Then bawled like a damn baby.

■ ■ ■ ■

PART TWO

■ ■ ■ ■

Night Stalkers never quit.
— U.S. Army SOAR motto

16

Monteleón, Central America
Eighteen months later

The Presidential Palace, which, unlike most architecture in the region, resembled the White House (had the home of every American president since John Adams been painted pink instead of white) sprawled atop a cliff overlooking the Caribbean Ocean. As if banished by presidential decree, the *garua,* a dense ocean mist that could roll in to cover the capital city of Ciudad Libertad for days at a time, had lifted, allowing spectacular views.

In one direction, the volcanic mountains that had given the country its name loomed, dark and forbidding. In the other direction, a tangerine sun sank into the sea, turning the water to a deep, burnished copper.

The gardens were a riot of color and scents. Servants, wearing embroidered white cotton shirts and black pants, moved silently, pouring wine, serving canapés, lighting the torches as dusk settled over the party. Torches that emitted an insecticide to keep the malaria-carrying mosquitoes away.

The waxy white night-blooming jasmine was beginning to open, its sultry, heady fragrance mingling with the expensive perfumes worn by the women guests and the aroma of sizzling slabs of beef, lobsters, and huge shrimp being grilled by native Indians, seeming of Mayan descent, over a wood-fired *parilla.*

While most barbecues Kirby had attended growing up back home in San Diego had been casual affairs, President General Juan Duarte Vasquez thrived on ostentation and conspicuous consumption; easy enough when you headed up a country that just happened to have been discovered to be sitting on one of the largest petroleum deposits in Latin America.

That it was beneath a reservation of the country's remaining indigenous tribes had not seemed to disturb either the president or the oil companies flooding into the country.

Unfortunately, the government — run by Vasquez's cronies and relatives — had never heard about the economic concept of trickle-down.

Which was why Kirby and the WMR were in Monteleón. As the government became richer, the ordinary people grew increasingly impoverished. Gazing around at the orchid centerpieces and gleaming crystal, china, and gold-plated cutlery, and having walked though the gilded nouveau-Graceland decorated interior to reach the garden party, Kirby decided that surrounded by so much sudden wealth and luxury, guests preferred to remain ignorant of what was happening outside the guarded gates of their palatial homes.

The dinner table conversation was much the same as Donald Trump and his pals might share in New York City. Stocks, bonds, deal making, polo, and shopping. And more shopping. From the blinding bling gracing the ears, throats, and wrists of all the women, Kirby figured diamond mines all over the world must've really had to kick into high gear since that first Monteleón gusher blew.

They did not, she noticed, discuss what had originally made them wealthy in the first place: the tall, innocent-looking cocoa plants and opium poppies that brightened up the mountainsides in brilliant streaks of red. Although oil had replaced cocaine and heroin as the biggest national source of income, these privileged few who owned the land allowed the peasants to continue to farm the "white gold" because it was far more profitable for farmer and landowner alike than growing vegetables or coffee.

If the government burned the fields, as the American government wanted, the farmers would become even more impoverished than they were now.

Which, the fear was, would drive all those poor people into the waiting hands of the rebel forces, thus endangering the lives and fortunes of this elite group sitting around the damask-draped table.

Heaven forbid, Kirby thought, they solve their socioeconomic problems by simply sharing some of those petroleum dollars with their countrymen.

She was wondering how gauche she'd be considered if she used this rare opportunity to lobby for funds to fight the current measles epidemic, when her host suddenly turned toward her.

As one of the two "honored guests," she had been seated on the president's left, while Dr. Rachel Moore, the physician in charge of the WMR clinic, had been given the higher honor position on his right.

"I am very concerned about you, Dr. Campbell," the president said in the nearly unaccented English she knew he'd acquired during his years in the States, studying law and political science at Harvard.

Kirby found it interesting that he had three accents: the English he used for CNN interviews or at the United Nations, a singsong very correct Spanish he was using tonight with his wealthy friends and hangers-on, and a rougher, more slang-spiced vernacular he used on local television or in speeches when he wanted to appear to his "people" as one of them.

She also couldn't quite decide if he'd chosen the dress-white military uniform to remind everyone present that he was in control of what several human rights groups had called one of the most brutal militaries in the world, or whether he believed the fruit salad of ribbons and medals adorning his jacket was more suited to a gathering of the rich and mighty than the military fatigues he'd gone back to wearing for his public appearances.

A slight breeze coming off the ocean blew some strands of hair across her eyes. Buying time, she tucked them behind her ear. "Why would that be, Señor Presidente?"

"You and Dr. Moore living alone out there in the jungle." He directed his response at her breasts, something she'd grown used to since they'd seemed to appear overnight the summer she turned fifteen.

Her blond hair drew enough attention in this country. But in a time when thin was in, even here in Central America, thanks to the influx of U.S. television programs and movies, her curves attracted male interest.

Even when, as now, they were modestly covered in the crisp white blouse she'd tucked into the navy knee-length skirt she'd bought for those rare occasions she was required to actually dress up.

The outfit, which Rachel had pointed out made her look as if she were about to join the U.S. Navy, wasn't exactly suitable for the occasion. But affairs such as this had never been on her list of fun ways to spend an evening. Formal dinner parties with a dictator were even worse, and Kirby had refused to buy a dress solely for the occasion. Especially when the money could, instead, buy so many more clinic supplies.

And the white blouse was certainly more appropriate than the T-shirt she'd jokingly suggested wearing. The one that read FIGHT HUNGER . . . EAT THE RICH.

"We're not exactly alone, señor," she said mildly. "Our clinic is in a village of nearly fifty people."

"Many of whom are not friends of this

government," he pointed out.

Meaning, she knew, rebels. Or terrorists, depending on whose definition you used. Unfortunately, the line between the two had become increasingly blurred as his propaganda machine continued to pump out misinformation while the leader of the rebel army was certainly no George Washington.

Monteleón had never been a wealthy country. But now, as the divide between rich and poor grew exponentially, more and more locals were daring to speak up. There were, unfortunately, also those with their own agendas willing to take advantage of the growing instability.

"WMR makes it a point not to get involved in local politics," she said mildly as she lifted a heavy cut-crystal glass and took a sip of ice water. "So I honestly couldn't tell you what our patients think of anything. Other than their health issues."

She took another sip.

Considered.

Then decided, What the hell? Go for it.

"Unless it's that they worry that their children might die of malnutrition. Or starvation. Or even, tragically, of measles, which, if we could only acquire much-needed funds, we could easily inoculate them against," she said on a rush of words before she could change her mind.

A fiftysomething woman gasped loud enough to be heard in the sudden silence that descended over the room. Her beringed hand flew to her pearl-and-emerald-draped breast.

Far below, the surf crashed against the cliffs; overhead parrots chattered amidst the purple blossoms of the jacaranda trees.

Around the table, everyone seemed to be holding their collective breaths, waiting to see how their president would respond to Kirby's appalling lack of etiquette.

The president's black eyes held a hard edge that reminded Kirby that, despite the luxuries he enjoyed now, this was a man who'd been honed by years of guerilla warfare against the previous dictator. Who'd conveniently been ousted by a CIA-engineered coup when *that* leader had threatened to nationalize the mining industry and kick out the American companies.

Finally, to Kirby's vast relief, he threw his head back and roared with laughter.

The others nervously, dutifully followed suit with noticeably less enthusiasm.

"You American women are always so deliciously outspoken."

Paying no heed to his wife, who was seated at the other end of the table, he skimmed a finger down the back of her hand, as if he had every right to touch her, however and whenever he wanted.

Which, Kirby considered, he probably thought he did.

"I'd forgotten how appealing that can be." His midnight black eyes met hers. "Under the right circumstances."

"I'm sorry if I spoke out of turn," Kirby murmured.

Actually, now that she realized she wasn't going to be arrested as an enemy of the people, she didn't mean a word of the apology, but while party manners might not be her strong point, she wasn't totally lacking in political skills.

"It's just that on the drive into the city, I was thinking about that speech you gave to the parliament last week."

After nearly two decades of running the country with an iron fist, he was campaigning to be elected president-for-life. Although he'd killed or scared off all his opponents, rumors persisted that the widow of an assassinated social-reformer husband was planning a return to the country to run against him. Currently living in Guadalajara, Mexico, Josefina Madrid was much beloved by her fellow countrymen.

At least those who weren't perched at the

very small top of the food chain.

"And what speech would that be, Doctor?" he asked.

She would have had to have been deaf not to hear the veiled warning in his tone. Or Rachel Moore's slight clearing of her throat. Rachel could not be more different from Kirby. Where Kirby could admittedly be impatient, and even impulsive, Rachel was even-tempered and far more likely to think before speaking.

But rather than cause friction, their differences were what made them such a good team. They complemented each other well. And, most importantly, they shared a common goal of helping people who couldn't help themselves.

Although Kirby had often been called stubborn, Rachel was the rock of WMR in Monteleón, admired for her unrelenting tenacity. Once the former Army National Guard physician made up her mind to do something, neither heaven nor hell, nor all the dictators' armies in all the world, were going to stop her.

"The speech where you claimed every citizen of Monteleón is deserving of dignity," she said. "And promised a plan to help the least of your citizens."

Although the palace may have resembled

the White House, the speech hadn't exactly gone as far as promising life, liberty, and the pursuit of happiness. But it *had* harked back to the revolutionary roots.

"Measles vaccine is relatively inexpensive," Kirby stressed. "As is mosquito netting to prevent children from contracting malaria. A healthy population is a stable population," she tacked on.

She didn't need to add that at the moment, Monteleón was anything but stable.

"I don't believe *el presidente* needs a civics lesson, Dr. Campbell," the American ambassador, who'd shown up with his female press secretary and had remained silent until now, chided. "Given his educational background."

"Of course he doesn't," Rachel agreed quickly, leaping in to keep Kirby from sticking her sandal even further into her mouth. "Dr. Campbell was merely quoting *el presidente*'s own words." She bestowed her warmest, most conciliatory smile on the dictator. "And, being one of the most charismatic speakers ever to hold elective office, of course he also understands the enormous power of words."

Yep, Kirby thought as the man visibly preened like the peacocks roaming the grounds. The longtime WMR doctor definitely won the tact medal.

"You are too kind, Dr. Moore."

He took Rachel's hand and lifted it to his lips. After holding it just a moment too long, he turned to his minister of health, who was seated across the table, next to the American ambassador.

"Tomorrow you must make a visit to the good doctors' clinic," he instructed. "Compile a list of everything they need. Then make certain that they receive it."

"That's extremely generous of you, Señor Presidente," the ambassador, whose press secretary, a brunet who'd accompanied him to take photos of the event, said.

Suck-up, Kirby thought darkly.

Everyone at the table knew that the offer was all for show. Hadn't she heard similar promises the entire six months she'd been in the country? But while Vasquez might talk the talk, his government had done nothing. *Nada.*

Meanwhile, the ambassador, who lived nearly as high on the hog as the dictator, never offered a single, solitary negative word.

Thus was the power of petroleum.

17

The dinner was followed by a concert by members of the Guardia de Hacienda, or house guards. The soldiers, handpicked by the president, had apparently been chosen for their good looks as well as their harmonic voices.

They were uniformly tall, dark, and handsome. Unfortunately, the oversized gold braided epaulets on their fitted red jackets and the gold-edged crimson stripes down their white trousers made them appear to be auditioning for Gilbert and Sullivan's *H.M.S. Pinafore.*

While Kirby found the rousing, patriotic Sousa-type war marches and American show tunes to be an odd mix, the rest of the guests seemed to enjoy the performance.

Not that anyone would dare not to, given that anyone who publicly criticized anything about the government tended to disappear.

Kirby nearly wept with relief when what

seemed the longest evening of her life finally came to an end.

Although their car had been searched on the way into the compound by grim-faced soldiers wearing green-and-brown jungle camouflage and armed with riot guns, they were forced to undergo yet another search on the way out. Only after the guards had thoroughly searched the trunk was the heavy red-and-white steel barrier pole raised.

"What did they think?" Kirby asked, as she and Rachel were finally allowed to leave. "That we were going to try to take off with the silverware? Or some sterling saltshakers?"

"I suspect it's routine security procedure," Rachel said, touching a finger to her lips to remind Kirby that their vehicle could have well been bugged while they were inside the palace having dinner.

They drove down Carretera Libertad, a broad esplanade bisecting the capital city to the Plaza de Armas — which featured a towering statue of Vasquez, arms outstretched, as if offering benediction to his people.

While hiding out in the mountains, forming his army, he'd named himself El Libertador, shamelessly stealing the title from the

George Washington of South America, Simón Bolívar, who'd actually liberated nearly an entire continent from the Spanish.

The one thing the two men *did* have in common was their harsh, autocratic rule once they achieved government power. Proving, as it always seemed to, that while power might corrupt, absolute power corrupted absolutely.

As they made their way across the circle, a delivery truck ran the red light, then cut through three lanes of traffic to pull in front of a bus. Horns blared, adding to the usual pandemonium. By the time she'd been in the country a week, Kirby had decided that driving in the capital entailed a type of Darwinian, survival-of-the-rudest logic.

The rusting city bus rumbled along, belching a noxious cloud of black fumes that smelled like burning tires, adding to air pollution considered by many environmentalists to be even worse than that of Mexico City.

Which partly explained the helicopters whirring overhead. While the majority of the people lived in abject poverty, the über-wealthy had begun choosing to avoid the smog and traffic snarls by flying above them.

There was also the little matter of Monteleón having become the kidnapping capital of Central America. While even an armored car could be run off the road, it was difficult to kidnap someone out of the air.

Rachel zipped around the bus with a daring that had Kirby gripping the edges of the seat. As she looked through the open windows — which were lacking glass — the passengers, crammed together like sardines in a rusting can, all had their heads down, not bothering to admire the statue of their leader. They did not look the least bit liberated.

"I've decided how we can make big bucks." Kirby forced herself not to close her eyes as a huge black Hummer headed straight for them.

"How's that?" Rachel deftly pulled back into their lane, earning a long blast of the horn and a rude gesture from the annoyed truck driver she cut in front of. The same one who'd crossed all those lanes of traffic earlier.

"We should start promoting driving in this city as an extreme sport. Make up some T-shirts we can sell on the Internet and have people pay us for the excitement of trying to make their way from one side of town to the other."

"The really strange thing is that you'd

probably have people take you up on it," Rachel said.

This time Kirby did close her eyes as a petroleum tank truck passed a car in the oncoming lane and, like the earlier Hummer, headed straight for them.

Following the unwritten "He who is larger wins the road" law of driving in Ciudad Libertad, she knew it wouldn't budge. Which forced Rachel to pull so far over the car's right wheels went up onto the sidewalk.

Which was another reason for those helicopters. As dangerous as it was to *drive* in the city, walking, except in a few select areas, was even more deadly.

The road continued through a wealthy community of gated homes, all surrounded by twelve-foot-tall walls. Broken bottles had been embedded in the top of the concrete walls like spikes. Which said a lot about the state of the country, Kirby thought as they passed the American ambassador's mansion, its gate guarded by U.S. Marines armed with automatic weapons.

The mansion's high walls were covered with bougainvillea, and while the red flowers were stunning, Kirby suspected they'd been planted more for their thorns, which provided an additional barricade against the unwashed masses, than their beauty.

Across the street, a ragged group of protestors waved signs and chanted "*Yanqui,* go home!" Monteleón had become so splintered, it was impossible to guess which of the many different factions they represented.

The neighborhood walls were broken up at intersections, leaving room for yet more heroic statues of El Presidente Vasquez.

"I'm sorry for mouthing off like that," Kirby said.

"Don't worry about it." Rachel slowed as they passed through the Zona Rosa, a neighborhood of pricey restaurants and nightclubs.

American pop music blared from open doorways, and well-dressed pedestrians crowded the sidewalk, safe in the knowledge that private police hired to patrol the area would turn away — or even, if given any trouble, shoot — any undesirables who might attempt to enter their comfortable zone without the proper windshield sticker.

Rachel turned left at the BMW dealer onto Avenida del la Reforma leading out of the city. "There are times I get frustrated, too."

"But you don't insult the dictator who has the power to shut you down."

Or arrest them. Or worse.

"I'm older." Kirby heard the reassuring smile in the other woman's voice. "And have more years dealing with uncooperative governments."

"Now, see." Kirby turned as far toward the other woman as her seat belt would allow. "That's what I don't get. Vasquez and all his pals are rolling in dough. The bunch of them have more tax-free money than their shopaholic wives could spend in several lifetimes, stashed away in Swiss and Caribbean banks.

"Meanwhile, because of their repressive tactics, they have rebel guerrilla groups popping up all over the place like crazed jack-in-the-boxes. So why aren't they willing to throw some of those bucks our way? Because it seems to me that people would be a lot happier if their children weren't starving or dying of easily preventable diseases."

She wondered if Vasquez was listening to their conversation, and since it wasn't anything different than what she'd said at dinner, hoped he was.

"In a perfect world, that would be the case." The traffic eased as they got farther from the city. Rachel glanced up into the rearview mirror, as if checking to see if they were being followed.

They wouldn't be the first relief workers

to disappear in Monteleón. Just last month the bodies of two nuns from Catholic Charities, who'd run a mission in the capital and had been like sand in Vasquez's oyster, had washed up onto the beach below the Presidential Palace.

The drive to the jungle village where their clinic was located would take an hour; something neither woman enjoyed doing at night, yet one did not turn down an invitation from El Presidente. Not unless you wanted a visit by the La Guardia de Seguridad, the most feared organization in the country.

Everyone knew that the guard not only ran the death squads; they were responsible for thousands of citizens being dragged from their homes. Mostly in the middle of the night. Some of the missing later showed up as mutilated bodies; most simply vanished, never to be seen again.

Not having to worry about bad press — the government owned the newspapers and television stations — the president's goons were experts at torture.

"How do you do it?" she asked. "Year after year. How can you stand seeing such misery?"

"I've honestly no idea."

Although they'd left the bright lights of

the city behind, Kirby could hear the shrug in the other woman's voice. It had begun to rain, the fog surrounding them adding an intimacy inside the car that encouraged the type of personal conversation they normally didn't have time to share.

"There are times I ask myself the same thing," Rachel admitted, "but the answer is always the same . . . that it's what I was born to do."

"I can't decide whether I'm envious or feel sorry for you."

"Ah." Rachel turned toward her, hazel eyes warm in the soft glow from the dashboard lights. "You sound as if you're suffering compassion fatigue. I think I should write you a prescription for a vacation."

"Yeah. Like I'm going to go off surfing while you stay here and handle a measles epidemic. So, how did you end up working for WMR in the first place?"

"It's a long story," Rachel said after they'd gone about three miles.

"It's a long drive."

"True."

Another silence settled over them. The only sounds were the drumming of the rain on the roof, the *swish, swish, swish* of the windshield wipers, and the hissing of the wet pavement beneath the tires.

"I know this sounds very cliché, but it was more a feeling of duty. That because since I'd been born, well, not exactly rich, but very comfortably off, I was brought up to believe I should give something back.

"Since I was already an ER doctor, when things started building up for Desert Shield, enlisting to serve my country seemed a natural thing to do."

"I can understand that."

Kirby might have needed the Army to help pay her way through medical school, but she'd learned traveling the world how fortunate she'd been to have been born in a middle-class suburban San Diego home to a schoolteacher father and librarian mother. Rather than in Iraq. Or the Sudan. Or the tragically beautiful Monteleón.

"Unfortunately, my husband —"

"You're married?"

Rachel never really talked about her personal life, but not mentioning a husband out there somewhere was really holding her cards close to her chest.

"Was. Past tense. In another lifetime.

"We met in medical school. His plan was that I'd go into a plastic surgery practice with him."

"Plastic surgery does a lot of good."

In fact, WMR had a program that re-

148

cruited surgeons to repair cleft palates and do skin grafts on bombing burn victims all over the world.

"True. But he's definitely more into nips, tucks, and boobs, which personally didn't interest me. I'd considered joining the regular military, but worried that a long-term deployment would put more of a strain on our marriage, so I opted for the Guard."

"And got deployed, anyway."

"Yes. But it wasn't as dangerous as it is these days. First of all, we were safe in Saudi Arabia, and my rotation was only supposed to be ninety days."

"But you got hit with a stop-loss," Kirby guessed.

The involuntary extension of a service member's active duty service under the enlistment contract in order to retain them beyond their initial end of term of service date was becoming all too common.

"Just the opposite. Treating soldiers was the greatest honor I'd ever had in my life. So, I checked around and managed to hook up with the 5th MASH unit, which became a forward operating clinic in Iraq."

"That probably didn't go over real well at home," Kirby guessed.

"Not well at all," Rachel agreed. There was another long moment of silence as she seemed lost in thought. "Looking back on it, although Roger blamed the problems on my service, he'd never honestly signed on to our marriage contract."

"He skipped the part about 'for better or worse'?"

"Well, that, too. But he also ignored the clause about infidelity being a deal-breaker. Even before I enlisted." She shook her head. "Our marriage was pretty much over when I shipped out. The only reason I didn't file for a divorce was that I knew my parents would be upset."

"But you were a grown woman. A doctor. And a soldier. It seems they'd trust your decision."

"You'd think so. And perhaps they would have. But I would've been the first divorce in our family. Ever."

"I can see how that would've been tough," Kirby agreed.

Having already witnessed the doctor's conciliatory nature, she could see how Rachel would have been reluctant to upset her parents with her marital problems when they were already worried about her surviving a war.

"Although they didn't say it, I knew they were concerned about their little girl going into battle," Rachel said, confirming Kirby's guess. "So I decided to wait until I got home."

"Makes sense. Besides, it's not as if you were going to find someone else while you were deployed."

Another silence.

Even longer than the others.

"Oh, wow. You did, didn't you?"

Okay, so it was prying. But Rachel *had* brought the subject up.

"I fell in love." Rachel dragged a hand through her shoulder-length hair she usually wore in a braid, but had left loose for tonight's dinner party. "For, I realized, the first time in my life. It was both the best and worst time of my life."

"Why? Was he married, too?"

"No." She shook her head. "He's an unrelentingly honorable man. Unlike me, he never would have committed adultery."

"Excuse me. But sleeping with a married woman doesn't exactly make him a saint," Kirby pointed out. "Not that I want to sound at all judgmental, because you'd already said your marriage was essentially over, but . . ."

"He didn't know I was married."

"What?"

"He didn't know," Rachel repeated. "Because I didn't tell him."

Since she hadn't exactly been a font of personal information these past months, Kirby could believe she'd kept her secret from her love. And understand why.

"Because you wanted him," she guessed. "And you knew your husband, who might be a husband in name only by that time, would've presented an obstacle."

"A huge one." Another sigh. "I don't know. Maybe Michael — that was his name — would have slept with me, anyway, but I didn't want to risk him feeling the need to be noble. Later, after we'd fallen in love, I kept trying to tell him, but I was a coward."

"There's not a cowardly cell in your body."

"We're all afraid of different things," Rachel said. "Anyway, I'd just decided to tell him when I received word my father had been diagnosed with cancer."

This was not where Kirby had expected the story to be headed. "I'm sorry."

"So was I. Fortunately, he didn't die. But it was tough going for a long while. The doctors had originally given him a year, maybe two, tops, to live.

"Perhaps it was because I was far from home, working in an unbelievably stressful environment after I'd moved to the Fifth, and was already feeling guilty about being unfaithful, plus desperately wanting to be

Daddy's 'good girl' so he wouldn't have anything to worry about but getting well, but I couldn't see how I could possibly get a divorce right then."

"But you were in love."

"Yeah. I was. Deeply. Thoroughly. But as I said, maybe Dad's diagnosis was the straw that broke the camel's back, so to speak, but the night I found out, I finally admitted to Michael that I was married."

"How did he take that little bombshell?"

"He was surprised, of course. But since he'd already told me that he loved me, and he was not the kind of man to treat such feelings lightly, I suspect we might have been able to move past it. If I hadn't also told him that when I got back to the States, I was going to try to repair my marriage."

"Wow," Kirby said again. "And here I was just thinking tonight at dinner how you don't do drama."

"You know that volcano looming over the village?"

"It'd be hard to miss, since it's been steaming ever since I arrived down here." Ixtab, named for the Mayan goddess of sacrifice, also created the most fabulously red sunsets Kirby had ever seen.

"Well, I suppose that's pretty much how I handle emotions. I keep them all bottled

153

up, then eventually the cork blows, and pow!"

"And it blew with Michael?"

"Sky-high." Another swipe of her hand through her hair. "Since then I've had a lot of time to think about it, and have come to the conclusion that the unpalatable but cold, hard truth was that I put off telling Michael about my marriage because our affair scared me."

Kirby had never seen Rachel afraid of anything. But she could understand this reasoning. "Because you felt out of control for the first time in your life."

"More than the first time I had to slice into a cadaver in gross anatomy class," Rachel admitted. "Although I didn't love my husband, our problems — not just his betrayal, but the fact that he'd never taken my work seriously — had hurt me. But worse, it had left me questioning my own judgment. I didn't want to go through that ever again."

She rubbed a hand against her chest in an unconscious gesture that suggested it still hurt to talk about it. Even after all these years.

"But after a night lying awake thinking about everything Michael had ever said to me, after all we'd shared, I knew that he was a man I could trust implicitly. I'd also come to my senses enough to realize Dad would never want me to be miserable on his account. But then a scud hit a group of our tents just as I was about to go try to mend things."

"You're kidding." At least she'd managed something besides "wow."

"I wish I were. They say I died, but I don't remember that."

"So you didn't see any white tunnel of light? Lots of relatives hanging around, welcoming you to green pastures?"

"No near-death experience. Michael saved my life." Her voice caught. "I'd already given him my heart. But that day he literally held it in his hands."

As amazing as Kirby found Rachel's story, she couldn't help thinking how it so echoed her own unhappy experience with Shane.

Why the hell hadn't she insisted they talk their situation out? Maybe not while he'd been in Landstuhl. But later, once he'd been transferred to Walter Reed and had had more time to adjust to the loss of his leg.

But no. She'd allowed herself to walk away.

The same as she'd done the first time after he'd flown off to Afghanistan.

"Anyway," Rachel continued, "after emergency surgery, I was airlifted to Germany."

"I've been to Landstuhl," Kirby said.

"They do amazing work there," Rachel said. "After a few weeks, I was sent back to the States, where my marriage finally broke up."

"What happened with Michael?"

"Let's say the window of opportunity had passed."

"He found someone else?"

"In a way. It's complicated. . . . Damn!"

The conversation came to an abrupt end as they turned a corner, their headlights shining onto the green-and-brown-camouflage-painted Toyota pickup parked sideways, effectively blocking the road.

18

Somersett, South Carolina

Wouldn't it be damn ironic, Shane Garrett thought, if he were to survive a helicopter crash in Afghanistan that had cost him his leg, only to end up dying of humiliation back here in the States?

"It's okay," the woman in whose bed he was dying assured him. "It happens to everyone."

"Not to me."

Hell. He hadn't really wanted to go on this blind date in the first place. After all, after all those months at Walter Reed and then in rehab, he'd gotten his life back on track. And it was a good life. All things considered.

His older brother, who'd taken over the day-to-day running of the family's Oregon ranch, had offered him a job. But while he liked being a cowboy on the rodeo circuit, Shane had never been all that jazzed about cows. Unless they were served up on a plate as bloody T-bones with crunchy steak fries.

Which is how he'd ended up here, in South Carolina, where — thanks to his former Navy JAG service — he picked up extra bucks by giving an occasional lecture on military law at the Admiral Somersett Military Academy. He also taught flying and spent time hanging with two guys whom he felt closer to than his own blood brother.

The problem was, more and more he'd realized that he was becoming the odd man out. Not because of his injury, which, thanks to a lot of hard work and way-cool twenty-first-century technology, he'd overcome pretty damn well. If he did say so himself. But the reason the dynamics of the three men had changed since they'd gotten back to the States was because Shane was the only single guy left.

After that goatfuck in Afghanistan, Zach Tremayne had come back home and married a woman he'd known most of his life. Sabrina Swann was beautiful, smart as a whip, and loaded. Not that Zach had ever cared about money. And, to Sabrina's credit, she never flaunted her wealth and was working damn hard on her goal of turning her family home and tea plantation into an inn.

Meanwhile, Quinn McKade, who continued to write his military novels while working with Zach at Phoenix Team — a high-risk international security company based on nearby Swann Island — had gone and gotten himself engaged to an FBI agent who was now also working with the team.

Apparently, the two women had gotten together with another friend, the wife of the Swann Island sheriff, and decided that what Shane's life lacked was female companionship. When he'd protested that he really wasn't interested in a relationship, his best friends had suggested that he was getting ahead of himself.

"We're not talking about registering for flatware, fly-boy," Zach had told him, over pints of Guinness at the Black Swan pub. "We're talking about getting laid."

"First of all, the fact that you would ever use the term 'flatware' in a sentence proves that Sabrina has domesticated you to a purely pitiful state," Shane complained. He'd bet dollars to Krispy Kremes that John Wayne never would've used that girly word.

"Sticks and stones." Zach wagged a dark brow and wiped the back of his hand across his mouth to get rid of the ale-foam mustache. "Don't knock domestication until you've tried it," he said. "At least I know

I'm going to have a sweet-smelling, sexy woman in my bed tonight."

"Believe it or not, frog boy," Shane countered, snagging a sweet-potato French fry from the basket in the middle of the table, "not every guy goes through life with sex on the brain every other minute."

"Which, if it's true, just shows that some guys need to prioritize," McKade said.

Shane cursed as the two men exchanged fucking satisfied grins and lifted their glasses to each other.

"How long has it been since you've had sex?" Zach asked.

"Not that long." Hell, he'd had it in the shower this morning, but he wasn't prepared to share that in public.

"Since that therapist in D.C.?"

"She wasn't my therapist."

His therapist had been a sadistic, muscle-bound Valkyrie named Helga, who'd definitely bought into the "What doesn't kill you makes you stronger" school of physical rehabilitation. Still, he knew he owed her big time. Without her, he might have gone through life as a helpless, one-legged gimp.

"She was my case manager in the Warrior Transition Unit."

Made of combat-experienced officers and NCOs, the brigade had been established to provide command and control, primary care, and case management for service members suffering wounds during deployment in the war on terror.

The goal was to promote said warriors' timely return to the force or transition to civilian life.

Apparently, his case manager took a hands-on approach to the situation, because his last night he'd been in D.C., she'd shown up at his apartment with a bottle of champagne, a pack of condoms, a Barry White CD and a hot-to-trot, skintight, crotch-length nurse's costume with thigh-high white lace stockings from Fredrick's of Hollywood.

By the time the sun had come up the next morning, Shane no longer worried about his ability to have sex as energetically and physically as he'd had before the crash. And he'd always be grateful for the fortysomething divorced lieutenant's generosity of spirit.

But the problem was, although he now had proof that all his important guy parts were in full working order, he'd yet to meet any woman who'd stirred him up enough to make the effort of dating — the movies, the dinners, the long getting-to-know you conversations — worthwhile.

Maybe it was due to having come so close to dying, but he no longer wanted to settle for the no-strings sex he'd once enjoyed.

Because he genuinely liked the matchmaking females, and because both Zach and Quinn had urged him to go along with the program so their women would get off their backs about his lack of love life, Shane had caved in and called the county prosecutor that the ladies had met at their Wednesday-night book group.

Gwyneth Giles was a tall, statuesque redhead whose body was nearly as ripped as his own, though not in any bulked-up steroidal way. The way the black silk dress clung to her magnificently toned body would probably have most guys panting before they'd made it through the fried calamari appetizers.

Although it had cost her a few points when Sabrina had mentioned she'd not only been Miss Buccaneer Days, but also first runner-up to Miss South Carolina while in college, Gwyneth didn't fit his admittedly prejudiced stereotype.

Just the opposite. It turned out she'd used the beauty contestant scholarship money to attend law school, and now spent her days putting bad guys behind bars. Her conviction rate was not only the highest in the

Somersett District Attorney's office, it was among the highest in the state, and although she'd just turned thirty-five, there was already talk of her being appointed to a federal judgeship.

So, she was gorgeous, intelligent, and smelled damn good, too.

Which was why, when she'd invited him back to her place for a nightcap, he'd decided, What the hell, only a saint or a madman would turn her down. Shane had been called crazy a few times in his life, most often by superior officers who complained about a few of his more daredevil flying stunts, but he'd always known the verbal reprimand was more for show.

And despite having been an altar boy at All Saints back in Oregon, he'd certainly never been bucking for sainthood.

After hanging her coat and his leather jacket cozily side by side in the front closet of the harbor-front town house, she'd grabbed hold of his hair, brought his head down to hers and gave him a gilt-edged, wet, open-mouthed invitation.

Looking back on it, Shane knew that's when he should've just called it a night.

Instead, he'd cupped her very fine butt and waited with fatalistic curiosity for his body to respond to her amazingly talented lips.

It didn't.

Seeming unfazed by his lack of response, she took him by the hand.

"Do you have any trouble with stairs?" she asked, revealing that she'd been warned about his injury.

Which perversely made him determined to forge on.

"No," he assured her. "I'm good to go." And determined to end the evening with a MISSION ACCOMPLISHED banner over her bed.

She smiled. Skimmed a look from the top of his head down to his wedge-heeled cowboy boots, then back up again. "Oh, I'd say you're a lot better than good, darlin'."

Twining her fingers with his, she led him up the stairs to the second floor and down a short hall to her bedroom.

Once again proving the problem with stereotyping, the room was not what he would have expected from the no-nonsense, law-and-order prosecutor image she showed to the world. It was pretty and feminine and smelled of flowers. It was the kind of room that a man would only feel comfortable in if invited.

Which he'd definitely been.

She kicked off her black alligator heels, then reached behind her back and lowered the zipper on her dress. The silk slid down her body to pool in a black puddle at her bare feet.

Her bra was the same color as her dress, and sheer, revealing taut, pebbled nipples.

For some weird reason, Shane's mind suddenly zapped back to Iraq. Even weirder yet was the way the seemingly safe memory of Kirby's practical white cotton bra did what that earlier hot kiss couldn't achieve.

It made him hard.

Dragging his mind from that trailer in Baghdad, he realized Gwyneth was waiting for him to say something.

"Nice," he obliged. Then, deciding that probably wasn't expansive enough, added "and really, really hot."

Obviously pleased, she unhooked the bra and let it fall to the floor with the dress. She was now down to a pair of black panties. "Why don't you take your pants off and stay awhile?" she suggested.

Shane stripped out of his own clothes as she walked around the room, lighting white candles. The mattress dipped as he sat on the bed and unfastened his prosthesis.

She tilted her auburn head, studying it for a moment with understandable curiosity.

"Wow. It looks real."

"It's pretty close," he said, not wanting to kill the mood by getting into specifics about it being an experimental model using computer chips, Bluetooth technology, myoelectric impulse, and transplanted nerves to create a closed loop between his brain and his leg. Which essentially made it as close as technology could manage to a real leg. And this one, which he liked to think of as his "formal" leg, and while not quite as maneuverable as the others he'd been given, even resembled actual human flesh.

"Well, I'm impressed."

But not overly intrigued, which suggested she wasn't turning out to be one of those "devotees" some of the other guys in rehab had told him about: women who got off on having sex with amputees.

Fortunately, as she pushed him back onto the mattress and began kissing her way down his chest, the sexy prosecutor showed no sign of such kink.

Rather, Gwyneth Giles actually seemed to like him for himself.

And he liked her just fine, too.

Over the next thirty minutes, the sexy prosecutor proved eager and talented and everything a guy could want in a bed partner.

So why the hell was his body betraying him?

The minute she'd curled her long, manicured fingers around him, his erection had softened like a deflated party balloon. And although she gave it her best shot, pulling out every female trick in the book, no amount of coaxing could achieve liftoff.

Shane tried telling himself his problem was only because this was his first time with a civilian. Although his leg might be part Robo-Cop, part Bionic Man, the rest of him, including his brain, was totally human. Totally guy.

Maybe it was the beer he'd had with dinner.

Which didn't make sense, since it was only a single bottle of Sam Adams, and he'd had more alcohol polishing off that bottle of Korbel with his case manager and hadn't any problems. But he'd gone into that more as an experiment, to get back into the swing of things, so to speak.

Even as he worked his way through a litany of possible excuses, as that hot flashback of Kirby in her white bra danced seductively in his mind, Shane had the nagging feeling that his inability to perform had a whole lot to do with the fact that the sexy prosecutor who'd left a red lipstick brand on his dick wasn't a certain sweet-tasting Army captain.

Which was when Shane realized, with full certainty, that he was well and truly screwed.

19

"Do you think it's the guards?" Kirby asked as Rachel braked.

Although it was difficult to see through the rain, there appeared to be people in the back of the truck.

"We're about to find out," Rachel said as she pulled to a stop.

Two boys, no older than fifteen, climbed out of the cab of the truck and swaggered toward them. They were wearing Rambo-style bandanas, .45 revolvers slung low on their narrow hips, like Western movie gun-fighters, and carrying Kalashnikovs on slings over their shoulders.

They were obviously members of *el ejécito de niños,* "the army of the children," a loosely organized branch of the rebel forces. Some had been kidnapped from villages; others orphaned or from impoverished families had joined willingly. They were also known as "little carts," transporting drugs and weapons. They could — especially the teen boys — be more dangerous than their adult counterparts, because they were more likely to feel the need to prove their machismo.

Rachel rolled down the window.

"What can we do for you?" she asked in the same perfect Spanish the president used with his friends.

"Salimos del coche," he demanded in a slurred voice.

That and the fact that Kirby could smell the beer on his breath was a clue that while they'd been dining at the palace, he'd been downing *cerveza.*

He also was chewing on something she suspected was a coca leaf. Keeping children soldiers slightly drunk and drugged was, unfortunately, a tactic used by the bad guys all over the world.

Rachel exchanged a quick glance with Kirby. It was obvious they were both thinking the same thing. That if they got out of the car they could easily end up dead.

Still, with the Toyota effectively blocking the road, and the soldier pointing the barrel of the automatic rifle through Rachel's window, it wasn't as if they had a whole lot of choices.

Wearing her usual calm dignity like a

shield, Rachel got out of the car. Trying to judge the distance to the trees lining the road, in case they had to make a run for it, Kirby followed.

Rachel held out a hand and introduced herself. Then Kirby.

Ignoring her hand, he did not — surprise, surprise — reveal his name. Instead he demanded the keys to their vehicle.

"Disculparme," Rachel said mildly. "Pardon me." *"Cómo se llama usted?"*

Rather than respond to her polite request for his name, he merely glared. And swayed, causing the barrel of the automatic rifle to go swinging in all directions.

He repeated the demand for their vehicle.

"No." Rachel tossed up her chin. She could've been a duchess looking down on an errant footman.

"Qué?" he asked, truly puzzled.

He exchanged a look with his younger compatriot, who thus far hadn't said a word. From the glazed look in his eyes, Kirby suspected he was even more tanked or high, or both, than the one who'd demanded they get out of the car.

Rachel repeated that she was not handing over the keys.

Kirby had learned, early in her days at WMF, that since, unlike when she was in

171

the military, she wasn't surrounded by lots of guys with guns who knew how to use them, the most important survival tool a medical relief worker possessed was the ability to never let them see you sweat. To not show fear, to look the other person straight in the eye, and say whatever it took — even if it took a lie — to extricate yourself from sticky situations.

And this was the stickiest she'd found herself in since treating that terrorist's son in Pakistan. The same day Shane had been carried into her refugee camp.

No. Don't think about that!

There were times for remembering, times for regrets and wondering about what might have been. This was definitely *not* one of them.

The kid exchanged another look with the younger one, who appeared even more flabbergasted.

"I am a close personal friend of Jesus Enrique Castillo," Rachel announced.

The lie had the effect of a flare of trumpets. Both boys actually stood up at something resembling attention.

"*Eso es verdad?*" the younger one spoke for the first time, glazed eyes wide as he questioned the veracity of this gringa not only knowing the rebel leader, but being a friend.

"Es absolutamente cierto," Rachel claimed with unquestionable veracity.

Then went on to spin a tall tale of how she'd once hidden their leader and treated him for a gunshot wound after he'd been shot in an ambush by Vasquez's army.

On a roll, she also implied that she and Jesus Castillo had shared far more than a doctor-patient relationship, and that since he'd assured her that if she ever needed anything all she had to do was ask and it would be given, she truly doubted the rebel leader would be very pleased to hear two members of his own militia had stolen his physician's — and close personal friend's — only means of transportation. She added a throaty tone to "personal."

They leered like two teenage boys who'd just logged onto the Internet to watch the Paris Hilton sex tapes, suggesting they were picturing their leader doing the medical relief doctor.

"Please give Jesus my best when you see him," Rachel said, her tone once again lingering sexily on the use of his first name.

"Sí," the older one said, apparently convinced. As they staggered back to the pickup truck, they were giggling and punching each

others' arms.

"That was a really good lie," Kirby said. "Not only did you manage to keep our wheels, you also put a stop to any ideas the idiots might've gotten about having themselves a gangbanger fiesta."

"They may have been drunk and stupid," Rachel agreed as the truck drove past, all the rain-soaked boys in the back leaning out of the bed, trying to catch a glimpse of their leader's alleged lover. "But fortunately they weren't suicidal. . . .

"There was a story making the rounds a few years ago about Castillo taking one of his fifteen-year-old girl soldiers as what they call a jungle wife," she revealed. "I've no idea if it's true. It may be the Monteleón version of an urban legend, but the way I heard it, the girl and one of the young boy soldiers fell into a Romeo and Juliet–type forbidden teenage love."

"Oh-oh."

"Oh-oh, indeed. As the tale goes, when Castillo caught them together, he turned the girl over to his soldiers. After they'd finished with her, he made her watch as he cut the boy into pieces and fed him to his pet jaguar. The girl, rumor has it, prostrate with grief, along with the trauma of being gang-raped and watching her young lover executed in such a brutal fashion, ended up hanging herself."

Kirby had seen terrible things. But that story still caused her flesh to pebble with goose bumps.

20

"There's something that's been worrying me," Kirby said, once she and Rachel had gotten back to the small house they shared at the clinic. "What's going to happen when those teenagers get back to camp and mention your name to Castillo?"

"I doubt they'll remember even having the conversation in the morning," Rachel said. "But even if they do, I'm covered. Because Jesus will vouch for me."

"Really?" Kirby was dying to ask.

"I'm nearly positive he will. And no, we weren't lovers," she answered the unasked question. "But I did take a bullet out of his shoulder last year." She glanced over at Kirby. "No lectures about working on the wrong side?"

"We don't do sides," Kirby said.

"True," Rachel agreed. "Yet over the years I've just worked with some people who brought more of a political bias to the job."

"Sometimes it's hard to stay impartial." The Sudan had been one of those places. "Especially when you're talking civil wars, which is a stupid name for them because there's nothing civil about them. But I certainly understand the importance of not openly taking sides."

"I know you do. Which is why I'm sending you to Washington."

"Well, you're just full of surprises tonight, aren't you? Washington State? Or D.C.?"

"D.C. After those nuns' deaths, the Senate Foreign Relations committee decided to hold hearings about the situation down here. They want views from people other than the usual suspects at the embassy, so I agreed to testify.

"But I think a break would be good for you. Not that it'd be an actual vacation, but a few days in the States might help you clear your head and get your bearings back. While deciding if you want to stay."

"What makes you think I wouldn't?"

"Most medical relief volunteers only manage, on average, two years before burning out. You've surpassed that. By a lot of years, if you include your military service."

She glanced over at Kirby again. "There's no shame in wanting a normal life. And it's certainly possible to use your medical degree to make an important difference in people's lives outside of war zones."

Some little voice in the back of Kirby's mind had been whispering the same thing the past few months. But she'd steadfastly ignored it.

"It seems, since you're the senior doctor and have been here the longest, you're the logical choice to testify," she said.

"Well, perhaps. But there's a slight problem with that idea."

She went over to a cabinet, took out a bottle of Chilean red wine. Although it was not unusual to end their days with conversation over evening glasses of wine, Kirby had the feeling she was stalling.

"My godfather's head of the Senate Armed Services committee," she revealed.

"Wow," Kirby said yet again. "Does Vasquez know that?"

"I don't think so. I've never gotten a hint that he does, anyway. I certainly try to keep it a secret."

"Because you'd make a good kidnapping target."

Since kidnapping had become a cottage industry in Monteleón, those same wealthy citizens who opted for helicopters to get around the city never traveled without bodyguards.

"Exactly. There are a lot of bad guys out there who might not realize the U.S. doesn't negotiate with terrorist kidnappers. I wouldn't want to put other WMR workers or the people I'm trying to help at risk."

"That's probably wise."

"It gets worse." Rachel sighed. "My mother's second cousin is president."

"The U.S. President?"

"Certainly not Vasquez." The doctor's tone was a great deal drier than the weather.

"How the hell do you keep that secret?"

"I joined WMR under my married name. There's never been any reason to connect me to politics. Which is why I'd just as soon keep a low profile in D.C. The last thing we need is some reporter discovering my political connections."

"When would I be leaving?"

"Day after tomorrow."

"That's not much time to come up with what to say."

"Simply tell the truth. It's usually the best policy. Except, of course, in those cases where you have to lie to save your life." Rachel took a long sip of wine and Kirby knew they were thinking how close they'd come to getting into serious trouble with those teenage soldiers. "So, would you be willing to do it?"

Kirby wasn't all that enthusiastic about making a public presentation, something she hadn't done since she ran for class president in high school. But it was for a good cause, and although she felt a little guilty even thinking about it, the idea of going back to the States, where she didn't have to deal with death on a daily basis and worry about getting shot or kidnapped, was admittedly more than a little appealing.

"Of course I will. If you think I'd be of help."

"You'll be fantastic. And while you're in the city, pick up a hunk staffer. Take him back to your hotel and have yourself some hot sex."

"I've sworn off men," Kirby said. "They're too high maintenance and not worth the trouble they cause."

"Yeah, that's what we all say," Rachel said knowingly. "Until we meet the one."

Not wanting to point out that she hadn't seen the other woman with a man the entire six months she'd been in Monteleón, Kirby didn't respond.

21

Kirby was given an indication about how important the government took the situation in Monteleón when she entered the subcommittee hearing room on the second floor of the Hart Senate Office Building. Barely ten by eighteen feet, the room was dimly lit. And nearly empty. It was definitely a long way from those huge, richly paneled, classically beautiful rooms she'd seen on C-Span.

She bet if only Brad Pitt or Angelina Jolie had shown up to testify about events in the Central American country, the entire damn building would be filled to the rafters with members of congress and reporters. Unfortunately, lone relief doctors weren't exactly on the Washington A-list.

Reminding herself that this trip wasn't about her, she took a deep breath and wet her suddenly dry throat with a long drink of water from the glass in front of her. Then, after the chairman introduced her, she began the statement she'd prepared with Rachel in Monteleón, honed on the plane, then polished yet again this morning before leaving for the hearing.

She was allowed to speak uninterrupted for twenty minutes, sticking to facts, avoiding conjectures or personal comments, and, although it wasn't easy, resisting the urge to criticize the Monteleón government for its corruption and cooperation with drug dealers.

Instead she told of the crushing poverty the majority of the people were suffering. "The indigenous people in the rural areas are among the poorest," she reported. "Unsurprisingly, the individuals we treat at our WMR clinic feel powerless to change their situation, which in turn leads to frustration. Especially when you factor in that the country has the highest mortality rate in Central or South America. Sixty-one out of every thousand children don't live to the age of five."

Knowing a mere recitation of numbers could make eyes glaze over, which indeed appeared to be happening, Kirby pulled out the heavy ammunition.

"To put that in perspective, taking into consideration that, with the House and Senate combined, there are five hundred and thirty-five members of congress, we're talking about thirty-three of those members having a child who does not live to the first grade."

She paused a moment to allow that to sink in. A couple of the men shifted uncomfortably in their chairs, while the sole woman committee member appeared stricken. Which was exactly what Kirby had been shooting for.

"Now imagine how you would feel if you watched your young son or daughter die of measles or malaria or typhus while the so-called intelligentsia drove Mercedes and BMWs and threw quinceañera parties for their fifteen-year-old daughters that can cost upwards of the equivalent of fifty thousand American dollars."

"Which explains the rebels." One of the senators nodded sagely.

"I'm not here to get into the political and military issues, Senator," she replied, trying to stay on message.

"The ambassador assures me the government is doing its best to help these native peoples," another senator said to her breasts.

"With all due respect, Senator," Kirby said, buttoning her navy jacket in an attempt to direct his wandering eyes back to hers, "if President Vasquez was sincere about wanting to help his people, a good start would be giving them at least part of their land back.

"Over the centuries, first during the coffee, mining, and timber-production booms, and now, of course, with the discovery of the oil, large parcels of land have been co-opted by the government.

"At present, more than seventy-five percent of the agricultural land is owned by less than two percent of the population, and those poor who have managed to hold on to some land own less than an acre, which is typically fragmented and unable to be tilled. Forty percent of the population owns no land at all."

Although some members of the committee were dutifully taking notes, Kirby could tell she was losing them again. Though his closed eyes might suggest he was deeply pondering her words, she suspected an elderly senator from Texas had actually dozed off.

She'd wanted to get into how deforestation, erosion, and the decline of traditional agriculture had, in turn, led to a decline in nutritional levels among the rural poor WMR was trying to help, but decided it was time for a little show-and-tell.

Opening a manila folder, she'd just begun showing the faces of those most harmed by decades of strife — widowed women, orphaned children — when the door to the hearing room opened and a young man in a snazzy navy suit entered and handed a note to the chairman of the committee.

"Thank you, Doctor Campbell," the chairman said briskly. "Your report has been very informative, and we'll be sure to take everything you said into consideration when we send our report to the other members. And, of course, to the president."

"Thank you, Senator." She gave him a small, polite smile. She gave a significant look at her watch. "But my time isn't up yet."

"I realize that, and we'll be certain to have you back at some later date." His tone let her know that the issue wasn't up for discussion. "If you'll just go with this gentleman, he'll accompany you to your next meeting."

Next meeting?

Rachel hadn't told her anything about any other meetings. Realizing that there was no point in asking for more details, Kirby gathered up her materials and followed the aide.

22

"Where are we going?" she asked, once they were out in the hallway.

"To Senator Sherman's office," the aide said.

"Why?"

"I wouldn't know, ma'am." He ushered her into an elevator and pushed the down button. "I was just sent to retrieve you."

He made her sound as if she were a bone someone had thrown to a dog.

Feeling like a student called before the principal's office for some misbehavior, Kirby was racking her brain, going through everything she'd done since arriving in the city, when she had a lightbulb moment, remembering Rachel's relationship to Sherman. Obviously, the senator was merely eager for news about his goddaughter.

The suite of offices was smaller than Kirby would have expected, given his stature in the senate. One wall was covered with the requisite "grip and grin" photo ops, showing him with movie stars, others she took to be famous people, some she didn't recognize, others — such as the Dalai Lama — she did, and various world leaders, including Vasquez, who had, Kirby noticed, worn his dress white uniform for the photograph. Balancing out the rich and famous were photos showing the senator visiting U.S. troops overseas. A few such pictures she recognized as having been taken in the Green Zone.

The wall behind the polished oak desk was covered in plaques; a third wall held landscape paintings of what she assumed were Connecticut landmarks.

The Stars and Stripes flanked one side of his bark brown leather chair; the blue flag with the Connecticut state seal the other.

He rose when she came in, and came out from behind the desk. He was a tall man with a shock of silver hair that provided the proper air of gravitas. He was deeply tanned, suggesting a lot of time spent outdoors. His dark blue suit, with the flag pin on its lapel, appeared to be custom-tailored; his crisply starched shirt was white, his tie red.

"Doctor Campbell," he greeted her, his voice deep and tailor-made for the lofty speeches for which he was famous. "It's good of you to come."

"It's good of you to invite me, Senator," Kirby replied.

Not that she'd been invited as much as dragged out of a hearing that meant a lot not to just her, but thousands of innocent victims of government. But since this was his office and he was Rachel's godfather, Kirby was determined to remain polite.

Also, given his position, he might actually be more help than the members she'd spoken with earlier. As head of the Armed Services Committee, he undoubtedly had the ear of the president.

She didn't want the U.S. military to invade Monteleón, which would only make matters worse, but perhaps if some sanctions were imposed, requiring Vasquez to share more of the oil wealth with all his countrymen . . .

"Please, sit down." He gestured toward the two chairs on the visitor's side of the desk. "May I offer you something to drink? Some coffee, tea? Soda?"

Having crawled out of her hotel bed in the dark at five this morning to go over her notes yet again, after a restless night spent chasing sleep, she was in definite need of caffeine.

"Coffee would be great."

He pressed a button on his speakerphone. "Mrs. Hansen, would you please bring in a pot of coffee?" He glanced over at Kirby. "Sugar? Cream?"

"Just black."

"Doctor Campbell takes hers black," he reported.

After placing the order with the unseen Mrs. Hansen, he leaned back in the chair and studied her.

"How was your flight from Ciudad Libertad?" he inquired.

"Other than a longer-than-scheduled layover, uneventful."

Kirby grew increasingly uncomfortable as he continued to study her with an intensity that was turning into a stare.

He began moving a gold pen back and forth from one hand to the other, his intense blue eyes on her face.

The pen kept moving.

Right hand. Left.

Then right again.

He was studying her. Looking for . . . what?

Kirby was relieved when his unblinking attention momentarily shifted to a middle-aged woman who'd entered the room, carrying two cups of coffee on a pewter tray.

"Thank you, Mrs. Hansen."

"No problem, Senator." She placed the tray on a table, handed Kirby a cup, and put the other on a coaster bearing the U.S. Senate seal on Sherman's desk.

She didn't say anything to Kirby, who also thanked her, but the deep look the staffer gave her before leaving the office, so similar to the senator's, was unnerving.

Sherman picked up his cup, which looked particularly small and delicate in his large, tanned hands, and eyed her over the rim.

It was all Kirby could do not to squirm.

"I've read your service record," he surprised her by revealing.

Of all the things she'd expected him to say, that wouldn't have even made the list.

"Oh?" She took a sip of the coffee. "May I ask why?"

"I wanted to know what kind of person you are. And what type of soldier you were."

" 'Soldier' is a relative term, given that there wasn't much opportunity to fire weapons while working in a combat support hospital."

"True. Yet you did have firearms training in Iraq."

"Although we were far safer than the medical staff working in the FOBs — forward operating bases — all the doctors in the Green Zone were required to learn how

190

to shoot."

"And you scored quite well."

"I did okay. But there's a big difference between being able to shoot *well* and being able to shoot *someone*."

"Your commanding officer's evaluations were consistently glowing."

"You've spoken with Colonel Walsh?"

"Early this morning. The term 'grace under pressure' was used more than once."

Kirby was beginning to suspect she hadn't been brought here solely to chat about this man's goddaughter. "I was merely doing my job, Senator."

"The colonel also said you'd say something like that."

He tossed back his coffee, put the cup down, picked up the pen, and began moving it back and forth again. "I've also been in contact with your supervisors at WMR."

"Oh?"

Understanding that the senator was used to commanding the stage, Kirby bit back her impatience and curiosity and let him do so now.

"Everyone I spoke with who knew your work considered it superlative. And told me that you're a remarkably intelligent, level-headed woman."

"That's very flattering." She decided not

191

to mention the dinner with Vasquez, where she certainly wouldn't have described herself as levelheaded.

"It's not flattery if it's true," he said briskly. "And I have the sense it's very true." The pen went right again. Left. "I was also told that while you work very well with others, you have a tendency toward stubbornness."

"I prefer to call it tenacity, sir."

He didn't return her slight smile. "I'm glad to hear that, Doctor Campbell. Because I've brought you here to ask for your help."

"I see," Kirby said, not seeing anything at all.

"It's my goddaughter, Rachel." His eyes narrowed. "I see you're not surprised by the revelation that we have a connection."

"Coincidentally, she told me that just the other night," Kirby admitted.

A horrible thought occurred to her. "Is Rachel alright? Did something happen?"

"I believe she is, at the moment, as well as can be expected under the circumstances."

His face turned stony, his eyes hard, and now that she looked at him closer, Kirby could see the shadows beneath his eyes, hinting at a lack of sleep. *This wasn't good.*

"I take it you haven't watched CNN this morning."

Not good at all. Her blood went cold as she braced herself for bad news.

"I was preparing for my testimony," she said. "Then I was in the hearing, when your aide pulled me out to bring me here."

"There's no easy way to say this." His deep voice, which had made him one of the senate's most influential speakers, turned as harsh as his expression. "Rebels stormed the WMR clinic in Monteleón during the night and took Rachel hostage. They've broadcast a video, showing her tied to a chair, with armed men, their faces covered in scarves like the stinking cowards they are, holding a machete at her neck."

"Oh, my God." Kirby pressed her fingers against her temples.

"They're demanding a million dollars from our government. Or they'll, in their words, 'declare her an enemy of the people' and execute her."

"But Rachel's no one's enemy. She even treated Jesus Enrique Castillo's bullet wound."

"Apparently, the bastard doesn't understand the concept of appreciation. Because he's accusing her of working for the CIA."

The audacity of that accusation cleared Kirby's head.

"That's ridiculous. She's the farthest thing

from a CIA operative possible. Besides, the government doesn't pay ransom."

"Not since the Nixon administration," he confirmed. "But that doesn't prevent a private person from paying it."

Kirby's first thought was that people who paid the rebels ransom were actually perpetuating the kidnappings by making them profitable in a country where so many people lived below the poverty line.

Her next thought, coming a second later, was that if she had a million dollars she wouldn't hesitate to hand it over right now.

"Are you talking about her parents?"

"They're comfortable, but they certainly don't have that sort of disposable income. I do, but given my position, not to mention her relationship to the president, if I pay it and the news gets out, it's going to look to many as if the United States government has changed its policy on kidnapping."

"Which would essentially put a target on the backs of every American visiting or working in an unstable country," she said flatly.

"Exactly."

"Surely you're not going to sit by and do nothing."

Kirby couldn't believe that both the leader of the free world and the powerful senator many considered a shoo-in to be the next president could actually be helpless in such a situation.

"Of course not." His brow furrowed at the idea she'd even think such a thing. "We merely need deniability. And a few degrees of separation."

He picked up his phone and pressed a button. "Please send Mr. Tremayne in, Mrs. Hansen."

A moment later, the office door opened and a tall, dark-haired man entered.

From his well-tailored chalk-striped charcoal suit, crisp snowy shirt, subtly striped rep tie, and spit-polished black shoes, he could easily have passed for a K Street lobbyist.

And although the last time she'd seen him he'd been sporting long hair and a beard, and had been dressed in native garb, Kirby immediately recognized him as that Special Ops leader who'd shown up at her refugee camp on the Pakistani border.

23

Somersett, South Carolina

The landing was rough, with a couple of bounces, but at least we stayed on the runway, Shane considered as the single-engine, high-wing Cessna Skyhawk taxied toward the hangar.

"That was pretty good," he said.

"Better than last week," the forty-year-old attorney said proudly.

"Absolutely." Last week a too-sudden twist of the controls had sent them into the weeds. Another few yards and they would've landed nose down in the marsh.

"So, when do I get to solo?"

"Let's talk about that next week," Shane suggested. "After you nail a three-point landing the first time around." They'd circled the field three times, having been forced to pull up at the last minute the first two tries.

As he climbed out of the Cessna, he

viewed the BMW parked on the tarmac. Not that he could have missed it, given that the car was fire-engine red and the ex-SEAL standing next to it was six-foot-five.

Shane led his student through the post-landing checklist beginning with chocking the main wheels and tying down the wing and tail, and ending with locking the door.

"So," Quinn McKade said as the lawyer drove away in a gold Lexus, "how long are you going to keep this up?"

"Keep what up?" Shane asked, knowing the answer, since they'd had this discussion countless times before.

"Teaching idiots with more money than sense how to fly these little-bitty toy planes."

"The Cessna's no toy. And its name just happens to be synonymous with 'light aircraft.' "

"Yeah, but *yours* isn't. Or do I have to remind you that it used to be synonymous with *big* aircraft?"

"Nobody's paying me to teach lawyers to fly Chinooks," Shane said with a shrug. "Besides, this gets me back in the air. I happen to like flying."

"What a surprise. Since you just happened to be the best SOAR jockey I ever flew with."

"That was then." Shane made some notes

in the training book. "This is now."

"Damn, that's profound. When you're done with that pen, can I borrow it to write that down so I won't forget it?"

"Or you could just kiss my ass," Shane said mildly.

"You're wasting your talents. 'The first thing to remember is these are called wings,' " Quinn said in a singsong voice that sounded ridiculous coming from a guy his size. " 'The second thing to remember is that it's important to have one on each side.' "

"It's not that bad." At least he was flying. Granted, in a plane his granny Garrett could've flown, but life in the air was always better than being stuck 24/7 on the ground.

"Maybe not. But it's not that *good,* either." Quinn, who'd always been the easiest-going guy — in or out of the military — Shane had ever known was clearly frustrated. As he was every time they had this conversation. "I can understand why you didn't want to stay in the Army —"

"I joined to fly." He'd given up a lot for that. Including a Navy commission. "Once I couldn't fly, there wasn't much point in staying in."

"The Army was willing to work with you on getting back up in the air again," Quinn reminded him.

"Yeah. Bad enough you guys had to drag me up a goddamn mountain. What if I crashed in a battle zone and something went wrong with my prosthesis?"

"Probably the same thing that would happen if you crashed in a battle zone and one of your teammates shattered a leg. You'd all work it out. The way we did up in those mountains."

He had a point. And one Shane had thought about a lot lately. But, having made the decision to separate with a medical honorable discharge, he couldn't exactly turn back time.

"It's not like you're an invalid," Quinn pressed his case. "You're always beating me at b-ball."

"That's because, despite your obvious height advantage, you could be the poster guy for *White Men Can't Jump.* Hell, an eight-year-old Girl Scout could probably beat you at a game of horse."

Shane didn't add that the additional spring from his titanium and carbon-fiber sports prosthesis helped out by giving his jump shot a bit more bounce than he'd had before the crash.

Quinn slapped a hand nearly the size of a baseball mitt against his broad chest. "I'm wounded."

"Just calling them like I see them. Besides, I'm a damn good instructor."

"I've not a single doubt you are. But when was the last time you had an adrenaline rush?"

"It's obvious you've never landed with a student pilot at the controls," Shane said dryly.

"How'd you like a real job?"

"I told you, if I'm not willing to fly birds for the Army, I'm not flying them for Phoenix Team."

"Look." Quinn blew out a breath. "Discounting the fact that you'd make enough to buy your own planes, hell, even a helo if you wanted one, I wouldn't be out here asking if it wasn't important. Like, for the good of the country."

Just as he was the most easygoing guy Shane had ever met, Quinn McKade had never been prone to exaggeration.

"Next you'll be putting on a pair of shiny tap dancing shoes, singing 'Yankee Doodle Dandy,' waving Old Glory, and baking me an apple pie," he said. But, dammit, he *was* curious.

"You've heard of Senator Sherman."

"Sure. Head of the Senate Armed Services Committee."

"Well, his goddaughter, Rachel Moore, is a medical relief doctor. For WMR."

Dammit. The other man knew Shane owed his life to Kirby Campbell, who just happened to work for WMR. Not that he felt obligated to the entire organization.

The hell he didn't. Which was why a sizeable donation to the organization automatically came out of his checking account every month.

"Good for her. And this should concern me, why?"

"I guess you haven't watched the news today."

"I've been a little out of touch. Like, at five thousand feet."

"Well, the good doctor's been taken hostage by rebels in Monteleón. They're demanding a million dollars' ransom."

"Shit." Shane raked a hand through his hair, which, while not as short as he'd worn it in the military, still didn't reach his collar. "So, for that amount of money, I guess they know who she is?"

"Not yet. They're asking for the money from our government. Who they're accusing of propping up President Vasquez's corrupt government."

"Can't argue with that," Shane said. "Since everyone knows the CIA helped get rid of his predecessor. And that was even before they struck black gold, which definitely vaulted the country into national-interest category. But she's an innocent civilian. What makes them think Uncle Sam's going to open the vault to get her back?"

"They're accusing her of being CIA."

Shane thought about that for a moment. Given that there were spooks working all over the world, including the ones who'd shown up with that bird in Pakistan, it wasn't an impossible scenario.

"Any chance it's true?"

"No. Zach's spent the morning on the phone, talking to a lot of people who know her well. She's actually not a real big fan of the CIA, since, like you said, they've had their fingers in the Monteleón pie for decades. Though scuttlebutt at Langley says the current agency station chief went down there with a new broom a few months ago and began cleaning house."

"Good luck with that."

"There's more. The doctor just happens to also be related to the president. Ours, not Vasquez."

Shane whistled. "That's one helluva can of worms."

"Which is why Sherman called Phoenix

202

Team. We're going deep, midnight black on this one, and if we're caught, needless to say, we're totally on our own. The government will deny all knowledge of our involvement, which would be true, since the senator's acting as a private person, not a member of congress."

"A distinction that wouldn't fly all that well if the press got hold of it."

"Exactly. Which is why we can't screw up. And in order to make sure we pull it off, we need the best bird jockey in the business. Who would be you . . .

"Oh, and before you turn me down again, there's one more thing you might be interested in. Zach just called from D.C. He's bringing back a new member of the team who's familiar with both the country and the players."

He paused, looking like a guy who'd just drawn a royal flush in a world championship game of Texas hold 'em.

"Well?" Shane asked. "You going to tell me who it is?"

"Doctor Kirby Campbell, who missed being captured in the raid only because she happened to be in D.C., testifying to a senate subcommittee."

Shane didn't have to think twice about it. "Count me in."

24

"Well, former Captain Campbell," Zachariah Tremayne greeted her. "We meet again."

"It appears so," she responded as her hand momentarily disappeared into his much larger, darker one.

The last she'd seen this man, he'd been climbing onto a Russian helicopter, risking his career and prison because of a brother-in-arms. She guessed he must not have ended up court-martialed and imprisoned in Leavenworth, since he was here in the office of the chairman of the Armed Services Committee.

"Zach Tremayne," he introduced himself. "I assume the senator's filled you in."

"He told me about Rachel."

There was more. Kirby wondered if the president, as Commander-in-Chief, was actually bringing in the military. While personally she'd love to send in the SEALs,

SOAR, Rangers, Delta Force, and all the Marines to save Rachel, surely there'd be a considerable fallout if the head of the country used the armed forces to rescue a member of his family.

"Mr. Tremayne is a former SEAL," Sherman revealed. "Now a member of Phoenix Team."

"I haven't heard of them." She wondered if it was some supersecret agency set up under the vast and complex Homeland Security umbrella.

"That's because we're private," Tremayne said. "Real private. We don't have a Web site, you won't find us in the yellow pages, and we only work on referral. We fly beneath the radar, doing the jobs the military can't, or won't, do." His eyes were flint, his jaw firm. "We're also the best in the business."

Having watched the way the men had maneuvered their way out of that refugee camp without a shot fired, Kirby believed him.

"And you're going to get Rachel out of Monteleón?"

"Yes, ma'am," he said. "We are."

Again, Kirby didn't doubt him.

"Good. And I'm going with you."

"What?" He shot a look at Sherman.

"Ms. Campbell," the senator began in a

cajoling voice.

"It's too dangerous," Tremayne said at the same time. "Besides, we've already got a doctor on board willing to work as team medic."

"It's not up for discussion." Kirby met his frustrated gaze with a firm one of her own. "If you recall, Mr. Tremayne, I wasn't exactly having high tea with the queen when we met. As an army physician, I was trained in self-defense and know how to handle a weapon." Since the senator had given that card earlier, Kirby decided to play it.

"There's also the fact that Rachel is my closest friend. And given the Special Ops motto to leave no man behind, I'm sure you'd agree that friends don't leave friends in the lurch."

"That's why I brought you here," Sherman said. "Since you and Rachel work together, you know the country better than anyone, including the ambassador, whom I suspect hasn't stepped outside the city limits of Ciudad Libertad."

"Not that I know of," Kirby agreed.

"Which is why the senator thought you could fill me in on the particulars of the location of the clinic and all the players," Tremayne said.

"Of course I will." Kirby agreed. "On the

way to Monteleón."

"That's not in the cards." The former SEAL's mouth grimly tightened.

Kirby could tell he was accustomed to people taking his orders without question. Tough.

"Then I suggest you deal yourself another deck, Mr. Tremayne," she said sweetly. "Because I'm going back to Monteleón. With or without you."

The back-and-forth motion of that wide jaw suggested he was grinding his teeth. Well, he could grind them to dust, but she wasn't giving in.

"As Senator Sherman has just pointed out, I know the country better than most Americans, and certainly better than anyone else in this room. I know where the rebel camps and marijuana farms are."

She folded her arms. No way was she going to stay behind. "I know the country. And I know the players. So whether you like it or not, Phoenix Team just took on a partner."

He dragged his hands down his face. Then looked at her, hard, trying to stare her down.

His unblinking eyes were a compelling kaleidoscopic combination of slate gray and blue, with a touch of hazel around the rim. They were also rife with frustration.

Having not wilted before those Afghan terrorists armed with AK-47s, there was no way Kirby was going to cave in now.

She met Tremayne's gaze. And waited.

His curse was brief and harsh and absolutely befitting the Navy SEAL he'd once been.

"You don't intimidate easily, do you, Doctor?" he asked.

"I haven't yet. And since we're going to be working together, you might as well call me Kirby."

"And you're not bluffing about going down there by yourself, are you?"

"I never bluff. I always speak my mind. Which," she admitted, thinking back to that dinner party, "has been pointed out to me isn't always prudent."

He studied her for another long time.

"If I allow you to come along, you'll have to work as a member of the team."

"Having spent the past several years in the Army, then working for WMR, I'm well acquainted with teamwork."

"While you may have outranked me in the military, you've been knocked down to a buck private in Phoenix Team," he warned.

"And here I'd always heard that one of the differences of the SEAL structure was that every member of the team is a leader," she said.

"True. In a traditional military structure, officers give the orders, and if there *are* no orders, there's no activity. In a SEAL platoon, the command is usually just 'Get it done,' and each member of the team sees what he needs to do to accomplish the mission, and does it.

"My point is that you are not a SEAL," he said through gritted teeth. "You've never been one, and never will be. So, here's how it's going to work. . . .

"I give the orders, you follow. I tell you to jump, you say 'Hooyah,' and ask me how high. I tell you to stay put and shut up, you don't even say 'Roger,' you just close your mouth and don't move a muscle until I give you permission. Is that clear?"

She simply looked at him.

He rubbed his forehead. He was wearing a gold band on his left hand that he hadn't had in Pakistan. Then again, it was unlikely a SEAL trying to blend into the local population would wear a wedding ring.

"Permission to speak," he said wearily.

"Roger," she said, snapping off a brisk military salute suitable for a four-star general.

His lips quirked, just a little. "Well, now that we've agreed on the rules of conduct, how soon can you be ready to leave for South Carolina?"

"As soon as I pick up my suitcase at the hotel, I can leave whenever you're ready. But am I allowed to ask a question?"

He blew out a harsh, frustrated breath. "This isn't a dictatorship, Doctor. Of course you're allowed to ask a damn question. It's just important I make sure, for everyone's sake, especially Dr. Moore's, that Phoenix Team isn't stuck with a loose cannon. So ask away."

"I realize you know more about covert activities than I do," Kirby allowed. She'd always believed in giving credit where credit was due. "Which means I was more than willing to follow your leadership before you decided to play Captain Queeg."

He still didn't smile. But she did see a fleeting glint of humor in his eyes.

"I'm just wondering why we're going to South Carolina."

"It's Phoenix Team's home base. Where the rest of the team, as you and I sit here arguing, is making plans."

"Well." She stood up. "I take that to mean you're ready to go."

"Roger that."

He said good-bye to the senator, assuring him that they'd do everything in their power to bring Rachel back safe and sound.

"I assume you booked a flight, knowing I'd be coming with you?" Kirby asked as they made their way down the green marble hallway.

"We've got a jet waiting to take us to South Carolina," he said.

"A private jet?"

"It's faster than waiting around a gate, hoping a flight isn't canceled."

"The security business must pay very well."

He shrugged. "The guy who created Phoenix Team has deep pockets. He's willing to spend when time is of the essence, like it is now."

"God, I can't believe this is happening," Kirby said while they walked across the expansive, skylit atrium, forced to weave through a clutch of tourists listening avidly to a lecture about the centerpiece of the marbled atrium, which apparently depicted mountains and clouds.

He glanced over at her. "Given the situation in Monteleón, you can't be all that surprised."

"Well, actually, I suppose not. But still, although Rachel and I have had a few unsettling incidents, I don't think anyone ever believes it's going to happen to you or anyone you know."

"Occupational self-denial," he said quietly.

From his flat tone, as they continued out of the surprisingly modern building onto the street, Kirby suspected he might be thinking back to that day they'd met in Pakistani mountains.

"There's something you should know," he said, after she'd retrieved her suitcase from the hotel bell captain. "In case you want to change your mind about coming along."

"That's not going to happen. So what is it?"

"I got a call from Quinn McKade while you were picking up your overnight case from the bell captain. He's the big guy who was with us that day."

She nodded. While all the Spec Ops guys had been impressive, that particular man was not someone anyone would meet and forget.

"He told me Garrett's signed on to be our pilot."

Even as her heart stopped, Kirby wasn't as surprised as she might have been. The men had undoubtedly had that band-of-brother thing going in order to make their way through those steep, snowy mountains filled with enemy fighters after the helicopter had gotten shot down. It only made sense that they'd continue such close team-work in their civilian lives.

It would also mean that she'd have to put in the deep freeze whatever feelings she had for the man. Something she'd have to remind her heart, which had begun beating again. Too hard and too fast, but that was undoubtedly only from all the coffee she'd drunk on an empty stomach.

"Well, that's reassuring," she said mildly.

Zach looked surprised by her response. "You mean that?"

"Of course. If I'm going to be risking my life, why wouldn't I want to fly with some-one who can land a helicopter in a snow-storm after it has been hit by an RPG? He must be doing well," she said with more casualness than she was feeling.

Although she'd wanted to be angry at him for sending her away, even though she'd guessed there was nothing Shane Garrett couldn't handle, that hadn't stopped her from worrying.

"Better than well. He's kicking butt with his new leg. Actually, it's kind of neat; he's got different ones for various situations."

"I've read the science is really taking off."

She'd spent hours on the Internet and reading every article in every professional journal she could unearth. Unfortunately, the rush to improved technology was partly due to the numbers of amputees returning home. Body armor could, as its name implied, only protect the body.

"He signed up to be kind of a guinea pig for the researchers," he volunteered. "Trying out some high-tech stuff that makes him a lot like the Six Million Dollar Man. Though with inflation, he's probably worth a lot more.

"He's back to running every day, working out, giving some lectures at ASMA — that's a military academy in Somersett, South Carolina — and teaching flying."

"That's good to hear."

"I figured you'd want to bail on the mission," he admitted. "Given the way he treated you in Germany. Which, by the way, not that you asked, but I told him I thought sucked."

At first she was surprised that he knew about that. Then decided that the fact that they were all still together in civilian life showed how close the men were.

"I told you. No way would I bail. As for Germany, it admittedly wasn't the easiest day I've ever spent. But, putting it in perspective, it wasn't the worst, either. And he'd been through a lot and was on heavy drugs when I showed up at Landstuhl. Plus, depression isn't uncommon after an amputation. It's perfectly understandable that tact wouldn't have been a real high priority at the time."

"Most women would be pissed off enough to still be holding a major grudge."

"I'm not most women," she said mildly, refusing to admit talking about that day still stung.

He shot her a look.

"I'm beginning to figure that out for myself," he said.

25

Swann Island, South Carolina
The worldwide offices of Phoenix Team
were set in the center of what Kirby guessed
must be at least ten wooded acres on a bluff
overlooking the Atlantic Ocean. A wall surrounded the property, and the tall iron gate
opened only after a visual scan of the
driver's pupil.

The building itself was a surprise. Designed along the lines of a traditional Lowcountry house, it was set on piers, with a
wide front porch boasting ceiling fans. The
siding had weathered to a silvery gray, two
stone chimneys rose high on either side of
the house, and double dormers contributed
to its homey appeal.

There was a helicopter landing pad to the
right of the circular driveway and small
parking lot, and basketball and racquetball
courts on the left, suggesting that members
of Phoenix Team took their play as seriously

as their work.

Unlike its homey exterior, inside the metal and veneer furniture could have come from DOD procurement. It wasn't any different from what she'd seen at military bases all around the world. Still, she supposed clients didn't hire Phoenix Team for its decorating savvy.

The floor-to-ceiling windows, however, offered a dazzling view of the water. But she had to wonder, given the building's purpose, if the glass was bulletproof.

"Bullet *resistant,*" Zach said when she asked. "There's no such thing as true bulletproof glass. At least not yet. When the company was founded, no one wanted to get rid of the view from when this was used as a family home, so the glass was replaced for security reasons. But there are also metal shutters that instantly lower at the touch of a button. Even if the power's off. Just in case."

Kirby decided not to ask what that "just in case" might be.

He introduced her to a young man behind the front desk, whose high-and-tight haircut, and the way he'd leaped to attention as he informed Zach that the other team members were waiting in the conference room, suggested he might be a Marine.

A fact Zach confirmed as he led her down a hallway. "New hires always work the desk until they get into the swing of things," he said. "But he proved his stuff with us up in the Kush. After his third tour, he decided he was ready for a new challenge. Since we currently have more work than we can handle, I think he's going to be a real good fit."

Kirby had assured herself during the hour-long flight here from D.C. that she was prepared to see Shane again. After all, forewarned was forearmed, and she'd certainly moved on with her life.

Well, okay, maybe moving on hadn't included sex. She might have made a huge mistake with the too-sexy-for-his-Wranglers Night Stalker pilot, but if there was one thing medical school had taught her, it was to learn from her mistakes. Of course, there was the little fact that she hadn't met a man she'd had the least interest in having sex with.

Until, heaven help her, she walked into the room, saw him sitting at the oval conference table, and felt her suddenly unruly pulse triple its beat.

His sable hair was longer than it had been in Iraq. Not as long as a lot of the Spec Ops guys had worn theirs, but still long enough to comb her fingers through. And to grab hold of. (Not that she had any intention of doing that.) It was streaked with gold she knew hadn't come from a bottle, but from being outdoors in the sun.

His body, clad in jeans and a snug blue T-shirt with SOMERSETT COASTAL AVIATION above a plane logo, stretched over broad shoulders and a chest that appeared as ripped as it had been their last time together, in her Green Zone trailer, when it had been gloriously naked.

"Some of you probably remember Doctor Campbell," Zach introduced her.

"There's a lot of stuff I've worked to forget about that day," Quinn McKade said. "But you're definitely not one of them, Doctor. In fact, if my breath hadn't probably tasted like a dead dog, I would've kissed you on the mouth."

"Well, you certainly hid your feelings well."

She couldn't remember him revealing any emotion. The SEAL had been as inscrutable and rugged as the mountain peaks looming over the camp.

"You know what they say about timing." His quick, sexy grin was nothing like the stone face she recalled.

"I certainly do," she said.

Deciding that the time had come to face the inevitable, she turned her full attention to Shane, who was, for some reason, shooting a steely stare at Quinn McKade.

"Hello, Captain Garrett." Even as she used his rank as a distancing device, Kirby prided herself on sounding supercasual, as if they were merely acquaintances who'd just seen each other yesterday. Rather than eighteen long months and fourteen days ago. Not that she was counting. "You're looking well."

Better than well. Dammit, he looked sinfully, unbearably good, his cowboy charisma oozing from every tanned pore.

"It's former Captain," he said, as if she hadn't known he'd left the Army. "And I'm feeling great." His Western baritone was still sexy as hell. "Thanks to you."

When he skimmed a look over her, in much the same way she'd checked him out while trying not to, Kirby was all too aware of her dark suit and starkly tailored white blouse she'd chosen because she'd wanted to look professional, so the senators would concentrate on her words instead of her body.

Unfortunately, that attempted bit of camouflage had her looking as if she were auditioning for the role of Will Smith's new partner in another *Men In Black* sequel.

"I was just doing my job," she repeated what she'd said that day in Germany.

She'd managed to mostly convince herself that she'd put his rejection behind her. Moved on with her life.

But as she felt that painful crack in her unruly heart opening up again, Kirby realized she'd been wrong.

"So," he said, "Quinn tells me you're helping plan this op."

She feigned calm. "I'm providing intel." She paused, realizing he hadn't been completely filled in. "Both here and in Monteleón."

"No way." He spun toward Zach. "She's not going into the jungle."

The other man shrugged. "Her information can be helpful. We need her on the team. Unfortunately, her staying behind in the States was a deal breaker."

"No way," Shane repeated. His biceps bulged as he folded his arms across his chest.

Grateful for the little flare of irritation that burned away her unexpected vulnerability, Kirby tossed up her chin.

"Way," she said sweetly.

He turned back to Zach, as if a man, especially a Navy SEAL, would have more sense than a blond female. Even one who'd saved his damn life.

"She's not going," he said through clenched teeth. "It's too damn dangerous."

"She insisted," Zach repeated. "Like I said, she can be helpful."

"She could also end up dead. Or worse."

"Excuse me," Kirby said, waving a hand. "But *she* just happens to be here in the room. And she can speak for herself."

It was her turn to fold her arms. If either of the men dialed up the macho level an additional notch, she'd be in serious danger of testosterone poisoning.

"If you're through pounding your manly warrior chest," she said to Shane, "I'd like to point out that, first of all, only a male would think there would be anything worse for a woman than death.

"I can tell you, as a physician, that dead is dead. And it's final. So, putting that issue aside, may I point out that I've been living in that very same jungle for the past six months?"

"Yeah. And look what happened," Shane argued. "If you'd been there when those rebels attacked the clinic . . ."

He paused. Drew in a deep breath, then let it out, as if attempting to garner composure.

"Christ, Kirby, if you hadn't been here in the States, it could be *you* we'd be running off to Monteleón to rescue."

Which was precisely what she'd been thinking about all the way on the flight from D.C. Instead of feeling relieved she'd escaped being taken hostage, she'd felt guilty for not having been there for her friend.

"Then it would be Rachel who'd be here helping you come up with a plan to rescue me," she said. "And I know damn well she wouldn't stay behind, either."

Refusing to give him the opportunity to argue that point, she pressed on. "I've been in a lot more dangerous situations. In fact, that day you were brought into the camp I'd just finished operating on the son of Imam Jalaluddin."

"Fuck that." He turned to Quinn, as if for confirmation.

What? Did he actually think she'd make something like that up? Besides, he'd been there. They'd even spoken, and although she hadn't mentioned the terrorists to him, surely the two SEALs had filled him in on their dicey situation as they'd made their way to the helicopter.

"It's true," both Quinn and Zach said at the same time.

"We saw him and his security force,"

Quinn said. "You saw them, too. Even insisted we give you back your M4."

"Shit." Shane pinched the bridge of his nose. "I don't remember anything about that."

"Have you had such instances before?" Kirby asked.

"A few." His tone suggested it wasn't his favorite subject.

Too bad.

"I'm sure your doctors have explained you could easily have had a TBI during all you went through which could have caused memory loss," she said. "Many people have head injuries and never realize it. Plus, it's not uncommon to have retrograde amnesia after surgery, due to certain anesthetics increasing central serotonergic activity."

"Yeah. That's what I've been told. But the gaps aren't that long and I can remember most of what went on."

"They're what's referred to as memory *islands.* And usually the forgotten memories return. But not always."

She wondered if he even remembered talking to her at the camp. And was it possible he'd forgotten sending her away? No. Not only would forgetting things that occurred after the injury involve anterograde amnesia, but Tremayne's comment about the former pilot's behavior having sucked indicated he'd shared their dismal conversation at Landstul.

Shane looked back at Zach. "I take it they didn't try to stop us from leaving."

"It was a Mexican standoff," Zach answered. "If they'd tried to shoot us, they risked getting the kid killed, and if they survived the gun battle —"

"Which they wouldn't have," Quinn broke in.

"Not in this lifetime," Zach agreed. "Still, things happen. They had a choice. Try to stop us from leaving in that CIA copter and risk heads literally rolling if they lost the kid, or stand down and save the battle for another day."

Shane looked back at Kirby with that same admiration she remembered seeing in his eyes that first night, when he'd shown up in her ER and she'd given him the keys to her trailer.

She could still feel the heat of him, his taste as he'd soul kissed her, making her realize that she'd never been truly, thoroughly kissed before. Then he'd taken her into the tiny bathroom, barely large enough for two people to turn around in, where they'd . . .

No. She would not, *could* not remember that day.

The only reason they were back together was because of Rachel. So long as she kept that thought in the forefront of her mind, she'd be fine.

"If that kid in the camp had died while you were working on him —"

"But he didn't."

Shane rubbed his cheek, obviously uncomfortable with the idea of her being in danger.

"I treated Iraqis all the time in the Cash," she reminded him.

"Sure. But you were surrounded by armed guards back in the Green Zone. Out there in the mountains you were on your own."

"Exactly." Check. And mate. She nearly smiled as he realized he'd just backed himself into a corner with that statement.

Satisfied she'd won that round, she turned to Zach, who'd taken his place at the end of the long table. "So, gentlemen," she said, folding her hands on the tabletop. "What's the plan?"

"Well, obviously we're now going to be making some adjustments, since you've joined the team," Zach said.

"Along with providing intel about the compound, I'll be able to take care of any medical problems that might crop up."

Which, in the jungle, were too many to count.

"We won't be needing your medical skills, Doctor," he said. "We've already got a team physician." He turned toward the man sitting next to Shane. "Doctor Michael Gannon."

The name rang an instant and very loud bell. Surely there couldn't be two men with that same name. Well, actually there probably could be. But what were the odds?

"Doctor Gannon? I thought you were a priest."

After they'd gotten back to the compound, Rachel had told Kirby that the reason she'd lost the man she loved was because after returning from Iraq, Dr. Michael Gannon had entered a seminary.

In contrast to Shane's well-muscled athleticism, the priest named for a fallen angel could have washed off the nave ceiling of a Renaissance cathedral. Lush black hair framed a poet's face; his eyes, set above slashing cheekbones, were an intense blue; and his beautifully sculpted lips had been designed to tempt both sinner and saint.

One look at him and she understood why Rachel had fallen fast and hard. And, apparently, had never quite gotten over him.

And couldn't Kirby identify with that?

"I was," the former Father What-a-Waste said. "I'm not any longer."

She thought it spoke a lot to his self-discipline that he didn't ask how she'd heard of him. Though he had to know.

"There's no TV in the jungle," she said. "Only occasional radio signals that bounce in from the city at night. Which is good, in a way, because it tends to give people time to talk."

He nodded, letting her know he'd received her message and understood that Rachel had shared their story.

At least part of it.

Since Rachel hadn't known why he'd become a priest after their time together in Kuwait, Kirby didn't, either. But she suspected the fact that he'd injected himself in this mission was an indication that he still had strong feelings for the WMR doctor.

"I was in touch with the CIA station chief while you were in Washington," Quinn told Zach. "Apparently, the general's concerned our government's going to send in Special Forces on a rescue mission. The way we did in Operation Urgent Fury back in the eighties to get those medical students out of Grenada."

"Why should that concern him?" Kirby asked. "It seems he'd be more than happy to have our Special Forces take on the rebels for him."

"You'd think so, wouldn't you?" Zach said. "But Vasquez is antsy these days because he's worried about Josefina Madrid's impending return to run against him in the upcoming presidential election."

"I've been hearing that for months," Kirby said. "But it's just a rumor. Isn't it?"

"I'm not exactly in the military intelligence loop these days," Zach said. "But nothing would surprise me about that place."

Which, Kirby decided, was as close to a confirmation about Madrid's return that she was going to get. What was already a volatile situation in Monteleón was obviously about to get a whole lot worse.

"Now that you've joined the team," he said, "I've got an idea on how to handle our potential problem with Vasquez."

"Which would be?"

"You're going to convince the president that he doesn't have anything to worry about. That there is no way the U.S. is sending troops into his country."

"Why would he believe me?"

"Because you've already earned a reputation for speaking your mind. Especially after that dinner the other night."

"And you say you're out of the loop."

Could they actually have the palace bugged? Or, more likely, she thought, one of those waiters — who no one, including herself, had paid that much attention to — must have been working for the CIA.

"Word gets out," he said. "Vasquez knows you left the country to go to D.C. to testify to congress. You can tell him that as soon as you learned about the kidnapping, you went from office to office in the Capitol, lobbying for help to rescue your partner.

"Unfortunately, you came away empty-handed, so now you're begging him for help."

"Which you just pointed out he won't want to do."

"He won't. But if we're lucky, he may just buy your story enough to let down his guard. Which will buy more time and make it easier for us to get into the country."

Kirby wished she were as sure about her persuasive powers as he was.

"Maybe it's because I'm jet-lagged," she said. "But I'm still having trouble with why Vasquez wouldn't be more than willing to invade the compound. It seems he'd love an excuse to use the full force of his army to kill Castillo and declare a military and moral victory."

"Jesus Castillo isn't at the compound," Shane entered the conversation. Obviously he'd been briefed before she'd arrived. "There's no point in Vasquez risking his men to take on some underlings. Especially since, if those whacked-out kids actually kill the doctor, the president gains the moral high ground."

He grimaced, obviously realizing he'd been too blunt. "Sorry," he said to Michael.

"Unfortunately, I believe you called it right," the former priest said. "As far as both Vasquez and Castillo are concerned, Rachel's merely a pawn." When his beautifully sculpted lips pulled into a tight, grim line, he looked far more warrior than priest. "An *expendable* pawn."

"I'll do whatever I can to help get her out of there," Kirby said fervently. It was, after all, exactly what Rachel would do if their situation were reversed.

"Okay. Welcome to the team." Zach stood up and went over to a large white board on the wall. "Let's get started."

26

Shane had assured himself that he'd prepared for Kirby's arrival. But, damn, he'd
forgotten how good she smelled. She'd
never gone in for that expensive stuff in
fancy bottles; it was her own unique scent
that somehow managed to still surround her
even after a long day working in the CSH.
It was sweet, without smelling like a funeral
parlor full of flowers, and green, but not as
pungent as new-mown grass. "Fresh" was
the only word he could come up with.

Doctor Kirby Campbell reminded him of
a mountain meadow after a spring rain.
They'd spent a lot of hours in bed, their
arms and legs tangled as he'd pressed his
lips against her hair and drank in the scent,
never quite placing it. But the one thing he
knew for sure was that he'd never smelled
anything before or since that could cause
such a knee-jerk jolt of lust.

He hated the fact that she was going to be

in danger. Which, in a way, was his fault. If he hadn't been such a shithead and lied to make sure she'd go away after she'd come all that way to visit him in Landstuhl, they might have actually gotten married. She hadn't come right out and said it — and sure, he'd been doped to the gills — but he could've sworn he saw a white-picket-fence fantasy shining in her remarkable eyes.

Not that being married gave a guy automatic veto power over a woman. Especially *this* woman. But wasn't marriage all about give and take? That's how it seemed to work with his folks, who were going on nearly forty years together.

If a husband calmly, rationally stated his case about wanting to keep his wife safe from doped-up killer rapists-terrorists, surely said wife would listen to reason.

Wouldn't she?

He watched Kirby intently listen to something Quinn was saying — it was difficult to hear anything with the blood roaring in his ears, as it had been doing since she stepped in the door, dressed like an impossibly sexy nun — and remembered that one of the things he'd always admired about her was that the lady wasn't a pushover.

She'd fight like a tiger for something she believed in. And obviously, as she'd proven with her trip to Germany, loyalty was one of her strongest traits.

So, no. Even if he hadn't been such an ass, and they had gotten hitched, she might have insisted on going to work for the WMR. Which, in turn, could have landed her in this same situation.

But not, Shane considered, as his mind wandered into a hazy, appealing fantasy, if he'd gotten her pregnant.

Although he liked his nieces and nephews a lot, he'd never given much thought to having any curtain climbers of his own before. Once he'd become a Night Stalker, he'd pretty much been married to Special Forces.

Still, call him a cowboy chauvinist, and a few women admittedly *had* over the years, but the idea of Kirby having his baby was suddenly more than a little appealing.

"Sorry." Realizing that everyone in the room was looking at him, Shane dragged his mind out of a hot fantasy of making love to a ripe and round Kirby Garrett on a fur rug in front of a blazing fire. "Would you mind repeating that?"

"I said," Zach repeated, giving Shane one of those hard-ass SEAL looks designed to encourage cooperation, "while Dr. Campbell —"

"Kirby," she said.

Zach didn't quite roll his eyes, but knowing how the former SEAL chief petty officer disliked being interrupted, Shane suspected he wanted to.

"While *Kirby,*" he corrected with overt patience, "is in the capital, reassuring Vasquez that our government has left Dr. Moore hanging out to dry, we'll be executing a covert landing."

"She's not going down there alone." Shane's mind was instantly, fully back on the mission.

"We're in full agreement there," Zach said. "Since all the air strips in the country are controlled by either the rebel forces or the Army, most of them built for the drug trade, I don't want to risk coming in by plane, because we wouldn't be able to hide any aircraft.

"So we'll do a beach landing in Costa Rica." He circled a section of coast on the map he'd taped onto the board. "And come into Monteleón, here, where the border's unguarded." He drew an X at the spot. "Meanwhile, you'll be with Dr., uh, Kirby in Ciudad Libertad."

"How am I going to explain showing up with a Special Ops guy in tow?" she asked.

"I'm not Spec Ops anymore," Shane said.

"Maybe not." Her gaze swept the room.

"But you all might as well be. You're just private these days."

"We're not mercenaries," Quinn said firmly.

"And I don't even work with these guys," Shane said.

"I wasn't calling you mercenaries," she swiftly corrected Quinn. "And perhaps I'm merely having a blond moment, but color me confused." Kirby batted her lashes and looked at Shane with mock perplexity. "If you're not a member of Phoenix Team, what are you doing here?"

"Freelancing. I owe a lot to WMR. Even more to you."

"I told you —"

"Yeah. I've heard it before. But it doesn't matter, because you're not going to change my mind. The bottom line is you saved my life, sugar. You know that old Chinese saying 'Save a life and it becomes yours'? Seems you're stuck with me."

"Not if you call me *sugar* again, I'm not," she warned.

He considered asking if she'd prefer *cupcake*, which she'd seemed to like well enough in Iraq. The question was right on the tip of his tongue.

Deciding, for now, that discretion was the better part of valor, Shane bit it back.

"Anyway, getting back to the subject at hand," he said, as he felt Zach's annoyance level rising, "I can pull off being a civilian. Especially a gimpy one. Being that I *am* one."

Her gaze slid unconsciously to his leg, which was under the table. But Shane knew she was curious. As a doctor? Or a woman?

"Still, won't he be suspicious? Since I left the country alone?"

"Shane's an old boyfriend," Zach said.

"Oh, please." She groaned.

"It'll work," Zach assured her. "You ran into him in D.C. while you were in the city to testify. Sparks rekindled, but then you heard about your friend being taken captive, so after striking out, trying to get help from our government, you rushed back down there to try to convince Vasquez to rescue her."

"And, being that I'm head over heels in love with her, and being a typical protective he-man alpha male — which any Latin guy can undoubtedly identify with — I refused to let the little lady go into a potentially dangerous situation alone," Shane picked up the story.

"Exactly." Zach nodded.

She frowned. "I think I hate 'little lady' worse than 'sugar.' You remind me of John

Wayne talking down to Maureen O'Hara."

Shane might not share his father's undying admiration for the actor, but having had to sit through countless showings of Wayne's movies over the years, he couldn't let that accusation pass unchallenged.

"You don't like the Duke?" Actually, he was surprised she'd ever *seen* a John Wayne movie, then decided they'd been popular among Green Zone military types.

"I have no idea about what kind of person John Wayne was. He might have been a gem of a guy. But it's hard to like a character who'd drag his wife across five miles of field with an entire village watching her humiliation."

"*The Quiet Man* was a dynamite movie," Shane argued. "And, the way I saw it, that quick-fire Maureen O'Hara always gave as good as she got."

She snorted.

"Ever see *McClintock*?"

"No." She didn't sound all that eager to, either. Like maybe she'd put it on her to-do list right after skinny-dipping with a school of piranha.

"You should. It has everything that made a Wayne movie great — cowboys, Indians, fistfights, not to mention some damn good brawling and hot lip-locks and clinches with

O'Hara. Their mud fight is a movie classic."

She actually rolled her eyes. "I believe I'll pass."

"Surely somewhere along the way you've read Shakespeare?"

"Of course. I was planning to be a lit major before turning to medicine."

He hadn't known that. Once again, Shane thought there was a lot about the sexy doctor he needed to learn.

"Well, you'd especially like *McClintock,* then, because it's a Western take on *The Taming of the Shrew.*"

"Which wasn't my favorite play, either."

Suspecting she wouldn't get the same kick out of the spanking scene at the end of that movie that he and his dad had, Shane decided against ever renting the DVD to share with her.

"So, Ebert," Zach said with obvious frustration, "if you're through giving us this week's movie reviews, can we get back to the topic at hand?"

"Aye, aye, sir." Shane grinned and saluted to show he didn't mind the reprimand.

Kirby shook her head. She did not appear amused.

"So, if I'm stuck pretending a reunion romance, what's the rest of our cover story?" she asked Shane. "What are you supposed to be doing? Surely you're not a former SOAR pilot?"

"Nah. Maybe I'm a congressional staffer. We met in the office building while you were testifying."

"Won't work," Quinn said. "Which just goes to show you flyboys don't spend enough time on the ground, mingling with the natives, to learn how to come up with a believable cover."

"Being a staffer smells too much of government involvement," Zach said. "Vasquez didn't get where he is by being stupid. Anything to do with the government would be bound to set off his internal bullshit alarms."

"Okay." Shane considered for a minute. "How about a lobbyist? Strike that," he said, before anyone could object to the idea. "Even if I did have time to go out and get an Armani suit and silk tie, even a banana republic dictator would never buy me as a member of the K Street Gucci brigade."

"It'd help if you had a job that would allow you to take this time of year off," Kirby mused.

Despite her objection to the romantic scenario, Shane noticed she seemed to be getting into the role-playing part of the gig.

"Well, that lets out Santa Claus," he said.

She ignored the admittedly lame comment. "What about a professor? Maybe from Georgetown."

"Closer." Zach nodded thoughtfully. "But Vasquez went to college in the States, so he's familiar with our culture. Think Georgetown, and the first things that come to mind are basketball, lawyers, and poli-sci majors. Which, again, risks a link to politics, which in turn suggests the government."

"It's obvious, with my artificial leg, I'm not a serious b-ball player. Though," Shane tacked on, "I've beat everyone in this room except Kirby at one-on-one."

"It's that damn carbon-fiber spring," both former SEALs said at the same time.

"Gives you an advantage," Quinn claimed.

"Like being six-five shouldn't come in handy from time to time, especially when you're trying to dunk," Shane countered. Though his sports leg was the coolest of the three prostheses he'd brought home from Walter Reed. "No way do I want to risk my karma even pretending to be a lawyer," he said, getting back to the topic at hand, "and again, a poli-sci professor would stink of government ties, particularly in D.C.

"So why don't I just teach history at Gallaudet? Since I minored in military history when I was pre-law, I should be okay if he decides to pull a pop quiz. We could've run into each other at Starbucks, which is definitely believable, since you can't throw a rock in the city without breaking one of their windows."

"That could work," Kirby said. "Especially if I went in there to use the wireless for my laptop to check my e-mail. But in case it's slipped your mind, there's a little matter of Gallaudet being a university for the deaf. It's possible Vasquez knows that."

"No problem. I don't want to boast or anything, but along with speaking Russian, Farsi, Spanish, Tagalog, and enough Cantonese to order Peking duck in Beijing, I just happen to be fluent in ASL."

To prove his point, he ran through a quick series of signs and finger spelling. The signing was much faster than anyone would ever use in normal conversation, and meant solely to impress.

It apparently worked.

Lowering the wall she'd erected between them from the moment she'd walked into the office with Zach, she stared at Shane. "How on earth do you know that?"

"My mother came down with scarlet fever when she was a toddler. Since she grew up on a ranch, even farther from town than the ranch she and my dad had, people tended to only go to the doctor in emergencies. Unfortunately, by the time her fever spiked and the rash broke out, her hearing had already been affected."

"I had no idea."

He could tell she was stunned by that revelation.

The reason she hadn't known was they didn't exactly waste much time talking about intimate stuff. Not that having sex at every possible opportunity wasn't intimate. It just hadn't been all that personal.

Hell, since the only choices in the Green Zone had been the dining hall, one Italian place, and two Chinese restaurants, he wasn't even sure he knew her favorite food. Or what she liked to do on a lazy Sunday morning when she didn't have to worry about helos bringing in wounded, or what movies she liked, and what she'd been like as a kid.

Although the timing wasn't perfect, Shane had learned the hard way that life didn't always wait for a plan. So, he decided, he might as well take this opportunity that had been dropped in his lap to make up for lost time.

"While I'm admittedly impressed by your signing skills, I'm sorry about your mother," she said.

He shrugged with what he hoped was the proper amount of aw-shucks response, and was glad she hadn't asked what he'd signed. Since he had the feeling she wouldn't be thrilled to learn he'd just silently told her how great she smelled and how hot she was, even in that ugly navy suit, and how he'd really, really like to have sex again. Like now. Right on top of Phoenix Team's glossy conference table.

"It didn't seem to be any big deal for her," he said, dragging his mind away from wondering if she still wore that white cotton underwear he'd been thinking about just the other night, and that, for some reason, had been such a turn-on.

Maybe because it had contrasted so much with the sexy inner Kirby.

"At least not by the time my brother and sister and I came along. She couldn't remember hearing. So, for Mom, I guess being deaf was normal. And, I gotta say, she could sure cuss like a sailor on shore leave when we kids screwed up."

As serious as the reason for them all being here was, the memory of a time when she'd hit the roof after he and his brother had put a parachute on a barn cat and dropped it from the top of the hayloft made Shane smile.

"It was also cool at school," he said. "My brother and I had a secret language."

"Well."

He could practically see the wheels turning in her head and suspected that she was thinking the same thing he just had. That they definitely had some catching up to do on personal stuff if they were going to pull off any questioning by Vasquez.

Quinn was right about him not being as up on the undercover stuff as those big bad SEALs or Delta Force boys might be, but he figured out that the closer they stuck to the truth about the day-to-day stuff, the better off they'd be.

"We'll keep our background info simple," he said. "Nothing that won't check out." He glanced over at Quinn. "Can that guy you know at the NPRC block access to my records?"

The National Personnel Records Center, outside St. Louis, held the military personnel, health, and medical records of every discharged and deceased veteran who served during the twentieth century.

The former SEAL nodded. "Consider it done. It's unlikely Vasquez's guys could hack in there. But like the saying goes, we'd better expect the best while preparing for the worst."

"I can get you listed on staff at the university," Zach said.

"Cool." Shane didn't bother to ask how, exactly, the chief was going to do that. SEALs had always seemed to have their fingers in a lot of covert pies. Including ties with the spooks. He suspected that along with all their military ties, the dough Phoenix Team seemed able to throw around when necessary helped open a lot of doors.

"We'll need a story for your leg," Quinn decided. "Although your hair's shaggy enough that you don't necessarily look military anymore, a missing limb could raise a red flag."

"Damn motorcycle," Shane said easily. "I should have known better than to ride that Harley in D.C. traffic."

"Works for me," Zach said. He turned to Kirby. "I'll need your passport."

"Why?" She'd kept her purse in her lap. Shane watched as her fingers unconsciously curled around the leather strap.

Obviously, she hadn't gotten the memo not to question the plan. Shane might not recall everything that had happened after his helo had been shot down, but he did remember Zach informing him, in that "I'm a big badass SEAL and you will not argue with me" tone of voice that pilots might be boss when they were up in the air, but when they were on the ground, SEALs ruled.

"Because, although I prefer using our own planes and pilots, you and Shane are going to be entering Monteleón just as you would under a normal situation," Zach said with forced patience, "so you don't raise warning flags. But someone else is going to be leaving in your place, while you remain behind in the country."

"You have someone willing to risk doing that?"

"I don't. But I'm assured by the CIA station chief that *she* does."

"And you trust she knows what she's doing?" Shane questioned him sharply.

"We wouldn't be sending either of you in if we didn't," Zach assured him. "Barbara Kirkland, that's the station chief's name, has set up her own network of NOCs. People she assures me she'd trust with her dear old granny's life."

NOCs, which stood for No Official Covers, were the most covert CIA operatives — men and women who worked in foreign countries without diplomatic protection. If they were caught, there was no guarantee the U.S. would admit to their true identities.

Knowing that the government only resorted to using them when an official cover could put a spy's work, or even life, at risk, Shane figured that something a whole lot bigger than the usual drug-interdiction stuff must be going on down there in Monteleón. Which again pointed to the rumors of the widow Madrid's imminent return.

He was uneasy about bringing outsiders in — after all, a secret started not being a secret as soon as more than one person knew it — but he had trusted the two SEALs with his life, and things had turned out okay.

"But if I give you my passport to give to that person, how am I going to get past immigration?" Kirby asked.

"We'll copy whatever entry and exit stamps are already in it in a duplicate you'll take down there in the lining of your carry-on bag."

"You can do that?" Shane asked. "Get one made so quickly?"

He wouldn't have been at all surprised by that assertion if they'd still been SEALs. Obviously, once again, he'd misjudged the scope of Phoenix Team's abilities. This was a helluva lot different from providing body-guards for CEOs and movie stars, which was pretty much what he'd assumed they did.

"We've got a guy on board who used to work at Langley," Quinn revealed. "In fact, he was the one on the helo who told us about your refugee camp," he said to Kirby. "Then called in his pals to bring in the Russian copter for the exfil."

"And this CIA agent makes fake passports?" Kirby asked.

"No. He's more a fixer with a lot of connections. In this case, he knows a guy who knows a guy who teaches at The Farm, who just happens to be a modern day Michelangelo," Zach said.

"The Farm's the CIA training center," Shane volunteered.

"I know that." Kirby smiled at Quinn. "I read it in your last thriller. Which was, by the way, riveting."

"Thanks."

Quinn always seemed a bit uncomfortable having his new career brought up. Having met him back when Quinn had been scribbling stories into spiral-bound notebooks every chance he got, Shane wasn't at all surprised that whatever fame he'd garnered hadn't gone to his head.

"There isn't anything this guy can't duplicate." Zach picked up the passport part of the conversation. "I called while you were inside the hotel getting your bag. I'm sending your passport to Virginia on the company plane this afternoon, and he'll have it back to us by oh-eight-thirty tomorrow morning."

Even Shane was impressed by that.

Apparently, Kirby was not. "Should we wait that long?" she asked. "Every minute Rachel's held captive is one more minute closer she could be to getting killed."

Nope. She definitely hadn't gotten that "Do not question the SEAL" memo.

"It's risky," Zach admitted. "But this is the best way to do it. Besides, we have a man in the compound with her. And he's armed to the teeth, with instructions to use all force necessary to keep her alive."

"Is this man tasked with keeping Rachel alive CIA?" she asked. "Special Forces? Or one of your own?"

Kirby impressed Shane by not appearing all that surprised to learn someone had infiltrated the rebel camp. Then again, she hadn't exactly been working at Disney World Pakistan the last time they'd met up. She had to have some knowledge of Special Operations.

And Quinn had told him that before going to that Pakistan earthquake zone, she'd been in Sudan, which had become a hellhole after twenty-five years of warfare.

"If we told you that, we'd have to kill you," Quinn said, flashing her a rakish grin that Shane had never seen *not* work on a female.

But, dammit, the SEAL had his own woman. Who, Shane admitted, Quinn was flat-out crazy about. He and Cait Cavanaugh had had themselves a history. Just like Kirby and him.

Well, maybe not exactly like it. He'd taken Kirby out on something resembling dates. Once in a while. At least a couple times, if you could call getting a take-out pizza from the Green Zone Italian café, then eating it cold much, much, later in bed, a date.

But at least it'd been more then Quinn and Cait, who'd shared a hot, nearly-set-the-hotel-room-sprinklers-on-fire one-night stand. Then she'd taken off, leaving Quinn holding the bag. Literally, after he'd gone out to get them breakfast.

But they'd gotten back together and were now looking at becoming a till-death-do-they-part couple. Shane knew Quinn would never cheat on Cait. And not just because she might shoot him with her Glock if he did. But because he was a stand-up guy who'd never break a vow. And was obviously besotted by the sexy redhead former FBI agent.

So, why didn't he just go home and use that smile on his woman?

Instead of Shane's?

Not that Kirby was actually *his* woman. But if Shane had anything to say about it — and he damn well did — that was absofuck-inglutely going to change.

"Can someone recommend a hotel for the night?" she asked.

"No problem," Zach said. "You can stay at my place."

She glanced down at his left hand, as if reassuring herself there was also a wife at his place. "I wouldn't want to put you out."

"It's no trouble. My wife, Sabrina, has been turning her family home into an inn. Sort of a combo bed and breakfast and wedding chapel. While she's got the tearoom up and going, she's still working on the inn part, so we don't have any guests yet. And believe me, there's plenty of room."

"If you're sure."

"Positive. So, with that settled, let's get cracking on the rest of the plan."

27

Rachel assured herself that she'd survived a lot worse in her life than a few ragtag teenagers.

Back during Desert Storm, she'd actually died.

Of course, having been unconscious, she hadn't been aware of that until she'd awakened in Landstuhl, where she'd been taken after Michael had brought her back to the living.

Michael. Why was it that she could never stop thinking of him? Not even now, when she needed so badly to keep a cool head.

"The government isn't going to pay ransom," she said quietly. Respectfully.

Although she wanted to make the man in charge of both the armed guards outside and these kids inside understand she wasn't a cash cow, neither did she want to piss him off.

She slapped at a mosquito that felt as big

as a B-1 bomber at the back of her neck. Which brought home the fact that her ultimate goal was to keep her cool head *on* her neck.

They'd already forced her to make the video in front of those masked, armed children, begging for the U.S. government to pay the ransom that would, if her captors could be believed, keep her alive.

During the sixty-second video, this man had held the blade of a machete against her neck while the other thugs, all wearing scarves to cover their faces, stood behind him. The only positive thing about the terrifying experience was that his hand had stayed steady. Having seen the bodies of victims who'd been hacked to death by machetes during the genocide in Rwanda, Rachel suspected there were very few more painful ways to die.

"Callate la boca," he snapped at her.

Not wanting to push her luck, she obeyed and shut her mouth, watching as he sharpened the machete on a whetstone.

Although the temperature was in the 90s, with humidity just as high, that idea raised goose bumps on her skin.

"May I have permission to ask one question?" she asked in Spanish, keeping her voice respectful.

His black brows plunged to his nose as he scowled darkly, but waved his hand in an impatient, go-ahead gesture.

"I'd like to speak to Jesus Castillo."

Castillo owed her, dammit. Given that he would have died without her treating that bullet wound, surely he'd harbor some gratitude. Hopefully enough to listen to reason.

"He's in the mountains," her captor surprised her by saying.

The rebel leader's whereabouts were usually kept secret on pain of death. In fact, it was rumored that Castillo slept in a different house every night to remain out of the hands of Vasquez's death squads.

Her captor shouldn't have told her, which made her worry that he might not be planning to let her escape this situation alive.

But even so, Castillo leaving the area made perfect sense. He had no real way of knowing that Vasquez wouldn't try to use this situation to assassinate him.

He also couldn't be absolutely sure what Rachel knew — that the U.S. wouldn't send in Special Forces to rescue her as they'd done for those medical students in Grenada. Of course, that country had been in the midst of anarchy, with fighting in the streets.

In this case, Rachel knew she was pretty

much on her own.

The one thing she had going for her was that her guard had been brought up in a Latino culture that encouraged machismo. Which meant — she hoped — that he wouldn't consider Rachel, a mere woman, to be any sort of threat.

She doubted he was as naive or stupid as those teenagers on the road had been. After all, he must have risen fairly high through the ranks to have been put in charge of guarding a million-dollar hostage. Not that they'd ever actually get the money, but apparently no one realized that.

"May I ask another question?"

His scowl grew darker. He glanced around at his fellow "soldiers," many of whom, already bored, were throwing dice against the wall, while others raided the hospital's food pantry. And no wonder. Many of them looked as if they hadn't eaten in a week.

"No mas."

"Please, señor." It did not take that great an effort to force a tear. Then another. "But I have to go." Trying to look embarrassed, properly chastened, and needy, all at the same time, she tilted her head toward the lavatory. "You know."

He gave her a long, considering look. His lips pulled into a grim line, but apparently he wasn't completely heartless, because he shrugged and gestured toward the bathroom.

Then followed her, fortunately allowing her to close the door between them.

It hadn't exactly been a lie. After quickly taking care of business, Rachel washed her hands, and with the water still running, climbed up on the closed toilet seat and tested the wooden frame window, which, no surprise, was swollen shut from all the moisture in the air.

Damn. Even if *she* had been able to open it, she wasn't sure she could wiggle through. But it was one possible escape option.

"Date prisa!" the harsh male voice shouted through the door.

"I'm hurrying," she called back.

Not wanting to risk him breaking the door down, she climbed off the toilet and turned off the water.

As she came out of the lavatory, Rachel thought at least there was one good thing about this situation.

Kirby wasn't here to give them two hostages.

28

Although Kirby wasn't thrilled about being thrown together with Shane, she had to admit that Zach Tremayne's plan sounded feasible.

While the two of them were in Monteleón, hopefully calming Vasquez's fears that American Special Operations troops might invade to free Rachel, the rest of the team — who'd take a Zodiac rubber boat in from a private yacht anchored offshore — would land in Costa Rica, where the coast was less guarded, then cross the border.

Meanwhile, she and Shane would meet up with the CIA station chief and the agents who'd leave the country in their place, then, after dyeing her hair — to more easily blend in with the general population — and pretending to be tourists, they'd drive to the Mayan ruin of Tzultacaj, where they'd rendezvous with the others. After which they'd head off through the jungle to the clinic.

And then, she was assured, the bad guys would be eliminated, and they'd all helo out, under the cover of darkness and below radar, across the border back into Costa Rica.

When Kirby asked where, exactly, they were going to acquire this helicopter, she was simply told not to worry, that they were experts at "getting stuff."

"We're going to need to get you something to wear," Shane said.

"I have clothes." Her suit and the jeans and T-shirt she'd worn on the plane.

"Wow, I never realized you were psychic," he said. "Or maybe you just believe in planning for any contingency, because bringing along a hat, gloves, boots, long pants, and long-sleeved shirts for trekking through the jungle with you to Washington, D.C., was really thinking ahead."

Damn. He had her there.

"All right," Kirby admitted. "You're right. All my jungle stuff is back at the clinic." Which, if she could get to, this entire mission would be unnecessary.

"We'll stop on the way to Swannsea," Shane decided.

Although she'd just as soon not spend all

that time alone with him, Kirby couldn't argue that it made more sense buying the clothes she'd need here, rather than waiting until she got down to Monteleón. Especially since Vasquez, who'd undoubtedly have his goons trailing them, would have to wonder why she was out buying jungle attire if she was planning to immediately return to the States.

"Good idea." Zach dug into the pocket of his suit trousers and pulled out the keys to the red Viper convertible he'd retrieved from the short-term parking at the Somersett airport. During the drive to these offices, Kirby had gotten a very good feeling what it must feel like to ride in a rocket. "Kirby's luggage is in my trunk."

"Would you mind getting it for me?" she asked Shane. "I'd like a minute to speak to Doctor Gannon." She glanced over at the doctor, who, apparently believing in ceding control to the former Special Ops experts, had stayed silent during most of the planning.

"I can wait," Shane said.

"Privately," she said.

He glanced back and forth between her and Michael Gannon, then shrugged. "Sure. I've got to bring the keys back to Zach, anyway."

Zach and Quinn obliged Kirby by suddenly finding other things to do, leaving the two of them alone

"How is she?" Michael asked. "At least when you last saw her yesterday morning?"

"Well. Better than well. Ever since the senator told me about what happened, I've been reminding myself that she's the most unflappable person — male or female — I've ever met."

Well, Shane had certainly remained equally unflappable both times she'd seen him injured. But there'd been nothing cool about the rest of their time together.

"She always was." A slight smile lifted the corners of those beautifully sculptured lips. "Most of the time, anyway."

Even if she hadn't already heard about their affair from Rachel herself, Kirby would have known exactly what he was thinking from the way his eyes warmed with what appeared to be sensual memories.

"She isn't married," she volunteered, trying to rid her mind of the sudden image of Rachel and the former priest making love on an army cot while bombs burst overhead. "Hasn't been for a long time."

This time the smile broke free. And it was stunning. "Thanks for not making me ask."

"She talked about you." Kirby paused,

wondering how much to tell. Then decided, What the hell. "She regrets how things turned out between you."

He immediately sobered. "Well, she's not alone there." He exhaled a long breath. "They're good." He nodded toward the door. "Those men. At what they do."

"I don't know what they've told you about their time in Afghanistan," she said carefully, not wanting to tell tales or share secrets, "but I've certainly never met anyone, before or since, who could have accomplished what they did that day."

Kirby knew that as worried as she was, it had to be worse for Michael. Because from what she could tell, he was still emotionally connected to the woman with whom he'd shared a wartime affair.

And couldn't she identify with that?

"That's good to know." He nodded. "I worked, in an advisory capacity, with Quinn and Cait — that's the woman McKade's going to marry — on a serial sniper case a while back. He was relentless. And highly intelligent."

"That's how I see him."

"I don't know the man who couldn't take his eyes off you as well as I know Zach, who I used to play football against back in ancient times when he went to school on

Swann Island and I attended St. Brendan's, or even as well as I've come to know Quinn. But from what I've witnessed, Garrett didn't merely recite that code of honor when he became a Night Stalker. He lives it on a daily basis."

Except when he was dumping a lover.

Which, Kirby allowed, wasn't entirely fair.

Bracing herself as the former priest's gaze shifted to the open door, Kirby slowly turned.

And felt her pulse skip a beat at the sight of Shane standing there.

"Ready?" he asked.

Yes, yes, yes! every mutinous body cell in her body screamed out.

"Ready," she said on what she thought was a remarkably mild tone, given that she had an almost overwhelming urge to jump his bones.

"So," Shane asked, as they walked out of the building side by side, "I guess you and Mike were talking about Dr. Moore."

"She still loves him," Kirby said. "I thought he'd like to know that."

"Well, since it's obvious he's still wild about her, there's all the more reason to get them back together."

He stopped beside a black pickup. Which was a bit of a surprise, since she would've expected him to have some hot sports car, like other pilots she'd met over the years.

"You know, maybe this will turn out to be a good thing," he suggested.

The truck beeped as he unlocked the passenger door. She found it telling that although it was parked in probably the most secure spot in the city, he'd still locked it. Then wondered, once you'd worked in Special Operations, if you could ever totally trust anyone.

"I fail to see how there could be anything positive about my friend being a hostage held by armed rebels in the jungle."

"Once we exfil her, since returning to the country will obviously be out of the question after this, you can come back and work here in the States."

"Although there's admittedly a great need for affordable, even free health care, WMR doesn't work in the U.S." She climbed into the truck, which was cleaner than many of the places she'd performed surgery. She wondered if it was his pilot's attention to detail that made him neater than most men. "So I guess I'll end up wherever they send me next."

She watched him walk around the front of the truck. Except for the faintest limp, she would never have guessed he was wearing a prosthesis. The doctor in her was dying to see it, to ask medical questions, but she decided to wait until he brought it up. After all, it seemed they were going to be spending a lot of time together.

"That's really admirable, what you do," he said as he settled into a charcoal gray bucket seat. Again, with seemingly little effort. She *really* wanted to see that leg. "Don't your parents ever worry about the way you put yourself at risk?"

"No more than they worried when I joined the Army," she said with a shrug. They'd been appalled at that decision. "Of course, I don't tell them everything."

She had learned, before rushing off to Pakistan, that her parents had stopped watching the TV newscast because the pictures from the Sudan were keeping her mother awake all night.

"That's probably best," he agreed, as he twisted the key in the ignition. "My dad was in 'Nam, so I don't really have to tell him how war is, because he already knows. And being a grunt in the jungle had to be a lot tougher than JAG or SOAR."

"JAG?"

"I told you I was in the Navy before I jumped ship to the Army," he reminded her.

"Because you wanted to fly," she remembered. "Which the Navy wouldn't let you do. But the Army would. You never mentioned being in the JAG corps."

Apparently, people leaving the Phoenix Team compound didn't need the same security pupil check as those entering, because after scanning a card he'd retrieved from the pocket of his jeans, the tall gate immediately opened.

"I guess it never came up."

Kirby was floored. JAG was more than just a sexy TV show. The Judge Advocate General's corps was one of the most respected units in the military. And, she'd heard, one of the most difficult to get into. Since it dealt with military legal issues, it was undoubtedly also one of the safest.

Yet he'd left behind the snazzy dress whites to end up flying night combat missions in Afghanistan?

"Why?"

"I suppose because we were otherwise occupied having sex like bunnies to talk all that much."

"No, I don't mean why didn't it come up, though it does seem that it was a fairly important bit of biography," she said. "I meant, why did you join JAG in the first place?"

"It's a long story." He glanced over at her.

"And one for another time, since I believe we were talking about you."

She considered keeping her thoughts, which she was still trying to sort out, to herself. Then admitted that if she wanted to know more about him — and she definitely did — then it was only fair she share something personal about herself.

"The longer I spent in Iraq, the more I started to feel as if I was just a cog in a machine. It was like working at McDonald's: Get the customers in, get them out."

"You were good at that," he remembered. "Working fast."

"I had a great team," she said. "But it was pretty basic medicine: stop the bleeding, put in an air tube, send the patients back to camp, or on to a better-equipped trauma center. There were times when things got really hectic — which they did on an almost-daily basis, since we were also treating Iraqi civilians, and even, in some cases, the insurgents themselves — that I never had the opportunity to learn my patients' names."

"I think you're being too hard on yourself. Don't forget, I saw you stop and pray with that one Spec Ops guy over a patient you couldn't save."

"That was a rough day." She remembered

it all too well. Partly because it was the day they'd first made love. "But we always tried to stop and acknowledge the ones we lost," she said, remembering the chaplain who welcomed every soldier to Landstuhl, unconscious or not. "And I doubt I'll ever forget any of their faces." Or what had been left of some faces. "But unless they returned with another injury, I never knew what happened to them after they left the Cash."

Shane had returned. Not because he'd been injured, but because he hadn't been able to stop thinking about her any more than she'd been able to stop thinking about him.

Kirby didn't believe in love at first sight. But she'd certainly discovered the power of instant lust.

"What I found at WMR was a way to reconnect with my humanity," she said. "I once worked with a male nurse who'd earned money for college fighting fires in the West. He claimed that being a relief worker was a lot like being a smoke jumper, which I suppose may be partly true, given that we're always the first in."

"Gotta be a rush in that."

She wasn't surprised he understood. Which, she considered, might be, along with the sex, why they hadn't talked all that much. They hadn't needed to, since, unlike if she'd tried dating a civilian, they "got" each others' worlds.

"There is. But in the beginning, being able to identify myself as a WMR doctor also gave me a sort of peace."

He glanced over at her again. Because he'd put on a pair of aviator sunglasses, she couldn't see his eyes. But she could tell that instead of just passing time with casual conversation, he was actually listening. Taking what she said — and didn't say — in.

"Hard to imagine finding peace in the kind of places relief doctors go."

"Not a quiet kind of peace, like sitting in a bubble bath, drinking tea while reading a romance novel." For some reason she found herself about to share something she'd never told to anyone. She didn't even like to dwell on it herself. "Or meditating." Like there'd been any time for that. "More an inner peace. Because whether I was inoculating a child against smallpox, or teaching a mother how to spoon-feed her child, or even supervising the digging of a latrine, I could see firsthand the value of what I was doing. Which was a gift."

"You say *was*."

And so she had, which had been a slip. He really didn't miss a thing.

She thought about how often she'd hated the way men would look at her curves, which had been the bane of her existence since her teens, and not bother to take time to realize that there were some pretty good brains inside her blond head. Then belatedly realized she'd been guilty of doing the same thing with Shane Garrett.

With his gorgeous George Clooney-meets–Brad Pitt looks and phemerones oozing from every male pore, along with the fact that if making love were an Olympic sport, she knew firsthand that he'd own the all-time record for gold medals, it was too easy to overlook the fact that Night Stalkers were the most intelligent unit in the Army, as this man's surprising JAG background definitely proved.

So he was not just a pretty face.

But that didn't necessarily mean he was the grand, all-consuming love of her life — Pitt to Angelina Jolie. Prince Eric to her Ariel. Bogie to Bacall.

More like Bogie to Bergman from *Casablanca*.

"Let's just say these days I'm more conflicted," she said mildly, wanting to change the conversation from a subject she hadn't yet worked out in her own head.

Kirby was grateful when, seeming to sense her reticence, he didn't push.

29

Their first stop was at a sporting supply store, where Kirby bought some long-sleeved shirts, pants, and boots. Since a tiny mosquito could be every bit as dangerous as a poisonous viper or jaguar, she was accustomed to wearing protective long sleeves, even in the sweltering heat of the jungle. She'd worn desert cammies in Iraq, but this was her first time in digital woodland camouflage.

And he thought my suit was ugly, she thought as she looked at herself in the dressing room mirror. The unflattering cut of the shirt, and the cargo pants, which while potentially useful with all those extra pockets, added at least ten pounds to her appearance. Which should be a good thing, because she wanted Shane to think of her solely as a team member. Not that sex-crazed woman who'd actually risked sharing a quickie with him in a CSH supply room closet.

Wondering when she'd become such a liar, and deciding she wasn't going to lose fifteen pounds in the next two minutes, she changed back into her suit. After paying for the clothes, including a pair of gloves and a billed cap, they moved on to the Somersett Piggly Wiggly, where they picked up packages of dehydrated packaged meals, dried fruit, PowerBars, and powdered Gatorade.

"Won't the others be bringing food in with them?" she asked as he added some processed cheese spread and crackers to the mix.

"Yeah. But you can never count on things working out the way you plan," he said, tossing in some peanut butter. "Their IBS could get swamped —"

"That's a Zodiac, right?" Kirby had often thought the entire military establishment would crumble if forced to abandon acronyms.

"It's SEAL-speak for 'inflatable boat, small,' " he agreed. "But it's not all that small. It'll hold eight people and a thousand pounds of gear. Anyway, it could get swamped, supplies could get washed overboard, they might even get caught in a gun battle on their way to the ruins and have to ditch the stuff."

They made their way through the aisles to the drug section of the store, where he started tossing a selection of over-the-counter medicines — antiseptic cream, antibiotic hand soap, wet wipes, and Motrin — into the cart.

"Like I said, anything can happen so it's best to be prepared."

Such attention to detail, she thought, as he snagged a box of Band-Aids, undoubtedly came from his days as a SOAR pilot, where failure to do a complete prefight check could end with a lot of troops dying.

They were at the checkout counter when, on impulse, Kirby tossed in a bag of M&M's.

It had been so long since she'd had American candy, it was all she could do to wait until she was back in the truck to tear into it.

"Oh, my God." She closed her eyes as the smooth chocolate melted deliciously on her tongue, and nearly wept. It was that good. "There have been times over the past few years I've fantasized about these. But reality is so much better."

Shane's fingers tightened on the steering wheel. Damned if she didn't look nearly the same way she looked whenever he'd made her come. He'd always known that the former Army doc had a deeply sensual side. However, if he'd known what a sucker she was for M&M's, he would have bought up every brown package in the Green Zone.

"Would you like one?" she asked.

"Sure." No way was he going to turn down anything this woman might offer.

The bag crackled as she dug into it, then pulled out a red candy. Reminding him a lot of Eve, when she'd held out that shiny red apple to Adam, she leaned across the center console and fed it to him.

"Damn. Some things never change," he murmured as he crunched the outer shell.

"I don't remember M&M's in the Green Zone."

Once again, he realized he should have bought her some. Courted her, like his mother always talked about his father having done.

He'd never much thought about his parents' having dated. Or, God help him, having sex.

His father was a typical rancher — laconic, never one to use two words when one would do, with a simple black-and-white morality that had served him well enough even as the world around him grew increasingly complicated. An outdoorsman who'd rather spend his rare free time hunting and fishing than reading a book, he'd never quite understood his younger son.

But Shane had never, for not a single moment, felt unloved. And looking back on it, he'd come to realize that while he might not recite sonnets, or drive into town for flashy bouquets of American Beauty roses on Valentine's Day — hell, half the time, if he hadn't had his kids to remind him, he would've forgotten the holiday altogether — Big John Garrett had adored his wife with the same all-encompassing emotion Peg Garrett had always shown him.

With his father not being all that talkative, and his mother being deaf, the sprawling log ranch house Shane had grown up in had probably been more quiet than most. But his parents hadn't needed verbal conversation for Shane to realize how close they'd been. Two very individual parts of a perfect whole.

Being a SOAR pilot hadn't allowed a lot of time for introspection. If Shane wasn't flying, he was practicing flying, or grabbing a few Zs before his next mission.

During his recuperation and all those months of being forced out of the cockpit, Shane had had plenty of time to think, and he'd come to the conclusion that while he might not have figured out exactly what he was going to do with the rest of his life, he didn't want to do it alone. He wanted that closeness his parents shared. That special intimate connection with another human being.

Which was the only reason he'd gone out on that blind date his friends' wives had set him up with.

Foolishly, he'd thought she might be the one.

The problem was he'd already *had* his *one.*

But thanks to his own dickheaded cluelessness and John Wayne, "A man's gotta do what a man's gotta do," tough hombre, go-it-alone pride, he'd lost her.

Shane had never been one to dwell in the past. It was one of the ways he'd managed to cope with the loss of his leg better than a lot of the amputees at Walter Reed.

Bygones, he'd told himself, when the pity party had gotten boring after a week. The thing to do was to get back on his feet, even if one was artificial, get the hell out of military hospitals, and get on with the rest of his life.

The funny thing was that while he'd moved beyond the amputation, he'd never completely figured out how to leave Kirby Campbell in the past.

He flashed her his most rakish smile, the

bad boy, "Wow, are you babelicious, and I so want to do you!" grin that, nine times out of ten, charmed. "I was talking about how easily you could always have me eating out of your hand."

"I think your mother misnamed you," she said, the edge in her tone suggesting this one of those rare times the grin had failed to work its bad-boy magic.

"Oh? How's that?"

He pulled away from the curb, slipping easily into the traffic. There were more cars downtown than usual. Shane figured they must be holiday shoppers. Damn. He'd promised his parents he'd be back at the ranch for Christmas. He'd have to call them before taking off tomorrow morning.

"I've never seen the movie, but wasn't Shane one of those strong, silent cowboy types?" she asked.

"That's the way I remember him."

Although Alan Ladd wasn't John Wayne, his dad had, on occasion, admitted to *Shane* being an even better movie than Wayne's iconic *Searchers*. Hence his name.

"You may have grown up on a ranch. But you're definitely not like the movie cowboy at all. In fact, you still seem to have the knack for always coming up with the perfect line."

He'd heard that before, too.

He glanced her over again. She looked exhausted. And oddly fragile, which tugged at some unseen cords and had him opting for honesty, even though she might not be ready for it. Or, more likely, not believe him.

"You want a laconic cowboy, when this op is over, I'll take you to Oregon and introduce you to my dad. Though, I've got to tell you right up front, he's taken, and I doubt Mom would want to share.

"As for me, hey, I'm a guy." He put a hand against his chest. "Which means I've been guilty of resorting to proven lines from time to time," he admitted. "But not with you." Shane was grateful for the sunglasses that hid his eyes, keeping her from seeing the naked need they undoubtedly revealed. "Never with you."

He hadn't even realized she could blush. But pink color, just like the flush that would warm her skin when they made love, bloomed in her cheeks.

"See," she said. "That's exactly what I mean."

His dad had always said that when you're deep in a hole, stop digging. Deciding that was damn good advice, Shane decided not to argue. When he'd been trying out for the 160th, he'd met a lot of pilots who could talk the talk, but fell down when it came to walking the walk.

So, better, he decided, to convince her with actions. Since he wasn't sure, after what he'd put her through, that she'd buy his words.

As she worked her way through the brown candy bag, a comfortable silence settled over the cab of the truck, broken only by Alan Jackson's smooth baritone advising Shane to stop running, to spin the wheel and try his luck.

Which wasn't such bad advice.

Because maybe the country singer was right. Maybe this time it'd be love.

Shane hadn't been ready to consider that possibility in Iraq. And especially in Landstuhl or during the long, hard months of rehabilitation.

But he sure as hell was now.

30

Just because Michael Gannon was no longer a priest didn't mean he couldn't still receive comfort in the cathedral where he'd spent so many years.

After leaving Phoenix Team's headquarters on Swann Island, he'd taken the ferry back to Somersett. Before returning to work at the clinic he'd started, he dropped into the church, slipping into a back pew.

The wood was a softly varnished yellow pine, milled from trees harvested more than a century earlier, the leather-topped kneelers worn to a buttery softness by generations of faithful. Including those of his former congregation, who, from what he'd been able to tell, bore him no ill will at having left them.

A sanctuary lamp glowed dimly in front of the tabernacle; votive candles flickered in red glass holders, sending prayers and the scent of burning wax upward. One of those candles in the back row was his.

Well, not really his, but one he'd lit for Dr. Rachel Moore.

Like that copter jockey had said, once you saved a life, it really was yours forever.

And he *had* saved Rachel's life. Not only had he held her heart in his hands, but he'd continued to hold it deep within his own heart.

Mike hadn't known Rachel had been married until their last night together. He'd been brought up to believe adultery was a sin. But at the same time, no way could he ever consider Doctor Rachel Moore a sinner.

She'd been a profoundly spiritual person. Not in the getting-down-on-her-knees-and-praying-every-night way, though, he considered, she might actually have done that. He'd have no real way of knowing, since they'd never been able to spend an entire night together.

It was more that everything she did was for reasons larger than herself. She considered herself merely an instrument to help others, and in the early days of Desert Storm, as a National Guard physician attached to the forward operating 5th MASH inside Iraq, she'd proven indefatigable.

When she'd been brought into the ER,

horribly broken and unconscious, as his team frantically worked to save her life, he'd begun making deals with God.

If she'd only open her eyes, he'd never take the Lord's name in vain again. If He'd only let her live, he'd never miss a Sunday mass, even while stationed here in a war zone. If her blood pressure would only, please, Jesus, rise, he'd give ten percent of his pay for the rest of his life to Catholic Charities.

But despite all his promises, despite putting her on a respirator, the woman he loved beyond reason kept sinking, sliding deeper and deeper into the void.

She was obviously suffering from internal bleeding, a diagnosis that was proven when an X-ray indicated internal hemorrhaging compressing her right lung and heart.

Which was when Michael opened her chest. The procedure was done only as a last-resort measure, but with her blood pressure plummeting and so much internal bleeding, the only other option would have been to pronounce her dead.

Which wasn't an option.

What he found caused his own heart to nearly stop.

Her left pulmonary vein, which carried blood to the heart, had ruptured.

The good news was the tear was small, which had kept her from bleeding out. More good news was that a piece of bone — undoubtedly from one of her three broken ribs — had lodged in the vein, slowing the flow of blood.

The bad news was that if not fixed quickly, the vein could fully rupture, causing massive loss of blood in a very short time. Also, due to its close proximity to the heart, air could get pumped into her system, risking an embolism.

Which made it extremely dangerous.

And deadly.

As a nurse prepared the suture and Michael clamped off the vein, her heart suddenly stopped.

Much, much later, when the last of the Scud victims had been treated, or their bodies taken away in heavy black bags to be cleaned up before being sent home to grieving families, Michael's entire body would tremble so badly it was as if he'd been taken over by a virulent form of palsy.

Shaking like a leaf in a hurricane, he'd spend the next five minutes puking up the MRE he'd eaten that morning before the Scud had hit. Which, all things considered, was actually probably the best thing he could have done with the rubbery, greenish ham-and-cheese omelet.

But, in the midst of crisis, his medical training kicked in, allowing his head to stay cool and his hand to stay steady as he deftly injected the epinephrine directly into her nonbeating heart.

It picked up again.

Lub as the atrioventricular valves closed.

Dup as the semilunar valves closed.

Lub. Dup . . .

Lub. Dup . . .

Lub. Dup . . .

It could be a helluva lot stronger, but at least it was beating.

He'd just repaired the vein, which stopped the hemorrhaging, when she went into full cardiac arrest yet again.

The nurse, as good as they came, immediately slapped another syringe into Michael's hand. He injected Rachel again.

Nothing.

The line on the EEG had gone even flatter than the landscape outside the surgical tent.

Knowing he only had four minutes before she began to suffer irreversible brain damage, Michael injected her again.

Lub . . .

Dup . . .

Lub.

Then silence.

If he'd only been a TV doctor, he could have shouted for the nurse to bring out the paddles, yell "Clear," and shock her enough to bring her back from the dead. Like jump-starting a car.

She would revive.

Weep tears of joy.

Then, after a beer commercial and a promo for the eleven o'clock news, as the credits rolled, they'd go on to live happily ever after.

Unfortunately, real life didn't work that way.

Since a defibrillator defibrillates, it only works when a heart is fibrillating. Or, in nonmedical terms, fluttering. But if that were the case, the line on the monitor would show a series of Vs.

This line was, once again, flat.

Which left him with two options. And since he'd already tried drugs, the next was internal massage.

Standard external cardiopulmonary resuscitation — CPR — typically only pumped about ten percent of the usual amount of blood.

But by massaging the naked heart directly, if it worked, Michael could achieve almost normal circulation.

As he literally took her warm and generous heart into his own two gloved hands, Michael played his last card in this life-or-death game with God.

If only Rachel would live and return to the marriage she'd told him she'd planned to try to put back together again, he'd give up medicine and do what his mother had dreamed of since he'd received his first communion at St. Brendan's cathedral.

He'd join the priesthood.

Which wasn't that great a sacrifice, he thought as he began to massage. Because the woman lying on this stainless steel table was the only one he'd ever want. The only one he'd ever love.

He'd no sooner made the promise when her heart resumed beating on its own.

Michael held his breath and prayed.

It stopped.

He repeated that sequence six times. And finally, after two hours of massage, the woman he loved more than life itself had stabilized enough for her heart to beat on its own.

Her blood pressure wasn't as strong as it could be. But high enough.

Her pulse, while still thready, was stronger, and increasingly steadier beneath his fingertips.

She was evacuated to Landstuhl. Although he didn't risk going to see her, Michael had called daily, using his medical pull to receive reports.

He also arranged for the florist across the street from the medical center to deliver flowers to her room once a week. But he instructed the cards be signed from the entire MASH unit.

After two months, she returned to the States.

Unable to let her just drift out of his life without a final word, he wrote her a brief note, wishing her well. And so she wouldn't feel guilty about having kept her secret from him for so long, only to dump him, he told her about his plans to enter a seminary. Which wasn't that much of a stretch, since along with his premed major at Notre Dame, he'd minored in theology.

Part of him had held his breath, waiting for a frantic phone call, or at least an e-mail or letter telling him that she'd made a terrible mistake, that he was the only man for her, and would he please reconsider his plans so they could set up a shared practice in some small bucolic town, where they would never again have to care for victims of war, and live happily ever after making babies.

But instead, all he received was an equally brief, polite letter thanking him for saving her life, and wishing him well in his new vocation.

And that was that.

If there'd been times when he'd wondered if he'd done the right thing, he'd pushed the doubts aside. He had, after all, been a good priest. He might not have the family he'd fantasized with Rachel. But he did have his flock.

Although the bishop had, on more than one occasion, accused him of being too independent-minded, too outspoken, and occasionally troublesome, his parishioners at St. Brendan's had liked him. And Michael had been proud of the job he'd been doing, which easily made up for the chiding phone calls from his superior.

Then Katrina came barreling through New Orleans. Unable to resist the scenes he was seeing on television in the rectory he shared with two other priests, Michael asked the bishop to temporarily transfer him to Catholic Charities, which the older man was more than happy to do.

He'd heard, through the diocesan gossip grapevine, that the cleric had claimed it was killing two birds with one stone by helping victims of the worst disaster in the nation's history while ridding himself of a pesky thorn in his side.

It had taken Michael only a week running a homeless shelter to realize that he'd rediscovered his calling. While he'd never really regretted taking Holy Orders, it had crossed his mind on more than one occasion that making deals with God under pressure wasn't exactly the same as a vocation.

His vocation was getting hands-on with people. Helping them physically at the same time he was helping them spiritually. Which was why, after returning to Somersett, he'd informed the bishop he was leaving to open a free medical clinic in an abandoned storefront across the street from the cathedral.

The bishop had not tried to talk him out of his decision.

So he'd been happy in his work.

Happier than he'd ever been. Happier, really, than he'd ever hoped to be.

There was only one thing missing. As he watched his brother, Joe, with his pregnant wife, Laurel, and his sister, Tess, with her husband, Gage, Michael had been thinking more and more about the life he'd once fantasized about with Rachel.

And now Rachel was single again.

Which meant she was available.

As soon as he and Phoenix Team rescued her from the rebels who were holding her hostage.

And this time, Michael vowed, as the candle flared, seeming to echo the strength of his conviction, he was going to keep her.

31

The sun was lowering as Kirby and Shane drove to Zach and Sabrina's home.

Swann Island appeared even greener than San Diego's Griffith Park, and really, really small. The village itself consisted of only four tree-lined streets arranged around a Victorian bandstand set in the middle of a green square.

Kirby suspected it was the type of place where everyone knew everyone. And their business.

A crescent beach curved around the southern tip of the island, then wrapped around the eastern coast that faced out to the Atlantic Ocean. Rows of houses, built on stilts, lined the beach. There was also a wooden pier from which a man and boy were fishing.

A panorama of wheat-hued marsh made up the west and north coasts.

"What are these fields?" she asked as they

passed row after row of waist-high green plants.

"Tea. And those trees over there are Swannsea's peach orchard."

Kirby immediately made the connection between the name of Zachariah Tremayne's wife's family home and these acres and acres of plants.

"Zach's wife is *the* Swann of Swann Tea?"

Which made her really, really rich.

Yet she'd married a SEAL, who might be a warrior hunk, but last time she'd looked, the Navy didn't pay its chiefs that much. Such a difference in economic status might be a problem for some couples, but from the way Zach Tremayne's eyes had gleamed when he'd talked about his wife, it was obvious that if it ever *had* been a problem, it definitely wasn't now.

Which made Kirby like Sabrina Swann Tremayne already.

"That's her. Small world, isn't it?" Shane asked mildly, letting her know that he hadn't forgotten that Swann's ginger peach herbal tea had always been her favorite.

And, in case she'd forgotten, which she hadn't, it was also a subtle reminder of the time he'd gone online and surprised her by ordering an entire case from the company's Web site to be sent to the Green Zone.

Which, now that she thought about it, was yet another indication that their relationship, despite what he'd claimed at Landstuhl, had been about more than sex.

"Zach said you're teaching flying." Which explained the plane logo on his blue T-shirt.

"Yeah. At an airfield over in Somersett."

"Do you enjoy it?"

He shrugged. "The planes we use aren't exactly extreme or challenging, but I enjoy being up in the air again."

"I've always thought it would be fun to learn to fly."

"Maybe, once we get back from Central America, I can give you a few lessons."

"Maybe," she said noncommittally.

"Shields up, Scotty," he murmured.

"That reference escapes me," she said, pretending a sudden interest in the waist-high tea plants outside the passenger window.

"Since we're going to have to work together over the next few days, I'm going to resist calling you a liar," he countered. "But I'm also not so clueless that I can't recognize when someone's put barricades up."

"I don't remember you being prone to exaggeration. I haven't put up any barricades."

Which wasn't exactly true. But they

weren't anywhere near as high or thick as the ones he'd erected between them in Germany.

"Look, I realize I owe you a huge apology."

His statement told her he was thinking the same thing. Which wasn't uncommon. Back in Iraq, there'd been countless times they'd say the same thing at the same time. Kirby didn't know whether the fact that things seemed to have stayed exactly the same between them was a good thing. Or bad.

"You don't owe me anything."

That was definitely true. Sure, she'd gotten hurt. But they'd both been equally responsible. If she hadn't put her heart on the line, he couldn't have broken it.

"Yeah." He blew out a quick, sharp breath. "I do. And we're going to have to talk about it."

"There's nothing to talk about."

Although she'd never admit it out loud, he was right. She *was* a liar.

"It's between us, Kirby," he said. "Now, if this was just about us, maybe we could ignore the way I screwed things up when you came all that way to Landstuhl."

"You'd been critically wounded. And were on heavy medication."

"Thanks for giving me an excuse." She thought she heard just a bit of laughter beneath the seeming regret. "But we both know that I've had plenty of time to make things right since then."

"Look." She turned back toward him. "I told you, I understand. My God, I'm a doctor. Don't you think I realize what you went through? What you've had to go through all these months in rehabilitation?"

A lump formed in her throat, clogging her words. "When I saw that report on the news about the deplorable conditions at Walter Reed . . ."

Unable to finish, she could only shake her head.

"Hey." He reached across the center console and took hold of her hand. "Those guys had it bad. Real bad, apparently. I lucked out because I never got moved into that building."

When she didn't pull her hand away, Shane returned to his original track. "The thing is, we've got to get what happened behind us. Because if the air in here was any thicker, we'd fucking suffocate.

"Vasquez didn't consolidate all that military and political power by being stupid. If we don't figure out a way to move on, there's no way he's going to ever believe we're long-lost reunited lovers."

He had a point. The problem was, in order to discuss it, so they could get it behind them, Kirby was going to have to open up and admit she'd been hurt. Which meant she was going to have to expose her vulnerabilities.

Which went against everything she'd been trying to do ever since she'd joined the Army and ended up a part of Operation Iraqi Freedom.

She'd had to hide the details about her life in Baghdad from her parents, who worried, and although they'd understood her need for money for medical school and were as patriotic as the next American, neither had ever quite been able to wrap their minds around their only daughter joining the military.

She'd definitely had to conceal her fear and concern from her patients in the CSH. They already had enough to worry about; her job had been to fix whatever she could, as fast as she could, and reassure her patients as well as she could before sending them back out the door.

Her WMR work was much the same. The only difference was, as in Afghanistan, and the other night on the road when she and Rachel were returning to the clinic from the presidential palace, showing weakness could very well have gotten her killed.

This situation wasn't the same. She might not be able to entirely trust Shane Garrett with her heart. But she knew, without a shadow of a doubt, that she could trust him with her life.

"You're right," she said. "Maybe this evening . . ."

She paused as she saw the muscle jerk in his tanned cheek. "Or not."

His reaction reminded her of all the months she'd waited around at the CSH for him to show up. On his schedule. Thought of all those really hard days when she could've used some emotional propping up.

Which really wasn't fair, she allowed as she tugged her hand away and felt an odd little prick of loss. The Army wasn't in the business ensuring her happiness. If she wanted emotional support, she could've e-mailed Dr. Phil.

"While you were talking with Mike, Zach decided we guys should run through the logistics once last time."

"Tonight?"

"We're leaving tomorrow," he reminded her unnecessarily. "And you know what they say: A failure to plan is planning to fail."

"Yeah. I seem to recall hearing that while

I was in the Army," she said dryly. "Interesting that you big strong men decided to leave the little lady out of the briefing."

"It's mostly military stuff. Like where and how we're going to get the copter, rendezvous locations, that sort of thing. Tactics we're used to doing and are good at. Now, if you and Dr. Gannon wanted to start talking about medical procedures, there'd be no reason for Zach or Quinn or me to hang around."

He had a point, she decided.

"Discussing down-and-dirty details of our past on the plane is definitely out," he considered. "Never know who might be sitting in front or behind of us. And Quinn warned me that our hotel room in Cuidad Libertad could be bugged."

"I have a hard time believing Vasquez has bugged every room in every hotel in the city."

"Probably not. But you've lived down there for six months. You know the guy better than I do. Do you think he'd miss the chance to eavesdrop on Americans? Especially since most of them are in the oil business and would probably love to figure a way to cut him out of some of those windfall profits."

"I hadn't thought of that," she allowed.

"But it's a good point."

"Why don't I pick you up a little earlier than planned tomorrow morning? You can sample a traditional Lowcountry breakfast; then we'll drive over to the coastal side and watch the F-18s from the Marine Air Corps in Beaufort while we work things out."

Kirby considered telling him that there wasn't anything to work out. But knew she'd be lying. And knew that he'd know it, too.

She also couldn't help noticing that he brought up the nearby air base. Flying was obviously in the man's blood. There'd even been those times when he'd shown up at the CSH or her trailer, still flying so high from a mission — most of which he couldn't give her any details about — when she'd wonder, if forced to choose, whether he'd wouldn't have picked his beloved helicopters over her.

After things had fallen apart, she'd reluctantly come to the conclusion that she obviously hadn't even come in a close second.

"I don't know," she dithered uncharacteristically.

Although she knew he had a point, she wasn't sure she wanted to be alone with him all that long in the cab of the truck. But while South Carolina wasn't exactly the

North Pole, a cold front along the tail end of a winter storm in the Great Lakes had pushed through the Southeast, bringing showers and thunderstorms. Which, if they hung around, precluded sitting somewhere less intimate outside.

"And here I thought you were big on tradition," he said.

"I am."

His words reminded her of the day they'd decorated a Christmas tree in her trailer.

It had not been a fragrant live fir, but an extraordinarily fake white plastic tree they'd bought from one of the local kids in the zone, who always seemed to have a collection of hard-to-find goods available at highway-robbery, black-market prices. She'd crafted the silver bows out of shiny duct tape Shane had contributed.

Although only tabletop size, it had still claimed way too much space in the tiny trailer, but it had lifted her spirits. As had the CD of carols Shane had surprised her with.

She didn't think she'd ever hear "The Christmas Song" without remembering making sweet, slow love to this man with Nat King Cole's voice as a soundtrack.

"Then how can you deny me a chance to park with my girl?" he asked. "After all, we never managed that American tradition in Iraq."

"There's just one problem," she said. "I'm not your girl."

"If you keep talking like that, we're going to slip up down in Monteleón," he warned. "While I'll be the first to admit I haven't had the on-the-ground undercover training Zach and Quinn had in the SEALs, I was still Spec Ops. We were taught enough for me to know that if we're going to be playing a role, it's vital to stay in character from the get-go."

She supposed that made sense.

Still . . .

"James Bond didn't stay in character when he and Vesper Lynd went undercover in *Casino Royale*," she argued.

"Yeah. And look how that turned out."

Once again, he'd won the damn point.

"There's not that much to go over," she insisted. "Although I really don't want to discuss it, I'll admit to making a fool of myself in Germany. Well, as you can see, I survived, while you made what appears to be a near miraculous recovery. We both moved on. End of story."

"You didn't make a fool of yourself. *I* did. By letting you walk away."

Hadn't she thought the same thing? Too

302

many times to count on those long, restless, *lonely* nights.

"They'd pumped you full of heavy medication."

It was what she'd tried to tell herself. At the time, then later.

But if she'd truly believed it, she would have looked him up after he'd been farther down the road to recuperation. When he'd had time to realize what he'd thrown away.

"Yeah. And since I normally only ever take vitamin M, they hit my system damn hard. But I'm not going to use drugs as an excuse for my shitty behavior. Because I knew what I was doing."

"I doubt that." She folded her arms and stared through moist eyes at the bare limbs of peach trees lined up in straight rows, like soldiers at parade rest. "You couldn't have possibly known how badly you crushed me."

There, she'd said it. And in doing so, felt a bit of the emotional shell she'd encased herself in since that day crack, just a little.

"Yeah. I did."

32

Stunned by the admission, Kirby turned back toward him. "Why?"

Shane might not have loved her, at least not in the all-encompassing way she'd loved him, but she never could have believed he'd be so purposefully cruel.

"I wanted to make sure you went away. And didn't come back."

"Why?"

"Because, dammit" — he swiped a hand through his hair — "there was no way in hell I was going to saddle you with a cripple!"

"You're far from a cripple," she said with far more calm than she was feeling.

"Maybe not now. But I sure as hell was back then."

She couldn't decide whether to burst into tears — which was so not her — or scream at him or just haul off and hit him. Hard.

"What gave you the right to make such a

unilateral decision about something that involved both of us? And what made you think I would have felt saddled?"

"You're a doctor."

"And you only figured that out when you got to Landstuhl? I just happened to be a doctor when you met me. And all those months we were, as you so colorfully put it, screwing like bunnies."

"Yeah. But during that time we were having sex at every opportunity, I was a pilot. A Night Stalker," he said stressing the credentials she knew he'd worked damn hard for. And was rightfully proud of. "If I let you stick around, you would've still been a doctor. But I wouldn't have been your lover. I'd have been your goddamn amputee patient."

His voice was rough. His expression even more tortured than it had been when he'd been lying in that hospital bed in Germany.

"It would've screwed up everything," he insisted. "So, not having anything else to do in those days before starting therapy, I gave our situation a lot of thought. And since it obviously would've put a burden on you that you hadn't signed up for when you gave me your keys to your hootch that day, I decided it'd be better to end things while we still had all those good memories to look back on."

Kirby couldn't believe he was serious.

"*You* decided?" Her voice rose high enough to shatter crystal. "That's the most ridiculous thing I've ever heard. You actually, purposefully broke my heart and didn't think *that* would be what I remembered whenever I looked back? Which, by the way, I damn well try not to do!"

Which hadn't worked out at all, because even on those days she kept him from her thoughts, Shane Garrett managed to infiltrate his way into her dreams.

He looked as surprised as she felt.

"I don't think I've ever heard you shout before. Scream, maybe, a couple times."

More than a couple, she allowed. But only during sex. Not that she was prepared to admit that.

"But you never shout."

"I'm not shouting!" she shouted.

He held up a hand. Blew out a long breath.

"Okay. Maybe, just possibly, I screwed up."

"Duh," she muttered.

He slanted her a look beneath those ridiculously lush lashes that had his brown eyes looking a lot like Bambi's. "I don't suppose I could claim having been in a pharmaceutical haze?"

"Too late. You already admitted the Demerol wasn't the reason," she reminded him.

"Yeah." He scrubbed a hand down his face. Momentarily lifted his eyes to the roof of the truck, as if seeking divine intervention.

"Maybe we ought to start over. Pretend this is the first time we'd ever met."

"Like that's going to work," she muttered.

"Probably not," he admitted. "Since I've been wanting to jump your bones since you walked into the office with Zach."

Kirby wasn't prepared to share that she'd been thinking the same thing. "It wouldn't be the same."

"No." He reached across the console again, recaptured her hand, and lifted it to his lips. "Because that day, in the Cash, I only suspected how hot you'd be. Believe me, sweetcakes, you definitely exceeded expectations."

It was *him*, Kirby thought, but refused to say.

No. It had been *both* of them. Together.

She thought about telling him not to call her that ever again. Then decided to play it light instead. "You weren't so bad yourself, cowboy."

He seemed to have moved on with his life.

Lecturing at the local military academy (she was still floored to learn he'd been a lawyer), teaching flying, playing basketball, and taking part in covert operations again.

Kirby wondered if moving on included women. It was impossible to imagine a man with such a strong sexual drive having embraced his celibate side all these past months. Since his injury hadn't affected his masculinity one iota, it wouldn't be surprising if all the available — along with some not available — women in Somersett would be more than willing to tumble into bed with him.

She'd expect that. Even understand it.

Even as she tried to convince herself she didn't care if he had sex with every female in the Lowcountry, Kirby hated the thought of him settling down with one special woman.

"I like to think I had some moves. At least back in the day," he said. "But it wasn't just my excellent Special Ops sexual prowess that made us good together, Kirby. It was *us*."

He looked over at her again with sex in his eyes. "You. And me. Together."

Damn. She hated that it was happening again. The two of them sharing the same thoughts.

How was it, if they'd been so in sync, things could have turned out so wrong?

"That was another life," she said on what she hoped looked like a casual shrug. "It'd be impossible to recapture it."

"Maybe," he said. But he didn't sound as if he meant it.

"I don't need this," she said on a flare of emotion that had her voice shaking. "*We* don't need it. Our focus should be on getting Rachel out of Monteleón."

"And we will," he said with a return of the cocky self-confidence she remembered so well. "One thing pilots have to be really good at is multitasking. I won't have any trouble focusing on two things at once."

The problem was, she didn't want to be one of his damn tasks. What she wanted now was the same thing she'd come to realize she wanted that last night together in Iraq. She wanted to be his *everything.*

Like, sure. That was going to happen.

Make me fall in love with you once, then dump me, shame on you.

Do it again, shame on idiot me.

"It's not going to happen," she insisted, folding her arms. "Sex between you and me," she elaborated, even as she doubted he believed that. "Besides, are you telling me there isn't anyone over in Somersett, or maybe here on the island, who wouldn't be ticked off by you playing house with another woman? Particularly a former lover?" she asked with what she thought was an offhand tone.

"Not a one," he said.

Okay. That was another surprise. Talk about having sex like bunnies. When it came to sex, Shane had been the Energizer Bunny times ten. He was also up for it, literally, anytime, anywhere.

Even more amazing was that while she'd been with him, she'd been the same way. Like pilots, physicians had to be good at multitasking, and Kirby had always considered herself one of the best. Which was why, during those times he'd be away from the Green Zone for more than a day or two, even while juggling half a dozen patients at once, there was a part of her brain counting the hours until the hunky pilot was back where he belonged.

In her bed.

In her.

There'd even been times when she'd worried she might be turning into a nymphomaniac. Which must not have been the case, since she hadn't really missed sex all that much since their affair had been one more casualty of a tragic war.

"Are you saying you haven't had sex since you were injured?" Having treated him, she knew his only injuries had been to his leg. Well, along with that seeming TBI.

"No."

Ha! She'd known it!

"I'm saying there isn't a woman in my life *now*."

"But there was?"

Hell. The minute she heard the question come out of her mouth, Kirby wished she could call it back. But, like so much of her experience with this man, she was too late. She had no right to be jealous of any woman he might have been involved with over the past eighteen months.

No reason to be upset that he'd moved on. Or hurt.

But, dammit, she was.

His broad shoulders raised and lowered as he sighed. Heavily.

"Not in the way you mean," he said.

Before she could decide whether or not she wanted him to elaborate on what, exactly, *he'd* meant, he turned off onto a narrow road.

"Oh, wow." Relieved to have something, anything, else to talk about, Kirby drank in the sight of the ancient oaks lining both sides of the narrow road. "This reminds me of that miniseries with Patrick Swayze. *The North and the South.*"

"Don't have big old trees like this out West," he said. "And that's the same thing I thought the first time I saw it."

She glanced over at him, surprised. "You actually watched that miniseries?"

"What, you think if it doesn't have cowboys, I wouldn't be interested? I always liked history."

She didn't doubt that. Especially since he'd claimed to have minored in military history.

But while the program had its share of battles, what she remembered was more Civil War soap opera than history.

The answer belatedly clicked in. "You only watched it because you were hot for Lesley-Anne Down," she accused.

He laughed. "Hey, what can I say? I was eleven. When I saw her in that corset, Christ, I nearly swallowed my tongue. It was also, by the way, when I first began to understand all that sex stuff my older brother and his friends were talking about all the time."

"Well, I guess I can't fault you," Kirby allowed. "Since I had a major crush on Patrick Swayze."

"Yet another thing we had in common,"

he said casually. "Not the Swayze thing. But it's kind of cool knowing that we were watching it at the same time — you down in San Diego, and me up in Oregon — for almost the same reasons. . . .

"Like I said, it's one more thing we have in common. If we were keeping track," he tacked on when she shot him a look.

"Which we're not."

He shrugged. "You'll just have to speak for yourself on that one."

The drive through the green alley was at least a mile long.

"I really hope Tremayne knew what he was doing when he invited me to stay here," Kirby murmured. "Not every wife would be all that wild to have a houseguest suddenly drop in on her."

"Sabrina's different," Shane assured her. "From the way she tells it, her artist parents traveled all the time, which left her staying either in boarding schools or hotels during vacations when she'd join them wherever in the world they were. I guess the staff at those hotels were more family than her folks."

"That's sad."

Kirby might have had some typical teen-age problems with her parents during those tempestuous years, but she'd never doubted that they loved her. Or that she was the most important thing in their lives.

"Yeah. I thought so, too, when I first heard the story. But I guess it all worked out for the best, because that's when she discovered that she really likes the hotel business."

"Which is why she turned her family home into a bed and breakfast?" Kirby asked. Another thought occurred to Kirby. "But if she has a family home, why did she live in hotels?"

"Like I said, her parents traveled a lot. But she spent summers at Swannsea, which is how she met Zach. Her grandmother passed on last year and left her the place. But before she ended up back on the island, I guess she really fast-tracked her way through the Wingate Palace Hotel chain. In fact, she'd just been appointed manager of their hotel in Florence, Italy, when a terrorist blew it out from under her."

"You're kidding!" As soon as she said the words, Kirby waved them away. "Forget I said that."

Terrorism was not anything anyone would joke about. Especially a man who'd spent so much time fighting terrorists. And who'd lost a leg to war.

"It was one of those life-altering events," he said.

And couldn't they both identify with that?

"So, afterward, she came back home for a little R&R and to figure out what to do next with her life. She and Zach had a history going back to when she'd spend summers here as a kid. They hooked up, fell in love, and except for a wacko who tried to kill her, everything's pretty much come up roses for both of them."

Tried to kill her?

She was about to ask for a few more details about *that* story when they turned a final corner and an alabaster, two-story house with Grecian pillars came into view.

"Oh, wow. You didn't tell me that Zach Tremayne was married to Scarlett O'Hara."

"It's really something, isn't it?"

"It's amazing. Next to the White House, and President Vasquez's pink monstrosity —"

"Pink?"

"You have to see it to believe it." Sort of like this antebellum mansion that looked as if it had been beamed in from MGM's back lot. "Well, thinking about it, I guess you will. See it, that is."

The white Doric columns rose two stories high. "How many columns are there?" she asked.

"Twenty-seven. I counted the first time I

was here," he admitted.

"So would I." It was a small thing, but one more item to put in the column of things they had in common.

If she were keeping score.

Which she definitely was not, Kirby reminded herself yet again.

"There are eight chimneys," he volunteered. "And the double front stairs are supposedly so men and women could go up different ones when they arrived for fancy dress balls. Because if a man caught a glimpse of a woman's ankle, according to the rules of Southern etiquette at the time, he'd have to marry her."

It was a good thing they hadn't lived back then, Kirby thought. Because Shane had seen a lot more of her than her ankle.

"Didn't Sherman make it down here?" she asked.

"He did indeed. In fact, Swannsea is one of the few antebellum homes outside of Savannah to survive the war.

"The way Sabrina tells it, although the Federal troops burned the gardens during the Civil War, or as they tend to say down here, the War of Northern Aggression, Annabelle Swann killed the plantation's last remaining chicken with her own two ladylike hands, then roasted it for the officer in command of the mission. She also served up two bottles of port she'd buried in the kitchen garden.

"According to legend and Annabelle's own diary, the colonel was so taken with Swannsea's hospitality, he chose to leave the house standing."

"Hmm," Kirby murmured. "I wonder if roast chicken and port were the only things the merry widow served up."

"Put another mark on that mental list you're making," Shane said, as he pulled into the circular brick driveway in front of the house. "Because the same thought occurred to me. Zach said rumors continue to this day exactly how far Annabelle had been willing to go to save her family home from those damn Yankees, but it's cool that she did."

"Yes. It is."

Athough Swannsea had undoubtedly been built by slaves and represented a dark time in the country's history, Kirby thought it would've been a great loss if such a magnificent house had been reduced to ashes. She'd never considered herself a fanciful person, but she would not have been the least bit surprised if Rhett Butler had come strolling out of that enormous, hand-carved front door.

Instead, Sabrina Swann Tremayne must have been waiting for them, because the door flew open and a slender blond wearing jeans and a red sweater came running across the porch and down the stairs.

33

"If it isn't my favorite flyboy," she said, throwing her arms around Shane. "It's been ages since you made the trip across the harbor to visit."

"Only about a month," he countered, as he lifted her off her feet. Without so much as swaying. Boy, did Kirby want to see that leg!

"That's far too long," she said.

Once he'd lowered her back to the brick semicircular driveway, she turned toward Kirby, her green eyes both smiling and appraising. "And you must be Dr. Campbell."

Her outstretched hand was smooth as a baby's bottom, the nails neatly trimmed and polished, making Kirby all too aware of how long it had been since she'd had a manicure.

Like, ten years? At least.

"It's Kirby."

"And I'm Sabrina."

Her smile was warm and every bit as gracious as Kirby imagined the late Annabelle Swann's must have been. As charmed as she was by it, she figured the Yankee colonel must have been a goner the moment he'd ridden up that long oak alley.

"You have a stunning house," Kirby said as they began walking toward the steps.

"It is beautiful, isn't it?" Kirby liked that the other woman didn't pretend to take it for granted. Which she doubted anyone could truly do. "When I was younger and would visit my grandmother on the island, I always expected Rhett Butler to come strolling out the door."

"That's exactly what I was thinking," Kirby admitted.

"There's a family legend that Margaret Mitchell was attending a party here when she impulsively decided to use Swannsea as a model for Tara," Sabrina confided. "But, as my grandmother Lucie use to point out, there are homeowners all over the South making the same claim, so, who really knows? Besides, there's another story that Mitchell was appalled by what MGM had come up with, because she'd written the house to be a rough-and-tumble plantation with no architectural planning at all."

"I read the book," Kirby said. "In the eighth grade. But I guess the image from the movie was so imprinted on my mind, that's how I saw it."

"Me, too," Sabrina said. "And I'd venture everyone else who ever read it envisioned a house like this."

"So, I suppose you're using it in your advertising?"

"No. It'd be much too presumptuous. But" — Sabrina's eyes lit with bright laughter — "we do just happen to have photographs of it stuck on every bit of promotional material."

Such photos, Kirby considered, would immediately bring Margaret Mitchell's blockbuster book to mind, allowing Sabrina Swann to appropriate the *Gone With the Wind* image without actually claiming it.

"That's very clever."

"Thank you."

"It's very generous of you to invite me to stay here," Kirby said.

"It's absolutely no problem," Sabrina bestowed a warm smile on Shane as he opened the heavy door, which had closed behind her as she'd come running down the steps. "As you can see, we've got lots of room. And you're just in time to taste test some new recipes my partner, Titania, and I are trying out."

Shane carried the suitcases into the house.

Walking beside him, Kirby drew in a sharp breath.

A chandelier the size of a Volkswagen dripped crystals and sent rainbows dancing across the walls.

White marble flowed underfoot like a glacier, and the doorways to each of the rooms leading off the foyer were festooned with intricate plaster detailing, while a fresco adorned the mile-high ceiling. The dramatic scale and architectural detail would be unimaginable today. Kirby doubted that even Donald Trump or even any of the Rockefellers could have afforded such grand attention to detail.

She'd been in entire apartments not as large as this entryway. Having spent so many years living in close quarters working for WMR, and earlier, when she'd been in the military, Kirby found the scale a bit unnerving and wondered how it would feel to live in a home the size of a hotel. Then remembered what Shane had told her about Sabrina having grown up in hotels.

"Why don't you take Kirby's luggage upstairs," Sabrina suggested. "Let her catch her breath for a bit. Zach says you've had a hectic twenty-four hours."

"It's certainly been eventful," Kirby agreed. Wasn't that an understatement?

"It's the fifth door to the right on the second floor," Sabrina instructed Shane.

"Take as much time as you need," she told Kirby. "Titania and I will be in the kitchen."

The carpeting on the stairs was faded, the pink roses nearly white. But rather than looking as if it needed to be replaced, Kirby thought it added to the sense of history of the home.

The walls were lined with gilt-framed oil paintings, lit by wall sconces, that she guessed must represent generations of Swanns. All the men appeared dashingly handsome, the women ravishingly beautiful. Kirby could see her hostess in several of their faces.

"Oh, it's exquisite," she said as she entered the room Sabrina had suggested. The silk-draped walls were the color of cream above a carved chair rail; the rich, deep hue of strawberry wine below.

The wonder of a bed — so different from the narrow one she and Shane had managed to make love in — with its four graceful rice posters at least eight feet tall, and so high she'd need the wooden steps beside it to climb up onto it, had to be an antique.

The quilted cover was ivory, trimmed with eight inches of exquisitely tatted lace. Lace that was echoed on the edges of the many pillows strewn over the mattress, and repeated at the windows, the latter slanting the sun into gold bars across the polished hardwood floor.

"Too bad we're not going to have time to try that out," Shane said, as they both took in that magnificent bed.

"Your ego is larger than that mattress," she muttered.

"Tell me that wasn't the first thought that came into your mind." He put her carry-on down and smoothed his palms over her shoulders, creating heat that slipped beneath her skin. "We both know you want me."

Annoyed at him, at herself, at *both* of them that she could be just as susceptible to him as she'd been in Iraq, Kirby shrugged off his touch and moved over to the window, staring out at the fields of tea and, beyond them, the glassy Atlantic Ocean.

Dammit, his accusation was too true.

While every fiber of her being would love to make him crawl naked on his hands and knees over broken glass, she knew if he touched her again, she'd be doomed. She shot him a look over her shoulder. "I take back what I said about your ego being bigger than the bed. It's actually bigger than this entire house."

A corner of his mouth turned up in that

cocky, Night Stalker grin she remembered all too well. "I remember a time you liked my ego just fine."

His timing, except for when he'd sent her away, had always been exceptional. It was now, as he paused just long enough to set up the punch line she could see coming like a stinger missile headed straight toward her. "But I sure as hell don't remember you complaining about size back in the sand-box."

She refused to acknowledge the double entendre. "That was then. This is now."

Wasn't that profound?

"Well," she turned back around. "Thanks for carrying up my suitcase," she said on the same brisk tone she'd have used to ask an ER nurse for a hemostat. "I'll see you in the morning."

"At oh-eight-hundred," he agreed. "Unless you want to take me up on that offer of breakfast before we go wheels-up at ten."

"If the smells coming from Sabrina Tremayne's kitchen are any indication, I'm probably at the place with the best food on the island, so I think I'll pass. Besides, I don't usually eat breakfast."

"Really?" He cocked a devilish brow. "And here I'd always thought you just had better things to do in the morning whenever we had a sleepover."

"Go. Now." She put her hands on his shoulders, turned him around, and marched him to the door.

He was nearly gone.

She'd managed to get him into the hall when he turned back and caught the edge of the door just as she was about to close it.

Then just stood there looking down at her.

"What?" she asked.

"I forgot something."

"What?" she repeated.

"This." And before she could slam the door, he was inside the room again, his fingers digging into her waist.

His head lowered.

And he took her mouth.

34

Doomed.

That was what she was, Kirby thought as her hand, which suddenly had taken on a mind of its own, moved to the back of his neck.

Absolutely, positively, unmistakably doomed.

This must be the downside of celibacy. It only made sense that if you kept anything bottled up too long, it would have to, well, pop its top. Explode. *Kaboom.*

It wasn't hottie Shane Garrett who had her hormones careening around like steel balls in a pinball machine.

He could be any reasonably sexy, available man.

But, oh, this one is good, she thought as he kicked the door shut behind him.

Really, really good.

Rather than ravish, the way he had the first time he'd kissed her, Shane took his time, brushing his lips against hers with a satiny, enticing touch.

"I've missed this." His breath was warm against her lips; his hands smoothed up and down her back.

He tasted of coffee from the gallons everyone had been drinking at Phoenix Team headquarters, of cinnamon gum, and of . . . well, Shane.

As hard as she'd tried, Kirby had never been able to forget the way he tasted, the way he smelled when he'd show up at her trailer after a mission — of heat and sweat and sex. The man was a walking, talking testosterone cocktail so potent it made her drunk whenever he got within kissing distance.

Which he definitely was now.

"Missed *you,*" he murmured. "So goddamn much."

His mouth brushed hers, then retreated, brushed, retreated, threatening to destroy her with his patience.

Doomed.

The word tolled in her mind like one of those huge bronze church bells that had been ringing over Landstuhl when she'd walked out of the medical center, tears streaming down her face.

Kirby had been trying to keep herself from

remembering. From wanting. She knew that all she had to do was to simply step away. And he'd stop.

But, Lord help her, his mouth was so amazingly clever. The almost kisses, as his lips drifted over hers in a slowly, lazy seduction, were so tempting, that although she knew it was medically impossible, Kirby felt her body melting.

Degree by enervating degree.

It was if her blood had turned molten, flowing hotly in her veins beneath his touch, which promised remembered carnal delights.

His lips were just as she remembered them, as she'd dreamed of them — smooth, soft, and delicious. They had always been the only soft thing about the man.

The fingers of his other hand brushed the back of her neck before sliding into her hair. Like everything else about Shane Garrett, the light touch proved scintillatingly seductive.

When Kirby would have hurried, Shane slowed the pace even more, as if intent to savor every moment.

She tilted her head, trying to fully capture his roving mouth, but his lips had already moved on, leaving only a lingering sense of pleasure and a steadily rising need as they skimmed up her cheek to her temple. Across her eyes, which fluttered closed at the feathery touch.

Without taking his mouth from her face, he turned her around, effectively trapping her between the door and his fully aroused body. "Tell me you missed it, too."

"I didn't want to."

"But you did." He nipped the lobe of her ear, creating a jolt of need that shot all the way to her toes, clad in a pair of sensible taupe pumps.

With every nerve in her body vibrating like the strings of a plucked harp, when he nuzzled her neck, Kirby tilted her head, giving his lips access to her throat.

When the tip of his tongue touched the little hollow where her blood was thrumming, her pulse leaped.

"It was *your* choice," she reminded him.

"It seemed like a good idea at the time." His hand, as it moved lower, lifting her butt to press her even closer against him, was both gentle and confident. His body was hard and fully aroused. "But I've had a lot of time to think about it, and I've pretty much come to the conclusion I made a mistake."

"Stop the presses." Despite all he'd been through, despite the surgeries and all those months in the hospital, he was every bit as powerfully built as ever.

At six feet even, he might not be as large as his brother-in-arms Quinn McKade. Nor did he possess Zach Tremayne's lean runner's body. Every bit as strong as the other men, his male sinew and powerful, muscled ridges had been molded into a more compact form.

Once, as she'd lain with him, arms and legs entwined, basking in the golden afterglow of lovemaking, her lips skimming over his damp chest, Kirby had found him perfect, even as it crossed her mind that he'd been designed to fit into the close confines of a cockpit.

"The hotshot pilot just admitted he's not infallible."

"I know." His other hand moved from her shoulder to her thigh, leaving a trail of sparks as it brushed against the side of her breast. "It's a helluva shocker to me, too. But it's true."

With a deft touch she hadn't even realized was happening, his other hand flicked open the first button of her blouse. Then another. A third. "I was an idiot."

"You won't get any argument from me there."

Her underwear wasn't the boring cotton

she'd worn in Iraq, rather some type of wickable material that made wearing a bra in the jungle actually bearable. But it still was a long way from the seductive black lace and silk she suddenly wished she was wearing.

Not that he appeared to mind as he skimmed a caress over the flushed crest of her breasts. "A dickhead."

She tilted her head back and looked up at him. "That absolutely works for me."

"But here's what I've been thinking. . . ."

He nudged the material aside, his caressing fingertips causing her foolish heart to flutter like a wild bird.

"Maybe this is our chance to make up for lost time."

His mention of lost time had her mind flashing to Rachel and Michael Gannon. What a waste, she considered. If all this didn't work out, if finally, now that they were both free of commitments, fate cheated them of the opportunity of the life they deserved together . . .

No. Kirby gave a swift, mental shake of her head. She would not allow herself to even contemplate this mission failing. Phoenix Team, including the man whose arms were so naturally, perfectly around her, would rescue Rachel. Then the doctor and the former priest would live happily ever after.

Meanwhile, as far as she and Shane were concerned, letting things get even this far had been risky.

But reminding herself that she'd always been a risk taker and desperate for more, Kirby rose on the balls of her feet, cupped her hands at the back of his neck, and finally dragged his mouth fully down to hers.

Jesus. He'd wanted to tease her, to let her start thinking about how it had been between them. Make her start wanting him again.

He remembered Dallas O'Halloran, while they'd been waiting around for the brass to get their collective asses in gear in Gardez, alleging that the best way to get a woman interested was to take things slowly, always leaving her wanting more and more until the anticipation became too much and she was literally begging you to do her.

Of course, the first flaw in that reasoning was that the Air Force Combat Controller had probably never had to worry about getting a woman interested, because from what Shane had seen, although there hadn't been all that many available females in Afghanistan, the few Americans and Europeans that *had* been downrange were always throwing themselves at him.

The second flaw was that backing off, just when things started heating up, required a helluva lot of self-control.

Something that had always been in short supply whenever Shane got around Kirby Campbell.

Okay, Shane thought as her tongue tangled sinuously, seductively with his.

Just. One. Kiss.

One rock-the-lady's-world kiss, then he'd leave. Because, he reminded his aching testicles, there was no way he was going to have sex with Kirby in his buddy's house, with Zach's wife downstairs. That would be just too freaking weird.

He pulled her against him, so tight he could feel her nipples pressing against his chest. His hand slid lower, gathering up her ugly navy skirt, lifting it high on her thighs so he could cup the damp crotch of her panties.

Oh, wow. She was incredibly hot.

And really, really wet.

As the earth shifted beneath his feet, alarm sirens began blaring, like when the Duke had called General Quarters in *In Harm's Way.*

Shane ignored them.

Instead of backing away now while he still

could, he captured both her wrists in his right hand and pinned them against the door above her head, then pushed between her legs and crushed his mouth against hers again.

He pushed his tongue past her teeth, deeper than he'd ever kissed anyone, even her, and stole her breath. He pressed against her, the metal button of his 501s gouging into his groin, which was one of the problems with going commando, grinding his hips in a slow, insistent rhythm.

At the same time, his stroking hand delved beneath the elastic of her panties, through the silky curls, to that place that was as hot and wet as her mouth.

As she gasped and arched against his touch, power and an urgent need to sink deep inside that moist heat slammed through him.

"Oh, God," she moaned against his mouth. "Please."

Captain Kirby Campell had never been a woman to beg for anything. Except for that day in Landstuhl. When he'd screwed everything up by trying to be noble, to do the right thing.

Which had, despite his best intentions, turned out to be the absolutely wrong thing.

So, although he figured his balls would be

blue for a week, even as he felt the familiar shudder of a climax rip through her, even as he wanted to take her hard and fast and deep, he forced himself to back away.

Now. While he still could.

"I didn't mean for that to happen," he said as he retrieved his hand.

She blinked. He watched her struggle to bring her eyes back into focus. She was obviously staggered by what had just occurred.

Don't feel like the Lone Ranger, cupcake.

"Didn't you?" she asked on a ragged, still shaky tone.

Glancing down, she seemed surprised that her skirt was still bunched up around her waist.

Which, as a vision of those smooth, tanned legs wrapped around him flashed into his mind, wasn't necessarily a bad thing.

Or wouldn't be, if they were alone in the house.

Unfortunately, they weren't.

He shrugged, pretending a nonchalance he was a long way from feeling. "I don't like to start things I can't finish."

He thought her lips quirked just a bit at that. "Well, that certainly wasn't a problem for one of us."

Having prepared himself for temper, or

Jesus, Mary, and Joseph help him, tears, Shane hadn't been expecting humor.

She directed a look at his groin, where his erection was still pressing against the front of his jeans. "I see all the important parts are in working order."

"Seem to be." At least with *you.* "I figure it's muscle memory."

The term usually referred to the reason troops drilled for hours, days, and months on end. So in the heat of battle, their bodies would remember what their scattered minds might forget. Shane figured it fit the definition in this case.

She surprised him again by laughing at that. Then disappointed him by shoving the skirt back down.

"I'd given up men," she said conversationally as she buttoned her blouse.

The ivory bra had been one of those sports deals you could see women wearing just about anywhere these days — in the gym, even jogging in the park. But for some reason he'd found it sexier than a Victoria's Secret commercial.

"Oh, have you?" Deciding that the best way to stay out of any more trouble was to follow her lead and keep things light, he said, "I'm guessing that's not your way of breaking the news that you've become a lesbian."

"No." His temperature spiked for an instant when she unbuttoned the skirt. But only to tuck the blouse back in. "I'm saying that I decided to embrace my celibate side."

"Yeah," he said, feeling a major twinge of regret as she refastened the button. "I could tell from the way you had your tongue down my throat that you've given up on sex."

"You're the one who started it."

"Wrong. You're the one who started it by being so damn sexy any guy with two working balls — hell, even one — would want to jump your bones."

She folded her arms across the front of the rumpled white blouse.

"You've always had such a way with words," she said dryly.

Shane shrugged. "You want a guy who talks pretty, go find yourself some long-haired, pale-faced, dickless poet who believes in embracing his feminine side. Me, I'd rather forego the poetry and concentrate on making sure my woman is sexually satisfied."

Which he sure hadn't done with that lawyer the other night. As horny as he still was, and as hard as it was going to be to walk away from Kirby right now, he was super relieved to discover that the problem really had been mental and not physical.

He'd adjusted to having lost his leg. Well, as much as he figured any guy ever could. But if he'd been unlucky enough to get his dick blown off, he'd rather have been left behind in the Kush, where the weather or bad guys could've finished him off.

"One flaw in that outrageously sexist statement is that I'm not your woman," she pointed out.

"Well, see, now this is where I give you fair warning that I'm going to be doing my damnedest to change that."

He waited for her to say that tangos would be ice skating in Fallujah before that happened.

For not the first time, she surprised him. "Consider me warned." She looked on the verge of saying something.

Maybe something personal.

Then the moment was lost as she glanced down at her watch. "You'd better be going if you're going to make that meeting," she said.

"Yeah."

He knew that wasn't what she'd been about to say. Letting out a breath Shane hadn't even been aware of holding, he stood there, just drinking in the sight of her, looking all mussed and soft, like a woman who needed to be dragged off to bed.

"What?" she asked when he didn't, couldn't, move.

"I was just thinking how goddamn gorgeous you are."

"Yeah. I'll bet." She dragged a hand through her hair. "Not only do I have jet lag; I'm probably carrying enough baggage beneath my eyes to fill the cargo hold of a C-17 and —"

He caught her hand as it made another swipe through her short, sleek hair. Lifted it to his lips and brushed a kiss across her knuckles.

"The first time we made love, you'd been on a twenty-hour rotation and were wearing BDUs and bloody boots, which wasn't exactly an outfit favored by a *Sports Illustrated* swimsuit cover model or *Playboy* centerfold," he reminded her. "But when you walked into your hootch, sweetcakes, damned if you didn't make me harder than an entire years' worth of naked Playmates."

Because he'd never said anything he'd meant more, he gave her his most sober, sincere look over their linked hands. "You still do."

Christ, that was corny. He wouldn't have been surprised to hear a bunch of violins start playing. No way was this woman going to buy that claim. Even if it were true, which it was.

"Well." Rather than call him a low-life scum liar who'd use any line he thought might work to get into her panties, she blew out a breath. Retrieved her hand and folded her arms across her breasts. "We can't let whatever this is between us screw up the mission. Rachel's too important."

"Agreed. But I don't think we necessarily need to put sex entirely off the table."

"Doesn't it just figure sex would be the uppermost thing in your mind?"

Finally. *There* was the scorn he'd been expecting.

"Not the uppermost."

Even back when they were having crazed monkey sex, when the time came to fly a mission, he'd been able to stay absolutely focused. Enough, he thought, to have successfully landed that broken helo on the side of a Afghan mountain in a damn blizzard, with terrorists with big guns turning it into a camouflage-painted colander.

"But we've always had this . . . thing — chemistry, attraction, whatever the hell you want to call it — going," he said. His voice had gotten deep and rough. It wasn't an act. It was a grinding woman-hunger that was turning his balls blue. "We're like TNT and nitroglycerin, Kirby. The question is not *if* we're going to get hot and blow up. But *when.*

"So," he said, noticing that she wasn't exactly rushing in to deny that statement, "it seems to me that trying to keep our hands off each other could prove more of a distraction than just going with the flow. And giving in to what we both know is inevitable."

She shook her head. But he could tell she was thinking about it.

"There's got to be a flaw in that reasoning somewhere," she said finally. "But I'm too wiped out to figure out what it is."

"Give it some thought." He skimmed a finger down her nose. Touched his lips to her frowning ones in a brief, hot kiss that ended way too soon.

Then, before he could change his mind and just drag her onto the too-inviting lacy bed, he left the room, forcing himself not to look back until he was in the truck and headed down that oak alley toward town.

35

After shutting the door behind him, Kirby could not resist going to the window, watching as he strode out to the truck, on much the same sexy, hip-forward way she remembered.

Again, she thought that anyone not knowing the details of his injury could well be unaware that he'd lost that leg.

Get him naked and you can see it, the doctor in her thought.

The problem with that, the woman in her countered, was that if she got him naked, his medical condition was going to be the last thing on her mind.

It wasn't fair. She'd never been comfortable showing emotion. Not because of any deep-seated childhood problems, or having grown up with cold, unfeeling parents. Just the opposite. Her mother and father were the most warm, loving, outgoing individuals she'd ever met.

Perhaps she'd been more reserved because she'd been an only child, which meant that much of her time had been with adults rather than kids her own age. Perhaps it was just her nature, the way her molecules had entwined together in her DNA. There'd actually been times growing up when she'd wondered if she could have been adopted. Or perhaps some absentminded nurse had made a critical mistake and mixed up the infants in the hospital nursery, sending the wrong one home with Kathleen and Duncan Campbell.

Whatever, that innate ability to emotionally distance herself had proven helpful during medical school, her internship, and residency. And even more so in her practice, particularly during her time at the CSH. Although inside she'd wanted to weep on a daily basis, often several times a day, she'd known that giving in to a crying jag was the last thing her patients needed. What they'd needed was for her to stay cool, calm, and decisive.

None of which she'd ever felt with Shane Garrett.

He'd had her from the moment she walked into that examining cubicle and seen him on that metal examining table. And, dammit, from the way she'd felt earlier, as if he'd lit a bunch of Fourth of July sparklers beneath her skin, that hadn't changed.

She'd given a lot of thought to their wartime affair over the past several months and come to the conclusion that, as much as she honestly believed she'd loved him, they were still pretty much a wartime cliché. If they had stayed together, the attraction undoubtedly would have grown old, the sex cooled.

"Yeah. Right."

God. She'd had an orgasm — the first in ages involving a partner — up against the bedroom door in the home of a woman she'd just met. With her clothes still mostly on.

And, if he'd even pushed just the slightest bit, she probably would have gone all the way with him right on that pretty, lacy bed.

Damn.

Kirby leaned her forehead against the glass and sighed as the truck headed down the road beneath the row of ancient oaks, away from the plantation house. Away from her.

He was right. Together they were as explosive as an IED. And definitely every bit as dangerous.

He might also be right that attempting to stay away from each other, to deny this sexual attraction that had always existed between them, could prove a distraction.

The good news was that they'd only be forced into close proximity for a few days. Once they hooked up with the others at the ruins, they'd be traveling with a team of chaperones.

As much as she appreciated the Army for her education and was grateful to have been able to experience so much more than she ever would have been able to in a civilian hospital in the States, Kirby had always chafed against all the rules and regulations.

During her work with WMR, she'd become an expert at punting. At going with the flow.

Which, she decided, as she went into the adjoining bathroom to freshen up before she joined Sabrina Swann Tremayne downstairs in the kitchen, was the best way to handle Shane.

Other than getting Rachel out of Monteleón safely, Kirby had no idea what was going to happen over the next few days.

So, she'd take things as they came. Or, as her superior, the golf-addict colonel used to say, play it as it lay.

Besides — she tried to justify her inability to resist the man — the more chemistry between them, the more likely Vasquez would be willing to buy their cover story.

The trick, she reminded herself firmly, was to remember that it was *just* a story. A game.

As long as she didn't lose track of that one constant, she should be able to come out of this adventure with her heart intact.

36

The meeting wasn't that different from other premission planning sessions Shane had taken part in. The difference was, this time, instead of Country Captain Chicken from a brown MRE bag — which, supposedly, were Meals Ready to Eat, but were better known as Meals Rarely Edible, Meals Rejected by Everyone, and even Meals Rejected by the Enemy — supper consisted of loaded pizzas with a side order of bread sticks. And the icy beer was a gazillion-percent improvement over a mix-it-yourself lemon carbohydrate electrolyte beverage.

"You know Kirby Campbell better than anyone else," Zach said to Shane. "How do you think she's going to react under pressure?"

"Like a rock," Shane said. "I watched her demonstrate amazing control during some brutally tough situations at the Cash in Baghdad. You probably remember a lot more about how she handled things at the refugee camp than I do, but she's one tough cookie."

"That sure as hell was my impression," Quinn agreed. "Not many people — male or female — could have stood up to those armed tangos."

"What about the history between you two?" Zach asked. "Will it get in the way?"

Shane thought about that kiss — and more — they'd shared. And how much it might have complicated an already dicey situation. But they were both experts at compartmentalizing. If he didn't think they could pull this off, there was no way he'd risk blowing the mission just because he didn't want to let her get away again.

"If she were a civilian, it might prove a problem," he allowed.

There was no point in holding back. Not when lives were at stake. Besides, he'd already shared the story while they'd all been hunkered down in a bunker shortly after the crash and firefight. A young Marine scout sniper had been fatally shot, but Christ, it had taken what seemed like forever for him to pass on.

So they'd all sat around shooting the bull, talking about women, like they were back in the barracks instead of an ice-cold bunker with a bunch of wild-eyed terrorists out there just waiting to kill them if they got the chance.

Quinn had talked about Cait, the woman he was now going to marry. And how she'd always seemed to hate him, except for when she'd gotten drunk at a wedding reception and they'd had their hot one-night hotel-room stand. Zach, who'd once dated her roommate, had ragged Quinn about Cait having always liked *him* just fine.

Shane had gone next, and while he'd never been one to kiss and tell, the situation seemed to call for it. So he told them about his and Kirby's time together in the sand-box.

Then Dallas O'Halloran had chimed in with his rules of female engagement. Which had pretty much been to figure out how to juggle his many lovers. "It's not an easy job," he'd said with his cocky, bad-boy wink. "But someone's got to do it."

After the SEAL medic Chaffee shared, it had been the wounded kid's turn.

He hadn't had nearly an easy time of it, with his mom dying of ovarian cancer when he was nine. Which was when he'd been sent to live with his grandmother in Salt Lick, Kentucky, because his dad was career Marine, like all the men in his family going back to the Revolution, and a gunnery sergeant couldn't very well defend America's freedom if he had to stay home to take care of Opie, which was what Zach had dubbed him, because he'd reminded them all of that freckle-face kid from Mayberry, USA.

Opie had a girl he planned to marry after his deployment, and they were going to have two kids and a couple bluetick hounds, because his granddaddy raised them and he wanted his boys to be able to go hunting with them, same as he had growing up.

They'd been laughing about how, if he and his girl had daughters, he might have to turn Catholic and send them off to a convent, like, yeah, a Kentucky Pentecostal was going to do that in this lifetime, when he'd suddenly, out of the goddamn blue, asked them to pray with him.

Thanks to his altar boy days, Shane had remembered the twenty-third psalm, which seemed appropriate, given its message of being comforted while walking through the shadow of death, which they all knew was the trip the young Marine was embarking on.

Then they'd recited the Lord's Prayer together, which made the kid smile.

Then he was gone. Just like that.

Although, despite his injuries and possible TBI, which seemed to be affecting some memories, Shane hadn't come home with PTSD like so many vets had, that particular event was still as vivid as if it had happened this morning. And it still slashed at a private place he suspected everyone who'd experienced war up close and personal had deep down inside themselves.

He realized everyone was looking at him. From the shadows in Quinn's and Zach's eyes, he suspected they were thinking back to that conversation, as well.

He shook off the memory and dragged his mind out of Afghanistan, back here to Lowcountry South Carolina and the matter at hand.

"Kirby might have been in the medical corps," he said, "but that didn't mean she wasn't military down to her fingertips. No way would she let personal stuff interfere with a mission. Especially when we're talking about rescuing her best friend."

"Okay. Good." Zach nodded and turned to Gannon. "I know it's been a lot of water under the bridge since you worked with Dr. Moore in a combat situation, but how do you think she's holding up? Might she unravel under pressure?"

"She thrived on challenge," the former

priest answered without hesitation. "Rachel Moore has the heart of a lion. And, if necessary, ice water in her veins. She's also going to be doing her best to figure out a way to escape. Which is why we need to get to her as soon as possible."

"We're working on it," Zach said.

"At least you should find some way to let her know you've got a man inside," Michael said.

Zach shook his head. "I don't want to do that. The fewer people who know he's our guy, the better the chances will be of him keeping her alive."

Shane could tell Gannon didn't like that idea. But apparently he'd spent enough time in the military himself to understand the chain of command. The members of Phoenix Team may be civilian these days, but Tremayne would be calling the shots for this mission.

Which, after seeing how the guy had handled that goatfuck in Afghanistan, was just the way Shane liked it.

He'd worked with enough SEALs to know the officers came up with the mission, which, to Shane's mind, was often the easier part.

Once the mission was decided upon, the chiefs figured out how to make the mission work. And Chief Zachariah Tremayne was the best Shane had ever worked with. In fact, were it not for the SEAL, he probably wouldn't be alive, sitting here.

The SEALs were daring, born risk takers, but they also were really, really intelligent. And Tremayne had always been one to plan down to the gnat's eyebrow. Which was a good thing, because when the plans went to shit, as they always did, at least there was some aspect of the larger picture they could cobble together to make things work.

"Another thing," Zach said to Gannon. "I totally understand how you feel. If anyone was holding Sabrina hostage, I'd want to torch the entire planet, if necessary, to get to her. But we've got enough dicey players already in the mix down there. I don't want to have to worry about you going Rambo on me."

"That's not going to happen."

Zach narrowed his eyes to what Shane always thought of as his Clint Eastwood squint, as dark and deadly as gunmetal.

Which was what they were now. Shane gave the former priest huge props for calmly meeting the look he'd seen plenty of men — even big, bad D-boys, and even badder tangos — squirm beneath.

"Okay," the former chief decided. He

swept his gaze over all of them seated at the table. "There's one more thing I need to say," he said. "I don't think it's any secret that I came home from that Operation Enduring Freedom Clusterfuck with some issues, as they like to call it these days."

No one responded, but every guy in the room knew the SEAL had returned Stateside with a rough case of PTSD. Partly, Shane had always felt, because he'd carried the guilt of responsibility. Which he shouldn't have, since he'd done better than any other guy Shane could think of to ensure the most men survived. But wasn't he proof that it could take time to sort things out in your mind?

"I've worked through that," Zach said. "The shrink at the V.A. said I'm good to go. Hell, I can even listen to The Doors without needing to get drunk, and I watched both *Apocalypse Now* and *Platoon* last week without wanting to shoot the TV. And I haven't had a flashback for months.

"If I wasn't absolutely positive that I'm qualified, in every way, to lead this mission, I'd bail. Because there's no way in hell I'd ever risk the lives of any of the members of this team."

Quinn raised his beer bottle. "Hooyah."

"Hooyah," Shane and Michael Gannon

corrected, repeating it in the Army way as they raised their bottles, as well.

"Okay." That uncomfortable bit of conversation behind him, Zack snagged the last piece of pizza from the box. "Looks like we're good to go."

37

Although Kirby had been given directions, she'd been afraid she'd get lost in the big house, but it turned out that all she needed to do was follow the amazing scents wafting up the stairs.

Sabrina was standing at a huge commercial stove, stirring something in a pot that looked large enough to cook for an army, while a stunning African-American woman wearing black leggings, calf-high boots, a bright color-blocked sweater, and sporting a very visible baby bump kneaded dough on a marble countertop.

"So," Swannsea's owner greeted her with a smile. "Did you get settled in?"

"I did, thanks. And the room's beautiful."

"If there's anything you need, just let me know."

"I think you've pretty much covered everything."

That was a decided understatement. The

woven sea grass basket in the adjoining bathroom held more luxury goodies — including a white origami washcloth — than what Kirby imagined could be found in a five-star Wingate Palace hotel. There was also an automatic coffeemaker featuring a fabulous selection of Swann teas, along with a variety of single servings of coffee.

And if all that wasn't enough, her hostess had included a carafe of springwater, a box of Swiss chocolate, and a stack of paperback novels and glossy magazines on a skirted table.

"Zach and I want you to be comfortable," she said with that smile Kirby suspected must have worked wonders calming down unhappy travelers.

"Well, you've certainly succeeded there. Shane said you managed a hotel in Italy?"

"I did. Well, for about an hour. Then a suicide bomber blew up the hotel, and that pretty much cut short my career in international hotel management." She put down the spoon to begin grating a block of rich, dark chocolate. "After the rescue crew dug me out of the rubble — miraculously, without any lasting injuries — I came back here to recuperate, went into business with my best friend, and fell back in love with Zach."

She smiled toward the woman. "This is my best friend and partner in crime and all things culinary, Titania Spencer."

As warm as Sabrina's smile was, the other woman's was so dazzling Kirby felt she should be wearing the shades she'd left upstairs in her purse. "Forgive me for not shaking your hand." Titania held up both two dough-covered hands. "But it's lovely to meet you."

"You, too," Kirby said. "Wow, it really smells fabulous in here."

"That's Titania's doing," Sabrina said. "She's the culinary genius; I'm just allowed to stir and do dishes."

The idea of the superrich tea heiress doing kitchen scut work was more than a little surprising.

"Are you hungry?" Sabrina asked.

Actually, since she'd been too nervous to eat this morning before the hearing, the only things she'd had to eat were those M&M's from the drugstore. The rest of the day had been so stressful, she hadn't realized she was starving.

Until now.

"I wouldn't want to put you out," she felt obliged to say.

"Nonsense; you're a guest," Sabrina countered. "And what kind of hostess would I be if I failed to live up to our legendary Southern hospitality?"

"Besides," Titania said with another of those blinding grins. "You're just in time to be our guinea pig."

"We're trying out new recipes," Sabrina explained. "Everything we make includes one of our teas as an ingredient, and we'd love an impartial opinion."

It was Kirby's turn to grin. "That's the best offer I've had all day." She sat down at the long plank table.

Thirty minutes later, she'd decided that if she hadn't died and gone to heaven, this surely had to be the next best thing.

The chicken breasts glazed with a sauce made of Swann orange spice tea, apricot and pineapple preserves, and a touch of red pepper flakes and soy sauce to give it bite was not only delicious, it was so tender it was falling off the bones.

The sesame seed oil added the perfect zing to the Earl Grey vinaigrette on the salad, and the fluffy rice, seasoned with Swann herbal green tea, could not have been more perfect.

"Wow," she said. "If the military could only hire you two as MRE contracts, not only would their recruiting problems disappear, but reenlistment numbers would go through the roof."

"Nate, he's my husband and a former Marine, swears the same thing," Titania said.

"Zach, too," Sabrina echoed as she topped off their wineglasses with a crisp Chardonnay while Titania stuck to iced sweet tea. "But then again, guys who'd actually eat the Four Fingers of Death and live to tell about it are not exactly going to be invited to judge *Top Chef*."

Just the memory of those gross mystery-meat things claiming to be hot dogs was enough to make Kirby groan. "Those things definitely lived up to MRE's 'Three Lies for the Price of One' reputation," she said. "It's not a meal, it's not ready —"

"And you can't eat it," both women joined in.

They all laughed.

"We were fortunate in the Green Zone to have a lot more options than the guys in the forward positions," Kirby said. "But I did do some rotation forward, and WMR buys a lot of surplus MREs, so I've suffered my share."

It had always amazed Kirby that the military could pinpoint targets with smart bombs, deploy thousands of troops to a flash point within days, and the Night

Stalker creed promised they'd arrive on target plus or minus thirty seconds, but they still hadn't figured out how to feed troops at the pointy tip of the spear.

The easy womanly companionship had Kirby thinking of Rachel again. Of the personal conversation they'd shared before Kirby had left for the States. Which, in turn, kicked up the worry factor times ten.

"She's going to be all right," Sabrina assured her, demonstrating the empathy Kirby figured was even more important than freebies in the bathroom if you were running a hotel. Even more so a smaller, more intimate inn such as the one she seemed to be planning here at Swannsea.

"Zach and Quinn are the best at what they do. And Zach's always claimed that there's not a better pilot in the military than Shane."

"So he always told me," Kirby agreed, which earned another laugh.

"He's also the most positive person I've ever met," Sabrina added. "A lot of people would be understandably bitter after what he's been through. Others might get depressed. But although I didn't know him until he came to town, Quinn, who visited him several times while he was in rehab, insists that he only let himself stay down a couple weeks. Then threw himself into regaining his life."

Kirby knew that the words were meant to reassure. But instead she found them depressing. If she'd only refused to leave and stuck around Landstuhl for a few weeks, would he have been willing to pick up their relationship?

Deciding there was no point in dwelling on the past, she turned to a more pleasant topic.

"When's your baby due?" she asked Titania.

"In May." The woman beamed, looking a lot like all those romanticized paintings on Italian cathedral ceilings of the Madonna. A very sexy Madonna. She unconsciously smoothed her hands over her belly.

"Being a genius at planning, you'll note that she cleverly scheduled the birth before the full heat of the summer," Sabrina said.

"Scheduled, hah," Titania scoffed. "It was all Nate's fault. He was the one who suggested we stay in Maui those extra days. If it's a girl, I think we should name her Mai. For the mai tais that were responsible," she explained at Kirby's puzzled look.

Her laugh was like silver bells. She was, hands down, the most stunning woman Kirby had ever seen who wasn't on a movie screen or in a music video.

"So you don't know if it's a boy or a girl?"

"No. We decided we want to be old-fashioned and be surprised."

"That's nice."

Kirby had occasionally given thought to having children. But the impracticality of her gypsy life in the military, then with WMR, had always precluded her becoming a mother.

There was always the problem of not having met anyone that she'd actually want to have children with. Or at least who wanted to father those hypothetical children — Shane coming to mind as he so often did.

"Do you have family here?"

"My mother died when I was born," Titania said.

"I'm sorry."

The boatneck sweater slid down over a caramel-hued shoulder as the other woman shrugged. "I've thought on occasion that was easier than having lost her later. Because I didn't have any memories, so it wasn't exactly as if I knew what I was missing."

Her doe-brown eyes took on a distant, somewhat sad look. Which she quickly shook off. "Besides, Nate's mother, who's now my mother-in-law, pretty much raised me while my father was working here at

Swannsea for Sabrina's grandmother."

The two women exchanged a look Kirby couldn't quite decode.

"So you've known your husband all of your life?"

"They took baths together," Sabrina offered.

"We were babies," Titania countered. "No more than toddlers."

"That's nice, though," Kirby said. "To have that history together."

Once again, it had her thinking about Shane. How they'd jumped into bed without knowing anything about each other. And how they hadn't known that much more when he'd dumped her months later.

It was her turn to shake off an unhappy feeling. "So," she said, with exaggerated brightness, "what about your father? He must be excited to be a grandfather. Is this his first?"

"And only," Titania said. She and Sabrina did that unreadable trading-look thing again. "He's been ill with Alzheimer's and used to confuse me with my mother a lot, so I was afraid he wasn't going to understand what's happening. But his doctor put him on new medication, which has him much more aware and less likely to suffer the hallucinations that used to seem real to him."

Another look.

There was definitely something going on here.

"Including a really difficult time when he wasn't sure I was even his daughter. Which is a long way of saying, that yes, Dad's over the moon at the idea of a new baby to continue the Davis family line. As are Nate and I."

The beaming smile was back, giving Kirby the idea that whatever family problems she and her father might have had — and with that tragic disease, they must be considerable — they appeared to be, at least for now, somewhat smoothed out.

"I think, since we've had a long day and worked really, really hard, we deserve a treat," Sabrina said, standing up and effectively putting an end to that line of conversation. "How would you like dessert?" she asked Kirby. "Titania's Swannsea chocolate mint brownies are absolutely to die for."

"Oh, my God," Kirby moaned, after taking a bite of the minty fudge dessert. "You were't exaggerating."

"I never do." Sabrina's smile was warm and lit up her lake blue eyes. "I like you," she said.

"Well, that would be mutual. Even if you hadn't given me the best meal I've had in months. Make that years."

"Titania, Cait — that's Quinn's fiancée — and I have been working on a project."

"Well, if you ever decide to take Swannsea Tearoom public, I want first dibs at the stock," Kirby said.

"Actually, it's not about food," Titania said.

"It's Shane," Sabrina said.

A second sinfully decadent brownie was on the way to Kirby's mouth when she paused. "Shane?"

My Shane? she thought, but did not ask.

"We've been trying to fix him up with a woman."

"Oh?" Her casual tone took a herculean effort, given that she doubted there was anything these two couldn't succeed in doing if they put their minds to it.

"But so far it's been a bust," Titania said.

"A total disaster," Sabrina added. "Of course, part of our problem is that he hasn't been at all cooperative."

Titania snagged another brownie from the plate in the middle of the table. "I'm eating for two," she announced. "And that's a decided understatement. I swear, I've never met a man I couldn't bend to my way of thinking."

Kirby had not a single doubt of that.

"But I've figured out why," Sabrina said.

"Oh?" Kirby asked.

"We've been using the wrong bait," Titania said.

Kirby was beginning to feel as if she were being tag-teamed by experts.

"It's obvious he's hot for you," Sabrina said. "I swear, I can't remember the last time I saw a man look at a woman the way he was looking at you."

"Like he wanted to start eating your toes and work his way up, is how Sabrina described it, to me," Titania said.

"I was afraid he was going to melt into a little puddle of need right there on the marble floor of the foyer," Sabrina said.

"That was before I'd told him I'd given up sex," Kirby found herself admitting.

Damn. It had to have been the wine that had her sharing that. She wasn't used to alcohol.

Neither woman looked any more convinced than Shane had appeared.

"And how's that going for you?" Sabrina asked after a pause.

"Fine."

She could tell neither of them believed

368

her. And why should they? When she didn't believe it herself.

"At least it was," she said. "Until a few minutes ago. Not that we actually did anything," she hastened to tack on, just in case her hostess might fear they'd been spreading bodily fluids all over that lacy bedcover.

"Ah." Sabrina lifted a brow. "So, that's why he didn't drop into the kitchen to say good-bye."

"Needed some time alone," Titania said knowingly. "Isn't it handy, since males so often are unwilling to share their feelings, how their bodies do all the talking for them?"

Even as she shared in the laughter, Kirby felt herself tingling again in places she'd forgotten she could tingle.

"You realize, of course, that all you've done by telling him that is present a challenge," Sabrina said. "SEALs are unbelievably competitive. They don't take no for an answer."

"Marines are the same way," Titania said knowingly. "The more I turned Nate down, the more determined he got."

"Just like Zach," Sabrina agreed. "Although, I have to admit that I'm the one who seduced him."

"Only because he let you," the other woman said. "I think, after the bombing, he probably wanted to let you make the moves. When you felt ready."

"If he'd made love to me when I was really ready for him, I would've given up my virginity in high school," Sabrina said. "It may have also been his PTSD. I think he may have worried that I'd have trouble dealing with it."

"But you didn't?" Kirby managed to keep her tone conversational while the mention of PTSD rang alarm bells.

"It helped when he had something else to focus on," Sabrina said thoughtfully. "Like falling in love."

"And then there was always the Swann Island Slasher to deal with," Titania said. "He had to get his act together for that one." She smiled at Kirby. "Funny what the power of love can do."

"It hasn't been that easy," Sabrina admitted. "But we've worked through it. And," she told Kirby, her expression serious, "if my husband had any worries about flashbacks on the mission, he wouldn't be going."

Kirby decided to believe her.

"I watched him in the Kush," Kirby said, wanting to ask about that so-called slasher, but deciding she could just Google it instead, rather than force her hostess to relive something that sounded as if it had been horrible. "After what had to have been some terribly difficult hours. And he was fully in control. I haven't a doubt he will be as cool and professional in Monteleón."

"Zach said you were the doctor who saved Shane's life when they went across the border into Pakistan." Sabrina's voice went up a little, turning the statement into a question.

"The doctors in Bagram and Landstuhl saved his life. I merely stabilized him so they could fly him out."

"That's not the way my husband sees it," Sabrina countered. "I doubt that Shane does, either."

"I don't want him to think of me as a doctor who saved his life."

"Oh, I didn't get the impression that was what he was thinking at all when he was fixated on your butt while following you up those stairs," Sabrina said.

"Well, it's why I didn't ask him about it directly," Kirby said. "But, since you brought it up, do you happen to know if he's displayed any PTSD symptoms since he's been Stateside?"

"Are you asking as a doctor? Or a

woman?"

"I'm not sure I can separate the two. But more as a woman."

"Well, I can tell both of you, the doctor and the woman, that he seems to have escaped any problems. Which seems to me somewhat surprising, given that of the three men, he's the one who suffered the most physically."

"But your husband was in charge," Kirby said. "Which had to have added burdens for him."

"That's exactly it," she agreed. "Plus, while I admittedly haven't known him that long, Shane seems to possess an unrelentingly positive attitude."

He always had.

Until Germany.

"Well," Sabrina said, picking up her wineglass, "this is skating close to a depressing topic. So, how would you like to be bored to tears looking at our wedding pictures?"

"We love to show them off," Titania said. "But everyone on the island has already seen them at least twice, and we're running out of victims."

"We had a double wedding," Sabrina said. "Cait, Quinn's fiancée," she reminded Kirby again, "was maid of honor."

"Which, when you meet her, you'll realize what a huge leap of girly friendship that was," Titania said. "Though it did take a bit of arm twisting."

"I don't believe anyone could say no to the two of you." They were a formidable pair. Kirby liked that about them.

"Cait's tough," Sabrina said. "But we won her over. Shane was an usher."

"And was to die for in his blues," Titania said.

She'd never seen the pilot in his dress uniform. But she'd certainly fantasized about it. Fantasized about them walking beneath crossed swords out of some pretty little church. Then fantasized about him taking it off and . . .

"I'd love to see the pictures," Kirby said.

38

"I knew, from some of the stunts you pulled in that flying Winnebago of yours, that you were nuts," Quinn said, as he and Shane sat at a table in the Stewed Clam, nursing beers and working their way through the bar menu. "But I never realized exactly how crazy you were until you got that leg blown off."

"Well, thanks for the vote of support." Shane took a bite of wing and felt flames scorch the roof of his mouth.

"Anytime. I just have one question."

"And that is?" Shane took a long pull on the beer bottle to put out the fire.

"How the hell did you let that female get away?"

Shane shrugged and snagged a fry from the red plastic basket. "Good question. And one I've been asking myself for a while."

"What took you so long?"

"It's only been eighteen months."

"Which is like a lifetime in idiot years," Quinn countered. "So, what are you going to do about her?"

"I'm going to get her back."

"Good idea." Quinn scooped up a handful of popcorn shrimp. "Seems rescuing her friend will win you huge points. Maybe save you from having to grovel too much."

"She's a female. Which, I suspect, means that some groveling's going to be in the cards."

Shane wasn't naive enough to think just because he'd given her an orgasm, she wasn't going to make him pay somehow.

"Probably," Quinn agreed. "But then you can kiss and make up. Which will make the effort worth it."

Shane certainly hoped so.

"You think we're going to have much trouble getting the doc out of the jungle?"

Even though, after hours of training and intensive PT getting used to it, his experimental bionic leg was working nearly as well as his real one had, Shane still hoped to hell that he wouldn't screw up his part of the mission.

"Let's see. On one side, we've got dozens of radical rebels who are probably drugged to the gills and armed with automatic weapons." Quinn lifted his right hand, palm up. "On the other side" — he held up his left — "we have two SEALs, a Night Stalker flyboy, and an Army doctor who hasn't held a weapon since Desert Storm, but just managed to beat both of us at the firing range."

"Gotta have been a fluke."

Shane was still stinging a bit from that. Especially since it hadn't been that long ago, at Walter Reed's FATS — Firearms Training System range — he'd actually topped what he'd been shooting before his helo had gone down. But when they'd all shot at the Phoenix Team range after the initial planning meeting, the former priest had beat him by one head shot.

"Or it's more personal for him," Quinn suggested.

"Yeah." Shane popped a deep-fried coconut shrimp into his mouth. "If anyone was holding Cait hostage, you'd undoubtedly tear heaven and earth apart to take them down."

"Then rip off their heads and piss down their necks," Quinn agreed.

"Works for me," Shane said.

39

For the next half hour, Kirby oohed and aahed over the pictures of the double wedding that had taken place in Swannsea's gardens. Sabrina and Titania were stunningly beautiful, as all brides should be, and their grooms — Zach in his Navy dress whites, Nate in Marine dress blues — handsome.

As was Quinn, who, like Zach, was wearing his dress whites with the choker collar. Cait Cavanaugh was stunning, the short black dress setting off her strawberry blond hair and porcelain skin.

But in every group photo, Kirby's eyes kept returning to Shane. She'd never seen him in anything but his flight suit, cammie BDUs, swim trunks, or naked. Looking at him in his Army dress blue uniform, with its shiny brass buttons and combat ribbons, nearly made her drool.

Both women kept up their tag-team conversation, sharing stories about their individual courtships, double wedding, but separate honeymoons — Titania and Nate to Hawaii, Sabrina and Zach to Italy. Although she'd worried that returning to Florence, where she'd almost died, would bring back bad memories, Sabrina apparently loved the country and had wanted to share it with Zach.

"Besides," she told Kirby, "if it hadn't been for that terrorist bomber, I wouldn't have come home to Swann Island and reunited with Zach."

As they'd looked through the album, Sabrina had literally glowed like a new bride. If Kirby hadn't liked Zach's wife so very much, she could have been jealous.

She couldn't remember the last time she'd sat around drinking wine and bonding with other women over conversations about men and sex and love. Even though she and Rachel had developed a working friendship, their hours were too long, their days too hard for them to do anything but collapse into bed at night, then get up at dawn and start working all over again. Which, except for the night they'd gone to dinner, didn't allow for much girl talk.

She'd had a few women friends in Iraq, but people were constantly getting rotated in and out of the CSH, and again, by the time she finished a shift, all she wanted was a shower and bed. Except for those months with Shane, when the shower and bed had come with a side of sex.

Even in medical school, while everyone had been focused on getting their degrees and planning active military careers, perhaps there'd been other people living a *Grey's Anatomy,* all sex, all the time, lifestyle, but she certainly hadn't known any.

Which hadn't left her much to talk about on those occasions the women students would get together.

Which was also why, although Kirby certainly didn't leave college a virgin, she'd actually begun to worry that she might be undersexed.

Then Shane had come crashing into her life and blown that concern to smithereens.

"You'll have to come back for some R and R after the mission's over," Sabrina said. "When was the last time you had a spa day?"

"Actually, never."

"Well, we'll just have to change that," Sabrina said.

"Absolutely," Titania agreed.

"You can meet Cait, and we'll all book a day at the Shores," Sabrina decided. Kirby could practically see her making the appointment on a mental BlackBerry. "The owner, Beatrice, promises 'a stress-free sanctuary from daily life,' which, I'll admit, when I first came back to town, sounded like a redundancy, since the island isn't exactly the big city, but her sea salt glow body treatment leaves your skin feeling like silk, and the hot stone massage is the next best thing to sex."

"Sounds interesting," Kirby said a little hesitantly. She figured, after all these years in the sun, it would take a lot more than sea salt and heated rocks to make her skin feel like silk.

Compared to these two ultrafeminine females, she was beginning to feel a bit like G.I. Jane.

Titania reached over and patted her hand. "Don't worry. You'll love it. And afterward we'll take the ferry over to Somersett, have ourselves high tea at the Wingate Palace, then go shopping. Because, girlfriend, I think you've been in cammies too long. You have a fabulously sexy body you're hiding beneath that nun's habit."

"Though we can understand why you wouldn't want to show off your sexuality down in your clinic in Monteleón, which could be dangerous," Sabrina said, "there's no reason why you can't polish the package just a bit."

She exchanged a look with Titania.

"Makeover!" they both said at once.

Oh, God.

"I'm not exactly an *America's Next Top Model* candidate." Kirby would rather be poked in the eye with a flaming sharp stick than be "polished."

"Who is?" Titania, whom Kirby thought could win that reality show without breaking a sweat, said with a toss of her dark, braided cornrows. "At least let us trim your hair a little. It looks as if you've been hacking away at it with a Swiss Army knife."

Kirby lifted a hand to the hair in question. "Actually, it was a pair of surgical scissors. I like to think of it as a shag."

"There are shags. And hatchet jobs." Titania leaned across the table, her fingers playing with Kirby's blond hair. "And you definitely fall into the second category." She turned toward Sabrina. "I'll cut it, while you do something with those nails."

"Oh, I really don't think —"

"Exactly," Sabrina jumped in as Titania's wingman, and cut off the planned protest. "It'll be painless. And fun."

"Like a sleepover," Titania said. "The way we used to when you'd come to the island for the summer in high school."

"Though without the 'N Sync and Back-street Boys tapes," Sabrina said.

"We don't need Justin Timberlake when we have Usher on my iPod," Titania said. "We'll just hook it up to your speakers, and we're set."

Which was how Kirby found herself wearing a white terry cloth robe, sitting on a padded stool in the bathroom adjoining the guest room, her bare feet soaking in scented water, a towel wrapped around her neck while Titania snipped away, and Sabrina smoothed some magical potion onto her hands to make her ragged cuticles disappear.

"I don't suppose you happen to have any makeup?" Titania asked as she added a fringe of bangs.

"It melts in the jungle." Kirby cringed as she watched a long piece of hair fall to the marble floor.

"Well, you're not going to be in the jungle all day tomorrow while you're on the plane," Sabrina said. "Trust me, men tend to have a certain image of us stuck in their brains. I know Zach was surprised to see I'd grown up when I came back to the island."

"So," Titania picked up the conversational thread, "you need a new look that will knock Shane's socks off."

"I'm not going on a date," Kirby complained, closing her eyes as Titania became more emboldened with the scissors. She'd never thought of herself as a coward. Until now. "I'm going down there to rescue a friend from terrorist rebels."

"Not looking like a frumpy nun and rescuing friends need not be mutually exclusive," Titania countered, unknowingly echoing Shane's multitasking claim.

Frumpy? Surely it wasn't that bad? Having hated the sexist comments boys had started throwing her way since her breasts had popped out during puberty, Kirby had always concentrated on being smart rather than sexy.

"Not that you're at all frumpy," Sabrina said soothingly, while looking up from applying polish to Kirby's now neatly trimmed and filed nails to shoot Titania a warning look.

"Well, okay, that may have been an overstatement," Titania allowed. "But still, entering into an affair with a hot guy is like going to war. A girl's gotta use all the weapons at her disposal. And you have a lot, girlfriend, that just have been sitting there rusting away from disuse."

"Not that you'd be one to push a metaphor," Kirby said dryly as the two women continued to happily play with her as if she were their own personal life-sized Barbie doll.

Two hours later, after they'd raided Sabrina's closet, Kirby was standing in front of the mirror, staring at a stranger.

No, not a stranger. She was still her. But better — make that sexier — than she'd ever looked before.

Although Sabrina was taller, Titania, proving herself a wizard with a needle as well as the scissors, had hemmed the midnight blue silk dress covered in white tropical flowers, so that it swirled romantically around her calves.

"The fit will be comfortable for traveling," Sabrina, proving herself the more practical of the two women, said.

"But still be hot enough to get your flyboy's juices flowing," Titania said.

Some more closet raiding unearthed a white cashmere cardigan sweater with a crocheted collar — for that obnoxious overhead airline air-conditioning, since the dress bared her shoulders, Sabrina said — and a pair of espadrilles that lifted her height nearly three inches.

"I'm going to fall off these and break my neck," Kirby complained.

"The ribbon ties will keep them on," Titania said. "And they're still sexy, but comfortable enough to wear through an airport."

"Just try them," Sabrina suggested. "You'll have your sneakers in your carry-on. So if they don't work, you can always change."

That made sense, Kirby decided as she turned sideways and skimmed her hand — with its newly white-tipped nails — over a hip. The dress flowed over her body like a silk waterfall. It really was stunning.

"The color exactly matches your eyes," Sabrina said. "I've no idea why I bought it, since mine are green and the color never worked on me, so I've never worn it." She picked up the scissors Titania had been using and snipped off the still-attached price tag. "But it was so gorgeous, I couldn't resist."

"This is incredibly generous of you." Kirby hadn't dared look at the tag, since she suspected the dress probably cost more than her monthly salary at WMR.

"Oh, it's been fun," Sabrina said.

"Like high school," Titania seconded.

The past two hours certainly hadn't resembled any of Kirby's high school experiences. Having been the class nerd, and pudgy to boot, she'd never experienced a sleepover. She'd assured herself that they were undoubtedly silly and a waste of time, while never quite convincing herself of that idea.

There'd always been a secret part of her who'd suspected that the pretty, slender girls, the ones who got elected to cheer squad and had the football stars drooling over them, had had all the fun. But until tonight, she'd never been sure.

Downstairs, she heard the front door open. Footsteps walked across the marble foyer floor.

"Sabrina?" the male voice called.

"We're up here, darling," Sabrina called back. "Come and tell us what you think of Dr. Campbell's magical makeover."

Kirby had been surprised by how much she'd enjoyed having the two women fussing over her. But now, as she heard the masculine footfalls on the stairs, her stomach clenched.

Then Zachariah Tremayne was standing in the doorway, his amazing kaleidoscope eyes skimming a judicial look over her.

"Well," Sabrina said with the first touch of impatience Kirby had heard from her since they'd met. "What do you think?"

He grinned at Kirby and winked. "I think," he said in his deep Lowcountry drawl, "that the Army flyboy's toast."

40

It hadn't gone according to plan. A plan that had been to knock Shane's socks off. To dazzle him with her new look. To stun him with the sexy new Kirby Campbell Titania and Sabrina had unearthed hiding inside her.

It wasn't that she'd forgotten the reason they'd been thrown back together again. Not at all. But somehow during last night's makeover, Kirby had come to the conclusion that Titania was right — looking hot and rescuing Rachel were not necessarily mutually exclusive.

An idea that had continued into her dreams, where Shane was stunned by her Cinderella-like transformation. Although there wasn't a ballroom anywhere in the jungle that she knew of — though there undoubtedly was somewhere in that enormous pink palace — in her dreams, they'd waltzed, beautifully, just like the couple who'd spin around on the jewelry box her parents had bought her for her eighth birthday. While she'd really wanted a junior chemistry set, she'd found herself charmed by the tiny prince and princess.

In the ethereal way of dreams, the vision morphed from that gilded ballroom to a waterfall in the jungle, which actually *was* real and not far from the village where the clinic was located. In her dream, they swam in the jade-colored waters and made slow, beautiful love while the sun-warmed water streamed over them.

The dream — and her plan — had stayed with her after she'd awakened, warming her from the inside out.

Until Shane showed up at the house, his expression as grim as she'd ever seen it. Even worse than when she'd visited him at Landstuhl.

"What's wrong?" The white tips of the new manicure she'd been so pleased with contrasted sharply with his dark tan as she caught hold of his arm. "Is it Rachel? Has something happened to her?"

"We don't know." He shook his head. "The news out of Monteleón's still sketchy. But that volcano that's been simmering —"

"Ixtab." She pushed the name past the lump in her throat.

"Yeah. Anyway, CNN's reporting it's taken out a village. There aren't any reports of any survivors."

Although she would have guessed it never snowed on Swann Island, a flurry of white flakes began swirling in front of Kirby's eyes.

■ ■ ■ ■

PART THREE

■ ■ ■ ■

De Oppresso Liber
To liberate the oppressed
— U.S. Special Forces motto

41

The damn woman wasn't playing fair. Bad enough that he'd found her hot even in cammies or that ugly suit she'd worn yesterday. But when Shane arrived at Swannsea to pick Kirby up and she'd come waltzing down those stairs, he'd nearly had to pick his tongue off that marble floor.

She'd always been gorgeous to him, both inside and out. But she'd downplayed her looks, which was, if he were to be perfectly honest, okay with him, because he'd just as soon not have had to fight off every other soldier or airman in the Green Zone. Not that they hadn't noticed, anyway.

Some women were just sexy to the bone.

Kirby Campbell was one of those women. The amazing thing was that she honestly hadn't seemed to believe that.

Until now.

A sensual aura, along with a new scent, surrounded her. And, Jesus, those shoes she was wearing, which weren't exactly fuck-me-big-boy stilettos, still had her hips swaying in a seductive way guaranteed to make a man drool.

But proving that timing was everything, just as he'd turned down Swannsea's oak alley toward the house, Zach had called with the news about that damn volcano.

And while he may not have Dallas O'Halloran's seduction moves, even Shane could figure out that hitting on a woman after telling her that her best friend might be lying dead beneath tons of volcanic ash was out of the question.

So they'd picked up their passports at the Phoenix Team offices, then, since it was important that their trip appear as normal as possible, suffered a bumpy flight on a sardine can of a cramped commuter jet to Altanta's Hartsfield-Jackson International Airport.

Not only would Shane not have been the least bit surprised if the pilot of that first jet had been wearing a leather helmet and scarf, when they'd finally arrived in Atlanta, they were informed that because of a plane being delayed somewhere in the Azores, their flight would be delayed. By at least two hours.

Terrific. One of the first things Shane had

learned after moving to the South was that even if you died and went to hell, you'd first have to change planes in Atlanta. And these days, getting anywhere on time without some glitch was a miracle right up there with Moses parting the Red Sea.

Although they kept their eyes glued to CNN, updates were not encouraging. Or verified. There were rumors that the volcano had been accompanied by devastating earthquakes that had left the entire country in ruins. Other reports had the rebels using the opportunity to seize control of all the power grids and communication networks.

Still other reports had Vasquez declaring martial law, and his goon squads not only shooting looters on sight, but using the opportunity to dispatch his political enemies.

Meanwhile, Kirby was as wound up as a cat on a hot tin roof. Unable to sit still, she paced the floor of the Crown Room, until he expected her to wear a path in the carpeting.

"You know, if you could only walk across water, you'd have probably reached Central America by now," he said.

"It's nice one of us can joke about this," she shot back.

"I'm just saying." He stood up, put his arm around her, and led her over to a couch at the far side of the room, away from all the businesspeople industriously tapping away on their laptop computers. One laid-back individual was practicing his putting on the miniature indoor green.

"You're not going to do your friend any good if you wear yourself out before you get there."

"I know." She threw herself down onto the couch and buried her face in her hands. "It's just that I'm so worried."

"You're not alone." He put his arm around her shoulder and resisted, just barely, taking a nip out of that smooth, fragrant skin.

He hadn't been lying when he'd told her he was an expert at multitasking. While one part of him was already thinking ahead about how the volcano might change the mission plan, or the ops tempo, another part of him was powerfully aware of her scent, which reminded him of the plant outside the window of his rental house in Somersett. It was exotic, seductive, and sexual.

"But Zach said as soon as he hears anything, he'd call."

"I know." Her pansy blue eyes — which, thanks to the smoky shadow she'd brushed onto the lids, looked even larger in her too-pale face — were bleak. "My parents have never understood why, if I had to become a doctor, I couldn't just settle down in some nice middle-sized city and set up a comfortable private practice."

"I can understand that, since I imagine most parents want their kids to be safe," he agreed, happy to turn the subject to something other than what might be happening to Dr. Rachel Moore.

"I suppose so. But there was also the little fact that I owed the Army for my education."

"Which you paid off with your service," he pointed out.

"True." She blew out a short breath. "But I'd go insane diagnosing skin rashes and writing steroid prescriptions for wheezy asthmatics."

"I'm not certain, but I suspect there's more to being a general practitioner than that."

"I'm sure there is. And I don't want sound dismissive, but the reason I chose trauma medicine is because I'm easily bored."

"I'll keep that in mind."

She'd done something to her hair. It framed her lovely, worried face and swung when she shook her head. He tucked a few strands behind her ear, enjoying the silk against his fingertips, remembering all too well how it had felt against his chest. And below.

"Don't worry," she assured him. "You have many flaws, flyboy." Shane thought it funny how the same name Zach and Quinn used to rag him sounded incredibly hot coming from those rosy pink lips. Which looked a lot wetter than they'd looked last night, making him wonder if whatever gloss the other women had pushed on her was flavored.

Strawberry, maybe.

Or, better yet, cherry.

Which brought back a memory of the time he'd traded all his Montgomery Gentry CDs to one of the flight crew for a jar of maraschino cherries from a care package the navigator's mom had sent him. Shane had taken them back to Baghdad.

Remembering how they'd spent the rest of the night licking the sticky, sweet cherry juice off each other was enough to make him hard as a rock.

"Since we've had other things on our mind, I held back saying anything," he said on a voice rough with need, "but you look great."

"Thank you," she said distractedly, looking back out the wall of windows toward the tarmac, as if wishing could make their delayed plane arrive sooner.

"Actually, better than great. You look really, really hot."

"It was Sabrina and Titania's doing. They took me on as a project last night, which just goes to show I must've looked even more pitiful than I felt. I've been buffed and polished." She held out a bare arm. "All over."

She might be worried to distraction about Rachel Moore, but Shane wasn't the only person in this lounge capable of compartmentalizing. He knew damn well she knew exactly what she was doing, inviting him to imagine her naked. Imagine and remember.

His fingers curled around her wrist as he brought the slender arm up to his nose. "You've changed your scent."

"That was Sabrina's idea, too." She trembled, just a bit, as he touched his lips to the crook of her elbow. "It's jasmine."

"Maybe a bit." Because he didn't entirely trust himself to behave, he backed away, just a little, and traced a wandering path down the inside of her arm with his index finger. "But underneath the flowers, it's still you."

That earned a faint smile, though she did reclaim her arm and inched a bit away from him. "You did that on purpose."

"What?"

"Distract me."

"Did it work?" The ploy had definitely boomeranged back on him.

"Doesn't it always?"

She didn't exactly sound happy by that admission. Not entirely unhappy, either, though, Shane reassured himself. More resigned, as she looked out the window again at the empty place on the asphalt tarmac where their plane should be.

"It goes both ways," he said.

He touched her cheek, turning her gaze back to his. She looked concerned. And not, he thought, solely because she was worried about whatever was happening down in Central America. This was personal, and they both goddamn knew it.

She was looking at him the same way she had in the CSH, just before she'd handed him the keys to her trailer.

He watched the mental wheels turn as she remembered that day, too. And wondered what she'd do if he went over to that bar and brought back a glass of cherries.

"We shouldn't be talking about this," she insisted. "Not now."

"Okay." His fingertips skimmed down her neck. "Maybe we should talk about what I want to do to you once we rescue your

400

friend. Who's going to be okay."

"You have no way of knowing that."

"I know that I'm not going to let anything make you cry. Ever again," he said simply, meaning every word as he continued to look in her eyes. He could easily drown in those deep, midnight blue depths. "Which makes it a given that we're going to get her out so she and the former Father-What-a-Waste can live happily ever after."

"How did you know that's what I thought when I met him yesterday?"

He shrugged. "I went to Catholic school for twelve years. And used to listen to my sister and her friends moon over Father Casey, who wasn't nearly as good-looking as Gannon.

"So putting that behind us," he continued, "we could talk about everything I want to do to you. With you."

"Shane —"

"Like how I'm going to touch you all over." He ran his hands over her shoulders. "Taste you all over. Including that tattoo."

He knew she'd gotten the tattoo — a caduceus, with its double serpent staff designating the medical corps — after a rare night out drinking until dawn with other medical school graduates.

It had been inked on the silky skin of her

back, below her waist and above her lush, round ass. He'd spent many a happy afternoon tracing the blue outline with his tongue.

That sexy blush stained her cheekbones again. "You can't talk about that. Not here," she complained, looking around the room.

"All those workaholic drones are too busy making money to pay any attention to us."

Though he had noticed more than a few of the harried businessmen watching the enticing sway of her hips as she'd paced. Each time he'd shot them his most intimidating Spec Ops glare, which had immediately sent their eyes back to their laptops.

"Still, it's not appropriate," she insisted.

Outside the window, the plane finally arrived. Hopefully, it wouldn't be much longer.

"So." She took a deep breath that did nothing to drag his mind away from sex, since all it did was have him noticing her breasts and fantasizing taking first one, then the other, in his mouth. "Why don't you tell me about how you ended up switching from JAG to the 160th Airborne?"

"It's not that interesting a story." Not nearly as intriguing as the nipples pressing against the flowered silk. "I'm a middle kid.

An older brother, a younger sister. I was also the first person in my family to go to college. When I got appointed to Annapolis—"

"Wait." She held up a hand. "You went to the Naval Academy?"

"Didn't I mention that?"

"Granted, we didn't spend all that much time talking. But I believe I would have remembered something as memorable as you being a naval cadet."

"Well, yeah. It wasn't any big deal. I got nominated by one of my state's senators after being elected governor of Boy's State. Anyway, ever since I was eight, and saw the Blue Angels perform at an air show, I wanted to be a Navy pilot.

"I'd already used my paper-route money and bucks I got doing odd jobs around the county during summer vacation to learn to fly small planes. But I wanted more. So I figured going to the academy would give me a better shot at getting into flight school."

"And you decided this at age eight?"

"Sure." He shrugged. "When did you decide to be a doctor?"

Her grin, the first smile he'd seen from her since he'd arrived at Swannsea with the news about her friend, was quick and lit up her entire face. "About the same age. When I had Dr. Barbie bandaging Ken."

"Sounds a bit like life imitating art," he suggested. "Or play."

"Hey, that was serious Barbie work," she said. "Besides, it was the only thing Ken was good for."

"Yeah. I remember that from my sister's doll," he said. "Not only were the guy's parts not in working order, he didn't *have* any parts."

"I know. I think it was from a terrible accident when Barbie ran over him in her pink Porsche. And you were telling me about how you went from flight training to the Judge Advocate General's Corps," she reminded him.

"I never got to flight training." Having dreamed of being one of those elite Blue Angels, the memory still stung, just a little. "The Navy docs ruled me out because of my astigmatism. I could've still been an airman, working in flight support, but watching other luckier guys flying off the decks of carriers would've been tough.

"So, since my mother had always wanted a lawyer in the family, and my adviser was pushing it because of all the personality-profile and career-assessment tests I'd taken, which supposedly pointed in that direction, I figured I might as well try JAG.

"Although it wasn't flying, I figured I'd be in court, defending seamen in court-martial trials, which could be fun. Or maybe go into international law. But no, I ended up in frigging contracts, which mainly meant going blind reviewing contracts for supplies and services."

"Ah, so you're the one to blame for the gold-plated toilets in the officers' clubs and the five-thousand-dollar screwdrivers."

"Very funny. Anyway, the upshot was when it came time for me to re-up, I jumped ship to the Army, which, after I'd gotten some laser surgery, let me fly helos. End of story."

"I have to admit, I can't imagine doing that. I suppose because I've always been one to stay on a set track."

"Yeah. I noticed that the way you jumped from the Army into WMR," he said dryly.

"Well, it's still sort of the same thing I was doing," she said. "Just with a few less administrative hoops to jump through, since we're such a small operation."

Before he could ask for more details about her work, his phone vibrated. At the same time their flight was called.

"Hey," Zach told him as they left the club and headed toward the gate. "We're about to be heloed out to that ship in the Gulf we're going to launch the IBS from. But I wanted to let you know that I got word from our man — or in this case, woman — on the ground. The clinic's village wasn't affected. And the report from inside the compound is that Dr. Moore's okay. But the general consensus is that the volcano's been building up for a long time to the big one. So the sooner we get in and out of the place, the better."

"Roger that," Shane agreed.

"Oh, that's the best news!" Kirby said when he relayed the information to her. Absolutely giddy, she lifted her hands to his face, went up on her toes, and kissed him.

Her lips hit his like liquid fire. Just as they'd always done. And, dammit, just as no other woman's ever had.

Shane tried to convince himself that he'd imagined the jolt.

But he'd been wrong.

She flooded his senses with her taste, her scent, the all-too-familiar but no less incredible way her body fit against his.

He wanted to drag her to the nearest horizontal place, even as he made a low, desperate sound deep in the back of his throat. To keep his hands out of trouble, he placed them on either side of her waist and kept them there.

God, I want you, his body was shouting, even as his brain tried to remind the aching, needy parts that they were in a freaking airport, about to get on a freaking plane, and although the idea of joining the mile-high club sounded cool — or in this case, hot — the reality was that when he finally made love to Kirby again, she deserved to have it done right. At the right time. In the right place.

Wanting a woman was one thing. *Needing* one was something entirely different.

It really was over for him, Shane realized as he forced himself to back away from temptation. As Zach had warned him when he'd come out of the kitchen to give him the passports and spending money, he was toast.

And the weirdest thing was, it felt just fine.

He'd never been looking for a woman, but he'd always known the time would come when he'd find her. The *one.* And he had, which is why he'd planned to track her down and propose to her as soon as he'd finished ferrying those SEALs and Rangers and Marines into the Kush.

He'd finagled some leave time. Even went on the Internet, found a ring he thought she'd like at a store back in Eugene, and sent his brother up there to check it out and make sure it was as shiny as it had looked online.

Amazingly, it had looked even better. It wasn't all that large — a carat solitaire — but with the same attention to detail he brought to his flying, he'd done all the research about the 4 Cs (cut, clarity, color, and carats) along with other factors like fluorescence, table percentage symmetry, and enough other stuff he'd probably driven the jeweler crazy with, quizzing him in back-and-forth e-mails.

Then, the day after the ring had arrived in Afghanistan, the helo had crashed, and while the woman was still the right one, the timing had been all wrong.

Shane may have let Kirby walk out of his life.

But he'd kept the ring.

Which was currently sewn into the lining of his duffle bag.

"We're going to finish this," he said.

"You sound awfully confident," she said with a toss of her head. Yep, she'd definitely done something different to it. Something sassy.

It fit.

"No point in beating around the bush," he said. "I told you, I want you. And I intend to have you."

She lifted her chin even as the line began to move around them. "Do you always get everything you want?" The minute the words came out of her mouth, he saw the regret in her remarkable eyes. "I'm sorry." She held up a hand.

"Don't worry about it." He caught the silky smooth hand and lifted it to her lips. "And no, I haven't always gotten what I wanted. At least it may not have seemed like it at the time. But some things — and some people — are worth waiting for."

She met his gaze over their joined hands, seeming oblivious to the crowds and the announcements being broadcast by disembodied voices, and the usual hustle and bustle and noise around them.

"You're not going to get any argument there," she said finally.

Things, Shane thought as they walked side by side down the jetway, were definitely looking up.

Now, he could only hope their luck held.

42

Kirby had worried that the long flight would be too much of a strain on his leg. When she'd asked, he'd merely shrugged and assured her it wouldn't be a problem.

Nor did it seem to be.

After the charter flight from D.C., she wasn't surprised to learn that they'd been booked into first class.

"Might as well take the opportunity to get some shut-eye while we can," Shane told her as the jet took off. "Because once we land in Monteleón, things could get real dicey, real fast."

That said, as soon as they'd hit cruising altitude, he'd put his seat back, folded his arms over his chest, and promptly fallen asleep.

She'd seen him do that countless times before, when he'd taken what he'd called combat naps, complete with jerky eye movements, body twitches, and irregular breathing, and, although she'd never actually checked his pulse, irregular heartbeat.

Even though she'd become accustomed to thirty-six-hour shifts during her residency, she'd never been able to manage this instant drop into REM sleep he'd told her that SOAR pilots, like other Spec Ops teams, learned to do. And she'd also been amazed, not only at how he could set an internal clock to wake himself up at the exact time he wanted, but that somehow he'd also managed to look, after ten minutes, as rested as most normal people who'd gotten their full eight hours.

She'd spent the past thee nights chasing sleep. The first in Monteleón, then the next in D.C. worrying about her testimony, and last night, at Swannsea, she'd been worried about Rachel. And, during those brief periods of time when she had drifted off, dreams of the man sleeping next to her had not proven at all restful.

Still wired, she tried to read the in-flight magazine, but her mind wouldn't focus. Nor could she concentrate on the novel she'd picked up in the airport bookstore. She spent a long time staring out at the clouds, wondering what was happening at the clinic, trying to hope for the best, and not to let her imagination drift to the worst.

But she couldn't help thinking about the story Rachel had told her, about what the rebel leader had done to those two young lovers. And when her exhaustion finally caught up with her somewhere over the Gulf of Mexico, this time her dreams were of jaguars tearing apart a boy soldier, beneath the body of a pretty, dark-haired girl — who kept morphing into Rachel — hanging from the limb of a yellow-flowered Gallinazo tree.

43

Even if their passports had been absolutely legitimate, Kirby still would have been nervous going through customs. Running the gauntlet of bored, granite-faced officers who, whatever the country, all seemed to have been cast from the same grim mold, was always her least favorite part of traveling.

It didn't help that this one was wearing a military uniform and armed to the teeth. Her nerves grew icier as the long line slowly snaked across the airport basement. Unlike the terminal upstairs, with its bright travel posters depicting colorful scenes of the country dating back to a time when tourists had actually made Monteleón a vacation destination, this dreary, institutional room, with its seven-foot ceilings and peeling army green paint, had all the ambience of a Third World prison.

Kirby watched, her pulse racing as the

officer grilled an elderly couple who, politely and with proper deference in German-accented Spanish, explained they were birders who'd come to the country in search of a rare, reclusive toucan.

The woman added that the bird was becoming endangered, and since they weren't getting any younger, they'd decided time was running out to see it in its natural habitat.

From the way the unsmiling man grilled them, backed up by two uniformed thugs carrying semiautomatic weapons, they could have been participants in a plot to overthrow the government.

Which was, of course, Kirby thought, precisely what Vasquez and his cohorts were afraid of. Why they'd do anything, including allowing the murder of an innocent aid doctor who'd never spoken a word about their despotic regime, but had only come to the country — and stayed through all the recent strife and upheaval — to help people too poor and too downtrodden to help themselves.

Apparently dissatisfied with their responses to his questions, the customs officer waved over the two soldiers, who strong-armed them down a long hallway. As they turned a corner, disappearing out of sight,

Shane took hold of Kirby's hand. Although meant to merely look like an affectionate gesture between lovers, from the way his thumb was pressing against her palm, Kirby knew he was warning her not to get involved.

Even as she wanted to leap to the German couple's defense, Kirby understood that they were playing for higher stakes. There probably wasn't anything she could do to help the elderly birders, but throwing herself and Shane into the midst of whatever trouble they might be in not only wouldn't do anything to help Rachel, it could only make things worse.

Finally, after nearly an hour in the crowded room smelling of mold, sweat, and fear, it was time for the inquisition.

"It'll be okay," Shane assured her as he brushed his lips against her ear, as if nuzzling it. "Just stick with the script, and we'll be out of here and on our way in no time."

She hoped that was the case. Not that she didn't have total faith in him, but there was the little fact that he hadn't been able to take his weapons onto the plane, so, although she suspected he could undoubtedly break necks with his bare hands, taking on all the armed-to-the-teeth soldiers marching around the room, glowering at the people shuffling along, might be more than even a Special Ops Night Stalker could pull off.

"Buenas tardes," she greeted the official as she handed over her passport.

Surprise, surprise. He didn't respond. Just typed her name into his computer. Then lifted a black caterpillar brow as he read whatever had popped up on the screen.

Even as every nerve in her body started to screech out warning sirens, Kirby kept the faint, hopefully innocent-looking smile frozen on her face while one of the soldiers standing behind him bent and said something in the man's ear.

This time both brows furrowed, diving toward his nose. She braced herself to be dragged off to wherever the elderly toucan hunters had disappeared to.

"Passaporte," he growled past her at Shane. Obviously, the soldier had told him they were together.

Unlike Kirby, Shane didn't bother greeting the bureaucrat. Nor did he smile. He merely handed over the navy blue passport the so-called Michelangelo at the agency had created for him.

The official studied the photo for a long time. Looked back toward Shane's face. Then at the passport again. He flipped through the pages, which bore enough stamps to appear as if Shane had traveled overseas, but certainly not enough to be suspicious. And, since she'd studied the passport when he'd first shown it to her, she knew the countries — Ireland, Italy, Australia, and New Zealand — weren't ones that would send up warning flags to Vasquez's government.

"Cuánto tiempo va a quedarse?" he asked Shane.

Rather than immediately respond in the Spanish Kirby knew he spoke, he opened the small booklet he'd picked up in Atlanta, when she'd bought her novel.

"Lo siento," he said with a total lack of the music the language was known for. He was pronouncing it as that German couple may have spoken it. "No, uh, *hablo Español.*"

The soldier leaned forward again and rattled off something at a rapid, machine-gun speed even Kirby, who'd taken Spanish in college and had spoken in this country for the past few months, had trouble keeping up with.

Something about his mother. And testicles, along with livestock and other cruder-sounding words that, from the appreciative laughter of a trio of soldier thugs walking by, Kirby didn't want to know.

Slanting a sideways glance at Shane, she noticed that his face remained politely perplexed.

"Lo s-i-en-to," he apologized slowly, more laboriously. "I'm sorry." He'd raised his voice as if the customs agents were the one who didn't speak the language and if he only said it loudly enough, he'd be understood. He flipped through the book again. *"No comprendo."* I don't understand.

Kirby suspected he knew exactly what had been said. She also began to understand how Special Ops teams could go behind the scenes. She'd never thought of a pilot as having the skills she'd heard SEALs or Delta Force operatives did, but then again, she considered, there was always the chance of getting shot down behind enemy lines.

Apparently, blessedly, buying the subterfuge, the man turned back to Kirby, asking her their purpose for coming into the country.

He was visibly unimpressed when she pointed out that she'd been living in the country for several months and was returning to work.

At which point he informed her that she may as well get back on that plane. Because the clinic had been taken over by terrorists. His knowing her connection to the clinic explained his apparent recognition of her name when he'd first taken her passport and checked the computer screen. Apparently, she'd landed on some government watch list.

She leaned forward, allowing her scent to envelope him in a heady, fragrant cloud of jasmine. Although Kirby had never — ever — been one of those women who used their femininity to gain their way, she suddenly, from the way his eyes kept drifting to her cleavage, realized she was now in possession of a powerful new weapon.

She explained, allowing a little trembling that wasn't entirely feigned into her voice, that she had heard about the rebels taking her dear friend hostage and had rushed back to the country to beg the president to help her in freeing the American doctor.

Then, remembering Rachel's ploy on the road, she said, "I am a close personal friend of El Presidente."

Just as it had with the teenage rebels, the lie garnered everyone's immediate attention. Several of soldiers who'd been slouching against the wall, appearing disinterested in the proceedings unless they might be allowed to start blasting away at innocent civilians, actually stood at attention, as if the dictator himself had suddenly appeared in the terminal.

"Eso es verdad?" the man asked. Again, just as on the road. Men were so predictable.

"Es absolutamente cierto," she assured him on a breathy, "Happy Birthday, Mr. President" Marilyn Monroe voice that had a flush rising up from the collar of his khaki shirt like a fever.

She went on to describe the house, the patio where the barbecue had taken place, the inside, which she knew this man had never seen. Then, grateful for the personal tour the president had insisted on taking Rachel and her on, she described his bedroom. Including the twenty-four-carat gold fixtures and shower large enough for three.

"Or," she'd added, looking up at him from beneath her lashes, "even four."

She shrugged, allowing the dress to slip, just a bit, baring a buffed, lotioned, and perfumed shoulder.

The men all exchanged leers. And began undressing her with their eyes.

Although he was continuing to pretend that he didn't understand a thing she was saying, Kirby knew Shane well enough to sense that he was less than pleased with her story. Or the cretins' response to it.

She also realized that she might have

pushed her luck, just a little. Because if any one of them got it into their heads to take her into a back room for a demonstration of what she might have been willing to share with the president in that marble shower, Shane would make sure all hell broke loose.

She backed up just a bit. Then took a bill from her purse, folded it, slipped it into his hairy paw, and assured him that the president would undoubtedly want to personally reward the official for having taken such good care of his very close personal friend.

Bingo. She watched ambition and greed replace the lust in his dark brown gaze. Heard the slight mutter from some of the soldiers.

After she'd told him that they wouldn't need a limousine, that they were, instead, renting a car, he snapped his fingers. Immediately, a soldier arrived with a cart.

"No es necesario," she assured him, lifting her bag to show she was more than capable of carrying it herself.

But he insisted, rattling off instructions to the soldier-turned-porter.

Kirby glanced over at Shane, who merely shrugged. When he handed over his bag, she followed suit.

The customs official stamped both their passports and handed them back, allowing his fingers to brush Kirby's as he did so.

A muscle jerked in Shane's jaw. But again, he maintained his cool.

It was all Kirby could do to keep from bursting into the "Hallelujah" chorus as they finally escaped the terminal. They'd made it past the first hurdle. And she liked to think that she'd played an important part.

With Shane's hand planted firmly on her back, they followed the porter down the sidewalk toward a kiosk with the yellow, red, and black sign depicting the national rental car company. A few months ago, the major companies — Hertz, Avis, National, Budget — had been represented. Then the president had nationalized public transportation, putting his brother-in-law in charge of all car rentals in the country.

Before they'd left Swann Island, Zach had reported that the CIA station chief had warned him since Vasquez suspected all Americans of being CIA, they could expect their rental car to come equipped with both a bug and a tracking device.

He'd also stated that he had that contingency covered; after they'd paid their visit to the president, the couple leaving the country in their place would drive the rental back to the airport. Kirby and Shane would be given a clean car to drive out of the city to the rendezvous point.

While making their approach into the airport, coming down from blue skies into a thick gray cloud, their pilot had assured them it was safe to land. That turned out to be true, but from the way it continued to belch smoke with its usual steam, it was obvious that Ixtab was not yet through with whatever it was intending to do.

Although the city was far enough from the volcano that the population, accustomed to sucking in massive amounts of auto pollutants, wasn't bothering to wear masks, the moment they left the terminal, Kirby's eyes began to burn and water.

"This isn't good," she said.

"No shit," Shane agreed.

The rental was a black Toyota two-door sedan. Knowing that the general's men might be listening to everything they said was more than a little unsettling.

Neither spoke as they drove toward the center of the city. A pungent, smoky, dark cloud hovered over the buildings, which was part volcanic pollution, part from the farmers slash-and-burn agriculture, and part from the cars crowding the narrow streets.

"This always reminds me of a destruction derby," Kirby said as a rusting truck piled high with green bananas blasted its horn at a stalled car, driving onto the sidewalk to pass it, which, in turn, sent a sidewalk taco vendor scrambling to escape serious injury or even death.

"Or the running of the bulls, with cars and trucks taking the place of bulls," Shane said, expertly swerving to dodge a car cutting diagonally across the traffic circle at the Plaza de Armas.

A middle-aged couple raced, hand in hand, across the road, barely missing being hit by a speeding taxi. Their shorts, the woman's designer bag, and the expensive camera around the man's neck practically shouted out, "Gringo tourists. Come rob us!"

"You're very good at this," she said.

"Thanks. Actually, this isn't all that different from driving in D.C.," he said, reminding her that they needed to stay in character.

"I'm so worried about Rachel." That was certainly true.

"Hopefully, we'll be able to get in to see President Vasquez," Shane said. "And he'll be able to intervene."

"I hope so," Kirby said, on cue. "It seems it would be in his best interest to send some of his army against Castillo's thugs." She sighed heavily, then said, "I'm still furious at our government for not helping."

"The U.S. doesn't negotiate with terrorists," Shane reminded her for their audience.

"I know. And the guerillas definitely fit into that category, since everyone knows they're getting funding from sympathetic terrorist groups. But WMR certainly doesn't have the funds to pay Castillo off."

"So, it all comes down to Vasquez," Shane said.

"That seems to be the case."

"What are you going to do if he turns you down?"

"I don't want to consider that."

"But it's a possibility, darling." He placed his hand on her leg. "You have to be prepared to be disappointed."

"The president's a reasonable man. I'm sure he'll listen," she argued, knowing nothing of the kind. Especially after the way she'd argued with him at the dinner only nights ago. But he'd probably enjoy making her beg.

"But if he doesn't?"

"Maybe we could go to the clinic ourselves," she suggested. "Try to negotiate on our own. Surely Jesus Castillo could be made to understand that harming an innocent American wouldn't help his cause any among the patients she's been serving for all these months."

"I doubt if any of those patients are going to leap up to defend her," Shane pointed out. "The rebels have a reputation for being brutal. If you were some peasant with a wife and five kids to feed, would you risk your life, and perhaps theirs, for a foreigner?"

She folded her arms. "I hate it when you get into that know-it-all professorial mind-set," she complained.

"I *am* a professor," he reminded her. "And you're a doctor. Neither of us has the skill set to take on terrorists."

"I know."

The sob in her voice was in no way feigned. For the first time, Kirby really understood, deep down, the meaning of survivor guilt. Because if Rachel was seriously injured, or, even worse, killed, because she'd taken her place before that subcommittee, she knew it would be a very long time, if ever, before she'd be able to forgive herself.

"But that's not going to keep me from trying to do everything I can."

"And it's not going to stop me from dragging you onto a plane back to the States if the president turns you down," he said.

"You're not the boss of me."

"No. But I *am* the guy who adores you,"

he said evenly. "And who is also willing to admit that I made a helluva mistake letting you get away. No way am I letting that happen again."

As he shot her a hard, don't-mess-with-me-look, Kirby couldn't quite decide whether or not he was talking for the hidden microphone's benefit. Or hers.

Although Kirby trusted Phoenix Team, she also knew that the odds were stacked against them. And while all three men who'd fought together that day in the Kush had assured her that they worked best against impossible odds, because it kept them at the top of their game, she was still having problems seeing this entire adventure as a game.

The hotel was in the Zona Rosa. It was also the priciest hotel in the city, probably the entire country. It was not one Kirby would have normally chosen, but Zach's CIA station chief friend had insisted on it, assuring them that they had "friendlies" working among the staff and on the security detail.

The liveried doorman was clad in a scarlet uniform adorned with gold braid and tasseled epaulets, which reminded Kirby a bit of the president's military uniform.

"Welcome to the Hotel de la Revolutión,"

he said in English, bowing low as he opened the passenger door of the rental car. He waved at a bellman, clad in a similar jacket but without the tassels, as Shane began to take the luggage out of the backseat.

"Your room is all arranged," the bellman murmured, for her ears only, as he gestured for Kirby to enter the revolving door ahead of him.

Although she resisted shooting a glance back, she did give him a quick, sideways look as he led her to the registration desk.

Was he one of the CIA friendlies? Maybe even an operative?

Or one of Vasquez's men, assigned to watch for her arrival and make sure the president knew where she went and whom she might meet with?

Wondering if Mata Hari had felt anywhere as nervous as she did now, Kirby pulled out her WMR credit card and greeted the desk clerk with her sweetest smile.

44

The guard couldn't watch her around the clock. Even he had to answer the call of nature occasionally, leaving Rachel alone with the armed children soldiers. As she watched a boy, no older than seven, killing time and apparent boredom by expertly taking his AK-47 apart, then putting it back together and reloading it, she worried they could be even more dangerous than her guard.

They were obviously more impulsive, and she knew from years of fieldwork in other impoverished countries that when abandoned children had no other way of getting the necessities of life — protection, food and even water — they'd bond together with other such children, who'd become their families.

Which, in turn, made it easy for evil adults to take on the role of parental figures, training them to obey orders and commit acts many adults would refuse to do.

However this little band had come to join the rebel army, whether voluntarily or having been swept out of their villages, entering such an armed, macho environment would have to prove frightening. Lacking any other survival skills, it was totally understandable that helpless children would use obedience as a strategy to stay alive.

Since they possessed an immature sense of mortality, they were often sent unprotected into minefields, reducing risks to the adult soldiers who'd follow them. They were also more likely to become conditioned to violence and the most brutal deaths than adults, regarding as normal such things as hacking limbs off a former schoolmate with a machete. Merely part of ordinary, everyday life.

She'd seen teenage boys in Sierra Leone, wearing Rambo-style bandanas, wildly dancing through the streets and shooting their guns into the air to celebrate their murderous sprees. Like some adults, those children appeared to have actually learned to enjoy killing.

When the boy with the Kalashnikov met her gaze, his eyes glittering with drugs and malevolence, Rachel decided that she didn't want to stick around and become a notch on anyone's gun belt.

Which was why, when her guard went outside to make yet another call on his cell phone (Is he talking with Castillo? she wondered) she took the opportunity to steal a scalpel from a drawer.

She didn't believe she could overpower the man, especially if the children decided to back him up, but first chance she got, she was going to make another try at prying open that bathroom window.

45

The doorman handed their bags off to a bellman, who carried them into the glass elevator that rose to the twentieth floor of the hotel. The rooms all surrounded a central courtyard planted with palm and banana trees and a variety of colorful plants designed to bring to mind the nearby jungle, even down to the brightly feathered birds flitting through their branches.

"Wow," Kirby said as the elevator passed a towering fake waterfall tumbling over a series of artificial rocks, into a tropical lagoon serving as the hotel's swimming pool, featuring a swim-up bar. "Too bad Sabrina isn't here to see this."

"It might be a bit over-the-top for her five-diamond taste," Shane said as he looked down onto the tops of a trio of coconut palms.

Which was exactly what Kirby was thinking.

"I wonder if there's a jungle ride," he murmured.

Once again, they were on exactly the same track. Despite the seriousness of the situation, Kirby laughed.

Shane flashed her a quick grin. And as she bathed in its warmth, enjoying this single, suspended moment and the company, Kirby found it almost possible to forget their reason for being here.

Until they entered a suite decorated with a haute Caribbean-resort-style flair, boasting shiploads of rattan and pink marble.

The dazzling view out to the Caribbean was actually better than that from the Presidential Palace. The suite was at the corner of the hotel, nearly all windows, with French doors leading out to a private balcony, and in the other direction, Kirby could see the green of the jungle and the mountains rising up from it, and, above all, Ixtab, ominously continuing to steam.

Which had her thinking about what Shane had said about the two of them being like TNT and nitro. Actually, they were a lot like the volcano, and the more time they spent together, the more she felt the pressure building.

The bellman — whose coppery brown skin, broad cheekbones, and black hair could have washed off the enormous Mayan frieze in the lobby — carried their luggage into the bedroom, which featured a king-sized bed with mosquito net curtains and canopy. Since the hotel was air-conditioned, Kirby decided the netting was merely decoration. Then again, if guests decided to sleep with the balcony doors open, they'd be wise to take precautions.

He returned to the living room, demonstrated the air-conditioning controls, showed off the minibar, the private safe, and the flat-screen television, which was hidden away in a whitewashed rattan armoire.

"The room's been swept," he said. Kirby wasn't as surprised as she would have been only two days ago to learn he was undercover CIA. "But I left the trackers the man at the airport put on your luggage to keep Vasquez's people from getting suspicious.

"That door" — he pointed toward one on the far side of the living room — "leads into the adjoining suite. The NOCs who'll be leaving the country in your place are already there, but I'd advise not mingling, since not all the maids or housemen are ours, and given the mix of bad guys in this country, you never know who's being paid under the table by whom."

He handed Shane a cell phone and a set

of car keys. "The unlisted number of the station chief, Señora Gwendolyn Patterson, as well as that of your teammates, has been programmed into the phone. Since the president is out of the city —"

"What?" Shane and Kirby said together.

"Since when?" Kirby asked.

"Since this morning. There are rumors Josefina Madrid has surreptitiously slipped into the country. Vasquez's goons have rounded up all the usual suspects and are interrogating them at the army barracks in Rio del Mar. He wanted to be present, undoubtedly to help convince her army of supporters to talk."

"Sounds like a fun guy," Shane said.

"Wait until you meet him," Kirby muttered, unable to believe this timing. "Since the president has other problems on his mind right now, and undoubtedly moved the possibility of a U.S. invasion down a couple notches on his to-worry-about list, why don't we just bail on meeting with him and head out to the pyramid and wait there for the others to meet us?"

"He is expected back late tonight. Tomorrow morning at the latest," the bellman said.

"Oh, great. Meanwhile, those rebels could being doing God knows what to Rachel."

"Dr. Moore is well," the bellman assured

her. "The clinic is closely guarded, which will give your Phoenix Team a challenge. But our man on the inside will keep her safe."

Kirby could only wish she could believe that.

"What are we supposed to do while we wait?"

"Señora Patterson is waiting to meet you at Casa de Don Quijote. It is a local seafood cantina, only two blocks away."

"How will we know her?" Shane asked.

"I've met her," Kirby remembered. "She accompanied the U.S. ambassador to dinner at the palace."

"She's the ambassador's press secretary," the man said. "You will go in. Order your drinks. Behave as if this is just a romantic holiday. Do not look around to try to detect which person in the restaurant might be one of us, or you will risk giving yourself away.

"Ten minutes after you sit down, Señora Patterson will arrive. She will be with friends, but when she sees you, she will break away and ask to join you. She will update you on what she knows of the doctor. She will also have instructions written in indelible ink on a paper cocktail napkin that she will slip under hers when her drink arrives."

"Geez," Kirby, stressed out and just wanting to get on with the program, said with more than a little sarcasm, "so when, exactly does Q show up to give us our Aston Martin with rocket launchers and our homing pills?"

When the man, obviously unfamiliar with one of America's greatest movie franchises, just gave her a blank look, Kirby was tempted to ask him what the hell kind of spy he was.

"Won't it seem suspicious if we're seen meeting with someone from the embassy our first night in the city?" she asked instead, trying to bite back her frustration. Her work at WMR had admittedly taught her some level of patience. But her problems had also never gotten this personal.

"The señora's light cover is as a press officer, which allows her to work undeclared while still providing diplomatic immunity in the event she finds herself in trouble. But she also freelances as a society reporter for *El Libertador.*"

"It's the national newspaper," Kirby told Shane. "Definitely a propaganda rag."

"True," the man agreed. "Her 'beat,' as you Americans call it, is stories and interviews with Americans and Europeans visiting the country."

"Which doesn't give her much to write about these days, with tourism being just about nonexistent," Kirby said. She'd never been one to focus on the society pages. Especially down here, where the gap between wealthy and poor was as wide as the Grand Canyon.

He favored her with the first smile he'd share so far. "All the more reason why it is only logical that she would be so eager to talk with you."

Shane nodded. "That's very good."

The brief friendly expression immediately vanished. His elongated eyes narrowed and his jaw thrust forward, just enough that Kirby, who'd grown accustomed to such displays in the Army, could sense a pissing contest coming on.

"Monteleón's freedom from tyranny may not be at the top of U.S. agenda at the moment," he said. His crisp tone sharpened the melodic accent. "But that does not mean we are second-rate. We have made blood oaths to bring down the dictator pig Vasquez and replace him with Josefina Madrid. Which makes us very good at what we do."

"If I didn't believe that," Shane replied, smoothly slipping his arm around Kirby's waist, "I would not have risked allowing Dr.

Campbell to accompany me on this mission."

Shane felt her stiffen, as if someone had just stuck a steel rod down the back of that dress. And hoped she'd manage to rein in her annoyance before the fake bellman left.

"Casa de Don Quijote," the man repeated. "She'll meet you there."

Shane walked him to the door, waited until he was in the hallway, thanked him, then handed him a folded bill, tipping him as he would any other bellman. Because, as the man had pointed out, you just never knew who might be lurking around corners.

46

The yacht was 148 feet in length and white as a glacier, with curved window frames, a swept-back radar arch, and triple portholes in the master stateroom giving it an elegant yet aggressive look.

The man who welcomed the group aboard *Finnegan's Wake* at their rendezvous point in the Caribbean Ocean echoed that appearance. Black Irish, as Michael Gannon himself was, his eyes were the same neon blue Michael viewed in the mirror when he shaved each morning, his hair just as jet-black, yet his face was more harshly hewn.

His body, too, was taller, more powerfully built. He could have stepped from the pages of one of the heroic Irish tales of kings and castles, battles and banishments that had so enthralled Michael both in childhood, then later in undergraduate school.

On a deep voice that carried a lilt of the auld sod, the man introduced himself merely as Conn. An ancient Irish name, derived from a Gaelic word meaning "hound," or "wolf". Conn Céthchathac had been one of Ireland's high kings.

Michael's maternal grandmother Reilly claimed ancestry to the man known as Conn of a Hundred Battles. The curved scar slicing from just below this modern-day Conn's eye down to his lip suggested he'd experienced at least one battle of his own. The whiteness of the raised flesh suggested it had been some time ago.

Michael had no idea if Conn owned the yacht or simply worked for its owner, but nevertheless, his pride, as he took the group on a tour, was evident.

It boasted twin elevated lounges, complete with teak tables, wet bars, ice makers, and a large-screen pop-up plasma TV, which could pick up signals from a satellite dish. If you preferred real life, the sliding doors and swept-back windows offered breathtaking views.

A large country kitchen, complete with a galley equipped with granite countertops, dishwasher, trash compactor, microwave convection oven, and Sub-Zero refrigerator had taken over what might have been the pilothouse. Another LCD television was attached to the wall, so anyone sitting at the granite table could watch TV while eating.

And if that weren't enough, a circular staircase led to the Sky Lounge, where two large window panels offered yet more amazing views. Including that of the touch-and-go-helipad, where, if everything went according to plan, Garrett would be piloting Rachel to safety once they'd rescued her.

"A man could easily live here," Michael murmured as he watched a school of dolphins frolicking a mere twenty yards away.

"I do," the Irishman said.

Michael envied this Conn his freedom. Before moving from Somersett to Swann Island, his brother, Joe, had, for a time, worked as an undercover drug agent, which had taken him all over the world. Granted, to dangerous countries where everyone always seemed out to kill him, yet still, he'd seen foreign lands and experienced more than most people would in a lifetime.

Even his sister was now happily married and living in California, in an amazing house overlooking the Pacific Ocean, both she and her husband providing a West Coast presence for Phoenix Team.

Of the three Gannon siblings, Michael was the only one still living in the city of his birth. Where, except for his time in Desert Storm, his seminary in New York State, and a year running that homeless shelter in New Orleans after Katrina, it appeared he'd never leave.

"Do you ever miss having a home?"

"*Finnegan's Wake* is my home."

"And a fabulous one it is," Michael agreed. Without being overdone with gilt and marble, as he suspected many of its kind might be. He'd seen a handful of crew members during the tour, which was only natural for a yacht this size. But they had a way of making themselves so unobtrusive as to be nearly invisible, which had him imagining you could almost forget they were there.

"But don't you ever miss land?" The moment he heard himself say the words, Michael regretted them. "Sorry. That was rude."

And totally uncharacteristic, which only showed how insane this situation was making him. During his years as a parish priest, he'd learned to choose every word with extreme care. But he was no longer a priest, and if he'd had his way, they would have used some of Phoenix Team's seemingly vast funds to just fly into the country like something out of *Apocalypse Now,* with guns blasting away at the bad guys holding Rachel hostage, and airlift her out. He had been forced to hold his tongue so many times during Tremayne's planning session, he was surprised he hadn't bitten it off.

"Don't worry about it," Conn said mildly. "And you'd be right: There are times when roaming the world like the Flying Dutchman isn't exactly heaven on earth — or in this case, heaven on the sea." The scar kept his mouth from fully smiling, but his eyes held humor that seemed to be directed inward. "But then again, what is?"

"Good point," Michael said.

The dolphins were moving on, riding a trail of water turned copper and gold by the setting sun.

"Tremayne told me that it's your woman who's to be rescued."

It was not a question, but Michael answered it, anyway. "She might not be fully aware of that yet, but yes. Rachel Moore is, indeed, my woman."

"She's a fortunate woman. To be so loved."

"Perhaps you'll vouch for me. Once we get her aboard."

"Aye. I could do that surely enough," Conn the Irishman agreed.

Both men fell silent as they stared out over the darkening sea. The moon had waned to a thin sliver crescent, but a new moon would have been more ideal for when they launched the Zodiac, which for some unknown reason, the former SEALs insisted on calling an IBS.

Michael was concerned they'd risk being seen, but although he'd been a doctor, his work at that forward MASH unit had taught him that there was no such thing as a perfect battle plan. Hadn't the damn scud that had hit Rachel's tent been proof of that?

"I envy you," Conn said finally, breaking the thoughtful dusk silence.

"Oh?" Michael might have found it odd that a man with such apparent wealth would envy him, who, thanks to the penury salary he'd received from the diocese over the years, could scarcely afford the single-bedroom apartment he was renting from Brendan O'Neill above the Black Swann pub. "Why?"

"It must be an incredible yet humbling thing to care about anyone so deeply."

His voice was flat. Rough.

And in those neon eyes, Michael viewed a desolation so deep and so unrelentingly dark, it chilled him to the bone.

47

"If I weren't a reasonable woman," Kirby said once the bellman had left them alone again, "I might be annoyed at the suggestion that you *allowed* me to come on this mission."

"It's a chauvinist country." Shane shrugged. "It's damn dangerous for a local to go against a dictatorial government. Especially one as brutal as this one. Everyone on this mission has to totally buy into the program, because we're talking life and death."

"Still —"

"Your head was covered in Pakistan," he cut her off. "Your arms, too. I may have a few blank spots concerning events after the helo went down, but that's one of the things I remember very well."

"It was the custom in that region."

"Exactly. Unless that bellman's playing both sides against the middle, which very well could be, he's risking his life for a belief. For his country. A Latin country, where males are not accustomed to females calling the shots. Especially on a matter as important as this."

"Yet the CIA station chief is a woman."

Shane couldn't recall her arguing as much as she'd done the past two days. Then again, their shared agenda — having sex as often as possible — had pretty much precluded disagreements. Then there was also the fact that she was worried about her friend.

"I'm not even going to attempt to get into official-spook mind-set," he said. "Zach and Quinn would know more about that than me, since I mostly spent my deployments in the air, where there's not much use for subterfuge and James Bond stuff," he said. "But I'm guessing that perhaps, since Patterson's under light cover, taking on such traditionally female jobs as a press officer and society reporter draws less attention to herself."

"And as an embassy employee, she can pick up gossip on the diplomatic circuit," Kirby allowed.

"While at the same time, her freelance job puts her inside the paper, where Vasquez undoubtedly has journalist sycophants cranking out pro-government propaganda, which gives her an inside track on what the guy's thinking. Perhaps even planning," Shane said.

"I suppose that makes sense. But —"

He put a finger against her lips to cut off her planned argument. "It'll be okay," he assured her.

He wouldn't allow either of them to think otherwise, because if they didn't pull this off, all of them, Kirby included, could end up in prison. Or dead.

While Shane agreed, intellectually, with what she'd said during the planning meeting about dead being the worst option, the Neanderthal male lurking inside him needed to protect his woman against all the bad men who might want to do terrible things to her.

"You can't know that," she argued. "Dammit, I was all pumped up to go one-on-one with Vasquez. I even had come up with all sorts of lovey-dovey ways to back up our story."

"Don't let me stop you," he said.

"Why am I not surprised that's the part of the plan you'd latch on to? After how hot you thought I was when I showed up at Phoenix Team, even in my ugly suit, and how you really, really wanted to have sex again."

Okay. She'd just managed to surprise the hell out of him.

He narrowed his eyes. "You're guessing."

Using a combination of finger spelling and gestures that might not be as fast and smooth as his own was, she signed, "And how you really wanted to have sex on the conference table."

She switched to oral speech. "During my pediatrics internship rotation, I was assigned a deaf kid. I only intended to learn enough to handle the basics, then it sort of became like learning Spanish or French. I just wanted to be able to communicate if I ever needed to. It's been a long time since I've needed it, but it came back. Enough to read what you were saying, anyway."

"I suppose this is where I should claim to be embarrassed for thinking such sexist thoughts."

"No." Her eyes crinkled a little at the corners. "Because I was thinking pretty much the same thing."

"Great minds," he said.

"Well, sex has always been the one thing we've been able to agree on." She began pacing again, as she had in the club lounge, her silk skirt swirling about her toned calves. "Did I mention that I hate, hate, hate Vasquez being away from the city now, of all times?"

"Like Prussian Field Marshal Helmuth von Moltke said, 'No plan ever survives contact with the enemy,' " Shane replied.

She paused, shooting him a look over her shoulder. "I thought General Patton said it." Kirby was sure she remembered it from the movie.

"It's often attributed to him," Shane agreed. "Others say it was Eisenhower. There are also votes for Napoleon. But it really did originate with old Helmuth in the mid-nineteenth century, though he wasn't nearly so succinct. Actually, his exact words were 'Therefore, no plan of operations extends with any certainty beyond the first contact with the main hostile force.'

"Like always happens, over time, his words got condensed into pithier phrasing, then put into more familiar mouths for the audience of the time.

"Hey," he said, when she stared at him, "I told you I majored in military history. That's pretty much Great General Quotes 101."

Well. She was definitely discovering that he was more than the cowboy pilot she'd first thought him to be. The hottie she'd figured was just into getting laid between missions. Which, at least in the beginning, she'd managed to convince herself that was all she wanted, too.

But she'd been wrong.

"Well, whoever said it, it makes my point." This was not the time to focus on their relationship, whatever it was. Her frustrated breath feathered the new spiky bangs Titania had given her, which she had to admit, set off her eyes. "We're not even going to be able to meet with the damn enemy until late tonight; more likely tomorrow at the earliest!"

But since she couldn't exactly go running out to the compound, she supposed she had no choice but to go along with the program.

"It'll be all right," Shane repeated.

"I'm just so worried," she complained.

"I know. But it's not as if we have any choice," he pointed out. "Meanwhile, since we're obviously being tailed by Vasquez's men, we might as well go out and make our cover look more convincing."

"Like I'd go partying with my friend being held hostage," she muttered.

"You have to eat. Besides, the guy doesn't exactly possess the same ethics you do. I'll bet that whenever he takes a break from waterboarding, he's got a willing woman waiting nearby to help him get his rocks off."

"You've such a way with words," she muttered. Though it was probably true.

"We'll call the palace switchboard," Shane said. "Request an audience. They'll tell you he's out of town. You'll beg — tearfully would be a nice touch — to speak with him as soon as he returns."

He shrugged. "It's the best we can do. Besides," he said, dancing his fingertips over her bare shoulders, "a sexy dress like this deserves to be taken out on the town."

"You're impossible," she said, even as she felt a little thrill beneath her skin.

"I know." He touched her, just a slow swipe of the knuckles up her cheek, as if he knew that if he kissed her they'd never leave. "That's one of the things you've always loved about me."

48

Neither Kirby nor Shane said anything personal or mission sensitive on the two-block drive to the restaurant. Instead, she pointed out a few scenic sights, all of which had been erected to honor the president.

All the tables on the outdoor patio were filled with twentysomethings seemingly unconcerned about the vast amount of pollution they were sucking into their lungs from the passing traffic. Then again, since they were all smoking, Kirby figured it didn't much matter.

There were also a few uniformed members of the army, drinking beer from dark bottles while flirting with young women who flirted back. American pop music filled the air, with Beyoncé singing about déjà, which Kirby figured somewhat fit her and Shane's situation.

The difference was that there weren't any mortars blasting in the background and so far no one had died. She could only hope it stayed that way.

The interior of the restaurant was dark and cooler than outside, with the fans overhead circling, stirring the air. A wall of windows looked out onto the sea, which was now a deep indigo with a single silver swath from the rising crescent moon. Kirby worried about the others being able to make their way from the yacht to the Costa Rican beach, but Zach had assured her that he'd accomplished more difficult missions, so she'd chosen to believe him.

When the hostess, a gorgeous J.Lo lookalike, led them to a table in the center of the room Shane flashed that killer smile and asked for one on the far side of the room. The woman instantly agreed. Kirby figured she'd also agree to strip naked and give him a lap dance on the spot, were he to ask for that.

She wasn't surprised when he took the chair that put his back to the wall. She'd seen that before with other military men, which definitely caused some table problems when a bunch went out together.

They ordered an Imperial beer for him, a piña colada for her, and at Kirby's suggestion, a selection of *platillos* — small plates of snacks including a vegetable and black bean *pupusa* (cousin to the quesadilla, but with corn dough replacing the tortilla), fried plantains, and *tamales de sal,* small chicken tamales wrapped in banana leaves.

"This is nice," she said with some surprise after their order had been delivered. She only wished they were here on a real date.

"We'll have to come back," Shane said.

Kirby had no idea if he'd said that for show or if he'd meant it. Which was impossible, of course, since after they rescued Rachel, the chances of her ever being allowed back into this country again were, oh, say, zilch.

"Definitely," she agreed, with a smile that was only partially feigned.

They chatted a bit about their plans to drive out to the Mayan ruins, just as any tourists would do, and although outwardly he seemed totally relaxed, Kirby suspected that, by the way he was peeling away at the black eagle label on the brown beer bottle, inside he was as tense as she was.

His eyes kept drifting not just to the door, but around the room, where more soldiers sat around, some in groups, others, like the ones on the patio, trying to charm young women with flashing dark eyes who appeared more than willing to be charmed. At

least as long as the frothy drinks kept coming.

On a small stage a trio of musicians played
while a woman performed an impressive
flamenco, heels clicking on the wooden
floor, colorful skirt swirling.

Outside, the laughter and sound of traffic
continued.

Kirby took a sip of the sweet rum drink,
barely aware of the screech of brakes outside.

Shane suddenly tensed.

She was about to tell him such sounds
were typical for the city when he yelled,
"Shit!"

Then knocked over the table, sending
drinks and appetizers flying. He dragged
her down behind it, his hand pushing her
head down as a dozen men with automatic
weapons stormed into the restaurant, shouting out liberation slogans and spraying gunfire.

49

The children — and despite their being armed and wild-eyed, Rachel could not think of them as anything else — were obviously starving.

Rather than hold her at gunpoint, they continued to raid the clinic kitchen devouring every bit of precooked things on the shelves.

When that was still not enough, she found herself in the odd position of making beans and tortillas for her captors.

She knew that food was often used to establish personal contact with another human being. Even an adversary. She'd realized that early on in her relief work, and had certainly seen it work on television police shows during those brief times she'd spent back in the States. Which was less and less, because with each year she stayed away, the more difficult it was to make the transition from the comfortable, even excessive lives so many Americans made to the way so much of the rest of the world lived.

Although the boys refused to participate in what they scoffed was women's work, the girls were willing to help. While the boys played cards and dominoes, or repeatedly cleaned their weapons, she worked on drawing some of them out.

Amando, one of the younger boys who could not be more than eight, had come over to sit on a stool next to the counter as she made corn tortillas. He told her how the rebels had come into his village one night and demanded that each family turn over one child to the guerilla cause.

"Our neighbor refused," the boy told her as she added the water to another batch of masa harina — corn flour — and began kneading the dough. "Because he only had daughters, and did not believe killing people was proper behavior for girls. So the soldier in charge shot the father in the head and took the oldest daughter. After that, everyone else chose who'd join the cause."

"And you were the one your parents gave up?" she asked, wishing she could be horrified, but she'd seen worse.

"I was the youngest. Too small to work in the fields," he said on a matter-of-fact tone that broke her heart. "When I got to the camp, the leader decided I was also too small to hold a gun, because it would drag on the ground when I carried it. So I was taught to make bombs."

"That sounds dangerous," she said mildly.

After covering the bowl of dough, she tore off a small ball from one that had been sitting for the past thirty minutes. Although the usual way was to put the ball in a tortilla press, having lost two iron ones and a wooden one to raiders her first month in the country, she'd given up and learned to pat them back and forth between her palms, creating a near perfect circle.

"It can be dangerous because you cannot mix the ingredients," he said in Spanish. "Or they could go off and kill many people.

"We use fertilizer liberated from the farmers, gasoline, diesel fuel, and gunpowder. The older boys break up metal from rusting cars and supports from houses, which we put in our bombs for shrapnel. Then it is set off by an electric charge.

"After I did not kill myself for six months, Tío Manuel, our leader, made me a teacher."

He puffed up a skinny chest clad in a blue Tennessee Titans T-shirt that had undoubtedly come from some other relief group. There'd once been a lot of missionaries setting up churches in the country. Most had fled upon advice of the U.S. government, as one entire group had been massacred, with both sides of the civil war blaming the other.

"That's very impressive." She tossed the circle of dough into a hot cast-iron pan, where it sizzled. "You must be a very smart and clever boy."

"I could read when I was only five years old," he boasted. "My mother wanted me to go to the city and become a doctor when I grew up."

"You could still do that," Rachel suggested.

"No, he can't." Another boy glanced up from his cards. "Unless we win the war. If El Presidente succeeds in destroying our movement, then we will all be executed. And even those allowed to live will always be outcasts in our villages for having committed murders."

From the mouths of babes, Rachel thought.

"Maybe Señora Madrid will come and bring peace," a teenage girl, who was folding black beans into the already made tortillas, suggested. "Then no one will ever have to die again."

"She's not coming," a third, older boy insisted.

The girl tossed up her chin. "People say she is."

"They've been saying that since I was this one's age." He nodded a head, covered in a tiger-striped wrap, toward the boy bomb maker. "Madrid is living the good life in Mexico. Why would she come back to this hellhole?"

"Maybe because she wants to help us," another girl, no more than eight, with black braids that fell down to her waist, suggested.

"She only wants to help herself," he scoffed. "Why else would she have run away after her husband was assassinated?"

"To gain support." Another boy, one of the eldest, whom Rachel guessed to be seventeen, suggested. "One person alone, especially a woman, cannot do anything against Vasquez. One woman with the backing of powerful countries could bring down a corrupt government."

"Then we would rule," the boy who doubted the possibility of the martyred leader's widow's return said.

"And Jesus Castillo would do exactly what this government would do to us," the teenage girl dared to say. "Kill everyone who did not agree with him." She placed the plate in front of the eldest boy and began filling another tortilla. "Which is not exactly

461

the democracy he preaches."

The room went absolutely still. So quiet, the only sound was the pop and sizzle of the corn tortilla on the propane stove.

"You would be wise to shut your mouth," the armed man, who'd returned after having taken food out to the guards surrounding the clinic, warned. "Unless you want me to turn you over to them." He gestured toward the night-black jungle outside the window. "And let them teach you what happens to traitors."

"It was merely conjecture," Rachel broke in quickly. "If you're going to use children as your army, you have to expect occasionally immature thoughts."

"Thoughts like that can get you killed." His midnight gaze raked the room. "You are, after all, no better than mangy dogs. Easily replaceable and not worth the food it takes to feed you."

Although it was not in Rachel's nature to hate, she hated this man. With a passion that went all the way to her core and had her trembling inside. If he was the only person she had to worry about, she'd risk her own life and pick up one of those butcher knives from the wooden block and drive it into that place in his chest where a heart should be.

But there were those other men outside, and while she certainly wouldn't look forward to it, she was prepared to die.

The problem was, she knew, without a single doubt, that if she did manage to kill, or even wound, her captor, the children would be executed like the stray dogs the man had called them.

She refused to allow that to happen.

And, although she'd nearly managed to unscrew the screen on the bathroom window frame with that scalpel, she now realized that the exercise had been pointless.

Because there was no way she would even attempt to escape the compound without taking this ragtag children's army with her to freedom.

50

The *bap-bap-bap-bap-bap* of the gunfire seemed to go on forever. People were screaming, plaster was falling from the floor and ceiling, overhead lights were blasted, sending glass flying.

More bullets shattered the bottles of liquor behind the bar; the smell of whiskey, rum, and tequila mixed with that of cordite and blood.

Fuck, fuck, fuck! Wasn't this just perfect? A reenactment of the shoot-out at the O.K. Corral, and him without a damn weapon. Which, Shane had been told, he'd receive during the car swap after his and Kirby's meeting with the president.

As much as he hated the idea of going into an op armed only with his fists and brains, Shane hadn't wanted to have to reveal weapons in a suitcase at the security check-point, since what the hell would a professor at a college for the deaf need with an automatic rifle?

There was some talk about having the guns already placed in the hotel suite, but since Kirby had told him about the cautiousness of the palace guards in searching for weapons, that precluded the possibility of taking them along on their little visit where she was supposed to beg for help.

And as Zach had pointed out, all too correctly, with Vasquez's iron-fisted hold on the country, it wasn't impossible to expect their room to be searched while they were at the palace.

No, it had been decided, the best time and place was when his and Kirby's look-alikes would return to the airport in their rental car, while they left in a "clean" car — with guns hidden beneath the wheel well in the trunk — to make their way to the rendez-vous point.

It hadn't been Shane's first choice. But he wasn't the one in charge of the mission, and he had to admit that it was probably the most fail-safe. Until you factored in that little adage about plans going awry.

"Are they shooting at us?" Kirby asked, as the bullets kept flying overhead. He wanted to get the hell out of Dodge, but so far Shane hadn't figured out the best way to accomplish that without getting them both shot full of holes.

"I think some of Castillo's boys, or some other rogue group, decided to do some target practice on Vasquez's goons. And we're just in the way."

"Lucky us," she said dryly.

A lot of women would be screaming bloody murder. Hell, a lot of men in the place were doing exactly that.

But not her. Shane wasn't all that surprised, having watched her keep her head in the midst of chaos in the CSH, but that didn't stop him from being damned impressed.

"You are fucking fantastic," he said, dodging as a spray of bullets shattered a pitcher nearby, drenching them both in a shower of beer.

"You're not so bad yourself, cowboy."

While not as experienced in street warfare as D-boys or Rangers, Shane had had enough Special Forces training to recognize that both sides were shooting AKs. Which should have given them a lull between the twenty-five to thirty rounds the weapons shot. But unfortunately, for that to work to their advantage, everyone would have to have begun shooting at the exact same time. Which, natch, wasn't the way it was working out.

"Okay," he said, "this could end up getting dicey."

Like it already wasn't? Holy shit, within seconds it had turned into a fucking kill zone.

No. The thing to do, Shane reminded himself, was focus on the positive. He had a ring waiting back at the hotel. A ring he had every intention of putting on this woman's finger.

But he wanted to do it right, with the entire get-down-on-his-knees-in-a-five-star-restaurant-where-you-had-to-put-on-a-jacket-and-tie-even-to-go-to-the-john grand gesture. He'd slip the maître d' some bucks to bring out the champagne at just the right minute. Maybe spring for some violins. And definitely flowers. Probably roses. If women didn't like red roses, why were they such a big deal with florists at Valentine's Day?

So, since he only intended to go through the marriage proposal deal once in his life, he wanted to get it right.

Which first meant getting out of here.

With both of them alive.

"How fast can you run in those shoes?" he asked.

"I don't know. Damn." She glared down at the wedged heels in question. Then looked up at him, regret written all over her face. A face splattered with someone else's blood. "I'm betting not all that fast. I'm sorry."

"You didn't have any way of knowing we were going out to have dinner at a shooting gallery." With them being the sitting ducks.

"That bellman could've set us up."

"Could have," Shane agreed as he lifted his shirt and used the tail to wipe at least some of those scarlet spatters off her cheek. "But I still think it's a wrong place, wrong time thing." If not, they were in a world of hurt, because even going back to the hotel could prove deadly.

"I'll take them off." She scooted around, trying to reach the ankle ties without lifting her head above the overturned table.

"Here." Since their positions had him closer, he pulled on the white bows, unlacing the ribbons. "The problem with this is that with all the broken glass, you could end up slicing up your feet."

He could carry her. Which would only end up making them a larger target. And slow them down. Plus, although so far his leg was holding up exactly how it was supposed to, and he'd lifted far more weight with it during PT, he was afraid of putting them at additional risk if it crumpled on him.

"I've been standing on my own two feet

for some time now," she assured him. "So, you give the count, tell me where to go, and I'll run like my hair's on fire."

He'd already given that thought, and although they might be able to blend into the crowd on the sidewalk, he'd bet most people had ducked into the nearest building, which, with all the flashing neon lights, could just put them in the bad guys' crosshairs.

"The beach won't be completely dark, because of the damn moon," he said. Something Zach had been a bit concerned about. "But it beats the alternative."

"Plus it's closer than the street," she said.

Yeah. By maybe two feet. Then again, the copilot who'd been killed in the Chinook's cockpit with him had been closer than that. Sometimes survival came down to inches. Shane could only hope it would this time.

"On the count of three."

"Roger that," she agreed.

Since he'd had to yell to make himself heard over the gunfire and shouting, he held up one finger.

Then a second.

Their eyes met. A silent message was exchanged: *We're getting out of here.* Because no way did either one of them want to die in this godforsaken country, smelling like beer, bullets, blood, and death.

He held up a third.

Then grabbed her hand. Ducking low, they raced through a blizzard of fire, leaping over bodies as they headed toward the open back doors leading out onto yet another terrace and the beach beyond.

At the same time, all his senses on full-battle-mode alert, in his peripheral vision, Shane saw one of the uniformed soldiers pull out a grenade.

What happened next was in that crazy blend of slomo and fast forward, where every bit of his focus was on the guy's hand as he pulled the pin and raised his arm, preparing to throw it.

But something went wrong, which wasn't all that much of a surprise when you bought crap, leftover Soviet weapons from unscrupulous arms dealers.

There was a flash of heat. A blinding light as Shane and Kirby were thrown through the air.

51

The mission was one Zach and Quinn had done numerous times before, both in practice and in real life.

The plan was to use *Finnegan's Wake* as a launch station, then take the IBS on an OTH (over the horizon) night transit of 41.5 kilometers, land on the beach, then cache the boat so it wouldn't be found. Then head across the border and link up with Garrett and Kirby Campbell.

They were both aware that this was easier said than done. Although he'd never considered himself a particularly religious man, abiding to the tenet that there were no atheists in foxholes — or Zodiacs — Zach accepted Mike Gannon's offer of a prayer before they set off. He may no longer be a priest, but there was always a chance that God might be more likely to listen to him than to either SEAL.

The inscrutable man known only as Conn

did not join them. Just stayed on the bridge, nearly invisible in his black sweater and black jeans. Had he not come well recommended, and just happened to own the only available yacht in the region, it wasn't as if they'd had a lot of choices. If it had been just him and Quinn, they might have done a helo drop from a Black Hawk onto the beach. But concerned that a copter might call more attention to them, and having no time to bring Gannon up to speed, this had seemed the most logical plan.

Unfortunately, the winds had picked up and the storm that the satellite weather maps had shown stalled over Costa Rica had moved east, barreling into the Caribbean.

The clouds covering the damn sickle moon was a good thing.

The drenching rain and rough seas kicked up by the wind were not.

Unlike Rangers or Delta Special Forces, SEALs worked in small teams, and were not designed to seize or hold a position, or fight a long-term battle. As a rule, their job was to seek out a target, destroy it decisively and silently, then disappear back into the ocean. Which was just the way Zach had always liked it. It was also, along with so many deaths, what had made that battle in the Kush such a bitch.

The rain was pouring, hitting the military assault suits they were wearing like bullets. Unlike the wet suits they'd worn during their long ago BUD/S training, the MAS was lightweight, boasting latex wrist and neck seals and a waterproof zipper. Meant to be worn over BDUs, it had been designed for surface swimming.

With the feet built into the dry suit, a SEAL could wear boots or even sneakers over it, then, rather than have to take the time to change into cammies when he hit the beach, he had only to peel off the MAS, stuff it into its bag, and, hooyah, he was all set for land travel.

The swells rose higher and higher, and Zach started getting worried about some of the supplies they were carrying being washed overboard. The MREs they could do without, especially in a jungle teaming with available food. The electronic equipment was another matter. Despite being lashed down, if the IBS swamped or tipped, it could be lost, which was exactly what had happened during Operation Urgent Fury in Grenada.

"Damn," Quinn said, pointing starboard. "We've got company at three o'clock."

What appeared to be a patrol boat, appearing an eerie green through Zach's NVGs, was running parallel to land, searchlights sweeping from shore to sea.

With the Zodiac trapped between the shoreline and the boat.

They were already running without lights. Zach immediately cut the gas engine. The Zodiac went silent. Bobbing helplessly on the rising, white-capped swells. All three men on the IBS, clad in black, held their collective breaths.

While Costa Rica's constitution banned an army, which was partly why Zach had chosen it for a landing zone, it did have a paramilitary security force mostly used to patrol the borders. It also had a coast guard, which, nearly a decade earlier, had entered into a maritime agreement with the U.S. Coast Guard, designed mainly to curtail drug trafficking into the United States.

While unfamiliar with the other country's cutters, Zach assumed, like so many U.S. patrol boats, it was carrying a single medium-caliber artillery gun and a variety of lighter secondary armaments, such as machine guns. In a worst-case scenario, it might also possess torpedo capabilities.

Since he doubted the patrol boat would be anywhere nearly as electronically equipped as one owned by the U.S. military,

Zach hoped that the wind, rain, and swells would combine to create enough sea clutter to confuse the boat's radar and allow them to remain undetected.

The patrol boat came closer.

Slowed.

Came closer still, near enough that Zach could see the crewmen on deck. And the lights on in the pilothouse, casting the captain into sharp relief.

While he suspected that Quinn was doing that spooky sniper thing, where he could control his heartbeat, allowing him to actually pause it long enough to nail his target, Zach's own heart was pounding so hard against his ribs he was amazed the men on that PB couldn't hear it even over the wind and surf.

The standoff — and it was indeed that, even if the other guys didn't know it — seemed to last forever.

Then, finally, the patrol boat moved on, continuing down the coastline. But not before its wake washed over them.

Which only made them even wetter.

Figuring that any time you were out on a stormy sea where you weren't supposed to be, in the middle of the night, and you didn't die was a good thing, Zach let out a long breath.

He wasn't the only one.

They waited, tossed violently around on the swells for another full five minutes. Zach fatalistically watched the MREs wash overboard. Fortunately, Gannon managed to nab the case with the radio right before it washed over the side.

Finally, when they seemed to be totally alone again, Quinn went to restart the engine.

"Shit," he shouted into the wind.

Then turned toward Zach, who hadn't seen the former SEAL sniper look that frustrated since the day they'd kept coming under attack while dragging Shane up the mountains to that refugee camp in Pakistan.

"The PB's wake flooded the engine," he reported. "We're fucking dead in the water."

52

They were on the beach. Shaken, not stirred, Kirby thought, which, despite the seriousness of their situation — or more likely because of it — made her giggle.

"Christ."

They'd run, for how long, Shane didn't know. Which was really weird, because he'd been trained to know such things. Then again, whenever he'd drilled, he hadn't been dragging along the woman he loved.

Finally winded, his hip aching like a bitch from running on the uneven slope down to the beach, he collapsed on the sand, Kirby right along with him.

"Well, so much for a relaxing seaside dinner," he said.

"I didn't even get to finish my drink," she complained.

"Just as well. Wouldn't have been all that helpful for either of us to have been drunk."

"Like one stupid girly drink could make

me drunk," she scoffed. Then took his face in her palms. "At least not anywhere near what I feel when I'm with you."

"Yeah," he said. "Can't say I don't bring a bang to the party."

She laughed. "God, I thought for sure we were about to get our tickets punched."

"Never happen," he said, turning his head and kissing her palm. Which was scraped from one of those times she'd stumbled to the sand. He vaguely remembered dragging her back up onto her feet so they could keep on running. "We're each other's good luck charms."

"That's a nice thing to say." She fell back onto the damp sand and looked up at the cloud-scudded midnight sky.

"It's true." He stretched out, as well, lying on his side, and drew her closer. "We make one helluva team, Dr. Campbell."

She snuggled closer, even as she looked back in the direction they'd come. Strangely, there were no flashing lights, nothing to indicate that any police or army officials (and in this country, they were the same entity) had shown up.

"Something's odd," she murmured. "Why do you think the guerillas had the balls to attack a place inside the city? In Vasquez's stronghold?"

"Maybe the balance of power's shifting." He plucked a piece of seaweed from her hair, which smelled of smoke and was damp from the beer and wet sand. "Something may have happened we're not up to speed on."

"God, if the president's losing power, what does that mean for Rachel?"

"I don't know," he said honestly. "I'm mainly just along to fly the copter when we get her out. And because Quinn told me you'd insisted on coming along."

As bad as things were, had been, and still could be, Kirby found herself smiling at that idea.

"You never should have let me get away."

"Roger that."

He rolled over on top of her, fitting his strong male angles against her curves, settling between her legs in a way that sent heat surging through her.

"This is just an adrenaline rush," she said, even as her hands fretted down his back. His shirt had scorched through, undoubtedly from the grenade blast, allowing her to feel the ridges of muscle beneath his warm skin. "A natural physical reaction to danger."

"Yeah, I've heard of the phenomenon. But in this case, it's a natural physical reaction to you."

Muscle memory, she remembered him saying.

Then, just as she'd wanted him to, he lowered his head and kissed her, a deep, passionate kiss that sent her reeling, tumbling helplessly, as if she'd been caught in a powerful riptide.

Kirby heard a low, throaty moan she didn't recognize as her own, was only dimly aware of his hands digging into her waist as he pressed his hard body against her, pushing her deeper into the soft sand.

"I hate to break this up," a droll female voice stated. "But I believe we had some business to conduct?"

Shane muttered a curse. Took time to give Kirby one last hard, tongue-tangling kiss before rolling off her now boneless body. He sat up and looped his arms around his bent knees.

"Agent Patterson, I believe?"

"That would be me."

"You were late."

"I was detained. Which was just as well, given that a war broke out in the restaurant."

"Yeah," Shane drawled as Kirby sat up beside him. "We sorta noticed that when the shooting started. So what the hell's going on?"

"I'm not sure." She was wearing a trim gray jacket that matched her silk slacks. Unlike Kirby, who'd fallen under the spell of those pretty shoes, she'd had the sense to wear flat-heel shoes, which had ended up much more practical for walking on the beach.

"Rumors are that Vasquez is trying to leave the country. Which, naturally, has things a bit destabilized."

"Yeah, I can tell the country's been real stable up until now," Shane said.

She shrugged. "There are levels of stability. Admittedly, this is the worst I've seen it."

"Why would he leave?" Kirby asked. "Castillo hasn't captured power yet, the heavy drug dealers are still in Vasquez's pocket, so except for the possibility of Madrid's return, it seems he's still holding a winning hand."

"He was. Until the photos of mass graves being discovered in the jungle showed up on CNN."

"His death squads have probably killed thousands," Kirby said. "As horrific as this is, why would it be different?"

"Because the graves are reported to be of an entire village of men, women, and children. Now, at this point, there's no way of knowing if the photos are fake or not.

"Hell, they could be graves from Iraq or Somalia or some country where its leaders practice mass genocide, and merely Photoshopped onto a jungle location to undermine Vasquez's power. They were also enough to get the U.S. government, along with several human rights organizations interested."

"Again, stories of the regime's brutality are not exactly news," Kirby pointed out.

"True again. But the ICJ just held an emergency press conference and announced they're sending people here to investigate."

"Well." Kirby tried to wrap her mind around how having the U.N. International Court of Justice investigating Vasquez would affect Rachel. "While the idea of trying the bastard in the Hague is appealing, that doesn't exactly solve our immediate problem."

"No." The station chief retrieved a set of car keys from the alligator bag she was wearing crossed over her shoulder. "Which is why you're going to continue on with your plan. These are the keys to a white Toyota parked in your hotel garage. It's on the second level, slot C-NINE. You'll find everything you need inside it."

She pulled out a key card. "Your room

has been switched with the one next door. We've seen that the necessities were taken from your luggage and transferred. We've also given you a bottle of hair dye, to make you less noticeable as you play tourist.

"The NOCs impersonating you will leave within the next two hours. To meet the rest of the team at the ruins, I suggest you leave right after breakfast at eight o'clock."

"That still leaves Dr. Moore in a precarious situation for another night," Kirby argued.

"At this point in time, Dr. Campbell, there's no one in the country who isn't in a precarious situation," Gwendolyn Patterson pointed out. "Dr. Moore is as safe as she'd be on the streets right now. And certainly safer than you were in that restaurant.

"But along with the eight armed guards who are definitely not friendlies, and an armed-to-the-teeth children's brigade inside, that leaves one lone man who's ours. Even if you and Garrett were to reach the clinic before morning, and that's doubtful, considering that roadblocks are undoubtedly going up as I speak, you'd end up getting yourselves killed."

She shook her head. "No. It's better, and safer, for all concerned, including all those who've gone out on a limb to help in this situation, if you wait here tonight, then catch up with your SEAL partners tomorrow.

"Meanwhile, the instability may in some way prove helpful, if the guards at the clinic hear about the photos and decide this is a good time to return to the civilian population. If it turns out Vasquez does get out of the country, you'll probably find a great many of his army headed for the borders, as well."

"What about the embassy?" Shane asked. "Are you staying?"

"For now. We have our Marine guards who are very, very good at what they do, and are well trained to give their own lives, if necessary, to keep us safe in the event locals decide to take to the streets and start riots.

"If we're fortunate enough to escape that, and the photos turn out to be real, we'll want to have our own people here overseeing the investigation."

"In order to orchestrate a cover-up about our own involvement in shady petroleum deals with the Vasquez government," Shane guessed.

She gave him a bland look. "The U.S. does not engage in internal politics in the countries where it maintains diplomatic agencies. However, it is also in our national

484

interest to see that Vasquez is deposed. With the least amount of disruption to the country's citizens or its economy."

"Oh, my God." Kirby combed a hand through her hair, dislodging sand and seaweed and she hated to think what else. "The rumors *are* true. You're bringing back Madrid to take over the leadership gap."

"The U.S. does not engage in internal politics in its host nations," she repeated.

Shane shook his head. "You people never learn, do you? You already replaced one despot with Vasquez —"

She tossed her head. "I was still in school when he took over."

"Only after the other guy was *deposed,*" Shane corrected. "Now you're about to do the same thing, having no way of knowing what kind of leader Madrid will even be. You know what they say —"

"Ah." The CIA station chief folded her arms. "This is where you fall back on the old cliché and remind me that those who do not remember history are condemned to repeat it."

"No. This is where I tell you that those who paraphrase George Santayana are condemned to misquote him. Actually, what he said was that those who do not remember the *past* are condemned to repeat it.

"It wasn't such a bad idea when the guy came up with it in 1905, and it's probably an even more important consideration during these days when we can't seem to get away from the urge to nation build."

"Excuse me." Her back stiffened. "There just happen to be those who believe the ideals of democracy, popular sovereignty, individual rights, and the rule of law are universal."

"Fuck it." Although it wasn't easy, and he was honestly worried about his leg folding and embarrassing the hell out of him, Shane pushed himself to his feet. "I cannot believe that after having been shot at, literally blown out of a building, I'm out on some beach in the fucking dark, arguing philosophy and international political policy with a government spook.

"Here's one more Santayana quote for you, lady, then Dr. Campbell and I are out of here: 'Fanaticism consists in redoubling your effort when you have forgotten your aim.' "

He held down a hand to Kirby. "Ready to leave?"

As she stood up, using Shane's hand for balance, without risking unsettling his balance, she rewarded him with the kind of "my hero" smile the girl always used to give the Duke at the end of the movie. "Actually, I was ready ten minutes ago."

They walked together, down the beach, hand in hand.

Neither looked back.

53

"That's why the Navy gives us paddles with these things," Zach yelled over the wind. The three men were drenched for the umpteenth time by a high, forceful wave as they fought their way onto shore.

There was a Navy saying — "You can't cheat the water."

Well, maybe they couldn't cheat it. But they could damn well make it work for them. Because while the name SEAL might stand for "sea, air, and land," every guy worth his trident would state that his real home was in the water.

The other SOF groups — Special Forces, Rangers, even the Air Force Tactics teams — conducted diving and small-boat training. But for all of them, water remained an obstacle. To a SEAL, water — both in and under it — was home.

Which was what made them different — and to Zach's mind, the goddamn best.

The patrol boat had disappeared over the horizon. The only thing he could see was the storm-tossed water, which swirled like green on a radarscope through his NVGs. They'd been spun around in so many circles as they'd sunk into the swells, only to be tossed back out again, that he probably would've become disoriented without his GPS.

But even then, they'd make it, because every SEAL was trained in dead reckoning, navigating with only chart, compass, and the known speed of your boat, which had, admittedly, slowed considerably since they'd lost the engine.

Then there was the little fact that Quinn had always accused him of having his own personal GPS in his head, which was partly true.

Zach always had been one of the best on the teams at knowing where they were at any given time, even out in the middle of the sandbox when they'd been tracking down insurgents and caches of weapons and ammo used by the Fedayeen Saddam, who'd turned out to be a helluva larger and stronger fighting force than any of the desk jockeys had expected them to be.

The second reason was simple. Failure was not an option.

He and Quinn were experts at OTB — over-the-beach — operations. A core skill of a Navy SEAL, they'd practiced it so many hours, Zach figured they could both do it in their sleep. Gannon might be the wild card, but he was fit, smart, and as determined as the rest of them to pull this off. He'd also, thank you, Jesus, proven to have been telling the truth when he'd said he could keep a cool head and not go Rambo on them.

He was as wet and cold as Zach himself was, but he hadn't uttered a word of complaint. Just kept his paddle stroking deep into the sea. Again and again.

"We're getting close to shore," Quinn yelled from behind him.

Which he really hadn't needed to announce, since the surf rising on the beach was full of bioluminescence.

Which could make them look like a giant green CHEMLITE.

The only easy day was yesterday.

With that familiar BUD/S refrain repeating in his mind, Zach kept paddling.

They were late hitting the beach.

More than an hour past the plan.

But at least the weather had cooperated, with the clouds dumping all the rain on them, keeping the moon mostly covered.

Once they ditched the IBS and got on the

road, they could call Garrett and change the time of the rendezvous. It wasn't a perfect plan. Then again, what was?

Right now, as they pulled the several-hundred-pound rubber boat onto the sand and dragged it into a nearby grove of coastal mangroves, where they buried, then covered it with branches and leaves, Zach was relieved to get this stage of the op behind them, seemingly without detection.

"Now," he said, as he peeled off his MAS, leaving him in a set of digital jungle BDUs, "let's go get Dr. Moore so we can all go home and get laid as a reward for all our hard work."

"Roger that," both Quinn and Gannon said together.

54

It had begun to rain. If the doorman was at all surprised to see them show up looking like wet rats, covered in sand, her limping a bit from the glass embedded in her foot from the race out of the restaurant, his expression didn't reveal it. Once more giving Kirby the impression that he might be in contact with Gwendolyn Patterson.

He did suggest they might feel more comfortable going in a side door and taking the servant's elevator to their suite. Which, when they agreed, he called forth their same bellman, instructing him to open the door that, for security reasons, was not accessible without a key from the outside.

They were no sooner in the new suite, which turned out to be a mirror image of their original room, when Shane noticed the blood on the white floor.

"Damn. I was afraid you'd cut your foot on all that glass."

"It's not that bad," she said. Though now that the adrenaline was wearing off, it was beginning to hurt. Just a little.

"Let me check."

He practically shoved her down onto the sofa, covered in a pastel seashell print, sat down beside her, and lifted her foot onto his lap.

"If you're thinking of sucking my toes, we might want to take a shower first," she suggested.

Their eyes met over her filthy foot, and from the flash in his she knew they were both remembering a time when they'd thought it might be sexy, but, given that she turned out to be ticklish, had only resulted in gales of laughter.

"Most of it's surface stuff. Sand, a bit of plaster." He brushed his palms over first one foot, then another. Then frowned. "But this doesn't look good."

"What?"

"You've got a shard embedded in your heel. Which is where the blood's coming from." He tried to pull it out with his fingertips, which didn't prove successful.

"I've got a pair of tweezers and some antiseptic cream in my carry-on," she said.

"Terrific." He lifted her feet so he could stand up, then put them back onto the sofa.

"This material is really going to need cleaning."

"At these prices, they can damn well absorb the cost of a little housekeeping," he said. "Stay here. I'll go get it and be right back."

"This is ridiculous," she said. "Don't you think we should be checking you out first? You're the one with the prosthesis, after all."

"Which seems to be holding up just fine," he said.

"Okay." Her gaze moved from his face to the leg in question. "Here's where I admit that I've been dying to see it."

"And you will," he said. "Because I intend for both of us to be naked in another ten minutes. But first things first."

Naked. With Shane Garrett. And, despite everything, wasn't that idea just exactly what she needed?

She leaned back, her head against the armrest, spread out the way he'd left her, and was trying to put that gun battle in the restaurant out of her mind when he returned. The wet T-shirt plastered to his body revealed a six-pack abdomen as impressive as he'd sported before his injury.

"I have to admit, I was surprised when, after we landed on the beach, your leg was capable of not just holding you up, but walking two blocks back to this hotel."

"I wasn't," he said. "Since it was put under all kinds of stress during those months of therapy. It's an experimental unit that's been tested six ways to Sunday long before I received it. They were just waiting for the right candidate."

"Who would be you."

"Yeah. Who would be me."

"I'm glad," she said, "that if you had to be so terribly injured, you at least got something positive out of it."

"My injuries weren't anything like a lot of the troops who ended up at Walter Reed," he said. "And actually, except for a two-week pity party, I came out of the entire experience the same as I ever was."

He rubbed his jaw, which was darkened with a sexy stubble of dark night beard. Reconsidered. "Well, nearly," he allowed. "Since, as you pointed out, I do have that memory glitch, which I've moved beyond."

He *had* seemed pretty much like the cocky cowboy she'd fallen for. Which, given all he'd been through, surprised her. Just a little.

"So, you haven't experienced any PTSD?"

"Nope. Not an iota."

"I guess you had a lot of talk therapy at Walter Reed."

"I went to a couple sessions, sure, since it was required. But they were depressing, so I quit."

"Just like that." She'd read that the best way for soldiers to avoid post-traumatic stress was to talk it out. But she also suspected it wasn't easy getting members of the military to let down their guard enough to admit to weaknesses. Especially psychological or mental ones.

"Yeah. But just because I didn't talk about it didn't mean that I didn't think about what happened. And you know what I figured?"

"What?"

"That I didn't have a problem with PTSD, because I already had NSDQ."

It took her a minute to figure the out the anagram. "Night Stalkers Don't Quit."

His grin was bold, and banished the earlier tension. "Roger that."

55

It was easier than either of them had thought it would be. After taking the glass out of her foot, Shane went into the bathroom and turned the water on in a jet tub large enough to swim laps in. There were bottles of various bath salts lined up on the shelf behind the tub. After a few sample sniffs, he chose one the closest to how he always had thought she smelled, like sunshine and meadows, and tossed in a handful.

Then, as the water streamed into the tub and the fragrant steam rose, he returned to the living room, stood in front of her, and held out his hand.

She went into his arms, lifting her face for his kiss. But needing to look at her, to assure himself that she wasn't a dream that would vanish upon waking, or a morning-shower fantasy, he traced the line of her cheek with a fingertip, surprised to find that his hand was as unsteady as his heart.

Reaching behind her, he lowered the zipper on the lovely, now ruined dress, feeling her shiver as his knuckles brushed down her spine.

"Cold?" he asked as the dress slid to the floor, leaving her clad in a wet pair of ivory panties that, like the others he'd seen her in, still didn't have any lace.

But these were of some slick, satiny material, cut low across her stomach, high on her legs, with little blue laces that tied at her hips. Hips that while still curvy, weren't as lush as they'd once been. He suspected that was due to the hard work and short rations that were undoubtedly part of a relief doctor's life. She was tanner than she'd been in Iraq. Not as dark as he was, but a pale, sun-kissed gold that seemed to shimmer in the overhead light.

Her bra matched the panties. The rest of her may have lost inches, but her amazing cleavage was still one of the great natural wonders of the world. It took every ounce of self-restraint Shane possessed to keep from burying his face in the enticingly soft flesh.

Wanting to make this last, to make love to her slowly, tenderly, for once, to try to make her understand how precious she was to him, he kissed her instead, slipping his tongue between her lips while creating soft suction within her mouth.

She moaned, a ragged vibration against his mouth as her lips clung to his. "More," she said as she caught hold of the hem of his wet shirt and pulled it over his head. Then stroked her hands back down over his rib cage, his abs, his stomach. When she reached the woven olive drab belt he'd kept from his SOAR days, her fingers busied themselves with the buckle.

"Soon." His tongue slid in and out of her moist, sweet mouth, hot and slick, penetrating her mouth the way he was aching to penetrate her body. Encouraged by her trembling, he untied first one satin ribbon, then the other, causing her panties to follow the dress onto the floor.

He pressed his hand against her mound. "I want to be inside you, Kirby. You've driven me crazy with wanting you."

"Ha, I haven't done a thing."

"You've never had to."

"And isn't that exactly what you were supposed to say." Her teeth nipped at his lower lips as she unzipped his jeans. "Gotta love a man who goes commando," she said as she found him naked beneath the denim. "It makes this undressing process one step simpler."

His flesh was jutting out like a damn flagpole, and actually jumped when she stepped back to give it a long look.

"I was beginning to think I'd imagined how magnificent you were." She closed her hands around his hot circumference, drawing a groan from deep in his chest. "You know what they say about time fading memory."

"Yeah. I've noticed that." Wanting to drive her as crazy as she was driving him, he unfastened the front clasp between her breasts, slid the lacy straps down her arms, and tossed the bra across the room. Then bent his head and kissed the rosy tip of a nipple. "But if I'd forgotten anything about how it feels to make love with you, Kirby, which I'm pretty sure I haven't, it sure as hell is coming back real fast."

"That was — oh, God," she moaned, as he rolled it beneath his tongue, then sucked. Hard.

"You were saying?" He moved to her other breast, taking it deep inside his mouth.

"That there's nothing wrong with my memory, either."

Christ, her thumb was skimming up and down the thick cord of his penis, and if she didn't stop squeezing him that way, they were going to have a lot more to wash off than sand.

She let out a little, very un-Kirby-like yelp as he lifted her off her feet and deposited her in the tub, feeling a tug of regret when the bubbles covered all that soft, golden flesh.

Deciding it was now or never, he kicked off his wet and sandy sneaks and then pushed the jeans down his legs. Both of them.

"Well." She tilted her head, taking in the titanium prosthesis he'd worn on the plane, because his dress one was bulkier and not as comfortable. "If I wasn't about ready to explode from pent-up lust, I'd love to check that out in more detail."

"Later."

"Much, much later," she said. Then twirled her hand through the fragrant bubbles, spreading them over her breasts, leaving her nipples showing like cherries on top of a particularly tasty dessert. "This is a very big tub." Her lips curved down in a little moue. "And very lonely."

He watched her switch momentarily into doctor mode when he sat down onto the lid of the toilet and pulled the top of the artificial leg from the receptor that had been buried into what was left of his real leg.

"It's the ultimate plug and play," he said.

She smiled. A slow, sexy, smile not unlike the ones he suspected sirens used to lure seamen to their under-the-ocean realms.

Then crooked a white-tipped finger as she flicked the switch with the other hand, turning on the jets. "Well, now that you've unplugged, why don't you join me in this hedonistic bathtub for some play?"

The scented water rose as he lowered himself into the tub, facing her. "I should've rethought putting this stuff in."

"Do you have something about bubbles?" She scooped up a handful and threw it at his chest.

"No. But not only is it not exactly a camouflage scent, the guys are never going to quit ragging me if I show up smelling like a girl at the ruins tomorrow."

"Don't worry." She picked up a cloth from the holder set in the tile and began running it up and down first one arm. Then the other. When she squeezed it, causing water to glide down her breasts, leaving wet trails in the white bubbles, he felt a hot, tortured anticipation rip through him. "By the time I finish with you, you'll be nice and manly sweaty again."

"You finish with me?"

"I owe you one," she reminded him.

"I didn't know we were keeping score."

"We're not." She scooted forward and began to massage the calf of his good leg. "It's just that after being nearly blown up this evening, I suddenly have this overwhelming need to feel in control."

She ran her hands up both his thighs, not only undeterred by disability, but seeming to sense that the nerve endings at the amputation point were some of the most sensitive in his body. Sometimes, when he wasn't wearing his prosthesis, like in bed at night, they were what caused phantom pain, a sharp tingling in a part of his leg that no longer existed.

But right now, while the sensations were definitely sharp, and certainly tingling, the only painful thing about her touch was that it left him dying for more.

"Did I ever tell you that I was on swim team the summer between my freshman and sophomore years in high school?" she asked conversationally, as she continued to torment him beneath the bubbles, trailing slow, sensual figure eights up and down the inside of his thighs.

"I don't remember it if you did," he said hoarsely, bucking when her touch grew more intimate again.

"I swam breast stroke." She skimmed a treacherous palm over the tip of his shaft. "My personal best time was one minute, nineteen and eight-tenths seconds for one hundred meters. It set a club record. There's still a trophy in the glass case in the high school's main hall."

"Good for you." His voice was rough. Almost strangled from lust.

"The trophy was nice enough. So was the blue ribbon with a gold seal on it. But want to know what my best thing was?"

Her fingers were now curled around him and she'd begun stroking his swollen flesh. Up. Down. Up again. "I'm beginning to get a good idea."

She wagged the finger of her free hand at him. "You've got a dirty mind. I'll have you know I graduated high school a virgin. No, what I was really known for was the fact that I could hold my breath longer than anyone on the team. Even the coach."

"Kirby." He grabbed her by the shoulders. "You don't have to —"

"But I want to."

Her eyes had grown so dark it was difficult to tell where the pupils let off and the irises began. But they sparkled with a sexual humor he remembered had been one of the best things about coming back to the Green

Zone. It had been more than the fact that he could eat real food. Have real hot showers and sleep with a sexy woman. It had been the way he unwound the moment he saw her. Coming back to Iraq, and to Captain Kirby Campbell, had always been like coming home.

"It's only too bad we don't have a stopwatch handy," she said. "Because I have the feeling I'm about to set a new record."

With that, she ducked her blond head beneath the bubbles, and as the warm water swirled around him and she took him deep into her mouth, he was lost.

Powerless, he bucked his hips, trying not to come. Not so fast. And not this way.

He tried to say her name. To tell her it was okay to stop.

But he couldn't talk.

Tangled his hands in her hair, intending, God, he didn't know what, but then she was sucking, and no longer able to hold back, his body spasmed.

His head fell back against the tile rim. He couldn't breathe. Couldn't move.

"Kirby." He managed to rasp out her name in a ragged expulsion of air.

She popped back to the surface. She looked wet and hot and utterly self-satisfied.

Still in a haze, he somehow remembered

patting her all over with one of the fluffy white towels, taking his time, until she was not only totally dry, but begging for him to take her.

They managed to make it to the bed. The details blurred, but as they lay on the cotton sheets that felt like silk beneath their heated flesh, they explored each other's bodies with a pleasure they'd never taken time for during those crazy wartime days and nights together.

The brush of her fingernail against his dark nipple inflamed; the caress of his lips against her softly rounded belly aroused, causing her to move her body sinuously against his, which made the flames rise higher.

Her sultry laughter shimmered over his moist flesh as her mouth nipped at his hip.

She wasn't laughing when he rolled her onto her back, put a pillow beneath her hips, slanting her pelvis toward him.

Then sat back, drinking in the sight of her. She looked wild. Wanton. And . . .

"You look good enough to eat," he said.

And proceeded to do exactly that.

As helpless as he'd been earlier, she writhed beneath him. When her back arched off the mattress, he cupped her sweet butt in his hands and pushed her higher, spreading her thighs wider, tongue thrusting, his beard, which he hadn't taken time to shave, scraping against her hot, wet flesh.

God, he loved her taste. And her scent. Hell with the meadow and the jasmine or orchids, or whatever that stuff Sabrina had given her. She was the most natural woman he'd ever known. And he knew if he lived to a hundred, he'd never get enough of her.

She was panting, faster and faster, and when she shattered, she turned her head, muffling her ragged cry into the soft down pillow.

Fired by the sight of her, spent, legs spread, her body flushed pink with orgasm, Shane sheathed himself with one of the condoms he'd brought along, then holding his erection, he slid partway into her, enough to bring forth a soft moan.

"You said it's been a while," he reminded them both, as he pulled almost completely out again. "I don't want to hurt you."

"That's the last thing you're going to do," she whispered against his throat. "And the only reason I'd given up men is that none of them were you."

He drew his head back. Looked deep into her eyes and saw the truth shining there. "Me, too," he said. "Not men, but —"

"I get it." She wrapped her legs around

his hips. "And while I'm always up for a good conversation, I'd really, really like it if you'd just put it back in. Where it belongs."

Truer words were never spoken.

He thrust in, deeper this time, then pulled out slightly, drawing a faint moan of complaint. Then a curse, which made him laugh out loud.

He thrust again. And again. Harder, faster, driving her deeper and deeper into the thick feather-top mattress, until they climaxed together.

"God," he said, rolling over and holding her tight against his chest, "now, *that* was a personal best."

She looked up at him as she trailed a finger down his damp and, yes, just as she'd promised, sweaty torso. "And just think — the night's still young."

56

Sometime before dawn, Kirby climbed out of the warm bed and finally got around to using the dye Gwendolyn Patterson had left for her. It was an ordinary brown, which, she decided, looking in the mirror, was exactly the point. If she and Shane stood out, the chances of them making their way to the clinic undetected could be compromised.

But still, after a night of fabulous sex that, except for a faint headache she put off to lack of sleep, had left her feeling feminine and sexy, she wanted to look that way, too.

Instead, she was back in the boring, utilitarian white blouse and navy skirt. She'd change into the cammies she'd bought on Swann Island once they reached the pyramid and hooked up with the others.

"Well? What do you think?" Shane was sitting at the table, studying a map. He looked up at her.

"You could be wearing a potato sack and you'd be beautiful to me."

"I was talking about my hair." She ran her fingers through the cut that no longer felt as carefree.

"It looks fine."

"Exactly."

"What's wrong with fine?"

" 'Fine' is just another word for 'boring.' "

"No." He leaned back and studied her more closely. "Fine is fine. Actually, it looks great."

"I'll bet you like me better as a blonde."

He took a long drink of the coffee he'd brewed while she'd been in the bathroom, then looked at her over the rim of the cup. "This is one of those trick female questions, isn't it? Whatever I answer, it's going to be wrong."

"It's not a trick. It's a simple question. Do you like me better as a blonde or a brunette?"

"Sweetcakes, I'd adore you if you decided to go back into that Taj Mahal of a bathroom, take my razor, and went for a Bruce Willis look. Not that it wouldn't probably draw some attention to us, which, I believe was the reason for the change in the first place, but hey, if that's what you want to do, go for it."

"I didn't say I wanted to go bald!"

Was she really shouting? What on earth was wrong with her? "I'm sorry. I guess I'm just nervous about today." She rubbed a finger between her eyes.

"Headache?" he asked.

"It's just a lack of sleep. Not that I'm complaining," she said quickly. "Or stress from that gunfight at the O.K. Cantina last night."

"Again, perfectly understandable. You also could be jet-lagged. You've done a lot of traveling in three short days."

"It seems longer."

"I know." He left the room, went into the bathroom, and came out with two tablets and a glass of water. "Take some vitamin M. You'll feel better."

"Ah, the Special Ops answer to everything."

"Sometimes simple works best."

"So says the bionic man."

He'd explained to her that his leg utilized computer chips, Bluetooth technology, and myoelectric impulses, all of which had been used in other prostheses before. But what made his leg so revolutionary was that each of *his* new prostheses literally plugged into a device embedded in his remaining limb, which allowed electronic signals from his brain to be rerouted through to his new leg through a process called targeted muscle reinnervation.

"The new grafted nerves grew into the muscles, and from there the doctors connected the dots, inserting electrodes that makes a closed loop between my leg and my brain. So it pretty much works like a real leg."

"We're going to have to rename you Steve Austin," she said, deciding that once she got back to the States, she was definitely going to do more research on this. The superior body armor prevented deaths, but left many of the troops with wounds that cost them at least one limb. To Kirby's mind, they were all heroes and deserved the best medical research could provide.

"I'm still the same guy I always was," he said. "Just 'cause I got lucky and got put into the program sure as hell didn't give me superpowers. Or make me better than any of the other guys who fought over there. Or anywhere else, for that matter."

Later, as they drove the white Toyota out of the city, Kirby was stunned at the devastation as they neared the ruins.

"All this was lush green farmland three days ago," she said, staring out over a gray desert, covered with ash.

The air was thick and hazy, the villages, with their shuttered markets and abandoned houses, looking like ghost towns.

Above the desolation, Ixtab was still smoking.

"I don't understand," she murmured, as they passed one village where people were gathered in the street, watching the ash spitting into the sky. Many were dancing in an attempt to appease the angry goddess. "I've only seen one minor eruption since I've been here, but the army closed the entire region off because of all the gas emissions."

"If it's true about Vasquez trying to leave the country, the army's probably in chaos," Shane suggested. "Which was why those guerillas last night felt free to bring their attack from the rural area into the city."

"Then we could well be looking at a civil war."

"I think you've already got one," he pointed out as they drove over a narrow wooden bridge. Women, their skirts pulled up and tied to their hips, were beating ash-laden clothes on the rocks, as women had been doing for centuries. "It's just now going to become really official."

"Which could definitely cause the few countries who have been trying to help to pull out completely."

"There is that," he agreed. "There's also the possibility that Madrid will be able to be a uniter."

"Yeah. Where have I heard that before?" she muttered.

Deciding to talk about something less depressing, she realized that there were years of his life when he'd been in the service that he couldn't talk about. Just as he hadn't been able to talk about missions when he returned to the Green Zone.

"So," she said, trying another topic, "what was it like, growing up on a ranch?"

"It had its good points. We were isolated, but we were independent. And although we never had much money, we never felt poor. There's an old saying that ranchers make over, make do, or do without. Which is pretty much the way it is."

"Do you ever think about going back?"

"Not really. My brother and brother-in-law have pretty much taken over the day-to-day running of the ranch. And, although it's probably heresy, I always found cows boring."

"Yet you rode bulls." She remembered him telling her that the night he suggested she save a horse and ride a cowboy.

"Yeah. Well, that was different."

"I was channel surfing one night when I

was back in the States, visiting my folks for Christmas," she said. "And caught the national championship bull-riding competition. It was amazing." She had no trouble imagining him atop those huge, bucking animals. "Is that what you did?"

"Mostly. When I was younger I did some steer wrestling, but I gave that up because I wasn't big enough."

She tilted her head as her gaze swept over him. "You're not exactly lightweight."

"The minimum weight of a competition steer is four hundred and fifty pounds," he said. "Along with a serious understanding of gravity, it helps for a cowboy to be strong enough to bring a steer down by sheer muscle force. If you can't do that, things can get dangerous real quick, since steers do not, as a general rule, appreciate being wrestled."

"Yet the announcer said that bull riding is the most dangerous rodeo sport."

"Yeah." He shrugged. "That's what they say."

"And you weren't afraid?"

"Not really. Beforehand, you're too busy feeling the bull out, running through the ride in your mind, to be afraid. Then, during the ride, there's too much to think about — staying on and winning points from the judges — to be scared. Then there's the adrenaline rush."

"But it only lasts, what? Ten seconds?"

"Eight. It just seems longer. Sorta like a slow-motion replay. Or jumping out of a plane."

"Or like last night at the restaurant."

"Exactly. There's nothing like thinking you might die to make you fully appreciate the value of living."

"Do you miss it?" she asked.

"Bull riding?"

"No. The Army."

"Yeah," he surprised her by saying. "I didn't think I would, especially since I was all the time bucking the rules. But yeah. I loved being in the air, and I loved flying those birds. So, sure, there are times I miss it." He reached between them and took her hand. "But not nearly as much as I missed you."

"That's nice."

"It's the truth," he said simply.

They'd left the ash-covered fields behind, driving through vast fields of tobacco that often hid marijuana between the rows. The same volcano that made living in its shadow so dangerous was also the cause of fertile soil.

They passed the banana plantations,

where *segadores* harvested the still-green fruit with swift swings of the razor-sharp machetes.

A convoy of army trucks passed, headed away from the volcano. The young, conscripted soldiers were dressed in jungle camouflage, much as Kirby had bought on Swann Island. They seemed to be coming down from the mountain villages, the truck drivers arrogantly taking up the center of the narrow dirt road, forcing Shane to pull the Toyota far to the right, nearly off the shoulder.

"They seem to be in a hurry," Kirby said.

"Something's definitely happening," Shane agreed.

With a maniac pounding away at her head, like those women had been pounding their clothes on the rocks, Kirby didn't even want to try to figure out whatever was going on could mean for Rachel.

They'd nearly reached their destination and were driving along the bank of Lake Itzamna when Shane's cell phone rang.

He looked at the caller ID.

"Yo." He frowned a bit as he listened, then nodded. "No sweat. We're about ten minutes away, so we'll just hang out and get something to eat while we're waiting."

He snapped the phone shut. "That was

Tremayne. They had a little trouble and are running about an hour behind. But they figure if they can pick up a ride, they'll make up the time."

"What kind of problem?"

"He didn't say."

"But everyone's all right?"

"Seems to be."

That, at least, was something, Kirby decided.

On normal days, fishermen from local villages plied the lake in dugout canoes, while boats ferried passengers from one town to another. Today, due to the impending storm and, perhaps, Ixtab's increased activity, the wind, known locally as *Xocomil,* had turned the usually placid waters of the crystalline lake into treacherous waves.

On the far side of the lake were the ruins of the once mighty pyramid built to honor Masaya, the Mayan goddess of fire and divination, who required that victims be thrown into volcanoes.

And conveniently, Ixtab, named for the protector of suicides, slain warriors, sacrificial victims, priests, and women who died in childbirth, just happened to be less than a kilometer away.

The first time she'd seen it, Kirby had stared up at it, looming over the landscape, mysterious, deadly, but still enthralling. It took no imagination at all to understand why volcanoes in mythology were either considered gods or goddesses or inhabited by gods, revered, worshipped, or feared as gateways to hell.

There was a cantina with a shabby motel attached for tourists. From the vinyl decals stuck on the doors of the various vehicles filling the lot, it appeared that most of today's visitors were volcanologists.

The sun had come out, leaving the temperature in the nineties, the humidity just as high. Last night's rain, rather than cooling things down, had only added to the stultifying discomfort.

The cantina was actually more of a shack, a far cry from last night's beachfront restaurant. The unpainted walls were caked with dirt and the floor was covered with what appeared to be ash.

An oppressive cloud of cigarette smoke hovered over the space, while a rusty paddle-bladed fan creaked overhead in a futile attempt to move the fetid air.

"We can wait in the Toyota," Shane suggested, as they took in the bartender who looked like an escapee from a chain gang. His dark eyes were as empty as a snake's, which complimented the red and blue tattooed reptiles wrapped around his bulky arms.

"No. It's like an oven in there."

"It's like a sewer in here."

Kirby shivered as a tarantula the size of her fist scuttled across the floor and up the screen door, escaping through a hole in the ratty black mesh. Although it was not yet ten o'clock, her blouse and skirt were clinging damply to her skin. At this moment, were it not for Rachel, she would have given anything to be back at the hotel, in that oversized tub. This time with it filled with ice cubes.

"We're tourists," he said. "Let's act like it." He went over to the bartender. "I don't suppose you'd have a guide to the pyramid?"

Reptilian eyes narrowed. "What the fuck do I look like," the guy, obviously an expatriot American or Aussie, shot back. "Fucking Fodor's?"

"Don't worry about it." Shane smiled. "We'll just figure it out for ourselves."

Having studied a bit about the ruins when she'd first arrived in the country, Kirby was able to do a reasonable tour-guide spiel.

"Like most pre-Columbian monuments, it was built in strict accordance with astronomical and astrological requirements," she said. "The nine terraces symbolize the nine heavens, and the four staircases stand for the four cardinal points. Each staircase has ninety-one steps. Or did," she tacked on, frowning. "Unlike a lot of other countries in the region, Vasquez and his predecessor didn't spring for the bucks to reclaim it. Or even try to keep people from climbing all over it and taking bits of stone as souvenirs."

She shook off the irritation. "Anyway, the number of steps adds up to three hundred and sixty-four. When you add the top platform, you get the total number of days in a year."

"Clever folks, the Maya," Shane said.

"And amazingly advanced for their time. While Europe was wallowing in the Dark Ages, these people practiced an astronomy so precise their calendar was as accurate as the one in use today. They plotted the courses of stars and planets, predicted the exact times of both the solar and lunar eclipses, calculated the path of Venus with an error of only fourteen seconds a year, and engineered the concept of zero."

She sighed. "Which makes it doubly unfair that their descendants should be treated like second-class citizens.

"What?" she asked when she dragged her eyes away from the towering stone pyramid to see him smiling at her.

"Anyone ever tell you that you're damn cute when you're being earnest?"

"Not recently."

"Well, you are. And where did you pick up all that stuff, anyway?"

"Once I gave up men, I gained a lot of extra reading time."

"Should I feel guilty about keeping you away from a good book last night?"

"Not at all." She went up on her toes and brushed her lips against his smiling ones. "I'd rather write my own story, anyway." With you and a happily ever after ending, she thought, but was not yet prepared to say.

57

They'd been humping through the jungle for the last three hours. Crossing the border hadn't been any problem, but by now Zach had figured there'd have been some sort of jeep or truck they could rent, or even liberate, if only for a few hours. It wouldn't be like they wouldn't pay for the damn thing.

But no. Once they entered the country, the only vehicles they saw on the road were convoys of army trucks, none of which seemed like a real good idea to hitch a ride on.

Zach was about to call Shane again, tell him he might have to add a bit more time to the plan, when they passed a gas station in an abandoned village covered in a layer of white ash. They would have passed it by, until Quinn said, "Talk about your small worlds."

Zach's eyes narrowed as he took in the man pumping gas into a camouflage-painted

Hummer. "Roger that."

He strolled over to the guy, who looked up at him, and nearly dropped the hose. "Oh, shit."

"Is that any way to greet an old buddy?" Zach asked. "One who probably saved your life?

"Since I saved your pilot friend's life, I'd say we're even." The CIA guy who'd been along on the Afghanistan mission put the nozzle back on its holder. "Nice to see you, Chief. But I've got places to go. People to see."

"That's a pretty big rig for three guys," he said, glancing into the Hummer at the two guys inside. Obviously Spec Ops. Maybe even SEALs. "What the hell is going on here? We've been seeing army troops moving all day."

"It's obvious you've been away from the news."

"Well, duh. Does it look like we're carrying a satellite dish with us?"

"Vasquez's plane is about to take off from the landing strip at his mountain retreat, if it hasn't already. Seems the rebel forces are moving into the city, while the infamous Guardia de Seguridad are acting like rats leaving a sinking ship. And if you're not up on that little bit of Latin American news, what the fuck are you doing down here?"

"It's personal. We're rescuing a WMR worker who's being held hostage by Castillo's guys. With, supposedly, one of your guys inside."

"Not one of mine. I just got here from Mexico, myself."

"Mexico?" The pieces clicked into place. Zach exchanged a look with Quinn, who, with Michael, had joined them. "Shit. You've got Josefina Madrid in that Hummer."

"I've no idea what you're talking about."

"Oh, cut the crap. Look, what you're doing is your own business. You want to stage yourself a nice little coup, super. Go for it. Just give us a ride down to the Masaya temple. It's not like you don't have enough room. Or aren't going that way."

"How do you know where we're going?"

"You're either stopping at Madrid's old hometown for a pep rally before she makes her triumphant return to the capital. Or you're taking her directly to Ciudad Libertad, where she can make her 'I have returned' speech to the little people. Either way, you're going to be passing right by where we need to be."

"Come on, buddy," said Quinn with a grin. "For old times' sake."

"Nothing personal, *buddy,*" the CIA agent said. "But I really, really hated our old times."

"Get us to Masaya, and I promise you'll never see us again." Quinn held up a hand. "Scout's honor."

Zach followed suit.

As did Michael.

"Who the hell is he?" the agent asked.

"We'd tell you," Quinn said.

"But then we'd have to kill you," Zach said. "Let's just say he's not anyone you want to have turned down when people start second-guessing this little black op you've got going."

Michael did his job by keeping his mouth shut and looking inscrutable. Like someone with a really big, very important, very dangerous secret.

"What the hell," the guy caved. "But you didn't see a thing."

"Who, me? All I see is a bunch of ash floating around in the air. And some troop convoys driving like they've got the hounds of hell on their tails. How about you guys?"

"That's about it," Quinn agreed.

"I didn't even seen the convoys," Michael said. "Guess that must've been when I was looking the other way."

"I knew I should've listened to my father

526

and become a chiropractor," the CIA agent muttered.

The three men scrambled into the Hummer before the less-than-enthusiastic driver changed his mind.

The SEALs who'd stayed inside didn't say anything to them. But from their nods, it was obvious that everyone knew who all the players were.

Including the woman dressed in cammies. The woman who had single-handedly — well, apparently with some help of this black ops team — done what the rebels hadn't been able to achieve in nine long years of fighting.

Send Vasquez running with his tail between his legs.

Which didn't mean she'd be able to piece her tattered country together again, but Zach wished her luck.

Not that this situation was all that helpful to their mission. Unless the guerillas got so happy they declared a national freedom day, abandoned their posts, and left Rachel Moore unguarded, the evacuation op was still on.

58

"Okay," Zach told Kirby. "What you want to keep in mind is BLISS."

"Yeah. That's not too hard to imagine," she said, sharing a look with Shane that had Quinn groaning and Zach rolling his eyes.

"If you two could quit looking like two teenagers after staying out all prom night, it'd be nice to have your attention," he said.

"Frogs rule on the ground," Shane told Kirby. "Now, if we were in the air, it'd be a whole different story. He'd be having to take orders from me."

"But we're not in the air, flyboy," Zach said through gritted teeth. "Here's the deal." He was crouched down with a can of camo makeup in his hand. "BLISS is an ancronym for Blend into your surroundings, have a Low silhouette, keep an Irregular shape, Stay small, and keep to Secluded areas.

"Now, as for your face, too many people

just smear a few streaks onto their face and call it done. I'm not suggesting you spend hours putting on your makeup, like you did the other night at Swannsea."

"The other night I wasn't going to be going through the jungle, trying to avoid bad guys," Kirby said, understanding he was suddenly being such a hard-ass, making her learn all this stuff she'd never need to know again, because he took his responsibility of getting everyone home safe extremely seriously.

She was also so damn hot she didn't think there was much point in putting all this green, brown, and black stuff on her face, since it would undoubtedly melt off in the first five minutes, out in the jungle.

"I get that," he said. "But here's the deal. . . . Poorly applied camo can end up drawing attention to you, which actually hurts your concealment efforts."

After handing her a plastic bottle of baby lotion to spread over her face (the better to take the stuff off once the mission was over, he explained), he scooped his fingers into the can.

"You want to make sure your nose, forehead, cheeks, and chin are well covered. You can use a blotch or line-pattern design of camouflage as you put it on. I prefer to cover high points of my face in black or dark brown. Also, it's a good idea to cover your eyelids, because they can be seen at night when light actually shines on them."

He held the can out to her, allowing her to do that herself. Kirby would love to see Sabrina and Titania's reaction to this makeover.

"Don't forget to cover your ears, both front and back. As well as your neck," he instructed.

"Don't you think this is overkill?" she asked.

"No," he said abruptly.

"Don't forget your hands and fingers," Shane offered. "They really stand out if the rest of you is camouflaged." He took her hand in his and applied the makeup to the webbing between her fingers.

"I don't even want to know what I look like," she muttered.

"Think about how you'll look tonight," Quinn suggested.

"And how will that be?"

"Alive."

Since there was no way to argue that point, Kirby didn't try.

59

The plan was fairly straightforward. Kirby would lead Michael, Quinn, and Zach to the compound, while Shane would liberate a small helicopter from a local airbase. When the mission had first been planned, this had seemed horribly dangerous to Kirby, but with the military in obvious disarray, she hoped the others were right about the base being less guarded.

Zach and Quinn would dispatch the guards, and while Kirby knew enough not to ask details about how that was going to be done, she couldn't miss the M4s, ugly SIG SAUER pistols and the knives stuck in their boots.

The rescue definitely wasn't going to be pretty. And it could well prove deadly for any and all of them.

The clinic compound was surrounded by a chain-link fence topped with rolls of razor wire. Although Rachel had always told her it made her feel as if she were living in a prison, there was also the fact that they kept drugs on hand. You'd think, with the thriving drug trade, that there'd be enough for everyone in the country to have their own personal stash, but when she'd first opened up, she'd discovered that certain people in the area had taken the "free" in "free clinic" literally, helping themselves to pharmaceuticals at night.

Patterson's man inside, if he could be trusted, which was always iffy in this part of the world, had said there were eight armed guards outside. Plus the kids. And — here was the kicker — three Rottweilers.

"Rachel's not going to be happy if you kill those dogs," Kirby warned as she led them through the jungle, which took longer than any of them would have liked, but as she'd explained back in Somersett, just deciding to cut through a drug patch could end up with them all dead before they even got to the compound.

"Maybe she'd be happier if we all just joined hands on the mountaintop and sang 'Kumbaya' and the Coca-Cola song," Zach said. "And, hey, you can count me in to sing harmony as soon as you and she get it organized. But if the dogs present a problem, they've got to go."

"How can they not?" she asked.

"I have a plan," Michael Gannon said. "Which hopefully will work."

"One you didn't choose to tell me?"

"Excuse me," Zach said. "I didn't realize you wanted to know every little detail. Like, maybe how, if I have to, I'll slit a bad guy's throat to keep him from calling out to the others. Or how Quinn's an expert at breaking a neck. One quick twist from the back, and the guy's dead meat. It's even better than a Vulcan nerve pinch, because it's permanent. Or —"

"I get the point." Kirby held up a hand. "But if you're trying to make me abhor the physicality of what you do, it's not going to work, because once you've gotten through gross anatomy, which is, by the way, appropriately named, there's not much that can, well, gross a doctor out.

"I don't want to hear details because I dislike the idea of violence. Even necessary violence. You may use it as a tool, which I can understand when it comes down to kill or be killed. But you also have also understand that I spent too many years seeing the results of that kind of violence.

"We've both watched a lot of people die. Too many. So, you can keep your damn details to yourself. But while it may not sound at all logical, I would like to know what you're going to do about the dogs."

"They're usually only let out at night. But if anyone sounds the alarm, they could decide to open the cages. So, hopefully they'll be asleep by the time we get there," the former priest said. "Patterson's guy's going to feed them some tranquilizers in their food. I'm no vet, but I can figure out weight versus dosage that should work."

"Thank you." It wasn't logical, Kirby allowed. But a lot of life wasn't. Such as love.

Much of the jungle had been clear-cut and burned, destroying the land for generations to come in the name of profits. But the area they were walking in now, along a river flowing to the sea, was still in its pristine state, almost cathedral-like.

If any cathedral was like a steam bath. Although few sunbeams could penetrate the thick canopy, there was no escaping the heat, even in the shade of the dense, tropical trees. And while there was a soft sough of breeze in the tops of some of the taller trees, down at ground level no breezes were stirring.

In such stifling heat, minutes seemed like hours. The long-sleeved shirt and long pants she'd bought to protect her from insects and stinging plants were soaked within minutes, leaving her feeling as if she were carrying an extra twenty pounds.

Time and time again, one of the men offered to carry her pack. Time and time again, she refused. Which might, admittedly, be hardheaded, but she didn't want anyone to accuse her of being deadweight just because she wasn't a SEAL or a Night Stalker, or even a former Desert Storm doctor-turned-priest-turned-doctor again.

What could have taken thirty minutes, had they traveled as the crow flies, ended up taking two and a half hours. But they finally reached the compound. It would have been better if they could have done the mission at night. But even Zach had agreed with Kirby that to wait any longer would present an even larger risk.

"Okay," he murmured, as they lay on their stomachs, watching the men leaning against the outer walls of the clinic, looking as hot as Kirby herself was feeling. "Game on."

60

Acquiring the helo, which Shane had been concerned about, turned out to be the easiest part of the plan. The base was fucking deserted, except for some villagers who were looting the buildings. While he didn't think it was a real good idea for angry civilians to have automatic weapons, Shane figured that problem would be something Madrid or Castillo or whoever the hell took over the country would have to deal with.

Right now, he just wanted to liberate himself a Black Hawk, get it over to the compound; evacuate Kirby, the other doctor, and the rest of the team; then get on with the rest of his life.

Which he was going to have to do.

Like, soon.

Unfortunately, two guys, dressed in the uniform of the rebel forces, had decided they had dibs on the copter.

"Oh, Christ," Shane said, as they spun

around toward him, AKs in their hands. "Just put the guns down, guys, and nobody's going to get hurt."

Apparently, his argument was unconvincing, because one of them lifted the gun and, holding it down at his side, like Rambo, began to fire, spraying the dirt a yard from from Shane's boots.

The first guy couldn't shoot worth shit and the second guy's gun jammed. But that didn't mean that one of the bad guys couldn't get lucky. Or hit one of the women or children who were also stripping the place bare.

Cursing, Shane lifted his own M4 and eliminated the threat.

Because sometimes a guy just had to do what a guy had to do.

Rachel had always heard that SEALs worked in the dark. At night, in and out before anyone knew they'd been there, the clandestine special teams of SOF.

Apparently, they worked differently by day.

She was talking with the small bomb maker about books he'd read and how he might become a doctor like her and return to his village and take care of his own people, when suddenly the door was kicked in and four men wearing camouflage battle uniforms, their faces painted like something from anyone's worst nightmare, shouted, "Go, go, go!"

Then to the startled children, *"Acostarse boca abajo,"* — telling them to lie facedown. Both startled and intimidated, they did exactly that. Several began crying.

"Don't worry, Rachel," one of the men said, "We're here to rescue you."

She stared. Blinked. Stared again. "Michael?"

"It's me. Don't worry." He had to shout to be heard over the screaming of the children, who were having plastic handcuffs strapped on them. "You're safe."

Which was when she slapped his gruesomely painted face.

Hard.

61

"What the hell?" Michael Gannon lifted his own hand to his face and stared at her. "What did you do that for?" he shouted.

"Because you scared these poor children to death," she yelled back.

"Ma'am," a huge man dressed and painted like her former lover said, "those poor children are carrying automatic weapons."

"They wouldn't have used them."

"You don't know that," another man, who was not a man at all, said.

"Kirby?" Rachel decided she must be dreaming. But this wasn't a dream. It was a nightmare.

"These are the men I told you about. From the Kush," she said. "And, well, I guess you know Michael."

"I thought I did." Rachel glared at him as the children, sensing a drama taking place, slowly quieted down.

"You were in danger," the former priest

539

insisted. "You've no idea what's happening out there. The entire fucking country is falling apart, and —"

"Did you just say 'fuck'?"

"I don't know." He dragged a painted hand through his long hair. "Maybe, but you've got me so —"

"Is a priest even allowed to use that word?"

"Probably. When provoked. But it's a moot point, because I'm not a priest anymore."

"You're not?"

"Excuse me, ma'am," the man who'd yet to speak said, "but we've got a helo coming in with an ETA of two minutes, so if you could just get outside —"

"Not without the children."

"What?" They all stared at her.

"Rachel," Kirby coaxed. "They're not hurt. They'll be fine. But you really do have to get out of here."

"They're coming with me."

"Back to the States?" the largest of the men asked in obvious disbelief.

"No. There's a place in Guatemala that helps kids recover from war. Helps them get their childhood back. We need to take them there."

"For Chrissakes," the man who'd told her

about the copter complained.

Rachel folded her arms. "I'm not going without them."

"Rachel," Kirby tried again.

"If there's room for me, there's room for them, as well. They'll need their restraints removed so they can protect themselves. Meanwhile —"

There was an explosion, like they'd suddenly been thrown into a battle zone.

"Oh, my God," Kirby cried, running outside. "If Shane was shot down . . ."

The others followed. All stared as Ixtab literally blew her top, sending molten lava high into the air and spilling down the side of the broken cone of the mountain.

The air filled with a dark cloud of soot.

"We've got to get out." The big man literally picked Rachel off her feet and began carrying her from the clinic.

Meanwhile, Michael, Kirby, and the other man began yanking the children to *their* feet, cutting the plastic straps, and dragging them outside, as well, where they all stood staring at the flaming lava flowing down the side of the volcano.

Even as she raced the children outside, Kirby was panicking about Shane. What if the explosion had caused him to crash? What if she were to lose him just as they'd finally gotten back together?

Her head was spinning from the ash she was sucking into her lungs as she stood with the others and stared up at the sky.

And then, out of the billowing dark cloud, a helicopter appeared.

Another minute and they'd be out of here.

Thirty seconds.

Just as Shane flared to land, the earth beneath Kirby's feet began to groan and tremble, the tremendous pressures seeking release.

62

Shane had always thought of himself a lot like that guy in *Titanic,* the one who thought he was the luckiest son of a bitch in the world. Until he drowned, of course, but at least he'd gone down being noble.

In all his years of flying, he'd only crashed one helo, and even that had turned out okay, except for losing his leg, which he'd come to decide sure as hell wasn't the worst thing that could've happened to him on that mountain.

And to top things off, Kirby was back in his life. For good.

But now, as he watched in horror as the earth began to split apart, unable to tell if the catastrophic rumbling was coming from the earth below or the volcano as it roared red streams of molten lava down its side, he was forced to wonder exactly how long "for good" was going to turn out to be.

If it was just the two women, he'd hover

low enough for Quinn and Zach to jump on board, and they could use the basket to pull Rachel Moore and Kirby into the Black Hawk. But the children were obviously panicking, and the way the earth was rocking and rolling, he feared that they didn't have time for that type of airlift.

Which meant he was going to have to land. Somehow.

He watched as a cleft opened up between Rachel and Michael. The doctor was fighting for a foothold as the fissure widened, threatening to swallow her into a maw of muck and stone. The same thing was happening to Gannon on the other side.

Amazingly, the army of children had formed a line, one of them holding on to Rachel's legs, as they all pulled, as if playing a deadly game of tug-of-war. Against Mother Nature. After managing to back away just in time, the former priest jumped the gap and helped the children pull the aid doctor out of the earth.

Afraid that if he touched his skids down, the helo could be swallowed, Shane hovered just inches from the ground, praying that the heavy ash wouldn't clog the engine and cause the bird to stall.

The three men and both women began dragging the children onto the bird. Rachel was next, and then it was Kirby's turn, but she stumbled, and when she tried to stand up, she risked getting decapitated by the whirling rotor, which wasn't anything like her at all.

It was Quinn who shoved her head down and literally threw her into the Black Hawk. Then he and Zach jumped on, as well, and Shane lifted off as the roar became deafening.

He was almost at treetop level when the earth opened, swallowing up much of the clinic as sparks of lava lit up the sky like tracers.

"Are you all right?" Shane managed to ask Kirby past the painfully large lump in his throat.

"I . . . oh, shit." As a red stain blossomed on the front of Kirby's jungle camouflage shirt, she passed out.

Rachel looked at Shane, who was trying to multitask between worrying about Kirby and fighting the roaring heat from the Ixtab and the heavy ash that was probably being sucked into his engines.

"I don't know who the hell you are," she said. "But you need to get us to a hospital. Because she's been shot."

63

After all the months he'd spent in hospitals, Shane could've lived the rest of his life without ever stepping foot in another.

But this was different.

Because Kirby was different.

The bullet had come close to killing her. She'd lost a lot of blood — even a drop was too much, to Shane's mind — and she'd been drifting in and out of consciousness for three days.

And all that time, despite coaxing from the others, and assurance that they'd take his place for a time, he'd refused to leave her side.

"Shane?"

The soft voice jerked him out of a restless combat nap.

"You're awake." Relief and the huge lump in his throat clogged and roughened his words. He pushed himself out of the chair he'd been living in.

"I seem to be." She glanced around. "I know this is a cliché, but where am I? And what happened?"

"You're in a hospital in Costa Rica. You were shot when one of those kids Rachel insisted on bringing along accidentally discharged his damn pistol in the scramble to get onto the bird. It was touch and go for a while."

He didn't mention that they'd all given blood. "But Rachel and Mike kept you stable until we could get you here. And they, along with the surgeon, assured me you'll be as good as new in no time at all."

She pressed her fingers against her temple. "I don't remember."

"Being a doctor, you should know that's not surprising," he said. Her other hand was lying at her side on the sheet. He covered it with his, linking their fingers together. "Plus, they've been giving you enough Demerol to knock out a Clydesdale, to keep you quiet so you could heal."

"Oh."

A little silence settled over them. The awkwardness was odd after having become so comfortable with each other.

"Rachel and Michael took those kids to the halfway house place." Shane figured she'd want to know that. "I guess it does a pretty good job of rehabilitating them so they can return to their regular lives."

"That's nice. It was horrible what was done to them."

"Yeah."

Another pause.

"What about the dogs?" she asked.

"Dogs?"

"The dogs that CIA inside man drugged. Did they make it out alive?"

"Oh, yeah." Funny that she'd remember that, Shane thought. But then again, she'd always seemed to care more about others than herself. "They ended up at some animal rescue place. Seems they really weren't very good guard dogs, anyway. The people there think they'll make okay pets for the right family."

"I'm glad."

"To catch you up on all things political, Madrid was sworn into office this morning. She's made Castillo part of her cabinet."

"Keeping her friends close, but her enemies closer," she murmured.

"Exactly."

"What about Vasquez? Did he get away?"

"No. He was picked up on the tarmac at his private airfield and delivered to the authorities in Mexico. Where, apparently, he has an outstanding parking ticket dating back to a vacation he took in Mexico City with a mistress a few years ago."

"You're kidding."

"Hey," he shrugged. "I'm just the messenger. And you know how strict Mexico is about their driving laws."

"About the same as Monteleón," she said dryly.

"Yeah. But they're extraditing him to the Hague."

"Oh, the news just gets better and better."

"I hope you will still think that when I tell you what I've decided. Well, sort of decided, anyway." He took a deep breath. "I placed a couple calls to some guys I know in the Army. In the 160th."

"Your old unit."

"Yeah."

Her brow furrowed, making him worry that he'd misjudged the situation. "I've got an offer to teach flying at Fort Campbell. I report for duty in a month."

"Oh, that's wonderful." Her smile lit up the room, its brilliance burning away a bit of the awkwardness. "Will you be able to fly, too?"

"Yeah. Just not in combat situations. They say I can, and the leg sure seems to work okay, especially after what we put it through, but . . ." He shrugged. "I'd still worry."

"Well, this is still a good compromise, I think. So, it sounds as if you've got your life back on track."

"Well, that's the thing."

He couldn't believe she didn't know where he was going with this. She was a smart woman, and while they might not know every detail about each other, like their favorite movies, songs — stuff like most people talked about on those early getting-to-know-you dates they'd never had — she knew his mind. And his heart.

The same way he knew hers. Which was the important thing. Shane figured they had the next fifty years to work their way through the details.

"Fort Campbell's in a real pretty place," he said. "It straddles the border between Tennesee and Kentucky."

"I've never been there."

No. She wasn't going to make it easy on him. But why should she? After what he'd done to her.

"Maybe, when you get out of here . . ."

But not right away. She'd need some time to get her strength back. Maybe go lie on some tropical beach, soak up some sun, make love, drink some mai tais, make love again. Maybe, he thought on a burst of optimism, make a baby.

"I'd like that," she said when he brought up the beach. But not being a total idiot, he decided to keep the baby part to himself for now.

"Great, great."

Jesus. Why was he so tongue-tied? He'd practiced this speech a million times. Even called the States and tried it out on Sabrina and Cait, both of whom had assured him it was irresistible. But his carefully thought-out words had gone flying out the window.

"I promised my parents I'd be home for Christmas."

"Isn't that funny? I'd forgotten all about the holiday."

"You've been a little preoccupied. And unconscious."

"Well, there was that," she agreed.

The silence hovered between them, as thick as early morning fog.

No mission had ever made Shane this nervous. Not even that last flight in the Kush, when he'd seriously thought he was going to die.

"I was wondering if you'd like to come with me. Unless you had plans of your own."

"My parents are doing Christmas in Germany this year. Apparently, there are lots of festivals in all these small towns. It's a big deal, they tell me."

"Sounds cool."

"Yes. Though I have to admit, Germany isn't exactly my favorite place."

Yep. Here came that crawling part Quinn had warned him about. Shane braced himself, fully prepared to grovel over his screwup when he'd sent her away.

"So, sure, Christmas on a ranch in Oregon sounds lovely," she surprised him by saying. "Will there be snow?"

"Probably."

"Growing up in San Diego, I've never experienced a white Christmas. And the only cows I've *ever* seen are the dairy kind, so that'll be different. If your parents won't mind the company."

"They'd love it. I told them all about you."

"Oh?" She tilted her head. She may have appeared cool and collected, but the way her fingers had begun gathering up the sheet, he realized he wasn't the only one who wasn't feeling exactly at ease with this conversation.

He wanted to drag her into his arms. But he didn't dare touch her. Not until he said what he needed to say.

"There's something else," Shane ventured. Just go for it. He shoved his hands through his hair, took a deep breath, and said, "Look, here's the deal. Remember when you suggested working at Landstuhl?"

"That would be a little hard to forget. Though I am trying," she said dryly.

"Well, I made a few more calls —"

"Nothing personal." She held up a hand. "Well, actually, it *is* personal. Did I mention Germany isn't exactly my favorite place?"

Because of him. But that might change down the road, too, Shane allowed himself to think on a little burst of enthusiasm. Maybe they'd take one of those Christmas tours. Maybe even a family trip with the kids.

"No. This was to Campbell. There's a hospital there. And with so many troops being rotated overseas, they have an opening for a civilian trauma physician. It's not traveling the world for WMR, but Rachel said you seemed like you were getting a little burned out on that —"

"You spoke to Rachel? About me?"

"Well, yeah. Because I figured she's your friend, and since she and Michael are going to be working together for WMR —"

"They are?"

"Didn't I tell you that part?"

"No. I believe you skipped a step."

"He's gotten someone to take over running his free clinic. Seems he has this yen to see the world and do good, and apparently she enjoys her work —"

"She loves it. Which makes her either a madwoman or a saint. Or maybe both."

"Well, anyway, I ran the idea of you maybe going back to trauma, which you seemed to enjoy. But in a regular hospital, where you can actually follow up on your patients. And since it'd be a civilian gig, you wouldn't have to worry about getting deployed anywhere. Like Germany."

"And we'd be at Fort Campbell together?"

"Shit." He dragged his hands through his hair again. "I'm not doing this very well, am I?"

"I suppose that depends on what *this* is."

He dug into his pocket. Pulled out the box he'd kept with him for all these months. "I bought this online. Well, not exactly online. I mean, I found it, but my brother, he actually went and checked it out for me first. I had it with me that day in the Kush. I was going to find you and ask you to marry me."

"You were?"

"Yeah. I was. Because as crazy as it was, because we sure as hell hadn't had any kind of normal, getting-to-know-each-other type of relationship, I loved you, Captain Dr. Kirby Campbell. I loved you then, and I love you now.

"And I want to marry you. And have

children with you, and grow old walking hand in hand on the beach, or a forest, or just rocking on the front porch, watching our grandkids throw sticks for the dog."

"We're going to have a dog?"

"Well, not if you don't want one. I mean, if you're allergic, or —"

"I love dogs."

"Is that a yes?"

"Of course it is," she said. "I love you, Shane. I've loved you forever. Since that very first day in the CSH."

"You just fell for my ass."

"It was a very fine ass. Still is, as a matter of fact. But I fell for rest of you, too. And now that I've decided to give up that giving-up-on-men idea, I can't think of anyone I'd rather make babies with.

"As for Fort Campbell, Tennessee and Kentucky sound lovely. But I'd be willing to go to Timbuktu. So long as we are together."

She opened the box. Drew in a quick breath as she took in the ring he'd never been able to get rid of.

"It fits," she murmured, slipping it onto her finger.

"Of course it does. Just like us."

"You certainly took long enough," she complained prettily.

"I know. And you can feel free to remind

me of that every year on our anniversary. But at least I had one thing going in my favor."

"And what's that?"

He lowered his smiling lips to hers. "Night Stalkers never quit."

ABOUT THE AUTHOR

JoAnn Ross lives with her husband and two fuzzy little rescued dogs in the foothills of the Great Smoky Mountains. Visit her Web site at www.joannross.com.

We hope you have enjoyed this Large Print book. Other Thorndike, Wheeler, Kennebec, and Chivers Press Large Print books are available at your library or directly from the publishers.

For information about current and upcoming titles, please call or write, without obligation, to:

Publisher
Thorndike Press
295 Kennedy Memorial Drive
Waterville, ME 04901
Tel. (800) 223-1244

or visit our Web site at:

http://gale.cengage.com/thorndike

OR

Chivers Large Print
published by BBC Audiobooks Ltd
St James House, The Square
Lower Bristol Road
Bath BA2 3SB
England
Tel. +44(0) 800 136919
email: bbcaudiobooks@bbc.co.uk
www.bbcaudiobooks.co.uk

All our Large Print titles are designed for easy reading, and all our books are made to last.

DATE DUE

BRODART, CO.   Cat. No. 23-221

THE POWER OF MONEY
IN CONGRESSIONAL CAMPAIGNS
1880–2006

Congressional Studies Series
Ronald M. Peters, Jr., General Editor

THE POWER OF MONEY
IN CONGRESSIONAL CAMPAIGNS
1880–2006

DAVID C. W. PARKER

UNIVERSITY OF OKLAHOMA PRESS : NORMAN

Library of Congress Cataloging-in-Publication Data

Parker, David C. W., 1973–
    The power of money in Congressional campaigns, 1880–2006 / David
C.W. Parker.
        p.   cm. — (Congressional studies series ; v. 6)
    Originally presented as the author's thesis (doctoral—University of
Wisconsin.
    Includes bibliographical references and index.
    ISBN 978-0-8061-3903-6 (hardcover : alk. paper)   1. Campaign
funds—United States—History.   2. United States. Congress—
Elections—History.   I. Title.
    JK1991.P37 2008
    324.7'80973—dc22
                                                                                    2007033996

The Power of Money in Congressional Campaigns, 1880–2006 is Volume 6
in the Congressional Studies Series.

The paper in this book meets the guidelines for permanence and
durability of the Committee on Production Guidelines for Book
Longevity of the Council on Library Resources, Inc. ∞

To the mother who gave me life,
the wife who sustains my life,
and to the girl who makes life funny:
Gloria, Hilary, and Sadie Sue

CONTENTS

LIST OF FIGURES

LIST OF TABLES

ACKNOWLEDGMENTS

I would like to thank the University of Wisconsin–Madison for providing me with a Dissertator Fellowship, which allowed me to focus on research and writing during my last year in graduate school. Generous financial support from the Manuscript Society, the Institute for Humane Studies, the Kosciuszcko Foundation, the Hoover Presidential Library Association, and the University of Wisconsin–Madison Graduate School paid for trips to the manuscript collections scattered across the country. Without this assistance, chapter 4 might not have been possible.

All the staffs at the many manuscript collections I visited provided quality assistance as I waded through the paper remains of lengthy and distinguished Senate careers. In particular, I am grateful to Terry Birdwhitsell at the University of Kentucky, Alan Virta at Boise State University, and Frank Mackaman at the Dirksen Center for providing me with helpful leads and tips.

Intellectually, I owe a large debt of gratitude to my teachers and mentors in the political science department at the University of Wisconsin: David Canon, John Coleman, Ken Goldstein, Ken Mayer, Virginia Sapiro, and Byron Shafer. Their inspiration is woven throughout the ensuing chapters, and any remaining mistakes or omissions are mine alone.

John Coleman and Ken Goldstein deserve special mention. John is a magnificent advisor, and his dedication to excellence both in teaching and the scholarly pursuit of knowledge is the proverbial beacon on the hill for all to follow. And Ken, who leads the Wisconsin Advertising Project, generated and generously supplied much of the data upon which chapters 5 and 6 rest.

The Undergraduate Research Scholars program at the University of Wisconsin matched me with a terrific research assistant, Mary Triick. Talented, bright, and energetic, Mary did much of the research for chapters 1, 4, and 7. I hope she enjoyed learning from me as much as I did from her, and I know she will succeed in whatever endeavor she chooses.

Steven Gerencser and Neovi Karakatsanis lent their advice and wisdom on marketing, and Elizabeth Bennion read a substantially revised theory chapter. The reviewers, Anthony Brown and John Pitney, provided excellent comments and feedback that strengthened the text immeasurably. Ron Peters, the series editor, was especially helpful in sharpening the theoretical contributions and shaping a dissertation into this book. I would also like to thank Matthew Bokovoy, the acquisitions editor at Oklahoma. His strong support for the project from the very beginning made it a reality.

My father-in-law, Doug Wilson, a lifelong student of history, cheerfully accompanied me on two research trips and provided able assistance. My parents, Charlie and Gloria Parker, encouraged my intellectual curiosity from an early age. Without their endless love, support, and dedication to education, I would never have had the courage to seek a graduate degree.

My wife, Hilary, has been with me since the beginning of this odyssey. She has read scores of drafts without complaint, tirelessly fixing my split infinitives and relentlessly pressing me to make opaque points crystal clear. This book's dedication is but a small down payment on all that I owe her. And to my young daughter, Sadie Sue, thank you for reminding Dad that more than resources rule.

THE POWER OF MONEY
IN CONGRESSIONAL CAMPAIGNS
1880–2006

CHAPTER ONE

THE PUZZLE

The standard story about congressional campaigns is that parties dominated the process in the nineteenth century, but lost control to candidates around the middle of the twentieth century. As the story goes, party dominance was once predicated on control of the nomination process, the production of ballots, the tithing of politicians, and access to voters. By the 1940s, progressive election reforms and the arrival of mass communication tools had loosened the party's grip on the electoral process. Party-centered campaigns became something altogether different. With open access to the airwaves, candidates had the ability to communicate their own personal merits and accomplishments directly to voters.[1] By the late 1960s and early 1970s, political scientists proclaimed the arrival of the new candidate-centered campaign where the candidate raised the money, made the decisions, formed the strategy, and ran a campaign downplaying party affiliations or party issues. The role of the political party—formerly nominator, bankroller, and campaign manager extraordinaire—diminished markedly.

This story is incomplete, however. Some candidates in the late nineteenth century raised money, sought nominations, and campaigned on their personal qualifications; at the midpoint of the twentieth century, some candidates still relied on the party to run the show. Parties did not lie prostrate before candidates in the television age; rather, parties underwent a period of revitalization. The following three narratives suggest the campaign picture is much more complicated than the standard story implies. Campaigns should not be thought of as candidate- or party-centered based on their historical setting. They should be considered something else entirely.

NEWLANDS: A PARTY OF ONE

Francis Newlands had been bitten by the political bug, and he desperately wanted to be a legislator. A native East Coaster who had moved to California as a young man, he had many attractive qualities. His immense fortune was one. It allowed him to purchase all the modern electioneering tools available. In preparation for a Senate bid, Newlands founded the California Democratic League, an organization designed solely to advance his candidacy.[2] Despite these advantages, his gambit failed. Sensing brighter political prospects in Nevada, he packed up and moved to Carson City.

Once there, Newlands wasted little time in pursuing elected office. Within a year of establishing Nevada residency, he ran for Congress as a Republican. It mattered not that the state's lone house seat already had a Republican occupant. Newlands boldly challenged him for the party's nomination. Losing did not deter Newlands, for he tried again just two years later. Leaving nothing to chance this time around, Newlands spent the modern equivalent of more than $1 million of his own money, sending out brochures detailing his issue positions to nearly every voter in the state.[3] The third time was the charm: Newlands won and went to Washington.

His political loyalties were always his own. A member of the Democratic Party while residing in California, he became a Republican because that party dominated Nevada. Later, having been sent to Washington as a Republican congressman, Newlands joined a third party in ascendance throughout the West. Once this third-party movement had been defeated resoundingly in the next presidential election, he returned to his Democratic roots. Notwithstanding his particular partisan affiliation at any given moment, Newlands never toed the party line. He forged his own political path, frequently taking stances at odds with his party of the moment, particularly on issues of monetary policy.[4]

Francis Newlands, by any measure, ran candidate-centered campaigns. He spent his own money, built his own organizations, made his own decisions, and maintained no partisan allegiance. His successful congressional bid took place in 1892, during the era of strong parties and partisan campaigns. How did Newlands escape the party's thumb so easily? In an age when parties dominated the provision of electoral resources, why did Newlands eschew the party and craft his own reputation, organization, and voting coalition? Existing campaign theories do not satisfactorily explain his actions.

PRIMARIES AS BACKROOMS

Of course, party leaders can exercise influence over candidates by controlling the nomination process. During the late nineteenth and early twentieth centuries, congressional district conventions composed of county and town delegates usually chose each party's nominee for Congress. Progressive activists, who viewed these nominating conventions as undemocratic and prone to the dominance of party bosses, pushed to open the process to the party rank and file with direct primaries. Some party leaders, on the other hand, found the convention process chaotic and difficult to control. Instituting direct primaries might be one way to break the control of local factions dominating conventions, reduce fraud, and incorporate a changing electorate into the party selection process while reasserting the party's authority.[5] The question is whether, at the close of the twentieth century, direct primaries had contributed to the decline of party bosses as Progressive reformers wished or had helped party bosses recover their influence.

The number of competitive primaries is one indicator of Progressive failure or success. In 2000, less than 30 percent of the Democratic and Republican nominations for Congress were contested by more than one candidate.[6] Why so many uncontested primaries? The power of incumbency is one explanation. Able to amass considerable election resources, sitting members of Congress simply deter the best challengers from emerging. As nearly all members of Congress seek reelection in a given cycle, many nominations leave the incumbent unchallenged within his own party. But another reason seems to be the involvement of the party power brokers whom the Progressives hoped to banish from the process. Today, Republican and Democratic Party leaders can secure nominations for favored candidates by clearing the field of prospective challengers. And perhaps more aggressively than even nineteenth-century party bosses dared, parties and candidates use the primary process to influence the selection of general-election opponents.

Party officials fear the primary free-for-alls about which Progressives dreamed. They might bruise the party's eventual nominee and unnecessarily drain scarce resources best devoted to the general election. In 2002 the National Republican Congressional Committee (NRCC) became mired in controversy when its chairman, Representative Tom Davis, played favorites in two primary elections in Kansas and Ohio. Hoping to knock off Democratic congressman Dennis Moore, Davis upset some Kansas Republicans by attending a fund-raiser for Jeff Colyer, one of three candidates for the Republican nomination. In Ohio, Davis publicly proclaimed that of all the candidates vying for the Republican nod in an open district, former Dayton mayor Mike Turner had the best chance of winning the general election.[7]

Hardly banished, party leaders maintain or create chamber majorities by boosting primary candidates deemed most competitive for the general election. Indeed, in the 2002 Louisiana Senate race, party leaders encouraged more Republican candidates to enter the primary not to give voters additional choices but to hold incumbent Democratic Senator Mary Landrieu to under 50 percent of the vote. In Louisiana, if a candidate receives more than 50 percent of the primary vote, there is no general election. By flooding the primary with additional Republican candidates, the party hoped to draw enough support away from Landrieu to guarantee a general election in the fall, which would present the best opportunity to retake the seat.[8]

Nor have the parties shied away from interfering in the other party's nomination process. California Democrat Gray Davis's advertising foray into the 2002 Republican Party primary damaged White House favorite and front-runner Richard Riordan just enough that the more conservative and less qualified businessman (and presumably weaker candidate) Bill Simon captured the nomination.[9] This tactic was by no means new, and in fact it may have been pioneered by the National Republican Senatorial Committee in 1996 when it launched a series of ads attacking both of Oregon's Democratic Senate candidates. The committee also sent mailers to Democratic voters in New York during the 2000 cycle, reminding them of former Republican-turned-Democratic representative Mike Forbes's frequent support of Newt Gingrich.[10]

While primaries could have freed candidates to forge independent links with the electorate, the Progressive vision failed. By 2000 the ability of parties to influence and control the nomination process, far from dwindling, took on new life. How did parties turn such an ostensibly decentralizing reform into an instrument of candidate control during an era of candidate-centered campaigns? If the communications revolution and progressive reforms provided candidates with the tools to pursue autonomy, why can parties exert so much influence over the nomination process? Existing party and campaign theory does not provide an answer.

THE RISE OF NATIONAL PARTIES

When political parties began to emerge in their modern form during the early to mid-nineteenth century, they mimicked the government's federal structure. Committees were formed at the local, state, and national levels—and their power relationship mirrored the government's. Local and state organizations controlled the bulk of the resources, decided who ran for office, and made the strategic campaign allocations. The national committees of both parties—and later the congressional campaign committees—merely redistributed funds aggregated from subscriptions paid by state committees (see chapter 3). Although the campaigns themselves reflected national issues and debates, their structure was decentralized, and power flowed from the bottom up. This was true especially during off-election years, when no national candidate topped the ticket.

As the national government grew in scope and authority during the 1930s, so too did the national party committees. The national committees accrued more and more power, with state and local committees losing much of their individual autonomy. Resources were gathered increasingly at the center, and decisions eventually followed. State and local parties had become, to a large degree, subordinate to each party's national committees, just as many states increasingly played second fiddle to the federal government.[11]

Contrasting with the late-nineteenth-century pattern, national Republicans, not local leaders, took charge of massive get-out-the-vote (GOTV) drives in 2000 and 2002. Speaker Dennis Hastert and Majority Whip Tom DeLay planned a campaign for the 2000 election cycle to "raise money for a new . . . multimillion dollar campaign to convince more Republicans to vote."[12] A similar effort was spearheaded by DeLay two years later that "transported some 8,000 volunteers to tight races across the country."[13] The Democrats engaged in similar national turnout initiatives. The extensive involvement of the national committees in an activity once well beyond their purview is one indication of their transformation into centralizing authorities.

During the 2002 midterm elections, the Bush White House made a concerted effort to develop a wholly coordinated national campaign making full use of the presidency. According to *Washington Post* reporter Dan Balz, "Tight coordination also means tight control. . . . The White House and the national party committees told Republican candidates that if they wanted to receive financial and other assistance, they had to include in their campaign plan a commitment, backed with money, to bid for the Latino vote, including the use of Spanish-language media where possible."[14] Democrats did not stand by idly. In both Arkansas and South Dakota, the Democratic Senatorial Campaign Committee transferred more money in 2002 to these candidates than they could raise independently.[15] Late-nineteenth-century committees never would have involved themselves in local campaigns so extensively.

The dominance of the national party committees at the close of the twentieth century departed significantly from the historic pattern of local control. The increased activity of national party organizations in congressional, state, and local elections has blurred the lines of authority between the various party units. With power radiating from the center to the periphery, the modern structure of American party organizations has more in common with European parties than with those of America's past. How could a centralized party structure, national in scope, rise successfully during a period of reputed party decline? And why, during the golden age of parties, were partisan structures so decentralized? The late twentieth century may be more appropriately labeled the parties' golden age.

PARTY-CENTERED, CANDIDATE-CENTERED, OR WHAT?

These three narratives present a series of puzzles left unexplained by existing party or campaign theory. The first describes what seems to be a mass-communications campaign. A candidate takes control of his own electoral destiny, raises his own money, constructs an organization to advance his candidacy, sends a direct-mail piece focusing on his qualifications and issue positions, and even challenges an incumbent for his party's nomination. But Newlands lived at the end of the nineteenth, not the twentieth, century. Existing theory holds this is not possible: parties ran campaigns, decided nominations, and summoned voters to the polls in the late nineteenth century. Only after a series of democratizing reforms such as the direct primary, the Australian ballot, and the invention of radio and television could a candidate have the wherewithal to seek elective office without the party's express support. And yet Francis Newlands used those same methods and tactics fifty years before many of these reforms had either taken place or established a firm institutional hold.

The latter two stories paint a colorful picture of party strength, vitality, and resurgence at the close of the twentieth century. Neither scholars nor longtime political observers anticipated the revitalization of America's political parties. The age of television advertising supposedly sounded the death knell of the political party machine.[16] But parties, as these stories demonstrate, turned a deaf ear to the prognosticators. They neither died nor skulked away at the close of the twentieth century. Today they strategize against the wishes of their candidates, dabble in nomination skirmishes, and rely on centralized hierarchical structures that are national in scope. As Gerald Pomper notes, political parties over the past twenty years have seemed more like those envisioned in E. E. Schattschneider's wildest dreams: responsible, responsive, and vigorous.[17]

Political actors do not campaign in isolation: they are affected by the strategies and behaviors of others. In contrast, much of the literature on the campaign strategies and behaviors of parties, candidates, and interest groups has itself evolved in isolation—or been developed, as Gabriel Almond might put it, by scholars "sitting at separate tables."[18] Congressional scholars take David Mayhew's proclamation that members of Congress are "single-minded seekers of reelection" as axiomatic.[19] It is not surprising that much of the literature on congressional elections explains electoral success or failure by focusing largely on the efforts and strategies of individual candidates. Party scholars would not necessarily agree with this candidate-centered campaign focus. Perhaps candidates did dominate campaigns in the late twentieth century, but candidates clearly took a backseat to the party throughout most of the nineteenth and early twentieth centuries. To understand campaigns, should one focus on candidates or parties?[20]

This book argues that neither party scholars nor congressional scholars have the story right. In some eras, political parties appear to dominate campaigns, whereas in others, candidates do. Why? The question is seductively simple, yet political science has had a difficult time explaining how the country moves from one pattern to another, why change happens when it does, whether the process is cyclical or linear, and how relationships between parties, candidates, and interest groups evolve. By combining the insights of congressional and party scholars with an emphasis on institutional rules, this book develops such a theoretical framework. Although this framework includes interest groups (their role in the campaign process is considered occasionally), I focus largely on the shifting relationship between political parties and candidates during congressional elections.

What distinguishes this book from the scores of others on campaigns? First, by spanning 120 years, this book is not about any one particular campaign, but many. As a result, these pages rely heavily on historical studies of congressional elections, biographies of members of Congress, and journalistic accounts of campaigns, in addition to the statistical analysis of roll-call votes, campaign advertisements, and voter surveys. Some students of history may find the depictions of certain campaigns, though informed by the past, less detailed than they might prefer. As my goal is to develop a theory of campaigns explaining the behavior of and strategies pursued by parties and candidates, broad brushstrokes are necessary. Second, unlike many works about elections, this book is not primarily about voter behavior. Although the perceptions of voters are the subject of chapter 6, the main focus is on elite strategies, tactics, and activities. Finally, the emphasis on electoral rules provides a more complete understanding of why candidates, parties, and interest groups pursue particular campaign strategies and which actor dominates at any given point and in any given campaign setting. Over the past two decades, political scientists have rediscovered the importance of institutions in shaping the behavior and strategies of political actors. This emphasis on institutions and rules preoccupies those who study the legislative process, and it has not stimulated as much work among those studying campaigns.[21] This is regrettable, as institutions provide the context within which political actors adopt campaign strategies. Indeed, if rules govern how legislators act within the House or Senate chamber, do they not also play a role in the decisions those actors make on the campaign trail? This book endeavors to fill this important gap by suggesting that resources and the rules producing them are the key to understanding when candidates or parties dominate campaigns and the strategies pursued by each.

THE ARGUMENT: RESOURCES RULE

Congressional candidates must gather resources to compete in elections. What are the resources at the heart of the theory? Although resources can be a variety of things, the resources of chief concern here are money and reputation. The ability of actors to gather these resources depends on the electoral rules. Put differently, rules can favor certain political actors in the resource race, and this affects candidate behavior on the campaign trail and the strategies that candidates pursue for victory. For example, party strength in the late nineteenth century was in part a function of parties' ability to tithe civil servants and control the nomination process via conventions. The introduction of civil service reform and primary elections undercut these enormous party advantages. Candidates responded by building personal organizations independent of parties and by taking stances at odds with their parties because the institutional changes allowed candidates to do so when it made sense in the district. Rule changes generate observable consequences, including how congressional candidates seek party nominations; how they organize, finance, and execute campaigns; and which issue reputations or agendas they choose to advertise to voters. Throughout the following pages, the important and oft-overlooked effects of changing election rules are considered by tracing these observable consequences.

As electoral rules evolve, the ability of political actors to accumulate the resources necessary to compete in elections is altered, benefiting some political actors over others. Campaigns are not universally party- or candidate-centered in a given era, but they are always resource-centered. For instance, campaigns can appear more or less candidate-centered depending on the resource situation facing ambitious office seekers. Resource-poor candidates readily accept party dominance if parties can bring favorable results. Otherwise, candidates will take matters into their own hands. This explains why candidates like Francis Newlands eschewed the party when running for Congress in the 1890s and why candidates during the Federal Election Campaign Act (FECA) regime campaigned on party issue themes and voted increasingly with the party in spite of having television and radio readily available to them for more candidate-centered appeals. By following the resources, our understanding improves as to why political actors engage in particular campaign behaviors or strategies. Existing candidate-centered and party-centered language tells us how campaigns should look at a particular moment, but it lacks a longitudinal component accounting for the host of anomalies in each period contradicting our theoretical expectations. The false demarcation of campaign eras—the late twentieth century as the age of the candidate, the late nineteenth century as the age of party-centered politics—has led scholars astray.[22] The resource theory in this book provides a new dynamic model that better explains these campaign anomalies.

The resource theory relies on the rational model of behavior. It assumes that political actors are goal oriented and pursue strategies designed to maximize their prospects of attaining those goals. Candidates run for office presumably because they want to win. Parties support candidates to achieve or retain majorities, which allow them to implement party programs. Interest groups desire to maximize influence with elected officials and legislative outcomes consistent with their preferred policies.

Some may consider the assumption of rationality problematic.[23] Certainly, candidates may have many reasons to run for office other than winning, and third parties often run candidates without any hope of winning. It is well known that congressional careerism did not emerge until the last few decades of the nineteenth century, so the reelection motive is a problematic assumption in earlier periods.[24] And political actors, while attempting to make rational decisions, can make mistakes. Lacking full information, they may underestimate their need for resources or misjudge their opponent's abilities, leading to what appear in retrospect to be irrational decisions.[25] In short, the assumption that all members at all times desire to maximize their election prospects is simply not valid under all conditions. Candidates might have goals other than winning, and even those who do can act irrationally. In defense of the assumption of rationality, the object of this or any other theory is to provide better explanation and prediction. The price of adopting a goal-centered assumption about candidate, party, and interest group behavior is lost specificity. What is gained, however, allows the creation of a dynamic theory that explains a certain amount of campaign behavior over the long term. This is a trade-off worth making, especially as the reelection goal for officeholders (or the election goal for candidates) is not far-fetched and has provided a sound foundation for congressional scholarship over the past three decades.

The book proceeds as follows. Chapter 2 briefly reviews the parties and campaign literature, providing the book's theoretical grounding. The inability of the party-, candidate-, or service-centered models of campaigns to explain satisfactorily the conflicting empirical evidence becomes apparent through this discussion. The resource theory of campaigns is then developed and offered as an alternative. A quick sketch of elections from the late nineteenth century through the close of the twentieth century, informed by this new approach, concludes the chapter and frames the discussion for the empirical chapters that follow.

The remaining chapters test the resource theory against a wide range of evidence, demonstrating that institutional rules affect the strategies of political players and the relationships between those players across time. Chapters 3 and 4 examine the mutual relationships between candidates and parties at the close of the nineteenth century and during the middle of the twentieth, using primarily qualitative and some limited quantitative data. Both test the proposition that the rules of the electoral game affect the party-candidate nexus by evaluating how state party organizational capacity affects the distribution of campaign resources. As will be shown, the "freeing" of candidates from party control, defined by some scholars as candidate-centered politics, was a less-than-uniform phenomenon and occurred unevenly during both periods. Whether candidates utilized "candidate-centered" tactics depended less on the arrival of new communication technologies than on each state's level of partisan institutionalization. The more established the partisan institutional environment, the better state parties are able to adapt to new electoral rules and campaign technologies to provide candidates with electoral resources.

Chapters 5 and 6 focus on FECA and contend that the federalization of the campaign process created incentives for political parties and interest groups to alter resource accumulation and dispersal strategies. As a result, resource-hungry candidates transformed their legislative behavior, and citizens began to perceive candidate and party reputations differently. Chapter 5 begins with an overview of FECA, detailing how it allowed for the nationalization of political parties and increased their financial strength. Do members of Congress respond to this renewed financial strength of parties? This question is examined first by testing the relationship between member support on unity votes and contributions received from the party. Finding that money does influence floor behavior, I examine the congressional television advertisement themes of the parties and their candidates during the 2000 campaign to determine whether parties can establish particular issue agendas and foist them on their candidates. In 2000 candidates and parties ran on similar issue agendas distinct from their opponent's (economics for Republicans, entitlements for Democrats). Furthermore, parties—especially the Republicans—set issue agendas onto which their candidates latched. The willingness both to back the party on unity votes and to use party-developed issue agendas in their advertisements is compelling evidence that candidates shape their campaign strategies in response to their individual resource needs.

The voter—missing from the story thus far—becomes the central focus of the last empirical chapter. Having found that parties can affect the advertising strategies of candidates, I ask whether voters notice. A brief discussion of the voting literature is followed by an exploration of the connection between political parties and candidates in the minds of voters. Contrary to the perceived wisdom, this connection has not weakened in the late twentieth century, as voters easily identify candidates with partisan issue messages. Coming full circle, I evaluate the relationship of party spending to voter perceptions, revealing that parties can use their financial muscle to shape their public persona.

The final chapter reflects upon the possible consequences of the Bipartisan Campaign Reform Act (BCRA) of 2002. With the U.S. Supreme Court upholding most of the provisions of McCain-Feingold in *McConnell v. Federal Election Commission* (2003), electoral rules have undergone their most sweeping change in nearly thirty years, drastically altering the resource landscape.[26] Here I consider how the new rules change the political fortunes of parties, candidates, and interest groups while creating a new set of unintended consequences for reformers. Finally, some thoughts are offered on how the new information environment engendered by reform might affect representative democracy. An epilogue offers some additional implications of the resource theory and considers its importance for understanding the mass-elite linkage.

Congressional campaigns are about convincing voters to choose one candidate over another. The result may have a particular policy or partisan consequence, but at their very heart, elections are about voters choosing someone to represent them. Presumably, those individuals who decide to go through the often arduous task of running for Congress want to win. Winning, of course, requires two essential ingredients. First, candidates must relay a message that convinces a majority of voters on election day that they are the best for the job. Second, they must have the money to communicate that message to voters. The message and the means to communicate it are the tools that candidates need to compete for the attention and commitment of voters. Without both, candidates simply cannot win.

As simple as all of this may sound, the desire of candidates to win elections and to craft a message and broadcast it to the voting public serves as the foundation of the resource theory. Candidates, seeking victory, carefully select campaign strategies designed to maximize their electoral fortunes. Should they create their own personal organization, raise money themselves, and run on their own biographies? Or should they rely on parties to provide the financial means and the political message? The following chapter offers the resource theory as an answer.

CHAPTER TWO

THE RESOURCE THEORY
OF CAMPAIGNS

To win elections requires adopting the appropriate strategy. Which voters should be targeted? When? And with what messages? The selection of the correct strategy, however, is only part of the winning formula. Strategy is affected by the available resources. The best strategy might require extensive polling and the saturation of television with negative ads during the final weeks of the campaign. If money is in short supply, however, the strategy requires modification. In brief, the strategies selected by political actors are related to their ability to accumulate electoral resources. The ability to gather resources successfully depends on the electoral rules that shape the resource environment facing candidates, parties, and interest groups. As these rules evolve, who can gather what resources in what amounts also changes. This is the heart of the resource theory of campaigns.

By acknowledging that electoral contexts change and modify campaign strategy, the resource theory builds on existing scholarship. While existing campaign models suggest that campaigns and eras are uniformly party-centered or candidate-centered, resource theory emphasizes a focus on resources to best explain the strategies selected and employed by political actors. Whether any given campaign is dominated by so-called candidate- or party-centered campaign activities depends on the resources available to the political players involved. This is determined by the constitution of electoral rules, the capacity of political actors, and the tools available to engage in voter communication and mobilization. The resource theory acknowledges that context matters, providing a more powerful and predictive theory of political behavior than current campaign models.

This chapter reviews the evolution of congressional campaigns and the historic relationship between candidates, political parties, and the electorate, as well as the role of institutional rules in shaping the electoral terrain. After evaluating existing models of campaigns, I have developed a dynamic resource theory to explain the campaign behavior of political actors. A sketch of congressional campaigns over the century demonstrates that the resource theory provides a better explanation of the historical campaign patterns. The chapter concludes with some thoughts on how the resource theory might offer new insight into the nature of the elite-mass linkage central to the functioning of democratic governance.

THREE MODELS OF CAMPAIGNS:
PARTY-, CANDIDATE-, AND SERVICE-CENTERED

Much of the existing literature on campaigns is derivative of scholarship on political parties, and this literature is difficult to present succinctly. Nevertheless, this body of work has contributed three basic campaign models: candidate-, party-, and service-centered. Party-centered campaigns have empirical and normative roots in early-twentieth-century work on political parties and the later writings of responsible-party advocate E. E. Schattschneider.[1] The candidate-centered campaign model, whose advocates include Barbara and Stephen Salmore, developed as an alternative to this party-centered model in the 1970s and 1980s largely to explain a wide range of empirical observations diverging from the expectations of the party-centered model.[2] The final model, the service campaign, is most fully articulated by Paul Herrnson. It argues that parties are adaptive institutions that have become auxiliaries to candidate-campaign organizations during the last quarter of the twentieth century.[3] These three models conceive of congressional campaigning differently, but they share the same basic flaw: lacking a dynamic element, they cannot explain the evolving strategies of political actors in response to new electoral contexts.

Campaigns are about strategic decisionmaking and emphasizing a particular "product." One way to explore the differences between the three models is to separate campaigns along the decisionmaking and product dimensions and then distinguish between strategic control in the campaign and the product emphasized by the campaign. Table 2.1 neatly summarizes most of the existing campaign literature.

Party-centered campaigns are those where parties make the strategic campaign decisions and are the actual product emphasized or sold to voters. The early descriptive literature on parties and the responsible-party literature fit in the lower-right quadrant of the table. Candidates hew the party line with clear and distinct positions, various party units (national, state, and local) provide a unified front to the electorate, and parties disperse funds and engage in activities assisting their respective candidates in party-centered campaigns.[4] In short, parties are the primary resource organizers and the centerpiece of the campaign itself.

Candidates are the main actors in candidate-centered campaigns: they make the decisions, and the campaign is about their skills, attributes, and issue positions. Candidates are largely self-recruited. They assemble their own organizations and have complete responsibility for the conduct of the campaign.[5] David Agranoff called this candidate-centered campaign a "new style" and outlined four key components: (1) The candidate is the focus of the campaign; (2) campaign management is undertaken by professionals independent of the party and responsible to individual candidates; (3) issue positions are tailored to individual electorates; and (4) communication is controlled by the candidate, dispensing candidate-generated messages through a variety of methods not controlled by the party.[6] Summarizing, candidates benefit from the collection and dispersal of resources according to the candidate-centered campaign, and parties do not play a large role nor are they the product being sold. In table 2.1, these campaigns are in the upper-left quadrant.

In the service model, parties are neither dominant nor irrelevant. Parties play a role in campaigns at the behest of candidates by providing resources and engaging in some strategic decisionmaking with, and occasionally independent of, candidates.[7] The product being sold, however, is still the candidate and his reputation rather than the party's reputation. Because of increased party involvement in decisionmaking, these campaigns fall in table 2.1's lower-left quadrant.

The party-oriented campaign approximates the resurgence of party in campaigns above and beyond the provision of resources to candidates noted in recent literature.[8] In this particular scheme, candidates largely

Table 2.1. Various campaign models

		Campaign is about?	
		Candidate	**Party**
Campaign run by?	**Candidate**	Candidate-centered	Party-oriented
	Party	Service-centered	Responsible-party/ Party-centered

dominate campaign strategy and resource gathering, but the campaign product presented to voters is the party's reputation and agenda. Perhaps the best example would be the 1994 congressional campaign. The House Republican leadership conceived of a bold plan to nationalize the election around a discrete number of issues. Many prospective members of Congress (but few incumbents) made this "Contract with America" a centerpiece of their campaign while retaining overall strategic control. In this case, the Republican Party became the campaign's product, but the candidate retained authority as a direct distributor coordinating the sales staff.[9]

THE LONGITUDINAL INADEQUACIES OF THE PARTY-, CANDIDATE-, AND SERVICE-CENTERED MODELS

The party-, candidate-, and service-centered campaign models generally describe and predict relationships between political actors during campaigns and the strategies those actors employ to seek electoral success only during particular eras. As electoral rules changed the nature of the resource game, political actors responded with new tactics and strategies altering the relationships between political parties, candidates, and interest groups.

These relationships, properly conceived, are fluid rather than static. The strengths and weaknesses of each model will be considered in turn.

In the late nineteenth century, party committees dominated the election process rather than individual candidates.[10] Local and state party organizations—not individual candidates—fueled get-out-the-vote activities, the production of propaganda, fund-raising, and campaign communications.[11] Interest groups, with rare exception, lacked the organizational might or resources to contest elections.[12] Formal party organizations held the keys to party nominations; direct primaries emerged slowly as a countervailing force. Candidates and interest groups bowed to the parties and futilely engaged in electioneering outside one of the two major parties.

Although the party-centered model accurately depicts the general conduct of campaigns in the late nineteenth and early twentieth centuries, parties collapsed as the electoral plates shifted beneath them. The Pendleton Civil Service Act of 1883 effectively denied parties a major source of financing. Until its passage, political parties at the federal, state, and local levels demanded that government workers give a percentage of their salary to the party organization. Despite the new protection provided to civil servants by Pendleton, parties still controlled the nomination process, produced ballots, and published position papers on which many candidates relied. Nevertheless, party machines needed new financial resources. No longer financially independent, parties were disadvantaged relative to candidates and interest groups after 1883. Additional progressive-style reforms, such as the Australian ballot and direct primary, further diminished the party's electoral authority. Interest groups and candidates soon began to play a larger role, and the party faded somewhat from the campaign picture.

Many party machines succumbed to progressive municipal reforms such as nonpartisan local elections, charter revision, and the institution of civil service exams. Others rotted internally, unable to husband the resources necessary to maintain their electoral coalitions. The rise of the New Deal administrative state further eroded machine support by making the provision of social services by local party bosses to immigrants and lower-class voters unnecessary.[13] Finally, many machines fell victim to the suburban exodus of the middle class.[14] Less mobilization, less voter contact, and less campaigning typified the political parties of the 1960s relative to their historical counterparts.[15] Unable to attract a core of committed supporters, parties contributed less to the electoral success of their candidates.[16] The binds of party loosened, allowing congressional candidates the opportunity to slip free.

Less significant as a recruitment and socialization mechanism, scores of congressional candidates opted out of long party tenure to make independent bids for office.[17] Electoral success no longer required climbing the party ladder and waiting in line. Many candidates eschewed partisanship and used reputations established in careers outside politics to advance their electoral prospects. Although labeled as Republicans or Democrats, these candidates ran their own campaigns, hired their own staff, and largely funded their own efforts.

New and improved communications technologies made contacting an electorate independent of the party easier. Older methods of campaigning—walking the ward, distributing party literature, holding party rallies, and the like—required strong parties to organize, demanded significant manpower, and transmitted largely partisan messages to a largely partisan audience.[18] Radio, television, phone banks, and mass mailings cost more than traditional methods, but required neither extensive labor nor party organizations to execute. Messages could also easily vary by tone, content, and appeal, which allowed candidates to create their own voting coalitions. Candidates relied increasingly on their own monetary resources and fund-raising abilities to acquire these new campaign tools.[19] Lacking the financial resources and finding the capacity to mobilize a partisan electorate less useful, the power of political parties diminished. Candidates held the upper hand because they could fund those activities most important to attracting increasingly independent voters. Resurrected by responsible party scholars as a normative ideal in the mid-twentieth century, the party-centered model as an empirical tool became less useful as time progressed.[20] The candidate-centered campaign developed as an explanation of observations at odds with the early literature on parties.[21]

As the Pendleton Act set into motion a long chain of institutional changes undermining parties and the party-centered model, time and new electoral contexts also undercut the empirical usefulness of the candidate model. Although it was an accurate picture of congressional campaigns between the 1940s and the 1970s when party power had eroded, the candidate model as a reflection of political reality declined in value thereafter.[22] Empirical evidence accumulating after the 1970s demonstrates the point.

If candidates dominate election finance, they should spend an ever-increasing share of money on their own election efforts when compared to other political actors. A glance at figure 2.1 suggests otherwise: party expenditures as a percentage of candidate expenditures have actually increased over time. In 1980, party expenditures on House and Senate candidates accounted for only 8 percent of the total spent by congressional candidates. With the advent of soft money in 1992, that figure jumped to 12 percent and soared to more than 28 percent by 2000. Party organizations have not withered on the vine. If campaigns are candidate-centered, then why do party organizations persist and indeed flourish?

If candidates compete locally rather than nationally, one might conclude that candidates generally vary their ideological appeals according to each district's individual ideological needs.[23] Members must explain and frequently defend legislative records to the public; therefore, their public records serve as a reasonable proxy for appeals generated during the campaign. Figure 2.2 plots the ideological distance between Democratic and Republican House members multiplied by the inverse of each party's standard deviation from 1960 to 2000. As the trend indicates, the parties increasingly polarized while simultaneously exhibiting less ideological variation internally.[24] In other words, House members within each party established increasingly uniform voting records. If these voting records are proxies for campaign messages, it appears that members of Congress broadcasted messages to a uniform distribution of voters. This implies national, not local, campaigns undertaken by congressmen. The candidate campaign model, predicting greater variability within the parties, does not clearly anticipate this outcome.

If campaigns are about candidates and candidate messages, a consequence might be declining partisanship among voters. In a campaign environment bombarded by messages centering on candidate characteristics and district-specific issue positions, party identification becomes a less-than-useful voter cue. With candidates constructing less partisan issue reputations, the electorate's party identification is no longer reinforced and might diminish over time. A cautious interpretation of the evidence indicates this might be the case. Figure 2.3 shows a steady decline in the public's identification with either of the two major parties from 1960 to 2000 during the period of so-called candidate-centered politics. Increasing candidate-centered activity coincides with declining mass partisanship.

Split-ticket voting, however, presents a different picture. If candidate-centered campaign advocates are right, any relationship between votes

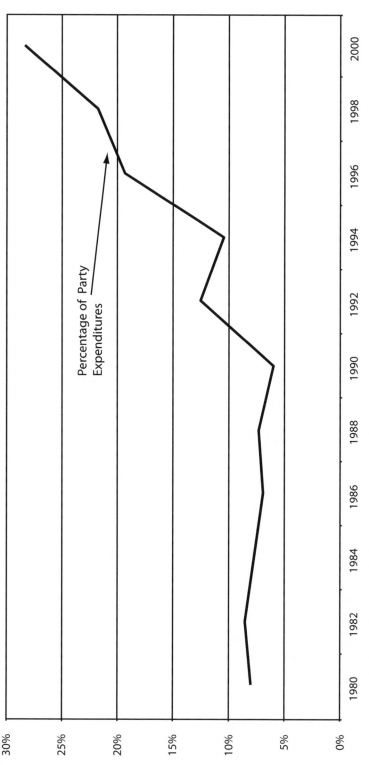

Figure 2.1. Party expenditures on congressional campaigns as a percentage of total candidate expenditures, 1980–2000. Compiled by the author from Ornstein, Mann, and Malbin, *Vital Statistics on Congress, 2001–2002*. Party expenditures include hard dollar contributions made by congressional campaign committees to congressional candidates, coordinated expenditures made on behalf of the candidates by those same committees, and committee soft money disbursements from 1992 onward. Candidate expenditure figures from which the party percentage is calculated were first adjusted by subtracting party contribution amounts. Adjusted for inflation to 2004 dollars.

23

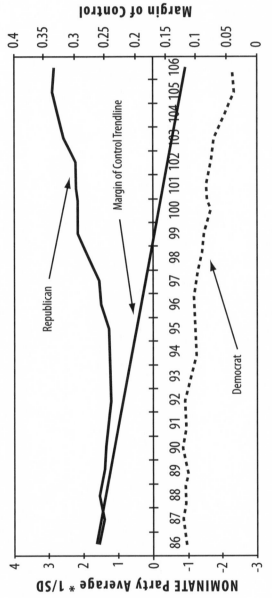

Figure 2.2. Interparty polarization and intraparty cohesiveness of the House of Representatives, 86th–106th Congresses, 1960–2000. The lines represent the average NOMINATE score for each party in the House of Representatives, multiplied by the inverse of that party's standard deviation. The Margin of Control Trendline is the seat margin by which the majority party controls the House and is expressed as a percentage of total seats. Compiled from NOMINATE scores provided by Keith Poole at http://voteview.uh.edu/, and information about historical partisan divisions in the House of Representatives provided by the clerk of the House at www.house.gov.

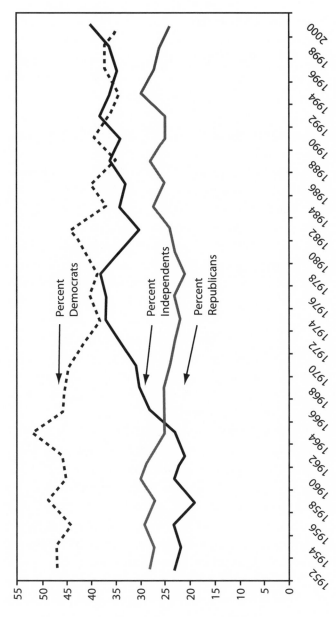

Figure 2.3. The declining partisan electorate, 1952–2000. Republican and Democrat identifiers consist of respondents self-identifying as either strong or weak partisans in the National Election Study. Independents are those who call themselves either true independents (a four on the seven-point Party Identification Scale) or a partisan flavor of independent (a three or a five). Compiled by author from the NES Cumulative File, 1948–2000, located at www.umich.edu/~nes.

cast for president and Congress should diminish over time. As each campaign is about a specific candidate, voting decisions should be made independently. Figure 2.4 is illustrative. It graphs the percentage of congressional districts that voted for one party for president and another for Congress between 1900 and 2000. In 1972, 43 percent of the congressional districts split their vote between a congressional candidate from one party and a presidential candidate from another. After 1972, with the exception of 1984, the percentage of split-ticket districts slowly declines. In 2000, the percentage almost equaled that in 1952. Similarly, the National Election Studies show a surge in split-ticket voting in the early 1970s and a slow decline thereafter (see figure 2.5). How can this decline be reconciled with the candidate-centered model? The candidate model of campaigns does not provide an answer.

According to service-centered campaign advocates, political parties in the 1970s and 1980s evolved into service organizations designed to supplement and aid congressional candidates during campaigns.[25] According to one chief proponent, Paul Herrnson, "Parties are malleable institutions that are continuously adapting."[26] What does this mean? In the 1980s and 1990s, national party organizations dominated local and state organizations, acting primarily as "aggregators, distributors, and directors of campaign services."[27] They began to recruit, manage, and raise funds aggressively for candidates in ways similar to the strong state organizations of the late nineteenth century. Parties, in short, had revitalized and adapted to a new campaign environment.

The service model does portray congressional campaigns in the 1980s and 1990s fairly accurately. Party organizations did reemerge to play a more vigorous campaign role, especially at the national level. Unfortunately, this newer campaign model shares the same problem with the party- and candidate-centered versions. Why and how do parties adapt? More specifically, can parties always adapt successfully? What, in particular, caused the institutionalization of national parties in the 1980s? Will parties always act as brokers, or might they revert to some other form? The service model also sheds little light on candidate, party, and interest group campaign dynamics over time. This is especially problematic as the recent passage of the Bipartisan Campaign Reform Act in 2002 might undermine the ability of parties to collect and dispense financial resources. Parties may be unable to continue to "convince, induce, or otherwise persuade state and local party organizations, political consultants, PACs, and

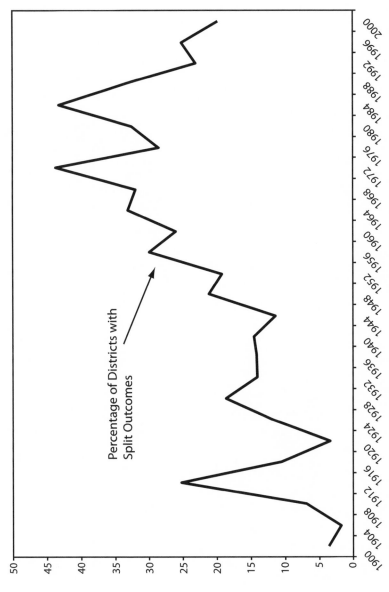

Figure 2.4. Split-ticket congressional districts, 1900–2000. Compiled by the author from Ornstein, Mann, and Malbin, *Vital Statistics on Congress, 2001–2002*. Data for 2000 obtained from the *Rhodes Cook Letter* at www.rhodescook.com.

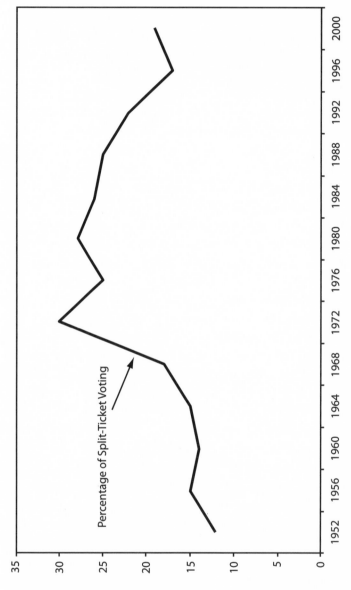

Figure 2.5. Split-ticket voting, 1952–2000. Compiled by author from data obtained from the National Election Study's table 9b.2 in *The NES Guide to Public Opinion and Electoral Behavior*, available at www.umich.edu /~nes.

candidates to follow their advice when conducting election-related activities."[28] The service-centered model again brings attention to the problems inherent with static campaign theories. It is clear that the campaign function of parties, candidates, and interest groups shifts according to new circumstances: the dominance of any one political player is neither constant nor a given. Something must explain the rise and fall of parties, candidates, and interest groups over time.

All three campaign models fall short because they do not consider changing institutional circumstances. They are descriptive accounts of a static campaign system, rather than models predicting relationships over time. An alternative theory based on competition for resources can better explain elite behavior during congressional campaigns both at a given point in time and longitudinally. Political actors make decisions about electoral competition and select strategies set against a background of institutional rules and contexts. By examining how those institutional rules create opportunities for and restraints on political actors, we can better explain how political actors communicate with voters and establish winning coalitions.

How can the pieces of the three competing models of campaigns build a new theory of congressional campaigns?[29] The literature on urban political machines provides a useful start. Some historians view political machines as service providers to individuals and subgroups either unsatisfied with or excluded by legally sanctioned governmental organizations and the "structural context."[30] This structural context, which affects the ability of city government to provide essential client services, includes things like the city's charter, the relationship of the city to the state's power structure, the city's financial wherewithal, and the urban growth rate. Essential services consist of urban necessities such as paved streets, sewage, and social welfare programs. Businessmen, native citizens, and immigrants are some of the many clients requiring these services. When a city's structural context in a city created a service gap, a political machine generally arose to fill it. The federalization of social welfare in the form of the New Deal closed many gaps established by structural contexts while the economic ascent of assimilated ethnics diminished the need for services among many subgroups.[31] The result? The widespread decline of urban party machines.

Steven Erie, in *Rainbow's End*, disputes the notion that New Deal led to universal machine decline. Why did some machines collapse shortly after the federal expansion of the welfare state, while others survived more or less intact?[32] The answer is the complex role of the New Deal in machine decline. Machine survival depended on the ability of bosses to gather and maximize resources. This allowed the provision of services to grateful clients who, in return, rewarded bosses with their political support. In other words, bosses collected resources to assemble and sustain the minimum winning coalitions, which allowed them to retain political power.

The expansion of the voting universe made successful resource management harder, making the size of minimum winning coalitions larger and more costly to obtain. Generally, bosses faced two options: they could restrict suffrage (keeping coalitions small and inexpensive) or increase the resource pool to meet the needs of the enlarged voting pool (paying for bigger minimum winning coalitions).[33] Machines able to strike the right resource balance retained some or all of their political power even after the New Deal diminished the need for the machine's social services.

BUILDING THE RESOURCE THEORY OF CAMPAIGNS

Erie's approach is an excellent way to theorize about campaigns more generally. A campaign can be defined as the process by which actors interested in government outputs and/or the control of government amass and expend resources to win elections, either individually or collectively. Like the bosses of urban machines, political actors who are engaged in election campaigns pursue the maximization of resources to enhance the prospects of victory. How successfully these actors play the resource contest affects the strategies and tactics they select during congressional campaigns.

A wide variety of things can be thought of as campaign resources: expertise, candidate quality, party popularity, the number of ads aired and pamphlets printed. All can be viewed as essential to successful electioneering. Winning an election, however, boils down to establishing a reputation, communicating it to the voters, and assembling a minimum winning coalition. The probability of winning an election equals a candidate's prospective share of voter support, which is a function of a candidate's share of monetary and reputation resources. In order to increase the probability of winning, candidates select campaign strategies that increase their share of monetary and reputation resources. These strategies depend, in part, on the electoral rules and electoral situation facing candidates.

Voter support and monetary resources are fairly easy to define and measure. Voter support essentially represents the campaign's prospective vote. In other words, what is the size and intensity of a candidate's public support at any given point during the campaign? Obviously, the greater the breadth and depth of a candidate's support among the electorate, the greater the probability of winning an election. A campaign's prospective vote can be estimated with public opinion polls and surveys.

Monetary resources are the expenditures made during a campaign by actors actively engaged in electioneering. Specifically, this includes expenditures made by candidates, the two major parties, and interest groups. Expenditures eventually become brochures, political ads, polls, and staff—in short, any good, service, or resource purchased in order to influence an election outcome broadly defined. Monetary resources may be easily visible and identifiable (such as those listed in FEC reports after 1974), or they can be partially obscured from public view (such as soft money expenditures and transfers). This includes money spent on so-called issue advocacy advertisements that are not designed to advocate expressly for or against the election of a candidate, but typically encourage a candidate to pursue a particular legislative action.[34] These ads are considered monetary resources because they can affect a candidate's reputation resources, either improving or diminishing the probability of winning the election.

The second resource concept, reputation, is multifaceted. It is similar to Gary Cox and Mathew McCubbins's "record" or John Petrocik's issue ownership.[35] According to Cox and McCubbins, the probability of winning an election is a function of individual and national party characteristics. It is important to distinguish between the two, as it is the interchange between party and individual reputations that can guide the selection of campaign strategies by political actors. Individual reputation resources are the bundle of issue stances and personal characteristics attributable to the candidates competing in any given election. What is the candidate's position on gun control, or his prior political experience? Personal characteristics might also include a candidate's ability to bring money and projects back to the district, something Congress scholars stress when discussing the incumbency advantage.[36] A party's reputation resources are a function of party characteristics separate from those of individual candidates bearing the party labels in a given race. These characteristics, according to Cox and McCubbins, can be thought of as "a summary of past actions, beliefs, and outcomes with which [a party] is associated."[37] For example, what is the party's record on taxes? Has the party successfully implemented its campaign promises? Has the party governed during a period of economic prosperity? Is the party tainted by scandals and corruption? Reputation resources are a sum of both parties' and candidates' public records in a given campaign.

A candidate and party record, however, is more than a summary of actual issue stances and characteristics. Citizen perceptions and beliefs shape party and individual candidate records. Additionally, a party record consists of "the central tendency in citizens' beliefs about the actions, beliefs, and outcomes attributable to the national party" that is distinguishable from the tangible party actions, beliefs, and outcomes.[38] Popular perception similarly conditions a candidate's record. In other words, the roots of reputation are the actual actions of candidates and parties, but public assessment further shapes reputation. To illustrate, a candidate may have voted against raising taxes, but voters might yet perceive that candidate as a tax and spender. Similarly, the Republican and Democratic Party platforms may contain similar language on federal conservation programs, but voters (rightly or wrongly) may perceive Republicans as the party of industrial polluters. Reputation is based on public actions by parties and candidates, but the perception of those actions by the public is an important manifestation.[39]

Crudely, there are two types of reputation indicators: those tapping public perceptions and those measuring the public record of political actors. Measures of the first might include questions in the National Election Studies (NES) asking respondents to place parties and individual candidates on 100-point feeling thermometer scales. These items indicate how a particular individual perceives a candidate or a party in light of that candidate's or party's record of achievements and attainments. There are many others, such as questions asking respondents to place parties and candidates on issue dimensions and the like.[40]

The second piece of reputation can be measured by canvassing party platforms, candidate voting records, or their actions while in office. Perhaps the best measure of party or candidate actions in the public sphere are campaign communications. These display the record of public actions in a manner that parties or candidates wish to be perceived. It is the rhetoric in the campaign itself that contains this aspect of the reputation resource. Items such as press releases, party platforms, candidate issue statements, leaflets, flyers, or television advertisements are all potential measures of the public record component of reputation resources. Reputation as a resource is particularly important in a campaign, as much of what political actors expend monetarily shapes reputations to the benefit or detriment of a particular party or candidate.

Money and reputation are critical to winning elections, but what about people power? In the late nineteenth century, well-oiled political machines consisted of party workers going door to door canvassing voters, while in the twentieth century volunteers engage in all sorts of campaign activities, ranging from manning phone banks, distributing literature, and participating in rallies. Today, parties, candidates, and interest groups have renewed their attention to the "ground game."[41] Why is people power neglected in the resource theory?

Volunteers are definitely an important part of campaigns, donating valuable time and talent for which political actors would otherwise have to pay. Indeed, volunteers may actually be more valuable than paid campaign assistance. Compare a phone bank staffed by workers paid nine dollars an hour with one run by ideological and passionate volunteers, and the difference becomes apparent. Should volunteers and free labor be treated as a separate resource? The ability to use people power effectively depends on monetary resources. Volunteers might give time and talent to a campaign, and they might be better than staff paid to do the same functions, but they need phones to man, letters to stamp, or signs to display to crowds. Volunteers also need to be effectively coordinated, generally by experienced and paid staff members. Ultimately, a campaign cannot be sustained on people power alone. The efforts of volunteers theoretically can be assigned a monetary value and require the use of material substances to be effective. For the purpose of the resource theory, it is not necessary or even desirable to distinguish volunteer activities and "people power" more broadly from the concept of monetary resources.[42]

RESOURCES, CONTEXTS, INSTITUTIONAL CONSTRAINTS, AND UNCERTAINTY

Money and reputation are essential campaign ingredients that political actors employ to win elections. The proportion of the ingredients depends on the relationship of reputation (individual and party) to monetary resources. This relationship is configured by three things. First, the need for and utility of resources vary according to electoral rules. Money might, for example, be the resource most critical to electoral success depending on how these rules are constituted in a particular period. Second, neither reputation (individual or party) nor monetary resources are independent. A candidate's reputation certainly can influence his ability to gather monetary resources, while the expenditure of monetary resources influences the perception of a candidate's reputation. Third, political geography itself affects how candidates and parties are perceived, the monetary resources available to them, and the resource amounts required to win. Although electoral rules provide the context within which political actors make strategic decisions and the need for particular resources in a given historical period, the utility of party, individual, and monetary resources vary considerably from congressional district to congressional district. Together, these three points suggest a complex and nuanced relationship between resources, prospective vote share, and the probability of winning an election. Each is worthy of further elaboration.

President Bush personally coaxed Congressman John Thune, who aspired to South Dakota's governorship, instead to challenge incumbent Senator Tim Johnson in 2002.[43] In a tight race, Thune lost to Johnson by 532 votes. Bush again pressed Thune to run for the Senate in 2004, this time against Senate Minority Leader Tom Daschle. Thune prevailed by accusing Daschle of being out of touch and attacking Daschle's use of obstructionist tactics to thwart the president's agenda. Reputation in 2004 seemed to be the key, and perhaps Daschle's partisan reputation dragged additionally on him during a presidential election year, unlike Johnson, who had the benefit of running for reelection during a midterm election. Thune had many useful personal qualities: he had political experience, widespread name recognition, the ability to raise funds, and popular support.[44] Thune's political attractiveness to the White House underscores an important point about the relationship between reputation and monetary resources: they do not operate in isolation. Thune's reputation as a hardworking legislator who remained in touch and popular with South Dakotans made him a serious contender. This reputation, which drew the sustained attention of the president and his political advisor Karl Rove, would also attract positive attention from donors. The point is that a candidate's individual reputation can improve the prospects of attracting the monetary means to run a competitive campaign.

A party's reputation as a collective likewise can depress or enhance a candidate's financial prospects. Senate Majority Leader Bill Frist's recent attempt to restrict the filibustering of judicial nominees may have proven wildly popular among the party's conservative base, but it may have hurt the party in the business community, which is so important to its financial well-being.

Monetary resources similarly condition candidate and party reputations. Candidates and parties spend money to achieve positive recognition with voters. As both political actors spend money, the presumptive goal is the improvement of that reputation relative to the opposition's. How successful campaign expenditures and advertisements are at moving voters is a topic of much heated debate.[45] Nevertheless, political actors implicitly assume that a campaign's sound and fury matters to voters. Why else would they spend so much time and energy raising and spending millions of dollars each campaign cycle? Candidates and parties believe that money affects reputations, so it is important to represent this in any model of candidate, party, or interest group behavior.

The ability of candidates to raise money and the reputation they enjoy (both individual and partisan) depends not only on their individual talents and standings. Monetary and reputation resources are also a function of one's electoral surroundings. Republican candidates campaigning in traditional Democratic strongholds face an uphill struggle compared with their counterparts in more Republican areas. Raising money is difficult, especially if the challenger faces a well-regarded incumbent. Donors—particularly those residing in the district—shy away from giving to such a Republican challenger unless the prospects of victory are enhanced by an incumbent scandal, demographic shifts, or a redrawn district. District voters, too, will be difficult for the Republican candidate to persuade. As voters will be favorably predisposed to Democratic candidates, Republican candidates will find that their party reputation is less useful in the district as a means to attract voter support. Even consciously avoiding the Republican brand name may not matter much. Simply carrying the party label may lower the candidate's own reputation among the electorate. At the very least, his reputation will probably be depressed relative to his Republican counterparts running in GOP-leaning districts. Unfortunately, a strategy of choosing to avoid Republican issue positions may carry a monetary risk: moving away from the party may make the candidate more attractive to independent and Democratic donors, but at the possible cost of losing some party dollars. Demographics alone suggest that Republicans running in poorer, blue-collar, and more urban districts will face an electorate less predisposed to hearing their message. This affects how they are perceived, the money they can raise, and ultimately their prospective vote share. The resource terrain for Republican candidates in Democratic fortresses, and Democratic candidates in Republican strongholds, is treacherous to navigate.

This discussion highlights the interdependent nature of reputation and monetary resources, as well as the importance of political context. It should be clear that the resource model sketched thus far requires three amendments in order to address the complexities of these resource relationships. First, money and reputation do affect voter support, but they are not purely exogenous variables; rather, the ability to raise money depends on reputations and vice versa.[46] Second, district characteristics can indirectly affect voter support because they provide the foundation on which reputation and monetary resources rest. In other words, Republican candidates find it easier to raise money and are better regarded in Republican-leaning districts than in those populated by Democrats. Third, these district characteristics can directly affect voter support for candidates. Electoral rules and the immediate political circumstances faced by political actors in individual congressional districts work together to affect how resource decisions are made.

Electoral rules are the final piece of the resource model. How these rules evolve over time affect the utility of resources for political actors and how these resources relate to each other. This resource relationship is not fixed: money may matter more in the FECA era than previously, while a party's reputation may increase the probability of a particular candidate's election more when the electorate strongly identifies with the parties. To represent how resources affect the probability of winning elections across time, each resource must be weighted to account for its variable impact. These weights represent the institutional constraints provided by electoral rules that define the relative importance of each resource element in a particular historical or political period. Electoral rules provide the boundaries within which actors engage in campaign activities. The constitution of those electoral rules and how they change affects the relationship of resources and actors to the overall probability of winning an election at a given point in time.[47] As these factors will vary across eras and across districts, generalizing is a challenge.

As an illustration, party reputation might trump monetary resources when electorates are highly partisan and active, and electoral rules such as strip ballots and party nominating conventions favor party over candidate-control in congressional campaigns. Electoral rules, in this scenario, emphasize reputation resources over monetary resources in a candidate's efforts to build winning coalitions among voters. Note the implications of this for a prospective congressional candidate in the nineteenth century. To build a winning electoral coalition, he needs to establish a reputation consistent with the party. As parties dominated the collection of monetary resources during the period, toeing the party line is even more important to the prospective candidate. A spotless adherence to party positions is a near necessity when facing an overwhelmingly partisan electorate.[48] Not only is the party important to securing a winning voting coalition of committed partisans, but the party is nearly the only way the candidate can communicate his reputation to the voters. Understanding how electoral rules affect the relationship between money and reputation is critical to understanding how the resource theory establishes the framework for resource allocation decisions made by political actors.

Although electoral rules shape a campaign's context, they do not always alter the resource-gathering decisions and strategies of political actors. Electoral reforms only affect the resource balance between actors if they are difficult to evade. Reforms cannot hope to influence the activities of political actors unless the costs of noncompliance are high enough to compel behavioral change. The Pendleton Act, for example, provided for the appointment of a commission to oversee implementation of the civil service reforms as well as stiff penalties for violators; those found contravening any provisions of the act faced fines up to $5,000 and three years in prison.[49] State party organizations continued to tithe state office workers, but the ability to reach federal civil service employees became difficult at best.

Later reforms either did not contain strong enforcement mechanisms or did not clearly designate responsibility for evasions. A particularly damning flaw hampering early-twentieth-century reform efforts permitted candidates to establish multiple organizations allowing easy contravention of reporting requirements and campaign contribution limits. The Tillman and Hatch Acts' corporate and labor contribution restrictions could be evaded easily. In the case of corporations, individual businessmen and their families simply gave their own money to candidates in lieu of company dollars. Labor countered by forming the first political action committees for the purpose of funneling member funds to candidates. Most important, the lack of an administrative agency with the capacity and ability to enforce penalties undermined the effectiveness of both laws. Political actors could openly flout the law because no one could stop them. Only electoral rules imposing high costs on those choosing to ignore the new regulatory reality will alter successfully the cost-benefit analysis of political actors.

Electoral rules are but one factor affecting the relative weight of resources on a candidate's probability of winning an election. Monetary resources may be weighed differently depending on the assets a candidate brings to the campaign. Considering that challenger spending may be more efficient than incumbent spending, money may matter less and personal reputations more for incumbents.[50] Even more important, however, is the variation in institutional capacity across campaigns, states, and time. For example, the ability of political parties to engage in electioneering not only is related to their resource capacity but is also a function of how deeply embedded they are institutionally and culturally in a particular locality or state. This is especially important in the late nineteenth through the mid-twentieth century when local and state parties had resource advantages unmatched by the national party committees. This "institutional thickness" can help buffer parties from the effects of changing rules, and the weights in the resource equation can also represent the density of the partisan environment in a given state. The institutional capacity of candidates and interest groups can also similarly vary.[51]

It is worth discussing institutional capacity in reference to political parties in some detail, as this is an important concept for the theory and the empirical chapters that follow. What is institutional capacity? Political parties develop processes to distinguish themselves from the external environment and to function with increased efficiency similar to other institutions. Nelson Polsby claims that an organization which is well-bounded, more complex, more universalistic in its procedures and automatic in its decisionmaking is institutionalized and has a high institutional capacity.[52] As parties in particular evolve and develop increased institutional capacity, they encourage and reinforce the development of partisan cultures and behaviors among the electorate, just as the institutionalization of Congress led to the creation of "norms of behavior" among its members. Party institutionalization provides stability for office seekers. Parties that have become institutionalized have established boundaries, procedures, and routines that, if effectively utilized and managed, lead to well-funded canvasses, get-out-the-vote efforts, and the guarantee of a certain percentage of voter support owing to a highly partisan electorate. The price for certainty is a loss of candidate flexibility: candidates stump for the party and advocate for the party's issue positions. This is generally worth the candidate's cost, as party reputation and resources weigh more heavily in the resource equation where and when parties exhibit a higher degree of institutional capacity.

In regions with infant party organizations, rapid population influxes, and weak norms of partisan behavior, the latitude for independent candidate action, however, is simply greater by definition as well as necessity. Parties faced with these circumstances find it more difficult to establish a strong financial base or partisan armies to secure the vote. In these situations, candidates must amass resources individually to compete successfully. They may still identify as Republicans or Democrats and seek party assistance, but their campaign behavior should reflect the uncertain political environment they face. They will often raise their own money, stump the district themselves, and espouse issue positions possibly at variance with their party's platform. Overall, their actions will exhibit the independence necessary in a less institutionalized partisan environment with more uncertainty. It is easy, in short, to defy or simply ignore the party when they have little to offer. It is much harder when parties dominate the resource environment. Conversely, parties cannot easily control candidate behavior when they lack effective carrots and sticks. The variability of party institutional capacity across states and localities in part explains the observed variability of candidate strategic behavior in some eras.

A final point: the resource model so far developed expresses the winning of elections as a function resource *share* rather than resource *amount*.[53] This construction is important, both practically and theoretically. Practically, political actors compete with one another for resources. Resources are meaningful when put into context. Spending a million dollars might assure a candidate a House seat. The same amount of money looks much less formidable when the opposition and his allies spend twice as much. In terms of reputation, a candidate can be well loved and regarded, but is he loved enough when compared to his opponent? Pollsters frequently ask which party or candidate is best able to defend the country or improve the economy, underscoring the point that candidates and parties compete for the biggest share of the reputation pie. The concept of resource share best models the concept of resource gathering as expressed by Erie in relation to political machines.[54] The more reputation and monetary resources a candidate marshals relative to his opponent, the more his probability of winning.

Resource share also reflects the larger theoretical point that, although the only measurable resources are actual dollars spent or election returns, there is a nearly boundless resource universe over which political actors compete. Actual voters are only a small piece of the voter universe. In the case of a House election, the voter universe consists of the entire voting-age population of the congressional district who are legally eligible to participate. Monetarily, the resource universe consists of the potential as well as practical amounts political actors can spend in a campaign—and in theory, could include the entire Gross National Product of the United States (since foreign contributions and expenditures are prohibited by law).[55]

Although somewhat exaggerated (what candidate, interest group, or political party can lay claim to the entire economic output in the United States for the purpose of electioneering expenditures), the point is worth considering: campaign actors operate in a resource universe with boundaries well beyond the actual resources employed in any given campaign. Resources are finite and practical boundaries do exist: all the money in the industrial world cannot change the fact that only twenty-four hours of television time can be purchased in a day on any one network. Still, the theoretically unlimited resource universe creates uncertainty. An actor never knows how much is enough to push the probability sufficiently in the winning direction. His opponent might raise more money or gather more voters. This uncertainty pushes political actors to expend more than what is absolutely necessary to win a given election. This might explain why incumbents greatly outspend even the weakest of challengers, even after the cost of "scare-off" tactics are subtracted.[56] This concept of resource uncertainty is best viewed as an error term.

How well actors mobilize monetary and reputation resources affects how these actors relate to each other. If parties, candidates, or interest groups have funding mechanisms they independently control satisfying their resource needs, the ability of one group to dominate the electoral process is minimal. If, however, an actor finds that their resource capacity cannot meet their resource need, other players are empowered relative to that actor. This returns us to the concept of resource share: actors who amass a sufficient share of resources are advantaged. Resources provide the building blocks for the campaign strategies adopted by parties, candidates, and interest groups during elections.

EMPIRICAL IMPLICATIONS OF THE RESOURCE THEORY

The resource theory of campaigns can predict the relationships between candidates, interest groups, and political parties in a given historical period with a particular set of electoral rules. Recalling the preceding discussion, the relative importance of monetary and reputation resources varies based on electoral rules and institutional capacity. Not only can a particular resource be more important than others to the winning of elections in a particular period, but the political actor most efficiently and effectively utilizing that resource within an electoral and institutional context has the advantage in the campaign.

By examining at any given point in time the capacity of political actors to provide the electoral resources they require for electoral victory, scenarios suggesting how interest groups, parties, and candidates might be helped or hurt in the electoral process at particular historical junctures can be developed. To expand on the previous example, consider the resource capacity of candidates against one measure of party capacity, institutionalization (see table 2.2).[57]

1860s–1940s

In the mid-nineteenth century, parties dominated politics by controlling the nomination process and the production of ballots. Candidates proved their worthiness of party support with their loyalty and by forfeiting a portion of their salary to fund the armies of voters and poll watchers necessary to maintain electoral coalitions. The official machinery of government cemented political loyalties further. Patronage and a host of social services were provided at the municipal level in exchange for electoral support. The ability of the party to create minimum winning electoral coalitions and maintain them with the official machinery of the state allowed them financial self-sufficiency. As a result, the need to gather electoral resources outside the party apparatus was low. As political participation was high and widespread, mass mobilization efforts were required to win elections. Parties and their local machines were well suited to provide the manpower and money to fund these activities with

Table 2.2. Candidate and party resource capacity

| | | **Candidate Resource Capacity** | |
		Low	High
Party Institutionalization	High	Party Reputation Resource Need High Monetary Need Low Candidate Reputation Resource Need Low Individual candidates and interest group strategies are generally party-centered owing to the relative weight of party-controlled resources Relative weight of party reputation benefits political parties relative to other political actors *1860s – 1940s*	Monetary Resource Need High Candidate Reputation Resource Need High Party Reputation Resource Need High Interest groups, parties, and candidates pursue a mix of party- and candidate-centered strategies to achieve electoral goals Relative weight of all resources provides for interest group, candidate, and party parity *1980s – 2002(?)*
	Low	Monetary Reputation Resource Need High Candidate Reputation Resource Need High Party Reputation Resource Need Low Candidates and interest groups utilize candidate-centered strategies to achieve electoral goals Relative weight of monetary and candidate reputation resources minimizes need for party resources, requiring candidate-centered strategies by parties *1940s – 1970s*	Monetary Need High Candidate Reputation Resource Need High Party Reputation Need Low Candidates engage in candidate-centered campaign tactics; interest groups bypass parties and candidates with direct appeals to the electorate Parties struggle to remain relevant as candidates have adequate resources; parties must develop new ways to gather resources and utilize strategies centered around candidates or interest groups *Post-BCRA(?)*

money from the state.[58] In a system of self-perpetuating party power and finance, interest groups were disadvantaged in their efforts to engage in electoral politics. Party politicians typically utilized their positions of power to extract resources from interest groups not for electoral purposes but to enhance their personal wealth.

The Pendleton Act's passage in 1883 put the funding of parties in doubt. No longer able to rely on the state to fund a mass-based politics, parties needed money. At first, the source was big business. Later, it became individuals and labor, as well as other assorted interest groups. The lack of financial security for political parties and candidates gave interest groups more political influence than they held in the earlier part of the nineteenth century. Political coalition building still required mass mobilization of voters, however. Voting rates, though lower than the mid- and late nineteenth century, were still high, and women's suffrage expanded the voting universe. Although some interest groups such as the Anti-Saloon League engaged in political activities directly, it made sense to channel power and influence through political parties because of their still impressive institutional capacity.

1940s–1970s

The era of mass-mobilized politics did not last forever. After the 1890s, parties were under siege. They could no longer sufficiently finance their activities: they no longer controlled the nomination process, and the erosion of patronage hurt the party's ability to mobilize voters. To make matters worse, the boom in radio and television allowed for communication to occur directly between the candidate and voters and even between interest groups and voters. These conditions made candidate appeals more sensible. Both the need for resources and the parties' ability to fund their candidates were affected. Candidates needed substantial sums to finance their individualistic appeals to the populace, and they built organizations to raise the necessary sums without extensive party assistance. With fewer voters participating and identifying less with the parties, mass-based mobilization efforts became less relevant to political success. Parties had become weak.[59] In this situation, resource-needy candidates sought interest group money to fund their campaign efforts. The legitimatization of special interests by FECA encouraged independent organizations to become more involved in electoral politics, as did the FEC's favorable decision regarding corporate and union monies funding PAC overhead costs. Special interest groups began to form PACs in substantial numbers and these became a major source of money for individual candidates. In a time when it mattered less to get everyone to the polls and more to get select groups activated, interest groups, with their funds and their established means for reaching specialized constituencies, flourished electorally.

1980s–2002(?)

The 1974 reforms and their subsequent interpretation by the courts ultimately shifted the balance between interest groups and parties. At first, parties seemed disadvantaged by the contribution limits, but their position would improve over time. Individual and PAC contribution constraints put candidates in nearly full-time fund-raising mode. PACs found that they faced a blizzard of funding requests from candidates, but many PACs were amateur operations without the political expertise necessary to deploy their funds for maximum effect. Ironically, the very demand for PAC funds that arose from the candidate-centered campaign provided an opening for the parties.[60] According to Paul Herrnson, FECA "allowed the [Congressional Campaign Committees] to become major brokers with the PAC community and devote staff and resources exclusively to the purpose of matching PACs with appropriate candidates for their donations."[61] Candidates realized that even if parties were not necessarily providing the funds, parties played a critical role in directing PAC dollars toward their campaigns. And parties, of course, could contribute directly to candidates as well.

The advent of soft money merely replicated this pattern at a much higher scale, because now interests could donate hundreds of thousands of dollars directly to the parties, which the parties could then deploy on behalf of specific candidates through issue advocacy and independent expenditures. Candidate dependence on parties and interests grew, though candidates still did substantial fund-raising on their own. Parties needed soft money to fund their new efforts, while interests needed to donate or spend independently ever-larger sums to be noticed in the ocean of soft money. Interest groups and political parties had reached a rough parity in campaign finance by the mid-1980s, and this parity continued at the onset of the twenty-first century.

These sketches of the party-candidate interest group relationships over time provide a broad picture of prevailing historical patterns. They do not, however, preclude the possibility of other resource relationships existing in a given period. In the late nineteenth and early twentieth centuries, party organizational capacity varied across states and localities due to the uneven institutionalization of partisan structures. Local and state parties with deeper cultural and institutional roots better withstood the winds of change brought about by electoral reform. In the late nineteenth century, parties dominated the conduct of congressional campaigns relative to the mid-twentieth century. Nevertheless, congressional candidates made their own appeals in areas with low levels of partisan institutionalization, while relying on parties in the mid-twentieth century where the party was strong. As resource needs and strengths differ from campaign to campaign, variability within historical contexts should be anticipated. And as the ensuing chapters will demonstrate, the variability is empirically verifiable.

CONCLUSION

The resource theory acknowledges that electoral contexts change, and this explains how political actors alter their campaign behavior over time. Unlike existing static theories tying political actors to one particular campaign strategy, the resource theory claims that strategies depend on campaign resources. Political actors—whether prospective members of Congress, parties, or interest groups—must amass and expend resources to achieve electoral objectives. The ability of a political actor to accumulate the resources necessary to undertake any particular strategy ultimately depends on a period's electoral rules. Rules favor certain political actors in the resource race, which determine how actors campaign and the strategies they choose in pursuit of victory.

What distinguishes resource theory from the existing literature on congressional campaigns? Existing typologies of campaigns do not explain change over time very well. As demonstrated earlier, the behavior of congressional candidates on the campaign trail changed in ways inconsistent with the expectations for party-centered, candidate-centered, or service-centered models. The resource theory, by emphasizing the importance of electoral rules, provides a vehicle to explain how, why, and when candidates might respond to an evolving campaign environment. It also provides predictions that can be empirically tested. Do electoral reforms alter the ability of parties to provide their candidates with resources, and if so, does this alter the behavior of candidates in response? The answer is yes: electoral rules can alter the resource terrain for candidates, and candidates campaign differently in response. This alone is an improvement over existing models that do not provide a ready answer for the shifting strategies employed by congressional candidates over the past 120 years.

Some might claim that the resource theory is not a theory at all but at best a more nuanced typology. There is substantial agreement between the resource theory and existing typologies concerning the characterization of particular campaign eras: the party-centered, candidate-centered, and service-centered campaign models do appear to get the big picture in the late nineteenth century, the mid-twentieth century, and the late twentieth century right. But the main virtue of the resource theory—and why it is a theory and not a framework—is the claim that variability can and does exist across congressional campaigns within a given era. And this variability exhibits a pattern that is predictable. For example, late-nineteenth-century congressional candidates do exhibit largely party-centered behavior, but some do not. The resource theory predicts that those congressional candidates running in territory hostile to their political party, or in areas where party institutionalization is low, will seek opportunities to raise their own monetary resources and run on their individual reputations. And as chapter 3 demonstrates, the variability observed in how candidates portray themselves to the electorate fits this expected pattern.

In this chapter, a theory of campaigns was presented along with some empirical expectations. The next four chapters provide empirical tests of this theory across a range of historical settings, with a focus on how electoral rules provide the context in which candidates make campaign decisions. Special attention will be drawn to the way in which these rules highlight the need for a particular resource and how specific actors are benefited in the provision of the critical resource. The following chapter begins with congressional campaigns in the late nineteenth century, the so-called golden age of parties. Taking advantage of the variability of party capacity across the states, it is demonstrated that candidate campaign strategies depended on the ability of parties to provide campaign resources to candidates even in an era where parties had significant resource advantages. Congressional campaigns did not shy away from campaigning on individual reputations, establishing independent campaign organizations, and paying for it out of their own pockets when parties simply could not muster the appropriate resources to communicate with voters.

CHAPTER THREE

Pomp, Circumstance, and Rationality in the Late-Nineteenth-Century Congressional Campaigns

A t first glance, congressional campaigns in the nineteenth century fit the party-centered model of campaigns advanced by many political scientists.[1] Candidates received party nominations at conventions dominated by party activists and leaders. With platform committees drafting the party's positions, issue agendas highlighted national problems and debates. From Maine to California, congressional, presidential, and even gubernatorial candidates talked, argued, and jousted over tariffs, monetary policy, or postbellum reconstruction policy. One could not mistake the two parties on issues: Republicans stood for sound money and high tariffs, while Democrats favored silver-backed currency and freer trade. The party, with its army of patronage-induced poll workers and assessment-filled coffers, organized and implemented the campaign. To the casual observer, strong parties contained individual candidate ambition, shaped national political discourse, and funded electioneering.

Scratch the surface, however, and anomalies appear. If the office sought the individual, why did some congressional candidates actively pursue their party's nomination? If campaigns revolved around national issues and party positions adopted at national conventions, why did other candidates disavow party positions on the stump? And if parties held the purse strings, why did a few candidates use their own funds to purchase personal organizations? In sum, why were some office seekers engaging in candidate-centered behavior while others relied on the party to conduct and control their campaigns?

The need for electoral resources, constrained by institutional and electoral landscapes, molded candidate behavior. Relying upon party machines and their issue reputations made sense for numerous office seekers. Partisanship remained the cultural norm; indeed, political independence was widely disparaged. "The neuter gender is not popular either in nature or society," sneered Senator John J. Ingalls in 1886. Independents are "effeminate without being masculine or feminine; unable to beget or to bear; . . . doomed to sterility, isolation, and extinction."[2] On some occasions, however, the party either could not or would not provide monetary or reputation resources necessary for candidates to win. Even in the era of so-called strong parties, rational congressional candidates desiring victory occasionally distanced themselves from their parties and went it alone.

In this chapter the resource theory is applied to congressional campaigns in the late nineteenth century. Electoral rules tilted the balance generally in favor of political party machines that controlled monetary and reputation resources to which candidates required access. Party organizations, however, were not uniformly strong. The capacity of state and local organizations varied greatly in their ability to provide electoral resources to candidates. By focusing on the importance of state party institutionalization, it is shown that the seemingly idiosyncratic behavior of congressional candidates interested in securing their electoral futures during the late nineteenth century is not idiosyncratic at all. Even in an era dominated by intense voter partisanship and strong party machines, how candidates organized their canvass, pursued nominations, and took issue stances depended on the institutional capacity of state party organizations, which are the product of electoral rules. Weaker organizations could not provide candidates with the resources required for victory. As a consequence, candidates seeking office in these states more likely engaged in the candidate-centered campaign techniques commonly ascribed to the late twentieth century. Using a range of qualitative and quantitative evidence, it is demonstrated that the resource theory provides a more complete picture of how congressional candidates campaigned during the late nineteenth century.

INSTITUTIONALIZATION: THE RESOURCE THEORY APPLIED TO THE LATE NINETEENTH CENTURY

Parties generally controlled access to elected office. In addition to regulating nominations and manipulating election machinery, partisanship shaped political culture. Partisanship was deeply ingrained and personal: "Most social groups found party identification a means of declaring and defending their cultural values."[3] The intensity of the period's partisan political style is best typified by Republican orator Robert G. Ingersoll's musings on his party's merits and Democratic shortcomings: "I belong to the party that believes in good crops; that is glad when a fellow finds a gold mine; that rejoices when there are forty bushels of wheat to an acre. . . . The Democratic Party is a party of famine; it is a good friend of an early frost; it believes in the Colorado beetle and in the weevil."[4]

The press reinforced this partisan worldview. "Day after day in the nineteenth century," writes Michael McGerr, "newspapers presented a political world and encouraged readers to view it in partisan terms. By reducing politics to black-and-white absolutes, the press made partisanship enticing. The committed Republican or Democrat did not need to puzzle over conflicting facts and arguments; in his paper he could find ready-made positions on any candidate and every issue." Strident party appeals helped pay the bills. Newspapers have always found profitability elusive, and the nineteenth century was no exception; indeed, the sheer number of newspapers vying for the public's attention made the printing business fiercely competitive. By 1875, six thousand journals were published in the North alone. Newspapers jockeyed for government printing contracts, with the most partisan frequently rising above the fray when their preferred party gained control of the federal administration. Parties even owned individual newspapers, ensuring that the partisan message remained undiluted.[5]

Patronage also reinforced the partisan tendencies of citizens. Ever since Andrew Jackson launched the spoils system, federal employment depended largely on one's party membership. From clerical positions in Washington to the nation's custom collectors and postmasters, politicians rewarded the party faithful at public expense. Patronage also provided parties with a significant resource advantage: parties tithed a percentage of government workers' salaries to pay for their electioneering activities.[6]

Nor was this phenomenon restricted to federal officeholders. State and municipal employees also faced the prospect of party assessment. Much more than a cultural curiosity maintained by habit and cues, partisanship was a practical necessity for many. Even presidential nominees and cabinet secretaries could not escape the parties' financial noose. They, too, received assessment notices requiring payment.[7]

The strength of the parties as a cultural and organizational force in campaigns tends, however, to exaggerate their function as nationalizing agents. Cohesiveness and unity did not characterize nineteenth-century Democratic and Republican Parties. Although campaigns revolved around national issues at all levels of government, state organizations had more political clout and power than the national party committees. The national committees sprang into existence at the presidential nominating conventions and quickly retreated at the conclusion of the November elections.[8] They played a role as fund-raisers and suppliers of literature and speakers. That was it. The state party, not the national committee, got out the vote, mobilized the base, and implemented a campaign strategy. "Most of the actual politicking and fund-raising took place through the efforts of local units of the party. . . . The leadership of both national parties during the last third of the nineteenth century consisted of alliances of bosses and local leaders."[9] Any money raised by the national committee went to state and local organizations.

Writing about the Republican Party, Robert Marcus described it as "a congeries of state and local organizations each of which named candidates, raised funds, conducted campaigns, distributed patronage and favors, and governed or sniped at the opposition scarcely disturbed from outside their immediate jurisdictions."[10] Both parties were "fragmented, decentralized, and perpetually conflicted, both internally and externally."[11] The national committees could provide resources to the various state campaigns, but they exercised only a minor influence over how those resources were disseminated. They were "very small drivers managing a very large team of horses."[12]

The passage of the Pendleton Act did remove a large source of funding for the national parties, further magnifying the role of state party organizations in a campaign system beset by decentralization. In the language of the resource theory, the main resource rivals to candidates in the late nineteenth century were state and local parties, not a centralized, hierarchical party organization stationed in Washington, D.C. While dominant in the provision of monetary and reputation resources, the decentralized nature of political parties meant they were not monolithic. The ability of parties and their institutional capacity varied substantially. This variation provides an opportunity to test the resource theory. Do congressional candidates vary their campaign behavior based upon the state parties' ability to provide monetary and reputation resources? In other words, do the strategies pursued by candidates depend upon what parties can do for them electorally? More specifically, congressional candidates should engage in more candidate-centered behavior when faced with underdeveloped parties that find it difficult to provide candidates with resources. State party institutional capacity is one possible measure of the party's ability to provide resources to candidates.

How can a party's institutional capacity be measured? Recall the four criteria by which Nelson Polsby judges the institutionalization of Congress: well-boundedness, complexity, the existence of universalistic procedures, and automated internal decisionmaking.[13] In an exhaustive study of party organizations during the 1960s, David Mayhew developed a measure of party organization for each of the fifty states. The resulting measure, traditional party organization (TPO), ranges from one to five— five being a state with substantial party organizations, and one being a state with little or no party organization. According to Mayhew, to rate a five, a state's parties must meet the following five criteria: (1) have substantial autonomy; (2) last a long time; (3) have an important element of hierarchy in its internal structure; (4) regularly try to bring about the nomination of candidates for a wide range of public offices; and (5) rely substantially on material incentives.[14]

Rhode Island is a good example of a state with a five rating. Party nominations were rarely contested, and the party organization utilized endorsements to indicate preferred choices to voters. State party organizations were distinct and separate from government, and most local communities had traditional machines with little or no civil service requirements. Those on "ward committees . . . were responsible for the orderly distribution of patronage jobs, of neighborhood improvements, [and] of a wide range of preferential treatments." Typically, a regular organization state also has a vibrant statewide organization maintaining a substantial degree of control over local party organizations. In Rhode Island, "the state's local Democratic organization served as building blocks for an organization at the state level exercising control over nominations and government." In short, states with highly institutionalized organizations dominate the candidate selection process, control access to government jobs, utilize armies of party regulars to organize the canvass, and generally run the campaign process. In contrast, states with little traditional party organization—such as Colorado—have no slating process, virtually no machine organizations in cities and towns, and "candidates doing things on their own."[15]

A state's TPO score is an ideal measurement of party institutional capacity because it captures all three elements. How well can a measurement based upon party organizational capacity in the 1960s reflect the capacity of parties in the late nineteenth century? Surprisingly well, according to Mayhew. Two separate accounts of turn-of-the-century party organizations "prove . . . to be . . . remarkably accurate organizational survey[s] when matched against more recent evidence of geographic particulars."[16] In other words, states with vigorous party organizations in the 1960s in many cases had vigorous party organizations in the late nineteenth century. Why? It seems that "there exist geographically rooted traditions of conducting electoral politics . . . [and] that institutional arrangements and politicians' practices have tended to persist rather stubbornly."[17] If one believes Mayhew, TPO provides a good indicator of state party institutionalization even in the late nineteenth century. Institutionalization provides a guide to how a state's electoral rules govern the provision of campaign resources. Candidates should behave more independently in states with lower levels of traditional party organization.[18]

THE CONGRESSIONAL CAMPAIGN:
THE QUALITATIVE EVIDENCE

Substantially altered at the presidential level, to the point where some scholars have seen the 1896 contest as the first candidate-centered campaign,[19] the evolution of political style trickled down to individual congressional campaigns slowly and inconsistently throughout the late nineteenth century.[20] Parties still exercised considerable control over the selection of congressional candidates, the conduct of the campaign, and the selection of issues, but hints of an embryonic candidate-centered style can be glimpsed.[21] Most significantly, the behavior of candidates and parties as measured by congressional candidate selection procedures, organization, and issue selection exhibit a pattern not easily explained by the party, candidate, or service models. The resource theory improves our understanding of late-nineteenth-century congressional campaigns by offering a definitive explanation for unexpected campaign-level variations: state party institutionalization. The greater a state's partisan capacity, the better parties can dominate resource collection and the more willing candidates will be to select party-centered strategies and behaviors. In those states where party capacity is low, as measured by TPO, candidates should exhibit more independence from the party, both financially and reputationally. In sum, low party capacity equates with more candidate activity in congressional campaigns.

A survey of the secondary literature on nineteenth-century congressional electioneering provides a test of these propositions. Although there is a highly developed Gilded Age presidential campaign literature, the congressional literature is neither as well organized nor as extensive. The following accounts were culled from works on presidential campaigns, broader surveys on Gilded Age politics, and a wide selection of congressional biographies.[22] More highly institutionalized states seem to be over-represented—both in the literature and this account—for a variety of reasons. By virtue of being older and having more developed partisan systems, these states might simply have more records and history for the scholar to scrutinize. A systematic survey of the literature was made, drawing anecdotes and examples from both low and high institutionalization states, while controlling for the threats to bias inherent in any project dependent upon the historical record.[23]

CONGRESSIONAL CANDIDATE SELECTION

The direct primary did not come into widespread use until early in the twentieth century. During the Gilded Age, conventions dispensed congressional nominations. Candidate involvement, if any, did not extend beyond canvassing delegates for support before congressional district conventions. The nomination system in Pennsylvania was typical of highly institutionalized party states. Each county had its own organization that nominated candidates for office at county conventions. Districts consisting of multiple counties or city wards had the counties select conferees who then met to determine the congressional candidate.[24] In many states, these conventions did not meet until a month or two before the election.[25]

In several cases, the nomination also rotated by custom between the various counties constituting a congressional district.[26] As New York

Democratic congressman Perry Belmont noted in his memoirs, "The Suffolk County delegates . . . insisted it was their turn to select a candidate from Suffolk whose nomination would be acceptable to the other two counties. As I was from Suffolk, it fell to my lot to be nominated and elected."[27] Deep roots in the community—a near prerequisite for candidates contemplating political careers today—were not necessarily required. Samuel "Sunset" Cox, a longtime Democratic congressman from Ohio, moved to New York City after failing to be reelected in 1864. In four short years, he was the Tammany organization's nominee for the Sixth District. Cox won the race and represented one of New York's several congressional districts intermittently over the next twenty years. The key to his success was the strong support of the party organization.[28]

Classic accounts of the nineteenth century depict candidates remaining aloof and distant from party conventions, restraining their ambitions.[29] True, party organizations did draft candidates, against their individual desires and wishes, to run for office. One example was ex-Confederate cabinet member and Democrat John Reagan in Texas's First District during the 1874 elections—nominated by the district convention despite his frequent protestations.[30] The implication that candidates could not or would not influence the nomination process is false, however. They did try, hoping to change the outcome with their actions.

Some candidates worked to secure delegate support in the months leading up to a nominating convention, refusing to leave their nomination to chance. This seemed particularly the case in less institutionalized party states. Knowing that the norm of county rotation worked against his congressional aspirations, Iowa Republican John Dolliver in 1886 "began quietly making plans to sound out the sentiment and win the support of politicians likely to be delegates to the congressional convention."[31] A recent arrival to Carson City, Nevada, in 1889, Francis Newlands began an active pursuit of the Republican congressional nomination the following year despite the prospect of opposing an incumbent from his own party.[32] This included circulating, "at some cost both to a great number of Nevadans and to many Western newspapers," a pamphlet detailing his Republicanism and views on silver coinage.[33] And in Ohio, a bastion of strong parties during the nineteenth century, Republican William McKinley found it necessary to bid actively for delegate support before the district convention.[34] Candidates could and did participate in a politics of personal ambition and candidate-centered campaigning despite facing a nomination process controlled by party officials. They did this even in the late nineteenth century. Typically, but not exclusively, candidates more actively pursued the nomination in states like Iowa and Nevada, states with less rooted party organizations and cultures.

CONGRESSIONAL CAMPAIGN ORGANIZATION

The involvement of candidates in the collection of campaign funds and control over those funds also depended upon levels of state party institutionalization. After the nominations had been decided, state party leaders often took responsibility for the general election campaign in highly institutionalized party states, during both the on- and off-year elections. This included raising funds, producing and distributing literature, scheduling and paying for speakers, conducting a canvass of voters, and providing poll workers for Election Day. Assistance included the provision of "walking around" or "election day" money; essentially, money for votes. This practice was common in the nineteenth century. Funds distributed by the party frequently went to "buying votes, paying leaders to influence their followers for a certain candidate, and keeping unfavorable voters from the polls."[35]

The Democratic State Central Committee of Virginia serves as a good example of the party's role during the period: it "controlled campaign tactics and policies, raised funds, and maintained close cooperation with and among lower district, county, and municipal organizations."[36] The state chairman of Pennsylvania's Democrats also had complete control over the 1882 campaign.[37] The Indiana Democratic State Central Committee's expense report in 1880 sheds additional light on a party's activities: line items include rent, telegraph charges, parade uniforms and badges, newspaper advertisements, posters, and copies of candidate speeches. Its primary role, however, seemed to be the organization and scheduling of rallies. "The two months after the adjournment of the Cincinnati convention in late June, 1880 were devoted [by the Indiana Democrats] to the mobilization and assignment of numerous distinguished speakers for concentrated campaign of near saturation during the last weeks in August."[38] Party-sponsored rallies still excited the passion of voters and encouraged their participation and loyalty through the fall campaign. Overall, the party's general election campaign sought to garner support for the ticket as a whole, rather than candidates individually.[39]

How did the party foot the bill? Some revenue still came from assessing government workers, especially in more highly institutionalized party states. The Pendleton Act's protections applied only to a portion of federal workers at first; state and municipal employees as well as those who did not receive civil servant status still found themselves subject to a party tax.[40] Pennsylvania Republican Matthew Quay's organization—an example of a highly institutionalized partisan machine—collected around $150,000 in assessments each year from congressmen, congressional secretaries, mint and customhouse employees, naval yard workers, federal court workers, and postmen, all during the last two decades of the nineteenth century in spite of Pendleton.[41] This $150,000 would pay for the Republican Party's campaign throughout the state.

Members of party committees chipped in their share, usually a considerable sum. Upon taking the chairmanship of the Democratic National Committee in 1872, industrialist Cyrus H. McCormick offered $10,000 to run the campaign in highly partisan Illinois.[42] Indiana's state party chairman and the Democratic vice presidential candidate, William English, paid some $15,000 to the Hoosier Democrats eight years later.[43] Others paid even higher fees: Benjamin Jones, the Republican National Committee chairman in 1884, chaffed at coughing up his $70,000 assessment.[44]

Candidates also fell prey to the party assessor. In Cook County, Illinois, the "canvass in behalf of the congressional, county, legislative, and local tickets . . . was financed almost entirely out of the candidates' own pockets. Congressional nominees were assessed by the campaign committee $1,000 each for this purpose."[45] The Hoosier Democrats demanded and received $2,000 apiece from their statewide candidates.[46] In Pennsylvania, officeholders made expected "voluntary contributions," and the personal wealth of an individual was considered a key factor in determining who would receive a party's nomination.[47] In all cases, these states had highly developed partisan organizations that congressional candidates ignored at their electoral peril.

Candidates often had little say in the distribution of these contributions. The funds supported the efforts of the entire ticket as opposed to the election needs of any particular candidate. This occasionally caused friction between party leaders and candidates. Pennsylvania congressman Samuel Randall, ex-Speaker of the House and a member of the Democratic Joint Congressional Committee in 1882, received a typical letter from a disgruntled congressional nominee decrying the party's lack of financial support:

"I am greatly disappointed. I don't know what to do. I paid my assessments to each county. I told you what I wanted with the money. Had you told me frankly that you couldn't aid me, I would not have been a candidate."[48]

Candidates traveled vigorously throughout the months preceding the election, serving the party by stumping wherever necessary in support of the entire ticket. Many congressional aspirants began their careers as party orators, traveling throughout their home state and beyond. Future Virginia congressman Claude Swanson started speaking on behalf of President Grover Cleveland. Iowan James Dolliver's rhetorical talents were in great demand long before he sought office in his own right in 1886; he traveled two months straight in 1880 at the expense of the Iowa Republican Party, rallying the party's troops. In 1884, he crisscrossed the country at the behest of the Republican National Committee exhorting the virtues of presidential candidate James Blaine.[49] Republican congressmen Thomas Reed and William McKinley worked their districts personally while finding time to travel to other districts and states to advance Republican principles, ideals, and candidates.[50] Republican William Hepburn, candidate for Congress in Iowa's Eighth District in 1892, found himself frequently absent from home, owing to his national reputation as a fine speaker.[51] Even though the Republican Party repudiated him, due to his heretical views on monetary policy in 1874, forcing him to run as an independent, partisanship still tugged at Pennsylvania congressman William Kelley. He remained loyal to the party and campaigned on its behalf during the 1875 off-year elections.[52] The practice was common, expected, and motivated somewhat by self-interest. A candidate could not achieve the party's nomination without working diligently for the party throughout the state, especially in states with highly institutionalized party structures such as Pennsylvania and Ohio.[53]

Although the fate of the entire ticket generally determined individual success or failure, some aspirants did take their electoral fate more firmly into their own hands. Again, candidates raising money and organizing independent efforts usually did so in those states with less developed partisan cultures and organizations. Congressional candidates could not always rely on the party for funds and occasionally developed their own independent sources of revenue.[54] When choosing to pursue the congressional seat in Iowa's Tenth District, Republican John Dolliver reported that he had raised $500 in preparation for the effort.[55]

Francis Newlands twice purchased an entire party organization out of his own pocket. In 1885, he established the California Democratic League ostensibly to foster harmony and unity in a party reverberating from a divisive campaign. In reality, the organization advanced Francis Newland's 1887 Senate bid.[56] After failing to fulfill his political aspirations in California, Newlands relocated to Nevada where (having abandoned the Democrats for the more politically advantageous Republicans) he again attempted to use his enormous wealth to construct an individual "party" organization.[57] Failing in his first attempt to wrest the Republican nomination from incumbent congressman Horace Bartine, Newlands succeeded in 1892 after spending, according to his own admission, more than $50,000.[58] To put this princely sum in perspective, Newlands spent the equivalent of nearly $1 million in 2002—the cost of a modern-day House election with television, radio, and all the trimmings!

After a decade in the House, Newlands again aspired to a seat in the Senate. To ensure widespread support, Newlands funded the campaign of the entire Democratic slate in 1902, having yet again switched parties. Unlike other congressional candidates, Newlands seemed uninterested in the ticket's success unless it had immediate consequences for him. An outspoken proponent of silver coining while serving in Congress, Newlands refused to campaign on behalf of William Jennings Bryan in 1896 despite his strong silver credentials. Newlands did not think Bryan could win, and presumably he did not want to risk his own reelection by sticking his neck out for Bryan.[59]

Again, generally in states with more established partisan traditions and organizations—such as Pennsylvania, Virginia, Indiana, and Illinois—candidates relied largely on the formal party organization to raise funds and organize the canvass. In states admitted to the union more recently, where a partisan culture had less time to fully ferment and prime party organizations, the story was somewhat different. Although party organizations aided the election efforts of candidates, they could not guarantee victory on election day; hence the independent efforts by candidates like Dolliver and Newlands. In both instances, the candidates raised their own money to pay for their electioneering efforts.

CONGRESSIONAL CAMPAIGN ISSUE SELECTION

National issues dominated congressional campaigns in the nineteenth century, with both national and state party conventions imposing the party's preferred stance upon its nominees. Most candidates happily sup-

ported the party platform as they campaigned, advocating for those beliefs regardless of their personal opinions. To do otherwise generally
made little political sense. Those who broke with the party found themselves branded as heretics, especially in states with deeply embedded partisan norms. Although focusing on the 1840s and 1850s, Joel Silbey's
depiction of independent-minded politicians still applied later in century:
"Any delegate or candidate who did not support the convention's decision was recreant to good faith and implied honor without which no party
or association can exist."[60] Politics in the late nineteenth century was much
the same. Congressional candidates widely supported the party's issue
positions on the stump, marching in lockstep with the party on its formidable issue reputation as opposed to staking out independent positions.
Loyalty to the party carried over into the legislature. "Elected less on their
own merits than on the basis of the party's organization, platform, and appeal, [members of Congress] felt obligated to support party leaders and
programs."[61] As political scientists David Brady, Joseph Cooper, and Patricia Hurley note, party unity was quite high among members of the
House of Representatives in the late nineteenth century, and in this respect the period was similar to the antebellum party period described by
Silbey.[62] Bucking the party usually led to dire consequences. Pennsylvania congressman William Kelley, one of the first Republicans elected to
Congress, was denied his party's nomination in 1874 because he had endorsed the Greenback Party's views on currency.

McKinley was the archetypal partisan warrior. In his campaign travels,
he traversed the country advocating for Republican policies, even when
he disagreed. "What the party thought best, he too thought best. However
questionable some Republicans might be, they were always better than
the Democrats, and his country was safest in the hands of his party."[63] Dis-
regarding his distaste for patronage politics, McKinley never wavered in
his support of President Benjamin Harrison's Dependent Pensions Act.
Henry Cabot Lodge hoped to run for Congress but found his stance on
free trade incompatible with the views of Massachusetts voters and the
Republican Party. He remedied this problem by abandoning his unortho-
dox views and embracing protectionism. His reward was a congressional
seat in 1886.[64] The strength of the party's pull even encouraged candidates
"to articulate party positions where none really existed."[65]

Not all candidates blindly adhered to the party platform and its national candidates even in the face of severe repercussions. Candidates

crafted their own personal issue reputations if political circumstances warranted. The silver issue in particular led congressional candidates to abandon their party. In 1896, California Republicans found it difficult to campaign on their party's monetary platform. Stressing the party's popular tariff position allowed some to avoid the contentious silver issue altogether, and ignoring the party's position and actively campaigning for the monetarization of silver became the tactic of choice in agricultural districts where the issue could not be evaded.[66]

The situation in Virginia during the 1890s mirrored California's. Democratic candidates faced an electorate favoring the Populist Party's position on silver and a presidential candidate (Grover Cleveland) publicly committed to gold. Party nominee Claude Swanson pledged to run on the Democratic Party's unpopular national platform, and he won. In 1894, however, the Fifth Congressional District convention, at which Swanson received the nomination by acclamation, repudiated both Cleveland and gold. The silver movement gathered momentum, overtaking the entire state convention where supporters of gold were effectively purged from the party. Swanson, in 1894 and 1896, advocated freely and openly for the silver position adopted by the Populist Party.[67]

Congressional candidates in both Iowa and Tennessee also had to find ways to square their party's currency stance with the electorate's. The incumbent congressman from Tennessee's Tenth District, Josiah Patterson, had been an outspoken proponent of Cleveland's gold policy. In 1896, he embraced silver, the national platform, and Bryan, announcing that "the currency question remained peripheral to the essence of the party." Prosilver Democrats could not swallow Patterson's conversion, so they nominated a true believer: Edward Carmack. Historian Marilyn Hutton argued that party unity in Tennessee collapsed owing to "the extreme instability of party organization in the 1890s."[68] Compelled to soothe pro-silver Republicans in Iowa, party leaders announced their support of silver and "emphasized as meaningless the statement in the Republican platform favoring an international agreement for the use of silver and gold as money."[69]

Even third party candidates, frequently elected in the nineteenth century, were not immune to the pull of local influences in their bid to keep and maintain their office. Indeed, third party candidates provide an illustration of the general resource principle that a lack of state party institutional capacity coincides with an increased willingness of candidates to jettison party positions in favor of their own individual reputations. Historian Karel Denis Bicha writes that Jerry "Sockless" Simpson, a Kansas Populist elected to Congress in 1890, "had no sense of party discipline." In particular, Simpson "devoted most of his attention to protectionism and militarism," two issues that were not central to the People's Party's platform. As Bicha notes, "The nature of the People's party insured that if discipline was to exist at all, it had to be imposed by leaders upon themselves; the party organization was too rudimentary and the rank and file too unskilled to force rigid adherence to the root principles of the movement."[70] In short, without deeply embedded roots and an established political culture, congressional candidates were free to buck the party if and when it served their purposes.

National, not local, issues dominated congressional campaigns in the late nineteenth century. Accepting the party's congressional nomination generally meant that the candidate embraced the party's national issue reputation. Contending with a partisan culture and the possibility of reprisals for abandoning the party line, resources favored generally partisan behavior by candidates. Even so, at times the party's reputation hurt a candidate's winning probability. In these cases, the candidate themselves—and local or state organizations—ran away from their party's issue reputation and attempted to craft their own.

Although certainly not frequent or even widespread, the fact that such behavior existed at all in an era of party strength requires explanation. State party institutionalization explains some of this behavior, but not all. Witness Henry Cabot Lodge embracing trade policy even though he ran for Congress in a weak party state. William Kelley endorsed Greenback monetary policy in highly institutionalized Pennsylvania.

From the bulk of the qualitative evidence, however, it would seem that the relationship between state party institutionalization and candidate campaign behavior is suggestive: candidates sought nominations, established independent political organizations, and were freer to establish independent issue reputations generally in states with less developed partisan landscapes. William Jennings Bryan, the agrarian and populist rebel who seized the Democratic Party nomination in 1896, fits this pattern. Having grown up in Illinois, Bryan moved to Lincoln, Nebraska, in 1887.[71] Within a scant three years, he became the Democratic nominee for the first congressional district. How did he obtain the nomination? He actively sought it. In a letter to his chief opponent, Bryan claimed he would step aside willingly in his favor should he wish to run, but only after

Bryan had already solidified enough support to make his nomination a foregone conclusion. He also drafted a radical party platform and then shrewdly manipulated the nomination process to have the convention adopt his platform before selecting its nominee. In this fashion, he pushed aside two other contenders who could not in good faith accept Bryan's more liberal platform.[72]

Throughout his campaign for Congress, Bryan exhibited a talent for keeping the correct distance from the party when it was politically expedient and changing his own political beliefs to suit his district. An avowed teetotaler, Bryan embraced the wet stance of the Democratic Party to attract immigrant voters. But he kept his Democratic mentor, J. Sterling Morton, at arms length, fearful that Morton's open free trade stance would drive away critical Republican support in an overwhelmingly Republican Nebraska. And, unlike other candidates during the period, Bryan took actively to the stump in support of his own candidacy, sometimes speaking as many as three times a day. As historian Louis Koening describes it, "Bryan seemed to reduce issues to mere political tools to be used or discarded as the necessities of his campaign dictated." In a more recent biography of Bryan, William Kazin picks up on this tendency, noting that Bryan freely and consciously avoided his and his party's support for bimetallism while speaking to labor organizations in Chicago during the 1896 presidential campaign.[73]

Bryan's behavior conformed classically to the candidate-centered model, and his success derived from Nebraska's lack of a firmly institutionalized two-party system—evidenced by the fact that the Populist Party easily captured the other two congressional seats in the 1890 election. Lack of party institutionalization created a vacuum that politicians have to fill in order to compete in elections. Frequently, this void was filled by carving a third path based on local conditions, local issues, and unique personalities. Parties dominated nineteenth-century campaigns by and large, but candidates had room to maneuver, especially when the parties could not provide their reputation or monetary resources.

CONGRESSIONAL CAMPAIGNS AND INSTITUTIONALIZATION: A QUANTITATIVE ANALYSIS

A more systematic test of the resource theory is provided by quantitative analysis. There is no easy way to develop measures of candidate involvement in the nominations process or the involvement of candidates in the funding and organization of their congressional campaigns. Records for the late nineteenth century are incomplete and fragmented. The candidate and party finance data that emerge are generally guesses, as financial disclosure laws did not exist.

It is possible to measure, however, the effects of institutionalization on the voting behavior of members of Congress. Assuming that members of Congress do establish records and issue positions with an eye toward reelection, their behavior on the House floor acts as a proxy for their campaign behavior.[74] In other words, voting against the party on a range of issues suggested that a member might be seeking to develop a distinctive issue reputation useful for reelection. Again, candidates faced with underdeveloped parties with little resource capacity needed to rely upon their own reputations to aid in their reelection.

To test this implication of the resource theory, roll call votes are used as a measure of partisan reputation for each member of the House of Representatives for the 47th through the 56th Congresses (1881–1903).[75] If a majority of the members of one party opposes the majority of members of the other party, this is classified as a unity vote by *Congressional Quarterly*. The same standard applies here, with an additional criterion: at least ten members from both major parties must record a yes or no vote on the roll call to be included. The resulting measure represents the member's support on party issues, ranging from nonexistent (zero) to complete (one).[76] Each Congress yielded between 109 and 500 party unity roll calls.

Party unity scores for members of Congress serving between 1881 and 1903 are used to explore the relationship between party institutionalization and member reputation. State institutionalization is represented by that state's TPO score, with a TPO score of one representing a state with a low level of state party capacity and a TPO score of five representing a state with a high level of state party capacity.[77] Of course, state party capacity is not the only factor that affects how a member of Congress might vote. These other factors cannot be ignored. First, any relationship observed between party capacity and unity voting alone might disappear when these other factors are taken into account. Second, any relationship between party capacity and member reputation must be observed within the context of these other factors in order to evaluate the magnitude of the effect. As a result, these other important factors possibly contributing to the voting behavior of members are included in the analysis. These factors, and an explanation of how they might affect a member's behavior, are described below.

"Vote" is the percentage of the vote the congressional candidate received in the last election.[78] The competitive nature of a member's district presumably affects how close they might want to be to the party. Candidates in more competitive districts might want to broaden their electoral appeal to capture more votes as opposed to those representing districts where one party is clearly dominant. Members in marginal districts should move away from their party's issue positions and move to the political center, while those in less competitive seats should feel free to hew closer to their party's stance.

How a member votes at a given point in time is strongly influenced by how they voted previously; indeed, it is perhaps the most powerful predictor of their voting behavior. Members of Congress are loath to "flip flop" for fear of being called to task for it by the voters. The support a member gives his party, therefore, should be closely related to the support he gave his party in the past. This tendency to vote in a similar fashion over time is addressed by including a member's previous unity in the analysis.[79]

Lack of competition in the general election due to the absence of Republican candidates and a tendency to vote together in support of racial and social issues led to increased unity voting among southerners during the late nineteenth century and less unity during the rise of the New Deal.[80] This tendency belies the South's overall low levels of party organization, and the "South" variable takes this tendency into account. This variable is known as a dummy variable, meaning that it takes a value of one when a member of Congress represents a former Confederate state and a zero when a member does not. In terms of interpretation, the coefficient value and its level of significance in the following regression results indicates whether Southerners behave any differently than congressmen from other parts of the country in terms of their willingness to support the party on unity votes.

Finally, the analysis includes the percentage received in the last election by the top third party congressional candidate in the member's district. The eruption of a strong third party movement in a state suggests an electorate that is politically independent and weakly tethered to the major parties.[81] Strong third parties in a district should lead candidates to seek a broader coalition of support, which should depress their support for the party. Conversely, states with weak third parties should feature electorates less willing to cross party lines.

"Term" indicates the number of terms the member has served in Congress prior to any given election cycle; zero indicates the member is running for the first time, while those running in their first reelection bid are coded as one. Incumbency should affect a member's party unity, but how it should is less than clear. Incumbents, who are more secure electorally, may be more able to support their party on a given vote. Alternatively, electoral security might encourage members to more frequently take independent views. As the pull of party was so important culturally and socially in the nineteenth century, members serving longer should support their party on unity votes more frequently.[82]

"Party," like "South," is a dummy variable. It is coded as zero for Democrats and one for Republicans. Cultural or social differences between the parties might lead Republicans collectively, for example, to support their party more on the House floor than Democrats. This may or may not be the case; nevertheless, the possibility that a difference between Republicans and Democrats as a whole might exist needs to be considered in the analysis. "Minority" is coded one if the member's party is in the minority during a session, and zero otherwise. Minority parties should be more cohesive than majority parties during the nineteenth century, utilizing their party reputations during elections to try to take over the House. Majority parties, on the other hand, should exhibit less party unity as members should be "freer" to vote the district. This means minority status should encourage members to vote along party lines more frequently than those in the majority.

Recapitulating, low state party institutionalization should be associated with lower levels of party unity according to the resource theory. Likewise, members representing states with higher levels of institutionalization should exhibit higher levels of party support on the House floor. Regression analysis is used to test this claim, and the results are reported in table 3.1.[83] The results provide strong support for the hypothesis that party institutionalization affects the behavior of congressional candidates.[84] In every case, the coefficients are positive or negative as anticipated and strongly significant statistically.

How should one interpret the findings presented in table 3.1? First, one should note whether the coefficient values are positively or negatively signed. A positive sign indicates that as the variable in question increases

Table 3.1. Party unity voting and strength of state organizations, 1881–1903

Explanatory Variables	Coefficient
Constant	.621*** (.021)
Previous Unity	.096*** (.021)
South	.076*** (.006)
Vote	.062*** (.017)
Term	.004*** (.001)
Minority	.034*** (.003)
TPO	.004*** (.001)
Party	.115*** (.005)
Third Party Voting	-.040*** (.014)
R–Squared	.240
N	3221

Unstandardized OLS coefficients with Huber–White robust standard errors reported in parentheses.

***p<=.01; **p<=.05; *p<=.10; two–tailed.

in value, so does party unity voting. A negative sign on the coefficient indicates an inverse relationship: as the variable in question increases, party unity decreases. Second, coefficients marked with stars indicate that the relationship observed between party unity and the variable is statistically significant. The more stars, the more statistically robust the relationship. Overall, the coefficients in table 3.1 have the correct signs (meaning that the relationship between the variables and party unity voting is as anticipated) and are strongly significant statistically.

There are a variety of interesting findings in table 3.1, but the most important for the purposes of the resource theory is the relationship between party unity voting and state party institutionalization.[85] Members representing more highly institutionalized party states vote more often with the party on unity votes. The magnitude of the shift, however, is small. The difference between a member's unity voting in the least institutionalized state and a member's unity voting in the most institutionalized state is slightly more than a percentage point. Although statistically significant, state party institutionalization seems to exhibit a rather small pull on a member's decisions to support the party on an issue. Compared to other variables, such as previous party unity, partisan affiliation, the vote percentage in the last election, and residing in the South, the effect of state party institutionalization on a member's vote is not large.

Although not large, the influence of a state's party institutionalization on the voting behavior of representatives is neither insignificant nor insubstantial.[86] The fact that party institutionalization exhibits the expected theoretical relationship, in spite of the measure's crudeness, testifies to the theoretical and empirical robustness of the finding. Furthermore, as party line voting occurred frequently in the late nineteenth century, it is all the more impressive that state party institutionalization performs at all, considering the small amount of variation to explain once regional effects are taken into account. Clearly, the institutional context in which congressional candidates find themselves affects both how they vote and the electoral strategies they pursue when seeking office. This was true even in the nineteenth century, the era of strong parties, when candidates supposedly remained in the background to let the party bosses run the show. Congressional candidates built individual reputations when the party could not provide either the monetary or reputation resources necessary to win reelection. This is supported by both a review of the literature on late-nineteenth-century congressional campaigns and a quantitative analysis of party unity voting.

CONCLUSION

The overall picture painted by party-centered theory during the late nineteenth century is not so much wrong as it is incomplete. Candidates for Congress did rely largely on partisan organizations to organize, fund, and develop the issues around which campaigns were contested. A closer look, however, leaves the viewer confused. Candidates did not lack individual initiative. They took charge of their electoral destiny, but only if the institutional landscape made such behavior necessary. If the party could not provide the resources (monetary or reputation) necessary to win, congressional candidates fended for themselves in areas with low levels of party institutionalization. As political reforms such as the Pendleton Civil Service Act in the late nineteenth century and the Tillman Act in the early twentieth century stemmed the flow of financial resources to political parties, candidate-centered campaign activities among congressional aspirants became increasingly the norm rather than the exception. This pattern merely replicated at a lower level what had been occurring at the presidential level as early as 1884: candidates relying more on their own skills and abilities to win elections as opposed to deferring to party experts and bosses.[87] Both nature and politics abhor vacuums; individual candidate initiative and efforts filled the resource gap when party organizations could not adequately meet candidate resource demands. The behavior of candidates—as party- or candidate-centered—depended not on the particular time period but on whether the level of state party institutionalization matched the particular needs of election-minded candidates.

In the next chapter, the analysis is continued by examining four Senate races between 1940 and 1960. Despite a host of electoral reforms designed to democratize the political process and the arrival of new communications technology, candidates still found themselves restrained by their local political environment. Senate candidates continued to use party organizations and campaign techniques when it made sense to do so. When parties were unable to provide campaign resources, however, Senate candidates abandoned the party in favor of candidate-centered techniques.

CHAPTER FOUR

Resources, the New Media, and the Race for the U.S. Senate, 1940–1960

I f the late nineteenth century's reputation as the Golden Age of Parties is somewhat exaggerated, then the collapse of parties beginning around 1940 and accelerating through the 1950s and 1960s is also an overstatement. True enough, parties at the century's midpoint had been weakened relative to their historical counterparts. The Pendleton Civil Service Act of 1883 instigated a series of reforms loosening the party's grip on candidates and the campaign process. The widespread adoption of the Australian ballot, nonpartisan elections, direct primaries, and the passage of the Seventeenth Amendment had the potential to shift monetary and reputation resources away from parties to candidates and interest groups. To the stew of Progressive reform add a dash of the New Deal and a pinch of new media technologies, and the ability of parties to control and dispense resources to candidates appeared to be under assault from every direction.

The assault was real, but the effect of these changes varied tremendously from state to state. Institutionally mature state party organizations successfully navigated the treacherous shoals of reform and the media revolution, maintaining their role as important resource aggregators in congressional campaigns. They retained the ability to collect monetary and reputation resources, and even embraced television and radio as useful tools. Candidates running for office still needed resources, and when party organizations successfully adapted to the new reform environment, candidates selected campaign strategies to secure party support. In those states with less-bounded partisan organizations, electoral reforms further hindered their ability to collect resources and utilize the new media effectively. Congressional candidates responded as one might expect: they created personal organizations, selected and debated their own issues, and assembled their own coalitions of voters. Some have argued that the mid-twentieth century marked the arrival of the candidate-centered campaign.[1] In reality, candidates structured campaigns depending on their particular situation. Some campaigns were "candidate-centered," while others were "party-centered." The "candidate-centered" politics associated with the mid-twentieth century merely replicated the pattern of the late nineteenth century: candidates selected campaign strategies based on the resource environment they faced.

In this chapter, the forces underpinning the rise of the candidate-centered campaign are examined. The "new" candidate-centered campaigns of Truman Newberry in Michigan and Frank Merriam in California are not revolutionary, but they are indistinguishable from campaigns in those states with weakly tethered partisan institutions during the late nineteenth century. Not by chance did senatorial and gubernatorial candidates resort to "candidate-centered techniques." Both Michigan and California had weak partisan traditions and organizations as defined by David Mayhew's measure of Traditional Party Organization (TPO), making a focus on a candidate's personal resources and assets sensible from a resource perspective.[2]

The following analysis draws extensively on primary source materials to evaluate the role of political parties in four Senate campaigns between 1940 and 1960. Each case represents a different level of state party institutionalization. Although the technology changed, the degree of partisan institutionalization played a significant role in the conduct of individual Senate campaigns during the "age of the candidate" as it had at the conclusion of the nineteenth century. The need for resources still conditioned the behavior of candidates, and institutionally vibrant parties withstood the tide of reform to retain their role as resource distributors.

Also investigated is the notion that the arrival of radio and television undermined parties and aided the arrival of a candidate-based politics, again by evaluating patterns of party support in Congress. As in the nineteenth century, higher levels of state partisan institutionalization coincide with increased unity voting by resource-hungry senators. And despite common scholarly wisdom, the findings indicate that a state's per capita television and radio stations inflates a senator's party unity score. Although television and radio may free candidates from their party by allowing direct communication with voters, their substantial cost pushes candidates into the arms of parties. Despite these enormous technological and regulatory changes, the rule of resources is undisturbed. As before, candidate access to resources independent of the party varies depending on the institutional capacity of state party organizations.

CANDIDATES ASCENDANT?

The rise of candidate-centered politics and techniques is ascribed, broadly, to two intertwined forces: a series of election reforms instituted by Progressives and the invention of new media and communication technologies such as radio, television, and direct mail. Election reforms served to displace parties from control of the ballot and the nomination process, undermining the party's role as gatekeepers to elective office. The advent of television and radio gave candidates the ability to communicate with voters without kowtowing to party bosses. With freedom to seek nominations and transmit unfiltered messages to voters, parties seemed all but irrelevant to candidates.

Three reforms in particular seem responsible for creating the atmosphere necessary for candidate-centered politics to flourish: the Australian ballot, direct primaries, and nonpartisan elections. Before the adoption of the Australian ballot, political parties printed their own ballots listing only their candidates. Voters would receive their ballot from the party and cast them in full view of precinct captains and ward officers. Splitting one's ticket required some effort, either scratching a candidate's name or attaching a portion of the other party's strip. This, as well as the public nature of the vote, made split-ticket voting undesirable. The Australian ballot—a ballot listing all office seekers together on a single strip of paper and printed by the state—made it physically easier to split one's ticket and to do so without repercussion.[3] The reform generally came with provisions that made voting secret, making it harder for parties to monitor the behavior of individual voters. Removing parties from the ballot business made the task of securing voter resources more difficult, while simultaneously creating incentives for individual candidates to craft independent reputations and issue stances to attract voters willing to split their tickets.

First implemented on a large scale by Wisconsin in 1903, the direct primary gave voters the power to select party nominees. This allowed "insurgents—candidates not championed by party organizations—a chance to appeal successfully to the majority of voters, who had weak ties to parties."[4] By opening the nomination process to voters, reformers also lessened the influence of party activists in the process, particularly in those states adopting open primaries. Why should officeholders pay attention to activists if they could achieve the nomination by appealing to the electorate at large?[5] And if officeholders provided no special access to activists, a powerful motive to hustle for the party, the rationale to become an activist was eliminated. The end result was a party that attracted fewer activists. Less manpower diminished the party's resource leverage over candidates, which encouraged candidates to move even further away from the party.

Some municipalities took the extreme measure of banning parties from ballots altogether, instituting nonpartisan elections for local offices. This had two potential consequences, both detrimental. First, by "denying parties the opportunity to nominate candidates and signal endorsements to partisan voters," reformers undercut the role of parties as political socializers. Second, the lower tier of elective offices—essential to recruiting party adherents, prospective candidates, and party workers—escaped the party's clutches.[6] Without the ability to socialize voters and workers into the party mold, parties found themselves less able to provide voting coalitions to office seekers. Candidates had to build these coalitions themselves or else seek interest group assistance.

If one judges by the attention received in the literature, the new media is the primary culprit of party decline. Almost universally television and radio are credited with shattering the foundation of America's political parties and displacing their traditional campaign role.[7] V. O. Key himself, as early as 1942, recognized the disruptive potential of the new media: "Political power has been based on a stable network of the party machine, around each member of which was clustered a little group loyal through thick and thin. For this there seems to be in the process of substitution a power structure broadly based on mass consent and support. The representatives and opinion-managerial function of the party machine become less important than it once was as leaders have available devices and methods for appealing directly to the great mass of the people. And in the midst of these changes in opinion manipulation the old-time politician is at sea and the men are bewildered and a little afraid."[8]

Why the focus on television and radio as harbingers of a new campaign style? Unlike the adoption of the Australian ballot, primaries, or nonpartisan elections, the new media directly challenged the party machine's *raison d'être*. Parties could survive electoral reforms if they maintained control of a communications apparatus. If the precinct captain and a partisan press provide the only access to voters, then candidates have little choice but to rely on the machine. As party regular Stimson Bullitt noted, "With mass media which use a common language that everyone can read, people no longer need party workers to advise them how to vote. . . . The media have done to the campaign system what the invention of accurate artillery did to the feudal kingdom—destroyed the barons and shifted power to the masses and the prince."[9] Now parties no longer held exclusive rights to the voter. The new media opened the voters' doors to candidates and interest groups. Television and radio allowed candidates to bypass the party and petition the voters directly.[10]

The California gubernatorial race in 1934, pitting author-social critic Upton Sinclair against incumbent governor Frank Merriam, is cited by some as one of the earliest examples of the new candidate-centered campaign.[11] Fearing that Sinclair's End Poverty in California program would lead to state ownership of private enterprises, several businesses and organizations banded together to form United for California. The organization exploited the new campaign style and media to the hilt, using targeted direct mail and radio.[12] Alarmed by Sinclair's remarks supporting a state role in movie production and screening, Hollywood produced movie shorts attacking Sinclair and his candidacy.[13]

Sinclair, a political newcomer, constructed his own organization, purchased radio time, published a newspaper, and traveled throughout the state during the primary and general election campaigns. Although Sinclair received the Democratic Party's nomination by a substantial margin in the gubernatorial primary, the party was rife with dissention. The San Francisco Democratic Club endorsed Sinclair's Republican opponent, and the party's central committee refused to support Sinclair. President Roosevelt decided to sit out the race despite several personal entreaties from the Democratic nominee. FDR considered Sinclair too radical for the Democratic Party. Without the party's aid, Sinclair had little choice but to go it alone and rely on his own political organization and effort.[14]

The Sinclair-Merriam race had all the ingredients of candidate-centered campaigns: a focus on the individual candidates, the cobbling together of voting coalitions independent of partisanship, the use of new methods of communication, and the extensive involvement of private interests. Party officials either stayed above the fray or, in the case of the Democrats, endorsed the other party's candidate.[15] It also featured campaign professionals using the modern publicity and advertising techniques. But was it really the first appearance of the "candidate-centered campaign"?

What about Truman Newberry's 1918 Senate primary campaign in Michigan? Facing three other candidates including a former governor of the state and Henry Ford, the inventor of the Model T, Newberry had comparatively few advantages. Unknown throughout the state and unable to leave his naval posting in New York City, Newberry's campaign expended vast sums of money on publicity, including newspaper advertisements and the production of a motion picture. By the end of the race the Newberry committee had a headquarters staff of twenty consisting of a campaign manager, field operatives, a public relations team, and an organization spread throughout the state. All told, the campaign spent more than $175,000 during the primary, with the bulk of it going to publicity.[16] The campaign certainly appeared to be candidate-centered, and yet it is (to the author's knowledge) rarely if ever cited as the progenitor of the candidate-centered campaign. Neither, for that matter, is Francis Newland's race for Congress in 1892 (see chapter 3).

Candidate-centered techniques did not erupt suddenly on the political scene after the implementation of Progressive electoral reforms or the invention of radio and television. To be sure, some scholars maintain that the transformation to candidate-centered campaigns was gradual and uneven,[17] but this still misses the point. Candidate-centered techniques have always been an option available to candidates. The use of those techniques, however, is governed less by whether parties dominate access to the ballot, the nomination process, or communication with voters and more by the institutional capacity of parties to meet the resource needs of candidates. Electoral reform and the new media *alter* the ability of parties to provide candidates with resources, but party organizations respond differently to these forces. As demonstrated previously, state partisan institutionalization determines the ability of parties to engage successfully in campaign activities. The more institutionalized—the more embedded—a party organization within a state's political fabric, the better it resists forces undermining its campaign capacity. State parties provided the main organizational presence during congressional campaigns in the mid-twentieth century. The national party organs still restricted themselves to presidential campaigns and politics. This division of labor had not been transformed by either Progressive reforms or the advent of radio and television.[18]

Nothing precluded parties from utilizing "candidate-centered" tactics and strategies. Indeed, where parties had the appropriate institutional capacity, they found ways around the new electoral rules. For example, parties in some states simply endorsed candidates during primaries. Others made use of television and radio to communicate directly with the electorate. Candidates took matters into their own hands when parties simply could not, but candidates more or less let parties run the show when the parties could provide the resources. This highlights the problem with labeling the mid-twentieth century as a "candidate-centered" era.

Resources governed the conduct of candidates and parties during campaigns in the late nineteenth and mid-twentieth centuries. Progressive reformers had not eviscerated all party organizations, and the age of mass communication had not left "the old-time politician" adrift at sea with his men "bewildered and a little afraid."[19] A state party's level of institutional strength, as measured by TPO, determined its ability to become involved in individual campaigns. The mid-twentieth century, supposedly the end of party-centered campaigns, is best described as a mix of party- and candidate-centered campaigning. The arrival of new communications technology and electoral reform provided opportunities for candidates and parties alike. How parties handled these opportunities depended on their organizational capacity.

FOUR SENATE CAMPAIGNS AT MIDCENTURY: STATE PARTIES AS RESOURCE PROVIDERS

Senate campaigns at midcentury provide a good opportunity to evaluate the claim of the resource model that the role and campaign behavior of candidates relative to parties depended substantially on state party organizational capacity. Senators received no reprieve from the reformers' zeal. Conceived as a saucer to cool popular passions, the widespread adoption of direct popular elections (later formalized by the passage of the Seventeenth Amendment in 1913) undercut to a degree the Senate's moderating influence on the legislative process.

The siren call of the new media tempted senators with a direct link to constituents that had always eluded them. "Unlike governors and mayors," write Barbara and Stephen Salmore, "senators did not have the services of the state and local party organizations, nor was it easy for them to practice at the statewide level the 'friends and neighbors' politics of the representative." They also did not have access to extensive patronage, particularly if representing the minority party in Washington. All of these factors made Senate careers a riskier long-term proposition relative to the House in an age of direct elections. Salmore and Salmore conclude that candidate-centered campaign techniques quickly found a receptive audience among senators.[20]

Without parties institutionally entrenched in Senate campaigns and with the reelection scenario facing senators favoring the use of television and radio, the campaign role of parties should be small as compared to House elections. By looking at Senate rather than House races at midcentury, the method effectively stacks the deck against the resource theory. If evidence is found that resources matter in Senate campaigns at midcentury and that this relationship is conditioned by state party institutional capacity, one can be reasonably confident in the resource theory's explanatory power.

The analysis in this section is restricted to four Senate races conducted between 1948 and 1956 (see table 4.1).[21] Each Senate race detailed below varies along the key independent variable of interest: party institutionalization as captured by Mayhew's TPO score.[22] As the modal TPO category, three, contains only one state (Louisiana), it is excluded from the analysis. In each of the four races selected, the analysis concentrates only on the winning candidate (see the italicized entries in table 4.1) in order to provide an in-depth look at the campaign's operation.[23] The analysis began by surveying the manuscript collections of each senator, focusing on the available campaign materials. A wide range of items, including campaign memoranda, letters from supporters in the field, banking statements, receipts, television and radio advertisements (actual as well as scripts), campaign literature, bumper stickers, and correspondence between the campaign and the state party organization were reviewed. As a picture developed of the party-candidate dynamics at work in each race, the search was expanded to include the manuscript collections of party officials and campaign managers and even oral histories of the candidates themselves or other key participants. In one instance, personal interviews with two campaign principals were conducted.[24] The snapshot provided by the archival materials came into sharper focus with the additional pe-

Table 4.1. The four Senate races, 1940–1960

TPO	Year	State	Contestants	Party	Incumbent	Vote
1	1956	Idaho	*Frank Church*	*(D)*	N	*59%*
			Herman Welker	(R)	Y	41%
2	1948	Tennessee	*Estes Kefauver*	*(D)*	N	*66%*
			B. Carroll Reece	(R)	N	34%
4	1956	Kentucky	*John Sherman Cooper*	*(R)*	N	*53%*
			Lawrence Wetherby	(D)	N	47%
5	1950	Illinois	*Everett Dirksen*	*(R)*	N	*54%*
			Scott Lucas	(D)	Y	46%

rusal of political biographies, journal articles, dissertations, and contemporary newspaper accounts.

All of this information had the potential of becoming unwieldy quickly, particularly when a detailed narrative was not the objective. In the four case studies that follow, the division of labor between state parties and candidates during Senate campaigns is evaluated. The focus is on three campaign processes: (1) the selection of nominees; (2) the management, organization, and funding of the campaign; and (3) the campaign's message and major issue themes. Across all four cases, the role of the candidate and party in each of these processes is examined, identifying the campaign roles and responsibilities of the state party organization and the candidate. In a state with a strong organizational presence, such as Illinois, the party should play a significant role in all three campaign processes. This includes slating of candidates in primaries, raising and distributing the bulk of the campaign funds, and dominating the issue landscape. In states with weak parties, like Idaho, candidates should dominate the process. Primaries will be crowded, candidates will not receive party endorsements, campaigns will be self-financed, and candidates will focus on personalities and issues not necessarily in keeping with the party line. As the analysis below demonstrates, this is indeed the case. Institutionalization matters. The more embedded a state's party organization, the more likely the party plays a significant role in deciding party nominations, managing and funding individual Senate campaigns, and dominating a campaign's issue message.

IDAHO: A WEAK PARTY, BUT A STRONG "CHURCH"

In late February 1956, Frank Church announced his candidacy for the U.S. Senate in his hometown of Boise, Idaho. The odds of winning seemed long. Church's opponent, Republican Herman Welker, won election to his first term with nearly 60 percent of the vote in a Republican-leaning state. Indeed, Church neatly fits the profile of a "hopeless amateur."[25] Although attractive, articulate, and a gifted speaker, Church was a young attorney who had never held elective office and had little name recognition beyond Ada County.[26] The presence of Dwight D. Eisenhower, a popular Republican president, on the ballot made an already difficult task even harder. Childhood companion Carl Burke, who served as campaign manager for all of Church's campaigns, bluntly informed his friend that he would not beat Welker.[27]

Church entered the fray without the party apparatus behind him. Idaho Democrats chose their candidates in primaries, heavily curtailing the party's control of the nomination process. In some primary states, party leaders play an informal role by seeking out candidates and encouraging them to run. Idaho's Democratic establishment, it suffices to say, did not beat a path to Church's door and beg him to run against Welker. It did not appear that the party regulars even had a preferred candidate. Church made the decision, with the considerable aid and support of his wife, Bethine, who had drafted a detailed letter outlining the pros and cons of a Senate run while offering her unqualified support should he decide to take the plunge.[28]

The sheer number of candidates vying for the Democratic nomination (at one point as many as six) demonstrates the party's inability to handpick its candidates. The situation on the Republican side appeared no better. Herman Welker, the incumbent, competed against four other aspirants in the primary, winning with only 43 percent of the Republican vote. Perhaps Welker's close association with Joe McCarthy drew more moderate Republican candidates to oppose him. In any case, neither party had a mechanism in place to formally endorse candidates before the primary.[29] As a result, neither party could effectively restrain candidates from running no matter how damaging a crowded primary might make the party's general election prospects.[30]

The inability of parties to control the nomination process is but one indication of their organizational weakness. Another sign is the inability of the Democratic Party to resolve its intraparty disputes. Church eked out a 170-vote primary victory over former U.S. Senator Glen H. Taylor. Convinced Church had won fraudulently, Taylor demanded a recount and Senate investigation. Denied both, Taylor announced he would not step aside and support Church; rather, he would run as a write-in candidate during the general election.[31] The Democratic Party was so weak and disorganized that Taylor could hardly fear a reprisal. Idaho's Democrats had no way to punish or discourage Taylor's unwillingness to get behind the party nominee.

Organizationally, if the party played a role in the Church campaign, it did so as an auxiliary to the Church organization. Without much money, a strong hierarchical structure, or even precinct committeemen and women operating in all of Idaho's counties, the party could not help.[32] The Church organization ran its own campaign. Staffed by volunteers, it operated autonomously from the Democratic Party. One of the campaign's first tasks was to build a Church statewide campaign organization; it did so by recruiting county chairmen in all forty-four of Idaho's counties. Some of these Church supporters worked in the state party organization, but for many, this was their first political campaign. As Church's campaign manager succinctly put it, "We ran our own campaign. Just basically ran the whole thing."

Frank Church, his wife, and manager-friend Carl Burke made all the major strategic campaign decisions together. A memorandum outlining the general election strategy, presumably written by Burke, focuses on television, radio, posters, billboards, and other devices designed to communicate directly with voters. There is no mention of a formal role for the Democratic organization in the coming campaign.[33] Burke's budget foresaw expenses totaling $57,000, with the bulk being spent on publicity in the form of television ($8,100), radio ($9,400), and print ($22,000).[34]

Although the Ada County Democratic Party paid for some television and radio time, much of the fund-raising responsibility fell to Church himself.[35] Frank and Bethine sold their home and used the proceeds to fund the campaign. The campaign also sent financial appeals to donors on their own. Outside contributors, such as the National Committee for an Effective Congress and labor unions, seemed to have targeted Welker for defeat, and they gave without an appeal from Church or the Idaho Democrats.[36] Apparently, an appeal was made by either Burke or Church to the Democratic National Committee, and an effort was made to send some money after Church secured the nomination.[37] However, the Church campaign financed its efforts from the wallets and purses of the Church family, their friends, and associates rather than the national or state Democratic Party.[38]

Television and radio played to Church's strengths and had the advantage of quickly introducing the inexperienced candidate to the public. Taking advantage of the new media, the Church campaign churned out a wide range of advertisements written, produced, and directed by the Churches and a few friends.[39] As "virtually the only Idaho candidate to use television" in 1956, Church was a political innovator.[40] His advertisements focused strictly on Church and his opponent.

Unlike candidates running in states with stronger partisan organizations, Church made little effort to link himself to other Democratic candidates, either locally or nationally. He did appear occasionally onstage with the state's Democratic congressional candidates, and he greeted presidential nominee Adlai Stevenson when he appeared at a rally late in the campaign.[41] But Church did not stress, in his literature or advertisements, the Democratic ticket as a whole. And there was no effort to coordinate a united Democratic campaign. Pamphlets exhorted Democratic primary voters to "unite behind Frank Church" and declared that "Idaho will be proud of Frank Church in the U.S. Senate." Although his campaign manager and wife stress that Church wore the Democratic label proudly and did not shun his party, one cannot help but notice the lack of prominence given to the party label in brochures, television advertisements, and radio announcements.[42] In such a Republican state, being a Democrat was a definite disadvantage. Combined with the organizational weakness of the party, Church had to focus almost completely on his personal strengths and qualities rather than on the party and its record.

The personalities of the candidates took center stage.[43] On the issues, Church avoided those favored by his party's standard-bearer. Stevenson discussed foreign policy, ending the draft, and eliminating atomic testing, while Church preferred jobs, farming, and natural resources. Church "declined to take up any of the issues raised by Stevenson. He even sidestepped Stevenson's effort to make an issue of the Near East crisis."[44] In a memo, Church asked national speakers to steer away from issues national in scope and to focus instead on "Idaho's Decade of Stunted Growth" and Herman Welker's "Deplorable Public Record."[45] Part of this record was Welker's once-close relationship with Republican Senator Joe McCarthy of Wisconsin, which included an active defense of McCarthy during his censure proceedings and praise for McCarthy's chief counsel, Roy Cohn, on his resignation.[46] It also refers undoubtedly to Welker's refusal to support federal aid for the Hell's Canyon water project, an issue important to farmers and the industrial development of the state, but in keeping with Welker's opposition to the federal government's growth and expansion.[47] The focus remained on the candidates and Idaho, not the Democratic Party and its national or state achievements.

Announcing the opening of the Citizens for Frank Church headquarters, Carl Burke invited "all persons, Democrats, Independents, and Republicans alike, to join forces to elect Frank Church to the United States Senate."[48] As a heavily Republican state, Idaho required a strategy of appeals to independents and Republicans. Although not expressly linking Church to Eisenhower, the campaign pointed out that incumbent Republican Senator

Herman Welker had been no Eisenhower friend, having offered the president scant support on the Senate floor.[49] A press release distributed early in the campaign, no doubt directed at Republican voters, notes that even Holmes Alexander, a national Republican columnist, called for Welker's defeat.[50]

In the end, Church overcame the odds, defeating Welker with 56 percent of the vote. Glen Taylor's third-party bid hardly mattered, garnering only 5 percent. The *New York Times* postelection coverage of the campaign neatly sums up the Democratic Party's campaign role: "He [Church] operated out of his own headquarters in Boise, hardly bothering to check in with the Democratic State Headquarters."[51] The Church campaign built an organization from scratch, communicated the candidate's strengths, discussed local issues, and virtually ignored the official party apparatus in Boise. The organizational weakness of the Idaho Democrats undermined their ability to cope with the new electoral reality, necessitating candidate-centered campaigns. Church blazed his own trail to victory by gathering monetary resources himself and side-stepping the party's reputation in favor of his own. His choice of campaign strategy was governed by the resources available to him but not his party.

TENNESSEE: NOBODY'S PET RACCOON

Unlike Frank Church, Estes Kefauver announced his Senate candidacy when he was already a seasoned political professional. Having been elected in 1938 to fill an unexpired term, Kefauver represented the Third Congressional District surrounding Chattanooga for nearly a decade. But like Church, Kefauver faced a tough election struggle. The national attention he garnered as one of *Collier Magazine*'s "ten best congressmen" had earned him widespread name recognition in his home state of Tennessee.[52] However, the state's long dominant political machine, run by E. H. Crump of Memphis, actively opposed Kefauver's bid for higher office. And Kefauver faced an incumbent senator for his party's nomination.

Like Idaho, no formal mechanism existed for Tennessee's political parties to select their nominees. The Democratic Party's state convention played no role in selecting candidates or adopting campaign platforms.[53] Party voters chose their Senate nominees through a direct primary held in August. Informally, however, the party apparatus had the opportunity to play a significant role in candidate selection. Party officials could and did endorse candidates for office, and in Tennessee, Crump's endorsement carried substantial weight.

"Boss" Crump headed an old-style political machine based in Memphis and Shelby County. From his perch on the Mississippi, Crump effectively ran Democratic politics in Tennessee from the early 1930s through the early 1950s. Politicians rarely achieved statewide office without his aid and support.[54] Crump "demonstrated his political influence innumerable times over the years by supporting senators, congressmen, mayors, and other elected and appointed officials," expecting "absolute capitulation to his will."[55] With a Crump endorsement, a candidate had the Democratic nomination and general election all but won.[56] The key to Crump's success lay both in his well-oiled Shelby county machine and willingness to impose "severe political and economic sanctions against those who dared oppose his will in his own bailiwick."[57]

Crump did not like Kefauver.[58] Even though Kefauver had joined a Crump-endorsed administration before serving in Congress, he resisted becoming an active machine supporter and participant. Kefauver had seriously contemplated challenging Senator Kenneth McKellar, one of Crump's key supporters, in the 1946 Democratic primary.[59] In the end, Kefauver declined to make the race. Had the matter ended there, all might have been forgiven. But Kefauver endorsed McKellar's opponent, Ed Carmack, and actively stumped for him. Crump could not ignore this heretical act. He would try to defeat Kefauver, throwing his organizational might into the effort. Crump's inability to clear the field for his favored candidate and ultimately to vanquish Kefauver indicates the limits of his political authority. It also demonstrates the weakness of a party system dependent on personalities and understandings rather than formal institutional foundations. Although stronger than the Democratic Party in Idaho, Crump had one problem as a political boss: his control over the party depended on keeping Shelby County in line. As the dean of southern politics, V. O. Key, noted, "Even the weakest opposition candidate for state office always made a respectable showing against his organization." A crack in Shelby County, as Key's analysis demonstrates, could prove to be his undoing.[60] The fact that Crump's death in 1954 led to the machine's collapse underscores the personal and fleeting nature of its organizational presence in Shelby County.

Kefauver knew he would receive little help from Crump and other professional politicians, so he worked "to form a campaign organization of people without a political past."[61] He turned to Charles Neese, a young Chattanooga attorney, rather than a party professional to run his Senate campaign. Traveling across the state for months before the primary, Kefauver visited old friends in an effort to build a grassroots organization bypassing the Crump machine. The plan called for organizations in every county and major city, with congressional campaign committees layered on top.[62] Most innovatively, the Kefauver campaign put substantial resources and energy into mobilizing the women's vote.[63] Neglected in many other campaigns, Kefauver and Neese knew they needed every vote possible, and so they made the women's vote a centerpiece of their strategy.[64] Even Crump-controlled Memphis was not immune to the Kefauver forces.[65] The cracks appearing at Crump's home base did not bode well for the coming campaign. In particular, Shelby County's business community did not fall in lockstep behind Crump: some dared to support Kefauver. [66]

The true burden of bucking the party appeared to be financial above all else.[67] To raise money for the primary, Kefauver put a third mortgage on his Washington residence. When the campaign had to buy radio time and pay in advance, Neese had to scrounge up the money. Neese frequently warned local Kefauver groups they would have to fend for themselves financially, as the campaign simply did not have enough money to go around.[68] Kefauver's extensive campaigning throughout Tennessee in the year preceding the August primary was an effort to increase his name recognition among voters and to compensate for the financial challenges he faced.

Despite all of Kefauver's work, he might never have been elected had it not been for a series of Crump miscalculations. Crump had handed incumbent Senator Tom Stewart his office, but Stewart's lackluster showing against Democratic challenger Edward Carmack in 1942 convinced Crump that he needed to find a new standard-bearer. He withdrew his support of Stewart and, without even personally meeting him, backed Judge John Mitchell for the nomination.[69] Unfortunately for Crump, Stewart refused to step aside, creating a three-way primary. Kefauver and Neese expressed concern that Stewart, having been shunned by Crump, would become the de facto anti-machine candidate.[70] Instead, the Stewart candidacy split the organization vote in half, allowing Kefauver to capture the nomination.

Kefauver had planned on running a positive primary campaign focused on "world peace, protection of TVA [Tennessee Valley Authority] . . .

and stabilization and reduction of cost of living."[71] Although he had the opportunity to combine his efforts with those of the anti-Crump gubernatorial candidate, Gordon Browning, Kefauver took the counsel of his advisers, kept his distance, and ran independent of Browning.[72] The Kefauver camp might have been content to continue largely in this vein had Crump not forced the anti-Crump mantle onto Kefauver's shoulders.

Beginning in early June, Crump resorted to a tactic he had previously employed with success: vicious attacks on his opponents in full-page newspaper advertisements. In the *Memphis Commercial Appeal*, Crump accused Kefauver of being "a pet coon." In the context of the ad, this meant that Kefauver straddled issues.[73] Particularly damaging was a further charge that Estes Kefauver voted frequently with Communist Congressman Vito Marcantonio.[74] Kefauver's response created a political legend. Giving a speech in Crump's Memphis, he donned a coonskin cap while boldly proclaiming he was nobody's pet coon.[75] The cap became the campaign's trademark, and Kefauver became the anti-machine candidate. Adorned with the slogan "Estes Is Bestes" and detailing Kefauver's accomplishments, campaign literature began to acknowledge the need to vote for a candidate not beholden to Crump.[76]

After Kefauver secured the party's nomination, the campaign underwent a dramatic transformation. Gordon Browning had also succeeded in capturing the Democratic Party's gubernatorial nomination. Neese, who had argued the perils of a joint anti-Crump primary campaign, noted in a memorandum that the fall campaign should be conducted separately but financed jointly.[77] Neese appears to have lost part of the argument, as the two forces effectively merged.[78] The Kefauver and Browning team appropriated state Democratic headquarters, and Neese became an assistant campaign manager serving under Browning's campaign manager, Robert Taylor.[79]

The general election campaign, organizationally, resembled those run in strong party states. Browning and Kefauver traveled together throughout the state, pitching the combined Browning-Kefauver ticket.[80] In the primary, the Kefauver campaign had focused on their candidate's individual attributes and qualifications. During the general election, Kefauver and Browning were packaged together with the Democratic ticket as a whole. This is apparent from the new campaign literature distributed in the fall, paid for by the state party rather than the individual campaigns, as had been the case during the primary.[81] Individuals previously neutral or actively endorsing the other candidates during the primary enthusiastically announced their support for the Browning-Kefauver ticket after the primary dust had settled.[82] Even Boss Crump could not swallow the prospect of endorsing the Republican ticket, begrudgingly giving his primary opponents his support.[83]

As one might expect in a factional party state with a shaky political infrastructure, the transition from primary to general election occurred with some difficulty. Emblematic of the problems facing the Browning-Kefauver leadership, who had to merge two previously autonomous organizations into a united effort, were those faced by Martha Ragland, chair of the campaign's women's division.[84] Ragland noted that some of the problems stemmed from lack of precedent: aside from the party's committeewomen, women had not been extensively involved in Tennessee's political campaigns.[85] Animosity left over from the bitter primary contests also hindered the closing of ranks behind Kefauver and Browning.[86] And there was a fear, among those women active in the Kefauver women's campaign during the primary, that committeewomen long active in the formal party organization would displace them.[87] On the other side of the ledger, some party women recoiled at the thought of being associated with Kefauver.[88] Ragland had the unfortunate job of smoothing ruffled feathers and encouraging those who had worked for Kefauver in the primary to put aside their past differences and work alongside former enemies for the good of the ticket.[89]

The Crump organization may have stepped aside for its opponents, but it offered little assistance.[90] It had drained the party treasury during the primary, so the Browning-Kefauver campaign found itself appealing to the national party for money.[91] This must have been awkward considering the candidates' desire to keep their distance from the presidential campaign and the national party on issues. The Truman administration had begun pushing positively on the issue of civil rights, proposing a Fair Employment Practices Commission to protect the occupational rights of minorities. This was anathema to southern candidates, and the joint Democratic campaign conspicuously neglected mention of Truman in its literature.[92] The campaign's support for the national ticket varied tremendously throughout the state. At the same time that Neese wrote reminding the Democratic National Committee of the campaign's efforts on behalf of Truman, the Shelby County committee for Browning and Kefauver decided to steer clear of the presidential race for fear of antagonizing the Crump forces favorable to Strom Thurmond's third-party candidacy.[93]

The Democratic Party's organizational strength during the general election belies Tennessee's low TPO score. Why? With the exception of eastern Tennessee, the Republican Party was not a factor in the state, and it had virtually no organizational presence during the entire region. Indeed, no Republican had won a Senate seat in the South since Reconstruction until John Tower won a special election to replace Lyndon Johnson in 1961. Tennessee Democrats did not lose a Senate election to the Republicans until 1966, when voters sent Howard Baker to Washington. The Democrats unified behind Kefauver and Browning because voting Republican was simply not an acceptable alternative, however unpalatable the Democratic nominees might be. The party brand name had value, even if the party organization was not strongly institutionalized.

Democrats also retained control of local election boards in Tennessee as they did throughout the South, even in scattered Republican strongholds. Key wrote that "state appointment results in Democratic control of local election boards even in counties with Republican majorities. . . . [I]n a few states central Democratic control of local election machinery provides a weapon of partisan advantage."[94] Because of the lack of competition and the ability to control the election machinery, the Tennessee Democrats appeared more organized and capable than might be the case during the general election. Nevertheless, these advantages did not translate into strength during the primary process, necessitating the use of candidate-centered strategies by congressional candidates. Indeed, in 1950, the Crump machine continued its downward slide as Senator Kenneth McKellar, a Crump ally, lost the Democratic nomination to Albert Gore, Sr.

In the general election, the joint canvass advocated by Browning and Kefauver fit Tennessee's increased level of partisan institutionalization. Unlike states with more advanced partisan structures, however, the Democratic Party in Tennessee rested on an unsound foundation. As in Idaho, the party had no control over the nomination process and only limited financial resources with which to conduct a general election campaign. The combined fall campaign consisted of cobbling together two separate organizations developed outside the party structure specifically to contest the primary election. As demonstrated particularly by the tensions within the women's division, this coalition acted uneasily. The fragility of the effort certainly precluded an enthusiastic embrace of the national ticket. Browning and Kefauver guardedly maintained their independence from the Truman campaign, finding it politically unpalatable to be linked to an administration pushing for the political advancement of blacks. Consciously blending both candidate-centered and party-centered tactics, the Kefauver campaign reflected its particular resource needs and the state party's ability to meet those needs. This meant a candidate-centered campaign during the primary, shifting to a partial reliance on party organizational forms and methods during the general election campaign.

Both Kefauver and Browning won easily in November. The outcome was never in doubt. While weaker organizationally than its Democratic counterparts in other states, the party brand name had a value in a one-party state like Tennessee above and beyond the state's low institutional capacity. Quite simply, Democrats outnumbered Republicans statewide, and supporting a Republican candidate was not an acceptable alternative. Even Boss Crump, who vehemently disliked Kefauver, endorsed him late in the campaign. Crump could have thrown his support to B. Carroll Reece, but it would have been meaningless and damaging in the long run to his reputation. Organizational strength can overcome many obstacles, but when a party enjoys an overwhelming reputational advantage, institutional capacity alone is not enough. Tennessee in 1948 provides a clear example of how a party's brand name can bring benefits to a candidate that institutional capacity alone cannot.

KENTUCKY: THE PERFECT STORM

On the last day of April 1956, Kentucky Senator Alben Barkley suffered a fatal heart attack after addressing a group of students. Barkley had been elected to the Senate after completing his term as Harry Truman's vice president, defeating John Sherman Cooper, who had been appointed in 1952 to complete an unexpired term. Barkley's death propelled Kentucky to the center of the country's political attention. Not only would the state be hotly contested during the presidential campaign, as Eisenhower had narrowly lost the popular vote there in 1952, but Kentucky voters would have the opportunity to choose not one but two United States senators in a single election cycle. Earle Clement, the occupant of the Senate seat Barkley had originally vacated to accept the vice presidency, sought re-election and was running against Republican Congressman Thruston Morton. The stakes could not be higher: Democrats clung to a one-seat majority in the Senate and could ill afford to lose Kentucky's two seats.

Kentucky Republicans had an incredible opportunity before them. The odds, however, were stacked against them. Republicans had not held both Senate seats in Kentucky since 1926. They lagged considerably behind the Democrats numerically, and the statehouse with all its crucial patronage and kickbacks from civil servants escaped their grasp. Democrats had selected Lawrence Wetherby, a former lieutenant governor and governor, as their nominee. To have a legitimate shot at winning, Republicans would have to attract a candidate equally qualified and talented. The White House and Kentucky Republicans agreed John Sherman Cooper fit the bill perfectly.

Cooper had a long list of political accomplishments. Starting in the state legislature, he quickly climbed the political ladder, serving a lengthy term as Pulaski County judge and running for governor in 1939. Although he lost the Republican primary, Cooper proved himself the good party man by selflessly stumping the state for his former opponent that fall.[95] In 1945, he ran for and won the right to complete Ben "Happy" Chandler's Senate term.[96] Three years later, he ran for the full term, but fell before a Democratic tide sweeping Republicans out of congressional control. When Virgil Chapman, the Democrat who had beaten Cooper in 1948, died in office, Cooper again ran for the seat and won. Unfortunately, he became the victim of circumstances a second time when running for the full term. Alben Barkley wanted his old job back after serving as vice president. Cooper put up a valiant fight, but he simply could not beat such a popular Democrat in an essentially Democratic state. Eisenhower named Cooper ambassador to India as a consolation.

Having been involved in four Senate races in eleven years, Cooper expressed little desire to try for the Senate again. He enjoyed his post in New Delhi. But when Barkley passed away, Cooper was overwhelmed by requests from Kentucky and Washington to leave his post and run for the Senate one more time. The Kentucky Republican Party establishment rallied behind Cooper, but it took a final plea from Eisenhower himself for Cooper to relent.[97] As Barkley's death occurred a day after the party primaries, in accordance with state law the party committee selected Cooper as its party's Senate nominee without visible or open dissent.[98]

Two organizations ran separate, but related, Senate campaigns for Cooper. During an election year, the Republican Party created a campaign committee responsible for the conduct of the canvass. In 1956, the Republican Party chairman selected Louie Nunn, a young attorney from Barren County, to run the show. He had considerable authority, as the Republican State Central Committee and its designees in Kentucky had complete charge of the campaign and the collection of funds. But Cooper also established his own campaign organization, headed by Frederick Sontag. Sontag served as a special counsel to Eisenhower's secretary of labor. The existence of a separate campaign committee for Cooper appeared to be unusual and caused Nunn some consternation. When Nunn first met Sontag and heard him say he was running the Cooper campaign, Nunn expressed his surprise to Cooper.[99] Cooper assured him this was not the case and indicated he would shut down his organization. This did not happen, and the two groups appeared to reach an understanding. They continued to operate independently, although representatives of the Cooper campaign attended meetings of the Republican campaign committee to represent Cooper's interest, and some coordination did occur.[100] The state campaign committee raised and provided funds for its canvass, while Sontag and Cooper actively solicited funds to pay for the Cooper campaign's activities. Both campaigns relied on a mix of literature, radio, and television spots to communicate with voters.[101]

Always considered a good party man, Cooper also had established a reputation as a liberal Republican representing a conservative state.[102] A bit of a maverick, he did not vote in lockstep with the party during his previous tenure in the Senate, and his campaign reflected these competing strategies.[103] The Republican Party's campaign literature advertised Thurston and Cooper together as a team with the Eisenhower administration.[104] "Eisenhower needs help in the legislature, so why not send him two people who will vote with him?" was the message. The Cooper campaign, in material it produced itself, did not avoid Eisenhower. Quite the contrary, the material always stressed Cooper's ties to Eisenhower through pictures of the candidate with the president and mentioned Cooper's support for the administration's foreign policy program.[105]

But Cooper wanted to have his cake and eat it, too. His own literature assiduously avoided the use of the Republican Party label and stressed his ability to work with Democrats and independents. For example, Cooper's stint as a Truman appointee to the United Nations delegation was often highlighted.[106] Cooper also made it clear that he did not want national speakers coming to the state on his behalf, as he felt this would undermine these efforts to attract non-Republican votes.[107] His own literature focused on his support for tobacco price supports, education, Kentucky's coal industry, and labor-friendly amendments to Taft-Hartley.[108] Civil rights and foreign policy stand alone as the major exceptions to this policy of avoiding Republican issue positions. Cooper openly proclaimed support for the Republican Party's pro–civil rights program, castigating Democrats for the segregationist policies of Mississippi Senator John Eastland.[109]

Why did Cooper embrace the Republican Party selectively? The answer is resources. Cooper knew from his previous campaign experiences and as a member of the state's minority party that Democrats and independents had to support him to win.[110] Cooper generally saw the party's issue reputation as a millstone around his neck, and he desperately tried to make more candidate-centered appeals to buoy his prospects. The two Republican issue themes he did stress, civil rights and foreign policy, could each help him win the general election. Foreign policy allowed him to latch onto Ike's popularity. Civil rights, while possibly turning off some white voters, if used selectively could attract African American support.

On the other hand, Cooper could not hope to construct a personal organization or following overnight—especially considering the Republican Party's organizational strength, the circumstances under which he found himself running for office, and the ability of the Democrats to rely on state employees for contributions and labor.[111] Cooper needed all the monetary and voter resources that the Republican Party could provide. As party manager Nunn put it, "I carried the water for [Cooper]."[112] As a result, Cooper relented to campaign appearances with Morton, allowed party headquarters to run a campaign on Republican issues, and linked himself to Eisenhower explicitly.[113] He certainly had no problem joining fellow nominee Morton in sending letters to party workers urging them to go all out for them during the campaign.[114]

Cooper could not ignore the benefits that the party's organization provided. As a result, he walked a tightrope between the party's campaign and his own efforts. And the party, despite its moaning over Cooper's liberalism, had a winning candidate.[115] Had the Republican Party been in a stronger demographic position, or had the party organization been less developed, Cooper probably would have behaved quite differently—or the party might have selected another candidate. In Kentucky, the seeds of candidate-centered politics fell on fertile soil but struggled against a strong-party apparatus. The Republican gamble paid off, and they captured both Senate seats.

Both Republicans and Democrats had strong party organizations in the state of Kentucky. In the case of John Sherman Cooper, his party's organizational vitality could not be ignored. Although Cooper selectively dissented from the party's issue orthodoxy and established a separate campaign organization, the party provided important campaign resources necessary for him to win. Eisenhower was popular, and he won Kentucky in 1956 after narrowly losing four years earlier. Connecting himself to Eisenhower and the Republican's reputation on key issues was a net positive for Cooper, as were the financial and manpower resources that the party could provide on election day. Although Cooper later became an independent Republican voice in the Senate, particularly on Vietnam, his victory would have been unlikely had he tried to utilize candidate-centered strategies at the expense of his party's support and resource base.

ILLINOIS: THE PARTY'S GOING STRONG

The 1950 Illinois Senate race pitted two talented political heavyweights in an expensive and pitched election battle. Scott Lucas had held the seat for two terms and hoped to win a third. As the Democratic Party's majority leader, Lucas carried the Truman administration's legislative program in the Senate. This presented Lucas with a double-edged sword: his loyalty had earned him the administration's full support in the coming campaign, while it tied him to programs increasingly unpopular at home, such as the war in Korea, universal health care, and the Brannan agricultural plan.[116] How the administration's support and popularity would factor in the swing state of Illinois remained to be seen; certainly the narrowness of his victory six years previous made Lucas vulnerable.

Lucas's close shave in 1944 had earned him a formidable challenger this time around: Everett Dirksen. Like Estes Kefauver, Dirksen had spent sixteen years in the House of Representatives before deciding to make a run for the Senate. As a congressman, he had received national recognition and admiration. The *Washington Post* considered him "one of the most powerful and highly esteemed leaders in the House."[117] Although Lucas had misgivings about his own party, the state of the Republican Party in Illinois surely gave Dirksen pause, too. The party had been thoroughly routed in the 1948 campaign, losing the governorship, a Senate seat, and the presidential vote.[118] Could the Republican organization recover sufficiently to aid Dirksen in his quest for higher office, or did its setback herald the beginnings of an organizational collapse?

The health of the Republican Party in Illinois was no small thing. Unlike Idaho or Tennessee, Illinois had one of the strongest partisan traditions in the country. Although Chicago's Democratic organization has received a goodly amount of attention from scholars, journalists, and historians, Illinois had a healthy, vibrant, and well-organized two-party system throughout much of the nineteenth and twentieth centuries. Any candidate for political office had to contend with the party organization in its many and varied forms during the primary and general election. Omnipresent, both parties throughout the state provided candidates with ample resources with which to contest elections.[119]

Dirksen chose not to run for reelection to the House in 1948 due to ill health. His eyesight had been deteriorating, and permanent blindness became a real possibility. Only a few months into retirement, however, Dirksen discovered his condition would eventually improve.[120] He could return to active political life. Eager to knock off Lucas, the Republican Party nearly salivated at the prospect of a Dirksen candidacy. Throughout 1948 and 1949, Dirksen received several delegations at his Pekin, Illinois, home asking him to make the race. Party officials pleaded with Dirksen to run.[121] Chicago alderman Alban "Stormy" Weber's pledge of full support in early 1949 was typical: "I have decided to go all out for you and your candidacy. This does not mean my best wishes for your success—it means that I merely wait the go signal from you to take any small part to which you may choose to assign me in the organization."[122]

Like Idaho, Tennessee, and Kentucky, Illinois chose its senators by direct primary. The parties influenced voters, however, by utilizing a slating mechanism. Local and county party organizations endorsed a slate of candidates for the party's nomination.[123] This slate would then be actively advertised and promoted by the party, with appeals sent to voters and activists to cast their ballots for the entire slate.[124] Although two other candidates besides Dirksen appeared on the Republican primary ballot, they represented token opposition.[125] Dirksen received the near-united support of the Republican organization in Illinois, from the state down to Chicago's precincts.[126] The party had cleared the field of any major opposition for Dirksen. Beyond this, the party had no official role in the primary process. Dirksen was responsible for running his own campaign and raising the funds to pay for it.[127]

The organizational picture of the campaign became complicated after the primary. The Republican Citizens Finance Committee enjoyed the status as the only official operation authorized to raise funds for the party organization, and it controlled much of the Dirksen campaign's finances.[128] This committee earmarked $70,000 specifically for the Senate race, although Dirksen's campaign manager, Harold Rainville, anticipated expenses exceeding $200,000.[129] Whether the Illinois Republican organization—at the state or local level—raised money in addition to the $70,000 pledged is unclear. Dirksen expressed satisfaction with the party's financial support, but he probably made up the budgetary shortfall from leftover primary funds, as well as monies donated by a series of "independent" Dirksen organizations. These groups included Irish Americans for Dirksen, Dry Cleaners for Dirksen, Bankers for Dirksen, and so forth. Their "independence" from the Dirksen campaign is questionable, as they shared a building with Dirksen's headquarters, corresponded with Rainville, and had their activities coordinated by a single individual.[130] It appears the groups had been established to avoid federal campaign spending limitations, but they probably worked in concert with Dirksen's campaign and perhaps with the rest of the party.

Although Dirksen retained Rainville's services as campaign manager even after winning the Republican primary, they did not run the show alone. Dirksen arranged meetings with his party's statewide, legislative, and congressional candidates on numerous occasions to discuss strategy, scheduling, and the division of labor during the canvass.[131] The party had a tradition of candidates touring downstate together, and Dirksen frequently joined the candidates for state supreme court clerk, treasurer, and superintendent of public instruction at rallies, picnics, and party meetings across Illinois.[132] The candidates also arranged to campaign separately to cover more ground effectively. Worried that separate appearances might be seen as evidence of a party division or squabble, Dirksen and his colleagues candidly discussed how to assure the media and public that no rift existed between them.[133]

The party played a role in much of the strategic and tactical decision-making. Agreeing to fund a statewide billboard purchase, the Republican Citizens Finance Committee pushed to include all the statewide candidates and communicated the preferred design and color.[134] The Cook County Republican Organization chided Rainville early in the campaign for scheduling an appearance in Chicago without prior authorization from the committee's chair; all later events received the local party's sanction first before appearing on Dirksen's schedule.[135] Indeed, campaign schedules and appearances generally received the input of party officials before being adopted by the Dirksen campaign.[136]

Dirksen explained the importance of the party in a letter to a supporter, writing that the "organizational and administrative work will be handled by the county chairman, the state central committee, the Cook County Committee, and the Federation of Women's Republican Clubs."[137] This included recruiting and reimbursing precinct workers responsible for getting out the vote on election day and holding rallies to energize precincts.[138] The Chicago Republicans even hired a publicity director in charge of creating radio programs and "spot announcements" promoting candidates individually as well as the entire Republican ticket.[139]

This team mentality shines through in the campaign literature produced by Dirksen and the Illinois Republicans at the state and local level.[140] On Dirksen's stationery, the declaration "Vote Republican" appears along the bottom. It also materialized on Dirksen for Senate campaign buttons.[141] Almost universally, party organizations advertised the Republican ticket, usually in the form of a sample ballot listing all the Republican candidates for office with checkmarks beside their names.[142] Fund-raising appeals also noted the importance not only of electing a Republican senator in November but also increasing the party's share of seats in the state legislature and congressional delegation, as well as returning those Republicans currently serving in statewide office.[143] "Voting the straight Republican ticket," exclaimed Cook County Republican chair John "Bunny" East to a packed crowd of Republican women, "is vitally important to this election."[144] Radio advertisements echoed these sentiments, calling for a Republican Congress to "clean up" the scandal and corruption in Washington.[145]

Unlike Kefauver or Church, who had to couch their support for the national ticket carefully, Dirksen found himself in the happy situation of running against an opponent linked to an unpopular Democratic presidential administration. The personalities, style, and characteristics of the two candidates did not factor heavily in the 1950 Illinois Senate race. The candidates focused instead on issues reflecting the substantive differences between the two parties. Dirksen made the campaign a referendum on the Truman administration with Lucas as its "symbolic surrogate."[146] Congressional Republicans nationally focused their assault on the loss of

China, communism, agriculture, socialized medicine, and foreign policy blunders.[147] Dirksen, following the plan perfectly, employed these same issues against Lucas, smothering him with the Truman administration at every opportunity. Indeed, Dirksen helped develop Republican issue strategy in September, playing a role in persuading the Republican National Committee to shift increasingly to the Truman administration's foreign policy shortcomings and "bunglings."[148] For his part, Lucas actively defended the administration and used a picture of Truman and himself on billboards throughout the state.[149]

In the end, the Republican Party prevailed, with Dirksen winning by 8 percent and even narrowly carrying Democratic Cook County. Journalists had proclaimed that a Lucas defeat would signal a repudiation of the Truman administration. This is a telling portrayal. The campaign had been waged by two partisan warriors, fighting on a partisan landscape employing a wide range of party resources at their disposal. Although the Truman administration had no place on the ballot, Lucas's close association with the president and the Republicans' skillful exploitation of that fact created such a referendum. The effort by the Republican Party to sell its candidates as a complete package may have contributed to the breadth and depth of its Illinois victory. Republicans increased their congressional delegation by four and even elected a Republican sheriff in Cook County. In Illinois, the Republican Party's vitality and institutional presence made running as part of a ticket sensible from a resource perspective. Running as a loyal team player gave Dirksen monetary, organizational, and reputational advantages difficult to collect alone. In the end, it propelled Dirksen to success against a sitting majority leader who had employed all the advantages of incumbency.

SUMMARIZING SENATE CAMPAIGNS
AT MID-TWENTIETH CENTURY

In all four races, Senate candidates engaged in campaign behavior consistent with the resource theory. Aware of the political necessity of gathering money and reputation resources to win elections, candidates carefully surveyed the political landscape when deciding how to conduct their campaign. When a vibrant partisan culture and a strong institutional presence were available, candidates hesitated to "go it alone" by building their own campaign organizations, prospecting for funds themselves, and

Table 4.2. Summarizing four Senate campaigns, 1940–1960

	Idaho	Tennessee	Kentucky	Illinois
	1	2	4	5
Was the primary contested by major candidates?	Yes	Yes	No	No
Did the party attempt to clear the nomination path for a candidate?	No	No	Yes	Yes
Did the party actively raise money and help fund the general election campaign?	No	Yes	Yes	Yes
Did the candidate campaign with other party candidates?	No	Yes	Yes	Yes
Did the party play a strategic role?	No	Mixed	Yes	Yes
Was the party ticket emphasized in publicity?	No	Mixed	Mixed	Yes
Did the candidate build a personal organization?	Yes	Yes	Mixed	No
Were the issue themes emphasized related to national or state party issue themes?	No	No	Mixed	Yes
Party Involvement Score	**0**	**3**	**6.5**	**8**
Was television or radio used?	Yes	Yes	Yes	Yes

abandoning party labels and issue positions in favor of advertising their own particular personalities and qualifications. When no strong partisan structure backed them, candidates took matters into their own hands. The mid-twentieth century cannot be typified clearly as candidate- or party-centered. Instead, the period exhibited a mix of campaign styles depending on each candidate's individual resource needs.

Table 4.2 summarizes the four Senate case studies examined in this chapter. Eight questions were posed concerning the primary process, campaign organization, and issue message. Each taps the party's role in each campaign. Party-centered responses—responses indicating party involvement—are coded as one and candidate-centered responses zero, with mixed responses receiving half a point. Totaling the responses across all eight questions yields a rough measure of party involvement ranging from zero to eight, and this value is reported in the penultimate row of the table.

As expected, party involvement in each Senate campaign is a function of the state's level of institutionalization. In Idaho, a state rating a TPO score of one, the party's involvement in Frank Church's Senate campaign was nonexistent. Republicans in Illinois, however, deeply involved themselves in Everett Dirksen's campaign to unseat Scott Lucas, which was not surprising, considering that Illinois had an active and organized partisan tradition quite unlike Idaho's. Tennessee and Kentucky, with parties stronger than Idaho's but weaker than those in Illinois, fall somewhere in between. The pattern is incontrovertible: candidate-centered strategies and behavior decrease with the concomitant increase in party institutionalization. On this point, the mid-twentieth and late nineteenth centuries do not differ.

Another important point is made by a final query: were radio and television used during each Senate campaign in that state? In all four races, television or radio appeared, sometimes funded by candidates, sometimes by parties, and sometimes by both. Campaigns employed these new communications technologies irrespective of institutionalization; indeed, parties used radio and television in the strong party states of Kentucky and Illinois as readily as candidate Frank Church did in the weak party state of Idaho. The use of television and radio did not signal the arrival of candidate-centered politics. Parties could, and did, use television to broadcast "party-centered" campaign messages to voters as ably as some candidates used the same medium to broadcast "candidate-centered" ones. Although Frank Church pitched himself and his qualifications to voters in 1956, in 1950 Illinois Republicans used Dirksen to tout the prospects of the entire ticket on statewide radio hookups. The new media did provide candidates with the ability to communicate directly to voters. But that meant little if candidates could not pay the hefty price to gain access to it. Candidates could hardly be set free of the party if they lacked monetary resources to take advantage of the new media.

Television and radio were simply new campaign tools that either candidates or parties could use. Its arrival on the scene did not spell doom for political parties and their ability to control the conduct of senatorial campaigns. Indeed, the fundamental logic of the resource equation still held: candidates engaged in candidate-centered behavior in areas lacking partisan institutionalization. Although this should be clear from the case studies, this proposition is also amenable to quantitative analysis. In chapter 3, party unity voting was used as a measure of a candidate's campaign reputation. Candidates run on their legislative records, and how much or how little they support the party is influenced by their need for resources. The party reputation can help gain votes during the general election. This was certainly the case for Kefauver in Tennessee, a state dominated by Democrats. In other situations, using the party reputation can be a useful way for candidates to ensure the party's organizational and monetary support during the campaign. John Sherman Cooper needed Eisenhower to help carry the state, and he needed to help Thruston Morton to persuade a more conservative state party to give him financial assistance.

In the late nineteenth century, high levels of party institutionalization in a state corresponded with increased support for the party on the House floor. Half a century later, the pattern in the Senate should be no different. Senators running for election in states with stronger state parties will consistently support their party on unity votes at a higher rate than those representing weakly institutionalized party states. The availability of television and radio, contrary to common scholarly wisdom, should have no effect on a senator's support for his party on the Senate floor.

To examine these two claims systematically, party unity scores are again used. The scores in question are from votes in the Senate between 1941 and 1961, representing the 77th through the 86th Congresses.[150] As in chapter 3, all votes where a majority of one party opposed the majority of the other are included and used to create a party unity score for each member in a particular Congress.[151] Senators not serving a full term and not representing one of the two major parties are excluded from the analysis.[152]

Many of the factors that affect voting in the House should also affect voting in the Senate. These factors were discussed in chapter 3 and are included in this analysis. These include the Democrat, South, and minority dummy variables, as well as seniority, previous vote percentage, previous unity, and TPO variables.[153] Of these factors, TPO is again central. Higher levels of party unity should be observed among senators representing more institutionalized states, after these other factors are taken into account. One other factor, state partisanship, is slightly different from the measure used in chapter 3, and two factors—election year and TV/radio per capita—are new to this analysis. These are explained below.

Third-party voting for the U.S. Senate happened rather infrequently during this period. It does not sensibly capture a state's political independence or partisanship as it had during the late nineteenth century. Instead, the percentage of the state's congressional delegation sharing the senator's party affiliation is substituted as a proxy for the electorate's partisanship.[154] The higher the percentage, the closer the electorate should be politically to the senator and hence the more likely he will support the party on unity votes. Conversely, the lower the percentage, the more likely a senator will want to carve an independent course when faced by a hostile electorate, resulting in a lower unity score.

Unlike the House, only a third of senators face election in any given election cycle. Presumably, senators facing an election in the immediate future will vote differently than those freshly elected to the chamber and sheltered from the immediate electoral consequences of their decisions. If a senator faces an election in the next cycle, the "Election Year" dummy variable is coded a one; otherwise, it is coded a zero. The coefficient value in the following regression results indicates whether senators facing re-election are less or more willing to support the party on unity votes. Whether there should be any difference in behavior is unclear. If senators are candidate-centered in their appeals, they should move away from the party going into an election cycle. This would produce a negative coefficient for the election year variable. If they need the party's support, however, they would want to increase their support on the Senate floor to guarantee the receipt of party resources. This would yield a positive election year coefficient.

Much of the campaign and parties literature argues that the appearance of radio and television signaled party-centered decline. As the diffusion of radio and television varies across states, this proposition can be tested easily. The number of television and radio stations indicates the degree to which a state has been penetrated by the new media; however, states are not equally populated. A per capita measure of television and radio for each state can be created by dividing the total number of radio and television stations in a given year by the state's total population. If the emergence of television and radio is associated with how senators portray themselves to the public, this television and radio variable will be marked by an asterisk in the following regression results, indicating a statistically significant relationship. As the resource theory anticipates no relationship, there should be no statistically significant relationship and no asterisk. If existing scholarship is correct, not only should the relationship be statistically significant but the value of the TV/radio per capita coefficient should be negative. This means that the emergence of television and radio is associated with senators moving away from the party on unity votes.

The results of the quantitative analysis appear in table 4.3.[155] Recalling the discussion at the end of chapter 3, one should note first whether the coefficient values are positive or negative. A positive sign indicates that the relationship between the variable in question is associated with higher levels of party unity voting. A negative sign on the coefficient indicates an inverse relationship. Second, remember that coefficients marked with stars indicate that the relationship observed between party unity and the variable is statistically significant. Nearly all the coefficients in table 4.3 have the correct signs (meaning that the relationship between the variables and party unity voting is as anticipated) and are strongly significant statistically.

While there are a number of interesting findings, it is worthwhile to pay the most attention to the coefficients directly related to the two claims being evaluated.[156] First, does state party institutionalization affect how senators voted? The answer is yes, as is denoted by the asterisks indicating a statistically significant relationship. Are higher levels of state institutionalization associated with higher levels of party unity? Again, the answer is yes. Senators hailing from states with a TPO of five and a unified congressional delegation of the same party have party unity scores six percentage points higher than those living in states with the weakest level of party institutionalization and no congressional allies. Senators who find themselves in hostile partisan territory, without a strong party apparatus to provide aid, duck the party and establish more moderate voting records in the candidate-centered tradition. Otherwise, senators contentedly support the party, hoping to reap the benefits of the party's voter and financial resources come election day. This demonstrates support for the resource theory.

What about the second claim? Is the emergence of television and radio associated with party unity voting in the Senate? Yes, as indicated by the asterisks in table 4.3, the relationship between the two is statistically significant. The claim that television and radio concentration bears no relationship to a senator's support of the party is not upheld because of the coefficient's statistical significance. But most surprising is the sign on the coefficient. Recall that the existing literature argues that the arrival of the new media signaled the collapse of traditional party organization. If correct, the TV/radio coefficient should be negative. It is not. Instead, it is positive. What does this mean?

Table 4.3. Party unity in the Senate and party organizational strength, 1941–1961

Explanatory Variables	
Candidate Characteristics	
Democrat	-.005
	(.014)
Minority	-.038***
	(.013)
Seniority	-.005***
	(.001)
South	-.049***
	(.014)
Vote Percentage	-.000
	(.000)
Previous Unity	.445***
	(.036)
Election Year	-.015*
	(.010)
Party Organization	
State Partisanship	.039**
	(.019)
TPO	.006**
	(.003)
TV/Radio per Capita	.005**
	(.002)
Constant	.401***
	(.034)
R-Squared	.314
N	917

Unstandardized coefficients based on ordinary least squares regression.
Robust standard errors reported in parentheses.
*** $p<=.01$, **$p<=.05$, *$p<=.10$; one-tailed.

The finding that television and radio density coincides with increased unity contradicts the claim that the new media spawned candidate-centered campaigns. Quite simply, the more television and radio per capita in a state, the more likely a senator will vote with his party on unity votes. Substantively, the effects have the potential to overwhelm state partisanship and organization combined. While maximum TV and radio per capita density can increase party unity voting by as much as fifteen percentage points, the effect is usually much smaller. An average amount of the new media's concentration accounts for an increase of party unity of only one percentage point.

The assertion made by many scholars concerning the new media's impact on campaigns is simply wrong. But why should a senator's partisan reputation be associated with media concentration? The resource theory offers the best explanation. The existence of television and radio did not alter the fact that candidates need resources to compete in elections. Without money, candidates can hardly make use of the ability to communicate directly with voters. If anything, the appearance of television and radio may have made it *more* likely for candidates to establish a partisan voting record, particularly in states with party organizations capable of providing the monetary resources with which to utilize this new campaign tool. Instead of encouraging candidate-centered techniques, television and radio may have actually hampered their adoption during the mid-twentieth century or at the very least slowed down the so-called demise of parties. And this pattern appears in the Senate, the institution where one might expect candidate-centered techniques and politics to be most instinctively appealing. In the most candidate-centered legislative environment with candidates the most likely to utilize the new communications technology, the rise of television and radio is related to increased reliance on partisan reputations. Resource need explains this otherwise unexpected and unintuitive finding.

CONCLUSION

Television and radio did not devastate parties, and candidates did not abandon their party organizations in the middle of the twentieth century. Parties undoubtedly faced some setbacks, but how each party weathered the storm depended on the depth of its roots. In states where parties had never taken a firm hold, the winds of change were felt the most harshly. Parties with roots burrowed deep in a state's political soil had less trouble withstanding the reform storm. The relationships observed in the late nineteenth century continued to hold at the mid-twentieth century, despite a New Deal undermining urban party machines and new electoral rules such as the Tillman, Corrupt Practices, and Hatch acts designed to restrict the flow of money into the political system. Senators relied as much on institutionally embedded state party organizations to conduct their campaigns as congressmen at the close of the nineteenth century.

Despite the uniqueness of their electoral situation, senators reacted as all candidates must: they carefully considered the resources laid before them before deciding on a campaign course. Television and radio played a role in that calculus, but no more so than any other campaign tool available to them. Senators relied on their parties for reputations, votes, and money when state party organizations could provide them. When they did not or could not, senators sought those resources themselves as had House candidates in the late nineteenth century. The appearance of television and radio did not alter that fundamental resource calculation. In fact, television and radio affirmed the resource strategy, pushing candidates to support the party in areas where the new media was most prevalent.

In this chapter, the versatility of the resource theory as an explanation of candidate campaign behavior was demonstrated. By looking at campaigns at the supposed height of candidate-centered politics and at an institution that encourages political independence, a difficult test of the theory was provided. A different type of evidence was utilized with which to assess the theory: archival data culled from Senate manuscript collections located across the country. The resource theory passed the test, as evidenced by the four case studies and the quantitative analysis detailed throughout this chapter.

Candidates sought party nominations, organized campaigns, and discussed political issues in ways consistent with their party's institutional strength in the mid-twentieth century as they had in the late nineteenth. In Idaho, Frank Church hit the ground running with nary an acknowledgment of the state's Democratic organization, built an organization centered on family and friends, fought fiercely for his party's nomination against six other candidates, and pitted his qualifications against those of the incumbent. In Illinois, where party still reigned supreme, Everett Dirksen received the nomination with its blessing, coordinated his strategy and fund-raising with the party, and made the campaign a referendum on the incumbent administration and its policies. The resource situation facing Church and Dirksen differed in one crucial respect: the state party's institutional strength. Idaho's Democratic Party was weak whereas the Republican Party in Illinois was strong, providing an explanation grounded in the resource for the very different campaign behaviors of Church and Dirksen. In both cases, television and radio were employed extensively, but Church funded these advertisements himself while Dirksen relied on his party to foot the bill.

In the next chapter, attention turns to congressional campaigning in the FECA era. Unlike previous electoral reforms, FECA had the potential to overturn the candidate-state party relationship governing campaigns since the late nineteenth century, transforming political parties into nationalizing agents with the ability to create unified partisan reputations with their new financial strength. Candidates responded as they always had by evaluating the effects of reform and modifying their campaign behavior to maximize resource collection.

CHAPTER FIVE

FECA AND NATIONAL PARTY RESURGENCE

The 1940s and 1950s marked the emergence of new campaign technologies and the rise of candidate-centered campaigns. Although state parties retained a significant campaign role where they were institutionally embedded, their ability to sustain themselves organizationally began to diminish in the 1960s, according to party scholars.[1] Rapidly disintegrating urban machines could no longer mobilize an unswerving partisan vote. Candidates, sensing the weakness of state party organizations, took the opportunity to build their own monetary and reputation resources to compensate. By the early 1970s, "the parties had largely lost control of campaigning, especially in national elections."[2]

The congressional campaign committees, although more substantial and institutionally autonomous forces by the mid-twentieth century, likewise seemed impotent. Unlike party organizations in an earlier era, they did not mobilize constituents or activists.[3] Their role was reactive and passive, channeling contributions to candidates and providing speakers and pamphlets on request.[4] Political parties by the 1960s seemed to have difficulty adjusting to a new era of direct voter-targeted campaigns.[5]

Candidates utilized candidate-centered tactics in the mid-nineteenth and the mid-twentieth centuries when parties could not provide campaign resources. It appears, from the apparent increase of candidate-centered activities in all congressional campaigns, that state parties were no longer relevant as independent political actors. In terms of reputation, party unity voting had declined precipitously. By 1969, Republicans and Democrats voted with their parties only 71 percent of the time (see figure 5.1) while unity votes constituted only 35 percent of all floor votes.[6] When placed in historical context, the decline is marked. Between 1881 and 1903, the average unity score of congressmen was 84 percent, with party unity votes making up 66 percent of all House votes between 1886 and 1900.[7] If these voting patterns were any indication, actual and prospective members of Congress found the development of less partisan reputations more beneficial to their electoral fortunes.

In areas with vibrant party organization, individual congressional candidates actively promoted the party slate and platform during the late nineteenth and mid-twentieth centuries. By the 1960s, this began to change. Congressional candidates increasingly divorced themselves from partisan efforts. Their campaigns became less about the ticket and more about their own issues and reputations.[8] The responsibility for campaigning devolved to an ever-larger group of independent committees and organizations as interest groups became more politically prominent.[9] These independent committees had more money to give directly to candidates. Increasingly, these same groups also conducted their own campaigns. Candidates no longer needed state parties for monetary or reputation resources. Parties, it appeared, had lost their grip on their congressional candidates. David Broder's 1972 book title, *The Party's Over*, signifies how far the fortunes of parties had fallen.

The party was not over, though. The decline of political parties reversed course sometime during the mid-1970s. This "party resurgence" has been amply documented by scholars.[10] What led to this revival? A change in the electoral rules invigorating parties. In the wake of Watergate, Congress arguably passed the most comprehensive law governing the conduct of federal elections since the Pendleton Act in 1883. By capping campaign expenditures and the amount contributors could give to candidates, the Federal Election Campaign Act (FECA) as signed into law in 1974 had drastically altered the resource equation for anyone seeking federal office. Later amendments also transformed the relationship between state and national party organizations. Although federal election reform had been attempted on several occasions after Pendleton and before FECA, new enforcement mechanisms and the closing of several loopholes appeared to create the critical mass necessary to change how political actors engaged in resource collection.

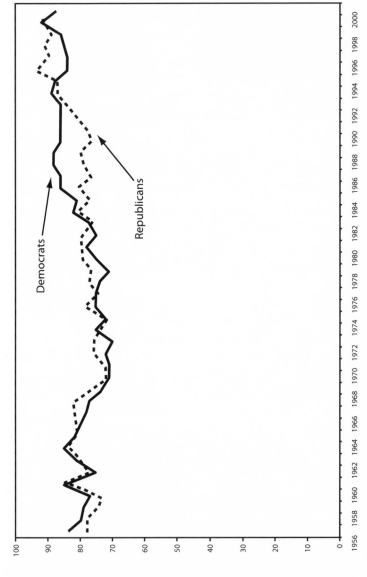

Figure 5.1. Party unity voting, 1955–2000. Compiled by author from party unity statistics between 1955 and 1988 as reported in Ornstein, Mann, and Malbin, *Vital Statistics on Congress, 1999–2000*, 202–203, table 8.4. Party unity scores for 1999 and 2000 calculated by author using CQ party unity votes as reported in CQ *Weekly*.

This chapter analyzes how FECA transformed congressional campaigns. It proceeds by discussing the federal campaign reform efforts in 1971 and 1974, the 1979 "soft money" amendments, and some key court decisions profoundly shaping the law's application. Two key points are highlighted. First, FECA, its subsequent amendments, and court interpretations revitalized the role of political parties in congressional campaigns. This forced candidates to reassess the role of party reputations and money in campaigns. Second, unlike earlier reforms, FECA subordinated state and local party organizations to newly strengthened national party committees. National party organs increasingly involved themselves in the conduct of congressional campaigns to an extent not seen previously.[11] State parties, on the other hand, became the vassals of the national parties, paying them fealty in exchange for resources. The relationship between state party institutionalization and candidate behavior faded in favor of a new dynamic between candidates and the national party.

To evaluate how this new nationalization of America's parties altered the resource strategies of congressional candidates, the various measures developed in chapters 3 and 4 are updated and revised. Whether party contribution strategies, the use of soft money, or independent expenditures affect how candidates develop partisan reputations is considered. The use of the parties' financial power to develop distinctive partisan reputations is also explored. A dataset of campaign advertisements from the 2000 election provides a more detailed look at how political actors employ partisan and individual reputations. Previewing the findings briefly, there is a relationship between party contributions and how candidates use partisan reputations during congressional campaigns. The television advertising done by candidates and the parties also corresponds surprisingly well in terms of issue content, with candidates broadcasting distinctly partisan issue agendas to voters. The chapter concludes by pondering how organization and candidate behavior might affect electorate opinion. This lays the foundation for the book's final empirical chapter.

THE FEDERAL ELECTION CAMPAIGN ACTS
OF 1971 AND 1974

The current federal campaign finance regime was the product of nearly five years of legislative effort in the short term, subsequent amendments in 1976 and 1979, and more than twenty years of judicial interpretation.[12]

This round of campaign finance, designed to replace the ineffective Corrupt Practices Act of 1925, began in 1971 when Congress passed the first Federal Election Campaign Act. What pushed Congress to act? Robin Kolodny notes that "the 1968 election was particularly important for motivating extensive reforms because of serious questions that arose regarding political advertising on television."[13] Previous campaign finance reform concentrated on driving special interests from the process. What made the 1971 reforms stand out, however, was the attention lawmakers paid to containing campaign costs. FECA circa 1971 restricted spending on television and radio advertising to five cents per voter and placed a $5,000 cap on individual campaign contributions. Also prohibited was any campaign spending not authorized by the candidate. This closed the most egregious loophole of the 1925 Corrupt Practices Act, as campaigns had previously evaded spending limits by establishing multiple campaign committees "independent" of the candidate's campaign committee. Other provisions also limited candidates' personal contributions to their own campaigns and strengthened public disclosure regulations.

Richard Nixon's 1972 campaign abuses prompted Congress to reevaluate many of the 1971 reforms. Corruption, graft, and undue influence rather than rising campaign costs provided the impetus for this new round. Unlike the 1971 legislation, the 1974 version of FECA focused on restricting the flow of money into the political process. It also contained major provisions dealing with how political parties and organized interests conducted electioneering activities.

Although the media limits imposed on candidates in 1971 were repealed, candidates were still restricted in what they personally could spend on behalf of their own candidacies. Their campaign organizations, too, had to abide by an overall spending limit. Unlike limits placed on contributions by candidates, parties, and political action committees (PACs), these overall spending limits were indexed to inflation.

Individuals could only give $1,000 per candidate per race and no more than $25,000 annually to federal candidates. PACs, which had operated since the 1930s, received express legal sanction for the first time, but could only give $5,000 per candidate per race.[14] Unlike individuals, PACs could give in aggregate to federal candidates as much as they could raise. Party organizations also were restricted to $5,000 in direct contributions to candidates, but could also coordinate the expenditure of an additional $10,000 with each of their House candidates. The amount that parties could coordinate with Senate candidates depended on a formula: $20,000 or two cents per eligible voter in the state, whichever was greater. These "coordinated expenditure limits," unlike the parties' direct contribution limit, were indexed to inflation.

In addition to how political actors could spend money, the law also established the Federal Election Commission (FEC) to oversee federal elections, implement its provisions, and enforce the new regulations. Candidates, parties, and PACs were required to report the names of their contributors to this new agency in a timely fashion. In sum, FECA was an incredibly comprehensive reform effort that greatly restricted the flow of money into the campaign process.[15]

The constitutionality of FECA's amendments was challenged immediately. As Congress had provided for expedited review, the Supreme Court handed down its decision a little more than a year after the amendments had been enacted. In *Buckley v. Valeo*, the Court held that overall limits on expenditures by campaigns violated the First Amendment. Conversely, the Court upheld the constitutionality of limits on contributions made by donors to campaigns.[16] It was a footnote, buried in the pages of the decision, which ultimately became the most important legacy of *Buckley*. The Court made a distinction between express advocacy and political speech more generally. If groups and individuals did not engage in campaign activities or advertising containing "express words of advocacy of election or defeat," they could spend freely. This subsequently became known as the "magic words" test.[17] Although FECA as written paved the way for legitimate special interest assistance to the candidates through PACs, the Court provided tacit consent to interest group activity that was political but not expressly seeking the election or defeat of a candidate. In a series of cases following *Buckley*, the courts further defined and expanded the ability of interest groups to raise money and spend it on these issue ads.[18]

The role of special interests in the campaign process, sanctioned by the recognition of PACs in FECA, was further expanded by the Federal Election Commission. In 1975, in its SUN PAC advisory opinion, the FEC ruled that corporations and unions could pay for the overhead costs of their political action committees.[19] This decision, according to Frank Sorauf, "removed the final impediment to the race of groups to organize PACs and enter electoral politics."[20] The decision encouraged corporate interests to establish PACs, something they had been largely reluctant to do despite labor's extensive use of PACs over the previous four decades.

In later amendments to FECA, Congress sought to protect the traditional role of local and state parties by allowing them to raise and spend unlimited sums on get-out-the-vote drives, voter registration activities, and other party-building efforts.[21] Through what would become known as "soft money" (in contrast to "hard money" contributions designated for candidate assistance), individuals, corporations, labor unions, and other organizations could now give money directly from their treasuries to fund party-building activities. Congress had legitimized another avenue by which private interests could influence the process. Issue advocacy advertisements required that interest groups spend money independently from candidates. Now interest groups could funnel money through parties to candidates courtesy of the soft money loophole. The ability of interest groups to engage in issue advocacy independently had shifted control of the electoral process away from candidates and parties; the 1979 soft money loophole seemed to tip the balance toward parity between the parties and interest groups potentially at the expense of candidates. Later, decisions by the FEC would clarify specifically what was and was not permissible under the rubric of soft money.

Most important, the FEC ruled that the parties could spend soft money dollars to run "issue ads" in 1995. These ads were clearly intended to influence election outcomes, but they avoided the use of magic words such as "vote for" and "vote against." An example is the advertisement Democrats launched against Congresswoman Heather Wilson, a New Mexico Republican running for her second full term in 2000: "Heather Wilson is on the ropes, throwing wild punches at John Kelly. Yet official records show under Kelly, New Mexico's district courts have one of the highest conviction rates in the country. But it's working families that Heather Wilson has hit the hardest. Wilson voted to use Social Security funds on tax cuts for the rich. She voted against guaranteed affordable prescription drug coverage through Medicare, and Wilson even voted against hiring 100,000 more teachers to reduce class sizes. Tell Heather Wilson to stop throwing punches at working families."[22]

An issue advocacy ad like this could be run without regard for the candidate's wishes. As the national parties took advantage of these thinly veiled campaign advertisements, the parties' demand for soft money grew along with concerns about the propriety of such funding. The Supreme Court, in *Colorado Republican Federal Campaign Committee v. Federal Election Commission*, further expanded the campaign role of the party committees.[23] This landmark decision allowed political parties to engage directly in independent expenditures and express advocacy ads. Unlike the amounts parties could contribute to candidates or could spend in coordination with candidates, these independent expenditures would not be restricted.[24] Parties, independent of candidates, could spend what they wished, with advertisements either favoring their candidate or criticizing his opponent. This ruling, combined with the FEC's opinion opening the airwaves to party issue ads paid for with soft money, gave parties a critical resource advantage in congressional campaigns.

RESOURCES AND FECA

FECA affected the campaign for resources substantially.[25] By restricting campaign contributions to candidates without indexing them to inflation, FECA pressured candidates to expand their donor bases as campaign costs increased. This made candidates more reliant on PAC donations and on discounted campaign services provided by political parties. Furthermore, parties acted as intermediaries by linking those who could contribute to those candidates needing financial assistance.[26]

When the Court dismantled the limits on independent expenditures, PACs, corporations, labor unions, and others were provided with a new electioneering tool and nearly unrestricted amounts of money with which to wield it. The effects of the Court's action were not limited to special interests. Candidates needed to raise ever greater amounts of money to inoculate themselves from potential attacks by these newly empowered groups. Who could help them raise this money? Parties could, especially when they began to exploit soft money, independent expenditures, and issue advocacy.

The soft money amendments also provided the national party organizations with a large pot of financial resources unavailable to them in earlier periods. Recall that national parties relied on state party organizations for money in the nineteenth century and the first half of the twentieth century. Much of this money simply got redistributed to state party organizations, and the state parties decided how to use that money. Soft money was different. It was a reliable source that the national parties could directly control. Even in the age of the new media, the national committees found they could meet and even exceed their resource needs. This freed a significant sum to be used on individual congressional campaigns—assistance that candidates certainly needed.

Where did all this soft money originate? Individuals, corporations, labor unions, and PACs all gave soft money directly to the parties. Restrictions on campaign donations to candidates limited the ability of interest groups to influence campaign agendas via candidates. Soft money, however, provided an opportunity to influence partisan agendas and reputations, with the hope for legislative payoffs. It is important to note that FECA, in some ways, pushed interest groups and political parties closer together. While interest groups continued to give money directly to candidates, the amount remained stable between 1984 and 2000: it was roughly a third of all campaign contributions received by congressional candidates.[27] Parties helped interest groups channel hard money donations effectively by sending signals with their own contributions.[28] Parties became yet another way for interest groups to channel dollars into campaigns by becoming soft money conduits. Although interest groups gave candidates in the 1960s and the early 1970s an opportunity to move away from parties, the movement of interest group dollars, courtesy of the soft money loophole, strengthened parties and their hold on resource-needy candidates.[29]

Overall, FECA, its subsequent amendment, and its interpretation by the courts revitalized the role of parties in the campaign for resources while candidates operated at a disadvantage due to contribution caps forcing them to build larger and more diverse donor bases over time. The role of PACs, interest groups, and individuals expanded as they received more tools with which to utilize their monetary resources. Candidates, seemingly liberated from parties in the 1960s and early 1970s, had to rely more than ever on the party to help them win campaigns. It was the national—not the state—organizations that controlled the resources that candidates required.

The relative importance of resources to winning also changed after the passage of FECA. In an age of low voter mobilization with the high costs of narrowcasting and voter targeting, money trumps individual reputation resources. If political parties or interest groups can use their monetary resource advantage to shape the issue environment, this affects the relative need for individual and party reputation resources. Recall the discussion of electoral rules in chapter 2. Electoral rules can shift an actor's need for resources generally. Electoral rules can also make a particular resource more useful. FECA made money more crucial to electoral victory than had previously been the case. By providing the national party organizations with an increased monetary capacity and undermining the ability of individual candidates to finance their own campaigns, FECA also altered the way candidates perceived their individual reputations. The need for money, and the ability of parties to provide it, pushed candidates once again to pay attention to their partisan reputations as an important resource. As many of the tools parties had available to them necessitated a focus on issues rather than on candidate qualities, candidates might find it useful to associate themselves and their own campaign efforts with the issue themes and stances that parties stressed in their own advertisements.

Partisan reputations were also useful to candidates because they would help them regain control of the campaign's issue agenda. Using independent expenditures and issue advocacy, interest groups can impose their own issue agendas on candidates and parties. With messages multiplying as more interests employ independent advertising and issue advocacy, individual candidates are less able to develop, hone, and transmit their reputations through all the clutter. In 2000 alone, interest groups spent $24.7 million on advertising in congressional races—17 percent of the $146 million spent by candidates, parties, and interest groups combined. Interest groups accounted for 21 percent of all advertising spots in the most competitive House races that same year.[30] With their campaign abilities similarly amplified by the advent of soft money and party issue advertising, political parties (in particular, the national committees) had the capacity to communicate a single reputation capable of slicing through the interest group din.[31] National party organizations began promoting their reputations actively in the 1980s, first with "generic campaign commercials." Examples include the "RNC's 'Vote Republican. For a Change,' 'Stay the Course,' and 'America's Back Again,' which aired in 1980, 1982, and 1984, and the DNC's 'It Isn't Fair, It's Republican,' aired in 1982."[32] Their efforts only grew over time. In the 2000 congressional campaign, parties spent $42.7 million on ads and aired 32 percent of all televised spots.[33]

Candidates can react to the party's financial and reputation power by tailoring their own campaign advertising to match the issue themes and agendas communicated by the parties. Unable to break through the glut of issue and independent expenditure advertising, candidates find themselves at a disadvantage in the dispersal of resources. Nevertheless, candidates must still communicate messages to voters in order to attract winning coalitions. With a resource deck stacked against them, candidates might find it advantageous simply to latch onto the party's issue agenda (and, more broadly, its reputation) rather than expend precious resources in an effort to communicate a separate and distinct reputation that might become overwhelmed. Put differently, candidates might use their own campaign resources to communicate an issue agenda indistinguishable from their party's in order to enhance their own electoral prospects.

Essentially, candidates would use the party's national brand reputation to sell themselves.[34] This is akin to a company promoting its name broadly rather than a particular product line. A good example is General Electric's "We bring good things to life" advertising campaign. Focusing on the innovations of General Electric broadly, the campaign built the company's name and image rather than any of its specific product divisions. The theory is that a company's reputation drives consumer choice and sells individual products, whether they are light bulbs, dishwashers, or hydroelectric generators.

The analogy is not exact, of course; few candidates explicitly reference their party in individual ads, and parties do not prominently display their own affiliation in their own ads.[35] Slightly different from the legislative cartel model promoted by Cox and McCubbins and discussed in chapter 2, the "brand name" here is not the party label per se but the cluster of issues on which a party has established its reputation. Parties "own" certain issues, communicate these agendas during campaigns in the hopes of focusing voter attention on them, and build support for their candidates.[36] Parties can and have used issue advocacy advertisements to create an association between the party and a particular issue agenda.

In 1996, National Republican Senatorial Committee chairman Alfonse D'Amato hired campaign strategist Arthur Finkelstein to control the party's media effort. Finkelstein is best known for his ads smearing Democratic candidates as "too liberal" and as reckless "tax and spenders." Not surprisingly, these themes emerged consistently in the commercials he produced for the NRSC. Democrats were branded as wasteful, while by implication Republicans were the party of fiscal responsibility and sanity. The themes were the same across the country; only the faces changed.[37] The tax and spend theme is one used by Republicans consistently, and it is certainly a part of their brand name.

Candidates can similarly run on the party's brand name by discussing these issues in their ads, press releases, and stump speeches. Essentially, party issues signify the party brand. Recall also that reputations, like Cox and McCubbins's party "record," consist of a party's true actions and the public perception of those actions (see chapter 2). Candidates might simply be trying to have the best of both worlds. By neglecting to mention party explicitly, they look like the independent politicians seemingly favored by voters. Simultaneously, by co-opting the party's issue agenda as their own, candidates can trade on an issue reputation established by their party to win votes.

Advantaged by FECA, national party organizations and interest groups can alter a campaign's issue terrain with their money, hurting or helping a particular candidate. Candidates must then respond to the issues that parties and interest groups introduce into the mix by either embracing them or dodging them. How they do so depends on their individual electoral needs. Candidates with the greatest resource needs, presumably those facing the most competitive election situations, will find it necessary to rely most on the party and its resources under the FECA regime. Although FECA altered the resource capacity of political players, this fundamental principle of the resource theory did not change.

Not only did FECA affect how candidates, interest groups, and parties relate to each other. It also affected the relationships between local, state, and national party organizations. Through the use of agency agreements and hard/soft money transfers, national party committees gained more authority over their state counterparts. National committees long had been subservient to state authority. This began to change after the enactment of FECA. Agency agreements "permit state party committees to transfer their spending quotas to the national party committees."[38] Transfers of hard and soft money from the national committees to the state parties "reversed the direction of resource flow since the 1970s." As a result, national parties gained leverage over state parties, sometimes placing constraints on transferred moneys or dictating institutional changes before money was dispersed. The consequence is increasingly integrated parties, run from the top down.[39] What does this mean for the resource theory? The institutionalization of state parties became increasingly less relevant to the resource decisions made by candidates. If candidates needed money or a partisan reputation to win an election, they turned to the national party for assistance. The new currency in the FECA era was dollars, and traditional party organization had little if any relevance to candidates.

TESTING THE RESOURCE THEORY:
THE DEMISE OF STATE PARTIES?

The rise of nationalized parties and the consequences for congressional candidate behavior can be demonstrated in a variety of ways. Earlier chapters focused on the relationship between state party institutionalization and the partisan reputations established by members of Congress. In this chapter, party unity is again used as one indicator of candidate reputation. Although a reasonable measure of how members of Congress present themselves to the public, it has been argued that the campaign messages communicated to the public in the form of advertisements are an even better measure. In chapter 4, we found that partisan institutionalization related to both message content of these ads and whether candidates or parties sponsored them. Unfortunately, archival data can be selective and incomplete. An extensive database of campaign advertisements from the 2000 election covering the top 75 media markets provides perhaps the best and most comprehensive measure of candidate reputations available. An examination of both party unity and campaign advertisements finds that the effects of FECA are unambiguous: the nationalization of political parties alters the resource strategies pursued by candidates.

As in previous analyses, party unity scores provide a measure of a candidate's reputation. As *CQ Weekly* reports scores at the conclusion of each congressional session that are not corrected for absences, these are the party unity measures for the analysis.[40] Members not serving the length of an entire Congress are excluded. As before, several other factors are included in the analysis, including "Vote," "Term," "Democrat," "Minority," "South," and "Previous Unity." All six have been described in chapter 3 and are simply updated for the FECA period beginning in 1976 and ending in 2000. Congressmen representing a southern state and serving in the minority should be less willing to support the party on unity votes. The dummy variable "Democrat," coded one for Democratic members and zero for Republicans, captures any behavioral differences that may exist between the two parties. Again, it is not clear that Democrats support their party any more or less than Republicans, but the possibility that they might needs to be taken into account. A member's previous unity should also signal a future willingness to vote the party's preferred position. All of these measures should already be familiar to the reader.

A candidate's need for resources is conditioned by his ability to collect resources relative to other political actors. After the passage of FECA, money became more important to winning elections, especially for candidates facing the most competitive election scenarios. Generally, scholars and pundits agree that the most competitive elections feature one or some combination of the following: no incumbent running for reelection, a freshman running for reelection, or an incumbent whose previous election margin was particularly close. From a resource perspective, these members need the most money and rely most heavily on partisan reputations in an era of independent expenditures, soft money, and issue advocacy advertisements. Members serving longer have had time to develop their own candidate reputations and to be more willing to use them. The longer a member serves, the less support he should give the party on unity votes. This means that the seniority coefficient in the regression results should be negative if this claim is supported. Indeed, recent work indicates that freshmen are more likely to support the party than their more senior colleagues.[41]

Median voter theory suggests that candidates in marginal districts will appeal to the ideological center to capture as many votes as possible. Resource theory argues that candidates facing competitive elections under FECA want to maximize their monetary and reputation resources to increase their probability of winning. When other political actors are better able to supply those resources than the candidate himself, the candidate will alter his campaign behavior to secure those resources. FECA provided national parties with a greater resource capacity than ever before. Candidates in tight elections should work hard to secure party support, so they should move closer to the party's preferred positions. The competitiveness of the district should affect the willingness of candidates to support the party, and according to the resource theory, those facing the stiffest challenge should utilize the party reputation more often. This means the previous vote share coefficient should be negative, which translates into more party unity voting by members representing more marginal districts.[42] A third party challenge to a candidate should create similar candidate behavior: candidates facing a significant third party threat should rely more heavily on the party's resources. The more substantial the challenge—as measured by a large third party candidates' vote share—the greater the need to utilize the party's reputation and financial resources, which should yield a positive "Third Party Percentage" coefficient in the regression results.[43]

Facing an intraparty challenge should also push candidates closer to the party's reputation. "Contested Primary," another dummy variable, takes a value of one when the member is challenged for the party's nomination, zero otherwise. A positive intraparty challenger coefficient value signifies that a nomination challenge moves a candidate closer to the party's preferred position on unity votes.

"TPO" represents state party institutionalization and is the same measure employed in chapters 3 and 4: David Mayhew's Traditional Party Organization score. Although reflecting party institutionalization in 1960, continuity argues for its inclusion. If FECA led to a nationalization of the parties that undercut the capacity of individual state organizations, candidates should now respond differently to state party capacity. State party institutionalization should no longer be crucial to a candidate's electoral success, so the relationship between TPO and party unity voting observed in earlier chapters should disappear and the coefficient will be insignificant from zero.[44]

Some might argue that the party organizational strength score compiled by Cornelius Cotter and his colleagues, which reflects the state of the parties in the early 1980s, better captures state party capacity in the FECA era.[45] The major shortcoming of using this measure, however, is its incompleteness. New Jersey does not have a score, and several states have only a score for the Democratic Party. The use of the TPO measure is less problematic in this regard. In addition, the relative institutionalization of parties across states should not change, as the strong correlation with a state's date of admission attests.[46] Substituting the Cotter et al. organizational measure for TPO in the regression analysis that follows does not substantially change the results.

"State Partisanship" and "TPO*State Partisanship" together help control for a possible relationship between a state's organizational capacity and ideology.[47] States with the highest level of partisan institutionalization, a "five" TPO score, include Rhode Island, Connecticut, New York, New Jersey, Pennsylvania, Illinois, Indiana, and Maryland. With the exception of Indiana, these high partisan capacity states have become more Democratic since 1974. Following the 2004 elections, Democrats held 3 of 8 governorships, 12 of 16 Senate seats, and 55 of 104 House seats.[48] Ideologically, the midwestern, northeastern, and mid-Atlantic states also appear to be more liberal in comparison with other regions.[49] Although no relationship between party unity and state partisanship is anticipated in this analysis, the relationship between state partisanship and organizational strength needs to be properly disentangled in order to be sure that the relationship between TPO and party unity is correctly represented.[50]

Four regressions appear in table 5.1. The first regression is simply a baseline that examines the relationship between state party institutionalization and candidate reputation without looking at the effects of party nationalization.[51] The remaining three regressions use slightly different measures to test the effects of party nationalization on party unity voting. As will become apparent throughout the discussion, the financial power of the national political parties does relate to the voting decisions of candidates: dispensing monetary resources in an effort to aid a candidate's election prospects consistently increases their propensity to support their party on the House floor. Conversely, the influence of state party organizations did not disappear. The effect of state party institutionalization, however, is overwhelmed by the national party's financial muscle.

Look first at model one in table 5.1 and the reported coefficients. As one can see from the many asterisks, nearly every coefficient is statistically significant. (With nearly 5,500 cases, this should not be surprising.) Looking at the signs on the coefficients, again one sees that most are signed (negatively or positively) as anticipated. The most attention should be paid, in terms of the resource theory and its claims, to the coefficients for vote percentage, term, and TPO.

Seniority depresses party unity voting, as indicated by the negative coefficient in table 5.1. Senior members of Congress have established individual reputations among voters and do not require as much campaign assistance from the party. Newly elected members without clearly established reputations, on the other hand, must make do with their party's reputation before slowly creating their own. As both the Democratic and Republican Parties are quite cohesive, the effects of seniority on unity are meaningful. To illustrate the effect of seniority, take a member of Congress serving ten terms. According to results presented in table 5.1, he would support the party only three percentage points less than a freshman (multiplying the seniority coefficient by 10). Junior members without clearly defined personal reputations do seem to cultivate a partisan reputation for display to the electorate, and this is clear from the fact that more senior members vote less frequently with their party than their less experienced colleagues.

Table 5.1. Party unity and party organizational strength, 1974–2000

Variables	Model One (1974–2000)	Model Two (1984–2000)	Model Three (1984–2000)	Model Four (2000)
Candidate Characteristics				
Democrat	-.013***	-.012***	-.011***	-.046***
	(.003)	(.003)	(.003)	(.006)
Minority	-.024***	-.026***	-.028***	---
	(.003)	(.003)	(.003)	---
Seniority	-.003***	-.003***	-.003***	-.001
	(.000)	(.000)	(.000)	(.001)
Vote Percentage	-.026***	-.003	.005	.011
	(.010)	(.011)	(.010)	(.024)
Previous Unity	.735***	.692***	.671***	.765***
	(.014)	(.018)	(.019)	(.031)
South	-.006**	-.006*	-.008**	-.010*
	(.003)	(.004)	(.004)	(.007)
Party Organization				
Third Party Percentage	.134***	.116***	.070**	-.082
	(.041)	(.037)	(.037)	(.064)
Contested Primary	.019***	.019***	.021***	.007
	(.003)	(.003)	(.003)	(.007)
TPO	-.003**	-.002**	-.002	-.005**
	(.001)	(.001)	(.001)	(.003)
State Partisanship	-.093**	-.060*	.001	-.104
	(.038)	(.042)	(.043)	(.095)
TPO * State Partisanship	-.003	-.012	-.024*	.028
	(.014)	(.015)	(.016)	(.028)
Party Expenditures				
Party Hard Money ($100,000)	---	.020***	.020***	.001
	---	(.008)	(.008)	(.016)
Soft Money Dummy	---	---	.025***	---
	---	---	(.003)	---
Party Advertising Expenditures ($100,000)	---	---	---	.002*
	---	---	---	(.001)
Constant	.277***	.299***	.302***	.269***
	(.015)	(.018)	(.018)	(.031)
R-Squared	.620	.591	.600	.687
F-statistic	432.29***	214.36***	222.42***	73.08***
N	(5418)	(3731)	(3731)	(413)

Unstandardized OLS coefficients with Huber-White robust standard errors reported in parentheses.

*** $p <= .01$; ** $p <= .05$; * $p <= .10$; one-tailed.

What about district marginality? In model one, members of Congress in marginal seats seem to adhere more to the expectations of the median voter theory than to the resource theory: the smaller the margin of victory, the less likely a member will support their party on the House floor. How much does a member's party unity decline? Not by very much. The difference between running unopposed and winning with only 50 percent of the vote is about a percentage point less of party unity. The relationship between district competition and party reputation will be discussed in greater detail later in the chapter.

The state partisan institutionalization coefficient is negative as expected, so higher institutionalized party states are associated with less party unity voting. The effect, however, is tiny. Representatives hailing from the strongest party organization states—coded a five—have party unity levels on average one percentage point lower than colleagues representing states with virtually no state party institutionalization. Although the relationship between party unity and TPO is not as anticipated, the weak effect supports the resource theory's expectation that state party organization should not greatly influence the voting behavior of members of Congress under FECA.

To summarize, without yet accounting for the financial power of the national parties, the simple model indicates that state partisan institutionalization pressures congressional candidates even in the FECA era. Stronger parties still move candidates ever so slightly away from support for the national party. The state's ideological position also matters: the farther from the national party mean, the less likely a member will support his party.

Model one, however, does not weigh the effects of national party power. Adding variables depicting the party's financial resources demonstrates how important the national party organizations have become as resource providers in the FECA era. Although high levels of state party institutionalization still drive candidates away from the party, the ability of national party organs to dispense enormous monetary resources can potentially overwhelm this effect. The consequence is increased party unity among congressional candidates who must increasingly rely on the national party to win elections.

Models two and three examine how the use of different financial tools by the national party committees can affect candidate behavior. Model two contains a measure of hard dollar contributions made by the political parties to and on behalf of congressional candidates.[52] The same variable is in model three, along with a dummy variable measuring soft money support by the party for congressional candidates.[53] The soft money dummy variable is zero for members of Congress serving before 1996 and one for those serving after 1996. Although the expenditure of soft money became legal immediately following the creation of the soft money provision in 1979, 1996 was the critical election year when soft money contributions to the parties exploded and parties utilized soft money on issue advocacy extensively. In both cases, members of Congress should react to the ability of national party organizations to provide additional monetary resources by increasing their propensity to support the party on the house floor.

A look at models two and three finds support for the argument that national party organizations, and their ability to generate significant monetary resources for candidates, affect how members behave on the House floor (see table 5.1). The two variables measuring the national party committees' financial strength are significantly related to the reputations that candidates construct.[54]

Receipt of hard dollar contributions is significant statistically in both models two and three, and the coefficient is positive. As hard dollar contributions from the party go up, so does a member's party unity score. It is important to put this finding into its proper context. For every $100,000 contributed by a party, a member's party support increases by nearly two percentage points. This seems like a lot, but party committees rarely contribute that much hard money to candidates. Between 1984 and 2000, the average party contribution to a member of Congress was slightly more than $10,000. On the other hand, one party contributed more than $600,000 to a candidate during the same period. Receiving the maximum contribution from the party equates with a jump of more than twelve percentage points in party unity. To put this in perspective, state party institutionalization at its highest level decreases candidate loyalty by only a single percentage point. The contribution of hard dollars can certainly alter the resource equation for candidates. The end result is greater party support by the candidate than otherwise might be expected.

The appearance of soft money on a widespread scale beginning in 1996 is also related to candidate behavior, as evidenced by the positive and significant coefficient on the soft money dummy variable in model three. Candidates running in the era of soft money exhibited a three percentage point increase in party unity when compared with congressional candidates running in election cycles before the soft money explosion. Again, this effect is substantive—larger than nearly every other coefficient listed in model three except previous party unity and the hard dollar contribution variable when parties give substantial sums. Using hard and soft money together, the national parties can change the resource terrain facing candidates. The response of candidates is ever higher levels of party unity. TPO is still significant in the third model, but its effects remain substantially uninteresting when compared with the effects of party contributions. In sum, models two and three support the notion that the party's monetary resources influence how members of Congress chose to present themselves to the electorate.[55]

Yet another way to evaluate the effect of party expenditures on candidate behavior is to look at campaign advertisements purchased by the parties and aired either as issue advocacy (paid for with soft money) or independent expenditure (funded with hard money) advertisements favoring or opposing a specific candidate. Fortunately, these data exist. The Wisconsin Advertising Project (WAP) has gathered information on the individual airings of all political advertisements shown in the top seventy-five media markets for all presidential, senatorial, congressional, and gubernatorial campaigns during 2000.[56] WAP identifies each advertisement's sponsor, regardless of whether soft or hard money paid for the ad.[57] A cost estimate for each airing is included, so an aggregate estimate of each party's advertising expenditures for each of their candidates can be computed.[58] The party advertising variable for each congressional candidate that results ranges from zero—indicating that the party spent nothing on advertisements for their candidate—to nearly $2.8 million. In 2000, the average candidate benefited from $50,600 in party advertising.

Model four includes this party advertising variable. Unlike models two and three, the analysis is restricted to incumbents winning reelection in 2000. As Democrats were in the minority in 2000, the party and minority variables are identical, so there is no minority coefficient reported. The soft money variable is also dropped; again, every race took place during the regime of party soft money. The resource theory anticipates a positive relationship between a party's advertising expenditures and a member's party unity. The more the party spends on behalf of a candidate, the higher a candidate's party unity.

The most important coefficient values to note are those for TPO, hard dollar contributions made by the party, and party advertising.[59] TPO is still statistically significant and negative, so higher levels of state party institutionalization are associated with decreased party unity. The hard dollar coefficient is statistically insignificant: the amount of money the party contributed directly to House candidates in 2000 had no effect on a member's unity voting. Most important, though, the party advertising coefficient is both positive and significant. The more parties spent on advertisements in support of their candidates, the more the candidates voted with the party. Again, party support is associated with higher levels of party unity among these members of Congress who benefit most from the party's assistance.

By comparing a party's hard dollar contributions to its advertising, one can observe which of the two strategies is most effective in generating the most unity. Look at the hard dollar coefficient in model two. A contribution of $50,000 is associated with an increase of 1 percent in a member's unity (multiply $50,000 and the party hard dollar contribution coefficient together). Compare this with the party advertising coefficient in model four. For a similar increase in unity, parties have to spend a half million dollars on television advertisements. This amount is much higher than the advertising support that the average candidate received from the party.

Of course, soft money dollars may have a greater potential to move candidates toward more partisan voting records as the ability to purchase advertisements with soft money is theoretically limitless. The maximum spent by the parties on television advertisements on behalf of a candidate was $2.78 million in 2000. This amount translates into an increase in party unity of almost six percentage points. This increase is not as large as that produced by the maximum hard dollar contribution, but parties could easily spend more soft money on issue advocacy ads. These effects overall are particularly striking after considering that party unity in the first session of the 107th Congress averaged 90 percent. Members already gave their party a high degree of support. In spite of this, monetary contributions and advertising expenditures are still associated with more party support.

The relationship between party money and unity voting is an important finding, but what does it mean for candidates and the resource theory? In the late nineteenth century, political parties dominated the campaign process in a variety of ways. Their ability to control access to party nominations was perhaps the most important, especially in areas with well-developed party organizations. Typically, the price for the nomination included the candidate's loyalty to the party. Can parties use campaign contributions to purchase party unity?[60]

In 1998, Senator Mitch McConnell took over the chairmanship of the NRSC. Political pundit Stuart Rothenberg ranked Senate races in Wisconsin and Washington as leaning Democratic in April that year.[61] The Republican Party funneled nearly a half million dollars to Wisconsin in support of Mark Neumann's campaign against Democratic incumbent Russ Feingold. Despite facing similar odds against first term incumbent Patty Murray, Washington Republican Congresswoman Linda Smith received less than half the support received by Neumann.[62] News accounts suggested that McConnell sought to punish Smith for openly supporting campaign finance reform, while hoping to defeat the Senate Democrat spearheading the reform.[63] In this case, one vote may have made the difference between receiving token and substantial party campaign assistance.

Aside from this one instance, it is probably not the case that parties actively punish those who fail to support House leaders. At least candidates and former members of Congress have not admitted openly as such. Typically, the primary goal for parties is to retain or gain congressional majorities. As Robin Kolodny's work on congressional campaign committees demonstrates, parties tend to funnel resources to the most competitive races. Ideology is typically not a factor in determining whether a candidate will receive party support.[64]

What is the relationship between party money and candidate behavior? What value is party unity for members if such loyalty is not rewarded with more financial support from the parties? Disentangling the relationship between party contributions and marginal districts provides some clues. The amount of hard dollar support given by parties to congressional candidates and marginality is strongly correlated.[65] Further illustrating the point, the Democratic and Republican Parties aired 51,497 ads in the most competitive House races during the 2000 cycle.[66] The number of ads aired in noncompetitive races, however, was only 1,147.[67] Or, put a bit differently, the competitive races on average saw the parties air 1,119 ads. Parties averaged only 9 ads aired in the noncompetitive House races. In the regression equations, competitiveness is not statistically significant once party contributions are added to the models. The reason is because parties target the most competitive races. And despite what median voter theory would predict, it is those candidates receiving the most party support who vote more regularly with the party on the House floor. This is reinforced by the fact that freshmen members are the most likely to vote with the party. The party reputation clearly has value for candidates struggling to get reelected.

Does restricting the regression analysis to marginal races alter the findings in table 5.1? The answer is no. In congressional districts where the winning candidate won with less than ten and five percentage points, respectively, the relationship between party unity voting and hard dollar contributions persists. Clearly, parties do give additional money to more loyal candidates. And yet they are unwilling to abandon disloyal members in competitive districts because of the need to retain (or gain) a congressional majority. Less loyal candidates receive fewer dollars from the party than they otherwise would, but they still receive enough money to beat their challenger. Parties can still have their cake and eat it, too.

Three maverick candidates who ran in competitive districts during the 1996 election cycle illustrate the point more clearly. Mark Neumann, a freshmen Republican from Wisconsin, may best be remembered for his singular commitment to balancing the federal budget. Irritating his party's leadership, he refused to support a "Republican-backed defense bill" that threatened his goal of quick deficit reduction. Appropriations chairman Bob Livingston, supported by Speaker Newt Gingrich, punished Neumann for his insolence by removing him from his seat on the appropriations national security subcommittee. Fellow freshmen came to his defense, and the leadership had to retreat, giving Neumann a seat on the budget committee as compensation.[68] Another freshman elected in 1994, John Hostettler, represented the bloody Eighth District in southern Indiana (so named for the intensively competitive nature of the district, which is split nearly evenly between Democratic and Republican voters). Hostettler refused to accept PAC contributions, recently pleaded guilty to attempting to bring a semiautomatic handgun through airport security, and was one of only ten House Republicans to vote against the use of force in Iraq.[69] Iowa congressman Jim Leach, first elected in 1976, has long been known for his independent streak. In 1997, he was one of nine Republicans who refused to support Newt Gingrich for Speaker.[70]

All three members faced tough reelections in 1996, and all won with less than 52 percent of the vote. All three also received financial support from the parties. In 1996, the average Republican member received $14,000 in hard money contributions from the party. Hostettler, Neumann, and Leach all received far more than the average. The "least" maverick of the mavericks received the most from the party. John Hostettler voted with the party 93 percent of the time on unity votes in the 105th Congress and received more than $85,000. Mark Neumann, supporting the party 83 percent of the time, got $80,000 and faced the stiffest challenge of the three. Jim Leach voted with the party far less frequently—only 67 percent of the time. The party gave him little more than $40,000 to support his reelection. This underscores the point that party unity seems to play a role not in the decision to give but rather in the amount given. Parties are loath to risk losing a seat. Nevertheless, a signal can be sent by the party to members by giving just a bit more to more loyal members.

It is possible that something else is going on here. Candidates are notoriously risk averse, which explains why they often raise far more campaign money than they otherwise might need to spend. Candidates facing competitive elections may play it safe by supporting the party more than they otherwise might, fearing that the party might choose to withhold crucial monetary support. Even though parties are unwilling to put a seat in jeopardy because a member is not optimally loyal, the party might encourage members to protect themselves from even this remote possibility.[71] Neumann and Hostettler may have positioned themselves more conservatively than their competitive districts might warrant, making sure the party did not forget them. Party money was especially important to them as freshmen legislators.

There are other reasons, too, why members of Congress are eager to support their party. As political scientist Thomas Stratmann notes, "Party support is important not only for winning an election but also for obtaining committee assignments, which are decided by each party's congressional caucus."[72] Speaker Dennis Hastert, as did Gingrich, prized loyalty over seniority in granting committee chairmanships.[73] Among the many ways candidates can develop their personal reputations is by bringing pork back to the district and touting their powerful positions on important committees. Ironically, as candidates seek over the long term to stay in Congress and develop valuable individual reputations that reap electoral benefits, they may need to position themselves in the short term as party loyalists to advance within the chamber.

Of course, party reputations may be valuable in their own right, beyond the financial support they can attract. At the same time Congress rewrote campaign finance law, David Mayhew wrote an article calling attention to declining marginal congressional districts.[74] After the reapportionment revolution set off by the Supreme Court's one man/one vote decision in *Baker v. Carr*, redistricting became predictable.[75] Before 1970, states generally did not redistrict unless they lost seats; after 1970, redistricting usually took place in the immediate aftermath of the decennial census.[76] The national party committees began to look more systematically at redistricting as an opportunity to redraw districts both to protect their incumbents and to create opportunities to gain seats. According to the authors of an important article on redistricting, the 1980s led to increasingly partisan gerrymanders designed to maximize one party's electoral prospects.[77] Indeed, first Republicans and later Democrats poured extensive financial resources into state legislative elections during the census year so as to take control of state legislatures governing the redistricting process.[78] It has been argued by some, such as *Washington Post* columnist David Broder, that redistricting has led to more safe seats for incumbents and fewer competitive districts.[79] It is true that marginal districts have declined. In the 2004 election, there were only thirty to forty competitive House districts.[80]

What is the relationship between party unity, party reputation, and redistricting? Some have argued that redistricting has been in part responsible for polarization and the rise of party unity in Congress.[81] Although many factors contributed to the rise of party unity, "there is evidence at the individual district level that more competitive seats lead to more moderate members and that 'cross-pressured' members are more likely to have more centrist voting scores."[82] Without the fear of a competitive general election, members of Congress have less incentive to make appeals to independent and moderate voters. In uncompetitive congressional districts, what matters the most is keeping party regulars happy to avoid a primary challenge. Is the rise of party unity less about resources and more about partisan gerrymanders?

It is difficult to disentangle the effects of redistricting from FECA. Some speculations can be ventured, however. First, party unity and polarization have increased in the House and the Senate during the same period, so it is hard to lay the blame entirely on redistricting when the Senate is never redistricted.[83] Second, if redistricting has led to an increase in safe seats, candidates should theoretically only need party monetary and reputation resources when they are challenged for the party nomination. Even after controlling for the effects of competitive primaries, party contributions still exhibit a positive and significant effect on a member's party unity.

And the relationship between party unity and party contributions occurs when members face competitive election scenarios, as the previous discussion suggests.

Third, how might a candidate react when facing the prospect of an intraparty challenge in a safe district? Anticipating the challenge, they will begin to move their reputations closer to their party's for fear of losing the party's active support. Although this dynamic is difficult to witness in House elections because of the short campaign cycle, the case of Senator Arlen Specter provides a nice illustration. In January 2003, the *Weekly Standard* reported that conservative Congressman Pat Toomey was "strongly considering" challenging Specter for the Republican nomination.[84] Arlen Specter was one of the Senate's few remaining moderates and consistently ranked as one of the most likely to vote against the party. How did Specter address the intraparty challenge? In 2003, his party unity score was 84 percent—its highest level since at least 1990. Only in 2004, presumably after dispensing with Toomey, did Specter's voting record return to form when he voted with the party 70 percent of the time. Candidates seek party assistance when they can provide the resources for victory. In this instance, Specter knew he was going to face a tough intraparty fight, so he circled the wagons, altered his floor behavior, and hoped it would pay dividends. It seems that it did, as the White House actively supported Specter during the primary.[85] In short, redistricting may have made districts less competitive, but the resource dynamic is still the same. When members of Congress find themselves without resources sufficient to win elections, they turn to political actors who can provide those resources.

FECA strengthened the hand of national party organizations, turning them into important political players in their own right. The increasing monetary pressures placed on candidates, and the freedom with which national committees could raise and spend soft money, made them attractive to candidates as resource providers. Parties gave candidates the help they needed in competitive elections. And candidates recognized the value of the party reputation as a means to—if not secure party support—make sure at the very least that the party had no reason to withhold contributions. Of course, party reputations have value beyond what they bring to candidates monetarily. They are important to how candidates are perceived, as winning is a function of both a candidate's reputation and his party's.

THE RESOURCE THEORY AND PARTY REPUTATION: CAMPAIGN ADVERTISING IN 2000

Party unity is a crude measure of congressional candidate reputation, but it has the virtue of being readily available. It has been argued that resource constraints can change how candidates develop their own reputation resources. In particular, the resource capacity of the national party organizations under FECA provides them with a resource edge that candidates need to be competitive electorally. The best test of this claim would be an examination of actual advertisements aired by the parties and congressional candidates during an election campaign to shed light on whether political actors seek construction of particular issue reputations. The Wisconsin Advertising Project (WAP), using the data obtained from the Campaign Media Analysis Group (CMAG), coded each political advertisement in the top seventy-five media markets during the 2000 election cycle for its issue content. Using this information, it is possible to determine the various issue agendas employed by congressional candidates and political parties in each race where television ads aired in the top seventy-five media markets.

Campaigns are coalition-building efforts in which candidates and parties attempt to communicate with voters. A large portion of effort is expended during a campaign communicating an agenda to attract enough votes on election day. John Kingdon, in his landmark study on agenda setting in policy making, defines agendas as "the list of subjects or problems to which governmental officials, and people outside of government closely associated with those officials, are paying some serious attention at any given time."[86] Campaign agendas are the subjects, problems, or issues to which political actors want voters to pay attention. Agendas are really nothing more than a bundling of discrete messages framing voter choices and decisions. The messages that constitute campaign agendas can be many or few in number. Conceivably, they can be anything that might be considered relevant to voters by the political actors constructing and communicating the agendas. Broadly, messages can be categorized into two types: issues and personal characteristics.

Issues deal with policy alternatives. Taxes, farm subsidies, and protection of Social Security are just a few examples. Personal characteristics focus more directly on candidates' qualifications for office: are they likeable, or do they have the right experience to do the job? They are devoid of issue content. Calling someone a "baby killer" because he favors abortion, for example, is an issue statement rather than a personal message. Agendas typically will mix both issues and personal candidate characteristics. Political advertisements, a bundling of agendas, can also contain a mix of the two. There are various ways that campaigns communicate messages and agendas to voters: press releases, candidate speeches, and television advertisements are but a few. WAP provides easy access to the television advertisements employed by candidates and parties, so their data are treated as a fair representation of a congressional campaign's agenda.

There is no doubt that candidate and party reputations are intertwined and somewhat correlated. One can, however, take advantage of the fact that both candidates and parties engage in campaign activities: each communicates an agenda to voters, each chooses the messages that make up those agendas, and each agenda carries a distinct tone. How does one measure a candidate agenda versus a party agenda? The source of the agenda is whoever paid for it and sponsored it. Candidate agendas are those appearing in advertisements sponsored by the candidate; party agendas are those appearing in ads paid for by the party.

Comparison of party agendas and individual candidate agendas—specifically their message content in television advertisements—allows a comparison of party and individual candidate agendas. If parties under FECA are merely service providers to individual candidates, the messages constituting the party's agenda in its communications should hew closely to those established and transmitted by individual candidates. These messages—both candidate and party—should also vary greatly across campaigns, taking into account the diverse views of candidates and district-specific issues. Voters in Idaho should see advertisements focusing on issues differently than voters in Indiana or New Hampshire. Essentially, party messages should serve to enhance candidate messages in each candidate campaign—what is referred to here as "bolstering." Party messages should causally follow candidate-established messages: party messages in effect grab onto candidate issue themes and provide candidates with issue support. Similarly, the mix of message types (candidate and issue) should be consistent between a party's agenda and a candidate's agenda in any given congressional campaign.

Alternatively, if party reputations are useful in their own right due to FECA, a variety of scenarios might be observed. If party and candidate campaigns talk "past" one another within a particular congressional race—the party's agenda and its messages are different than the candidate's agenda and messages—this might be an example of parties attempting to build a partisan reputation but failing to affect the strategic behavior of its candidates.[87] For the candidate, the party agenda may not be a useful way to build a winning coalition. Alternatively, political parties may be doing the "heavy" lifting for its candidates, such as talking about issues that the candidate would rather avoid but needs to discuss to enhance his election prospects. Most frequently, this means the party is attacking the candidate's opponent while the favored candidate talks about other issues and runs a positive campaign. This would happen if individual reputations were more important in the reelection campaign and would be evidence of bolstering. It would also suggest that the party is acting in a service capacity.

Observing message consistency between parties and candidates in a specific congressional race is trickier to classify. This might be an example of parties bolstering individual candidate agendas and messages, providing support for the candidate-centered campaign model. Alternatively, if parties are establishing the agenda within a race and candidates acquiesce to that agenda (again, leading to messages that are indistinguishable between candidates and parties), this suggests that the party-centered model is more appropriate. Here this is referred to as "latching"—candidates "grab" onto party agendas and issues.

The empirical difference between the two scenarios is timing. If candidate messages follow party messages, this would suggest that candidates are latching onto party themes.[88] If, however, party messages follow candidate messages, this would suggest bolstering. When a race is competitive, the party and candidates will probably begin advertising immediately. This makes bolstering and latching observationally equivalent. In practice, parties and candidates rarely begin advertising at the same time. Generally, either the party or the candidate advertises first; this was the case in the 2000 election campaign according to WAP data.[89] Under FECA, the electoral value of partisan reputations should have increased for candidates. If this is the case, then candidates should use those reputations in their own television advertisements to help them win election.

WAP coders had four opportunities to describe the issue content of each advertisement. If a spot discussed multiple issues (as they frequently do), these were captured and coded separately. Each airing of an advertisement, then, has four issue mention variables associated with it. For example, a spot may have mentioned four issue areas; hence it received four separate issue codes, one for each issue mention.

The types of issues that respondents could code were quite specific: Clinton, campaign finance reform, farming, tobacco, and a lottery for education, to name but a few. To make the analysis more tractable, the four issue mention variables, each containing one of the fifty-three possible issue statements, were combined into nine issue theme variables. These issue themes are social, economic, education/childcare, foreign/defense policy, trade/immigration, entitlements, environment, biography, and miscellaneous.[90] Essentially, each of these variables ranges from zero to four—zero if the ad did not mention a particular issue theme, and four if the ad mentioned the issue theme at least four times. An issue theme can be mentioned multiple times in an ad simply because that theme can be mentioned in a variety of ways. For example, the entitlement theme variable includes the issue mentions of health care and Social Security. Clearly, a political advertisement could mention both; the entitlement variable for that spot would be coded a two.[91]

To develop a measure of candidate and party agendas in each congressional race, each of the issue theme variables for all of the congressional districts represented in the WAP data were aggregated.[92] These aggregate variables contain the number of times that an issue theme was mentioned in each congressional campaign's television advertisements. These variables are then broken down between the Democratic and Republican Parties and their respective congressional candidates. To summarize, each candidate and each party have nine issue theme variables associated with them that denote the number of times each particular theme was mentioned in all of the candidate's or party's television advertisements. From these variables, each political actor's issue agenda was established.

Did political parties talk past each other or discuss the same issues?[93] In 2000, it seems as if the two parties ran completely different campaigns. The Democratic Party stressed entitlements in its ads. The following advertisement, paid for by the Democratic Congressional Campaign Committee, criticized Republican House candidate Mike Rogers's record on elderly care and is typical of the entitlement genre: "When families can no longer care for the elderly, we trust nursing home professionals to protect our loved ones, but sometimes that trust is violated. Seniors are mistreated, forgotten, even abused. So we don't understand why State Senator Mike

Rogers voted five different times against adding new nursing home inspectors. It's true. The record shows Mike Rogers even voted against improving nursing home quality standards. Can working families trust Mike Rogers to protect our seniors?"[94]

Nearly 30 percent of Democratic ad mentions concerned health care, Social Security, welfare, and other social programs. Entitlements were mentioned even more times than candidate characteristics; personal or biographical attributes made up almost a quarter of total ad mentions. Rounding out the top issue areas, this was followed by the catchall "other" category at 19 percent and economic issues at 14 percent of total mentions (see figure 5.2).

Republicans focused their ads overwhelmingly on individual candidate characteristics, with more than 30 percent of mentions falling in this category. The number one issue area for the Republican Party was the economy, and almost 25 percent of the total mentions in 2000 were about taxes, economic growth, or the size of government. The next most frequently mentioned issue area was "miscellaneous"—accounting for 20 percent of mentions—with education trailing with 11 percent. Entitlements, the number one issue area for Democrats, barely registered in Republican ads. Only 8 percent of all mentions discussed entitlement programs. The following Republican Party ad, launched against Minnesota Congressman Bill Luther, demonstrates how one ad can tackle a variety of issues. Note that while the candidate's record, education, and taxes are mentioned, the dominant issue theme is taxes (mentioned three times): "Why is Bill Luther running negative attack ads? Maybe so you won't think about his real record. Luther voted for three of the largest tax increases in Minnesota history. And when he had a chance to help our families by opposing the marriage penalty and death taxes, he wouldn't. Luther also voted against the Straight A's Plan, a pilot program that returns decision making power to parents and local school boards because we should decide on new school construction and more teachers, not government bureaucrats. Call Bill Luther. Tell him he's lost touch with Minnesota."[95]

At first blush, it seems that the Republicans and Democrats used very different advertising strategies. Although the differences appear slight, Democrats discussed issues more than candidate characteristics, while Republicans discussed the personal characteristics of their candidates. Why the difference? The resource theory suggests that political parties

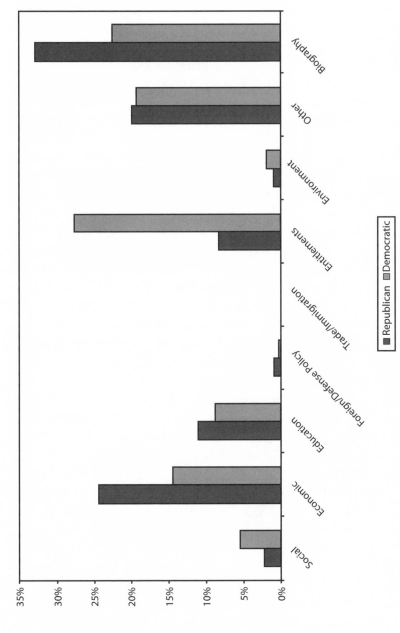

Figure 5.2. Democratic and Republican Party ad themes in 2000: percentage of total mentions. Calculated by author from data provided by the Wisconsin Advertising Project, available at www.polisci.wisc.edu / ~tvadvertising.

focus on building party reputations for their candidates when it increases the probability of their candidates winning an election. In 2000, of course, Republicans held a majority of House seats and wanted to protect its incumbents. Democrats, on the other hand, hoped to capture a majority by defeating an appreciable number of Republican incumbents. Their strategies differed. The resource disparity explains why. Challenger candidates are relatively unknown, especially when compared with incumbent members of Congress. Building a reputation is difficult and expensive. It is far easier to emphasize an already known product to the electorate and hope that voters associate a party's challengers with that reputation. The Democratic Party has a long history of supporting and protecting entitlement programs, so they highlighted this reputation advantage in advertisements in an effort to help their challengers defeat Republican incumbents.[96] In this case, a party reputation trumps a candidate reputation because of resources, so the Democratic Party acted accordingly. The Democrats had more challengers than incumbents, so issues sensibly dominated their advertisements.

Conversely, incumbents have established reputations separate and somewhat distinct from their parties, courtesy of their serving in elective office. Their reputations do not have to be created from scratch and are something with which voters may already be familiar. As Republicans held more seats than the Democrats, Republican advertisements rationally should use candidate reputations to the party's collective advantage when appropriate. With the protection of majority status as the foremost goal, the Republicans sought to bolster the individual reputations of their candidates through its television advertising. Candidate personalities should dominate Republican Party messages and agendas.

Presumably, then, Republican Party ads focused largely on candidate characteristics because of its incumbency advantage, but would mimic the Democratic strategy in open and Democratic-held seats. Similarly, Democratic Party ads presumably stressed the records of its incumbents when holding the seat. Figures 5.3 and 5.4 look at the ad themes of the Republican and Democratic Party advertisements, but this time they are separated by the seat's competitive status. Sure enough, party advertising strategies varied depending on the strategic situation faced by political actors.

In open and Republican-held seats, Democratic Party ads focused on issues rather than the personal qualities of its candidates. Entitlement programs were the primary issue theme for Democratic Party ads in seats held by a Republican incumbent. In open seats, it was second only to the catchall "other" category. Conversely, candidate biographies dominated in the party ads aired in Democratic-held seats: nearly 50 percent of all mentions discussed a candidate's attributes. Education was a distant second, managing only 13 percent of mentions in Democratic-sponsored advertisements.

Republican advertising generally followed the same pattern, but not completely. In open seats, issues also dominated Republican ads: 34 percent of all ad mentions in open seats fall in the economic issue theme, followed by personal characteristics with 21 percent. Republican Party ads also exploited candidate reputations when the seat was occupied by a Republican. Half of all mentions pertained to the candidate, more than twice as often as the "other" issue theme. Strangely, Republican ads most frequently mentioned the candidate in Democratic-held seats as well with 35 percent of mentions falling in this category. As the biography issue theme contains mentions of personal attributes for any candidate running, it is possible that Republicans ads discussed the characteristics of Democratic opponents in their ads. The fact that the vast majority of Republican Party ads in 2000 were negative in tone lends credence to this supposition. Republican Party ads probably attacked Democratic opponents for perceived character flaws.[97]

Did the political parties have a national issue agenda? Although political parties varied in how much they mentioned personal characteristics in their advertising based on seat status, party advertisement issues exhibited some degree of consistency across House races. Restricting the analysis to issue themes other than candidate characteristics, Republican Party ads mentioned the economy more frequently than any other issue in open and Democratic-held seats. Only when the Republican candidate was an incumbent did the economy slip from the top three issues, falling to fourth place behind other, entitlements, and education.[98] Among Democratic Party ads, entitlements were the major issue in Republican-held seats and a close second to other in open seats. Again, only in seats held by Democratic incumbents did entitlements fall to third place behind other and education.

Summarizing, it seems that parties did communicate issue agendas representing the party's reputation, as suggested by the relative issue theme consistency in Democratic and Republican Party ads across strategic environments. Second, parties employed the use of party issue agendas

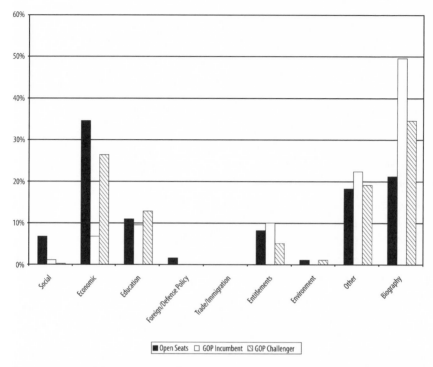

Figure 5.3. Republican Party ad themes by seat status in 2000: percentage of total mentions. Calculated by author from data provided by the Wisconsin Advertising Project, available at www.polisci.wisc.edu/~tvadvertising.

carefully. Parties provided their reputations to relatively unknown challengers, both when the challenger was running in an open seat and when he was running against an incumbent. The presence of an incumbent alters the equation; in these cases, parties bolster their candidate by relying on personal characteristics of the incumbent to retain the seat. In other words, party reputations matter most for challengers and less so for incumbents, and this is reflected in party advertising strategies.

How do party ads compare to those sponsored by their congressional candidates? Candidates and parties communicate largely the same issue agendas to voters. Figures 5.5 and 5.6 compare the percentage of mentions in each issue theme category for each party and its respective candidates. Two things stand out. First, parties and candidates spoke the same issue language in their television commercials. The top five issue themes were the same for the Republican and Democratic Parties as well as their respective candidates: personal characteristics, the economy, other issues,

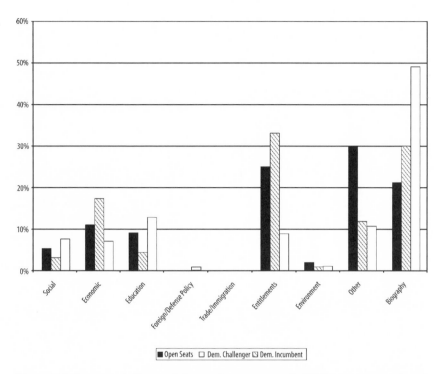

Figure 5.4. Democratic Party ad themes by seat status in 2000: percentage of total mentions. Calculated by author from data provided by the Wisconsin Advertising Project, available at www.polisci.wisc.edu/~tvadvertising.

education, and entitlements. Second, although each party prioritized these issues differently in its own television advertising, near-agreement existed between each party and its respective candidates on the emphasis of issues. In its ads, the Democratic Party and its candidates stressed entitlements first, followed by personal characteristics, other issues, economic considerations, and education. The Republican Party and its candidates discussed personal candidate characteristics and the economy more than any other issue, but Republican candidates emphasized entitlements and education slightly more than the party.

The relative message consistency between party and candidate advertisements presents the possibility that parties are lending their party reputation to candidates who latch onto it during the campaign, both to attract a coalition of voters large enough to win and to wrest control of the issue agenda from outside interests cluttering the airwaves. Alternatively, the observed message consistency between party and candidate advertisements

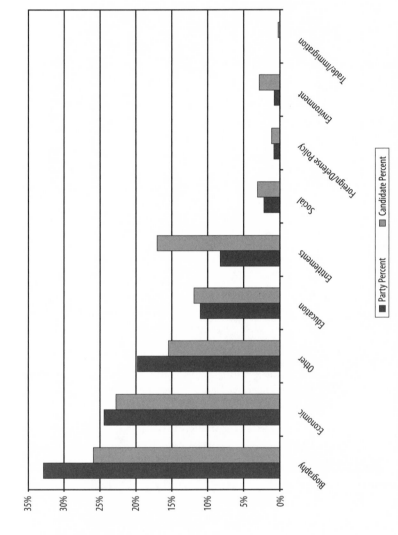

Figure 5.5. Republican Party and House candidate advertising by issue theme in 2000: percentage of total mentions. Calculated by author from data provided by the Wisconsin Advertising Project, available at www.polisci.wisc.edu/~tvadvertising.

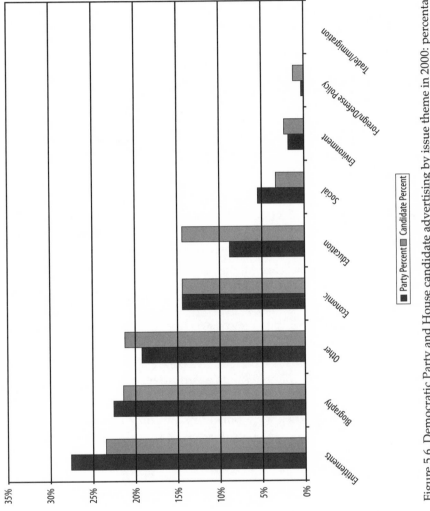

Figure 5.6. Democratic Party and House candidate advertising by issue theme in 2000: percentage of total mentions. Calculated by author from data provided by the Wisconsin Advertising Project, available at www.polisci.wisc.edu/~tvadvertising.

could be the result of parties bolstering individual candidate agendas and messages. The primary distinguishing characteristic between the two scenarios again is timing. Latching occurs when candidates follow party advertising and the messages match. Bolstering occurs when parties follow candidate advertising and the issue agenda is indistinguishable. Ever conscious of the resources necessary to obtain victory, candidates and parties act strategically. Parties only lend the party's reputation to candidates when it aids a candidate's election efforts. And candidates will only latch onto the party's reputation when they require party resources for victory.

In 2000, there were thirty-one House races where the parties and their respective candidates spent money on television advertisements in the top seventy-five media markets. What kind of races attracted the attention of parties? Competitive races did. Forty-five percent of the seats where parties outspent their candidates had no incumbent from either party running. The average margin of victory for the winner was less than 10 percent; compared with the average House candidate in 2000 who won with nearly 70 percent of the total vote.[99] Parties carefully husbanded their resources, using them where their effect would be felt the most.[100]

Table 5.2 divides these races into four categories: parties outspent their respective candidates, neither party outspent its candidates, and either the Democratic or Republican Party outspent its own candidates. Cell entries are the percentage of races falling into that category. Fully 65 percent of the House races where the party and candidate spent money on television advertising saw one or both of the parties outspending their candidates.

More than half of the time a party chose to invest advertising resources in a campaign, it actually spent more than the candidate. But, in order to determine whether parties were bolstering or allowing candidates to latch, one must know when the candidate and the party aired their respective ads. The Democratic Party aired the vast majority of its ads before its candidates' own ads appeared, whereas the opposite is true of Republicans (see table 5.3). Again, cell entries are simply the percentage of races falling into each category. The Democratic Party had the largest number of opportunities to set the issue agenda for the candidates onto which candidates could latch. Did parties use the opportunity to set campaign agendas?[101]

The Republicans seemed to set the issue table with their own campaign ads despite having fewer opportunities to do so (see table 5.4). The cell entries indicate the percentage of time the party and its candidate agreed on

Table 5.2. House races where the candidate and the party aired ads in 2000

	Republican Party $ *> GOP Candidate $*	*Republican Party $* *< GOP Candidate $*
Democratic Party $ *> Dem. Candidate $*	29% (9)	15% (5)
Democratic Party $ *< Dem. Candidate $*	18% (6)	33% (11)

Total number of races: 31

Percentage of races where only one party or both parties outspent their candidate(s): 65%

(N=20)

Entries in parentheses are number of cases in each cell.

Source: Calculated by author from data provided by the Wisconsin Advertising Project, available at www.polisci.wisc.edu/~tvadvertising.

the most frequently mentioned issue theme in advertising.[102] Although the Republican Party held its advertising fire—going on television after its own candidates nearly 30 percent more often than the Democratic Party—when it did choose to launch its salvo first, its candidates seemed to follow. A majority of the time, the Democratic Party and its candidate talked past one another. Why?

Looking a bit more closely at the congressional races where parties spent more money than their candidates *and advertised first* is illuminating. When parties spent before their candidates, they usually did so to help a challenger's campaign regardless of whether the candidate agreed with the party on the issue agenda. In eight out of eleven races where the candidates agreed with their party on the issues, the party was spending in favor of a challenging candidate. The percentage is almost the same when candidates and parties disagree.

What distinguishes between races where candidates "latch" versus those where they do not? The competitiveness of the race. Although parties funneled the bulk of their resources to competitive races generally, it was in the *most* competitive races where candidates agreed with the party on the issue agenda. The average margin of victory in races where the candidate and

Table 5.3. House races where the party outspent its candidates on ads in 2000

	Republicans	Democrats
Candidate advertises first	56%	27%
	(10)	(4)
Party advertises first	44%	73%
	(8)	(11)
Total	(18)	(15)

Source: Calculated by author from data provided by the Wisconsin Advertising Project, available at www.polisci.wisc.edu/~tvadvertising.

parties discussed the same issues was 6 percent; in races where they disagreed on the primary issue, the margin of victory widened to 10 percent. Candidates seem to latch onto party reputations when their electoral prospects are in the most doubt. This comports well with earlier findings on the relationship between party advertising expenditures and party unity voting. In the most competitive districts, the expenditure of party resources actually alters the resource equation for candidates, making it more likely that they will adopt an individual reputation in line with the parties and campaign on that reputation to win elections.

The campaign for the open seat in Florida's Eighth Congressional District during the 2000 election provides a window into how candidates and parties employ similar themes in their advertisements. Linda Chapin, clerk of the court and former county chairwoman, faced off against political newcomer Ric Keller. Keller was a conservative who had defeated a more moderate state legislator in the primary. According to the *Almanac of American Politics* summary of the race, Keller focused largely on an anti-tax message during the general election while Chapin stressed her moderation.[103] The WAP data contain CMAG storyboards for three Keller spots: two from the general election and one from the primary. These three spots confirm the almanac's summary of the race: all mention lowering taxes. Chapin may have stressed moderation, but in terms of actual issues, it seems that she focused on her party's reputation: entitlements. A majority of Chapin's advertisements stressed or mentioned Social Secu-

Table 5.4. Issue agreement when the party outspends its House candidates
on ads and advertises first

	Republicans	Democrats
Candidate and Party Agree	88%	36%
	(7)	(4)
Candidate and Party Disagree	12%	64%
	(1)	(7)
Total	(8)	(11)

Source: Calculated by author from data provided by the Wisconsin Advertising
Project, available at www.polisci.wisc.edu/~tvadvertising.

rity, Medicare, prescription drugs, or health care more generally—all sta-
ples of her party's national reputation. In a race decided by a margin of
2 percent, both candidates chose to advertise on their party's reputation
in their own commercials.

Much of the argument in this chapter rests on whether candidates can
find the resources necessary to compete in elections. When they cannot,
they look to other political actors—in particular, to political parties during the FECA era. Of course, if candidates have adequate resources, then
they should be less willing to rely on the party. Do candidates who can adequately self-finance their elections need the party reputation? This is an
important question, as it addresses whether partisan reputation is useful
to candidates beyond its ability to attract monetary resources from the
party.

In 2000, five House candidates spent more than $1 million of their own
money on their campaigns: businessman Darrell Issa (R-CA), lawyer
Philip Sudan (R-TX), businessman Roger Kahn (D-GA), lobbyist Terry
Lierman (D-MD), and former state senator Jim Humphreys (D-WV). All
but Issa lost, and only two of the races were truly competitive with margins of victory of less than 10 percent.[104] Nevertheless, it is striking how
closely these five candidates adhered to their parties' issue agendas. Combined, there are fifty-three spots representing the five candidates in the
WAP data. In thirty-two of those spots, there is issue agreement between

the candidate and his party. It would seem that the need for monetary resources alone does not necessarily drive the candidate's decision to utilize the partisan reputation. Instead, it seems to have some additional electoral value. This is explored further in chapter 6.

CONCLUSION

FECA has produced the possibility for national parties to overshadow state organizations through the use of contributions and soft money expenditures. Most significantly, parties have a potent tool in the form of party advertising expenditures with which to alter the behavior of their candidates. Lacking the resources guaranteeing victory at the polls, it is those candidates facing the most competitive races that need party assistance the most; ironically, they appear the most susceptible to polarizing partisan persuasion when their marginal districts suggest a strategy of cobbling together an independent and distinctive reputation.

Why do candidates act this way? Why should they vote more frequently with the party and latch onto party reputations during campaigns? What these candidates lack—money—matters more in the FECA era. As parties can contribute or expend substantial sums on behalf of their candidates, candidates are forced into a difficult situation. They can accept party assistance, but this might mean pursuing a strategy of latching onto party reputations. Certainly, as congressional races become more competitive and interest groups clutter the airwaves, party reputations are useful. Unable to spend enough money to establish a reputation distinct from the party, candidates must latch onto the party's issue reputation in order to compete successfully. But even self-financed candidates, who have enough money to avoid the party reputation if they so choose, can find party reputations useful. Perhaps the party reputation helps candidates beyond the monetary assistance it might bring from the party.

Thus far, the relationship between electoral rules and candidate behavior has been explored. But do changes in the electoral rules affect democratic discourse? The fact that parties can change the issue priorities of candidates in their television advertising and voting records suggests that they do. A true evaluation of the relationship between electoral rules and democratic discourse, however, requires turning to the final piece of the resource equation puzzle: the voters themselves. Does the need for resources, structuring how candidates campaign for Congress, affect how individual voters perceive political parties and candidates for office? If political parties increasingly can control the conduct of congressional elections after the 1974 campaign finance reforms, are voters aware?

In the next chapter, the analysis moves from political actors exclusively to the electorate more broadly to see whether elite level activities translate into changes in the mass electorate. The National Election Study has asked questions concerning congressional candidates and political parties from the mid-1970s onward. The nexus between reputation and voters resources is examined next by tracking the relationship between parties and congressional candidates in the FECA era. Can parties use their financial resources to create reputation advantages in particular issue areas? And if voters are able to perceive such advantages for parties, does a party's reputation play a role in shaping voter impressions of candidates? Using candidate and party ideology scales, open-ended questions allowing respondents to express their likes and dislikes of the parties, and the candidate-feeling thermometers from the NES, we will investigate the possible effects of spending on public opinion.

If voters do not respond to the issue agendas that parties and candidates advertise, then the ability of parties to set issue agendas during congressional campaigns is of little consequence. If party expenditures do alter the perceptions of voters, then this is powerful evidence that rules have concrete implications for the political behavior of the general public. It would also demonstrate how partisan reputations can reap electoral benefits for candidates other than additional party assistance. Both implications serve to reinforce candidate decisions to pursue partisan advertising strategies, closing the resource circle.

CHAPTER SIX

RESOURCES, STRATEGIES, AND VOTER PERCEPTIONS

Rules affect political actors' ability to gather and distribute resources. Rules also establish which resource is most important to success at different points in time. Utilizing these two simple principles, it was demonstrated in the last three chapters how party institutionalization, campaign contributions, and partisan reputations shape the voting behavior, advertising strategies, and campaign tactics employed by congressional candidates. Candidates alter their behavior to secure monetary or reputation resources when their own efforts cannot guarantee them.

Does the resource race have consequences reaching beyond elite behavior and strategy? Presumably, campaigns are more than games played by political actors: they try to influence opinion and attract votes by dispensing information. How voters react to candidates, parties, or interest groups during a campaign influences both the immediate decision inside the polling booth and the nature of the democratic linkage following the election. If candidates alter their campaign strategies by latching onto party-determined issue agendas, then the electoral rules governing resource availability indirectly shape the information environment that is most accessible to voters.

Campaigns are full of sound and fury signifying something. The issue agendas that parties and candidates communicated during the 2000 congressional campaign fell on receptive ears. Citizens quite capably credited the two parties and their candidates with the primary issue messages they conveyed in television advertisements: the economy for Republicans, and entitlements for Democrats. And money mattered: the more a party spent, the greater the party advantage perceived by respondents on its signature issue. This reveals the importance of party reputations to congressional candidates in their pursuit of office, and it further illustrates the party's potential as an agenda setter.

Voters feel more positive about a candidate when they recognize the candidate's party as having an advantage on its signature issue. By creating an issue advantage with advertisements, parties can indirectly form voter evaluations of congressional candidates. This strengthens the resource hand of parties relative to candidates.

INFORMATION, VOTING, AND RESOURCES

Campaigns shape the information environment available to voters, giving them the means to identify candidates and change the ways in which candidates and parties are evaluated.[1] Campaign tone can affect voting turnout and individual levels of campaign knowledge.[2] Spending by candidates influences the recognition and recall of candidate names, as well as voter knowledge of candidate ideology and issue stances.[3] These findings collectively do not contradict the notion that voting is primarily a function of social characteristics and attitudinal predispositions.[4] Rather, they reaffirm the early literature's conclusions that campaigns can change voting decisions, but generally at the margins and for those most susceptible to persuasion.[5]

Voters make decisions by using information. That information can be a particular issue position (taxes should be raised), the view of a candidate (the candidate seems to lack intellectual prowess), or an enduring commitment (long-standing support for Republican candidates and philosophy). Campaigns are one source of information that voters may resort to when making decisions, and political actors meticulously sculpt that information. Their ability to do so is a function of the resources at their disposal.

One resource available to parties and candidates is their respective reputations: actual and perceived records of their past actions, stances, and commitments. Perception is critical. Along with highlighting particular aspects of candidate or party reputations, political actors can change the perception of those reputations and, in so doing, can alter weights that voters attach to preferences bearing on their decisions. Political actors can "shape the alternatives from which the choice is made."[6] They can also "change the salience of an issue . . . by increasing the perceived difference between candidates [or parties] on an issue." Drawing upon party and candidate reputations, political actors can create the terms of electoral choice for voters by deciding what to highlight during the campaign. "The important effects of the campaign," writes Sam Popkin are "not in changing attitudes, but in changing priorities."[7] Campaigns can reorder voter priorities by stressing partisan messages and themes, focusing on candidate qualities, or raising relevant issue concerns.

When choosing how to present a reputation to voters, political actors recognize the need to reach two distinct audiences. First, there are the supporters, those who are predisposed to see the world as the political actor presents it. Second, there are the potential supporters, those who see the world as the political actor does some of the time but, because of attitudinal or social commitments, find themselves cross-pressured. Supporters need to be reminded of how a candidate's or party's reputation matches their worldview.[8] Potential supporters need to be persuaded that their worldview aligns with a candidate's or party's reputation on a particular issue and why this issue outweighs other issues, commitments, or concerns. This distinction is important because campaign effects on individual decisionmaking can be grossly underestimated by focusing on a campaign's persuasion function at the expense of its reminding function. Persuasion may provide the winning margin for candidates, but is a smaller portion of the appeals universe. Most voters need to be reminded simply to stand pat. If reminding is successful, the base should not move. Campaign effects are small because candidates and parties may only need to shift—to persuade—a small fraction to win.

Political consultants use similar language when discussing voter targeting strategy. Ron Faucheux, a frequent contributor to *Campaigns and Elections*, recently wrote that the best campaign plans incorporate "seven winning components." One of these components is strategy. Candidates must decide how to allocate resources between efforts to persuade undecided voters and those designed to mobilize the base of existing supporters.[9] Whether a candidate will need to mobilize, create a base, or persuade a significant portion of undecided voters depends on the district's characteristics, his individual party's reputation, and the monetary resources he has available.

The race for Congress in West Virginia's Second District demonstrates the importance of developing coherent message strategy. The incumbent congressman, Bob Wise, retired, and the seat was open. Like the rest of state, the district trends Democratic. Republican candidate Shelley Moore Capito had to expand beyond her base and attract Democrats and independent voters to win. For her, a persuasion strategy was more important than mobilizing the base. Her opponent, state senator Jim Humphreys, had substantial personal money he could contribute to the race. Capito had to rely heavily on outside groups, especially the Republican Party, to launch advertisements on her behalf. The party's campaign strategy was simple: attack Humphreys's credibility on taxes, the one issue on which Republicans had a clear reputation advantage. In her own advertisements, like many candidates running in districts where the majority of voters do not share the same partisan affiliation, Capito avoided mentioning that she was a Republican. She stressed instead her ability to find independent solutions while simultaneously capitalizing on the Republicans' partisan advantage on taxes.[10] The party used the Republican reputation advantage on taxes, while Capito carefully cultivated her own reputation as an independent and made use of her party's issue reputation. In this way, she could hope to attract crossover voters.

Humphreys used the Democratic tilt to his advantage by linking Capito to Republican efforts to privatize Social Security. The effort was a classic attempt to remind voters that Republicans cannot be trusted to protect entitlement programs. It was also an effort to appeal to his party's reputation, especially as his own reputation was tarnished. A high level of absenteeism in the state legislature and a request for immunity in a criminal case had hurt his credibility with voters. He even introduced himself as "Democrat Jim Humphreys" in his television ads—an unusual tactic, but clearly designed to remind West Virginia voters of their commitments. In the end, Republican efforts to undermine his individual reputation worked. His base crumbled, and Capito capitalized, winning a tight race. Republicans had poured money into the race, even advertising in the Washington television market. She has been a strong supporter of her party in Congress despite her efforts to tout her independence. In her first term, she supported her party 89 percent of the time on unity votes. This compares favorably with the Republican average of 90 percent for the entire 107th Congress.[11]

Campaigns are not always effective at reminding or persuading. Campaigns succeed, or they fail. Political actors can make strategic errors, choosing to highlight the wrong aspect of a candidate or party reputation. They can lack the resources necessary to communicate their messages effectively. Past commitments can be so strong that persuasion efforts are unsuccessful, or attempts to remind supporters cannot activate prior commitments. More important than whether campaigns do matter at a particular time and place is the belief among political actors that they might.[12] Their choice of campaign strategies and tactics are made with this in mind.

In short, political actors wish to define their own and their opponent's reputations in ways that either remind supporters of past commitments or persuade potential supporters to downplay their existing commitments in favor of more pressing concerns.[13] A Democratic Party–sponsored advertisement praising their candidate's record on the environment reminds supporters why they should remain steadfast to their Democratic commitments, while it may potentially persuade cross-pressured voters to abandon past Republican commitments in favor of a party and a candidate sharing a stance on an issue personally important to them. Similarly, a Republican Party ad attacking a Democratic congressional candidate on economic policy highlights the perils of abandoning commitments for supporters, while offering the cross-pressured voters, concerned about government's scope, cognitive comfort to ease their ballot box conversion.[14]

"Parties," notes Popkin, "use ideologies to highlight critical differences between themselves, and to remind voters of their past successes. They do this because voters do not perceive all the differences, cannot remember all the past performances, and cannot relate all future policies to their own benefits."[15] Candidates and interest groups behave no differently. They stress candidate quality and abilities, past commitments such as partisanship or social characteristics, and issue-specific concerns as it suits them. In every case, they do so in a way to best portray the electoral choice on their terms.

When political actors cast a candidate or party reputation in a particular light, and voters perceive this and (possibly) act upon it, they have altered the electoral terrain. This provides the actor with a reputation resource advantage that does not go unnoticed by other political actors. Reputation advantages guide the strategic behavior of other actors. Either they accept the presentation of the reputation and capitalize upon it, or they try to redefine the reputation more suitably to their own electoral goals.

Returning to the previous example, suppose taxes are not salient to voters and voters do not perceive a Republican advantage on the issue. The

Republican Party launches a series of tax ads, taxes become salient, and the public now perceives a Republican tax advantage. This creates a reputational advantage for the Republican Party. Alternatively, a party may advertise on an issue that is already salient and on which they already have an advantage. The ad may simply "bolster" or "remind" voters of the issue's salience and the Republican's issue advantage. A Republican congressional candidate may seek to "latch" onto the tax issue provided by his party in either case. The Democratic candidate, however, responds by airing several environmental ads to change the debate. He may wish to make the environment salient, create an issue advantage on the environment, or advertise on an issue perhaps even more salient to voters than taxes. In each case, the Democratic candidate seeks to redefine the issue terrain in a way favorable to his reputation and unfavorable to his opponent's. The most important points are who "owns" a particular issue and how each political actor decides to influence the issue agenda.[16] The advantages that parties have on issues have consequences for the way members of Congress advertise themselves to voters. These advantages are a reflection of the distribution of reputation resources. Under the right circumstances, a candidate's closeness to his party can reap electoral benefits.

THE 2000 CONGRESSIONAL CAMPAIGN REVISITED: PARTISANSHIP, VOTING, AND REPUTATIONS

The Federal Elections Campaign Act and its subsequent interpretation by the courts strengthened political parties after 1974 relative to candidates and interest groups—at least monetarily. But the role of parties since the early 1970s is less clear in terms of the voting public. Several references have been made in previous chapters to the alleged collapse of partisans in the electorate: the percentage of voters identifying with either of the two major parties has fallen from 75 percent in 1952 to 58 percent in 2000 (see figure 2.4).

In particular, Martin Wattenberg observed several trends suggesting that the evaluation of candidates and issues by voters occurs through a less partisan lens. Increasing neutrality of citizens toward the Democratic and Republican parties is a case in point. Wattenberg cites the rise of the neutral-neutrals: those individuals who have no net like or dislike of the two major parties. The National Election Studies (NES) asks people if they have any likes or dislikes about the Republican and Democratic Parties.

Wattenberg simply sums the number of likes an individual expresses for the two parties and subtracts from this sum the total number of dislikes about the parties. If the net result is zero, he classifies the individual as neutral-neutral. In 1952, 13 percent of NES respondents fell into the neutral-neutral category; by 1980, this had risen to nearly 37 percent.[17]

Another measure of party relevancy is whether individuals can express an opinion on the parties at all. The NES has developed a measure of party salience, which is simply the total number of likes and dislikes expressed by a respondent about both major parties, ranging from zero to twenty. The higher the score, the greater the salience. For our purposes, parties are considered to be salient by respondents if they can express any number of likes or dislikes concerning the parties.

Figure 6.1 reports the percentage of respondents falling into the salient and not salient categories from 1952 through 2000. The mid-1970s, the end-point of Wattenberg's analysis, represents a low point in the party salience trend. In 1952, more than 90 percent of respondents could express either a like or dislike about at least one of the two major parties. By 1978, this figure had declined substantially to less than 60 percent. After 1978, however, party salience recovered. By 2000, nearly 80 percent of respondents perceived the major parties as salient, a level not achieved since 1972.

Other general measures of affect and salience suggest that voters in the aggregate associate political parties with their candidates. This association has strengthened since the late 1970s. The correlation between party and presidential candidate like/dislike measures declined between 1952 and 1980, but the trend reversed sharply in 1984 and has since achieved levels consistent with the earlier portion of the time series (figure 6.2). And although the NES did not ask the like/dislike questions in reference to congressional candidates until 1978, the correlation trend between congressional candidates and parties (with the exception of 1992) also demonstrates a clear upward trend (figure 6.3). Finally, the correlation between respondent placement of parties and congressional candidates on feeling thermometer scales intensifies over the same period, as does the party-candidate ideological correlation (figure 6.4).

As chapter 5 demonstrated, partisan reputations are useful to candidates because they cut through crowded airwaves. They might also have a monetary value for candidates. But the deliberate projection of partisan reputations also may help candidates to build partisan voting coalitions. Candidates, in the years following the 1974 reforms, may deliberately

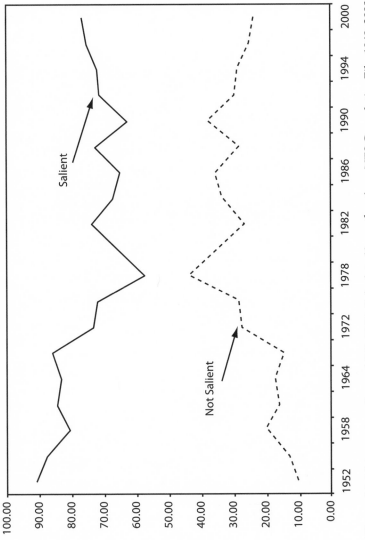

Figure 6.1. Major party salience, 1952–2000. Calculated by author from NES Cumulative File, 1948–2000. File located at www.umich.edu/~nes.

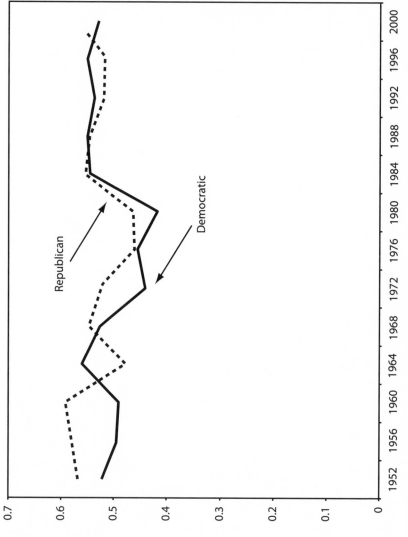

Figure 6.2. Party and presidential candidate affect correlations, 1952–2000. Calculated by author from NES Cumulative File, 1948–2000.

158

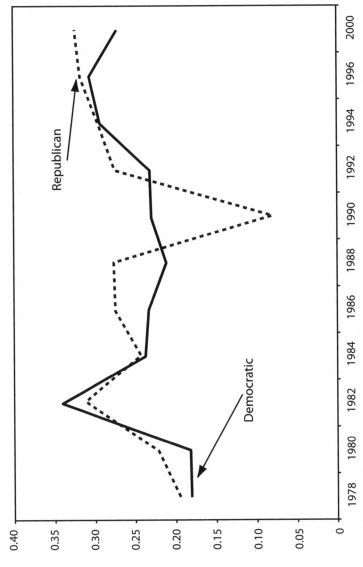

Figure 6.3. Party and congressional candidate affect correlations, 1978–2000. Calculated by author from NES Cumulative File, 1948–2000.

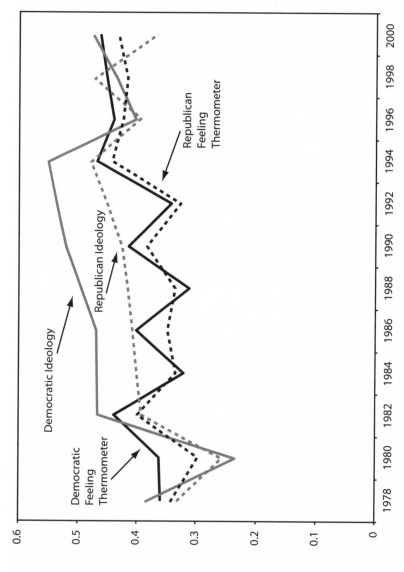

Figure 6.4. Correlations between party and congressional candidate on ideology and feeling thermometer placements, 1978–2000. Calculated by author from NES Cumulative File, 1948–2000.

project increasingly partisan reputations as a means of securing particular voting coalitions. Recall that mobilization efforts include both reminding and persuasion messages. Historically lower levels of turnout have encouraged campaigns in recent years to stress more frequently the ability to activate a candidate's or party's base—those who have actively supported a candidate in the past and are likely to do so in the future—at the expense of persuading either active opponents or the uninvolved.[18] The communication of partisan messages is an efficient and effective way to remind the base of its previous commitments. The increasing association between the parties and their respective candidates perceived by the public in the aggregate may reflect a calculated strategy by candidates and parties to rally their bases in anticipation of election day.

Candidates and parties can generate or reinforce existing partisan reputations by spending monetary resources; the hope is that supporters will notice. Moving from aggregate trends to the individual ones, does the spending by parties and candidates affect individual perception of the candidates? Other studies have explored whether incumbents and challengers can alter the perceptions of incumbent voting records and issue positions,[19] but the question remains open of whether party and candidate dollars have independent effects.

This is an important distinction. Parties and candidates can pursue either complementary or competing electoral strategies. If there is a concerted effort by parties to create a partisan reputation for their candidates to utilize in elections, the amount of money spent by the parties should affect how the public views candidates in relation to their respective parties. If candidates are actively turning to their parties for issue cover, then their individual spending should similarly create an impression of increased ideological closeness to their party. Alternatively, candidates may wish to spend themselves away from their parties to establish independent reputations, and parties may aid them. Finally, candidates and parties may engage in competing strategies: one pushing away from the party, the other pushing toward it.

MONEY AND IMPRESSION FORMATION

The 2000 National Election Studies asks respondents to place themselves, congressional candidates, and the two major parties on a seven-point ideology scale ranging from strongly liberal (coded as zero) to strongly conservative (coded as six). Taking the absolute distance between a party and that party's congressional candidate creates a measure of ideological distance. The greater the gap, the more distant a candidate is perceived from his party. Conversely, the narrower the gap, the closer the party and the candidate. One question of interest is whether the campaign expenditures of political parties can reduce the candidate-party ideology gap perceived by citizens. Another is whether the expenditures of candidates also affect how they are perceived by citizens.

In the 2000 election, parties and candidates pursued complementary advertising strategies highlighting partisan advantages and disadvantages (see chapter 5); that is, parties and their candidates bound themselves to a common issue agenda while driving the opposing party and candidate apart. The more a party and its candidate spends, the more alike they should seem to respondents. The more the opposing party and candidate spend, however, the greater the chasm between them.[20] The candidate spending variables, as in chapter 5, include all campaign contributions reported to the FEC minus party contributions and coordinated expenditures. Party spending includes those contributions and coordinated expenditures excluded from the candidate variables in addition to television advertising funded with soft money and tracked by the Wisconsin Advertising Project (WAP).[21] The actions of candidates and parties during a campaign certainly are affected by the opposition's activities. As a party spends money on advertisements highlighting a particular issue, it might affect how the candidate chooses to position himself on a unity vote, which in turn can affect the party's strategy. This is known as endogeneity, and it creates a host of problems in statistical analyses. The solution is to use estimates of the spending totals, and these estimates are used in the regression equations that follow rather than the actual spending amounts.[22]

It is important to consider how candidate and individual characteristics can influence the perceived party/candidate ideology gap. "Previous margin of victory" is the absolute difference between the Democratic and Republican vote percentages in the 1998 congressional election. Chapter 5 demonstrated that as races become increasingly competitive, parties are more likely to create issue agendas onto which candidates latch. A probable consequence is a smaller ideological gap between a candidate and his party in more competitive races. The "previous margin of victory" variable takes this effect into account. Incumbency certainly influences how respondents perceive candidates relative to their parties: presumably Democratic and Republican incumbents are most able to establish individual reputations distinct from their parties' reputations. Incumbency may also influence respondent perceptions of challengers: the longer an incumbent serves, the less knowledge and experience respondents have with the opposing party, its candidates, and their records. Lacking information, respondents in districts with long-serving incumbents may simply be unable to distinguish between the opposing candidate and his party; therefore, they view the two similarly. Two "year in office" variables represent these incumbency effects: a Democratic year in office variable and a Republican year in office variable.

The ideology of a candidate certainly affects how citizens perceive a candidate relative to his party: the more extreme a candidate, the greater the gap observed between him and his party.[23] Ideology is represented by Poole and Rosenthal's common space scores, which range from positive one to negative one. Positive values represent the conservative end of the ideological spectrum, and negative values represent the liberal end. Challengers, unfortunately, have no voting records on which to base an ideological measure. Using a three-step procedure similar to that employed by Berry et al., who produce measures of state ideology, an admittedly rough challenger ideology score can be calculated and substituted.[24]

The final candidate characteristic measure, "candidate ideological extremity," is a dummy variable, coded one if a candidate is very liberal or very conservative.[25] Particularly conservative or liberal ideological records might distort respondent perceptions of candidates, leading them to place candidates even further from the party. The coefficient value reported in the table below should be positive if this is indeed the case.

How individuals perceive themselves relative to the parties and the parties relative to the political spectrum itself also determines how they view candidates relative to their parties. Respondents who believe that a party is far from the political center may also perceive candidates as extreme collectively. Those who see themselves as close to a party, on the other hand, should perceive that party and its candidate as nearly indistinguishable. The scale gap between the party and respondent and the scale gap between party and the median scale values take these possible placement effects into account.[26] An individual's partisanship, too, influences how they view the political world. "Folded party identification" represents how strongly partisan an individual is, with greater values

Table 6.1. Spending and creation of general partisan reputations, 2000

Variables	Democratic Candidate-Party Ideological Gap	Republican Candidate-Party Ideological Gap
Spending		
Republican candidate spending ($100,000)	-.021	.017
	(.017)	(.024)
Democratic candidate spending ($100,000)	.007	.005
	(.017)	(.023)
Republican Party spending ($100,000)	.060	.048
	(.060)	(.063)
Democratic Party spending ($100,000)	-.045	-.045
	(.070)	(.072)
Candidate Characteristics		
Previous margin of victory	-.281	.330
	(.359)	(.511)
Democrat year in office	-.004	.016
	(.008)	(.015)
Republican year in office	-.008	.002
	(.011)	(.012)
Candidate ideology	1.954	2.384**
	(1.947)	(1.373)
Candidate ideological extremity	-.175	.040
	(.225)	(.175)
Individual Characteristics		
Folded party identification	-.092**	-.031
	(.051)	(.056)
Politics not complicated	.026	.015
	(.036)	(.040)
Scale gap between party and respondent	.051*	.158***
	(.037)	(.041)
Scale gap between party and median value	.273***	.180***
	(.070)	(.074)
Political knowledge index	-.080***	-.136***
	(.031)	(.033)
Attention to campaign	.025	-.148**
	(.072)	(.083)
Education * Candidate ideology	-.050	-.315
	(.263)	(.276)
Constant	.701***	.161
	(.292)	(.409)
R-squared	.11	.15
F-statistic	2.48**	3.39***
N	492	475

*** $p<=.01$; **$p<=.05$; *$p<=.10$; one-tailed. Unstandardized coefficients with robust standard errors in parentheses .

indicating increasing partisan strength. The more partisan an individual, the less distinct ideologically the parties and candidates should appear.

The final four variables measure the political awareness of individuals: "Politics not complicated," the "Political knowledge index," "Attention to campaigns," and "Education-candidate ideology."[27] Generally, the more politically aware and educated an individual, the closer candidates and parties should appear to that individual. This may seem contradictory: presumably, political sophistication increases sensitivity to ideological differences. True enough, but candidates of the same party have become less distinguishable from one another empirically over the last thirty years (see chapter 2); therefore, the politically aware should perceive candidates close to their parties ideologically.

Does candidate spending relate to an individual's ability to distinguish between candidates and their political parties? Party spending and candidate spending appear to have no significant bearing on how individuals perceive candidates relative to their parties (see table 6.1).[28] The four spending variables in both the Democratic and Republican candidate-party ideology gap equations are not statistically significant.[29] In fact, few variables manage to achieve statistical significance at all, and the few that do are not central to the discussion. The aggregate trends noted earlier, suggesting a closer association between parties and candidates in the public mind since the late 1970s, do not appear to be related to party and candidate spending and the formation of individual perceptions of parties and candidates at the individual level in 2000.

MONEY AND ISSUE REPUTATIONS

Campaigns do not seek conversion of worldviews or the abandonment of long-standing partisan commitments, so these findings regarding spending and the relationship of parties relative to candidates in the minds of voters are not unanticipated.[30] Rather, campaigns want to change issue priorities, in particular the issues upon which respondents evaluate parties and candidates. The aggregate trend from 1978 to 2000 denoting an increased connection between parties and candidates on a range of measures is probably the artifact of many campaigns spending money through the years on developing stronger issue links between candidate and party agendas. This movement occurs glacially over time and is most likely invisible at the micro-level during any one campaign or any one election year.

If, however, candidates establish particular issue reputations for themselves and their opponents in any given campaign, respondents should be able to discern them. That is, if campaigns truly concern themselves with shifting voter priorities on a discrete set of issue concerns, and campaigns actually affect voter perceptions, voters should be able to identify and match particular issue reputations to each candidate. If the concept of issue reputation is more than a signaling game played by political elites, citizens should be able to distinguish between issue reputations that parties create, and those issue reputations should influence how citizens order their priorities.

The 2000 congressional campaign traversed a narrow issue terrain. The Republican Party and their candidates highlighted economic issues in their television advertisements, while the Democratic Party and their candidates stressed entitlement issues such as Social Security, health care, and welfare. These themes matched those employed by the presidential candidates: Bush talked tax cuts, and Al Gore supported a Social Security "lock box." As demonstrated in chapter 5, the Republican Party successfully set the issue agenda for its candidates, particularly in competitive congressional races. In races where the Republican Party launched its advertising first, Republican candidates responded by latching onto the economic themes established by the party. Democratic candidates latched on as well, but they did so less frequently.

Parties influenced the campaign strategies of their candidates, especially those most vulnerable to defeat: freshmen members and those engaged in competitive races. In the aggregate, voters perceived a stronger relationship between the parties and their candidates generally over time, but could voters identify the issue terrain as landscaped by the parties and candidates? Did the public equate Republicans with economic and Democrats with entitlement issues? Did citizens in 2000 view the Republican Party favorably on economic issues and the Democratic Party on entitlements, as both parties hoped they would? Similarly, did they view the parties negatively with respect to the opposing party's issue agenda: Republicans adversely on entitlements, and Democrats less positively on economic concerns?

The NES asks respondents if there is anything they like or dislike about each of the two major parties. In each case, they are allowed five responses, for a maximum of twenty (ten total likes and dislikes of the two parties combined). Totaling each respondent's likes about a party and subtracting the number of dislikes about a party can create an individual affect score for the party indicating how much a respondent likes or dislikes that particular party. If a respondent answered negatively or "don't know" to the screening question inquiring whether there was anything they liked or disliked about a party, this was coded as a neutral response.

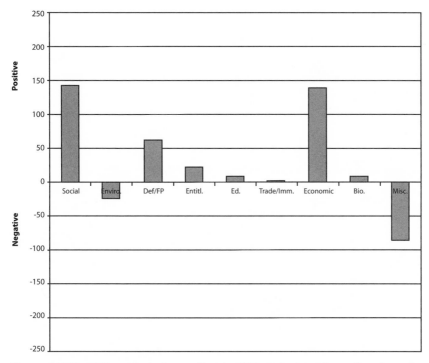

Figure 6.5. Republican Party issue affect in 2000. Calculated by author from the 2000 NES file located at www.umich.edu/~nes.

If an individual only volunteered one like or dislike and no other, the other four response opportunities were also coded neutrally at zero.

Similarly, a party issue affect score can also be created by adding the total number of individual likes and then subtracting the total number of dislikes. By issue area, this allows evaluation of the particular reasons each respondent or the public as a whole likes or dislikes a party and creates issue affect scores for each party. The NES categorizes responses to the like/dislike questions. These are used to create nine issue categories analogous to those detailed in appendix A and employed in chapter 5.[31] This allows one to match how respondents perceive the parties on issues to the actual campaign themes used by parties and candidates in advertisements. Appendix B provides a list of the NES likes/dislikes categories sorted into the issue classifications utilized in this chapter.

Public perceptions of the parties matched the reputations that parties advertised (see figures 6.5 and 6.6): economic issues benefited Republicans,

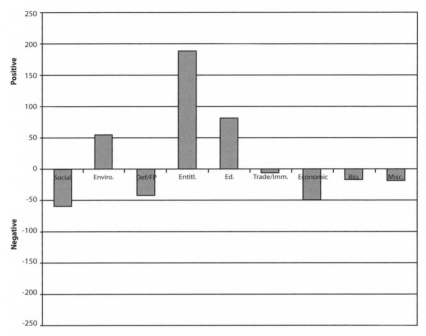

Figure 6.6. Democratic Party issue affect in 2000. Calculated by author from the 2000 NES.

and entitlements favored Democrats. The general public also rated the two parties poorly on the opposing party's issue reputation. Democrats received a negative affect score on Republican-owned economic issues, while Republicans received little credit on entitlement issues.

Issue affect only measures the like/dislike statements made about one party in a particular issue area. Issue advantage, however, measures how a respondent perceives the parties relative to each other on a particular issue. Advantage is calculated first by summing a respondent's dislikes about one party and his likes about the other party in a given issue area. From this summation, the total number of likes about the party and the total dislikes about the other party can be subtracted, creating a score ranging from negative ten to positive ten on the issue. Positive values indicate a Republican advantage on a particular issue, and negative values indicate a Democratic advantage. For example, if a respondent mentioned two dislikes about Republicans, five likes about the Democrats, one like about the Republicans, and two dislikes about the Democrats—all concerning the economy—the respondent's economic advantage score would

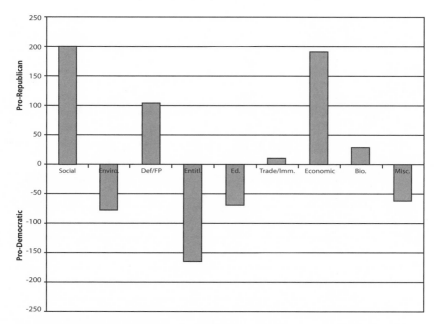

Figure 6.7. Republican and Democratic Party issue advantages in 2000. Calculated by author from the 2000 NES.

be a negative four. This would indicate that the respondent perceived a Democratic advantage on the economy.

In 2000, Republicans enjoyed a large issue advantage on economic and social issues while Democrats enjoyed a similar advantage on Social Security, Medicare, welfare, and other entitlement issues (see figure 6.7).[32] The Republican and Democratic parties engaged in virtually two separate campaigns in 2000, and the electorate noticed.

One of the important connections made in chapter 5 concerned the timing of party advertisements and the themes utilized by congressional candidates: when parties advertised first, candidates followed by latching onto their respective party's issue reputation. Republican candidates latched onto economic issues, and Democratic candidates latched onto entitlements. This pattern should persist in the likes/dislikes responses of the public. In congressional districts where the parties and candidates spend money, citizens should associate particular issue likes/dislikes with each of the parties. And indeed they do (see figures 6.8 and 6.9). Republicans are most positively perceived on economic issues when both the Republican Party and candidate spent money. The expenditure of money by

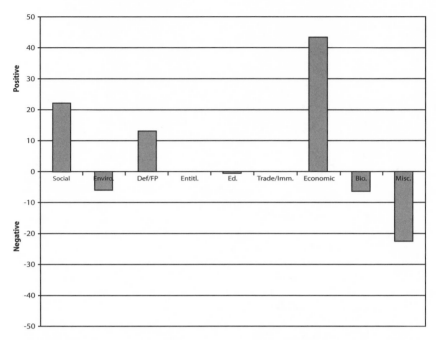

Figure 6.8. Republican Party issue affect where Republican Party and candidate spend money. Calculated by author from 2000 NES and Wisconsin Advertising Project data.

the Democratic Party and its candidate is likewise associated with a positive image on entitlements. Where parties and candidates spent money, the public's issue perceptions matched those being advertised.

The spending patterns of the parties are also associated with how citizens view the parties on issues relative to each other. Republicans enjoy an issue advantage over Democrats on economic issues among citizens in districts where both parties spend money (see figure 6.10). Television advertisements by the Democratic Party generated an entitlement advantage in the same districts. Parties may have manipulated their images successfully, although it is difficult with these data to demonstrate a causal relationship. It is no coincidence, however, that the public says little about the parties—positively or negatively—on issues of trade and education. These were not major issue themes in candidate or party congressional campaign advertisements.

As V. O. Key famously opined, "The voice of the people is but an echo. . . . As candidates and parties clamor for attention and vie for popular support, the people's verdict can be no more than a selective reflec-

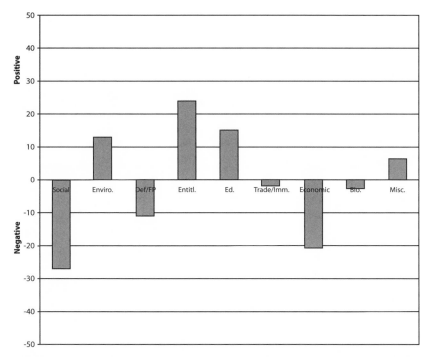

Figure 6.9. Democratic Party issue affect where Democratic Party and candidate spend money. Calculated by author from 2000 NES and Wisconsin Advertising Project data.

tion from among the alternatives and outlooks presented to them."[33] The echo of candidate and party advertising seemed to reverberate strongly in the public perception, providing the issue terrain of taxes and Social Security on which parties were assessed.

THE ROLE OF PARTY REPUTATION ON INDIVIDUAL IMPRESSIONS

In 2000, the Republican Party and its candidates staked their issue ground on economic policy (Bush and tax cuts). The Democrats, on the other hand, marked their territory on entitlement issues (Gore and his lock box). Parties and candidates hoped to shift citizen issue priorities by creating or maintaining particular issue advantages and then translating these issue advantages into positive electoral outcomes. Through careful and targeted spending on television advertisements focused on their respective issue agendas, parties and candidates planned to accomplish these goals.

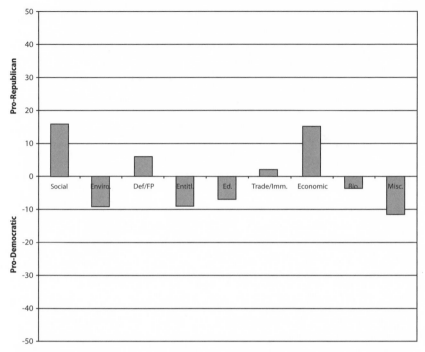

Figure 6.10. Republican and Democratic issue advantages where both parties spend money. Calculated by author from 2000 NES and Wisconsin Advertising Project data.

The issue advantage measure introduced earlier is a perfect way to evaluate party advertising efforts at the individual level. As before, each respondent's likes/dislikes about a party can be converted to advantage scores on each of the nine issue areas.[34] As the Republicans focused on economics and the Democrats on entitlements, I combined the number of positive mentions about a party and the number of negative mentions about the opposing party in each issue area, then subtracted from this total the number of negative mentions about the party and the total number of positive mentions about the other party in each issue area. As before, a no response to a like or dislike opportunity, don't knows, and those answering no to the initial like/dislike screening question were all coded neutrally at zero. Both hypothetically range from negative ten to positive ten, but actually both the economic and entitlement advantage variables range between negative four and positive five.[35] Positive values of the economic advantage variable indicate a Republican issue advantage, while positive values on the entitlement advantage variable indicate a Democratic advantage. Negative values reflect a Democratic and Republican disadvantage on the economic and entitlements, respectively. These issue advantage scales and their connection to candidate and party spending are the subject of the following regression analysis.

It is important to take into account other factors that may be related to the perception of a partisan issue advantage. Some of these factors, such as the "political knowledge index," "attention to the campaign," "seniority," and the "previous margin of victory" have been described previously. Most important for our concern is how party and candidate spending are related to partisan reputation advantages. The total amount spent by a party or candidate does not translate easily into a measure of spending on economic and entitlement issues: campaign expenditures represent staff salaries, consultant fees, travel and event costs, and a host of other advertisements that may or may not specifically focus on a party's or candidate's primary issue agenda. To reflect the dollar volumes spent on economic and entitlement advertisements, the total dollar amounts spent on these advertisements by the parties and candidates in each congressional district can be calculated using estimates drawn from WAP data. Using these figures in combination with the spending totals provided by the FEC, the percentage spent by each campaign on entitlement- and economic-themed television advertisements can also be computed. To avoid the problem of endogeneity discussed above, these percentages were then multiplied by the two-stage spending estimates calculated earlier.[36] Increased spending by a candidate and his party should widen a party's issue advantage, while spending by the opposing candidate and his party should narrow that advantage.

A variety of demographic, media, and issue variables control for other important relationships affecting whether citizens perceive a partisan reputation advantage. More Democratic generally, women and nonwhites should perceive a greater Democratic advantage on both economic and entitlement issues, hence the inclusion of "Race" and "Gender" dummy variables that are coded one for nonwhites and women. The coefficient on both variables should be negative in the economic advantage table (and positive in the entitlement table). "Family income" as reported to the National Election Study by respondents is also included in both equations. The variable ranges from low income to high income. The wealthier a respondent's family, the greater the Republican advantage on economic issues and the smaller the Democratic advantage on entitlement concerns.

Democrats should view their party as providing the best economic and entitlement solutions. Republicans should behave no differently with reference to their own party and its policies. "Party identification" represents this, with strong Republicans and Democrats anchored at the positive and negative ends of the scale. The coefficient on the partisanship variable should be positive in the economic advantage table (the more Republican, the greater the economic advantage) and negative in the entitlement advantage table (the more Democratic, the greater the entitlement advantage).

"Union household" and "unemployment," included only in the economic advantage table, are dummy variables coded one for unemployed respondents and those living in union households. Although entitlement policies do have consequences for union members, their families, and the unemployed, economic policies more directly involve the concerns of unions and the jobless, which explains why they are included only in the economic advantage analysis. Again, both union household and unemployed coefficients should be negative, reflecting a perceived Democratic advantage on economic issues by union members and the unemployed. The logic behind including age only in the entitlement equation is the same: age more directly involves concerns about retirement and medical care than general economic policy. The older a respondent, the more likely he will perceive a Democratic advantage on entitlements.

Presumably, individuals who pay more attention to the news by reading the paper and watching television will have a better sense of the images that candidates and parties are attempting to portray for themselves and their opponents. The NES asks how many days a week individuals read a newspaper and watch both the local and national news. Combining these three measures (local news, national news, and newspaper consumption) creates a media use index ranging from zero to twenty-one. The more attention individuals pay to the news, the more likely they can accurately discern the issue advantages that parties and candidates wish them to distinguish. The greater the news intake, the greater the Republican economic (a positive coefficient) and Democratic entitlement advantage (a negative coefficient).

Another set of variables control for particular issue concerns voters have that might influence their perception of a partisan issue advantage. "Guaranteed jobs" and "Clinton job approval" denote individual support for government involvement in the economy and how respondents rate the outgoing administration's performance.[37] "Support for government health care" and "delayed medical procedures" tap a respondent's desire for the federal provision of medical care and their own immediate need for treatment.[38] "Delay medical procedures" is a dummy variable coded one if the respondent had to put off a medical procedure for financial reasons. The more conservative a respondent's view on the economy, the greater the perception of a Republican advantage on economic issues. Likewise, the more in need of medical care and more desirous of government-sponsored health care, the greater the Democratic advantage on entitlements.

The relevance of economic and entitlement issues to individuals can also be measured by whether respondents feel the issue is important to them personally. NES respondents are asked what is the most important problem facing the nation today. Using a procedure similar to the one matching the likes/dislikes questions to issue themes, the economic most important problem and entitlement most important problem variables can be created.[39] People viewing economics or entitlements with utmost concern should give the party advertising and talking about the issue an advantage on that issue.

Those who are economically vulnerable should view the parties differently on both economic and entitlement concerns. People do not necessarily envision the state of the national economy and their own personal economic concerns, and the political relevancy of both varies.[40] As the Republicans ran the 2000 campaign on economic concerns, those who are most dissatisfied with the present economic arrangements (both personal and national) should respond by perceiving a greater Republican advantage on the economy. Correspondingly, those are the same people who should perceive a Democratic advantage on entitlement issues: being vulnerable, they are willing to listen to calls for greater government involvement in the provision of a social safety net.[41]

RESULTS

Spending on economic and entitlement issues is associated with citizen perceptions of the parties on those issues, but not completely as anticipated (see tables 6.2 and 6.3). Candidate spending had neither a substantial nor a significant effect on whether individuals saw a partisan issue advantage on either the economy or entitlements—note that the coefficients for candidate spending are not starred. And neither did party spending work to increase their advantage on their own issue turf. The

Democratic and Republican parties do not gain additional advantage on entitlement and economic issues, respectively, by spending more money.

Co-opting issues, however, is one way in which parties can persuade cross-pressured voters of opposing partisan persuasions to jump ship or appeal to cross-pressured supporters to come home on election day. For example, in Connecticut's Fifth District, the National Republican Congressional Committee launched a series of ads against Democratic incumbent Jim Maloney. Like many Republican ads, this one focused on Maloney and his record of raising taxes.[42] How did Democrats respond? They attempted to use the tax issue—normally a Republican strength—to their advantage in order to neutralize the issue. The Democratic Congressional Campaign Committee attacked the Republican challenger, Mark Nielsen, on taxes. These ads claimed that Maloney had voted against taxes while Nielsen "support[ed] raising taxes on middle-class families, including eliminating deductions for home mortgages and charitable contributions."[43] This is classic issue co-opting.

When a party chooses to co-opt the opposing party's issue, spending does affect how respondents perceive the parties on that issue (refer to tables 6.2 and 6.3). That is, the more parties spend advertising on the opponent's issue terrain, the less of an advantage the opposing party is perceived to have on that issue. The more entitlement spending by the Republican Party, the less of an entitlement advantage the Democratic Party enjoyed. The same is true for Democratic Party spending on the economy: the Republican Party's issue advantage declines as more money is spent. To be sure, the effects are slight: the Republican Party needs to spend a million dollars on entitlement ads to move a respondent roughly one point on the entitlement advantage scale, and the Democratic Party needs to spend about half as much for a similar movement on the economic advantage scale. And the Democratic and Republican parties did not co-opt their opponent's issues often: entitlements consisted of less than 10 percent of total ad mentions for Republicans and economic policy less than 15 percent of total ad mentions for Democrats (see chapter 5). By comparison, economic-related ad mentions accounted for 32 percent of the Republican total, and entitlements accounted for 27 percent of the Democratic. Nevertheless, parties can utilize their financial resources to affect the perceptions of voters on issues and can do so if they engage in particularly concentrated issue spending.[44]

But these findings make sense for another reason. Individuals who are already supportive of a party because of sociological, attitudinal, or philo-

Table 6.2. Spending and the Republican economic reputation advantage, 2000

Variables	Republican Economic Advantage
Spending	
Republican candidate spending ($100,000)	.000
	(.055)
Democratic candidate spending ($100,000)	.039
	(.052)
Republican Party spending ($100,000)	.046
	(.066)
Democratic Party spending ($100,000)	-.203*
	(.143)
Candidate Characteristics	
Previous margin of victory	-.237
	(.201)
Democrat year in office	.001
	(.005)
Republican year in office	.013**
	(.008)
Individual Characteristics	
Race	.068
	(.085)
Gender	.001
	(.060)
Party identification (–Democrat, +Republican)	.146***
	(.016)
Income	.011
	(.010)
Union household	-.070
	(.062)
Unemployment status	-.099
	(.181)
Media usage	.002
	(.005)
Political knowledge index	.082***
	(.021)
Attention to campaign	.038
	(.044)
Guaranteed jobs	.018
	(.020)
Clinton job on economy	.037*
	(.024)
National economic conditions	.051**
	(.025)
Personal economic conditions	-.017
	(.025)
Most important problem is economy	-.043
	(.074)
Constant	-.281**
	(.138)
R-squared	.21
F-statistic	8.76***
N	875

*** p<=.01; **p<=.05; *p<=.10; one-tailed. Unstandardized coefficients with robust standard errors in parentheses.

sophical commitments should be difficult to move away from those commitments. In other words, their worldview is colored by their partisan lenses: they stand pat and continue to view the party as the parties wish to be perceived. The direction and strength of the party identification coefficient is evidence of this: individuals see the world through a partisan filter, and their issue judgments of the parties are colored by that filter. Advertising strategies reinforce this but do not change it.

By spending money on economic issues, the Democratic Party accomplishes two things. First, it gently reminds Democratic supporters persuaded by the Republican economic message of their own party's accomplishments and record on taxes, spending, and budgets. Second, it communicates to independents and Republican adherents that the Democrats are not the tax-and-spend bogeymen the Republican Party and its candidates would lead them to believe. In a sense, the Democratic Party is giving those who view Republican economic policy favorably permission to vote Democratic. The same is true for Republican entreaties to voters on entitlements. By dipping into the issue strength of the other party, each party is attempting to neutralize the issue advantage and force the debate onto terrain favorable to them.[45]

The other finding worth discussing concerns incumbency. Only Republican incumbency has an effect on the party's issue reputation: the longer a Republican serves in Congress, the more substantial the Republican Party's economic advantage. The average Republican incumbent in 2000 served two terms in the House. This accounts for a modest half point increase in the party's advantage on economic issues. Democratic incumbency does not give the party a similar advantage on entitlements. Why the difference between the two parties? Perhaps Republican incumbents do a better job of credit claiming and position taking over time on their party's key issue than Democratic incumbents. Maybe Democratic incumbents spread themselves too thin in terms of issue reputation: Republicans may be more single-minded in the pursuit of downsizing government (or at least in advertising this) than Democrats are at protecting and expanding the welfare state. Although district competitiveness alters the issue strategies pursued by candidates and parties, it has no apparent bearing on the public's issue evaluation of the parties.[46]

Campaigns may alter the way in which individuals weigh various issue concerns, and they may even increase or decrease the advantage given to a party on a particular issue. The ultimate hope, however, is to influence

Table 6.3. Spending and the Democratic entitlement reputation advantage, 2000

Variables	Democratic Entitlement Advantage
Spending	
Republican candidate spending ($100,000)	.007
	(.043)
Democratic candidate spending ($100,000)	.014
	(.026)
Republican Party spending ($100,000)	-.153*
	(.099)
Democratic Party spending ($100,000)	-.000
	(.029)
Candidate Characteristics	
Previous margin of victory	.098
	(.149)
Democrat year in office	-.002
	(.004)
Republican year in office	.001
	(.004)
Individual Characteristics	
Race	-.069
	(.067)
Gender	.012
	(.047)
Party identification (–Democrat, +Republican)	-.077***
	(.012)
Income	.008
	(.007)
Age	-.002
	(.001)
Delayed medical procedure	.032
	(.061)
Media usage	-.002
	(.004)
Political knowledge index	.031**
	(.014)
Attention to campaign	.025
	(.032)
Support for government health care	-.014
	(.015)
National economic conditions	-.031**
	(.019)
Personal economic conditions	-.014
	(.019)
Most important problem is entitlements	.016
	(.052)
Constant	.077
	(.112)
R-squared	.08
F-statistic	3.36***
N	875

*** $p<=.01$; **$p<=.05$; *$p<=.10$; one-tailed. Unstandardized coefficients with robust standard errors in parentheses.

an individual's vote. The perception of an economic or entitlement advantage means nothing if citizens do not translate it into action. Once partisanship, demographics, and candidate affect are controlled, however, there is little room for issues to alter a person's vote. More recent work on information processing and political psychology suggest, however, that available and accessible attitudes can influence behavior.[47] In other words, "salient" concerns—such as a particular issue—may affect one's vote. By spending money to make particular issues accessible and available to voters, campaigns seek to change the issue priorities of voters. This in turn affects their perceptions of candidates. By changing issue priorities and issue reputations, then, political actors influence the vote by affecting how citizens perceive candidates.

Virtually all studies of voting recognize the importance of candidate evaluation upon the vote decision. Respondents in the NES have been asked, since the early 1970s, to rate candidates on a feeling thermometer scale ranging from zero to one hundred, with fifty the median value. Responses of fifty are neutral, with those greater than fifty meaning that the respondent feels warmly (positively) toward the candidate and below fifty coolly (negatively). Voting studies have treated this measure as an important independent variable, but few if any have evaluated it as a dependent variable.[48]

This neglect is unfortunate, as the strategies of candidates and parties are designed precisely to alter how citizens view candidates during campaigns. This is an important point. Political pundits and strategists frequently talk about and measure the favorability rating of a candidate: presumably, the less favorably a candidate is viewed by the public, the less likely they are to vote for him. Campaigns hope to create impressions, which are then translated into votes. Chiefly this is done by massaging a candidate's image. In a sense, we have been looking for the effects of campaigns in all the wrong places: campaigns exert influence on the antecedents to voting and not on voting itself. The causal chain works thusly: campaign spending and advertising alters a voter's issue priorities by making particular issues accessible and available; this shapes the evaluation of candidates and party, and finally—along with previous partisan and social commitments—determines vote choice. Resources, then, are once-removed from the ballot box. Resource imbalances affect issue reputations, which then alter candidate impressions.

Resources have been shown to affect the issue reputations of party. If the causal ordering set out above is correct, then partisan issue advantages should have a significant effect on the evaluation of congressional candidates. Feeling thermometer placements of the House Democratic and Republican candidates as reported by respondents in the 2000 NES represent a measure of candidate evaluation similar to the favorability rating used by political professionals. How is a voter's evaluation of a candidate affected by party issue advantages? A perceived Republican economic advantage should produce more positive evaluations of the Republican candidate and more negative evaluations of the Democratic candidate. The reverse is the case for a perceived Democratic entitlement advantage: the Republican candidate should be more negatively evaluated and the Democratic candidate more positively evaluated.

The party and candidate estimates used in table 6.1 are included in the final regression analysis. Generally, there should be no relationship between party spending and evaluation of candidates. Direct candidate spending should, however, affect feeling thermometer placements. Candidates wish to establish positive images of themselves with their spending, and they generally cultivate a negative image of their opponents. A candidate's spending, therefore, should be positively related to their own image and negatively related to their opponent's.

The other variables included in the analysis (margin of victory, Democrat and Republican year in office, candidate ideology, candidate ideological extremity, party identification, attention to campaign, and the education-candidate ideology interaction) have been described elsewhere. Generally, the more information that voters have and the more attention paid to campaigns, the more positive the evaluation of the candidates. Likewise, those candidates who are ideologically extreme and not sharing a respondent's partisanship should be viewed more negatively by respondents. The final variable, political trust, is simply the standard NES trust in government index.[49] More trusting individuals should perceive individuals generally, and candidates specifically, in a more positive light than those who are more suspicious of government.

Issues do shape how respondents evaluate candidates (see table 6.4). Three out of four of the issue advantage variables are significant, as denoted by the asterisks. More important, the issue advantages act as one would expect. A Republican advantage on the economy creates a more favorable impression for the Republican candidate and a more negative impression for the Democratic candidate. An advantage on entitlements favors the Democratic candidate, with respondents feeling more warmly about the Democratic House candidate when the Democrats have an entitlement advantage. Only the Democratic entitlement advantage variable is insignificant in the Republican candidate feeling thermometer equation.

The positive pull of an issue advantage outweighs a perceived disadvantage on another issue: an extreme Democratic advantage (a placement

Table 6.4. Partisan issue advantages and candidate reputations, 2000

Variables	Democratic Candidate Feeling Thermometer	Republican Candidate Feeling Thermometer
Spending		
Republican candidate spending ($100,000)	-.359*	.882***
	(.238)	(.268)
Democratic candidate spending ($100,000)	.218	-.206
	(.262)	(.267)
Republican Party spending ($100,000)	.923	-1.230*
	(.792)	(.903)
Democratic Party spending ($100,000)	-.825	.753
	(.978)	(1.040)
Candidate Characteristics		
Previous margin of victory	1.130	6.756*
	(5.179)	(4.603)
Democrat year in office	.155	-.094
	(.116)	(.123)
Republican year in office	-.123	.118
	(.139)	(.182)
Candidate ideology	4.286	14.004
	(20.862)	(11.334)
Candidate ideological extremity	.236	-6.110***
	(2.925)	(2.162)
Republican economic advantage	-.940*	1.093**
	(.629)	(.629)
Democratic entitlement advantage	1.573**	-.423
	(.870)	(1.059)
Individual Characteristics		
Party identification (–Democrat, + Republican)	-2.867***	2.865***
	(.314)	(.329)
Trust in government	.627***	.373**
	(.231)	(.206)
Attention to campaign	1.213*	1.744**
	(.869)	(.833)
Education * Candidate ideology	3.261	-3.217
	(3.893)	(2.835)
Constant	52.263***	47.585***
	(3.973)	(3.944)
R-squared	.20	.20
F-statistic	17.82***	15.83***
N	831	821

*** p<=.01; **p<=.05; *p<=.10; one-tailed. Unstandardized coefficients with robust standard errors in parentheses .

of five) on entitlements generates a nearly eight point jump in a respondent's placement of the Democratic candidate on the feeling thermometer. The perception of an extreme Republican advantage on the economy, however, decreases Democratic placement by less than five points. The magnitude of economic advantage on a respondent's evaluation of Republican candidates is similar: an extreme Republican economic advantage generates five degrees of candidate warmth, while a Democratic advantage on entitlements has no significant bearing on the Republican candidate's temperature. Incumbency has no effect on how voters evaluate candidates.

The key, of course, is whether voters perceive a partisan advantage on the issue. Efforts by candidates and parties to co-opt the issue strength of the opposition can obscure many voters from discerning a partisan issue advantage. It is likely that those voters who do perceive one party or the other as having a particular issue advantage are voters who are already particularly interested in that issue and weigh it heavily in their voting decision. It is not surprising, then, that exit polls taken in 2000 correspond with the finding that the agendas of voters affect candidate perception. Those respondents who indicated that taxes were the most important issue to them voted overwhelmingly (80 to 17 percent) for George Bush. Voters who were most concerned about Social Security supported Al Gore (58 to 40 percent).[50] Whether party and candidate advertisements raised the salience of taxes and Social Security for voters or these issues were already important to voters cannot be determined here. What is important, however, is that the use of monetary and reputation resources do appear related to voter evaluations of candidates.

As anticipated, partisanship impacts the evaluation of candidates and is similar to the issue advantage effect. A strong Democrat (a negative two) is warmer toward Democratic House candidates by almost six degrees, while a strong Republican (a positive two) is also warm to candidates sharing his political persuasion. Ideological extremism hurts only Republicans, as conservatism cools the ardor for Republican candidates by six degrees.

Respondents also warm to Republican candidates who win by a wide margin: those winning by twenty points gain more than four degrees when compared with those winning with only 50 percent of the vote. More trusting and more attentive voters also view both Democratic and Republican candidates more positively: the trust and attention to campaign variables are positive and, with one exception, strongly significant. Trust in government and familiarity breeds favorability among citizens.

Finally, the effects of campaign spending are not limited to establishing or reinforcing existing partisan issue impressions. Democratic candidate and party spending have no apparent direct effects on respondent impressions of candidates. Republican candidate spending, however, acts as anticipated. The more Republican candidates spend, the warmer respondents rate them and the cooler they feel toward the Democratic candidate.

The Democratic candidate spending coefficients, on the other hand, are not significant. Republican Party spending negatively impacts respondent ratings of the Republican candidate. The more the Republican Party spends, the less the Republican candidate is liked. There is no apparent reason why Republican Party spending might create negative impressions: Republican advertising was slightly more negative in tone during the 2000 campaign.[51] In any case, this serves as a cautionary note for parties and candidates: Spending can have the anticipated and desired effect, but it can also create a backlash hurting the very candidate it is intended to help. The positive effect of Republican candidate spending on a candidate's feeling thermometer is more than offset by the negative effect of Republican Party spending. Granted, party spending in a particular race does not often approach that of the candidate's individual spending. Nevertheless, the potential is there for parties—in an attempt to generate or reinforce a particular partisan reputation—to undermine a candidate's reelection by creating an overall negative impression for one's candidate. The spending decisions and strategies of parties must be carefully considered and weighed with this effect in mind.

CONCLUSION

Parties provided a link in the 2000 election between voters and governing elites. The ability of parties to set issue agendas, communicate those agendas to voters, and alter the basis upon which voters evaluate candidates indicates the extent to which resource imbalances affect political outcomes. This ability to create or reinforce partisan reputations and have the public react to them further strengthened the resource hand of parties relative to their candidates. Candidates needed party money to compete successfully electorally and needed to latch onto partisan reputations to which the public responded, and that shaped how the public evaluated them. Creating or reinforcing a reputation complementing one's party brings not only financial rewards but also a more positive image with which to attract votes.

The concepts of resource and issue advantages also suggest new avenues of inquiry for scholars studying voting behavior. Campaigns can alter the decisionmaking calculus of voters—if we carefully look in the right places. Gelman and King smartly noted that the chief effect of campaigns was to provide information to voters to allow them to act accurately upon their true preferences.[52] This is certainly correct. Campaigns serve first to remind voters of their commitments. They also remind voters of candidate and party records on particular issues. Although party and candidate spending in general has little influence upon how citizens view parties and candidates on their marquee issues, by co-opting the other party's issues, parties can remind supporters of their previous commitments and give other voters "permission" to abandon their party. Most important, by establishing particular partisan issue advantages, spending can change the terms by which citizens evaluate candidates. This, in turn, can alter their voting on election day.

By landscaping the issue terrain and altering how candidates are evaluated, parties provide a critical bridge between the electorate and the governing elite. Their ability to do so boils down to their ability to provide the resources necessary for candidates to win elections. Without resources, parties could not shape the issue terrain. They could not establish issue advantages, and they could not advertise these advantages to voters. The ability of the parties to connect voters to candidates, at least in 2000, was very much a function of their ability to amass monetary resources which, in turn, allowed them to establish partisan reputations upon which candidates may have latched during campaigns.

"May have" is important. The causal arrows are difficult to sort, especially because the 2000 NES only asked respondents their likes and dislikes about the parties during the preelection survey, while the post-election survey contained the only feeling thermometer measures of congressional candidates. This analysis does not indicate whether party or candidate advertisements definitively altered voter perceptions because the NES does not provide benchmark measures with which to compare post-election changes. The evidence presented in this chapter is suggestive; future work will have to more rigorously test the relationships uncovered here using either panel surveys or experimental methods.

The final chapter returns to the initial question: the effect of rules on the resource equation. FECA governed the conduct of elections from 1974 through 2002, but the rules have changed. In 2002, Senators John McCain and Russ Feingold, after more than five years of effort, succeeded in passing the Bipartisan Campaign Reform Act (BCRA). This law, designed to alter radically the ways in which parties collect and disperse resources, was immediately challenged in the federal courts courtesy of an expedited review process written into the statute. In late 2003, the Supreme

Court handed down its decision in *FEC v. McConnell*. In general, the Court deferred to Congress, upholding the law as passed, leaving it primarily intact. The rules of the resource game had been once again been greatly altered. The concluding chapter speculates as to BCRA's effect on the ability of candidates, parties, and interest groups to amass campaign resources and engage in electioneering activities. It also evaluates whether the resource theory, in light of this reform, is still a useful way to think about congressional elections.

CHAPTER SEVEN

RESOURCES RULE

The previous two chapters evaluated the effect of the Federal Election Campaign Act of 1974 on the resource capacity of political actors and on voter perception. But FECA no longer governs the conduct of federal campaigns. In 2002, Congress instituted yet another round of campaign finance reform: the Bipartisan Campaign Reform Act (BCRA). Initially introduced in the 105th Congress by mavericks Russ Feingold and John McCain, the act signed by President Bush was a watered-down version. Nevertheless, its provisions curtailing the use of soft money alter the existing electoral regime. This represents a significant change in how political actors will finance campaigns. As the Pendleton Civil Service Act ended the practice of assessing federal officeholders and FECA limited the hard dollar contributions of individuals, BCRA affects how political parties and interest groups engage in electioneering by restricting the use of soft money.

BCRA provides another opportunity to assess the explanatory power of the resource theory. Does BCRA change the fundamental relationship between resources and campaign strategies? The short answer is no. Although the relationships between political actors will probably change, the anticipated effects of BCRA's provisions demonstrate that the need for resources still plays an important role in how candidates, parties, and interest groups select campaign strategies. This chapter concludes by detailing the changes made by the 2002 law, then specifically examining whether three likely outcomes of the new campaign finance regime affect the fundamental premise that political actors alter strategies based on the resource landscape. BCRA, like FECA and the Pendleton Act, further demonstrates that campaigns are resource-centered. Following the chapter's conclusion, some additional thoughts on the broader implications of the resource theory for American politics are offered in an epilogue.

THE RESOURCE THEORY AND BCRA

How does BCRA differ from FECA? In short, campaign finance reform supporters hoped to close the soft money loophole that Congress opened in 1979. Concerned that the FECA limits on party and individual contributions would undermine the traditional organizational activities of parties, Congress allowed parties to raise and spend money on party-building activities without the limits imposed by FECA. The loophole was then expanded both by judicial fiat and by the entrepreneurial activities of interest groups and political parties alike until the law became almost meaningless. Parties, interest groups, corporations, and labor unions used soft money to support and attack candidates in ways nearly indistinguishable from advertisements funded with regulated (hard) dollars.[1] Millions of dollars that were not subject to FECA's restrictions or its more stringent reporting requirements flooded into the political system.

BCRA addressed these concerns by placing tight restrictions on the use of soft money in future campaigns. Most significantly, the law displaces parties from their role as collectors and dispensers of soft money. After 2002, parties could not solicit any money not subject to the provisions of FECA.[2] This meant no more unrestricted corporate, labor, or individual donations for issue advocacy, party building, or any other activity. All electioneering would have to be funded using hard dollars raised under and subject to FECA contribution limitations and reporting requirements. The power of corporations and labor unions was similarly curtailed; they could no longer fund broadcast communications with funds from their corporate treasuries. Now all political advertisements sent over the airwaves would have to be financed by their affiliated political action committees.[3]

Congress also desired to make candidates, groups, and parties more accountable for the advertisements they air by making sponsorship more readily apparent to voters. All electioneering communications identifying a federal candidate falling within a thirty-day window before a primary and a sixty-day window before a general election would have to be paid for with hard money and subject to strict public disclosure requirements. These advertisements would be required to carry clear sponsor identification and, in the case of candidates, would have to feature the candidate's voice and image acknowledging approval of the advertisement and its message. By forcing candidates to take clear responsibility for their advertisements, sponsors hoped to elevate the tone of political discussion by making negativity less desirable and harder to air without repercussions. Early indications suggest the tone of the debate may not have been elevated by the reform, but voters may have found it easier to vent their anger at sponsors of negative spots. It appears Howard Dean and Dick Gephardt suffered a voter backlash in Iowa after launching a series of attack ads leading up to the Democratic caucus in 2004.[4]

In return for these restrictions, Congress increased the amount of hard money available to political actors by raising individual and party contribution limits. Furthermore, the reformers avoided one of FECA's chief pitfalls: these limits would be indexed to inflation. This would help guard against the development of unforeseen consequences, such as pushing candidates toward parties or political action committees, which could provide additional resources as the value of individual contributions lessened with the passage of time. House and Senate candidates would also be allowed to raise monies from individuals beyond the statutory contribution limits if running against a self-financed candidate.[5]

Acknowledging that BCRA would face a constitutional challenge immediately after passage, a provision granted expedited judicial review to resolve constitutional questions before the 2004 election cycle. In December 2003, the Supreme Court handed down its decision in *McConnell v. FEC*. Somewhat surprisingly, the Court stepped back from nearly two decades of legal precedent protecting the "magic words" distinction, holding nearly the entire act constitutional in its existing form.[6] The majority opinion in *McConnell v. FEC* held that a less rigorous standard of constitutional review applied to contribution limits, and a clear governmental interest existed in preventing "both the actual corruption threatened by large financial contributions and the eroding of public confidence in the electoral process through the appearance of corruption." The Court deferred to Congress's ability to weigh properly the competing constitutional interests in an area in which it enjoys particular expertise. Most significantly, the Court greatly weakened the "magic words" distinction it made in *Buckley*, indicating that subsequent events had demonstrated that the distinction between issue advocacy and direct advocacy (which the majority claimed was never a constitutional mandate anyway) was impracticable.[7]

What are the consequences of BRCA for the resource theory? At its core, the resource theory argues that the strategies selected by political actors depend on their ability to gather the resources necessary for victory. Congressional candidates chose their strategies based on their district's composition, the ability to raise the money necessary to be competitive, and the ability of other actors to provide reputation and monetary resources. Who can best provide those resources to candidates depends on how the electoral rules are shaped. Does BCRA change this in any way?

As candidates still need to find the money to communicate with voters, and the probability of their election is still a function of their individual and partisan reputation, the answer is no. All BCRA does is change the relationship of political actors to each other and their ability to provide electioneering resources successfully. BCRA is but another example of how electoral rules constrain the campaign decisions of political actors. Indeed, BCRA yet again demonstrates the relevance of the resource theory.

Like FECA before it, BCRA profoundly affects the ability of candidates, parties, and interest groups to compete for resources. Will BCRA change the strategies and behaviors of political actors engaged in electioneering activities? It takes time for the effects of rules to be felt. Political actors need to respond and adapt, so the consequences are not immediate. In addition, the effectiveness of BCRA depends on how vigorously the Federal Election Commission upholds its provisions. Until it is known how those responsible for enforcement will respond, any conclusions about BCRA's effects remain tentative at best. With these caveats in mind, it is possible to engage in some informed speculation.

INTEREST GROUPS INCREASE THEIR FINANCIAL STRENGTH

Political parties certainly benefited under FECA. Using soft money, the national parties undermined the independence of state party organizations. The ability to organize traditionally was trumped by the need for monetary resources, and the national committees could easily respond to the ever-growing needs of candidates. The result was more cohesive political parties, with candidates and parties communicating similar issue agendas to the public.

BCRA does not change the fact that candidates need money. In fact, they need it now more than ever. Television advertisements are still expensive, and an increasing emphasis on voter mobilization by using careful micro-targeting also costs a substantial sum of money. BCRA does, however, change the relationship of parties to interest groups. In particular, interest groups will have fewer incentives to coordinate their activities with parties under BCRA, overtly or otherwise. They will be able to act more independently of political parties that no longer serve as soft money conduits.

With soft money removed from their clutches, parties will have fewer resources with which to fund their electioneering activities. On the other hand, interest groups should (and did) proliferate under two organizational forms, the 501 and the 527, created by the IRS for tax purposes.[8] A 501 is a nonprofit organization and a 527 is a for-profit political organization whose sole purpose is to collect and disperse funds to influence elections. These organizations argue they are not subject to the same campaign finance restrictions placed on parties, candidates, and political action committees. They can continue to raise unlimited amounts of soft money and spend it on issue advocacy broadcast advertisements or virtually any other political activity without needing to abide by any disclosure provisions. This creates the potential for the resource balance to shift in favor of interest groups.

In 2004, seventy-three 527s participated in federal elections with disbursements exceeding $100,000, with combined expenditures exceeding $416 million.[9] More than half of the total contributions raised by 527s registering with the Internal Revenue Service were made by nearly 1,900 individuals who, on average, gave almost $136,000. By comparison, federal 527s raised only $151 million in the previous election cycle.[10] It appears that BRCA did indeed spur political actors to move beyond parties and candidates financially to achieve their electoral objectives. Does this mean that candidates will begin to select campaign strategies that divorce them from parties in favor of establishing closer connections with interest groups and their issue agendas?

Interest groups, parties, and candidates, it appears, operated at near-resource parity in 2004, and candidates did not seem to forsake the issue agendas and reputations of their parties during this campaign cycle. Political parties still had a formidable array of reputation and monetary resources at their disposal, so it made sense for candidates largely to stand pat and utilize partisan resources. Of course, monetary resources have not yet tipped decisively in favor of interest groups. But this balance may not last. If the history of campaign finance tells us anything, it is that political actors are risk-averse and may react timidly to changing electoral circumstances initially. The PAC as a form of interest group influence was pioneered by labor organizations in the 1930s, only coming into its own legally after the Federal Election Commission issued an advisory opinion (known as SUNPAC) clarifying the PAC's permissible campaign role in the 1970s. Although 527s have been the subject of numerous FEC advisory opinions, their long-term fate is not immediately clear. Members of Congress have begun a crusade to undercut the ability of 527s to operate, but it remains to be seen whether this will succeed.[11]

How will candidates respond in future election cycles? They will continue to follow the resources. Although the growth of 527 organizations under BCRA is impressive, and advertisements sponsored by the Swift Boat Veterans for Truth and Moveon.org generated extensive press coverage, it is much too early to proclaim the immediate demise of parties. For the moment, political parties have been able to replace now-illegal soft money donations with hard dollar contributions. In 2000, the federal party committees of both parties raised nearly $1.2 billion in inflation-adjusted 2004 dollars—in soft and hard contributions combined. Four years later, they raised $1.4 billion, but all of it in hard dollars as dictated by BCRA.[12] For all the attention given to 527s, political actors still preferred the time-proven political action committees. The 4,800-plus registered PACs spent twice as much as 527s in 2004, contributing and making independent expenditures to the tune of $842.9 million.[13]

The response of candidates depends largely on the ability of parties to remain monetarily relevant under BCRA. If parties can continue to raise money to meet the monetary needs of their candidates as they did in 2004, the relationship between candidates and parties will not change very much. Indeed, it may even be strengthened. As interest groups continue to bombard the electorate with an increasingly diverse array of issues, the need grows for candidates to use the party's brand to be heard above the din. Candidates would need parties more than ever, especially their brand name. This book confirms the notion that parties are adaptable institutions, and there is no reason to think that BCRA will cause them to cease functioning.[14]

If parties for some reason cannot continue to compete financially, candidates will need to respond to the increased monetary strength of interest groups and their ability to influence the issue agenda. To satisfy the more diverse ideological and issue needs of interest groups, candidates will most likely drift from their partisan moorings. Party unity should decrease, and appeals to the electorate made by the candidates should move away from the party's core issue agenda. Candidates will seek monetary and reputation support directly from a range of interest groups as befits their individual reputations, and parties will find it harder to enforce party unity in the House or Senate. As party reputations become less distinctive, their usefulness as a resource will diminish. In short, BCRA does strengthen interest groups. Whether parties will suffer is an open question. In any case, the rule of resources still governs the relationship between political actors.

THE INCUMBENCY ADVANTAGE IS ENHANCED

One of the most interesting findings in the previous chapters was the power of political parties under FECA in the most competitive campaigns. Candidates in these situations require the most substantial monetary and reputation resources. Should BCRA provide incumbents with increased electoral security, decreasing the total number of competitive races, the tendency for resources to flow to marginal districts and open seats should be magnified in the House. Under FECA, these candidates relied on their parties to provide resources. Does BCRA affect the electoral landscape by reducing competition, and if so, does this alter the resource relationship between candidates and parties observed under FECA?

Alarmed by the prospect of facing well-financed challenges, incumbents used BCRA to protect themselves. House candidates running against opponents who are spending more than $350,000 of their own money will be permitted to raise $6,000, rather than $2,000, from individuals. National and state parties also will be allowed to spend unlimited amounts in coordinated expenditures on their behalf. The Senate formula is more complex, as the maximum individual contribution allowable depends on the number of eligible votes in a state and the amount by which the $150,000 threshold amount is exceeded. In states where a candidate spends more than ten times the threshold amount plus .40 times the voting age population, the maximum individual contribution limit for the opposing candidate increases to $12,000 and parties can engage in unlimited coordinated expenditures.

In 2002, thirty-three House incumbents did not face a challenger—major party or otherwise. This was true for thirty-four House incumbents in 2004. Although BCRA has not discouraged challengers from emerging, it may have altered the competitive landscape by diminishing the quality of challengers choosing to face incumbents in 2004. BCRA's millionaire provision eliminates some of the advantages that self-financed candidates have against incumbents. Generally able to raise money from a range of individuals and political committees, incumbents should have ample monetary resources available to them without the fear of threshold penalties being levied. Unable to rely on their own financial resources without being penalized, self-financed challengers are less likely to emerge. This provides for fewer quality challenges and competitive congressional campaigns. More important, it suggests that quality challengers will rely even more on political parties or interest groups as a direct consequence of BCRA's self-financing provisions.

The average challenger facing a House incumbent personally contributed or guaranteed loans totaling nearly $80,000 to his campaign in 2002. Two years later, in the first election held under BCRA's self-financing restrictions, this amount was cut nearly in half.[15] Table 7.1 demonstrates how damaging these provisions might prove to be over the long term to the challenger prospects against the weakest incumbents. In races where the victorious candidate wins with less than 10 percent of the vote, the amount that challengers contributed to their own campaigns plummeted between 2002 and 2004. The pattern persists in races where a candidate wins more securely, with a margin between 10 and 20 percent. Only in the least competitive races, where a candidate wins with more than 20 percent of the vote, does the candidate contribute roughly the same amount to his losing campaign.

Of course, challengers may replace their own dollars with contributions from interest groups or political parties. Indeed, table 7.2 indicates that challengers facing incumbents in the most competitive races (with the winner receiving 20 percent or less of the vote) saw personal funds as a percentage of total disbursements decline between 2002 and 2004. Among challengers running in less competitive races, however, the percentages remained stable between the two election cycles.

Table 7.1. Self-financing of House challenger campaigns, 2002 and 2004

Year		Winning Candidate's Margin of Victory				
		0–10 percent	11–20 percent	21–30 percent	31+ percent	Total mean
2002	Candidate contributions and loans	$176,089	$559,897	$76,677	$9,608	$78,764
	Number of races	(22)	(29)	(57)	(231)	(339)
2004	Candidate contributions and loans	$66,776	$112,012	$63,186	$13,343	$39,834
	Number of races	(20)	(45)	(84)	(217)	(366)

Source: Figures compiled by the author from candidate summary reports available from the Federal Election Commission at www.fec.gov.

These data suggest that challengers facing weakened incumbents—those with the best shot at winning—adapted their campaign strategies as the resource theory predicts, relying less on their own fortunes and more on contributions made by individuals, parties, and PACs. Assuming that challenger disbursements remained relatively constant between 2002 and 2004, this is a reasonable conclusion. Challengers spent more in 2004 than in 2002 in races where the margin of victory was ten percentage points or less (1.3 and 1.1 million, respectively)—roughly a constant level of campaign spending. Challengers in less fortuitous campaign circumstances—running in races that were ultimately decided by a margin greater than 10 but less than 20 percent—spent far less in 2004 than in 2002: $625,000 as opposed to more than $1 million.

Table 7.2. Self-financing as a percentage of total challenger disbursements, 2002–2004

		Winning Candidate's Margin of Victory				
		0–10 percent	11–20 percent	21–30 percent	31+ percent	Total mean
2002	Candidate contribution as percentage of disbursements	16%	23%	22%	23%	23%
	Number of races	(22)	(29)	(57)	(231)	(339)
2004	Candidate contribution as percentage of disbursements	9%	14%	22%	23%	21%
	Number of races	(20)	(45)	(84)	(217)	(366)

Source: Figures compiled by the author from candidate summary reports available from the Federal Election Commission at www.fec.gov.

In the final analysis, the millionaire provision of BCRA provides strong evidence that the resource terrain affects the decisions made by congressional candidates, a key argument of the resource theory. When incumbents facing a well-financed challenger were given additional money, those candidates in the most competitive congressional races opted to rely less on their individual fortunes and more on interest groups and parties to fund their campaigns. This is exactly what the resource theory would predict. For those who have only an outside chance of ousting an incumbent, however, the prospects of success have become much grimmer. They cannot rely on their own funds to compete, and it appears they are unable to obtain the necessary financial resources from alternative sources. This inability to secure resources should discourage challengers from emerging in the post-BCRA era, providing incumbents with greater electoral security.

If for some reason parties cannot provide sufficient monetary resources to their candidates in competitive elections under BCRA, the resource theory indicates that interest groups should gain at their expense. The demise of parties, however, is not a foregone conclusion. With fewer competitive races to target, candidates will find it even harder to be heard above the racket. This makes partisan reputations even more valuable to them and reinforces the findings in earlier chapters that freshmen in the most competitive districts should support the party more than the median voter theory might suggest. Reputations are useless, however, without monetary resources to communicate them. If parties adapt to the financial constraints of BCRA, it is very likely that the relationship observed during the FECA era will persist under BCRA. The fact that parties will have to spread their money over fewer races provides them with a crucial advantage, making it more likely they will be able to continue providing their candidates with monetary resources. As partisan reputations provide candidates with the best opportunity to reach the electorate, this continues to provide parties with a privileged position relative to candidates, confirming the vitality of the parties in the political system under BCRA.

NARROWCASTING DOMINATES CAMPAIGNING

Soft money did not disappear wholly from the resource scene after BCRA's implementation. Its use merely was curtailed and restricted to certain groups. In particular, 527s (and to a more limited degree 501s) can continue spending unregulated money on electioneering activities much the way parties and PACs did under FECA. Most interesting, however, are the electioneering provisions restricting soft money expenditures on broadcast advertising but not on Internet or print media. Corporations and labor unions, restricted from using soft money on broadcast advertisements, can continue using money from their corporate or union treasuries to fund issue advocacy advertisements via newspapers and the Internet. Provisions requiring clear identification of a television advertisement's sponsor may also provide incentives for interest groups, parties, and candidates to avoid the airwaves in favor of these alternative media outlets. This encourages political actors to engage in narrowcasting and stealth politics.

Does the rise of these new tactics undermine the relationship between resources and campaign strategies? Narrowcasting is not new. Through the use of polling, direct mail, and telemarketing, political actors have sought for some time to craft messages appealing to particular segments of the population in ways similar to corporate advertisers selling a product. Using membership lists, political actors have targeted members of organizations like the National Rifle Association or the Sierra Club on specific issues. The dialogue may be very different from the one occurring on the stump or over the airwaves. In a direct mail piece, Senator Joe Smith might tout his tough antipollution legislation, but in his television advertisements reaching a much larger population segment he might stress the tax incentives he pushed to encourage industry to relocate to the state.

The 2004 presidential contest is a case in point. The Bush campaign consciously avoided the strategy of appealing to undecided voters. Polls indicated that few voters had undefined opinions on and feelings about the president. Republican strategists, led by Karl Rove, targeted instead so-called soft Bush supporters: those who were predisposed to particular Republican messages, but needed persuasion to make the effort to get out and vote. Using data frequently employed by commercial marketing organizations, Republican pollsters and consultants "determine[d] 'anger points' (late-term abortion, trial lawyer fees, estate taxes) that coincided with the Bush agenda for as many as 32 categories of voters." Unlike earlier get-out-the-vote operations that provided voters with, in the words of Republican consultant Alex Gage, "a tape-recorded voice of Ronald Reagan telling you how important it was to vote," soft Republican voters received issue messages specifically tailored to them and their "anger points."[16] Rather than bring a fragmented electorate together under one banner, the Bush campaign used the many fissures in the American electorate to its advantage.

Business organizations also employed BCRA's Internet loophole to engage in a largely underground campaign operation. *Washington Post* reporters Jeffrey Birnbaum and Thomas Edsall found that "91 of the Business Roundtable's 160 member companies took part in a program that gave employees political information via the Internet. The program ... attracted 6.5 million visits to BIPAC [Business-Industry Political Action Committee] sites and produced about 25 million page views." Even more impressive were the "800,000 voter registration forms . . . downloaded" from the site. Dirk Van Dongen, president of the National Association of Wholesaler-Distributors, remarked that "the effort in this election was truly huge. It was several times bigger and broader than anything done by business before."[17] As labor unions, 527s, and other corporations take note of these successful Internet ventures, the use of the Internet as yet another tool to hone messages to receptive audiences will surely grow.[18]

How does the rise of narrowcasting relate to the resource theory? Political party scholars have long argued that the rise of television and radio spelled the end of political parties in the twentieth century. Television and radio provided the means by which candidates could communicate directly with the electorate, so why would candidates need the party any longer? As we discovered, the spread of television and radio actually pushed candidates closer to political parties. The high cost of the new media might have been the reason: in states where the party organization had sufficient institutional capacity, parties had the funds to pay to use television and radio. As a result, candidates continued to need the party to help communicate their messages to the public. Frequently, this meant holding onto and using the party's reputation.

The rise of the Internet and reemergence of print advertising may have similar effects. The parties can help candidates develop, coordinate, and their Internet and print messages. Although narrowcasting allows one to send tailored messages to carefully targeted groups, the messages sent by parties and candidates will probably tap into issues already identified with the parties. Democrats will probably still make appeals to voters based on Social Security, but they will target seniors more directly. And Republicans will probably still use their low tax, small government messages. Nothing prevents parties from using a new communications tool except monetary limitations. Assuming again that parties can continue to raise money, there is little reason to assume that candidates will drift far from their parties. The larger point is this: if electoral reform suggests a particular method of communicating with voters, the response of candidates should be to select strategies that allow them to best employ that method. At the moment, it appears parties continue to serve a useful monetary and reputation need for candidates despite (or because of) the increasing usefulness of narrowcasting and stealth politics. The rule of resources is still in operation.

CONCLUSION

As has been stressed throughout these pages, campaigns are not universally party-centered or candidate-centered in a given era, but they are always resource-centered. Campaigns look more or less candidate-centered depending on the resource situation facing ambitious office seekers. Candidates readily accept party dominance if parties can bring favorable results. Otherwise, candidates will take matters into their own hands. This explains why candidates like Francis Newlands avoided the party in the 1890s when running for Congress, and why candidates during the FECA-regime campaigned on party issues and voted increasingly with the party in spite of having television and radio readily available to them for more candidate-centered appeals. By focusing on the resources, our understanding of why political actors engage in particular campaign behaviors or strategies improves. The resource model better explains how and why political actors pursue particular strategies by focusing on the evolution of electoral rules. It also details the implications of these strategies on both legislative outcomes and voter perceptions.

The ability to gather resources is a function of the electoral landscape. Rules provide political actors with advantages and disadvantages as they pursue monetary, reputation, and voter resources. The effects of rules, however, are spread unevenly among political actors. Over the long term, the Pendleton Civil Service Act of 1883 put parties at a disadvantage relative to candidates and interest groups in the collection of monetary resources. In the short term, however, parties with strong institutional structures built on a culture of partisanship found themselves less at a disadvantage relative to unbounded parties in states with little tradition of partisan politics. The result was overwhelmingly party-centered campaigns during the late nineteenth century with pockets of candidate-centered campaigning appearing where resource needy candidates abandoned resource-deficient parties.

In the same way, FECA changed how political actors approached campaign strategy. Because of contribution limits not indexed to inflation, the rising costs of campaigns, and an inability to dominate issue agenda, candidates needed to find new monetary and reputation resources. The national party committees, long relegated to second-class status by state organizations, now had the capacities to help candidates. FECA provided them access to nearly limitless soft money and the ability to coordinate its use. This allowed them to exert increasing influence on the campaigns of individual candidates, by telling candidates how and where to spend money. Furthermore, by creating nationalized campaigns based on a discrete set of issues, parties could more effectively communicate a message to voters bombarded with appeals from countless interest groups. Candidates took note and became increasingly likely to adopt partisan themes and strategies in their own advertising. FECA invigorated political parties on a national scale, and perhaps more cohesive parties emerged as a result. To top it off, it appears that voters respond to partisan message agendas and themes, further cementing the strategic relationship between congressional candidates and their parties.

The Bipartisan Campaign Reform Act demonstrates the continued validity of the resource theory. Although BCRA will undoubtedly change the relationships between candidates, political parties, and interest groups, it does not affect the fundamental need that political actors have for reputation and monetary resources. As other election reforms have demonstrated, the political actor who has an advantage in resource collection very much determines the strategies selected by congressional candidates on the campaign trail. BCRA is no different in this regard from the Pendleton Civil Service Act or the Federal Election Campaign Act. Provisions removing political parties from the soft money game, discouraging the emergence of self-financed candidates, and encouraging narrowcasting together suggest that political parties might be disadvantaged in the long run relative to interest groups and candidates. If this is indeed the case, candidates will alter their behavior—most notably, in how they present themselves to voters on the House floor and in their campaign advertisements. In the short term, because political parties have been able to remain financially powerful and relevant, this has not been the case. The moment parties falter monetarily, however, candidates will notice and quickly adapt to the financial realities presented to them. This is exactly what the resource theory would anticipate and expect.

EPILOGUE

RESOURCE THEORY AND CONTEMPORARY AMERICAN POLITICS

This book has focused on how electoral rules affect the behavior of political elites. But changing electoral rules have implications well beyond elites. Indeed, electoral rules affect the quality and shape of democratic discourse itself. Fundamentally, elections link governing elites and individuals. When citizens vote, they indirectly decide both the shape and scope of public policy as well as who will be charged with its implementation through the next campaign cycle. The policy implications of elections are not always immediately clear, even if the vote overwhelmingly favors a particular candidate. Essentially, though, *how* voters decide at the polls is as important as the specific alternative selected. When voters face a choice, they rely upon their past experiences and predispositions in addition to some set of information for guidance. This information can include perceptions about the candidate's leadership capabilities, opinions about the party's or candidate's issue positions, or knowledge gleaned from an interest group's flyer. Electoral rules, by shaping the tactics and strategies employed by candidates, parties, and interest groups, shape the information environment available to voters when making decisions.

As we have seen, before FECA, the need for monetary and reputation resources encouraged congressional candidates to adopt party issue themes in states with institutionalized party structures. Since FECA, the role of state parties has diminished as national parties have established national partisan reputations and used their monetary resources to encourage candidates to adopt these issue agendas in the most competitive elections. Rules governing the acquisition and dispersal of resources constrain the decision calculus of candidates and parties during the campaign. The residual effect is a different menu of informational cues available for citizens to canvass when making electoral choices; that is, they are different from those informational cues presented by candidates governed by hypothetical electoral rules guaranteeing their resource needs without relying on parties or interest groups for assistance.

Elections also perform an indirect linkage function between government and citizens. Public needs, wants, and desires can be transmitted through an organization distinct from elected elites such as a political party or interest group. Put another way, interest groups and political parties can serve as mediators between the people and their government. The nature of the democratic linkage—whether it is to be direct or mediated by some group—depends upon the sources of information on which citizens rely when making voting decisions in elections. Candidates, political parties, and interest groups compete for resources necessary to provide information to voters during elections. The champion among them determines whether the nature of the democratic linkage is direct or mediated through some group. More succinctly, elections determine how responsive government is and *to whom*. If elections are the cornerstone of republican governance in the United States, then the campaign for resources underlying the dispersal of information is the keystone to responsiveness.

Denise Baer and David Bositis state that the political party is "a distinctive social formation whose purpose is to link the elites who govern with the masses who do not."[1] But elections are not fought by parties alone. Candidates run for office on their own merits, individuals give time and money both through and outside of the parties to make their preferences known, and interest groups also advertise certain issue positions to influence the partisan composition of legislative and executive bodies. The nature of the democratic linkage—whether it is to be direct or mediated by some group—depends upon the sources of information on which citizens rely when making voting decisions. How the electorate is engaged or activated conditions the character of the linkage. The capacity of political actors to communicate with the electorate is fundamentally a function of their ability to gather and dispense resources. This is the heart of the resource theory of campaigns.

Parties are but one way to link the elite and masses. Candidates or interest groups can also mediate between the governed and the governing. Whether candidates, parties, or interest groups provide this linkage depends largely on which actor has the resource edge. Parties are not always the harbingers of elite responsiveness. E. E. Schattschneider was only partly right in *The Semisovereign People:* parties do not always seek expansion of the conflict scope. Two things determine whether parties or other political actors seek to expand the scope of conflict: resource capacity and whether such an expansion is necessary for victory. The problem is the cost of such an expansion—and perhaps the ability of parties to do it more efficiently and effectively. Interest groups and candidates, therefore, usually seek to expand conflict through political parties—and can do so only if political parties are unable to provide the resources for mobilization activities. Alternatively, political parties might be just as apt to minimize conflicts, as Schattschneider claims interest groups always do, if this leads to favorable electoral consequences. The rise of narrowcasting and microtargeting, increasingly used by all political actors including political parties, are examples of minimizing the conflict's scope.

All of this is to say that the information voters receive, and from whom they receive it, is important and a function of the resource theory. Changing electoral rules guide both elite and mass behavior. As chapter 6 demonstrated, the effects of electoral rules on the information environment are powerful. Resources affect the options that elites present to voters. In turn, those options alter the perceptions of citizens. This provides a cautionary note to reformers: beware campaign finance reform efforts absent a clear understanding of the possible consequences for democratic discourse.

In this vein, it should be noted that the increase in narrowcasting by political parties, candidates, and interest groups over the past decade—which will likely accelerate further under BCRA—has possibly negative implications for democratic discourse. Television and radio advertisements may or may not have negative consequences, but both are very public forums through which candidates, parties, and interest groups can engage in a political discussion. Using selective targeting, discourse can become gradually more fragmented and private, which might serve the electoral needs of candidates, parties, and interest groups, but might have crippling effects for governance. If the American electoral system already makes it difficult to understand the will of the people and govern with a mandate, then a politics based upon particularistic appeals will make governing nearly impossible. The policy implications of an election will become even muddier, and the building of policy coalitions will be hampered by a factionalized electorate. A vigorous public debate of issues and policy allows for the possibility of consensus building. BCRA's broadcasting, Internet, and print provisions have the potential to undermine the creation of such a consensus.

Although it is a debatable proposition that politics in recent years is any more partisan or vicious than it has always been in the United States, the requirement that broadcast advertisements carry a clear visual and audio acknowledgment of sponsorship will push political actors not to avoid negative attacks altogether but to be more creative in how they are distributed.[2] Meaner, nastier, more partisan appeals will simply show up in people's electronic inboxes, mailboxes, and the magazines or newspapers they read.[3] Using these channels allows political actors to avoid clear responsibility for the content of their appeals while simultaneously hiding them from the public and press at-large. "There's more degrees [sic] of freedom for these types of communications to be more aggressive because they'll be under the radar," says Internet strategist Jonah Seiger.[4] In this way, these Internet advertisements can have the maximum effect desired by their sponsor: they excite supporters enough to come out at the polls without reaching the segment of the population turned off by such tactics. Political actors will be able to have their cake and eat it, too, while further undermining the prospects of a healthy political discussion necessary for elites to govern successfully. The resource theory demonstrates that changing electoral rules affects the behavior of political actors and suggests that voters notice. It is worrisome that BCRA, a noble effort to "cleanse" politics from unseemly soft money, might actually serve to further undermine the pursuit of open and free political discourse in the public square. This is something which reformers might wish to consider when embarking on the next inevitable round of campaign finance reform.

This project was inspired by both the paucity of empirical theory on political parties and the need for a theory of congressional campaigns. Much of the early literature on parties is trapped in a normative world of what ought to be, and more recent literature—empirically rich—conspicuously lacks theoretical grounding. Scholars of the American party system have created detailed accounts of what parties actually do and what they should do, but have been unable to square reality with existing theory or unwilling to construct their own predictive and explanatory theory.[5] Why do parties do what they do, why do they look as they do, and how do they change over time? By starting with a fundamental goal of parties, candidates, and many interest groups—the successful contestation of elections—this book is a first attempt at answering these questions. The need to gather resources to compete in elections, governed by changing electoral rules, explains why political actors behave as they do in campaigns, indicates how the balance of power changes between them longitudinally, and determines which group provides the elite-mass linkage so important to democratic governance.

Scholars of Congress, on the other hand, have focused intensively on the electoral connection to explain legislative behavior and outcomes. They have also spent considerable time on the effect of institutional rules. Less time, however, has been devoted to understanding why and how political actors make campaign decisions and how rules affect those decisions.[6] More problematic, however, is that the emphasis on members of Congress as single-minded reelection seekers without consideration of electoral rules may have led scholars astray.

For example, this book has focused on the importance of political parties in certain electoral contexts. Political parties produce collective goods that overcome collective problems faced by officeholders and office seekers.[7] Parties allow office seekers and officeholders to overcome institutional arrangements hampering the pursuit of office. In short, they channel ambition and competition for office, prevent majority cycling in legislatures, and overcome the collective problem of mobilizing voters and supporters on Election Day.[8] Additionally, parties can be thought of as "legislative cartels" designed to sidestep electoral inefficiencies that "overproduce particularistic-benefits legislation and under-produce collective-benefits legislation."[9] Because parties solve these problems, officeholders and office seekers inevitably engage in some actions that might be irrational from their individual electoral perspectives but that are designed to enhance the party as a whole. Viewed in terms of their reputation resources, individual candidates might have to vote against the needs of the district (damaging their individual reputation) in order to protect or enhance the party's collective reputation. This requires a delicate balancing act for many members that is not always predicated on the need to claim the credit or take a position.[10] The need for resources complicates the electoral connection for representatives and suggests a more nuanced dynamic may be at work.

The resource theory is but a beginning. As the BCRA regime takes hold and political actors campaign under its aegis, new opportunities will arise for scholars to test the resource theory. BCRA's more robust reporting requirements make tracking the flow of money easier than ever. Using databases like those created by the Wisconsin Advertising Project, the Federal Election Commission, and the Internal Revenue Service, scholars can now follow the issue dialogue of the campaign, understand who is saying what, and track how political actors respond to one another. Now that we have better tools with which to measure a campaign's outputs, we can better evaluate its effects on voters.

CONSTRUCTION OF ISSUE THEME CATEGORIES

C oders for the Wisconsin Advertising Project were given four opportunities to describe the issue content of each political advertisement aired in 2000 in the top seventy-five media markets. The
issue statements provided to coders were placed into nine issue theme
categories as follows. The numbers next to each issue statement represent
the code in the original Campaign Media Analysis Group data as obtained
from the Wisconsin Advertising Project.

Table A.1. Issue theme categories

Economic
10 Taxes
11 Deficit/surplus/budget/debt
12 Government spending
13 Minimum wage
14 Farming (e.g., friend of)
15 Business (e.g., friend of)
16 Employment/ jobs
17 Poverty
19 Other economic reference

Education/Children
40 Education
41 Lottery for education
42 Child care
43 Other child-related issues

Defense/Foreign Policy
50 Defense
51 Missile defense/Star Wars
52 Veterans
53 Foreign policy
54 Bosnia
55 China
59 Other defense/foreign policy issues

Other
60 Clinton
61 Kenneth Starr
62 Whitewater
63 Impeachment
64 Sexual harassment/Paula Jones
78 Government ethics
95 Other
99 None

Social
20 Abortion
21 Homosexuality
22 Moral values
23 Tobacco
24 Affirmative action
25 Gambling
26 Assisted suicide
28 Other reference to social issues
76 Civil rights/race relations

Biographical/Personal
1 Background
2 Political record
3 Attendance record
4 Ideology
5 Personal values
6 Honesty/integrity
7 Special interests

Environment
70 Environment

Trade/Immigration
18 Trade/NAFTA
71 Immigration

Entitlements
73 Social Security
74 Medicare
75 Welfare

Conversion of
NES Party Likes/Dislikes
into Issue Theme Categories

T he 2000 NES asked respondents if there was anything in particular they liked or disliked about each of the two major parties. Respondents were given the opportunity to mention five likes and five dislikes for both the Republican and Democratic parties. The NES later assigned codes to these open-ended responses and organized them into categories grouped by issue themes. The NES provides a list of the party-candidate master codes in the appendix to the 2000 NES.

The party-candidate master codes assigned by the NES were matched to the issue category themes employed in this study. Below, the reader will find the codes assigned by the NES to each open-ended like/dislike response matched to the issue theme categories listed in chapter 5 and detailed in appendix A. One additional issue theme category was necessary to accommodate specific personal and biographical remarks made in reference to liking or disliking the two parties. Those interested in the content of the specific categories can refer to the party-candidate master code listing, available for download at http://www.umich.edu/~nes.

Table B.1. Conversion of likes/dislikes into issue themes

Social: 805–10, 829–30, 837–38, 847–49, 946–51, 980–81, 985–87, 979, 991–96, 1013–15, 1022–24, 1043–45

Environment: 957–64, 1004–1006

Defense: 813–14, 965–67, 1101–56, 1170–99, 1300–1304

Entitlements: 905–13, 920–25, 1001–1003, 1025–26, 1027, 1038–40

Education/Kids: 914–19, 1019–21, 1047–49, 1059–61

Trade/Immigration: 1016–18, 1164–69, 1196

Economic: 601–602, 605–606, 627, 811–12, 901–904, 926–42, 943–45, 952–58, 1007–1009, 1031–33, 1035–37, 1046

Biographical/Personal: 1–97, 201–97, 301–97, 401–98, 500–597

Miscellaneous: 101–97, 603–604, 607–97, 701–97, 801–803, 815–28, 831–36, 841–46, 900, 1010–12, 1028–30, 1050–58, 1201–97, 5001–5004

NOTES

CHAPTER 1

1. See Mayhew, *Congress: The Electoral Connection;* Fenno, *Home Style.*

2. Lilley, "Early Career," 171–75; Rowley, *Reclaiming,* 38–40.

3. Rowley, *Reclaiming,* 69; Lilley, "Early Career," 222.

4. Lilley, "Early Career," 219–22; Rowley, *Reclaiming,* 79–80, 106.

5. Ware, *Political Parties and Party Systems,* 37–94, 196–224.

6. McGillivray, Scammon, and Cook, *America Votes 24.* Republican and Democratic candidates could contest 870 primaries in 2000. If more than one candidate actively sought a party's congressional nomination, the primary was labeled contested. The election was labeled as contested for the party if two party candidates were listed on the ballot in blanket primary states. Primary "elections" without a major party contestant are labeled as uncontested.

7. Berke, "GOP Gives Help to House Hopefuls"; Quaid, "National GOP Involved in Kansas Congressional Race."

8. Cillizza, "The More the Merrier."

9. Rothenberg, "You Can Pick Your Friends, but Can You Pick Your Opponent?"

10. Rothenberg, "How a Democrat Won California's Republican Gubernatorial Primary." Democrats also accused Republicans of helping to oust liberal Democratic congresswoman Cynthia McKinney of Georgia's Fourth District during the 2002 Democratic primary. See Kintisch, "The Crossover Candidate."

11. A brief overview of the rise, fall, and reemergence of the parties' national committees can be found in Herrnson, "National Party Organizations." For a

detailed look at congressional campaign committees, consult Kolodny, *Pursuing Majorities*.

12. VandeHei and Chappie, "DeLay Allies Seek $25 Million Group."

13. Crabtree, "Revamped DeLay PAC May Fund STOMP."

14. Balz, "Republicans Strive for Dominance with 2004 Race."

15. Oppel, "The 2002 Campaign: Finance Campaign."

16. Salmore and Salmore, *Candidates, Parties, and Campaigns*, 41–56.

17. Pomper, "Alleged Decline of American Parties"; Schattschneider, *Party Government*; Schattschneider, *Semisovereign People*.

18. Almond, *Discipline Divided*.

19. Mayhew, *Congress: The Electoral Connection*, 5.

20. See Epstein, *Political Parties in the American Mold* for a review. Schattschneider, *Party Government*, and Herring, *Politics of Democracy*, provide two competing theoretical visions of American parties.

21. For exceptions, see King and Ellis, "Partisan Advantage and Constitutional Change," and Crook and Hibbing, "A Not-So-Distant Mirror."

22. See Silbey, "Beyond Realignment Theory" for the pitfalls of slicing up history willy-nilly.

23. There are many critiques of rational choice and formal model. The most widely cited is Green and Shapiro, *Pathologies of Rational Choice Theory*.

24. Polsby, "Institutionalization of the U.S. House of Representatives."

25. A good defense of the rationality assumption and a discussion of rational error are provided by Downs, *Economic Theory*, 8–11.

26. *McConnell v. Federal Election Commission* 124 U.S. 619 (2003).

CHAPTER 2

1. Ostrogorski, *Democracy and the Party System*; Sait, *American Parties and Elections*; Bruce, *American Parties and Politics*; Bone, *American Politics and the Party System*; Schattschneider, *Party Government*; Schattschneider, *Semisovereign People*. See Ranney, *Doctrine of Responsible Government* or Epstein, *Political Parties in the American Mold* for a lucid discussion of the party-centered model and responsible-party literature in its formative years. As Ranney notes, conflicting notions of party function make it difficult to understand party responsibility (8–9). Early-twentieth-century scholarship on parties was largely descriptive. Later, more normative responsible-party scholarship as typified by E. E. Schattschneider meant what parties "ought to do," since the normative vision did not match empirical reality.

2. Agranoff, *New Style in Election Campaigns*; Blumenthal, *Permanent Campaign*; Sabato, *Rise of Political Consultants*; Herrnson, *Party Campaigning in the 1980s*; Salmore and Salmore, *Candidates, Parties, and Campaigns*. Hints of the candidate-centered model appear in earlier scholarship. Pendleton Herring, disagreeing with the responsible notion of parties based on a mandate view of democracy, claimed parties served to aggregate a number of competing interests with the goal of winning elections. Parties were to be judged by their leaders, not their issue

stances. See Herring, *Politics of Democracy*, 112–14, 116. Herring suggests that the weighing of candidate merits in campaigns is the essence of the candidate-centered model. Rational choice theory also provides the raw materials for a candidate-centered model. The ideological positioning of parties is a function of the "numerical distribution of voters along a political scale."

Parties in a two-party system, faced with an electorate clustered around the midpoint of the political spectrum, construct "vague and ambiguous" platforms in order to capture the maximum number of voters without losing votes to the other party. Because voters cannot distinguish between parties based on issues, voters are in effect "encouraged to make decisions on some basis other than issues." Downs, *Economic Theory*, 136. Again, this implies a politics where candidates campaign on their own records and characteristics to provide voting cues to an electorate faced with parties with homogeneous issue preferences.

3. Jacobson, *Politics of Congressional Elections*; Salmore and Salmore, *Candidates, Parties, and Campaigns*; Herrnson, *Congressional Elections*; Herrnson, *Party Campaigning in the 1980s*.

4. American Political Science Association, *Toward a More Responsible Party System*; Ostrogorski, *Democracy and the Party System*; Bruce, *American Parties and Politics*, 21–32; Sait, *American Parties and Elections*; Bone, *American Politics and the Party System*.

5. Herrnson, *Party Campaigning in the 1980s*, 18–19.

6. Agranoff, *New Style in Election Campaigns*, 4–5.

7. Cantor and Herrnson, "Party Campaign Activity"; Salmore and Salmore, *Candidates, Parties, and Campaigns*; Herrnson, *Party Campaigning in the 1980s*; Herrnson, *Congressional Elections*.

8. For example, see Coleman, "Resurgent or Just Busy?" and Pomper, "Alleged Decline of American Parties."

9. Gimpel, *Fulfilling the Contract*; Killian, *Freshmen*. Another prominent example is the Republican campaign to retake the House in 1980. The Republican Party sponsored advertisements with the tagline "Vote Republican: For a Change." Kolodny, *Pursuing Majorities*, 143.

10. Ostrogorski, *Democracy and the Party System*; Bruce, *American Parties and Politics*; Sait, *American Parties and Elections*, 155; Bone, *American Politics and the Party System*.

11. Pollock, *Party Campaign Funds*; Merriam and Gosnell, *American Party System*, 365. Parties also provided the funds for congressional campaigns. No law required political parties, candidates, or interest groups to file campaign finance statements, so most of what scholars know about the financing of congressional campaigns is fragmentary. Chapter 3 examines nineteenth-century congressional campaigns and agrees with the conventional political science wisdom that parties dominated congressional campaign finance. This conclusion rests on an evidentiary foundation of diary entries, newspaper accounts, and scattered ledgers containing records of party receipts and expenditures during election campaigns. To a significant degree, the nineteenth-century canvass integrated local, state, and

national campaigns into a unified whole, especially during presidential election years. See Summers, *Rum, Romanism, and Rebellion*. For accounts of specific congressional races in the nineteenth century, see Shelton, "William Atkinson Jones, 1849–1918"; House, "The Democratic State Central Committee of Indiana in 1880"; Rathgeber, "The Democratic Party in Pennsylvania"; Josephson, *Politicos*; Kolodny, *Pursuing Majorities*; Polakoff, "The Disorganized Democracy." David Mayhew provides a dissenting view in *Placing Parties in American Politics*.

12. The Anti-Saloon League specifically and the Prohibition movement generally are exceptions to the low levels of interest group involvement in campaigns during the late nineteenth and early twentieth centuries. Odegard, *Pressure Politics*; Kerr, *Organized for Prohibition*.

13. Merton, "Latent Functions of the Machine"; Shefter, "Emergence of the Political Machine"; Shefter, *Political Parties and the State*. For an alternative view, see Erie, *Rainbow's End*.

14. See Wade, "Periphery versus the Center."

15. National party and congressional campaign committees traditionally acted as resource brokers. They gathered funds, produced campaign materials, and provided a speakers' bureau during election campaigns. Resources were then dispersed to state parties or individual candidates during the campaign (see chapter 3). The role of national committees declined after the turn of the century, particularly in the 1930s, largely due to a lack of funds. Ever more money was funneled to support the efforts of the presidential candidate at the expense of congressional candidates. See Caro, *Years of Lyndon Johnson* for an account of congressional campaign financing in the 1930s and 1940s. Combined with the collapse of many urban machines, the monetary shortfall among national committees encouraged candidates to depend less on the party for financial support. For an account of campaign financing in the mid-twentieth century, see Heard, *Costs of Democracy*. For a discussion of urban machine collapse, see Erie, *Rainbow's End*.

16. Dwight Eisenhower's campaign benefited from an unprecedented volunteer effort to organize and fund the canvass. Although the Republican National Committee financed television commercials to nationwide audiences, Eisenhower clubs sprang up in all fifty states and contributed significant money and volunteer resources. This was independent of party campaign efforts and became a commonplace tactic at the congressional level as well. See U.S. Congress, Subcommittee on Privileges and Elections of the Committee on Rules and Administration, *1956 Presidential and Senatorial Campaign Contributions and Practices*.

17. Scott and Hrebenar, *Parties in Crisis*,15.

18. Michael McGerr calls this political style, which is the "different fashions in which people perceive, discuss, and act in politics." McGerr, *Decline of Popular Parties*, 9.

19. Salmore and Salmore, *Candidates, Parties, and Campaigns*; Kolodny, *Pursuing Majorities*; Agranoff, *New Style in Election Campaigns*; Agranoff, "New Style of Campaigning," 230–40.

20. Party scholars did not miss the changing fortunes of parties: the responsible-party school of thought was a response to party decline. See Schattschneider, *Party Government*; Schattschneider, *Semisovereign People*. Even those long trumpeting the role of political parties recognized the rising fortunes of congressional candidates: "The party organizations, at least, find it difficult to control the selecting of candidates, the taking of stands on issues, the fixing of campaign strategies, even the raising of money. Those aspects of the contesting of elections are controlled, in the name of the whole party, by its candidates." Sorauf, *Party Politics in America*, 198.

21. The maturation of a theoretical tradition distinct from the responsible party mold aided the creation of the candidate model of campaigns. As the campaign landscape evolved during the 1950s and 1960s, political science gradually shifted from examining institutions and laws to evaluating individual political behavior. The quantification of the social sciences in the postwar era also helped the transformation. See Farr, "Remembering the Revolution."

22. Students of voter behavior might disagree. The authors of *The American Voter* found that party identification was the best predictor of voice choice. No single variable performed as well. Nevertheless, the Republican Eisenhower used his attractive personal characteristics to draw substantial crossover votes in 1952. See Campbell, Gurin, and Miller, *Voter Decides*; Campbell et al., *American Voter*.

23. Generally, electoral rules provide a context in which political actors compete for resources. How political actors benefit from the collection of resources determines the strategies they pursue in elections. The electorate responds to these strategic outcomes and changes its behavior accordingly. As the electorate follows shifting elite strategies, these mass changes influence electoral contexts. Elite behavior generally drives mass behavior, but mass behavior provides a feedback mechanism that either reinforces existing elite behavior or factors into the strategic decisions of elites. See Carmines and Stimson, *Issue Evolution*. In the case of the electorate's weakening partisan identification and resulting congressional campaign strategies, the initial loosening of partisan ties may have been a product of the electorate following cues provided by elites during campaigns. This then reinforced the use of candidate-centered campaign techniques by prospective members of Congress.

24. Polarization increases simultaneously with competitiveness after the mid-1970s, contrary to the expectation of the median voter model. See Downs, *Economic Theory*. This suggests that distinct party reputations might have some value for candidates.

25. Jacobson, *Politics of Congressional Elections*; Salmore and Salmore; *Candidates, Parties, and Campaigns*; Herrnson, *Party Campaigning in the 1980s*; Herrnson, *Congressional Elections*; Cantor and Herrnson, "Party Campaign Activity"; Herrnson and Dwyre, "Party Issue Advocacy." But see Cotter et al., *Party Organizations in American Politics*.

26. Herrnson, *Party Campaigning in the 1980s*, 120.

27. Ibid., 48.

28. Ibid., 47.

29. This section is influenced by Parker and Coleman, "Pay to Play," 145–49.

30. Merton, "Latent Functions of the Machine," 29.

31. O'Connor, *Last Hurrah*.

32. Erie, *Rainbow's End*, 110–11.

33. In the first case this meant placing additional registration burdens on newly arrived immigrant voters, instituting lengthy residency requirements, and / or failing to publicize polling locations. In the second case, resource expansion generally meant the annexation of suburbs to create new city revenues, increasing the tax burden on middle- and upper-class voters, or dispensing federal welfare largesse in the post–New Deal Era themselves. See Erie, *Rainbow's End*, 191–235.

34. These advertisements were defined and protected in *Buckley v. Valeo* 424 U.S. 1 (1976), and their use was further explicated by a series of rulings including *Federal Election Commission v. Massachusetts Citizens for Life, Inc.* 470 U.S. 238 (1986), *Austin v. Michigan State Chamber of Commerce* 494 U.S. 652 (1990), and *Colorado Republican Federal Campaign Committee v. Federal Election Commission* 518 U.S. 604 (1996). Technically, they are not supposed to advocate for or against the election of a particular candidate. But by associating a candidate with a particular issue position, candidate and party reputations can be altered. Therefore, in this formulation, they are considered resources utilized by interest groups, parties, or individuals designed to influence the probability of election.

35. Cox and McCubbins, *Legislative Leviathan*, 109–11; Petrocik, "Issue Ownership in Presidential Elections." Cox and McCubbins do not develop a term explicitly for their "record" concept; this is a simplification of their more complicated notion.

36. See Mayhew, *Congress: The Election Connection*, or Fenno, *Home Style*.

37. Cox and McCubbins, *Legislative Leviathan*, 110–11.

38. Ibid., 110.

39. One might object, saying voter support and reputation resources are highly collinear. Their relationship is more complicated. Just as money does not buy reputation, reputation does not necessarily bring votes. On average, one might expect candidates with higher levels of voter support will also attract more reputation resources. One can conceive of candidates who are respected and have a high amount of reputation resources and yet do not attract voter support for a variety of other reasons. For example, the candidate might not be able to communicate that reputation, hence voters do not know about it. Or a candidate may have a low reputation and receive many votes, as may happen in a highly partisan district where partisan reputation trumps individual or monetary reputation.

40. This includes NES questions tapping respondent perception of the parties ideologically on defense spending, an equal role for women, government aid to blacks, government spending and services, and the provision of abortion services, to name just a few that have been included in studies over the past forty years.

41. Harris and Farhi, "Taking the Campaign to the People."

42. To be sure, this is not a wholly satisfactory construction. There are situations when people power can trump money. For example, the author managed Wyoming state senator Mike Enzi's successful campaign for the Republican nomination to the U.S. Senate in 1996. Two candidates spent twice as much as Enzi in the primary, and yet Enzi eked out a victory in part due to his superior organization and ground game. Looking at the amount Enzi spent, it is clear that the dollar value underestimates the true monetary might of that largely volunteer organization. For the purposes of a campaign theory, however, it is not clear how volunteer resources could be easily estimated. In short, monetary value underestimates the resource need of some candidates and the success some candidates have in meeting that need.

43. Dewar, "Senate Power Shift Intensifies Battle for '02"; Dewar, "Minn. May Be Key to Senate's Helm."

44. Grow, "South Dakota Boots Sharp-Dressed Liberal"; Stolberg, "Gracious, but Defeated, Daschle Makes History."

45. See chapter 6 for a discussion the literature on this subject. See also Goldstein and Ridout, "Measuring the Effects of Televised Political Advertising in the United States"; Converse, "Assessing the Capacity of Mass Electorates."

46. The direction of this arrow depends upon the constitution of electoral rules in a given era.

47. It could be argued that the political (i.e., party) system—defined in part by electoral rules—is itself shaped by political parties, interest groups, and candidates. William Chambers wonders whether political parties should be treated as independent or dependent variables in party systems: "Probably the most nearly precise way to summarize the relationship between political parties and the course of political development in general during the last hundred years and more is to say that the role of parties and party systems has changed to one of adaptation and adjustment rather than one of innovation." Chambers, "Party Development and the American Mainstream," 22–23. In short, political parties are properly a dependent variable. For the changing role of political parties as a nationally integrative force, see Skowronek, *Building a New American State*.

48. What about Newlands? As will be discussed in chapter 3, Nevada was a state with feeble partisan organizations and voters weakly attached to either party. Newlands thrived in this situation as a candidate-centered politician.

49. *United States Statutes at Large*.

50. Jacobson, *Politics of Congressional Elections*.

51. Chapter 3 provides a more detailed discussion. See also Mayhew, *Placing Parties*.

52. This is an application of Nelson Polsby's work on Congress. See Polsby, "Institutionalization of the U.S. House of Representatives."

53. What about a resource threshold? Having the most money does not guarantee victory. What is important, however, is having enough money to be competitive and get one's message out. This would suggest that a threshold might be more appropriate than share conceptually, and the congressional campaign literature

notes that challengers do not have to outspend incumbents (for example) but raise and spend enough to be competitive. See Jacobson, *Politics of Congressional Elections*. The threshold amount, however, depends on political circumstances. For an incumbent without a challenger, $500,000 might be an appropriate threshold, but that threshold probably increases in the face of an experienced challenger with a substantial war chest. The point is that context matters, and resource share best approximates the effect of context on resource need in terms of the theory developed here.

54. Erie, *Rainbow's End*, 221–29.

55. Monetary resource does not explicitly capture the notion of free media. Free media is an admitted objective of congressional campaigns, but it is nearly impossible to measure. That said, certain aspects of free media can be captured by the monetary resource concept. For example, a negative advertisement is aired and receives attention during nightly newscasts. While the value of the nightly newscast is not captured, the initial expense of producing the ad and airing it captures a portion of the ad's effect. How to capture the value of free media is elusive and, at the moment, beyond this study's scope.

56. Jacobson, *Politics of Congressional Elections*, 36–37; Cox and Katz, "Why Did the Incumbency Advantage Grow?"

57. Thanks to Michael Franz for helping to develop this two-by-two schema.

58. Yearley, *Money Machines*.

59. The decline of political parties and the rise of candidates is well documented. See Salmore and Salmore, *Candidates, Parties, and Campaigns*; Scott and Hrebrenar, *Parties in Crisis*; Sorauf, *Party Politics in America*.

60. Kayden, "Nationalization of the Party System."

61. Quoted in Kolodny, *Pursuing Majorities*, 132.

CHAPTER 3

1. Sait, *American Parties and Elections*; Ostrogorski, *Democracy and the Party System*; Bruce, *American Parties and Politics*; Merriam and Gosnell, *American Party System*; Bone, *American Politics and the Party System*; Schattschneider, *Party Government*; Schattschneider, *Semisovereign People*. An earlier version of this chapter was presented at the 2003 meeting of the Social Science History Association. Thanks to Timothy Nokken and Jack Reynolds for their feedback.

2. Quoted in Summers, *Rum, Romanism, and Rebellion*, 17.

3. Argersinger, "Democracy, Republicanism, and Efficiency," 121.

4. Quoted in Josephson, *Politicos*, 289.

5. McGerr, *Decline of Popular Parties*, 14–22, 109–10. See Summers, *Press Gang* for an account of the partisan press in the early Gilded Age.

6. Morgan, "Congressional Career of William McKinley"; Schiesl, *Politics of Efficiency*, esp. chap. 2; Yearley, *Money Machines*; Skowronek, *Building a New American State*; McGerr, *Decline of Popular Parties*; Summers, *Rum, Romanism, and Rebellion*, 21.

7. Abraham Lincoln's secretary of the navy, Gideon Welles, on assessments: "Judge Edmunds and Senator Lane called on me Monday morning for funds. Showed me two papers, one with Seward's name for $500. On another was Blair's (Postmaster-General) and Secretary Usher, each for $500, with some other names for like amounts. Told them I disapproved of these levies of men in office, but would take the subject into consideration. . . . Something should, perhaps, be contributed by men when great principles are involved, but these large individual subscriptions are not in all respects right or proper." Pollock, *Party Campaign Funds*, 113–14.

8. Summers, *Rum, Romanism, and Rebellion*, 164.

9. Dobson, *Politics in the Gilded Age*, 37. Also Marcus, *Grand Old Party*, esp. vii and 22.

10. Marcus, *Grand Old Party*, 22.

11. Kornbluh, *Why Americans Stopped Voting*, 47.

12. Summers, *Rum, Romanism, and Rebellion*, 255.

13. Polsby, "Institutionalization of the U.S. House of Representatives." See chapter 2 for a discussion of institutionalization and institutional capacity.

14. Mayhew, *Placing Parties*, 19–20.

15. Ibid., 25–26, 143.

16. Ibid., 210.

17. Ibid., 236. This suggests that strongly institutionalized parties require a particular environment to establish their roots. Lacking such an environment, parties will be weak and unable to exert much political influence. Certain changes in electoral rules might hinder the development of vibrant parties. In other words, it is hard to establish a new party machine in an environment with nonpartisan elections, primaries, and Australian ballots because party leaders have few incentives to grant party activists or candidates. Existing party organizations can survive these electoral changes if they are embedded in the state's political fabric. Admittedly, this is a slippery argument, but the patterns of political organization noted by Mayhew are hard to refute. See Mayhew, *Placing Parties*, chap. 8, for elaboration on the nexus between traditional party organization, history, urbanism, and ethnocultural factors.

18. A useful substitute for TPO is a state's date of admission. With only three exceptions, every state with an organizational capacity of two or more was admitted to the union before 1821. See Mayhew, *Placing Parties*, 204. TPO and a state's date of admission is strongly correlated ($-.507$, $p < .01$). Using age as an indicator does not substantially change the qualitative findings that follow.

19. Epstein, *Political Parties in the American Mold*. A historian of the Gilded Age argues that the candidate-centered style appeared even earlier. See Summers, *Rum, Romanism, and Rebellion*.

20. "Style," writes Michael McGerr, "is one part of political culture—the manner in which people think and behave politically." McGerr, *Decline of Popular Parties*, 19.

21. These indicators are merely an operationalization of the responsible party's electoral function as defined by party scholars such as Alan Ware: "A strong party

organization is one which, at the very least, can determine who will be the party's candidates, can decide (broadly) the issues on which electoral campaigns will be fought by its candidates, [and] contributes the lion's share of resources to the candidate's election campaigns." Quoted in Schier, *By Invitation Only*, 46.

22. There is very little specifically written on congressional campaigns during the late nineteenth century. Many accounts focus on political machines in various cities, while others focus on presidential politics. More generally, there exist many works that characterize the politics and campaigns of the period. Even congressional biographies pay scant attention to the election of their subjects. I have attempted to provide the most accurate picture of campaigning for Congress during the period with this in mind. The examples that follow are at best an approximation of the campaign landscape. It should be noted that candidates did appear to adhere generally to the expectations of the party-centered model; however, the very fact that stories emerge of candidates behaving in a more candidate-centered fashion from such a sparse literature is in itself telling.

23. Two bias threats are noticeable. The first is the reliance upon biographical accounts. The tales of mavericks make for more interesting reading than those of party regulars and simply might be overrepresented in the historical record. The second bias possibility is the historical record itself: Illiterate people do not leave behind a written record, some people are simply more interested in preserving their legacy for posterity, and records can be lost, destroyed, or fall victim to the vagaries of nature. See Lustick, "History, Historiography, and Political Science."

24. Rathgeber, "Democratic Party in Pennsylvania," 10–11; Dobson, *Gilded Age*, 25.

25. Procter, *Not without Honor*; Kornbluh, *Why Americans Stopped Voting*.

26. For examples, see Ross, *Jonathan Prentiss Dolliver*, 68; Bartholomew, *Indiana Third Congressional District*, 81; Morgan, "Congressional Career of William McKinley," 40.

27. Belmont, *American Democrat*, 215.

28. Lindsey, *Sunset Cox*, 108.

29. The conception of the self-sacrificing representative comes from the memoirs and diaries of politicians, scarcely unbiased and dispassionate accounts. Benedict, "The Party, Going Strong," 46–49.

30. Procter, *Not without Honor*, 184.

31. Ross, *Jonathan Prentiss Dolliver*, 63.

32. Newlands lost the nomination to the incumbent, Horace Bartine.

33. Lilley, "Early Career," 222.

34. McKinley's tactics compare favorably to those of a more candidate-centered era: "He was in his buggy mornings before dawn, touring through the countryside or driving to a distant meeting. He shook hundreds of hands, kissed his share of babies, tasted an endless procession of good and bad pie, and smiled his way through dozens of meetings, hoping to gain local delegates to the district convention." Morgan, *Congressional Career of William McKinley*, 5–6.

35. Shelton, "William Atkinson Jones," 61.

36. Ibid., 53–54.

37. Rathgeber, "Democratic Party in Pennsylvania," 73. The Philadelphia Democratic Central Committee's accounts from 1882 show receipts of $25,662—with $6,700 coming from city, congressional, senatorial, and legislative candidates and more than $18,000 from citizens—undoubtedly, assessments on government employees. Of this, almost half ($10,000) was spent to pay for the poll taxes of citizens, and another 19 percent went to "election day" or "walking around" money. Ibid., 82–83.

38. House, "Democratic State Central Committee," 191–95.

39. Kornbluh, *Why Americans Stopped Voting*, 44.

40. The president had the ability to extend civil service protections to federal workers and effectively "blanket in" his party's supporters. As the nineteenth century progressed and party control of the White House alternated between the two parties, each president would take the opportunity to further extend civil service to an additional class of employees to prevent their removal when a hostile administration took control. Skowronek, *Building a New American State*, 65.

41. Josephson, *Politicos*, 411.

42. Polakoff, "Disorganized Democracy," 145.

43. House, "Democratic State Central Committee," 188.

44. Summers, *Rum, Romanism, and Rebellion*, 165.

45. Polakoff, "Disorganized Democracy," 172–73.

46. House, "Democratic State Central Committee," 189.

47. Rathgeber, "Democratic Party in Pennsylvania," 13, 82. Congressional nominee William L. Scott supplied $50,000 to the national committee in 1884 when it had run out of money. Ibid., 133.

48. Letter from Alexander H. Coffroth to Samuel Randall, October 31, 1882, quoted in Rathgeber, "Democratic Party in Pennsylvania," 80.

49. Ferrell, *Claude A. Swanson of Virginia*, 11; Ross, *Jonathan Prentiss Dolliver*, 43–57.

50. Offenberg, "Political Career of Thomas Brackett Reed," 43, 53; Morgan, "Congressional Career of William McKinley," 7, 66.

51. Briggs, *William Peters Hepburn*, 165.

52. Nicklas, "William Kelley: The Congressional Years, 1861–1890," 365–76.

53. Benedict, "Party, Going Strong," 50–51.

54. Summers, *Rum, Romanism, and Rebellion*, 167.

55. Ross, *Jonathan Prentiss Dolliver*, 67.

56. Rowley, *Reclaiming*, 38–40; Lilley, "Early Career," 171–75.

57. Newlands claimed he abandoned the Democrats when he fell out with the Cleveland administration on monetary policy. Lilley, "Early Career," 219.

58. Rowley, *Reclaiming*, 69. After his first successful campaign, Newlands even had his own campaign song (ibid., 75):

Our Congressman is Newlands, who loves Nevada true
He says our lonely deserts yet shall bloom as roses do,
He'll irrigate our valleys, and get free coinage through,

So come along to victory.
Come all Nevada silver men, we'll have a glorious song,
The tune will be free coinage, sung by every voter strong,
And 'though we're weak in number, we'll win the fight ere long.
For we're marching to victory."

59. Ibid., 79–80, 106. There is much confusion surrounding Newlands' party identification. Having switched from the Republican to the Democratic Party, he later switched back after having been identified with both the Silver and Populist parties. Lilley, "Early Career"; Williams, *Democratic Party and California Politics, 1880–1896.*

60. Silbey, *American Political Nation, 1838–1893,* 67.

61. Argersinger, "Democracy, Republicanism, and Efficiency," 125–26.

62. Brady, Cooper, and Hurley, "Decline of Party in the U.S. House of Representatives, 1887–1968."

63. Morgan, "Congressional Career of William McKinley," 161.

64. Dobson, *Politics in the Gilded Age,* 92–97.

65. Benedict, "Party, Going Strong," 49.

66. Williams, *Democratic Party and California Politics,* 247.

67. Ferrell, *Claude A. Swanson,* 15, 25–32.

68. Hutton, "The Election of 1896 in the Tenth Congressional District of Tennessee," 43, 65.

69. Ross, *Jonathan Prentiss Dolliver,* 128.

70. Bicha, "Jerry Simpson: Populist without Principle," 295, 300.

71. Kazin, *A Godly Hero,* 18.

72. Koenig, *Bryan,* 65, 71–72.

73. Ibid., 74, 78 ; Kazin, *A Godly Hero,* 26, 69.

74. David Mayhew posits that members are motivated largely by reelection. In particular, candidates engage in credit claiming and position taking to please their constituents. Position taking is the most relevant here: If members of Congress vote in order to present a particular record and/or reputation to the district, then it is reasonable to assume that record could serve as a "proxy" for the message a member might wish to communicate to voters during the campaign. Mayhew, *Congress: The Electoral Connection.*

75. Roll call votes for the period were obtained from the Inter-university Consortium for Political and Social Research, located at www.icpsr.umich.edu.

76. If the member voted with his party's majority, the vote was coded a one. If the member opposed his party's majority, the vote was coded zero. These totals were then summed and averaged by the total number of party unity votes taken during each Congress. The biggest problem with roll call analyses in the late nineteenth century is absenteeism. Prior to the creation and adoption of Reed's Rules in the mid-1890s, members of both parties commonly engaged in dilatory tactics to obstruct House business. See Davidson and Oleszek, *Congress and Its Members,* 6th ed., 156–57. In many cases, this meant refusing to answer a roll call to prevent a quorum despite being physically present in the chamber. Additionally, absence

from a session did not necessarily mean a member was ducking a politically difficult vote. Train travel between California and Washington, D.C., took weeks rather than days, so a representative might be absent simply because he was unable to reach the Capitol in a timely fashion. Unlike *Congressional Quarterly*, the measure adopted here does not count an absence against a member for the purposes of calculating his individual party unity score. This means that any one party unity vote is calculated in an individual member's unity score only if he recorded either a yea or a nay. Substantively, this means that the denominator used to calculate the party unity score varies from member to member.

77. For those uncomfortable with TPO as a measure of institutionalization, the regression results reported in table 3.1 do not substantially change when age is substituted for TPO. The older the state, the more a member supports his party on the House floor.

78. Previous vote was obtained from *Congressional Quarterly's Guide to U.S. Elections*.

79. Previous unity is included for theoretical reasons, but there is also a more practical need for the variable: the possibility of serially correlated errors. A previous unity variable helps alleviate this problem. See Neter, Kutner, Nachtsheim, and Wasserman, *Applied Linear Regression Models*, chap. 12, for a discussion. Another remedy is Generalized Least-Squares. Running the model with GLS does not substantially alter results. Construction of this variable posed two problems. First, rarely did members in the late nineteenth century serve more than three or four terms. The requirement of a previous unity variable based solely on a member's previous legislative record would prevent a test of other theoretically interesting propositions, such as the relationship between freshmen legislators and their propensity to support the party. To overcome this issue, the previous unity variable utilized is simply the unity score of the member previously occupying the seat. This is defensible because marginal districts will have representatives who are less likely to support their respective party on the House floor, while districts that are less competitive should produce members with high levels of unity.

The second major issue concerning the construction of the previous unity variable concerns the nature of late-nineteenth-century congressional redistricting. Unlike the twentieth-century redistricting experience, late-nineteenth-century state legislators did not redraw congressional boundaries with any great regularity. State legislators would often repair to the drawing board to redraw congressional districts when the partisan balance shifted. See Engstrom, "Stacking the House." Practically, this means that the construction of a previous unity variable is not easily accomplished. Using maps of congressional districts and census statistics, I was able to trace a congressional district in a given congress to its antecedent in the previous congress, in spite of the frequent changes that took place during the time period. I expect that the resulting previous unity variable is associated positively with a member's level of party support in the next congress.

80. V. O. Key notes the propensity of the South to stick together on roll call votes. See Key, *Southern Politics*. During the nineteenth century, this meant aligning

closely with the Democratic Party leadership as the party remained substantially pro-states' rights, anti-black, and conservative in its outlook. See Kazin, *A Godly Hero*. During the rise of the New Deal, southerners still voted as a bloc, but they began voting more frequently with Republicans in a conservative coalition on social and civil rights legislation. See Brady, *Critical Elections and Congressional Policy Making*.

81. Again, this was retrieved from *Congressional Quarterly's Guide to U.S. Elections*.

82. This is a hypothesis generated from the socialization literature. Matthews, *U.S. Senators and Their World* is representative of the genre.

83. As party unity is continuous and ranges from zero to one, the method of estimation is ordinary least-squares regression. Unstandardized coefficients with robust standard errors are reported in table 3.1.

84. Another problem in a pooled data set with individual and state-level variables is the possibility of heteroscedasticity. A Cook-Weisberg test indicated that this is a problem; hence the use of robust standard errors as a remedy.

85. Members representing marginal districts, for example, tend to buck their parties more often than those in safe districts. Southerners do tend to stick together, and members of the minority party are more unified than those serving in the majority. Finally, length of service is associated with higher levels of party unity. As congressional careerism was not widespread in the late nineteenth century, this effect is quite minimal: the average Republican served just over one and a half terms, which increased his unity by barely one percentage point.

86. Is the concept of party institutionalization amenable to a threshold? Once a certain level of institutionalization is achieved, then the effects of party kicks in. This was tested by collapsing the TPO variable into a series of dummy variables, with each variable taking on the value of one at different TPO levels. For example, the first dummy variable would take a value of one if the state exhibited any degree of institutionalization (a TPO score of 2, 3, 4, or 5). A second variable would be coded one if the state's TPO was 3, 4 or 5. And so on. The regression was run four times, and each time the TPO variable was replaced with one of these dummies. In every instance, the results were the same. This is consistent with the characterization that increasing levels of TPO have a greater pull on a member's voting behavior. A threshold characterization would only be appropriate if dummy variables representing less institutionalization were insignificant and suddenly dummies representing substantial institutionalization were significant. This was not the case.

87. Summers, *Rum, Romanism, and Rebellion*.

CHAPTER 4

1. For example, see Salmore and Salmore, *Candidates, Parties, and Campaigns*, 19. Party scholar Frank Sorauf noted in 1968, before the explosion of PACs, that "parties appear to have lost at least part of their dominance over the mobilization

of political power in the American polity. . . . In short, parties appear to have suffered an overall net decline in their competitive position among the political organizations." Sorauf, *Party Politics in America,* 426.

2. Mayhew, *Placing Parties.*

3. The effect of the Australian ballot on split ticket voting depended on the ballot form adopted by a state. The office-bloc form lists candidates by office sought, while the party column arranges candidates by party affiliation. The office-bloc form discourages straight-ticket voting, while the party column form encourages it. Rusk, "The Effect of the Australian Ballot Reform on Split Ticket Voting"; Bass, "Partisan Rules, 1946–1996"; Harris, *Election Administration in the United States;* Walker, "Ballot Forms and Voter Fatigue."

4. Salmore and Salmore, *Candidates, Parties, and Campaigns,* 34. Not all scholars agree. Alan Ware argues in *The American Direct Primary* that primaries were instituted by party elites attempting to regain control of the nomination process. Frank Sorauf notes that in some cases primaries "effectively neutralized the political party as nominator; in others it clearly has made little difference to parties." Sorauf, *Party Politics in America,* 220.

5. Maisel, "American Political Parties," 111–12.

6. Menefee-Libbey, *Triumph of Campaign-Centered Politics,* 15.

7. Silbey, "From 'Essential to the Existence of Our Institutions' to 'Rapacious Enemies of Honest and Responsible Government'"; Herrnson, "National Party Organizations"; Sorauf, *Party Politics in America;* Salmore and Salmore, *Candidates, Parties, and Campaigns;* Blumenthal, *Permanent Campaign;* Agranoff, "New Style of Campaigning"; Menefee-Libbey, *Triumph of Campaign-Centered Politics;* Sabato, *Rise of Political Consultants.*

8. Key, *Politics, Parties, and Pressure Groups,* 570–71.

9. Sorauf, *Party Politics in America,* 224.

10. Agranoff, "New Style of Campaigning."

11. Kelley, *Professional Public Relations and Political Power;* Salmore and Salmore, *Candidates, Parties, and Campaigns.*

12. Mitchell, *Campaign of the Century,* 291, 344, 469.

13. Ibid., 63, 369–72, 423–24, 434–35, 499–501, 510–11. According to the *New York Times,* much of this effort was coordinated by Louis B. Mayer, state chairman of the Republican Party until future governor and Supreme Court chief justice Earl Warren was selected in mid-September. Mayer, of course, ran MGM studios. "Resources to Fight Sinclair," *New York Times.* Hollywood's use of the new media in conjunction with the Republican Party casts some doubt on the relationship between the rise of the new media and the collapse of parties.

14. Mitchell, *Campaign of the Century,* 35, 95–100, 154–55, 406, 417, 441–42.

15. The fear of Sinclair did not equate with love of Merriam. Independent organizations largely ran an anti-Sinclair campaign rather than a pro-Merriam effort.

16. Ervin, *Henry Ford vs. Truman H. Newberry,* 7–12, 15, 20, 21. In 2005 dollars, this amounts to more than $2.5 million.

17. Salmore and Salmore, *Candidates, Parties, and Campaigns*; Agranoff, "New Style of Campaigning," 235; Silbey, "From 'Essential to the Existence of Our Institutions.'"

18. Kolodny, *Pursuing Majorities*, chaps. 3 and 4.

19. Key, *Politics, Parties, and Pressure Groups*, 570–71.

20. Salmore and Salmore, *Candidates, Parties, and Campaigns*, 47.

21. Excluded are any Senate races where either of the candidates receives their party's future nomination for president. The size of the historical record available for any one Senate candidate or campaign might be correlated with the future aspirations of the Senate contestants. Most serious is the possibility that candidate-centered behavior in a Senate campaign is related to the presence of a "progressively ambitious candidate." Schlesinger, *Political Parties and the Winning of Office*. In other words, those campaigns featuring a future presidential candidate are more likely to have an extensive historical record documenting the congressional campaign and are more prone to exhibit candidate-centered behaviors. Although the bias cannot be completely eliminated, it can be minimized by restricting the analysis to those Senate races where neither of the candidates actually receives their party's future nomination for president.

22. Unlike large n-quantitative studies relying upon the rules of statistical inference, the four cases here are not randomly selected, as this may introduce bias in a small n study. See King, Keohane, and Verba, *Designing Social Inquiry*. When cases are purposely selected, an important bias threat is the possibility that a selection rule is correlated with the dependent variable (in this case, the degree of party involvement in the campaign). To minimize selection bias, races were chosen from each category with multiple states by considering the quality, amount, depth, and range of secondary and primary sources regarding a particular race.

23. Does the analysis, by focusing on the winning candidate, create any problems? Although the research here focuses on the winning candidate, evidence gathered from archival collections or newspapers suggests that the losing candidate in each Senate race selected resource strategies similar to the winning candidate. Both candidates in the 1950 Senate race in Illinois depended heavily on their parties' organizational capacity to conduct their campaigns. In contrast, both candidates in Idaho and Tennessee seemed to rely more on candidate-centered techniques (although in the case of Herman Welker, Idaho's incumbent senator, this is difficult to substantiate satisfactorily only because his senatorial papers were destroyed upon his death).

24. Bethine Church and Carl Burke generously spoke with the author during his visit to Boise in September 2003.

25. Canon, *Actors, Athletes, and Astronauts*.

26. His short political resume included a stint as chairman of the state's Young Democrats, an unsuccessful run for the state legislature as a write-in candidate in 1952, and membership in Ada County's Democratic organization.

27. Burke interview.

28. Ashby, "Frank Church Goes to the Senate"; Ashby and Gramer, *Fighting the Odds.*

29. Indeed, Mayhew notes that the parties in Idaho experimented with a variety of selection processes between 1918 and 1960. Mayhew, *Placing Parties*, 179–80.

30. The Church campaign encouraged supporters to persuade his opponents to withdraw from the primary field. See unknown author to Nell Robinson, April 24, 1956, series 5.1, box 1, f. 48, Frank Church Papers, Special Collections Library, Boise State University (hereafter cited as FCP).

31. Some suggested the Taylor campaign received financial assistance from the Welker forces. See "Taylor Denies Backing," *Idaho State Journal,*

32. What little organization existed in the state had taken root in northern Idaho. Tom Boise "had developed a pretty good Democratic organization in North Idaho" of which the Church campaign made use. Burke interview, 7. But the organization did not control the state party, and at times it acted very independently, to the point of actually helping to elect moderate Republicans. See Stapilus, *Paradox Politics*, 86–87. One interesting indication of a party's institutional strength and depth is whether county organizations have their own stationery. In states with well-developed and entrenched partisan organizations, counties and even ward organizations have their own stationery, whereas in states like Idaho, the county is lucky to even have a chairperson, let alone the money to create their own letterhead.

33. "Short Memorandum Concerning the General Nature of the Projected Campaign of Frank Church against Herman Welker for the U.S. Senate from Idaho," n.d., series 5.1, box 2, f. 30, FCP.

34. Memorandum, "Budget for Citizens for Church," n.d., series 5.1, box 1, f. 10, FCP. There is some dispute as to whether this was the actual amount spent by Church. Bethine Church remembers something in the neighborhood of $59,000 for the entire campaign, while Stapilus pegs the amount at $40,000. Church interview; Stapilus, *Paradox Politics*, 91. Campaigns in this period frequently had more than one campaign committee raising and spending money to avoid limits proscribed by the Corrupt Practices Act of 1925. In the case of Church, there was the Church for Senator Committee and Citizens for Frank Church, both run by Burke. But there was also a Church for Senator Supporters group that may or may not have been controlled in some fashion by the Church campaign.

35. See "Agreement Form for Political Broadcasts," various dates, series 5.1, box 1, f. 4, FCP.

36. Church and Burke interviews; Church, *Lifelong Affair*; Ashby and Gramer, *Fighting the Odds*, 51.

37. George H. R. Taylor to Frank Church, September 10, 1956, series 5.1, box 1, f. 59, FCP; George Smathers to Church and Carl Burke, September 10, 1956, series 5.1, box 1, f. 10, FCP. Senator Smathers, chair of the Democratic Senatorial Campaign Committee, thought the Church campaign committed too many of its resources to television and newspaper advertising. The national party did send money, but how much is unclear.

38. Corlett, "Politically Speaking," *Idaho Daily Statesman*, September 27, 1956.

39. The Church campaign apparently had an advertising agency (Hanawald) working with it to place the advertisements. See Richard K. Mooney to Randolph Gretes, October 15, 1956, series 5.1, box 1, f. 4, FCP.

40. Ashby and Gramer, *Fighting the Odds*, 57.

41. Corlett, "2,000 Hear Stevenson Address."

42. Pamphlet, "United behind Frank Church," n.d., series 5.1, box 1, f. 7, FCP; pamphlet, "Idaho Will Be Proud of Frank Church in the U.S. Senate," n.d., series 5.1, box 1, f. 7, FCP; various newspaper advertisements, n.d., series 5.1, box 1, f. 3, FCP; films, "Church for Senate," 1956, series 11.1, campaigns, FCP; audio recordings, "Church for Senate," 1956, series 11.2, campaigns, FCP. The word "Democrat" is set in conspicuously smaller type both in the print and television advertisements when compared with Church's name and the campaign's slogan.

43. Martin, "The 1956 Election in Idaho."

44. Corlett, "Politically Speaking," *Idaho Daily Statesman*, November 4, 1956.

45. "Memorandum Concerning Certain Issues of Local Importance to Idaho in the Coming Election Campaign," n.d., series 5.1, box 2, f. 12, FCP.

46. Hinton, "Now GOP Senators Shy from M'Carthy"; "Welker Praises Cohn"; "Welker Recalls Senators Who Have Been Unsteady."

47. "Church of Idaho Noted as Speaker," *New York Times*.

48. Untitled news release, September 14, 1956, series 5.1, box 2, f. 37, FCP. This appeal to voters of all stripes appears in a television spot in which Henry "Scoop" Jackson—another independent-minded senator from an organizationally weak state—endorses Church. Jackson emphasizes that Church will support all the people of Idaho. Film, "Church for Senate," 1956, series 11.1, campaigns, 56016, FCP.

49. See memorandum, "Herman Welker," n.d., series 5.1, box 2, f. 30, FCP; film, "Church for Senate," 1956, series 11.1, campaigns, 56006, FCP; memorandum, script for twenty-second political telecasts, n.d., series 5.1, box 1, f. 3, FCP; memorandum, "Eisenhower vs. Welker," n.d., series 5.1, box 2, f. 30, FCP; untitled news release, October 12, 1956, series 5.1, box 2, f. 37, FCP.

50. Untitled news release, September 28, 1956, series 5.1, box 2, f. 37, FCP.

51. "Church of Idaho Noted as Speaker." See also Ashby and Gramer, *Fighting the Odds*. Two weeks into the general election campaign, Burke wrote to his candidate asking him to call the chair of the Idaho Democratic Party, John Glasby, noting, "Glasby would like to hear from you from time to time and I think it good relations that you give him a buzz." Burke to Church, September 29, 1956, series 5.1, box 1, f. 59, FCP.

52. Neese, "Estes Is Bestes."

53. Goodman, *Inherited Domain*.

54. Through the years, Crump had built alliances with several smaller political organizations throughout the state, using state and federal patronage. In addition, for a share of the federal patronage, Republican Congressman B. Carroll Reece of East Tennessee guaranteed his organization's support of Crump candidates dur-

ing the Democratic primary. See Fontenay, *Estes Kefauver*, 152; Neese, "Estes Is Bestes," 52. The entire apparatus, based on loose arrangements and understandings, paled in comparison with more formally institutionalized partisan organizations in other states.

55. Langsdon, *Tennessee*, 34.

56. Neese, "Estes Is Bestes," 21.

57. Fontenay, *Estes Kefauver*, 137.

58. Neither did President Truman, despite Kefauver's impressive support (for a southerner) of administration policies on the House floor. Apparently, Truman, a protégé of the Pendergast machine in Kansas City, found Kefauver's independence from Tennessee's Democratic organization unsettling. Fontenay, *Estes Kefauver*, 118.

59. See Gardner, "Political Leadership," 24; Neese, "Estes Is Bestes," 42–49; Fontenay, *Estes Kefauver*, 129–32.

60. Key, *Southern Politics*, 62, 65–67.

61. Gorman, *Kefauver*, 40.

62. Gardner, "Political Leadership," 47, 51, 52. And the Kefauver campaign largely succeeded, establishing a campaign group in nearly every county across the state. Memorandum, May 10, 1948, series V: Political, 1948 Political Files, box 8, Estes Kefauver Papers, University of Tennessee Special Collections, Knoxville (hereafter referred to as EKP). Unless otherwise indicated, all materials cited are located in the 1948 Political Files of series V.

63. Martha Ragland chaired the women's organization during the primary and ran her campaign separately from the main effort under Neese's supervision in Nashville. Gardner, "Political Leadership," 52–54.

64. Memorandum, Charles Neese to Estes Kefauver, "Factors Opposing," n.d., box 16, EKP.

65. Neese, "Estes Is Bestes," 72–74.

66. Key, *Southern Politics*, 64.

67. The Crump forces allegedly received their money from the party treasury, as well as "voluntary" contributions from state employees and businessmen. Gardner, "Political Leadership," 57.

68. Neese, "Estes Is Bestes," 107. Gardner writes, "When bills had to be paid, the bucket would be passed at a rally, often a necessity to pay for gasoline to the next town." Gardner, "Political Leadership," 58. Some expenses incurred by Kefauver and his team during the primary still had not been paid well after the November general election. Harve M. Duggins to Neese, March 7, 1949, box 8, EKP.

69. Gardner, "Political Leadership," 44.

70. Gorman, *Kefauver*, 43.

71. Gardner, "Political Leadership," 41. In addition to women, Kefauver targeted farmers and veterans in his appeals. Pamphlet, "Kefauver Fights for the People of Tennessee," n.d., box 14, EKP; memorandum, Neese to Kefauver, "Factors Opposing"; pamphlet, "Estes Is Bestes," n.d., box 8, EKP.

72. Gardner, "Political Leadership," 48, 70, 100. See also memorandum, Neese to Kefauver, "Factors Opposing." The Browning forces likewise hesitated to consummate an alliance. See E. N. Eggleston to Major Herbert McKee, August 2, 1948, box 8, EKP.

73. One might also suspect that this language carried a more pejorative connotation. The term "coon" was and still is a derogatory term for African Americans. Crump played on white racist stereotypes by sticking Kefauver with this label.

74. Advertisement, "Estes Kefauver Assumes the Role of a Pet Coon," *Commercial Appeal*, June 10, 1948, box 16, EKP. For another example of Crump's methods, see advertisement, "Kefauver's Slick Trick," *Memphis Press-Scimitar*, July 6, 1948, box 11, EKP.

75. Gorman, *Kefauver*, 52; Fontenay, *Estes Kefauver*, 148; Neese, "Estes Is Bestes," 75–80.

76. Pamphlet, "If You Believe," n.d., box 8, EKP; cf. pamphlet "Estes Is Bestes."

77. Memorandum, Neese to Kefauver, "Factors Opposing."

78. Gordon Browning to Kefauver, August 28, 1948, box 8, EKP. The campaign constructed a list with all the primary managers working for each campaign in all the counties and congressional districts on one side of the page and the newly merged team for the general election on the other side. Memorandum, "First Congressional District," n.d., box 11, EKP.

79. "Candidates Open Uptown Headquarters," *Nashville Tennessean*. The letterhead for the new fall campaign tells the whole story. Neese to Frank Brizzi, October 12, 1948, box 11, EKP; c.f. Neese to Kefauver, May 31, 1948, box 11, EKP.

80. "State Political Drives Speed Up This Week" and "Democrats Plan Woods-Shelling for Big Vote," *Nashville Tennessean*.

81. See pamphlet "You Must Choose," n.d., box 14, EKP; pamphlet, "Get Out the Vote for the Democratic Nominees," n.d., box 9, EKP.

82. John Mitchell agreed to campaign with the ticket on his home turf, while campaign managers for both McCord (Browning's opponent) and Stewart wrote letters endorsing the Democratic ticket for the November election. Neese to Mitchell, October 5, 1948, box 14, EKP; Gardner, "Political Leadership," 128.

83. Gorman, *Kefauver*, 62. Crump's endorsement came late in the game, and rumors abounded that he and his organization would actively support the Republican coalition ticket. See Palmer Weber to Kefauver, n.d., box 8, EKP; Neese to Edmund Orgill, September 30, 1948, box 8, EKP.

84. It appears the campaign spent considerable time overseeing the unification. Neese to Horace Alsup, October 25, 1948, box 14, EKP; Earle Hendren to Robert L. Taylor, September 24, 1948, box 14, EKP; Dallas A. Hall to Neese, October 25, 1948, box 14, EKP; Kefauver to Neese, October 17, 1948, box 14, EKP.

85. Martha Ragland to Carrie M. Pace, October 10, 1948, box 14, EKP.

86. Mary Holmes to Ragland, September 21, 1948, f. 49, Martha Ragland Collection, University of Tennessee Special Collections, Knoxville (hereafter referred to as MRC).

87. Holmes to Ragland, September 19, 1948, f. 49, MRC.

88. Ragland to Taylor, October 8, 1948, f. 32, MRC. Ragland underscores some of the tension inherent in all coalition tickets, noting "repeated complaints that the men push Mr. Browning and neglect Mr. Kefauver."

89. Neese to Howard McGrath, October 25, 1948, box 14, EKP; Ragland to Edith Honks, September 14, 1948, f. 42, MRC.

90. Jennie Gardner to Marion, n.d., f. 50, MRC.

91. Gardner, "Political Leadership," 127. Also Kefauver to Leslie Biffle, September 27, 1948, box 8, EKP.

92. Despite having joined organizationally with the Dewey campaign forces, Republicans Acuff and Reece kept their distance from the presidential campaign because of civil rights. Asked for campaign literature by workers on the ground, Neese replied due to "complications regarding the National ticket, there would not be any literature." The reason why is not wholly clear, as Neese requested pamphlets from the Democratic Senatorial Committee advertising the achievements of the Truman administration and Democratic Senate candidates. It appears that the campaign lacked funds to continue production of its own literature and decided after Neese's request that it did not want materials linking Browning and Kefauver to the national ticket. Neese to R. L. Taylor, October 19, 1948, box 14, EKP; Neese to Biffle, October 5, 1948, box 9, EKP.

93. Holmes to Ragland, September 10, 1948, f. 50, MRC.

94. Key, *Southern Politics*, 451.

95. Smoot, *Cooper*, 78.

96. Chandler had resigned to become commissioner of Major League Baseball.

97. Nunn interview, 36; Schulman, *Global Kentuckian*, 79; Smoot, *Cooper*, 165–66. According to Louie Nunn, manager for the Republican Party's state campaign, the national party promised Cooper election day money as an incentive to run.

98. No formal mechanism existed to object to the party's choice, although members of the state party could have expressed their displeasure at the state committee meeting that selected Cooper. There is, as far as the author could determine, no evidence of open dissent or disapproval from party members of Cooper's selection. Had any dissent arisen, the nomination process would have been classified as contested for the purposes of table 4.2.

99. Jewell and Cunningham, *Kentucky Politics*, 79; Nunn interview, 20, 30–32.

100. Unknown author to John Sherman Cooper, n.d., box 863, John Sherman Cooper Papers, Wendell H. Ford Research Center and Public Policy Archives, University of Kentucky, Lexington (hereafter referred to as JCP). This appears to be a memorandum addressed to Cooper from Frederick Sontag, Cooper's campaign manager. See also memorandum, Sontag to Andrew Duncan, October 24, 1956, box 863, JCP.

101. Nunn interview, 61, 64. Also see unknown author to Cooper, n.d., box 863, JCP. Sontag established a special finance committee directing appeals to liberal Republicans as well as Democrats and Independents. The "George" referred to in the memo appears to be George Agree, chairman of the National Committee for

an Effective Congress, a center-left organization endorsing Democrats and liberal Republicans for the U.S. Senate during the 1956 election that also raised money nationally on their behalf. The liberal mayor of Cincinnati, Charles Taft, also helped the Cooper campaign financially. Nunn reports they had raised $50,000 (Nunn interview, 31). See also memorandum, Sontag to Mayor Taft, October 19, 1956, box 863, JCP; memorandum, Howard to Sheila, September 4, 1956, box 860, JCP.

102. Smoot, *Cooper*, v–vi, 30; Nunn interview, 119.

103. In his first Senate address, he opposed his party on tobacco price supports. See Smoot, *Cooper*, 114.

104. The entire state ticket was promoted, including congressional candidates. See John S. Greenebaum to Friends, n.d., box 864, JCP; "Eisenhower-Morton-Cooper," n.d., box 860, JCP; pamphlet, "Ike Plus Two," n.d., box 860, JCP; Rogers Morton to Andrew Duncan, October 26, 1956, box 860, JCP; pamphlet, "Here's What President Eisenhower Says," n.d., box 860, JCP.

105. Pamphlet, "For Distinguished Service," n.d., box 861, JCP; pamphlet, "John Sherman Cooper," n.d., box 861, JCP; Cooper to Friend, October 31, 1956, box 861, JCP; Cooper to Friend, November 1, 1956, box 861, JCP.

106. Pamphlet, "Cooper Gets Things Done for the People of Kentucky," n.d., box 861, JCP; pamphlet, "John Sherman Cooper"; Cooper to Friend, October 28, 1956, box 861, JCP. See also unknown author to Cooper. Cooper specifically sought out the names of influential Democrats and independents throughout Kentucky so he could write to appeal for their vote. Cooper to Sheridan Barnes, October 13, 1956, box 860, JCP.

107. Unknown author to Cooper; memorandum, "Points to Go Over with Senator," n.d., box 863, JCP.

108. Cooper to Friend, October 28, 1956, box 861, JCP; pamphlet, "The Working Man Likes John Sherman Cooper," n.d., box 861, JCP; pamphlet, "The True Friend of Coal Miners," n.d., box 861, JCP.

109. Pamphlet, "A Vote for Stevenson Is a Vote for Eastland," n.d., box 861, JCP.

110. Thruston Morton reported that Cooper believed "that no Republican in Kentucky could afford to become too partisan." Schulman, *Global Kentuckian*, 40.

111. Fenton, *Politics in the Border States*, 20.

112. Nunn interview, 95.

113. Cooper on rare occasion did plug his fellow Republican candidate Thruston Morton in his own literature and letters. Cooper to Friend, October 31, 1956, box 861, JCP. His staff, however, did not appear to like the idea. See Sontag to Duncan, October 20, 1956, box 863, JCP.

114. Cooper and Morton to Committeemen and Committeewomen, August 7, 1956, box 863, JCP; Cooper and Morton to Friend, October 17, 1956, box 863, JCP; memorandum, Sontag to Duncan, September 29, 1956, box 863, JCP; memorandum, Sontag to Don Cooper, September 19, 1956, box 863, JCP.

115. Nunn interview, 34, 94.

116. Both President Truman and Vice President Alben Barkley campaigned

with Lucas. See Deason, "Scott Lucas, Everett Dirksen," 33–51; Eckel, "Lucas' Re-election Linked to Freedom"; "Barkley Attacks GOP 'Isolation,'" *New York Times*; Eckel, "Lucas and Dirksen Run Nip-and-Tuck."

117. Deason, "Scott Lucas, Everett Dirksen," 33.

118. Schapsmeier and Schapsmeier, *Dirksen of Illinois*, 58.

119. Recall that in Idaho and Tennessee few county organizations had their own stationery. In Illinois, however, nearly all county and ward organizations had individual stationery listing the organization's officials. A good example is Cook County's, which lists not only all the officials but the entire Republican ticket from the state offices down to local offices. See Lorraine Ford Riley to Harold Rainville, August 23, 1950, Politics series, f. 222, Everett M. Dirksen Papers, Dirksen Congressional Center, Pekin, Illinois (hereafter referred to as EDP). Unless otherwise noted, all items cited can be found in the Politics series.

120. Dirksen, *The Education of a Senator*, 203–205, 217–18; Deason, "Scott Lucas, Everett Dirksen."

121. MacNeil, *Dirksen: Portrait of a Public Man*, 85; Schapsmeier and Schapsmeier, *Dirksen of Illinois*, 54. "Springfield and Chicago leaders and party workers are anxiously awaiting your announcement," wrote one supporter to Dirksen. Browel to Everett M. Dirksen, May 14, 1949, f. 15, EDP. See also Frank M. Kalteux to Dirksen, July 6, 1949, f. 23, EDP; William H. Reid to Dirksen, August 19, 1949, f. 32, EDP; Clarence N. Bergstrom to Dirksen, August 19, 1949, f. 32, EDP; Karl E. Mundt to Dirksen, April 27, 1949, f. 12, EDP.

122. Alban Weber to Dirksen, March 28, 1949, f. 12, EDP.

123. Ranney, *Illinois Politics*, 16.

124. Diana Brinkerhoff to Neighbor, n.d., f. 127, EDP; pamphlet, "Vote at the Republican Primary," n.d., Chicago Office series, f. 3884, EDP.

125. The seriousness of Dirksen's opposition can be gauged from a letter sent in late January 1950, apparently after the filing deadline had passed. The chairman of the National Republican Senatorial Committee wrote to Dirksen congratulating him on "escaping opposition in the primaries in Illinois." Owen Brewster to Dirksen, January 24, 1950, f. 96, EDP.

126. Schapsmeier and Schapsmeier, *Dirksen of Illinois*, 58.

127. This did cause some tension between the party and the Dirksen campaign. In particular, the party feared that an extensive fund-raising effort by Dirksen leading up to the primary would hamper the party's effort to raise money for the general election campaign. See Kent S. Clow to Harry Hedlund, October 27, 1949, f. 59, EDP; Clow to Dirksen, November 2, 1949, f. 62, EDP; Henry A. Gardner to Dirksen, November 14, 1949, f. 65, EDP. Harold Rainville, Dirksen's campaign manager, hoped to boost his candidate's general election prospects with a strong primary showing and to provide an insurance policy against the possibility the party would fail in its responsibilities during the fall campaign. Rainville's concerns probably stemmed from the party's poor showing in 1948. Rainville to Mrs. Peter "Bazy" Miller, February 13, 1950, Chicago Office series, f. 3899, EDP.

128. See Schwartz, *Party Network*, 38; Ranney, *Illinois Politics*; Harry J. Neumiller to J. E. Countryman, October 3, 1949, f. 50, EDP; Neumiller to Harold W. Osgood, March 30, 1950, f. 124, EDP.

129. George Williamson to Dirksen, May 5, 1950, f. 141, EDP; memorandum, "Budget," n.d., Chicago Office series, f. 3915, EDP.

130. Dreiske, "Capt. Dan's Advertising Missing Fire?" The headquarters of Dirksen for Senate campaign operated from 10 South LaSalle Street, as did the Executive Committee of Illinois Insurance Men for Dirksen, Irish-American Organizations for Everett M. Dirksen, and the Affiliated Home Owners and Taxpayers Action Committee for Dirksen, just to name a few. Andrew Helmick to Illinois Insurance Men, October 27, 1950, f. 309, EDP; cf. Dirksen to Friend, November 1, 1950, f. 319, EDP. Also Perry John Ten Hoor to Rainville, November 2, 1950, Chicago Office series, f. 3908, EDP.

131. See Charles M. Burgess to Dirksen, May 6, 1950, f. 141, EDP; Charles W. Vursell to Dirksen, June 11, 1950, f. 156, EDP; John W. Spence to Rainville, February 20, 1950, f. 119, EDP; Dirksen to various members of Republican congressional delegation, June 9, 1950, f. 156, EDP; Dirksen to various state and county candidates, July 1, 1950, f. 169, EDP; Dirksen to various state legislative candidates, various dates, fs. 180–82, EDP.

132. Kanady, "Lucas Is Man on Flying Trapeze, Dirksen Says." The Democrats also campaigned in this fashion. Governor Adlai Stevenson joined Lucas on the stump, and junior Senator Paul Douglas toured the state on behalf of Lucas during the last six weeks of the campaign. See Tagge, "Douglas Ready to Stump for Lucas' Election."

133. Vernon L. Nickell to Dirksen, July 13, 1950, f. 178, EDP.

134. Clow to Rainville, June 8, 1950, f. 155, EDP; Clow to Rainville July 6, 1950, f. 173, EDP.

135. Riley to Rainville, October 11, 1949, f. 52, EDP.

136. Rainville to Peyton Berbling, June 15, 1950, f. 159, EDP; Rainville to John B. Anderson, April 27, 1950, Chicago Office series, f. 3903, EDP. Other statewide candidates also sent schedules and appearance commitments to Dirksen headquarters to aid in coordination. See Nickell to Dirksen, July 13, 1950, Politics series, f. 178, EDP.

137. Dirksen to Fred A. Burt, June 1, 1950, f. 150, EDP. The major exception was a direct mail campaign launched by the various "independent" Dirksen for Senate committees and targeted at particular business and ethnic groups.

138. Logan, "GOP Earmarking $30 for Each Precinct Here"; "GOP Precinct Captains to Go to Rally Friday," *Chicago Tribune*.

139. Dreiske, "Local GOP Hires a Drum Beater." Apparently, other county organizations also hired public relations consultants. See Warren L. Anderson to Dirksen, August 9, 1950, f. 210, EDP.

140. For example, pamphlet, "Everett M. Dirksen," n.d., f. 159, EDP; pamphlet, "50th Ward Regular Organization," n.d., f. 323, EDP.

141. "Everett Dirksen for U.S. Senator" surrounded an inner circle on the button with the inscription "Vote Republican." Dirksen Campaign Button, n.d., box 169, f. 1, Scott W. Lucas Papers, Illinois State Historical Library, Springfield.

142. Joseph F. Novotny to Neighbor, November 3, 1950, f. 323, EDP; pamphlet, "Do Not Forget These Candidates They Merit Your Support," n.d., f. 323, EDP; pamphlet, "Welcome to Our Annual Picnic," n.d., f. 579, EDP; pamphlet, "The Illinois Republican Reporter," August–October 1950, f. 586, EDP.

143. Pamphlet, "1950 Republican Citizens Finance Committee of Illinois," n.d., box 179, f. 2, Scott W. Lucas Papers. The committee hoped to raise $700,000 for the party's statewide campaign.

144. Fitzpatrick, "1,500 Women Rally behind GOP Crusade."

145. See various radio scripts, n.d., Chicago Office series, f.3885, EDP.

146. Schapsmeier and Schapsmeier, *Dirksen of Illinois*, 59; Deason, "Scott Lucas, Everett Dirksen," 45.

147. *Congress and the Nation, 1945–1964*, 11.

148. Tagge, "Republicans Blast Foreign Policy Bungles"; Dreiske, "GOP Sidetracks Red Issue."

149. Tagge, "Lucas Campaign Is Called Most Lavish in the State"; Deason, "Scott Lucas, Everett Dirksen," 35–36. The notable exception is the president's health care plan, which Lucas openly advertised he did not support. See Deason, "Scott Lucas, Everett Dirksen," 37.

150. For the 85th and 86th Congress, party unity scores as reported by *Congressional Quarterly* in its annual almanacs were used. Unlike the late nineteenth century, absenteeism resulting from transportation difficulties is less likely, so scores uncorrected for absences are employed. Before the 85th Congress, *CQ* does not consistently report unadjusted party unity scores. Using Senate roll call data obtained from ICPSR, uncorrected party unity scores were created for the 77th through the 84th Congress using the *CQ* definition as a guide. See Interuniversity Consortium for Political and Social Research, United States Congressional Roll Call Voting Records, 1789–1990, parts 1–202. Data can be obtained at the ICPSR website. The definition of party unity can be found in chapter 3.

151. This also differs from the measure employed in chapter 3. Dilatory motions, used to delay House procedures in the late nineteenth century, created many votes with fewer than ten members voting. This was not a problem in the Senate between 1941 and 1961, as dilatory motions were procedures used in the House, and all unity votes had a substantial portion of the membership participating.

152. The analysis was run with those senators serving incomplete terms included and a dummy variable indicating that fact. The dummy variable was significant and negative (not a surprise), but the results reported in table 4.3 did not change either significantly or substantially.

153. See chapter 3 for a review of variable construction.

154. Third party house members are excluded from the calculation.

155. Again, OLS regression is employed, with unstandardized coefficients and robust standard errors reported in table 4.3.

156. Previous unity and state partisanship are both associated with high levels of party unity among senators, while seniority, running for reelection, representing the South, and serving as a member of the minority party all correspond with lower levels of unity voting. Margin of victory and party affiliation are both insignificant, and other than the decline in unity among southerners, the results appear substantially similar to those presented in chapter 3. Unlike the late nineteenth century, southern Democrats and the North did not see eye to eye on social issues, especially on civil rights. The national leadership had moved decisively to the left during the New Deal, and a conservative coalition between southern Democrats and Republicans emerged. This is widely documented in the literature. For example, see Key, *Southern Politics*, chaps. 16 and 17.

CHAPTER 5

1. Sorauf, "Power, Money, and Responsibility"; Silbey, "From 'Essential to the Existence'"; Herrnson, "National Party Organizations"; Salmore and Salmore, *Candidates, Parties, and Campaigns*; Sabato, *Rise of Political Consultants*.

2. Sorauf, "Power, Money, and Responsibility," 84.

3. Epstein, *Political Parties in the American Mold*, 123.

4. Kolodny, *Pursuing Majorities*, 125; Herrnson, "National Party Organizations."

5. Agranoff, *New Style in Election Campaigns*.

6. The years 1970 and 1972 hold the record for lowest percentage of party unity votes between 1953 and 2003: 27 percent. Ornstein, Mann, and Malbin, *Vital Statistics on Congress, 2001–2002*, 201.

7. The average unity is based on the party unity scores calculated by the author and utilized in chapter 3. The percentage of total unity votes between 1886 and 1900 is provided by Brady, Cooper, and Hurley, "The Decline of Party in the U.S. House of Representatives, 1887–1968."

8. Salmore and Salmore, *Candidates, Parties, and Campaigns*.

9. For examples, see Sorauf, "Power, Money, and Responsibility," 84–85; Herrnson, *Congressional Elections*, 146–49.

10. Cotter et al., *Party Organizations in American Politics*; Herrnson and Dwyre, "Party Issue Advocacy"; Kayden and Mahe, *Party Goes On*; La Raja, "Political Parties in the Soft Money Era"; Herrnson, *Party Campaigning in the 1980s*; Herrnson, "National Party Organizations"; Pomper, "Alleged Decline of American Parties"; and Blumberg, Binning, and Green, "Do the Grassroots Matter?" See Coleman, "Resurgent or Just Busy?" for a dissenting view.

11. La Raja, "Political Parties in the Soft Money;" Blumberg, Binning, and Green, "Do the Grassroots Matter?"

12. This section draws upon Parker and Coleman, "Pay to Play," 136–41.

13. Kolodny, *Pursuing Majorities*, 127.

14. PACs are the campaign finance arm of corporations, unions, and groups but are legally separate from these organizations. A corporation cannot directly contribute to a House candidate, for example, but the corporation can establish a PAC, and that PAC can contribute.

15. For more extensive information about the reforms and the changes they underwent, see Corrado, "Money and Politics."

16. *Buckley v. Valeo* 424 U.S. 1 (1976).

17. Corrado, "Money and Politics, 43n52.

18. For example, *FEC v. Massachusetts Citizens for Life, Inc.* 470 U.S. 238 (1986); *Austin v. Michigan State Chamber of Commerce* 494 U.S. 652 (1990).

19. SUN PAC also allowed corporations to form limitless numbers of PACs, each with its own $5,000 maximum individual contribution limit. The 1976 amendments to FECA changed this by summing the total contributions across an organization's PACs and applying the statue's PAC maximum contribution amount per election to that total. Even if a corporation had thirty PACs, it could still contribute no more than $5,000 total to an individual candidate.

20. Sorauf, "Political Action Committees," 124.

21. Corrado, "Money and Politics." When the original 1974 amendments were drafted, House Republicans had expressed concern about their effect on political parties in a minority report. They felt that the new regulations would undermine the traditional role of political parties in the American system. See Committee on House Administration, *Federal Election Campaign Act Amendments of 1974*.

22. New Mexico Democratic Party, "NM/NMDP Wilson Wild Punches," a storyboard provided by the Wisconsin Advertising Project.

23. *Colorado Republican Federal Campaign Committee v. Federal Election Commission* 518 U.S. 604 (1996).

24. In June 2001, the Court in *FEC v. Colorado Republican Federal Campaign Committee* upheld the coordinated expenditure restrictions contained in FECA (533 U.S. 431 2001).

25. Why did FECA change the resource balance for political actors when so many other campaign finance reforms had not? The establishment of an agency responsible solely for enforcement of its provisions, fines for violations, strict public disclosure regulations holding political committees responsible for violations, and the elimination of multiple candidate committees gave FECA teeth. Unlike the earlier reform efforts, the high costs of noncompliance imposed by these features forced political actors to change how they gathered and dispersed resources.

26. Herrnson, "The Revitalization of National Party Organizations"; Sabato, *PAC Power*.

27. Ornstein, Mann, and Malbin, *Vital Statistics on Congress, 2001–2002*, 99–105.

28. Herrnson, *Party Campaigning in the 1980s*, 123.

29. One might argue that the power of parties rested on the willingness of interest groups to use parties as conduits of influence. Marianne Holt wonders "how many party leaders become indebted to large soft-money donors because of their contributions." Holt, "Surge in Party Money," 37. What effect do the increasingly

close connections between interest groups and parties have on partisan reputa-tions? If interest groups affect how parties communicate issue advantages to the public, then one might see party reputations vary greatly nationally. Interest groups, in short, would pull parties to tailor their advertising and reputations to match their own interests. As will become clear at the end of the chapter, this does not seem to be the case. The Republican Party and its candidates universally pre-ferred economic and tax themes, while the Democratic Party and its candidates fo-cused on entitlements.

30. Franz and Goldstein, "Following the (Soft) Money," 145, 151.

31. For example, see Herrnson and Dwyre, "Party Issue Advocacy."

32. Herrnson, *Party Campaigning*, 60.

33. Franz and Goldstein, "Following the (Soft) Money," 145.

34. Cox and McCubbins, *Legislative Leviathan*.

35. Franz and Goldstein, "Following the (Soft) Money," 149.

36. Petrocik, "Issue Ownership."

37. Baden and Hamburger, "Political Consulting."

38. Sorauf, "Power, Money, and Responsibility," 89.

39. Bibby, "State Party Organizations," 37–42; Herrnson, "National Party Or-ganizations"; La Raja, "Political Parties in the Soft Money Era"; Blumberg, Binning, and Green, "Do the Grassroots Matter?" According to Frank Sorauf, FECA's main effect is the "functional fragmentation of political parties" with "each party com-mittee and each organized group of party officeholders increasingly stand[ing] by itself . . . funded by itself, and . . . largely responsible to itself." Sorauf, "Power, Money, and Responsibility," 93–94. Sorauf underestimates the centripetal effects of soft money transfers on the national state party nexus.

40. Formerly known as *Congressional Quarterly Weekly Report*. As before, party unity ranges from 0 to 100 percent, and the score used is the session average.

41. Stratmann, "Congressional Voting over Legislative Careers," 670.

42. A Durbin-Watson test run on the following regression models prior to the addition of the previous unity variable was inconclusive regarding the presence of autocorrelation. The previous unity variable helps alleviate a portion of the problem should serially correlated errors be present. See Neter, Kutner, Nacht-sheim, and Wasserman, *Applied Linear Regression*, chapter 12. See chapter 3 for the construction and discussion of this variable.

43. Using *America Votes*, the third party vote cast in each district was tallied and divided by the districtwide vote total for Congress. This total included all candi-dates running under a third party label, as well as those candidates listed as in-dependent if they received five hundred votes or more.

44. There may be no relationship if TPO is a poor measure of current party de-velopment. Again, this should be of little concern since TPO is a measure of broad party institutionalization that changes gradually rather than abruptly over time.

45. Cotter et al., *Party Organizations in American Politics*.

46. See chapter 3 and Mayhew, *Placing Parties*.

47. "TPO*State Partisanship" is an interaction term. Basically, all this means is TPO is multiplied by State Partisanship, and this additional term is included in the regression.

48. One seat was vacant due to Robert Menendez's appointment to the Senate.

49. As one example, the Republican senators representing these three regions as defined by the National Election Study in the 94th through the 107th Congress voted consistently to the left of their western and southern colleagues. Their average NOMINATE score was .187 compared with .396 for all other Republicans. The difference is statistically significant (p < .001, one-tailed test).

50. To create the state partisanship variable, the mean NOMINATE score for all Democratic and Republican House members between 1976 and 2000 was computed. Next, each state congressional delegation's NOMINATE average in the previous session was calculated separately for Republicans and Democrats. Those state delegations falling below the mean of the absolute distance between the delegation and its party's national averages were coded as ideologically close to the national party. Those above the mean were coded as far from the national party. This measure controls for the apparent relationship between organizational strength and the ideological distinctiveness of northeastern Republicans uncovered in bivariate analysis (not included here).

51. As before, the possibility of heteroscedasticity is present. A Cook-Weisberg test unambiguously indicated that this is a problem, so Huber-White robust standard errors are reported in this table.

52. Using candidate summary files obtained from the Federal Elections Commission and ICPSR, a variable was created representing the party's contributions to each member of Congress and the coordinated expenditures made on the candidate's behalf. As financial figures prior to 1984 seemed unreliable upon inspection, the analysis is restricted to 1984 through 2000 in models two and three. Candidate summary files between 1992 and 2000 can be downloaded. Files from cycles before 1992 are available from ICPSR. The files used are titled "Campaign Expenditures in the United States," with each file covering a separate election cycle between 1984 and 2000.

53. Soft money statistics are not readily available from the FEC, so the dummy variable was constructed. In 1992, the six national party committees disbursed more than $79 million in soft money. This nearly tripled in 1996 to $271 million. See Ornstein, Mann, and Malbin, *Vital Statistics on Congress: 1999–2000*.

54. The stability of the model is demonstrated by the fact that nearly all the control variables retain the level of significance and sign direction when compared with the baseline model.

55. Party unity does increase in general between 1974 and 2000, so how do we know that there are not other factors besides party financing that are responsible? There are three other plausible explanations for the increase in party unity: the capture of the South by the GOP, which removes a significant conservative element from the Democratic Party; the creation of fewer and fewer competitive

House districts courtesy of increasingly sophisticated gerrymandering; and structural changes in the House itself that encourage more unity among members. The biggest factor is probably the arrival of the GOP South, which is controlled for by the inclusion of the South variable. The measure of marginality—district vote percentage—helps control for the appearance of fewer competitive districts throughout the period. The one factor that is not easily addressed is the subcommittee reforms undertaken in the early 1970s, which gave the leadership increased power over individual members. As these changes took place at the same time that FECA passed, it is plausible that these reforms and not FECA are responsible for the increase in party unity.

56. These data were obtained from a joint project of the Brennan Center for Justice at New York University School of Law and Professor Kenneth Goldstein of the University of Wisconsin–Madison, and includes media tracking data from the Campaign Media Analysis Group in Washington, D.C. The Brennan Center–Wisconsin project was sponsored by a grant from the Pew Charitable Trusts. The opinions expressed in this article are those of the author and do not necessarily reflect the views of the Brennan Center, Professor Goldstein, or the Pew Charitable Trusts. A full description of these data is available at the Wisconsin Advertising Project website. For a full discussion of WAP data mechanics, see Goldstein and Freedman, "New Evidence for New Arguments"; Goldstein and Freedman, "Campaign Advertising and Voter Turnout." The validity and reliability of WAP data are detailed in Ridout, Franz, Goldstein, and Freedman, "Measure the Nature and Effects of Campaign Advertising." Information on the date and time of commercial airings, the location of airings, and cost estimates for each advertisement were obtained by the WAP from the Campaign Media Analysis Group (CMAG). WAP coders provide contextual information, such as sponsor type, ad tone, and issue content by examining a storyboard of each advertisement provided by CMAG.

57. The CMAG coding does not distinguish between local, state, and national party committees, so the total advertising expenditure variable includes ads sponsored by all these committees.

58. According to Franz and Goldstein, "CMAG estimates the cost of an ad buy on the basis of market and cost of a regular advertisement in a particular time slot." Franz and Goldstein, "Following the (Soft) Money," 143. They caution, however, that the CMAG underestimates the actual money spent on ads since "in the heat of an election . . . television stations tend to overcharge parties and candidates." Any connection uncovered between party advertising expenditures and party unity voting should actually *understate* the true effects of the relationship.

59. With only 413 cases, many of the relationships previously observed are no longer significant.

60. There are two conflicting accounts of whether parties can buy member loyalty. See Cantor and Herrnson, "Party Campaign Activity"; Leyden and Borrelli, "Party Contributions and Party Unity: Can Loyalty Be Bought?"

61. Rothenberg, "Rothenberg's 1998 Senate Ratings."

62. Federal Election Commission, "Party Support for Senate Campaigns—1998."

63. "The Soft-Money Dodge in 1998," *New York Times.*

64. Kolodny, *Pursuing Majorities*, chaps. 4 and 5.

65. The correlation is .43 and is significant (p < =.001, two-tailed).

66. Franz and Goldstein, "Following the (Soft) Money," 151, table 7.7.

67. The races are the forty-six House seats identified by political commentator Charles Cook as competitive. See Franz and Goldstein, "Following the (Soft) Money," 162n9.

68. Abrams, "Unlikely Rebels Make Life Difficult for GOP Leaders"; Killian, *Freshmen.*

69. Leonard, "Ex-Coach Jennings Seeks Seat in Indiana: Candidate for House Is Former Clinton Aide"; Salvato, "National Briefing South."

70. Merida, "Agony with Little Ecstasy."

71. The author is grateful to John Pitney for suggesting this dynamic.

72. Stratmann, "Congressional Voting over Legislative Careers," 666.

73. VandeHei and Eilperin, "GOP Leaders Tighten Hold in the House."

74. Mayhew, "Congressional Elections: The Case of the Vanishing Marginals."

75. *Baker v. Carr* 369 U.S. 186 (1962).

76. Cox and Katz, *Elbridge Gerry's Salamander.*

77. Cain, MacDonald, and McDonald. "From Equality to Fairness," 28–30.

78. Edsall, "Contests over Legislative Power Turning into Political Street Fights"; Roberts, "Fight for Legislature Stirs National Action"; Janofsky, "Redistricting Puts Fire into Legislative Races."

79. Broder, "No Vote Necessary."

80. "Making Votes Count," *New York Times.*

81. But see Oppenheimer, "Deep Red and Blue Congressional Districts." Oppenheimer argues that residential self-selection might be the chief cause of the decline in marginal house districts.

82. Cain, MacDonald, and McDonald, "From Equality to Fairness," 21.

83. Ibid., 20.

84. "Judge Pickering, Arlen Specter, and More," *Weekly Standard.*

85. Hayes, "A Challenger Haunts Specter."

86. Kingdon, *Agendas, Alternatives, and Public Policies*, 3.

87. Geer, "Campaigns, Party Competition, and Political Advertising."

88. Herrnson and Dwyre, "Party Issue Advocacy."

89. As each advertisement in the WAP data has a time/date stamp indicating when it aired, it is easy to distinguish between latching and bolstering.

90. Unfortunately, with the exception of the seven specific items lumped into the other issue theme, other literally means *other* as this category was not broken down into more specific issue content types by the WAP. See appendix A for additional information.

91. The issue statements provided to WAP coders are detailed in appendix A, in addition to a breakdown of the specific issue statements included in each issue theme category.

92. The 2000 WAP data covered 168 congressional races. The sample is fairly representative, with a slight bias toward competitive races and against districts in the northeastern and mid-Atlantic states. As congressional campaigns in urban areas air fewer ads (since the media markets are inefficient), this is sensible. In 2000, the average winning margin of victory in all House races was 41 percent. The winning candidate received 68 percent of the vote. In the WAP sample, the average margin was only 28 percent, but the vote received is closer to the national mean at 62 percent. In 2000, 399 House incumbents were reelected: 200 Democrats, 197 Republicans, and 2 independents. There were 36 seats open. The WAP data include 32 open seats, 55 with Democratic incumbents, and 87 with Republican incumbents. Republican incumbents and open seats are overrepresented at the expense of races with Democratic incumbents. Although slightly tilted against the Mid-Atlantic and Northeast, the congressional sample drawn by the WAP is fairly representative regionally: 30 percent of the congressional districts are in the South, 27 percent in the West, 26 percent in the Midwest, and 17 percent in the Mid-Atlantic and Northeast. Nationally, the breakdown was, respectively, 29, 25, 24, and 22 percent. The focus of the WAP on the top 75 media markets, however, probably seriously underrepresents rural congressional districts.

93. Geer, "Campaigns, Party Competition, and Political Advertising."

94. Democratic Congressional Campaign Committee, "MI/DCCC Rogers Nursing Homes," a storyboard provided by the Wisconsin Advertising Project.

95. Minnesota Republican Party, "MN/MNGOP Luther Attack Ads," a storyboard provided by the Wisconsin Advertising Project.

96. See Petrocik, "Issue Ownership."

97. Franz and Goldstein, "Following the (Soft) Money," 147, fig. 7.4.

98. This, quite possibly, was the result of conscious issue inoculation by incumbents fearful of Democratic attacks on this issue.

99. Calculated by the author from the data used for the analysis in this chapter.

100. These thirty-one races were the most competitive in 2000. In the WAP data set, the margin of victory was less than 5 percent in twenty races (12 percent) and less than 10 percent in forty-three (26 percent). Twenty-two of the races where both parties and their respective candidates spent money had margins of victory less than 10 percent (71 percent), fourteen with margins less than 5 percent (45 percent). Twenty-six percent (forty-three candidates) of the WAP sample saw candidates win with less than 55 percent of the vote; seventy-eight candidates (46 percent) won with less than 60 percent. All thirty-one of the races where both parties and their respective candidates spent money had the winner taking less than 60 percent of the vote; twenty-three (74 percent) received less than 55 percent.

101. Herrnson and Dwyre, "Party Issue Advocacy."

102. If the number one issue theme mention was biography for either the candidate or party, then the most frequently mentioned issue theme used for this cal-

culation was the top issue theme other than biography or personal. The goal is to assess the issue agenda in terms of policy alternatives rather than personal characteristics.

103. Barone and Cohen, *Almanac of American Politics 2002*, 389.

104. Lierman lost to Connie Morrella by eight points, while Capito bested Humphreys by two.

CHAPTER 6

1. Ridout, "Presidential Primary Front-Loading"; Johnston, Blais, Brady, and Crete, *Letting the People Decide*; Bartels, *Presidential Primaries and the Dynamics of Public Choice*; Gelman and King, "Why Are American Presidential Election Campaign Polls So Variable"; Popkin, *Reasoning Voter*; Zaller, *Mass Opinion*; Layman and Carsey, "Party Polarization and 'Conflict Extension' in the American Electorate"; Spiliotes and Vavreck, "Campaign Advertising"; Petrocik, "Issue Ownership."

2. Ansolabehere and Iyengar, *Going Negative*; Finkel and Geer, "A Spot Check"; Freedman and Goldstein, "Measuring Media Exposure and the Effects of Negative Campaign Ads"; Lau and Pomper, "Accentuating the Negative?"; Lau and Sigelman, "Effectiveness of Political Advertising"; Wattenberg and Brians, "Negative Campaign Advertising"; Goldstein and Freedman, "New Evidence for New Arguments"; Goldstein and Freedman, "Campaign Advertising and Voter Turnout"; Kahn and Kenney, "How Negative Campaigning Enhances Knowledge of Senate Elections"; Coleman and Parker, "Congressional Campaign Spending and Election Involvement."

3. Coleman and Manna, "Congressional Campaign Spending and the Quality of Democracy."

4. But see Zaller, *Mass Opinion*.

5. Two of the foundational voting behavior texts conclude that while social structure, demographic characteristics, and partisan affiliation are the primary factors guiding vote choice, campaigns could also play a role. Berelson and his colleagues found that cross-pressured individuals—that is, those belonging to multiple social groups with conflicting political preferences—tend to be less consistent in their vote choice throughout the campaign and to make up their minds later than those belonging to politically homogenous social groups. Berelson, Lazarsfeld, and McPhee, *Voting*, 129–31. It is the cross-pressured and less interested voters who find themselves less rooted by their social obligations and hence more likely to be buffeted by campaign winds. In *The American Voter*, Campbell and his fellow authors found that Eisenhower overcame a decided Democratic numerical advantage by projecting a strong personal image and stressing the foreign policy concerns of voters. This allowed less attached and less interested Democratic adherents to overcome their predispositions and cast a vote for Eisenhower.

6. Johnston et al., *Letting the People Decide*, 4.

7. Popkin, *Reasoning Voter*, 15.

8. Ibid., 51; Gelman and King, "Why Are American Presidential Election Campaign Polls So Variable."

9. Faucheux, "Writing Your Campaign Plan."

10. For example, the Capito ad titled "Jobs" attacked Humphreys for supporting the expansion of federal government and new taxes to pay for it.

11. Basu, "Shelley Moore Capito's Uphill Climb."

12. Fenno's work illustrates the point. Congressmen and senators develop a presentation of self to communicate their work in Washington to particular constituencies back home. Fenno, *Home Style*; Fenno, *Senators on the Campaign Trail*. In so doing, members of Congress feel that by simply making the folks back home understand how their time in Washington benefits them, they will be rewarded with reelection.

13. Put differently, political actors provide "the contextual information needed to translate their values into support for particular policies or candidates." Zaller, *Mass Opinion*, 25.

14. Although this book does not examine the tone of political advertisements specifically, negative advertising is an important part of developing a candidate's reputation resources. Political parties and candidates use negative advertisements to paint a picture of their opponents, typically on a set of issues, to either persuade supporters of the other candidate to jump ship on Election Day or to remind their own supporters of the risks of refusing to stand pat. For example, negative ads might be used by the Democratic Party to link a candidate to the party's brand—and perhaps that party brand is not favorable among the voting public at the moment. The candidate might wish to find a way to avoid the party brand name (as Republicans are presently doing in the 2006 midterm) or to co-opt the issue reputations of the other candidate and party to inoculate themselves from these attacks. Co-option is an important part of branding and is discussed below.

15. Popkin, *Reasoning Voter*, 51.

16. Petrocik, "Issue Ownership."

17. Wattenberg, *Decline of American Political Parties*, 61, table 4.4.

18. Scholars have found evidence that parties have shifted their mobilization efforts over the past four decades, emphasizing likely voters and committed partisans rather than independents and nonvoters. See Goldstein and Ridout, "The Politics of Participation."

19. Coleman, "Party Images and Candidate-Centered Campaigns in 1996"; Franklin, "Eschewing Obfuscation?"

20. The introduction of substantially similar variables into a regression equation creates the possibility of multicollinearity. This is certainly the case with four spending variables. Standard multicollinearity tests fell within acceptable limits.

21. See chapter 5 for discussion of WAP data scope, method of collection, and representativeness of the 2000 congressional campaign.

22. Any study examining the nexus between money and campaign outcomes needs to grapple with endogeneity. See Green and Krasno, "Rebuttal to Jacobson's 'New Evidence for Old Arguments'"; Jacobson, "Effects of Campaign Spending in

House Elections: New Evidence for Old Arguments"; Coleman and Manna, "Congressional Campaign Spending." Endogenous predictors bias regression coefficients; the corrective remedy is to employ an instrument of party unity purged of the endogenous component. Using a two-stage procedure, four sets of spending instruments were created. The correlation between the original spending variables and the instruments generated by the two-stage procedure are Democratic Party spending .610, Republican Party spending .699, Democratic candidate spending .732, and Republican candidate spending .629.

23. Poole and Rosenthal, *Common Space Scores for the 1st through the 107th Congress*, Common space scores are essentially a measure of ideology that are related to NOMINATE scores. Common space scores are used instead of the more common D- or DW-NOMINATE values because of the need to estimate the ideology of challengers, as they allow direct comparisons between House and Senate members. D- or DW-NOMINATE values do not.

24. Berry, Ringquist, Fording, and Hanson, "Measuring Citizen and Government Ideology in the American States, 1960–93." A mean common space score for both the Democratic and Republican parties in each state was calculated from the mean of each party's House delegation. This state party common space mean is used as the challenger's ideology score. If the challenger's party holds none of the state's House seats, the mean value of the party's Senate delegation was substituted. As D-NOMINATE and DW-NOMINATE scores are not comparable across chambers, this explains the need for common space scores. See "Description of NOMINATE Data." Finally, in a few instances, the challenger's party holds neither of the state's Senate seats. In these instances, the mean common space score of his party's House or Senate delegation from the nearest state with a similar political culture serves as the challenger's ideology score. This procedure is far from ideal. Perhaps the best solution is to use the donations made by interest groups to calculate challenger NOMINATE scores. See Franz, "Choices and Changes: Interest Groups in the Electoral Process."

25. Very conservative or liberal is defined as being more than one standard deviation from the party's mean.

26. See Coleman, "Party Images and Candidate-Centered Campaigns."

27. "Politics not complicated" ranges from zero (politics very complicated) to three (politics not complicated at all). The "Political knowledge index" is composed of six objective questions of political fact and is simply the number answered correctly by the respondent. People were asked six questions: which party has the most seats in the House of Representatives, which party has the most seats in the Senate, and who is the majority leader of the Senate, the chief justice of the Supreme Court, the attorney general, and the prime minister of the United Kingdom. Correct responses are coded as one; all else (including don't know) are coded as zero. "Attention to campaign" is how closely the respondent followed the congressional campaign in his district, ranging from not very much (zero) to very much (two). Finally, the "Education-candidate ideology" variable is an interaction between a candidate's ideology score and the respondent's level of education.

Individuals who are more educated are more likely to know a candidate's issue stances, hence the inclusion of the interaction term controlling for this effect. As education alone, theoretically, exhibits no clear independent relationship to whether an individual perceives a larger or smaller gap between a party and its candidate, it is not included separately in the regression equation. This follows from Coleman, "Party Images and Candidate-Centered Campaigns."

28. As the variables in the regression equation represent different levels of analysis (individual and congressional district), heterogeneity becomes a possible issue. Therefore, robust standard errors are reported.

29. This confirms the findings of Coleman, "Party Images and Candidate-Centered Campaigns."

30. See Popkin, *Reasoning Voter*, 51–71.

31. Actually, there are ten issue categories, only nine of which are displayed in figures 6.5–6.10. The final category consists of respondent likes and dislikes about the party referencing candidates or individuals. This category had no clear counterpart to the Wisconsin Advertising Project's coding scheme and seemed significantly different from the responses included in the miscellaneous category to merit its own classification. This category is excluded from the figures for the sake of clarity; including it would have no bearing on the substantive interpretation of the results.

32. As the candidate representing the incumbent administration, how did Gore not have an advantage of economic issues considering the existence of a budget surplus and unprecedented economic prosperity? Gore actively disassociated himself from Clinton, and perhaps as a result, he suffered at the hands of the voters on economic issues. Republicans, on the other hand, argued that while economic times were good, they could be even better, especially if the surplus were given back to the taxpayers.

33. Key, *Public Opinion and American Democracy*, 2.

34. Appendix B details the conversion of the NES likes and dislikes into the Wisconsin Advertising Project's issue themes employed in chapter 5.

35. The mean and standard deviation of the economic advantage variable are .105 and .899, respectively. The mean and standard deviation are .092 and .686, respectively, for the entitlement advantage variable.

36. This is similar to a procedure adopted by Coleman and Parker, "Congressional Campaign Spending and Election Involvement."

37. "Clinton job approval" ranges from strong approval (zero) to strong disapproval (four).

38. The guaranteed jobs and health care trade-off questions are coded from zero to four, with zero being the liberal (pro-intervention, pro-government health care) response. The entitlement measure is certainly broader than health care, as it includes welfare and Social Security issues. The NES does not provide good measures tapping respondent opinion in these areas. There is a question asking whether the surplus should be used to shore up Social Security and Medicare, but this seems to be a question about economic and budget policy rather than entitle-

ments. Inclusion of this variable in the entitlement equation does not substantially alter the reported results, as the variable is statistically insignificant from zero.

39. The Most Important Master Code distribution for the economic and entitlement advantage variables is as follows: Economic Advantage: 010, 013, 400–453, 491, 496, 498, 499; Entitlement Advantage: 010, 020, 030, 035, 040, 050, 060, 090, 091, 092. If respondents mentioned that an economic or entitlement issue was the most important problem, then the appropriate variable was coded as one. If no concern was mentioned, a don't know was given, or some other concern besides economic or entitlement was forthcoming, the variables were coded zero.

40. Kiewiet, *Macroeconomics and Micropolitics*; Kramer, "Short-Term Fluctuations in U.S. Voting Behavior, 1896–1964."

41. The economic variables are scored from zero to four, with positive values indicating an increasing dissatisfaction with the state of the national or their personal economic situation. The personal and national economy variables should be positive in the economic reputation equation and negative in the entitlement equation.

42. The RCCC charged that "Maloney voted against cutting the marriage tax penalty and the death tax." It also claimed that "Maloney was the principal architect of the effort to slap an 8% sales tax on gasoline." See "CT/NRCC Maloney Skyrocketing Taxes," a storyboard provided by and available from the Wisconsin Advertising Project.

43. See "CT DCCC Maloney Voted against Taxes," a storyboard provided by and available from the Wisconsin Advertising Project.

44. Although I generally do not place much stock in the R-squared statistic, it does offer the reader a guide to how much variance the regression model explains. In this case, the R-squared of .08 is quite low when compared with the R-squared of .21 obtained in the economic reputation model, meaning the entitlements model does not explain much variance. First, there simply is not much variance to explain: a bulk of respondents view both parties neutrally on economic and entitlement concerns (see Key, *Public Opinion and American Democracy*). Second, although the 2000 NES has several nice measures tapping economic concerns of voters, there are few tracking entitlements such as Social Security, Medicare, or education, thereby making the resulting model less robust.

45. Co-opting is most important in the districts where parties are apt to concentrate resources: competitive districts.

46. Political knowledge and the state of national economy also influenced issue assessments. The politically knowledgeable had no trouble identifying the parties' issue strengths; this fact should be comforting to candidates, party strategists, and democratic theorists. Among those with increased political awareness, Republicans scored better on the economy and Democrats on entitlements. Americans, if sufficiently tuned in, can evaluate the terms of the issue debate in the way that political actors desire. Individual assessment of the nation's economic health also affects how respondents evaluate the parties on economic and entitlement issues. Those who are unhappy with the country's financial health saw the Republicans

as better on economic and entitlement issues. Other demographic, candidate, and issue characteristics show no statistical relationship to economic or entitlement issue advantage.

47. For a review, see Aldrich, Sullivan, and Borgida, "Foreign Affairs and Issue Voting"; Kinder, "Communication and Opinion."

48. Little is known about the feeling thermometer measure because it has received scant scholarly attention. See Weisberg and Rusk, "Dimensions of Candidate Evaluation"; Wilcox, Sigelman, and Cook, "Some Like It Hot"; Wlezein, "A Note on the Endogeneity of Ideological Placements of Government Institutions."

49. The trust index is created from the following questions: How much of the time can you trust the government? Would you say the government pretty much is run by a few big interests? Do you think people in government waste a lot of money? Do you think that quite a few people running the government are crooked? All variables were recoded from less to more trusting. The resulting index ranges from zero to twenty-four, with higher values indicating greater trust.

50. Exit polls for the 2000 election were conducted by the now-defunct Voter News Service. The results presented here were obtained from MSNBC.com.

51. According to the WAP, contrast or attack advertisements constituted 87 percent of Republican Party ads during the 2000 campaign, compared with 85 percent for the Democrats. This is a slight difference, but perhaps it is substantially significant considering the dataset contains more than 50,000 party ads from the 2000 congressional campaign.

52. Gelman and King, "Why Are American Presidential Election Campaign Polls So Variable."

CHAPTER 7

1. Krasno and Goldstein, "The Facts about Television Advertising and the McCain-Feingold Bill"; Krasno and Selz, *Buying Time.*

2. Levin funds are the notable exception. According to the Campaign Finance Legal Center website, "Levin funds are contributions to state, district, or local political party committees that are permitted under federal law for specific purposes and are limited to $10,000 per year per donor, so long as allowed by state law. If state law allows, they can come from sources ordinarily impermissible under federal law, like corporations or labor unions. . . . Levin funds may only be spent in conjunction with federal funds and may not be used to pay for broadcast advertising."

3. BCRA defines electioneering communications as "any broadcast, cable, or satellite communication which . . . refers to a clearly identified candidate for federal office . . . [and] is made within 60 days before a general, special, or runoff election for the office sought by the candidate or . . . 30 days before a primary or preference election." *Federal Election Campaign Act of 2002,* U.S. Code 2 434 (2004).

4. Rutenberg, "Strategists Use Iowa Lessons."

5. This is the millionaire provision. In 2004, congressional candidates triggered increased individual contribution limits in eight Senate races (one general and seven primary campaigns) and nineteen House races (seven general and twelve primary campaigns). See Steen, "The Millionaire's Amendment," 209–12.

6. *FEC v. Massachusetts Citizens for Life, Inc.* 470 U.S. 238 (1986); *Austin v. Michigan State Chamber of Commerce* 494 U.S. 652 (1990); *FEC v. Colorado Republican Federal Campaign Committee* 518 U.S. 604 (1996).

7. *McConnell v. Federal Election Commission,* 26, 27, 47–49, 59, 62–63, 83–87.

8. According to the Internal Revenue Service website, 527s are "political organizations and operated primarily to accept contributions and make expenditures for the purpose of influencing the selection, nomination, election, or appointment of any individual to Federal, State, or local public office, or office in a political organization or the election of Presidential electors." The 501s are nonprofit organizations that can engage in political activities but are not organized primarily for that purpose. The 501(c)(3)s are nonprofit organizations to which contributions are tax-deductible, while the 501(c)(4)s are charitable organizations seeking promotion of social welfare but to which contributions are not tax-deductible.

9. Center for Public Integrity, "2003–04 National or Federal Race 527 Activity."

10. Weissman and Hassan, "BCRA and the 527 Groups."

11. The Federal Election Commission has been reluctant to bring 527 organizations under the umbrella of federal campaign finance law. See Potter, "Current State of Campaign Finance Law." Reformers in Congress, however, are involved in a two-pronged assault on 527 organizations and issue ads. Congressmen Christopher Shays and Marty Meehan have sought to compel the FEC to tighten its regulation of independent political organizations, 527s, and the use of issue advocacy ads. In July 2005, a federal appeals court agreed with suits that the FEC had been too lax, ordering the FEC to "rewrite and tighten regulations instituted under the 2002 McCain-Feingold campaign finance law." Edsall, "Court Orders Tougher Campaign Finance Rules." On a second front, Senators John McCain and Russ Feingold have introduced legislation requiring 527s to register with the Federal Election Commission and abide by the soft-money contribution limits by which parties, corporations, and labor unions must abide. An amended version passed the Senate Rules Committee in May 2005 but never reached the Senate floor. Several of the amendments have drawn harsh criticism, including those which increase individual contribution limits to PACs and additional flexibility for corporate and trade association PACs to solicit donations from employees. See Edsall, "Panel Backs Bill to Rein In '527' Advocacy Groups."

12. Federal Election Commission, "Party Financial Activity Summarized for the 2004 Election Cycle," news release, March 14, 2005. Malbin predicted as much, and he argues that BCRA will not displace the role of the parties from the political process. This remains to be seen, however. Malbin, "Political Parties under the Post-McConnell Bipartisan Campaign Reform Act."

13. Federal Election Commission, "PAC Activity Increases for 2004 Elections," news release, April 13, 2005.

14. See Herrnson, *Party Campaigning*; Kolodny, *Pursuing Majorities*.

15. Figures calculated by the author from candidate summary reports available from the FEC.

16. Edsall and Grimaldi, "On Nov. 2, GOP Got More Bang."

17. Birnbaum and Edsall, "At the End, Pro-GOP '527s' Outspent Their Counterparts."

18. As this was written, the nomination campaign for President Bush's Supreme Court appointee, John Roberts, was under way. After Justice Sandra Day O'Connor announced her retirement from the court, the author received at least two or three e-mails a week from both left- and right-wing organizations telling him how he should feel about Judge Roberts and the effect Roberts will have on the court's ideological balance.

EPILOGUE

1. Baer and Bositis, *Politics and Linkage in a Democratic Society*, 21–22.

2. See Summers, *Rum, Romanism, and Rebellion*.

3. Indeed, the Bush campaign's use of the term "anger points" in crafting its targeting appeals amply demonstrates the point. Edsall and Grimaldi, "On Nov. 2, GOP Got More Bang."

4. See Faler, "Presidential Ad War Hits the Web."

5. Notable exceptions are Cox and McCubbins, *Legislative Leviathan*; Keith Krehbiel, *Pivotal Politics*; and Aldrich, *Why Parties?*

6. Dick Fenno's fantastic work is an exception.

7. Schlesinger, *Political Parties and the Winning of Office*; Aldrich, *Why Parties?*

8. Aldrich, *Why Parties?* 21–25.

9. Cox and McCubbins, *Legislative Leviathan*, 125.

10. Mayhew, *Congress: The Electoral Connection*, 52–73.

BIBLIOGRAPHY

MANUSCRIPT COLLECTIONS

Burke, Carl P. Papers. Special Collections Library, Boise State University, Boise, Idaho.

Church, Frank F. Papers. Special Collections Library, Boise State University, Boise, Idaho.

Cooper, John S. Papers. Wendell H. Ford Research Center and Public Policy Archives, University of Kentucky, Lexington.

Dirksen, Everett M. Papers. Dirksen Congressional Center, Pekin, Illinois.

Kefauver, Estes. Papers. MS0837. Special Collections Library, University of Tennessee, Knoxville.

Lucas, Scott W. Papers. Illinois State Historical Library, Springfield.

Neese, Charles G. Papers. MS1834. Special Collections Library, University of Tennessee, Knoxville.

Ragland, Martha. Papers. MS883. Special Collections Library, University of Tennessee, Knoxville.

DATA FOR QUANTITATIVE ANALYSES

Adler, E. Scott. "Congressional District Datafile [78th through the 105th Congresses]." University of Colorado, Boulder.

Almanac of American Politics. Washington, D.C.: National Journal Group, 1972–2000.

America Votes: A Handbook of Contemporary Election Statistics. Washington, D.C.: Congressional Quarterly, 1956–2001.

Broadcasting Year Book. Washington, D.C.: Broadcasting Publications, 1940–60.

Burns, Nancy, Donald R. Kinder, Steven J. Rosenstone, Virginia Sapiro, and the National Election Studies. *American National Election Study, 2000: Pre- and Post-Election Survey*. Ann Arbor: University of Michigan, Center for Political Studies, 2001. Downloaded from www.umich.edu/~nes on September 15, 2003.

Congressional Quarterly Almanac. Washington, D.C.: Congressional Quarterly, 1956–2002.

Congressional Quarterly's Politics in America. Washington, D.C.: Congressional Quarterly, 1984–2002.

Congressional Quarterly's Guide to U.S. Elections. 1975. Washington, D.C.: Congressional Quarterly.

Congressional Quarterly Weekly Report. Washington, D.C.: Congressional Quarterly, 1972–2000.

Cook, Rhodes. *Rhodes Cook Letter*. Available at www.rhodescook.com.

Federal Election Commission. *Campaign Expenditures in the United States: Freedom of Information Act (FOIA) Data*. 1984–90. Washington, D.C.: Federal Election Commission; Ann Arbor: Inter-university Consortium for Political and Social Research (distributor), 1988–92. Downloaded from www.icpsr.umich.edu on January 30, 2003.

Federal Election Commission. *Campaign Expenditures in the United States*. 1992–2000. Washington, D.C.: Federal Election Commission, 1994–2002. Downloaded from www.fec.gov on January 15, 2003.

Goldstein, Kenneth, Michael Franz, and Travis Ridout. "Political Advertising in 2000." Combined file [dataset]. Final release. Madison: Department of Political Science at the University of Wisconsin–Madison and Brennan Center for Justice at New York University, 2002.

Inter-university Consortium for Political and Social Research. *United States Congressional Roll Call Voting Records, 1789–1990, Parts 1–202*. Ann Arbor: Inter-university Consortium for Political and Social Research, 2001. Downloaded from www.icpsr.umich.edu on February 1, 2002.

Lewis, Katy, Robert Moore, Leah Rush, and MaryJo Sylwester. "Undisclosed: Half of States Fail to Keep Public Informed of State Party Campaign Activity." Downloaded from www.publicintegrity.org/dtaweb/index.asp?L1=20&L2=9&L3=0&L4=0&L5=0 on April 17, 2003.

National Election Studies, Center for Political Studies, University of Michigan. *The NES Guide to Public Opinion and Electoral Behavior*. Ann Arbor: University of Michigan Center for Political Studies, 2002. Downloaded from www.umich.edu/~nes/nesguide/nesguide.htm on February 9, 2002.

Ornstein, Norman J., Thomas E. Mann, and Michael J. Malbin. *Vital Statistics on Congress, 1999–2000*. Washington, D.C.: American Enterprise Institute for Public Policy Research, 2000.

———. *Vital Statistics on Congress, 2001–2002*. Washington, D.C.: American Enterprise Institute for Public Policy, 2002.

Parsons, Stanley B., William W. Beech, and Michael J. Dubin. *United States Congressional Districts, 1843–1883.* New York: Greenwood Press, 1986.

Parsons, Stanley B., Michael J. Dubin, and Karen T. Parsons. *United States Congressional Districts, 1883–1913.* New York: Greenwood Press, 1990.

Poole, Keith T., and Howard Rosenthal. *NOMINATE Scores for the 1st through the 107th Congress.* Downloaded from voteview.uh.edu on August 15, 2002.

———. *Common Space Scores for the 1st through the 107th Congress.* Downloaded from voteview.uh.edu on December 10, 2003.

Roberds, Stephen C., and Jason M. Roberts. "Are All Amateurs Equal? Candidate Quality in the 1992–1998 U.S. House Elections." *Politics and Policy* 30 (2002): 482–501.

Sapiro, Virginia, Steven J. Rosenstone, and the National Election Studies. *American National Election Studies Cumulative Data File, 1948–2000.* 11th ICPSR version. Ann Arbor: University of Michigan, Center for Political Studies, 2002.

SRDS Television and Cable Source. 2000.Wilmete: Standard Rate and Data Service.

U.S. Bureau of the Census. *Statistical Abstract of the United States: 1950.* 71st ed. Washington, D.C.: Government Printing Office, 1950.

———. *Statistical Abstract of the United States: 1960.* 81st ed. Washington, D.C.: Government Printing Office, 1960.

———. *Statistical Abstract of the United States: 1962.* 83d ed. Washington, D.C.: Government Printing Office, 1962.

———. *County Business Patterns.* Alabama–Wyoming. Washington, D.C.: Government Printing Office, 2000.

U.S. Congress. House. Office of the Clerk. "Political Divisions of the House of Representatives, 1789 to the Present. Downloaded from www.clerk.house.gov/histHigh/Congressional History on February 9, 2002.

DATA SOURCES

Abrams, Jim. "Unlikely Rebels Make Life Difficult for GOP Leaders." *Associated Press and Local Wire*, August 17, 1998.

Agranoff, Robert. *The New Style in Election Campaigns.* Boston: Holbrook Press, 1972.

———. "The New Style of Campaigning: The Decline and the Rise of Candidate-Centered Technology." In *Parties and Elections in an Anti-Party Age: American Politics and the Crisis of Confidence,* ed. Jeff Fishel, 230–40. Bloomington: Indiana University Press, 1978.

Aldrich, John H. *Why Parties? The Origin and Transformation of Political Parties in America.* Chicago: University of Chicago Press, 1995.

Aldrich, John H., John L. Sullivan, and Eugene Borgida. "Foreign Affairs and Issue Voting: Do Presidential Candidates 'Waltz before a Blind Audience'?" *American Political Science Review* 83 (1989): 123–41.

Almond, Gabriel A. *Discipline Divided: Schools and Sects in Political Science.* Newbury Park: Sage, 1990.

American Political Science Association. Committee on Political Parties. *Toward a More Responsible Party System*. New York: Rinehart, 1950.

Ansolabehere, Stephen, and Shanto Iyengar. *Going Negative: How Attack Ads Shrink and Polarize the Electorate*. New York: Free Press, 1995.

Argersinger, Peter H. "Democracy, Republicanism, and Efficiency: The Values of American Politics, 1885–1930." In *Contesting Democracy: Substance and Structure in American Political History, 1775–2000*, ed. Byron E. Shafer and Anthony J. Badger, 117–48. Lawrence: University of Kansas Press, 2001.

Ashby, LeRoy. "Frank Church Goes to the Senate." *Pacific Northwest Quarterly* 1 (1987): 17–31.

Ashby, LeRoy, and Rod Gramer. *Fighting the Odds: The Life of Senator Frank Church*. Pullman: Washington State University Press, 1994.

Baden, Patricia L., and Tom Hamburger. "Political Consulting." *Star Tribune*, August 20, 1996.

Baer, Denise L., and David A. Bositis. *Politics and Linkage in a Democratic Society*. Englewood Cliffs: Prentice Hall, 1993.

Balz, Dan. "Republicans Strive for Dominance with 2004 Race; Strategy Is to Feed Base, Reach Out to New Voters." *Washington Post*, June 22, 2003.

Balz, Dan, and Thomas B. Edsall. "Kerry May Delay Party Nomination." *Washington Post*, May 23, 2004.

"Barkley Attacks GOP 'Isolation.'" *New York Times*, November 4, 1950.

Barone, Michael, and Richard E. Cohen. *Almanac of American Politics 2002*. Washington, D.C.: National Journal, 2002.

Bartels, Larry M. *Presidential Primaries and the Dynamics of Public Choice*. Princeton: Princeton University Press, 1988.

Bartholomew, Paul C. *The Indiana Third Congressional District: A Political History*. Notre Dame: University of Notre Dame Press, 1970.

Bass, Harold F., Jr. "Partisan Rules, 1946–1996." In *Partisan Approaches to Postwar Politics*, ed. Byron E. Shafer, 220–70. New York: Chatham House, 1988.

Basu, Sandra. "Shelley Moore Capito's Uphill Climb." *Campaigns and Elections*, May 2001.

Belmont, Perry. *American Democrat: The Recollections of Perry Belmont*. New York: Columbia University Press, 1940.

Benedict, Michael L. "The Party, Going Strong: Congress and Elections in the Mid-Nineteenth Century." *Congress and the Presidency* 9 (1982): 37–60.

Berelson, Bernard R., Paul F. Lazarsfeld, and William N. McPhee. *Voting*. Chicago: University of Chicago Press, 1954.

Berke, Richard L. "GOP Gives Help to House Hopefuls." *New York Times*, March 3, 2002.

Berry, William D., Evan J. Ringquist, Richard C. Fording, and Russell L. Hanson. "Measuring Citizen and Government Ideology in the American States, 1960–93." *American Journal of Political Science* 42 (1998): 327–48.

Bibby, John F. "State Party Organizations: Strengthened and Adapting to Candidate-

Centered Politics and Nationalization." In *The Parties Respond,* 4th ed., ed. L. Sandy Maisel, 19–46. Boulder: Westview Press, 2002.

Bicha, Karel Denis. "Jerry Simpson: Populist without Principle." *Journal of American History* 54, no. 2 (September 1967): 291–306.

Birnbaum, Jeffrey H., and Thomas B. Edsall. "At the End, Pro-GOP '527s' Outspent Their Counterparts." *Washington Post,* November 6, 2004.

Blumberg, Melanie J., William C. Binning, and John C. Green. "Do the Grassroots Matter? The Coordinated Campaign in a Battleground State." In *The State of the Parties,* 3d ed., ed. John Green and Daniel Shea, 154–70. Lanham, Md.: University of American Press, 1999.

Blumenthal, Sidney. *The Permanent Campaign: Inside the World of Elite Political Operations.* Boston: Beacon Press, 1980

Bone, Hugh A. *American Politics and the Party System.* New York: McGraw-Hill, 1949.

Brady, David W. *Critical Elections and Congressional Policy Making.* Stanford: Stanford University Press, 1988.

Brady, David W., Joseph Cooper, and Patricia A. Hurley. "The Decline of Party in the U.S. House of Representatives, 1887–1968." *Legislative Studies Quarterly* 4 (1979): 381–407.

Briggs, John E. *William Peters Hepburn.* Iowa City: State Historical Society of Iowa, 1919.

Broder, David S. *The Party's Over: The Failure of Politics in America.* New York: Harper and Row, 1972.

———. "No Vote Necessary; Redistricting Is Creating a U.S. House of Lords." *Washington Post,* November 11, 2004.

Bruce, Harold R. *American Parties and Politics: History and Role of Political Parties in the United States.* New York: Henry Holt, 1927.

Burke, Carl. Interview with the author. Transcript. September 26, 2003.

Cain, Bruce, Karin MacDonald, and Michael McDonald. "From Equality to Fairness: The Path of Political Reform since *Baker v. Carr.*" In *Party Lines: Competition, Partisanship, and Congressional Redistricting,* ed. Bruce Cain and Thomas Mann, 6–30. Washington, D.C.: Brookings Press, 2005.

Campaign Finance Legal Center. "Levin Funds." Downloaded from www.campaignfinanceguide.org/f-levin.hmtl on July 26, 2005.

Campbell, Angus, Philip E. Converse, Warren E. Miller, and Donald E. Stokes. *The American Voter.* Ann Arbor: University of Michigan, 1960.

Campbell, Angus, Gerald Gurin, and Warren E. Miller. *The Voter Decides.* Evanston: Row Peterson, 1954.

"Candidates Open Uptown Headquarters." *Nashville Tennessean,* September 14, 1948.

Canon, David T. *Actors, Athletes, and Astronauts: Political Amateurs in the United States Congress.* Chicago: University of Chicago Press, 1990.

Cantor, David, and Paul S. Herrnson. "Party Campaign Activity and Party Unity in the U.S. House of Representatives." *Legislative Studies Quarterly* 22 (1997): 393–415.

Carmines, Edward G., and James A. Stimson. *Issue Evolution: Race and Transformation of American Politics.* Princeton: Princeton University Press, 1989.

Caro, Robert A. *The Years of Lyndon Johnson: The Path to Power.* New York: Knopf, 1982.

Center for Public Integrity. "2003–04 National or Federal Race 527 Activity." Downloaded from www.publicintergrity.org/527/db on July 21, 2005.

Chambers, William N. "Party Development and the American Mainstream." In *American Party Systems: Stages of Political Development,* ed. William N. Chambers and Walter D. Burnham, 3–32. New York: Oxford University Press, 1975.

Church, Bethine. *A Lifelong Affair: My Passion for People and Politics.* Washington, D.C.: Francis Press, 2003.

———. Interview with the author. Transcript. September 29, 2003.

"Church of Idaho Noted as Speaker." *New York Times,* November 7, 1956.

Cillizza, Chris. "The More the Merrier." *Roll Call,* May 23, 2002.

Coleman, John J. "Resurgent or Just Busy? Party Organizations in Contemporary America." In *The State of the Parties,* 2d ed., ed. John Green and Daniel Shea, 367–84. Lanham: University of American Press, 1996.

———. "Party Images and Candidate-Centered Campaigns in 1996: What's Money Got to Do with It?" In *The State of the Parties,* 3d ed., ed. John Green and Daniel Shea, 337–54. Lanham, Md.: University of American Press, 1999.

Coleman, John J., and Paul F. Manna. "Congressional Campaign Spending and the Quality of Democracy." *Journal of Politics* 62 (2000): 757–89.

Coleman, John J., and David C. W. Parker. "Congressional Campaign Spending and Election Involvement." Manuscript.

Congress and the Nation, 1945–1964: A Review of Government and Politics in the Postwar Years. Washington, D.C.: Congressional Quarterly Service, 1965.

Converse, Phillip E. "Assessing the Capacity of Mass Electorates." *Annual Review of Political Science* 3 (2000): 331–55.

Corlett, John. "Politically Speaking." *Idaho Daily Statesman,* September 27, 1956.

———. "2,000 Hear Stevenson Address." *Idaho Daily Statesman,* October 10, 1956.

———. "Politically Speaking." *Idaho Daily Statesman,* November 4, 1956.

Corrado, Anthony. "Money and Politics: A History of Campaign Finance Law." In *The New Campaign Finance Sourcebook,* ed. Anthony Corrado, Thomas E. Mann, Daniel R. Ortiz, and Trevor Potter, 7–47. Washington, D.C.: Brookings Institute Press, 2005.

Cotter, Cornelius P., et al. *Party Organizations in American Politics.* New York: Praeger, 1984.

Cox, Gary W., and Jonathan Katz. "Why Did the Incumbency Advantage Grow?" *American Journal of Political Science* 40 (1996): 478–97.

———. *Elbridge Gerry's Salamander: The Electoral Consequences of the Reapportionment Revolution.* Cambridge: Cambridge University Press, 2002.

Cox, Gary W., and Mathew D. McCubbins. *Legislative Leviathan: Party Government in the House.* Berkeley: University of California Press, 1993.

Crabtree, Susan. "Revamped DeLay PAC May Fund STOMP." *Roll Call,* November 14, 2002.

Crook, Sara B., and John R. Hibbing. "A Not-So-Distant Mirror: The 17th Amendment and Institutional Change." *American Political Science Review* 91 (1996): 207–26.

Cummings, Jeanne. "Companies Pare Political Donations." *Wall Street Journal*, June 7, 2004.

Davidson, Roger H., and Walter J. Oleszek. *Congress and Its Members*. 6th ed. Washington, D.C.: CQ Press, 1998.

Deason, Brian. "Scott Lucas, Everett Dirksen, and the 1950 Senate Election in Illinois." *Journal of the Illinois State Historical Society* 95 (2002): 33–51.

"Democrats Plan Woods-Shelling for Big Vote." *Nashville Tennessean*, October 5, 1948.

Dewar, Helen. "Senate Power Shift Intensifies Battle for '02." *Washington Post*, June 3, 2001.

———. "Minn. May Be Key to Senate's Helm." *Washington Post*, May 12, 2002.

Dirksen, Everett M. *The Education of a Senator*. Urbana: University of Illinois Press, 1998.

Dobson, John M. *Politics in the Gilded Age: A New Perspective on Reform*. New York: Praeger, 1972.

Downs, Anthony. *An Economic Theory of Democracy*. New York: Harper, 1957.

Dreiske, John. "GOP Sidetracks Red Issue, Puts Korea 'Bungling' First." *Chicago Sun-Times*, September 16, 1950.

———. "Capt. Dan's Advertising Missing Fire?" *Chicago Sun-Times*, October 6, 1950.

———. "Local GOP Hires a Drum Beater." *Chicago Sun-Times*, October 20, 1950.

Eckel, George. "Lucas' Re-election Linked to Freedom." *New York Times*, August 18, 1950.

———. "Lucas and Dirksen Run Nip-and-Tuck." *New York Times*, October 27, 1950.

Edsall, Thomas B. "Contests over Legislative Power Turning into Political Street Fights." *Washington Post*, November 2, 1990.

———. "Republican Soft Money Groups Find Business Reluctant to Give." *Washington Post*, June 7, 2004.

———. "Panel Backs Bill to Rein In '527' Advocacy Groups." *Washington Post*, April 28, 2005.

———. "Court Orders Tougher Campaign Finance Rules." *Washington Post*, July 16, 2005.

Edsall, Thomas B., and James V. Grimaldi. "On Nov. 2, GOP Got More Bang for Its Billion, Analysis Shows." *Washington Post*, December 30, 2004.

Engstrom, Erik J. "Stacking the States, Stacking the House: The Partisan Consequences of Congressional Redistricting, 1870–1900." Paper presented at the annual meeting of the Midwest Political Science Association, Chicago, April 2003.

Epstein, Leon D. *Political Parties in the American Mold*. Madison: University of Wisconsin Press, 1986.

Erie, Steven P. *Rainbow's End: Irish-Americans and the Dilemmas of Urban Machine Politics, 1840–1985*. Berkeley: University of California Press, 1988.

Ervin, Spencer. *Henry Ford vs. Truman H. Newberry: The Famous Senate Election Contest.* New York: Arno Press, 1974.

Faler, Brian. "Presidential Ad War Hits the Web." *Washington Post,* March 15, 2004.

Farr, James. "Remembering the Revolution: Behavioralism in American Political Science." In *Political Science in History: Research Programs and Political Traditions,* ed. James Farr, John S. Dryzek, and Stephen T. Leonard, 198–224. Cambridge: Cambridge University Press, 1995.

Faucheux, Ron. "Writing Your Campaign Plan: The Seven Components of Winning an Election." *Campaigns and Elections,* April 2004.

Fenno, Richard F., Jr. *Home Style: House Members in Their Districts.* New York: Longman, 1978.

———. *Senators on the Campaign Trail: The Politics of Representation.* Norman: University of Oklahoma Press, 1996.

Fenton, John H. *Politics in the Border States.* New Orleans: Hauser Press, 1957.

Ferrell, Henry C. *Claude A. Swanson of Virginia: A Political Biography.* Lexington: University Press of Kentucky, 1985.

Finkel, Steven E., and John G. Geer. "A Spot Check: Casting Doubt on the Demobilizing Effect of Attack Advertising." *American Journal of Political Science* 42 (1998): 573–95.

Fitzpatrick, Rita."1,500 Women Rally behind GOP Crusade." *Chicago Tribune,* October 14, 1950.

Fontenay, Charles L. *Estes Kefauver: A Biography.* Knoxville: University of Tennessee Press, 1980.

Franklin, Charles H. "Eschewing Obfuscation? Campaigns and the Perception of U.S. Senate Incumbents." *American Political Science Review* 85 (1991): 1193–1214.

Franz, Michael M. "Choices and Changes: Interest Groups in the Electoral Process." PhD diss., University of Wisconsin–Madison, 2005.

Franz, Michael, and Kenneth Goldstein. "Following the (Soft) Money: Party Advertisements in American Elections." In *The Parties Respond,* 4th ed., ed. L. Sandy Maisel, 139–62. Boulder: Westview Press, 2002.

Freedman, Paul, and Ken Goldstein. "Measuring Media Exposure and the Effects of Negative Campaign Ads." *American Journal of Political Science* 43 (1999): 1189–1208.

Gardner, John B. "Political Leadership in a Period of Transition: Frank G. Clement, Albert Gore, Estes Kefauver, and Tennessee Politics, 1948–1956." PhD diss., Vanderbilt University, 1978.

Geer, John G. "Campaigns, Party Competition, and Political Advertising." In *Politicians and Party Politics,* ed. John G. Geer, 186–217. Baltimore: Johns Hopkins University Press, 1998.

Gelman, Andrew, and Gary King. "Why Are American Presidential Election Campaign Polls So Variable When Votes Are So Predictable?" *British Journal of Political Science* 23 (1993): 409–51.

Gimpel, James G. *Fulfilling the Contract: The First Hundred Days.* Boston: Allyn and Bacon, 1996.

Goldstein, Kenneth M., and Paul Freedman. "New Evidence for New Arguments: Money and Advertising in the 1996 Senate Elections." *Journal of Politics* 62 (2000): 1087–1108.

———. "Campaign Advertising and Voter Turnout: New Evidence for a Stimulation Effect." *Journal of Politics* 64 (2002): 721–40.

Goldstein, Kenneth M., and Travis N. Ridout. "The Politics of Participation: Mobilization and Turnout over Time." *Political Behavior* 24 (2002): 3–29.

———. "Measuring the Effects of Televised Political Advertising in the United States." *Annual Review of Political Science* 7 (2004): 205–26.

Goodman, William. *Inherited Domain: Political Parties in Tennessee.* Knoxville: Bureau of Public Administration, University of Tennessee, 1954.

"GOP Precinct Captains to Go to Rally Friday." *Chicago Tribune,* September 22, 1950.

Gorman, Joseph B. *Kefauver: A Political Biography.* New York: Oxford University Press, 1971

Green, Donald P., and Jonathan S. Krasno. "Rebuttal to Jacobson's 'New Evidence for Old Arguments.'" *American Journal of Political Science* 34 (1990): 363–72.

Green, Donald P., and Ian Shapiro. *The Pathologies of Rational Choice Theory: A Critique of Applications in Political Science.* New Haven: Yale University Press, 1994.

Green, John C., and Daniel M. Shea, eds. *The State of the Parties.* 3d ed. Lanham, Md.: University of American Press, 1999.

Grow, Douglas. "South Dakota Boots Sharp-Dressed Liberal." *Star Tribune,* November 7, 2004.

Harris, John F., and Paul Farhi. "Taking the Campaign to the People, One Doorstep at a Time." *Washington Post,* April 18, 2004.

Harris, Joseph P. *Election Administration in the United States.* Washington, D.C.: Brookings Institution, 1934.

Hayes, Stephen F. "A Challenger Haunts Specter." *Weekly Standard,* April 26, 2004.

Heard, Alexander. *The Costs of Democracy.* Chapel Hill: University of North Carolina Press, 1960

Herring, Pendleton. *The Politics of Democracy: American Parties in Action.* New York: W. W. Norton, 1940.

Herrnson, Paul S. *Party Campaigning in the 1980s.* Cambridge: Harvard University Press, 1988.

———. "The Revitalization of National Party Organizations." In *The Parties Respond: Changes in American Parties and Campaigns,* 2d ed., ed. L. Sandy Maisel, 45–68. Boulder: Westview Press, 1994.

———. *Congressional Elections: Campaigning at Home and in Washington.* 3d ed. Washington, D.C.: CQ Press, 2000.

———. "National Party Organizations at the Dawn of the Twentieth-first Century." In *The Parties Respond,* 4th ed, ed. L. Sandy Maisel, 47–78. Boulder: Westview Press, 2002.

Herrnson, Paul S., and Diana Dwyre. "Party Issue Advocacy in Congressional Elections." In *The State of the Parties,* 3d ed., ed. John Green and Daniel Shea, 86–104. Lanham, Md.: University of American Press, 1999.

Hinton, Harold B. "Now GOP Senators Shy from M'Carthy." *New York Times*, July 1, 1951.

Holt, Marianne. "The Surge in Party Money in Competitive 1998 Congressional Elections." In *Outside Money: Soft Money and Issue Advocacy in the 1998 Congressional Elections*, ed. David Magleby, 17–40. Lanham: Rowman and Littlefield, 2000.

House, Albert V. "The Democratic State Central Committee of Indiana in 1880: A Case Study in Party Tactics and Finance." *Indiana Magazine of History* 58 (1962): 179–210.

Hutton, Marilyn J. "The Election of 1896 in the Tenth Congressional District of Tennessee." PhD diss., Memphis State University, 1978.

Jacobson, Gary C. "Effects of Campaign Spending in House Elections: New Evidence for Old Arguments." *American Journal of Political Science* 34 (1990): 334–62.

———. *The Politics of Congressional Elections*. 4th ed. New York: Longman, 1997.

Janofsky, Michael. "Redistricting Puts Fire into Legislative Races." *New York Times*, October 28, 2000.

Jewell, Malcolm E., and Everett W. Cunningham. *Kentucky Politics*. Lexington: University of Kentucky Press, 1968.

Johnson, Glen, and Patrick Healy. "Kerry Rules Out Delaying Tactic." *Boston Globe*, May 27, 2004.

Johnston, Richard, Andre Blais, Henry E. Brady, and Jean Crete. *Letting the People Decide: Dynamics of a Canadian Election*. Stanford: Stanford University Press, 1992.

Josephson, Matthew. *The Politicos, 1865–1896*. New York: Harcourt, Brace, 1938.

"Judge Pickering, Arlen Specter, and More." *Weekly Standard*, January 20, 2003.

Kahn, Kim Fridkin, and Patrick J. Kenney. "How Negative Campaigning Enhances Knowledge of Senate Elections." In *Crowded Airwaves: Campaign Advertising in Elections*, ed. James A. Thurber, Candice J. Nelson, and David A. Dulio, 65–95. Washington, D.C.: Brookings Institution Press, 2000.

Kanady, Johnson. "Lucas Is Man on Flying Trapeze, Dirksen Says." *Chicago Tribune*, October 13, 1950.

Kayden, Xandra. "The Nationalization of the Party System." In *Parties, Interest Groups, and Campaign Finance Laws*, ed. Michael J. Malbin, 257–82. Washington, D.C.: American Enterprise Institute, 1980.

Kayden, Xandra, and Eddie Mahe, Jr. *The Party Goes On: The Persistence of the Two-Party System in the United States*. New York: Basic Books, 1985.

Kazin, Michael. *A Godly Hero: The Life of William Jennings Bryan*. New York: Knopf, 2006.

Kelley, Stanley. *Professional Public Relations and Political Power*. Baltimore: Johns Hopkins University Press, 1956.

Kerr, K. Austin. *Organized for Prohibition: A New History of the Anti-Saloon League*. New Haven: Yale University Press, 1985.

Key, V. O. *Politics, Parties, and Pressure Groups*. New York: Thomas Y. Crowell, 1942.

———. *Southern Politics in State and Nation*. New York: Knopf, 1949.

———. *Public Opinion and American Democracy*. New York: Knopf, 1960.

Kiewiet, D. Roderick. *Macroeconomics and Micropolitics*. Chicago: University of Chicago Press, 1983.

Killian, Linda. *The Freshmen: What Happened to the Republican Revolution?* Boulder: Westview Press, 1998.

Kinder, Donald R. "Communication and Opinion." *Annual Review of Political Science* 1 (1998): 167–97.

King, Gary, Robert O. Keohane, and Sidney Verba. *Designing Social Inquiry: Scientific Interference in Qualitative Research*. Princeton: Princeton University Press, 1994.

King, Ronald F., and Susan Ellis. "Partisan Advantage and Constitutional Change: The Case of the Seventeenth Amendment." *Studies in American Political Development* 10 (1996): 69–102.

Kingdon, John W. *Agendas, Alternatives, and Public Policies*. Boston: Little, Brown, 1984.

Kintisch, Eli. "The Crossover Candidate: Did the GOP Take Down Cynthia McKinney?" *American Prospect*, September 23, 2002.

Koenig, Louis W. *Bryan: A Political Biography of William Jennings Bryan*. New York: Putnam, 1971.

Kolodny, Robin. *Pursuing Majorities: Congressional Campaign Committees in American Politics*. Norman: University of Oklahoma Press, 1998.

Kornbluh, Mark L. *Why Americans Stopped Voting: The Decline of Participatory Democracy and the Emergence of Modern American Politics*. New York: New York University Press, 2000.

Kramer, Gerald H. "Short-Term Fluctuations in U.S. Voting Behavior, 1896–1964." *American Political Science Review* 65 (1971): 131–43.

Krasno, Jonathan S., and Kenneth M. Goldstein. "The Facts about Television Advertising and the McCain-Feingold Bill." *PS: Political Science and Politics* 35 (2002): 207–12.

Krasno, Jonathan S., and Daniel Selz. *Buying Time: Television Advertising in the 1998 Congressional Elections*. New York: Brennan Center for Justice, 2000.

Krehbiel, Keith. *Pivotal Politics: A Theory of U.S. Lawmaking*. Chicago: University of Chicago Press, 1998.

Langsdon, Phillip. *Tennessee: A Political History*. Franklin: Hillsboro Press, 2000.

La Raja, Ray. "Political Parties in the Soft Money Era." In *The Parties Respond*, 4th ed., ed. L. Sandy Maisel, 163–88. Boulder: Westview Press, 2002.

Lau, Richard R., and Gerald M. Pomper. "Accentuating the Negative? Effects of Negative Campaigning in U.S. Senate Elections." Paper presented at the annual meeting of the American Political Science Association, Boston, September 1998.

Lau, Richard R., and Lee Sigelman. "Effectiveness of Political Advertising." In *Crowded Airwaves: Campaign Advertising in Elections*, ed. James A. Thurber, Candice J. Nelson, and David A. Dulio, 10–43. Washington, D.C.: Brookings Institution Press, 2000.

Layman, Geoffrey C., and Thomas M. Carsey. "Party Polarization and 'Conflict Extension' in the American Electorate." *American Journal of Political Science* 46 (2002): 786–802.

Leonard, Mary. "Ex-Coach Jennings Seeks Seat in Indiana: Candidate for House Is Former Clinton Aide." *Boston Globe*, October 27, 2003.

Leyden, Kevin M., and Stephen A. Borrelli. "Party Contributions and Party Unity: Can Loyalty Be Bought?" *Western Political Quarterly* 43 (1990): 343–65.

Lilley, William, II. "The Early Career of Francis G. Newlands, 1848–1897." PhD diss., Yale University, 1965.

Lindsey, David. *Sunset Cox: Irrepressible Democrat*. Detroit: Wayne State University, 1959.

Logan, Hub. "GOP Earmarking $30 for Each Precinct Here." *Chicago Sun-Times*, October 18, 1950.

Lustick, Ian S. "History, Historiography, and Political Science: Multiple Historical Records and the Problem of Selection Bias." *American Political Science Review* 90 (1996): 605–18.

MacNeil, Neil. *Dirksen: Portrait of a Public Man*. New York: World, 1970.

Maisel, L. Sandy. "American Political Parties: Still Central to a Functioning Democracy?" In *American Political Parties: Decline or Resurgence?* ed. Jeffrey Cohen, Richard Fleischer, and Paul Kantor, 103–21. Washington, D.C.: CQ Press, 2001.

———, ed. *The Parties Respond: Changes in American Parties and Campaigns*. 4th ed. Boulder: Westview Press, 2002.

"Making Votes Count." Editorial, *New York Times*, January 18, 2004.

Malbin, Michael J. "Political Parties under the Post-McConnell Bipartisan Campaign Reform Act." *Election Law Journal* 3 (2004): 177–91.

Marcus, Robert D. *Grand Old Party: Political Structure in the Gilded Age, 1880–1896*. New York: Oxford University Press, 1971.

Martin, Boyd A. "The 1956 Election in Idaho." *Western Political Quarterly* 10 (1957): 122–26.

Matthews, Donald R. *U.S. Senators and Their World*. New York: Vintage Books, 1960.

Mayhew, David R. "Congressional Elections: The Case of the Vanishing Marginals." *Polity* 6 (1974): 295–317.

———. *Congress: The Electoral Connection*. New Haven: Yale University Press, 1974.

———. *Placing Parties in American Politics: Organization, Electoral Settings, and Government Activity in the Twentieth Century*. Princeton: Princeton University Press, 1986.

McGerr, Michael E. *The Decline of Popular Politics: The American North, 1865–1923*. New York: Oxford University Press, 1986.

McGillivray, Alice, Richard Scammon, and Rhodes Cook. *America Votes 24: 1999–2000, A Handbook of Contemporary American Election Statistics*. Washington, D.C.: CQ Press, 2001.

Menefee-Libbey, David. *The Triumph of Campaign-Centered Politics.* New York: Chatham House, 2000.

Mercurio, John. "Looking Ahead GOP Maps Future Plans." *Roll Call,* November 15, 1999.

Merida, Kevin. "Agony with Little Ecstasy." *Washington Post,* January 8, 1997.

Merriam, Charles E., and Harold F. Gosnell. *The American Party System: An Introduction to the Study of Political Parties in the United States.* 4th ed. New York: Macmillan, 1949.

Merton, Robert K. "The Latent Functions of the Machine." In *Urban Bosses, Machines, and Progressive Reformers,* ed. Bruce M. Stave, 27–37. Lexington: Heath, 1972.

Mitchell, Greg. *The Campaign of the Century: Upton Sinclair's Race for the Governor of California and the Birth of Media Politics.* New York: Random House, 1992.

Morgan, H. Wayne. "The Congressional Career of William McKinley." PhD diss., Syracuse University, 1960.

———. *From Hayes to McKinley: National Party Politics, 1877–1896.* Syracuse: Syracuse University Press, 1969.

Nagourney, Adam. "Political Parties Shift Emphasis to Core Voters." *New York Times,* September 1, 2003.

Neese, Charles G. "Estes Is Bestes." Series 5: manuscripts, box 5, folders 6–12, Charles G. Neese Papers. MS1834. Special Collections Library, University of Tennessee, Knoxville.

Neter, John, Michael H. Kutner, Christopher J. Nachtsheim, and William Wasserman. *Applied Linear Regression Models.* 3d ed. Chicago: Irwin, 1996.

Nicklas, Floyd W. "William Kelley: The Congressional Years, 1861–1890." PhD diss., Northern Illinois University, 1984.

Nunn, Louie B. Interview with Terry Birdwhistell, February 12, 1998. Louie B. Nunn Oral History Project, University of Kentucky Special Collections.

O'Connor, Edwin. *The Last Hurrah.* New York: Bantam Books, 1956.

Odegard, Peter H. *Pressure Politics: The Story of the Anti-Saloon League.* New York: Columbia University Press, 1928.

Offenberg, Richard S. "The Political Career of Thomas Brackett Reed." PhD diss., New York University, 1963.

Oppel, Richard A., Jr. "The 2002 Campaign: Finance Campaign." *New York Times,* November 5, 2002.

Oppenheimer, Bruce I. "Deep Red and Blue Congressional Districts: The Causes and Consequences of Declining Party Competitiveness." In *Congress Reconsidered,* ed. Lawrence C. Dodd and Bruce I. Oppenheimer, 135–58. Washington, D.C.: CQ Press, 2005.

Orren, Karen, and Stephen Skowronek. "Political Learning and Political Change: Understanding Development across Time." In *Dynamics of American Politics: Approaches and Interpretations,* ed. Lawrence Dodd and Calvin Jillson, 311–30. Boulder: Westview Press, 1994.

Ostrogorski, M. *Democracy and the Party System in the United States: A Study in Extra-Constitutional Government.* New York: Macmillan, 1910.

Parker, David C. W., and John J. Coleman. "Pay to Play: Parties, Interests, and Money in Federal Elections." In *The Medium and the Message: Television Advertising and American Elections,* ed. Kenneth Goldstein and Patricia Strach, 127–54. Englewood Cliffs: Prentice Hall, 2004.

Peterson, David A. M., Lawrence J. Grossback, James A. Stimson, and Amy Gangl. "Congressional Response to Mandate Elections." *American Journal of Political Science* 47 (2003): 411–26.

Petrocik, John R. "Issue Ownership in Presidential Elections, with a 1980 Case Study." *American Journal of Political Science* 40 (1996): 825–50.

Polakoff, Keith I. "The Disorganized Democracy: An Institutional Study of the Democratic Party, 1872–1880." PhD diss., Northwestern University, 1968.

Pollock, James K., Jr. *Party Campaign Funds.* New York: Knopf, 1926.

Polsby, Nelson. "The Institutionalization of the U.S. House of Representatives." *American Political Science Review* 62 (1968): 144–68.

Pomper, Gerald. "The Alleged Decline of American Parties." In *Politicians and Party Politics,* ed. John Geer, 14–39. Baltimore: Johns Hopkins University Press, 1998.

Poole, Keith T., and Howard Rosenthal. *Congress: A Political-Economic History of Roll Call Voting.* New York: Oxford University Press, 1997.

Popkin, Samuel L. *The Reasoning Voter.* 2d ed. Chicago: University of Chicago Press, 1994.

Potter, Trevor. "The Current State of Campaign Finance Law." In *The New Campaign Finance Reform Sourcebook,* ed. Anthony Corrado, Thomas E. Mann, Daniel R. Ortiz, and Trevor Potter, 48–90. Washington, D.C.: Brookings Institution Press, 2005.

Procter, Ben H. *Not without Honor: The Life of John H. Reagan.* Austin: University of Texas Press, 1962.

Quaid, Libby. "National GOP Involved in Kansas Congressional Race, Redistricting." *Associated Press State and Local Wire,* February 23, 2002.

Ranney, Austin. *The Doctrine of Responsible Government: Its Origin and Present State.* Urbana: University of Illinois Press, 1954.

———. *Illinois Politics.* New York: New York University Press, 1960.

Rathgeber, Lewis W. "The Democratic Party in Pennsylvania." PhD diss., University of Pittsburgh, 1955.

"Resources to Fight Sinclair." *New York Times,* November 4, 1934.

Ridout, Travis N. "Presidential Primary Front-Loading, the Information Environment, and Voter Learning and Choice." PhD diss., University of Wisconsin–Madison, 2003.

Ridout, Travis N., Michael Franz, Kenneth Goldstein, and Paul Freedman. n.d. "Measure the Nature and Effects of Campaign Advertising." Working paper. Downloaded from www.wsu.edu/~tnridout/reliability.pdf on March 13, 2004.

Roberts, Steven V. "Fight for Legislature Stirs National Action." *New York Times,* November 3, 1980.

Ross, Thomas R. *Jonathan Prentiss Dolliver: A Study in Political Integrity and Independence.* Iowa City: State Historical Society of Iowa, 1958.

Rothenberg, Stuart. "Rothenberg's 1998 Senate Ratings." *CNN.com,* April 13, 1998. Available at www.cnn.com/ALLPOLITICS/1998/04/13/spotlight/rothenberg/index2.html.

———. "How a Democrat Won California's Republican Gubernatorial Primary." *Roll Call,* March 7, 2002.

———. "You Can Pick Your Friends, but Can You Pick Your Opponent?" *Roll Call,* July 15, 2002.

Rowley, William D. *Reclaiming the Arid West: The Career of Francis G. Newlands.* Bloomington: Indiana University Press, 1996.

Rusk, Jerrold G. "The Effect of the Australian Ballot Reform on Split Ticket Voting, 1876–1908." *American Political Science Review* 64 (1970): 1220–38.

Rutenberg, Jim. "Strategists Use Iowa Lessons in New Ads in New Hampshire." *New York Times,* January 23, 2004.

Sabato, Larry J. *Rise of Political Consultants: New Ways of Winning Elections.* New York: Basic Books, 1981.

———. *PAC Power: Inside the World of Political Action Committees.* New York: Norton, 1984.

Sait, Edward M. *American Parties and Elections.* New York: Century, 1927.

Salmore, Stephen A., and Barbara G. Salmore. *Candidates, Parties, and Campaigns: Electoral Politics in America.* 2d ed. Washington, D.C.: CQ Press, 1989.

Salvato, Albert. "National Briefing South." *New York Times,* August 25, 2004.

Schapsmeier, Edward L., and Frederick H. Schapsmeier. *Dirksen of Illinois: Senatorial Statesman.* Urbana: University of Illinois Press, 1985.

Schattschneider, E. E. *Party Government.* New York: Holt, Rinehart and Winston, 1942.

———. *The Semisovereign People.* New York: Holt, Rinehart and Winston, 1960.

Schier, Steven E. *By Invitation Only: The Rise of Exclusive Politics in the United States.* Pittsburgh: University of Pittsburgh Press, 2000.

Schiesl, Martin J. *The Politics of Efficiency: Municipal Administration and Reform in America, 1800–1920.* Berkeley: University of California Press, 1977.

Schlesinger, Arthur, Jr. Letter to the Editor. *New York Times,* May 22, 2004.

Schlesinger, Joseph A. *Political Parties and the Winning of Office.* Ann Arbor: University of Michigan Press, 1991.

Schulman, Robert. *John Sherman Cooper: The Global Kentuckian.* Lexington: University Press of Kentucky, 1976.

Schwartz, Mildred A. *The Party Network: The Robust Organization of Illinois Republicans.* Madison: University of Wisconsin Press, 1990.

Scott, Ruth K., and Ronald J. Hrebenar. *Parties in Crisis: Party Politics in America.* New York: Wiley, 1979.

Shefter, Martin. "The Emergence of the Political Machine: An Alternative View." In *Theoretical Perspectives on Urban Politics*, ed. Willis Hawley and Michael Lipsky, 14–44. Englewood Cliffs: Prentice-Hall, 1976.

———. *Political Parties and the State: The American Historical Experience*. Princeton: Princeton University Press, 1994.

Shelton, Charlotte J. "William Atkinson Jones, 1849–1918: Independent Democracy in Turn-of-the-Century Virginia." PhD diss., University of Virginia, 1980.

Silbey, Joel H. *The American Political Nation, 1838–1893*. Stanford: Stanford University Press, 1991.

———. "Beyond Realignment Theory." In *The End of Realignment? Interpreting American Electoral Eras*, ed. Byron E. Shafer, 3–23. Madison: University of Wisconsin Press, 1991.

———. "Divided Government in Historical Perspective." In *Divided Government: Change, Uncertainty, and the Constitutional Order*, ed. Peter F. Galderisi, Roberta Q. Herzberg, and Peter McNamara, 9–34. Boulder: Westview Press, 1996.

———."From 'Essential to the Existence of Our Institutions' to 'Rapacious Enemies of Honest and Responsible Government': The Rise and Fall of American Political Parties, 1790–2000." In *The Parties Respond*, 4th ed., ed. L. Sandy Maisel, 1–18. Boulder: Westview Press, 2002.

Skowronek, Stephen. *Building a New American State: The Expansion of National Administrative Capacities, 1877–1920*. Cambridge: Cambridge University Press, 1982.

———. *The Politics Presidents Make: Leadership from John Adams to Bill Clinton*. Cambridge: Belknap Press, 1997.

Smoot, Richard C. "John Sherman Cooper: The Paradox of a Liberal Republican in Kentucky Politics." PhD diss., University of Kentucky, 1988.

"The Soft-Money Dodge in 1998." Editorial, *New York Times*, October 8, 1998.

Sorauf, Frank J. *Party Politics in America*. Boston: Little, Brown, 1968.

———. "Political Parties and Political Analysis." In *American Party Systems: Stages of Political Development*, ed. William N. Chambers and Walter D. Burnham, 33–55. New York: Oxford University Press, 1975.

———. "Political Action Committees." In *Campaign Finance Reform: A Sourcebook*, ed. Anthony Corrado, Thomas E. Mann, Daniel R. Ortiz, Trevor Potter, and Frank J. Sorauf, 121–64. Washington, D.C.: Brookings Institution Press, 1997.

———. "Power, Money, and Responsibility in the Major Political Parties." In *Responsible Partisanship? The Evolution of American Political Parties since 1950*, ed. John C. Green and Paul S. Herrnson, 83–100. Lawrence: University of Kansas Press, 2002.

Spiliotes, Constantine J., and Lynn Vavreck. "Campaign Advertising: Partisan Convergence or Divergence?" *Journal of Politics* 64 (2002): 249–61.

Stapilus, Randy. *Paradox Politics: People and Power in Idaho*. Boise: Ridenbaugh Press, 1988.

"State Political Drives Speed Up This Week." *Nashville Tennessean*, October 4, 1948.

Steen, Jennifer A. "The Millionaire's Amendment." In *The Election after Reform: Money, Politics, and the Bipartisan Campaign Reform Act,* ed. Michael Malbin, 204–18. Lanham, Md.: Rowman and Littlefield, 2006.

Stolberg, Sheryl. "Gracious but Defeated, Daschle Makes History." *New York Times,* November 4, 2004.

Stratmann, Thomas. "Congressional Voting over Legislative Careers: Shifting Positions and Changing Constraints." *American Political Science Review* 94 (2000): 665–76.

Summers, Mark W. *The Press Gang: Newspapers and Politics, 1865–1878.* Chapel Hill: University of North Carolina Press, 1994.

———. *Rum, Romanism, and Rebellion: The Making of a President, 1884.* Chapel Hill: University of North Carolina Press, 2000.

Tagge, George. "Republicans Blast Foreign Policy Bungles." *Chicago Tribune,* September 15, 1950.

———. "Douglas Ready to Stump for Lucas' Election." *Chicago Tribune,* September 20, 1950.

———. "Lucas Campaign Is Called Most Lavish in the State." *Chicago Tribune,* October 25, 1950.

"Taylor Denies Welker Backing." *Idaho State Journal,* September 25, 1956.

U.S. Federal Election Commission. "Party Financial Activity Summarized for the 2004 Election Cycle." March 14, 2005. Press release. Downloaded from www.fec.gov on September 17, 2005.

———. "PAC Activity Increases for 2004 Elections." April 13, 2005. News release. Downloaded from www.fec.gov on September 17, 2005.

———. "Party Support for Senate Campaigns—1998." Press release. Downloaded from www.fec.gov/press/senpty98.htm on July 20, 2006.

United States Statutes at Large. Washington, D.C.: Government Printing Office, 1883.

U.S. Congress. House. Committee on House Administration. *Federal Election Campaign Act Amendments of 1974: Report of the Committee on House Administration to Accompany H.R. 16090.* 93d Cong., 2d sess., 1974.

U.S. Congress. Senate. Subcommittee on Privileges and Elections of the Committee on Rules and Administration. *1956 Presidential and Senatorial Campaign Contributions and Practices: Hearings before the Subcommittee on Privileges and Elections of the Committee on Rules and Administration.* 84th Cong., 2d sess., 1956.

———. Committee on Rules and Administration. *Federal Election Campaign Amendments of 1974: Report of the Committee on Rules and Administration to Accompany S3044.* 93d Cong., 2d sess., 1974.

VandeHei, Jim, and Damon Chappie. "DeLay Allies Seek $25 Million Group: Will Emulate Union Strategy." *Roll Call,* May 24, 1999.

VandeHei, Jim, and Juliet Eilperin. "GOP Leaders Tighten Hold in the House." *Washington Post,* January 13, 2003.

Wade, Richard C. "The Periphery versus the Center." In *Urban Bosses, Machines, and Progressive Reformers,* ed. Bruce M. Stave, 75–79. Lexington: Heath, 1972.

Walker, Jack L. "Ballot Forms and Voter Fatigue: An Analysis of the Office Bloc and Party Column Ballots." *Midwest Journal of Political Science* 10 (1966): 448–63.

Ware, Alan. *Political Parties and Party Systems*. Oxford: Oxford University Press, 1996.

———. *The American Direct Primary: Party Institutionalization and Transformation in the North*. Cambridge: Cambridge University Press, 2002.

Wattenberg, Martin P. *The Decline of American Political Parties, 1952–1994*. Cambridge: Harvard University Press, 1996.

Wattenberg, Martin P., and Craig L. Brians. "Negative Campaign Advertising Demobilizer or Mobilizer?" *American Political Science Review* 93 (1999): 891–900.

Weisberg, Herbert F., and Jerrold G. Rusk. "Dimensions of Candidate Evaluation." *American Political Science Review* 64 (1970): 1167–85.

Weissman, Steve, and Ruth Hassan. "BCRA and the 527 Groups." In *The Election after Reform: Money, Politics, and the Bipartisan Campaign Reform Act*, ed. Michael J. Malbin. Lanham, Md.: Rowman and Littlefield, 2006.

"Welker Praises Cohn." *New York Times*, July 21, 1954.

"Welker Recalls Senators Who Have Been Unsteady." *New York Times*, November 17, 1954.

Wilcox, Clyde, Lee Sigelman, and Elizabeth Cook. "Some Like It Hot: Individual Differences to Group Feeling Thermometers." *Public Opinion Quarterly* 53 (1989): 246–57.

Williams, R. Hal. *The Democratic Party and California Politics, 1880–1896*. Stanford: Stanford University Press, 1973.

Wlezein, Christopher. "A Note on the Endogeneity of Ideological Placements of Government Institutions." National Election Studies, Center for Political Studies, University of Michigan, Ann Arbor, 2002. Electronic resources from www.umich.edu/~nes.

Yearley, Clifton K. *The Money Machines: The Breakdown and Reform of Governmental and Party Finance in the North, 1860–1920*. Albany: State University of New York Press, 1970.

Zaller, John. *The Nature and Origins of Mass Opinion*. New York: Cambridge University Press, 1992.

INDEX

References to illustrations are in italic type.